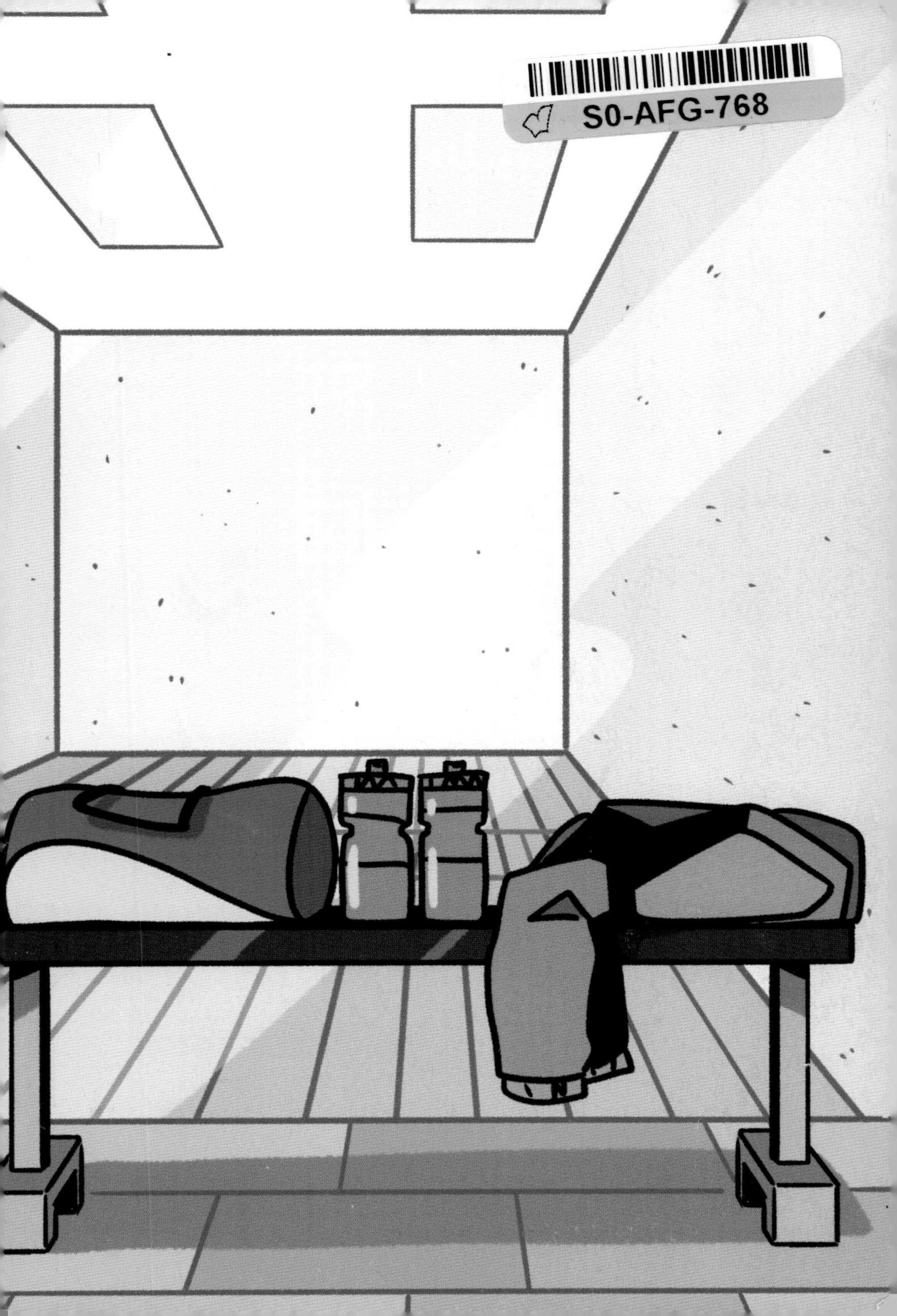

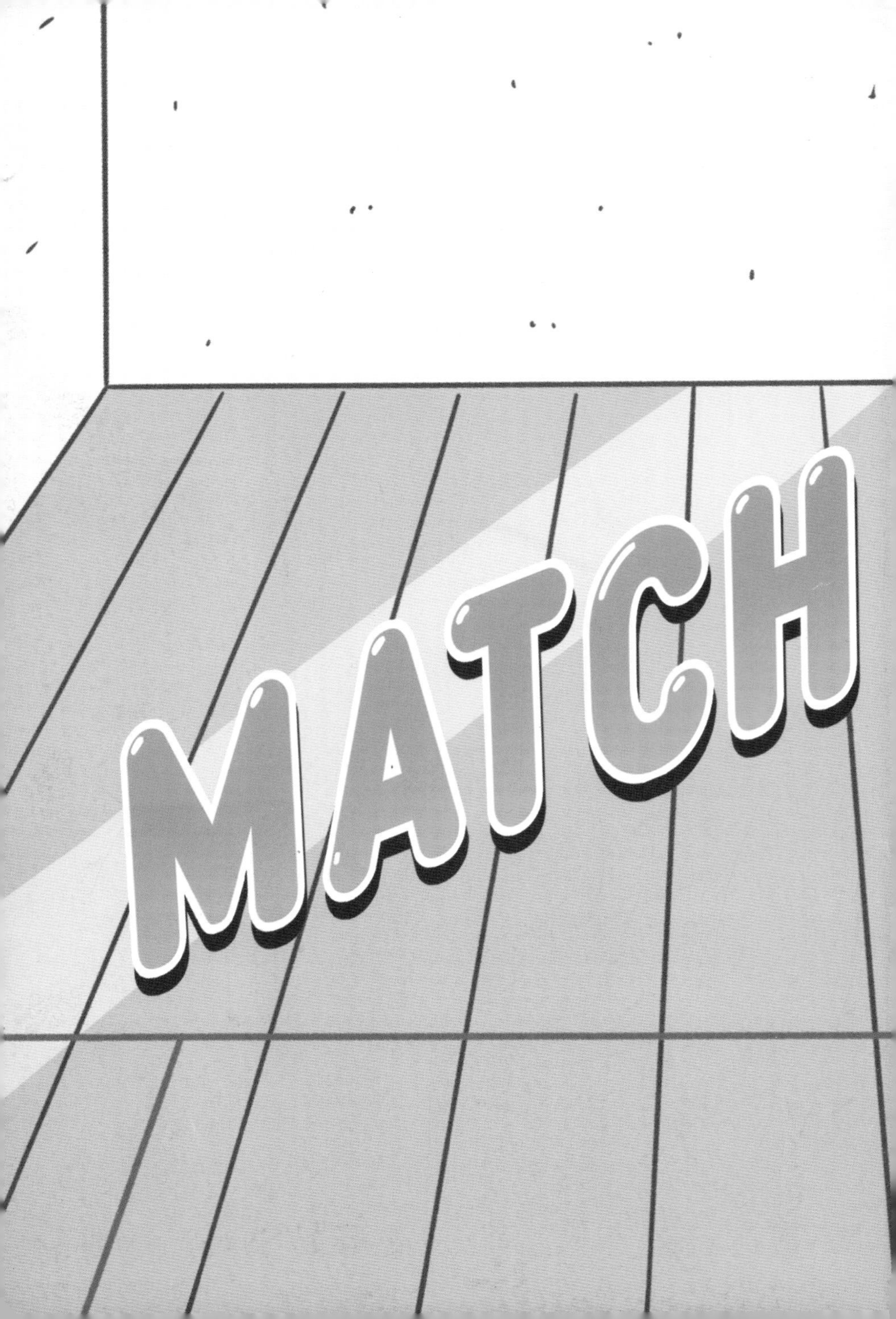
MATCH

POINT!

MADDIE GALLEGOS

:01
First Second
NEW YORK

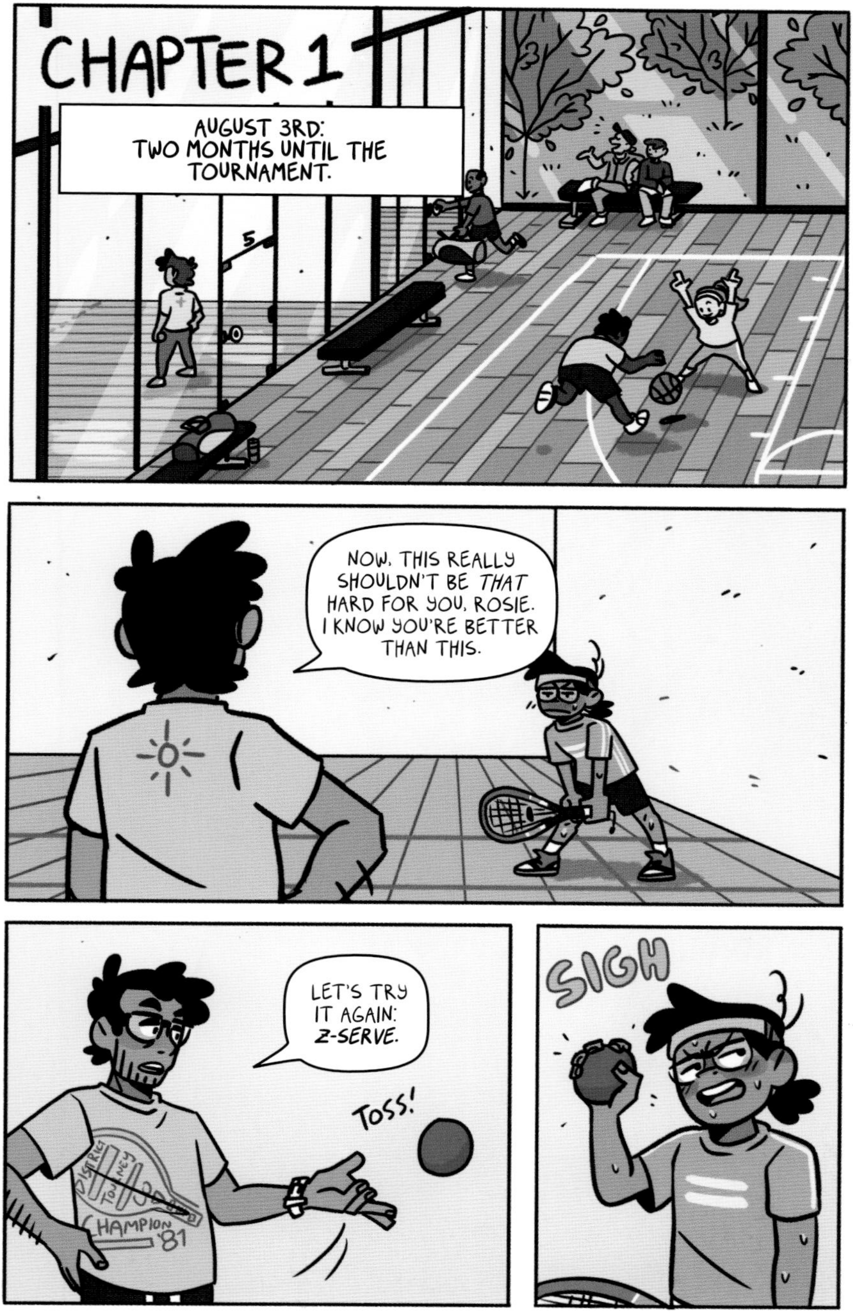
CHAPTER 1
AUGUST 3RD: TWO MONTHS UNTIL THE TOURNAMENT.
NOW, THIS REALLY SHOULDN'T BE *THAT* HARD FOR YOU, ROSIE. I KNOW YOU'RE BETTER THAN THIS.
LET'S TRY IT AGAIN: **Z-SERVE.**
TOSS!
CHAMPION '81
SIGH

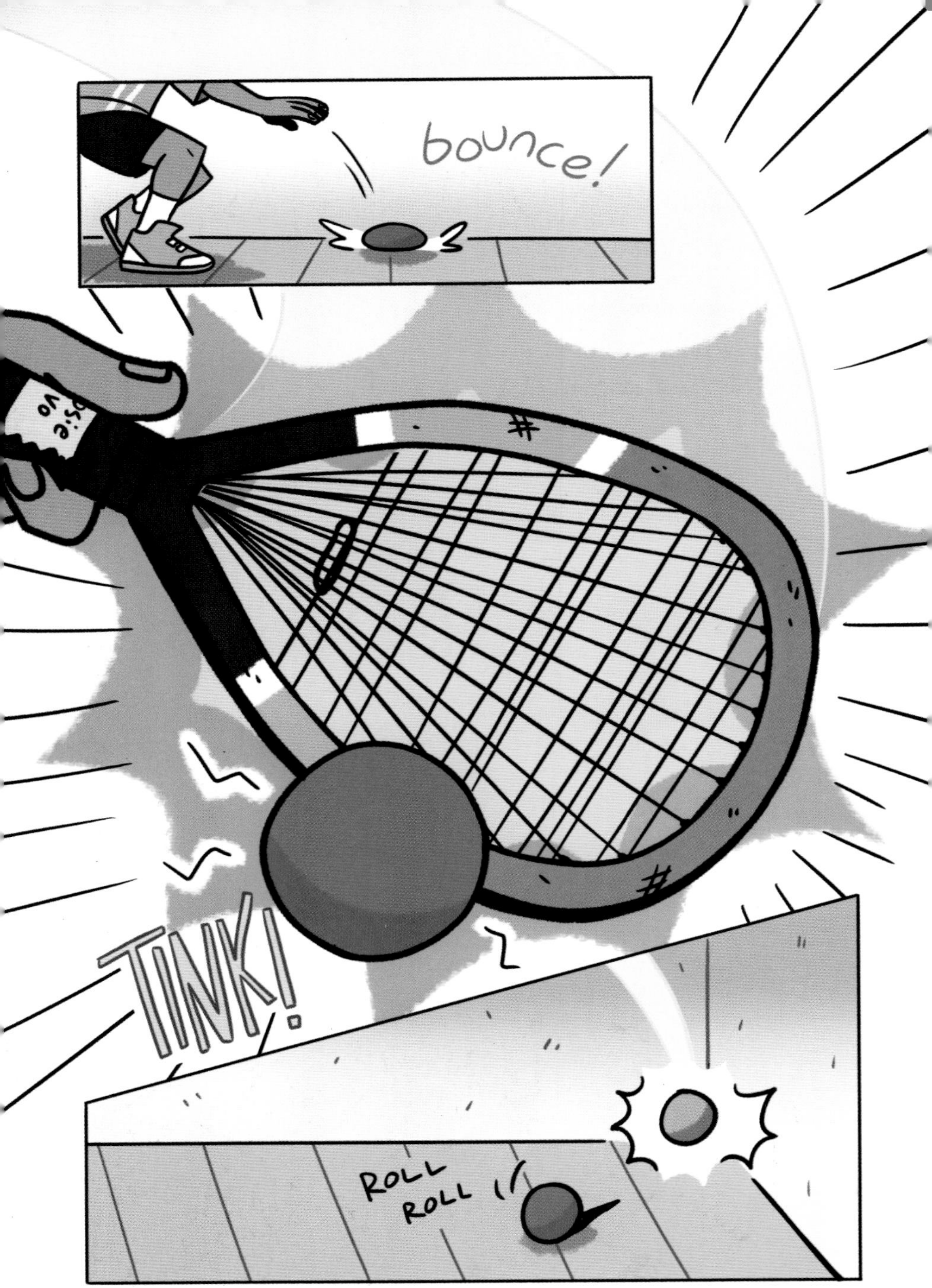
bounce!
TINK!
ROLL
ROLL

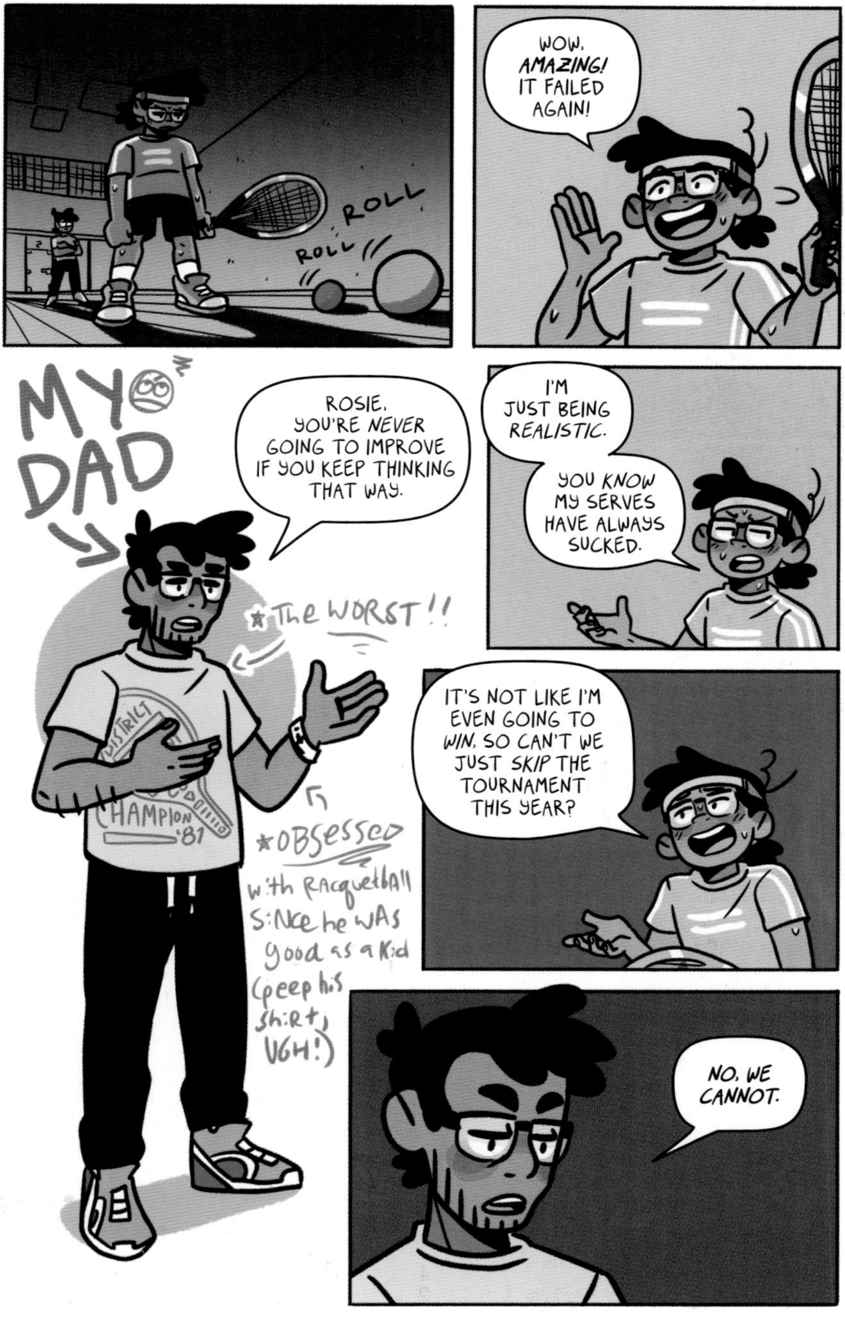
ROLL
ROLL
WOW, AMAZING! IT FAILED AGAIN!
MY DAD
ROSIE, YOU'RE NEVER GOING TO IMPROVE IF YOU KEEP THINKING THAT WAY.
*The WORST!!
DISTRICT CHAMPION '81
*OBSESSED with Racquetball since he was good as a kid (peep his shirt, UGH!)
I'M JUST BEING REALISTIC.
YOU KNOW MY SERVES HAVE ALWAYS SUCKED.
IT'S NOT LIKE I'M EVEN GOING TO WIN, SO CAN'T WE JUST SKIP THE TOURNAMENT THIS YEAR?
NO, WE CANNOT.

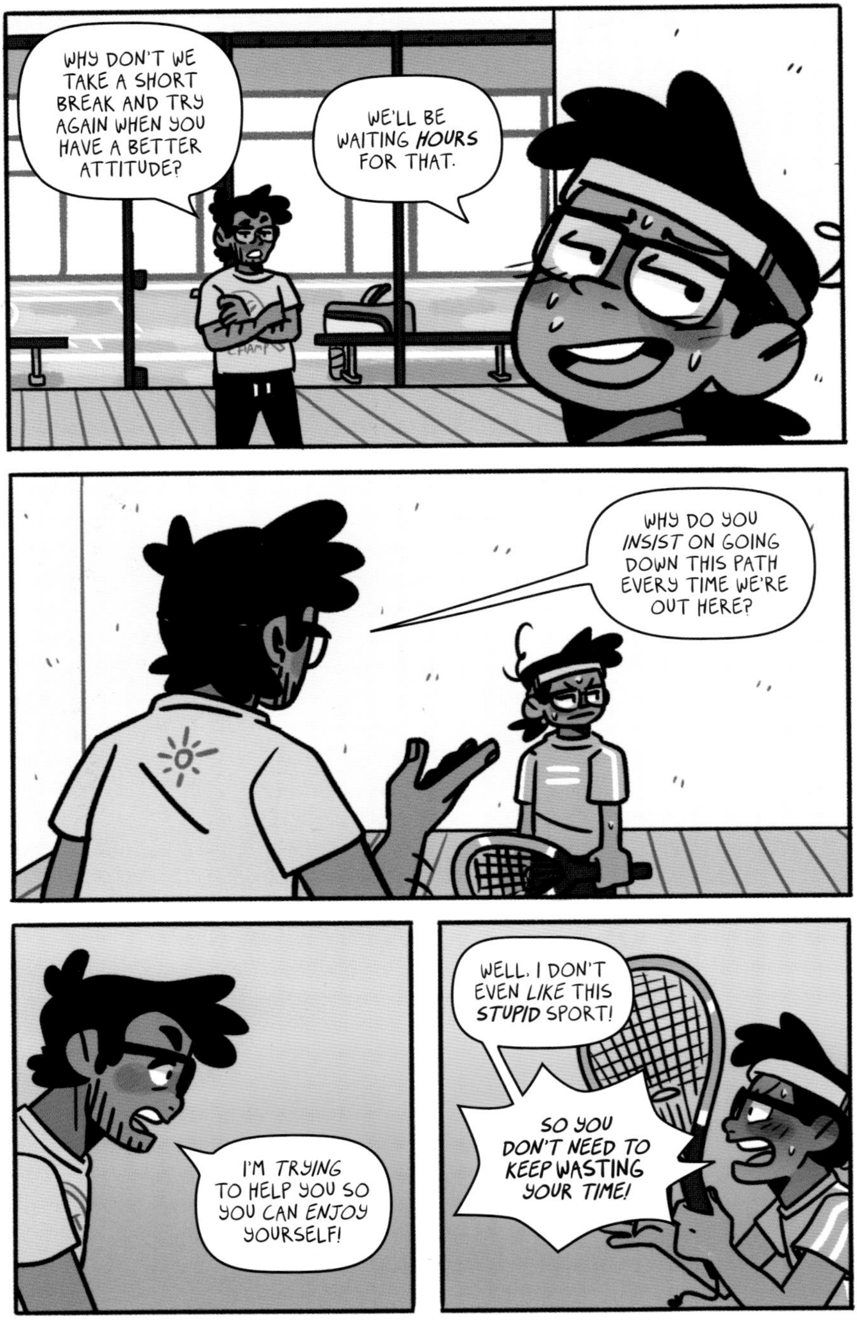
WHY DON'T WE TAKE A SHORT BREAK AND TRY AGAIN WHEN YOU HAVE A BETTER ATTITUDE?
WE'LL BE WAITING HOURS FOR THAT.
WHY DO YOU INSIST ON GOING DOWN THIS PATH EVERY TIME WE'RE OUT HERE?
I'M TRYING TO HELP YOU SO YOU CAN ENJOY YOURSELF!
WELL, I DON'T EVEN LIKE THIS STUPID SPORT!
SO YOU DON'T NEED TO KEEP WASTING YOUR TIME!

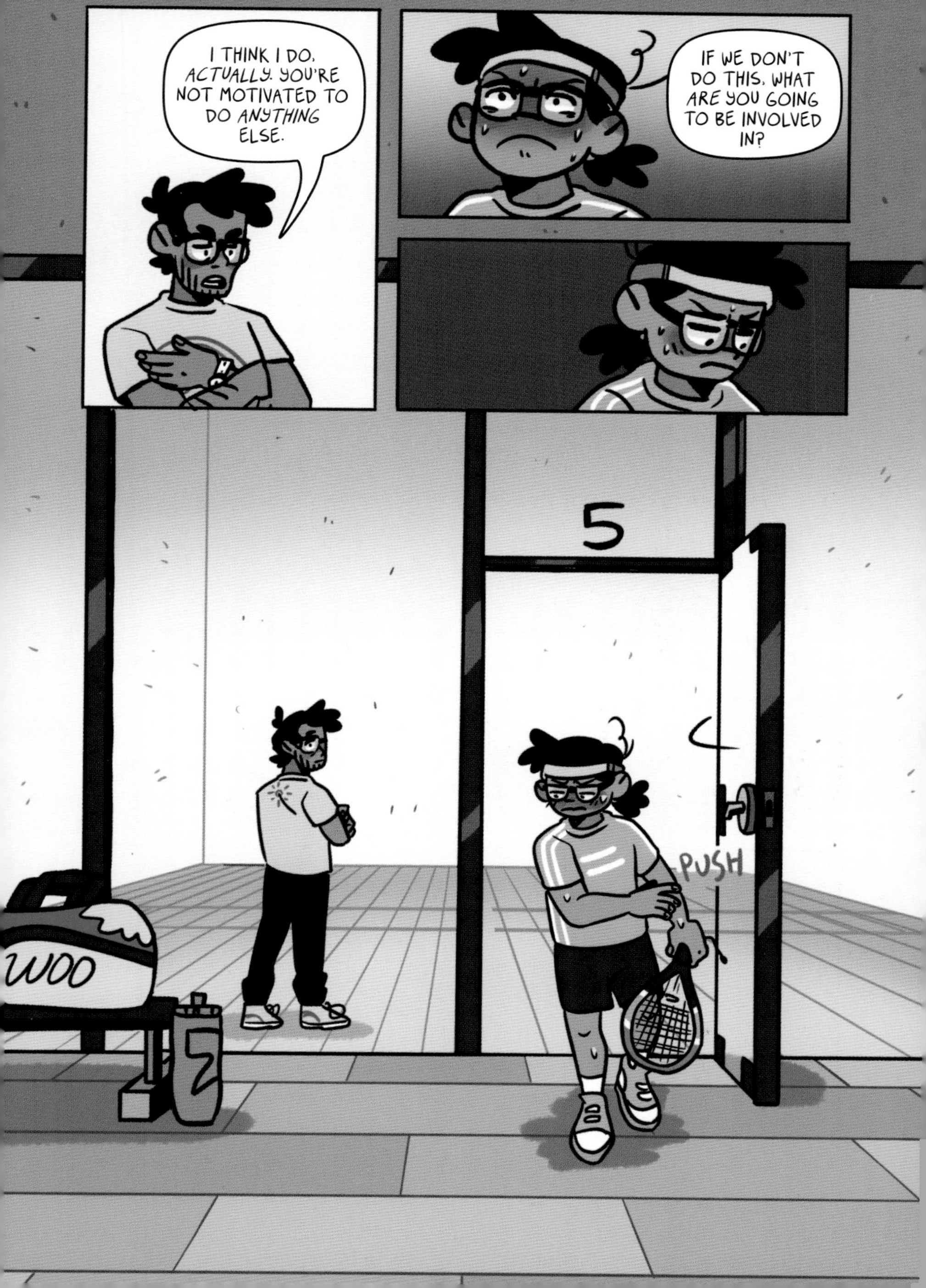
I THINK I DO, *ACTUALLY.* YOU'RE NOT MOTIVATED TO DO *ANYTHING* ELSE.
IF WE DON'T DO THIS, WHAT ARE YOU GOING TO BE INVOLVED IN?
5
PUSH
WOO

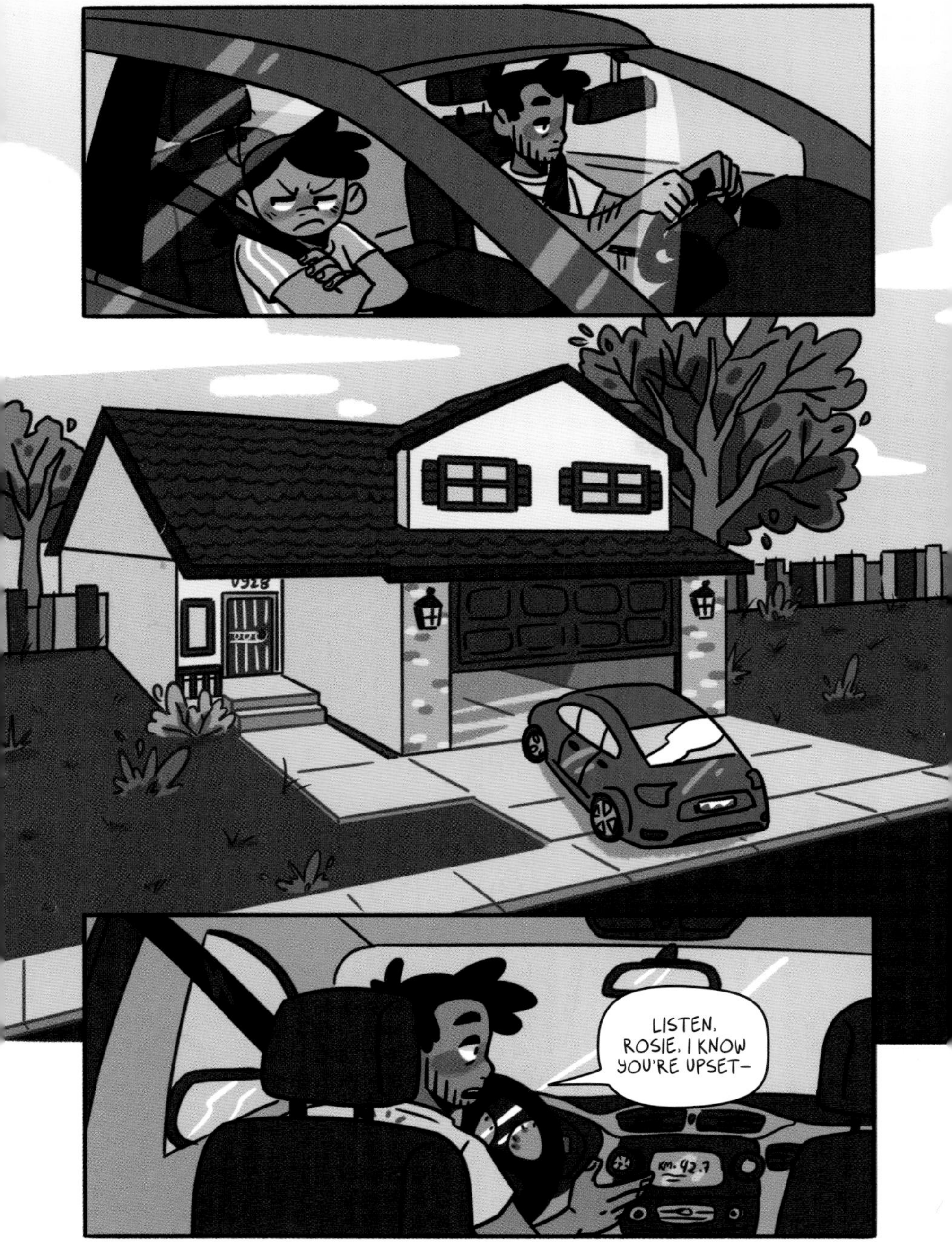
LISTEN, ROSIE, I KNOW YOU'RE UPSET—

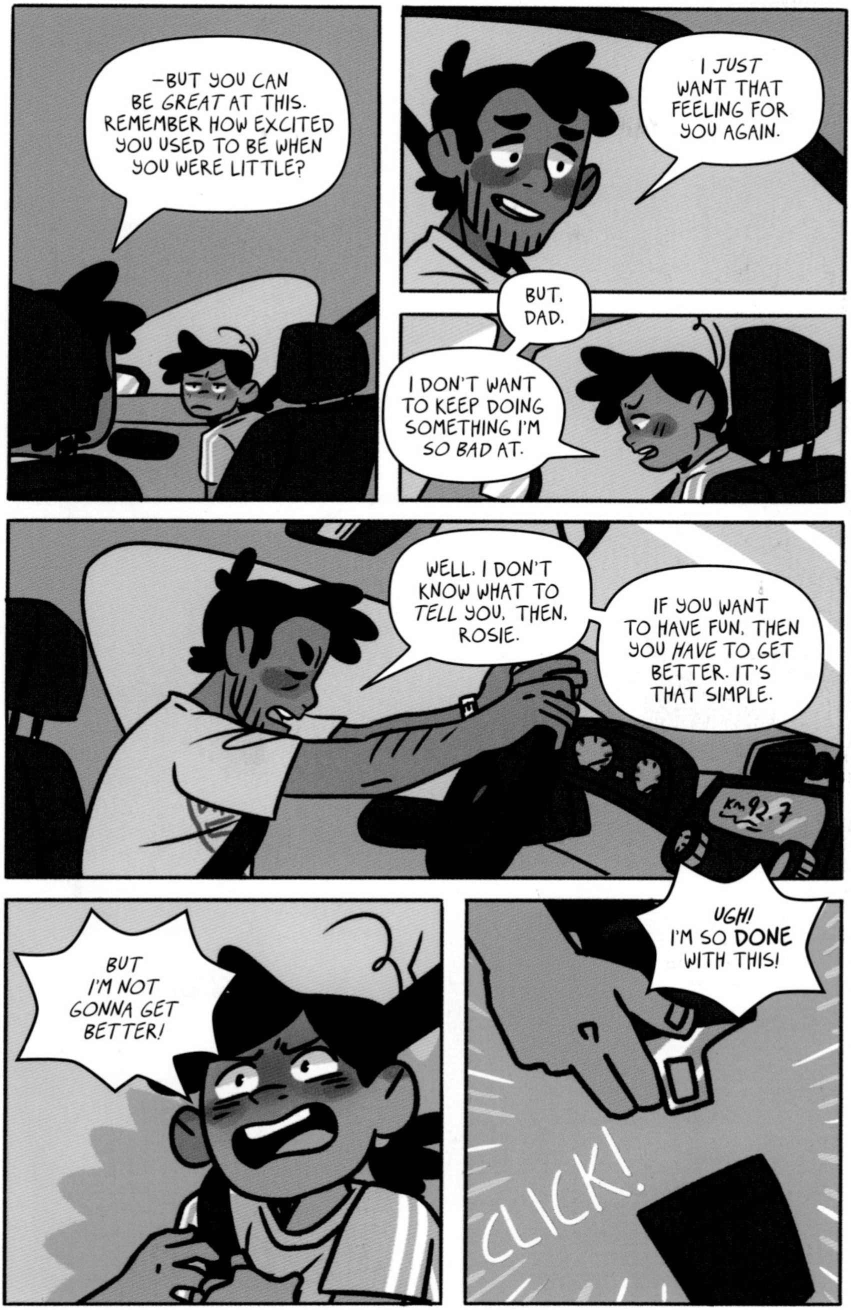

—BUT YOU CAN BE *GREAT* AT THIS. REMEMBER HOW EXCITED YOU USED TO BE WHEN YOU WERE LITTLE?
I JUST WANT THAT FEELING FOR YOU AGAIN.
BUT, DAD.
I DON'T WANT TO KEEP DOING SOMETHING I'M SO BAD AT.
WELL, I DON'T KNOW WHAT TO *TELL* YOU, THEN, ROSIE.
IF YOU WANT TO HAVE FUN, THEN YOU *HAVE* TO GET BETTER. IT'S THAT SIMPLE.
92.7
BUT I'M NOT GONNA GET BETTER!
UGH! I'M SO **DONE** WITH THIS!
CLICK!

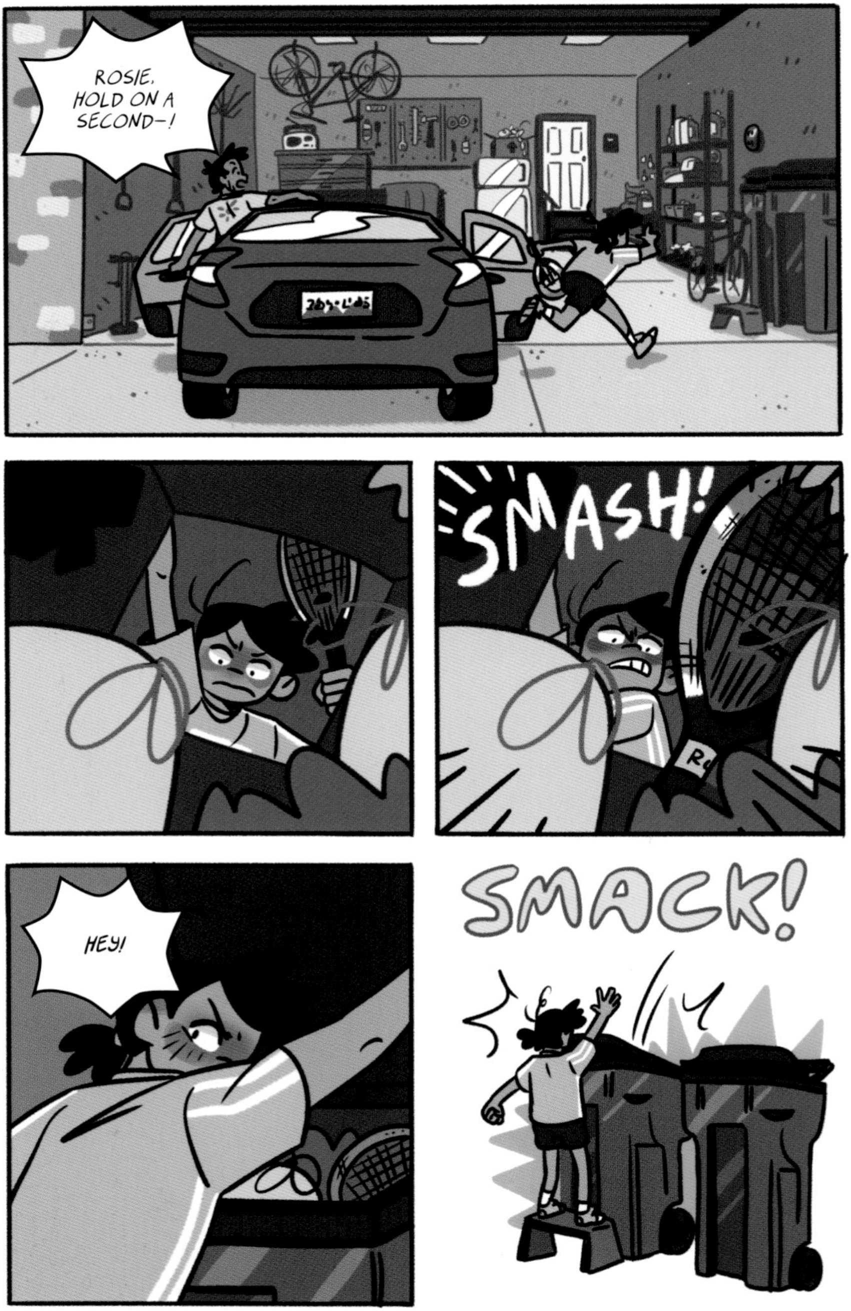
ROSIE, HOLD ON A SECOND–!
SMASH!
HEY!
SMACK!

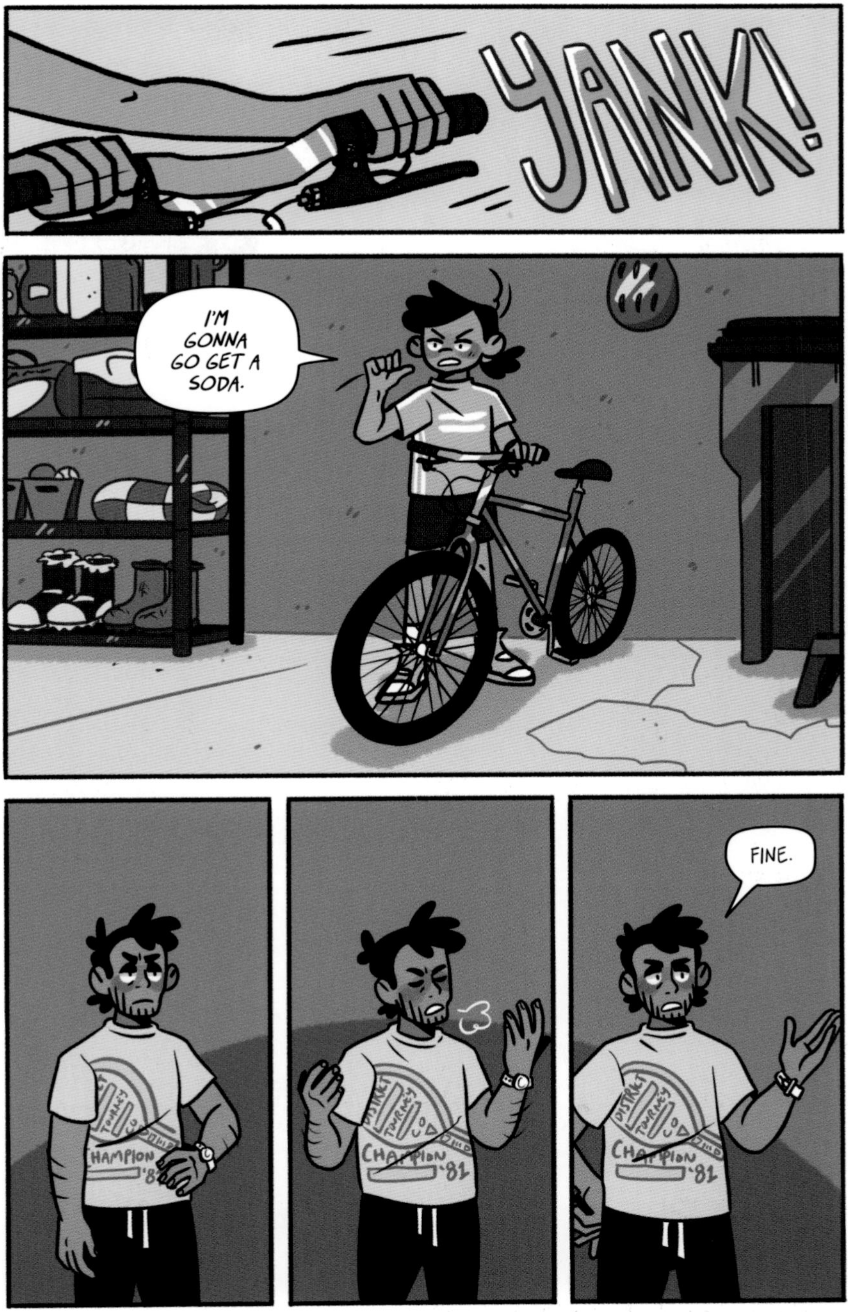
YANK!
I'M GONNA GO GET A SODA.
DISTRICT TOURNEY CO CHAMPION '81
FINE.

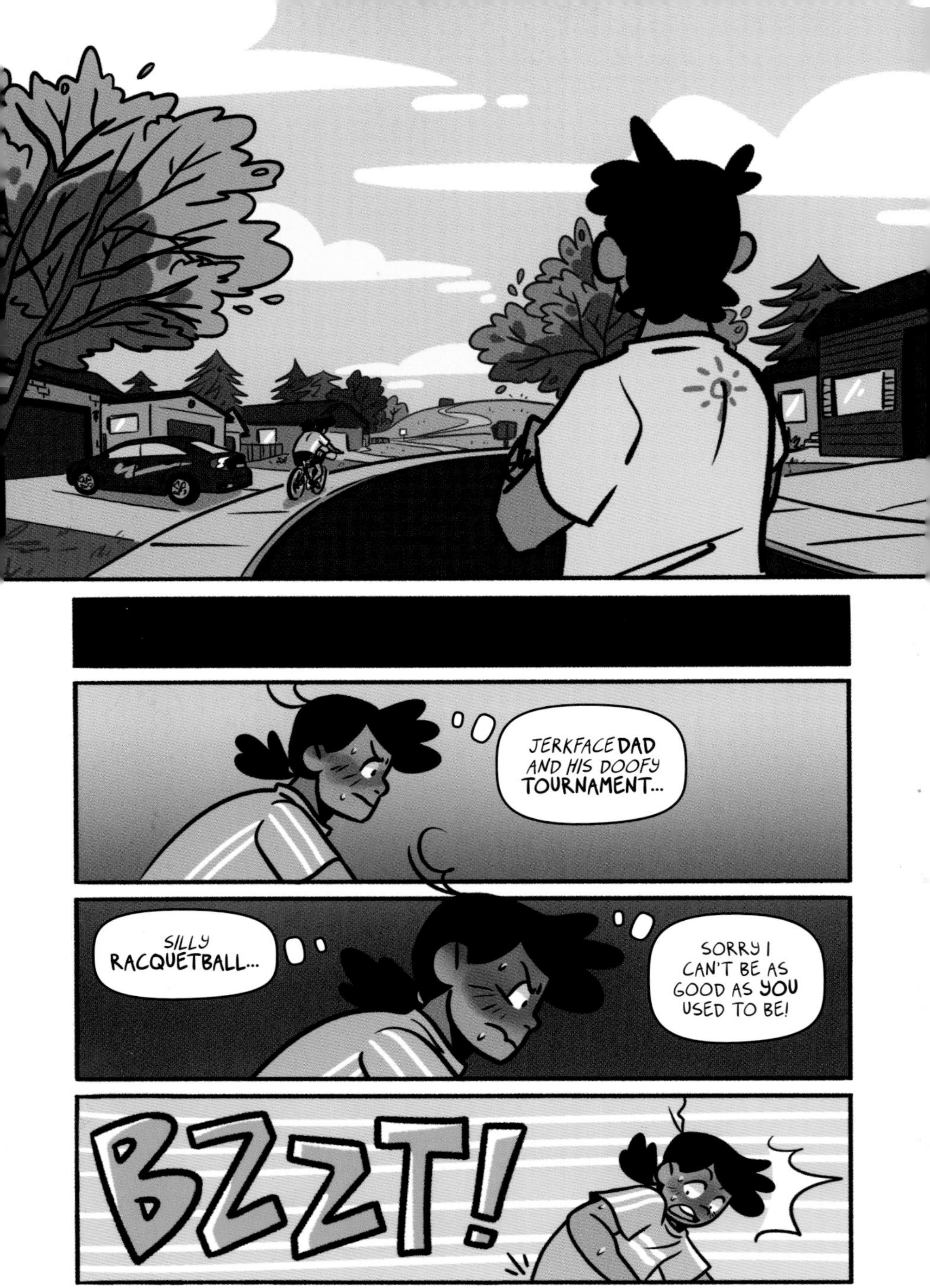
JERKFACE DAD AND HIS DOOFY TOURNAMENT...
SILLY RACQUETBALL...
SORRY I CAN'T BE AS GOOD AS YOU USED TO BE!
BZZT!

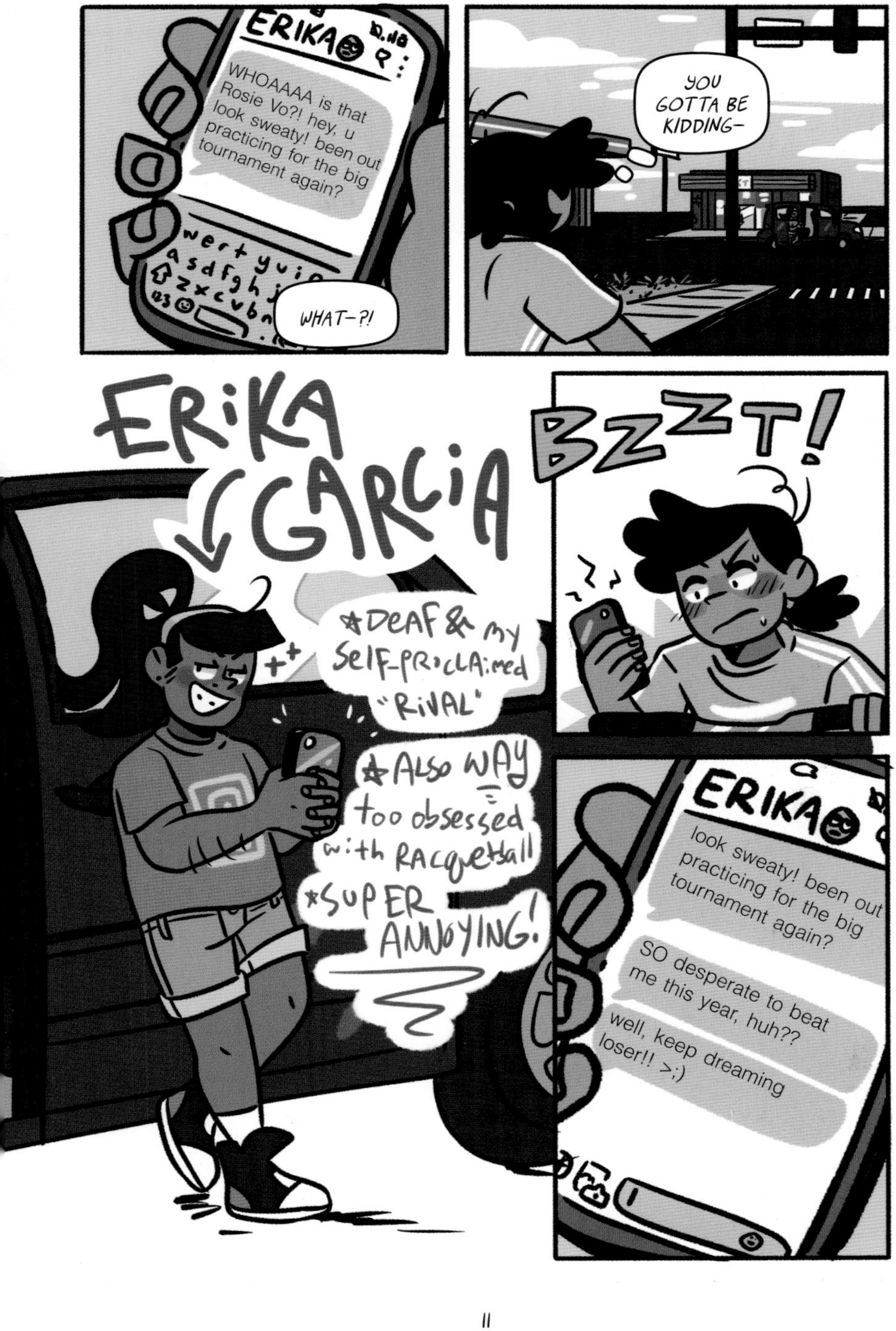

ERIKA
WHOAAAA is that Rosie Vo?! hey, u look sweaty! been out practicing for the big tournament again?
WHAT-?!
YOU GOTTA BE KIDDING-
ERIKA GARCIA
*DEAF & my SELF-PROCLAIMED "RIVAL"
*ALSO WAY too obsessed with RACQUETBALL
*SUPER ANNOYING!
BZZZT!
ERIKA
look sweaty! been out practicing for the big tournament again?
SO desperate to beat me this year, huh??
well, keep dreaming loser!! >;)

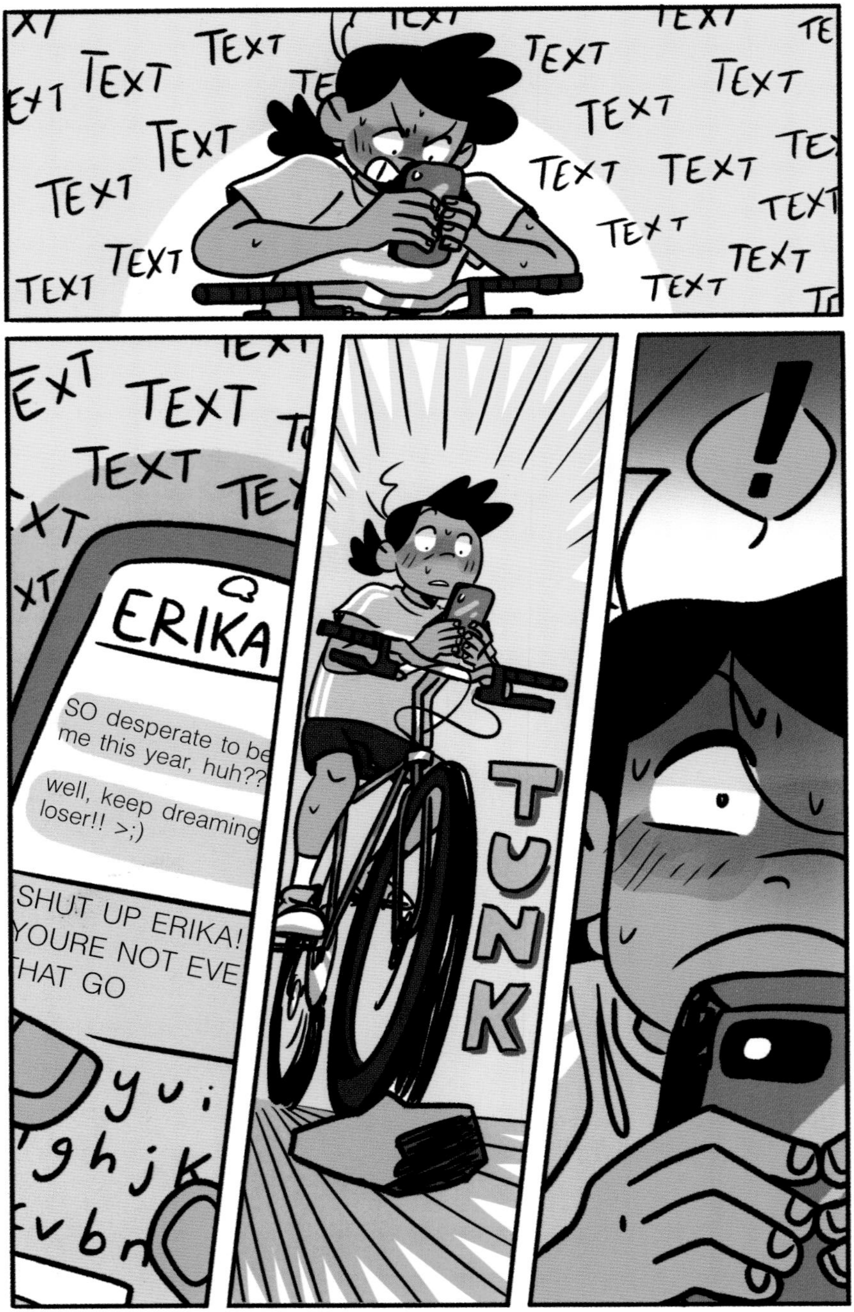
TEXT TEXT TEXT TEXT TEXT TEXT TEXT TEXT TEXT TEXT TEXT TEXT TEXT
TEXT TEXT TEXT
ERIKA
SO desperate to be
me this year, huh??
well, keep dreaming
loser!! >;)
SHUT UP ERIKA!
YOURE NOT EVE
HAT GO
TUNK
!

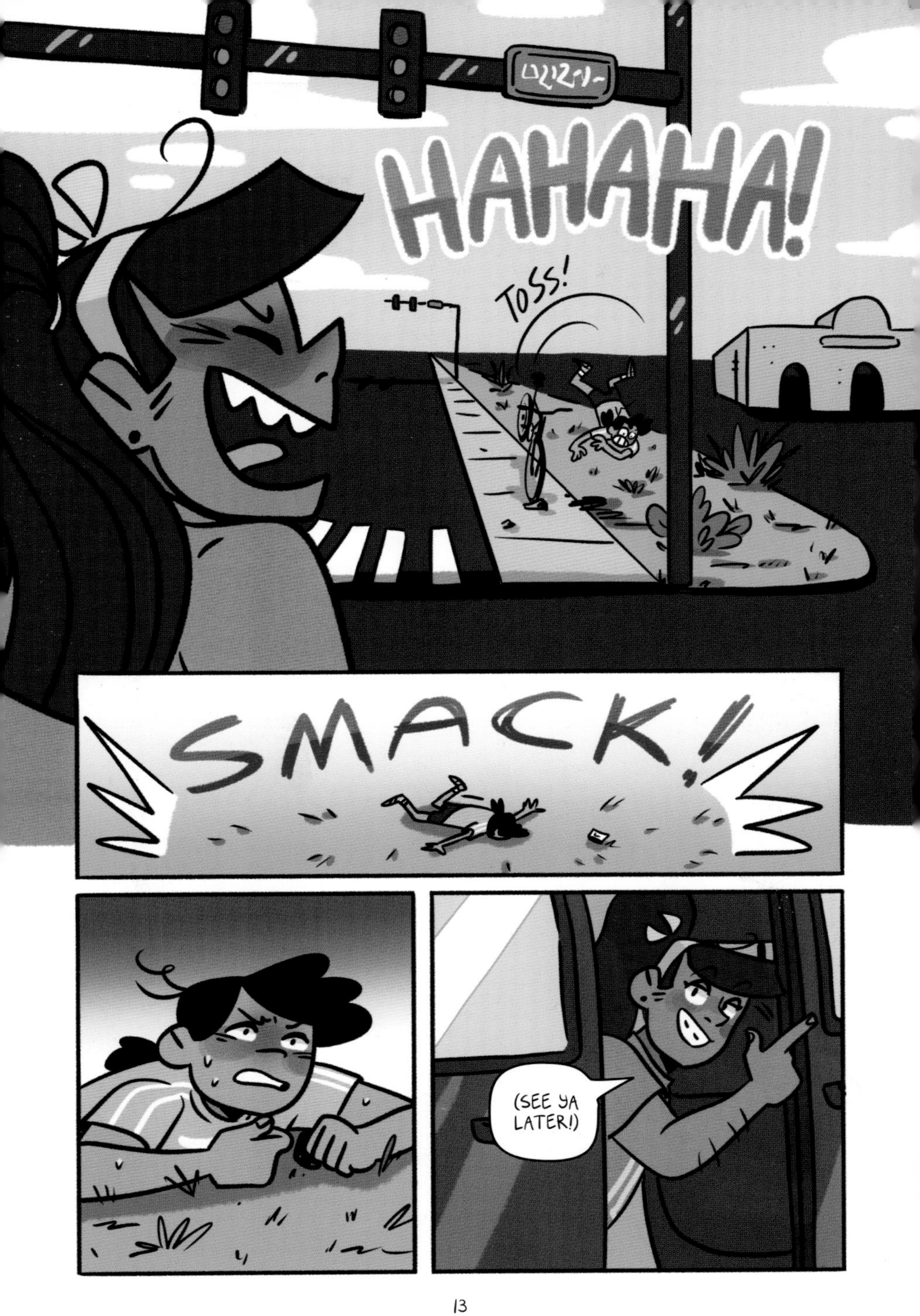
HAHAHA!
TOSS!
SMACK!
(SEE YA LATER!)

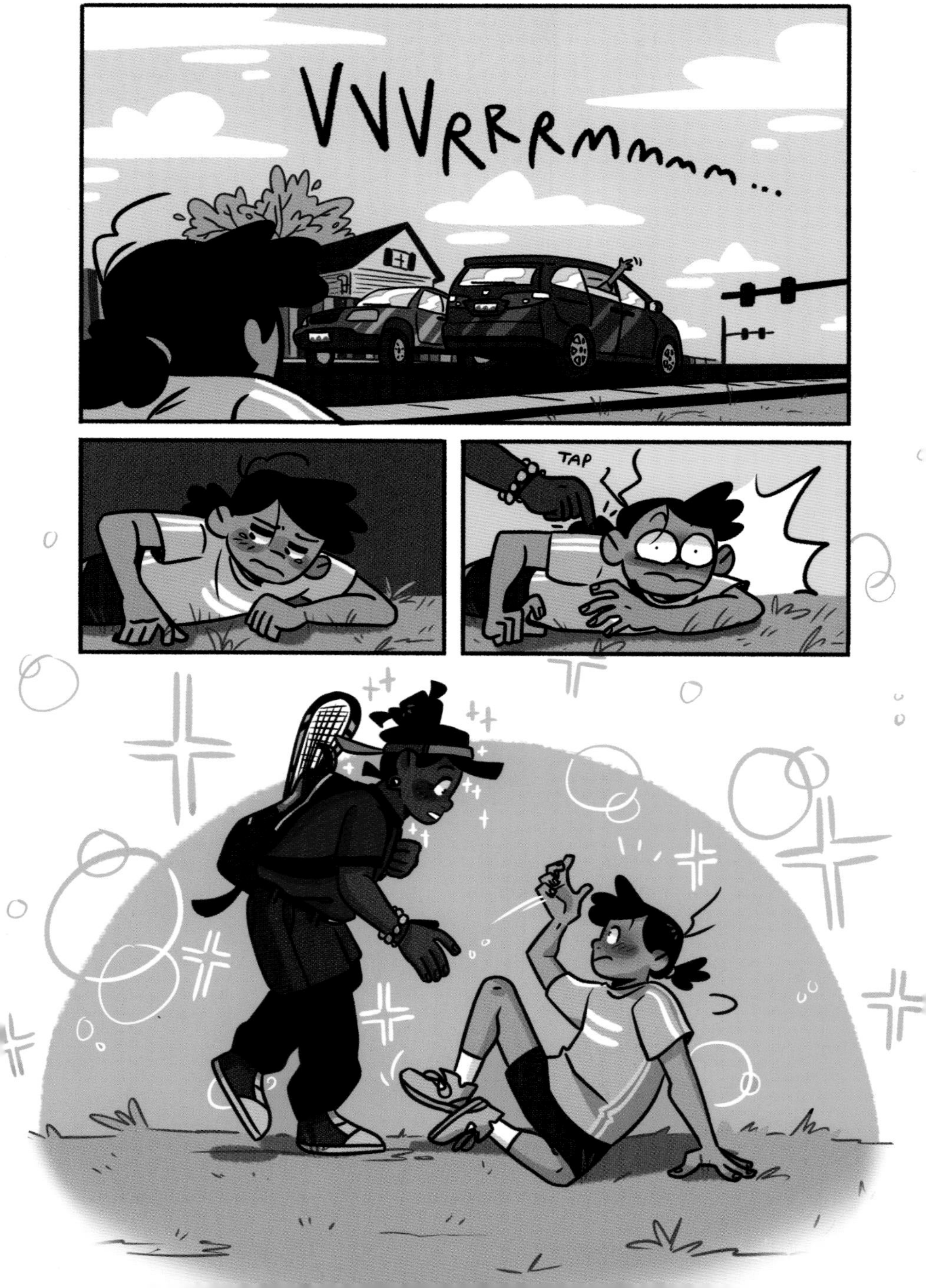
VVVRRRMmmm...
TAP

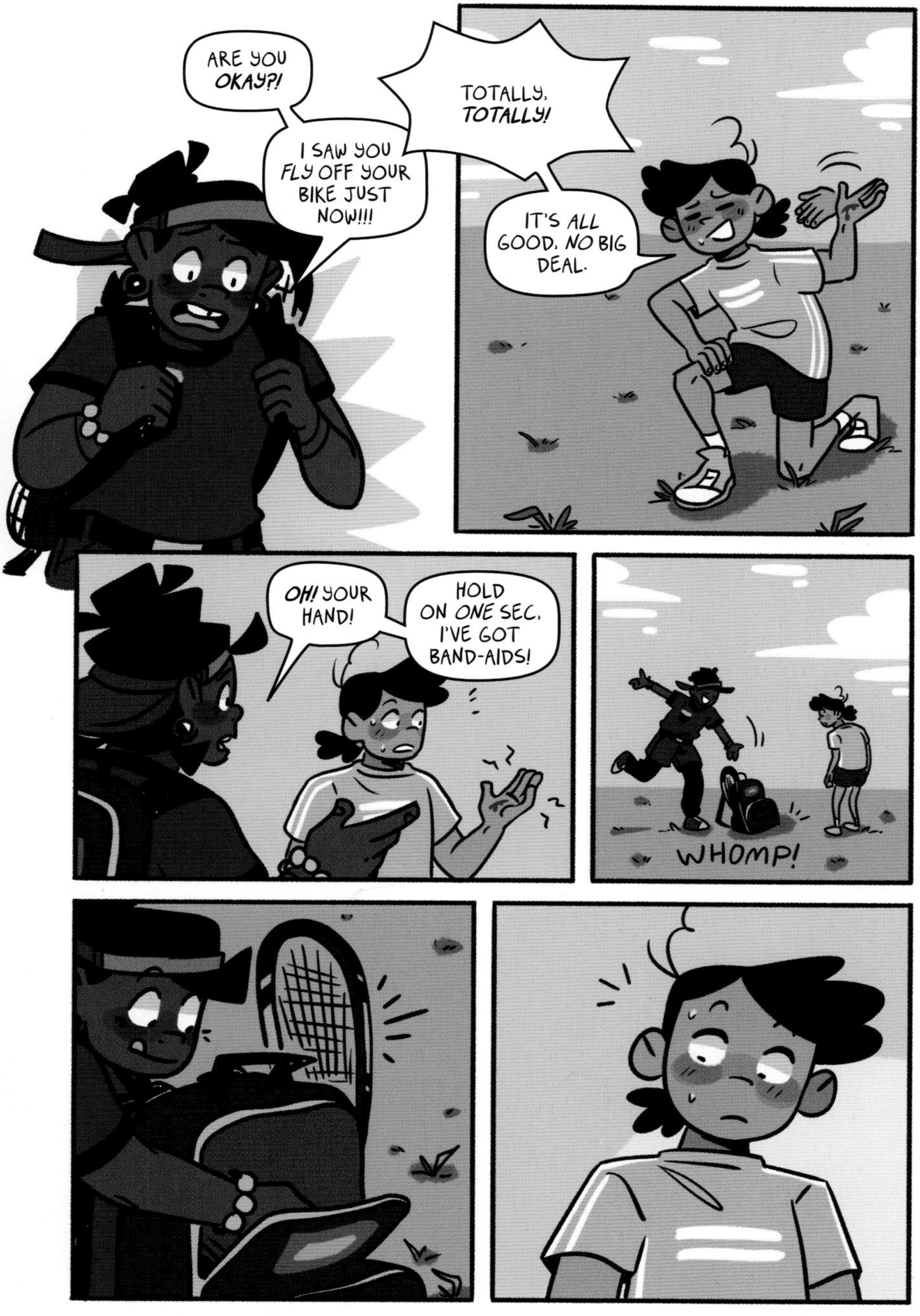
ARE YOU OKAY?!
I SAW YOU FLY OFF YOUR BIKE JUST NOW!!!
TOTALLY, TOTALLY!
IT'S ALL GOOD, NO BIG DEAL.
OH! YOUR HAND!
HOLD ON ONE SEC, I'VE GOT BAND-AIDS!
WHOMP!

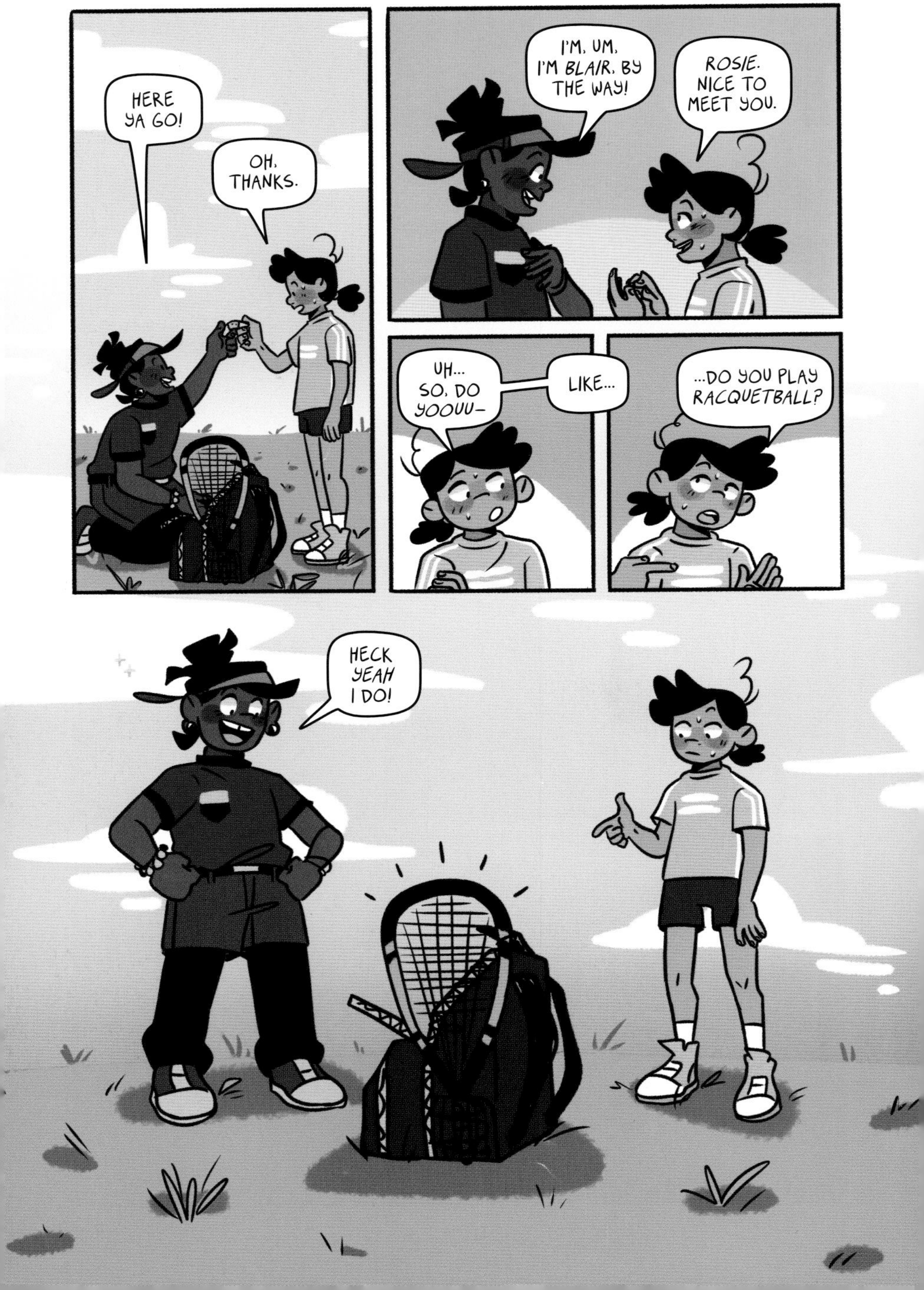
HERE YA GO!
OH, THANKS.
I'M, UM, I'M BLAIR, BY THE WAY!
ROSIE. NICE TO MEET YOU.
UH... SO, DO YOOUU–
LIKE...
...DO YOU PLAY RACQUETBALL?
HECK YEAH I DO!

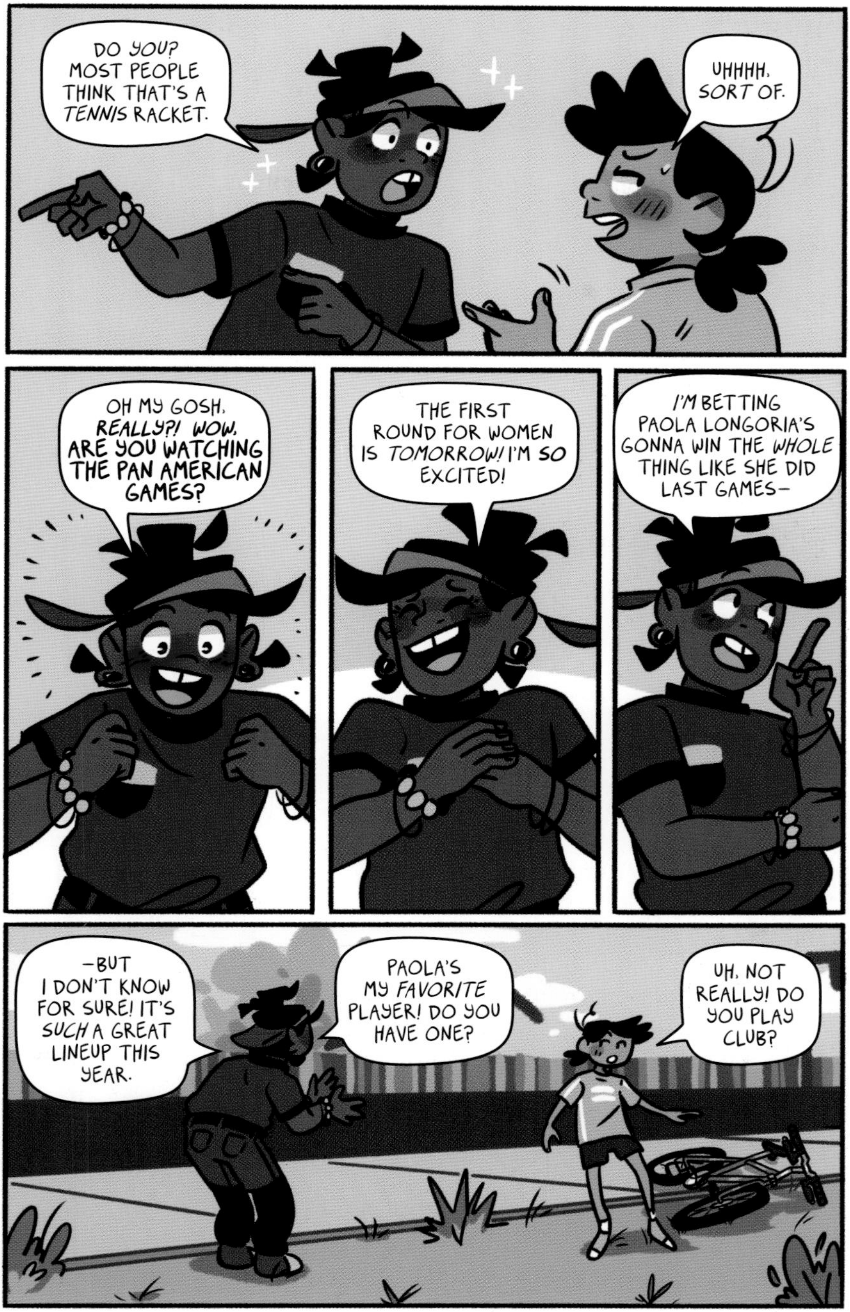
DO YOU? MOST PEOPLE THINK THAT'S A TENNIS RACKET.
UHHHH, SORT OF.
OH MY GOSH, REALLY?! WOW, ARE YOU WATCHING THE PAN AMERICAN GAMES?
THE FIRST ROUND FOR WOMEN IS TOMORROW! I'M SO EXCITED!
I'M BETTING PAOLA LONGORIA'S GONNA WIN THE WHOLE THING LIKE SHE DID LAST GAMES—
—BUT I DON'T KNOW FOR SURE! IT'S SUCH A GREAT LINEUP THIS YEAR.
PAOLA'S MY FAVORITE PLAYER! DO YOU HAVE ONE?
UH, NOT REALLY! DO YOU PLAY CLUB?

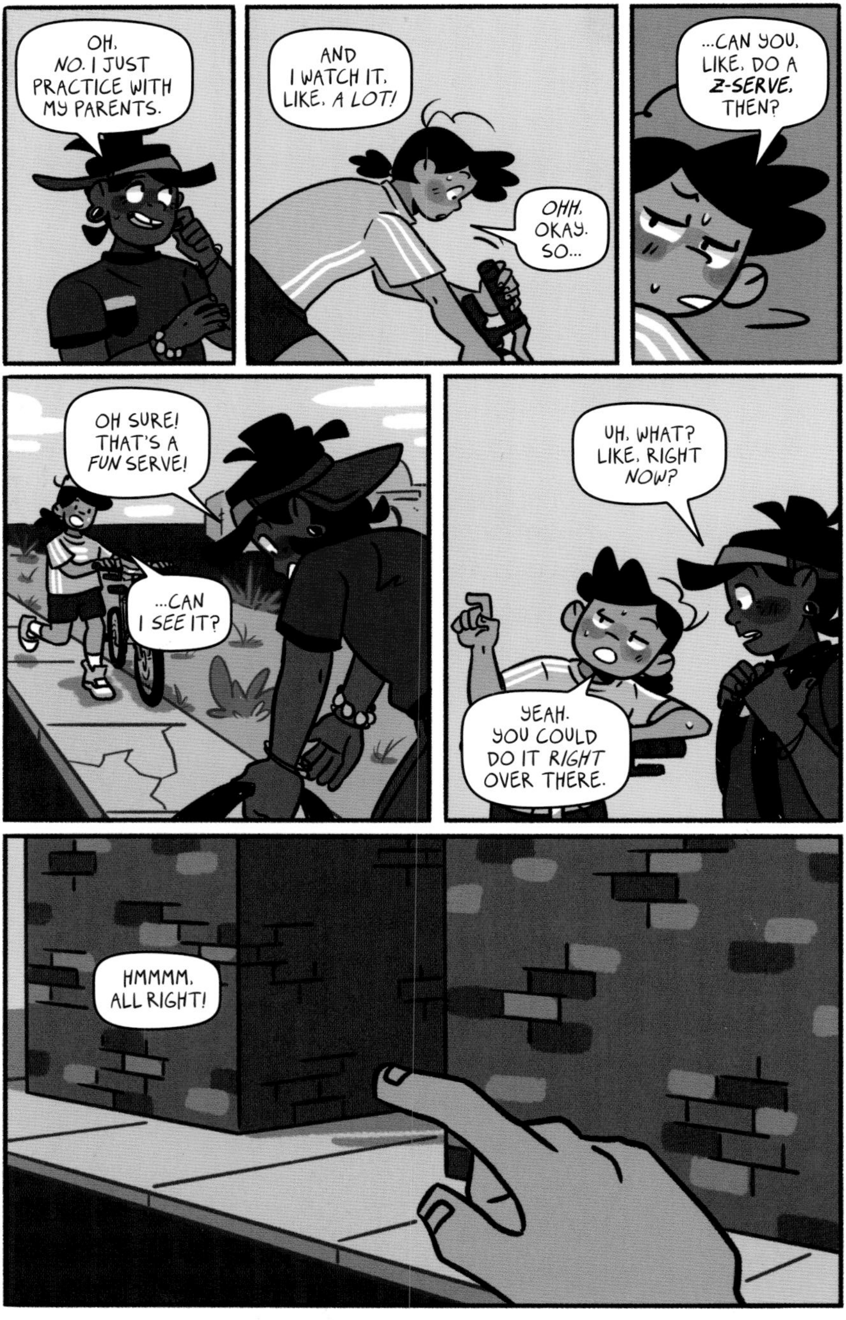
OH, *NO.* I JUST PRACTICE WITH MY PARENTS.
AND I WATCH IT. LIKE, *A LOT!*
OHH, OKAY. SO...
...CAN YOU, LIKE, DO A **Z-SERVE,** THEN?
OH SURE! THAT'S A *FUN* SERVE!
...CAN I SEE IT?
UH, WHAT? LIKE, RIGHT *NOW?*
YEAH. YOU COULD DO IT *RIGHT* OVER THERE.
HMMMM. ALL RIGHT!

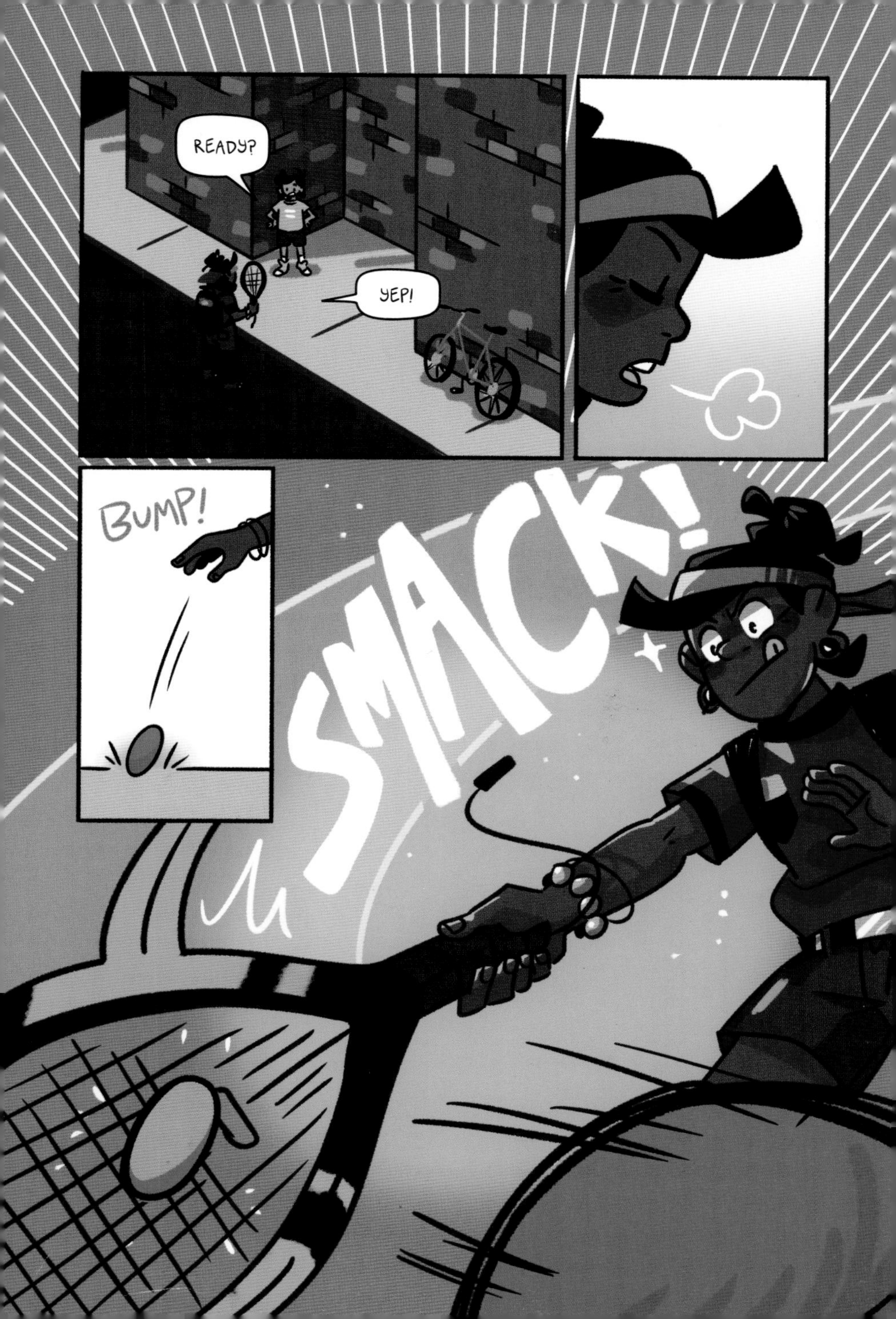
READY?
YEP!
BUMP!
SMACK!

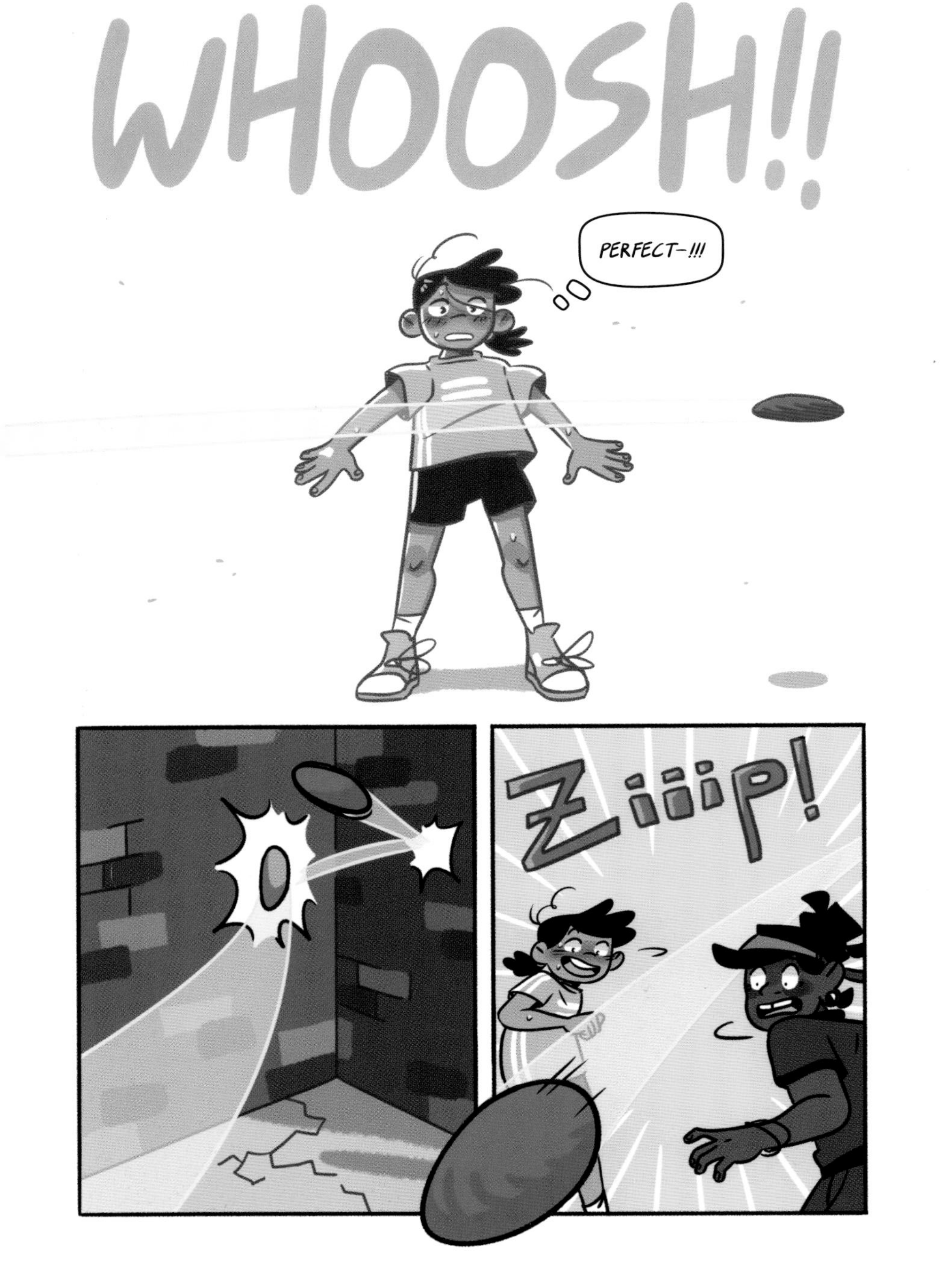
WHOOSH!!
PERFECT-!!!
Ziiip!

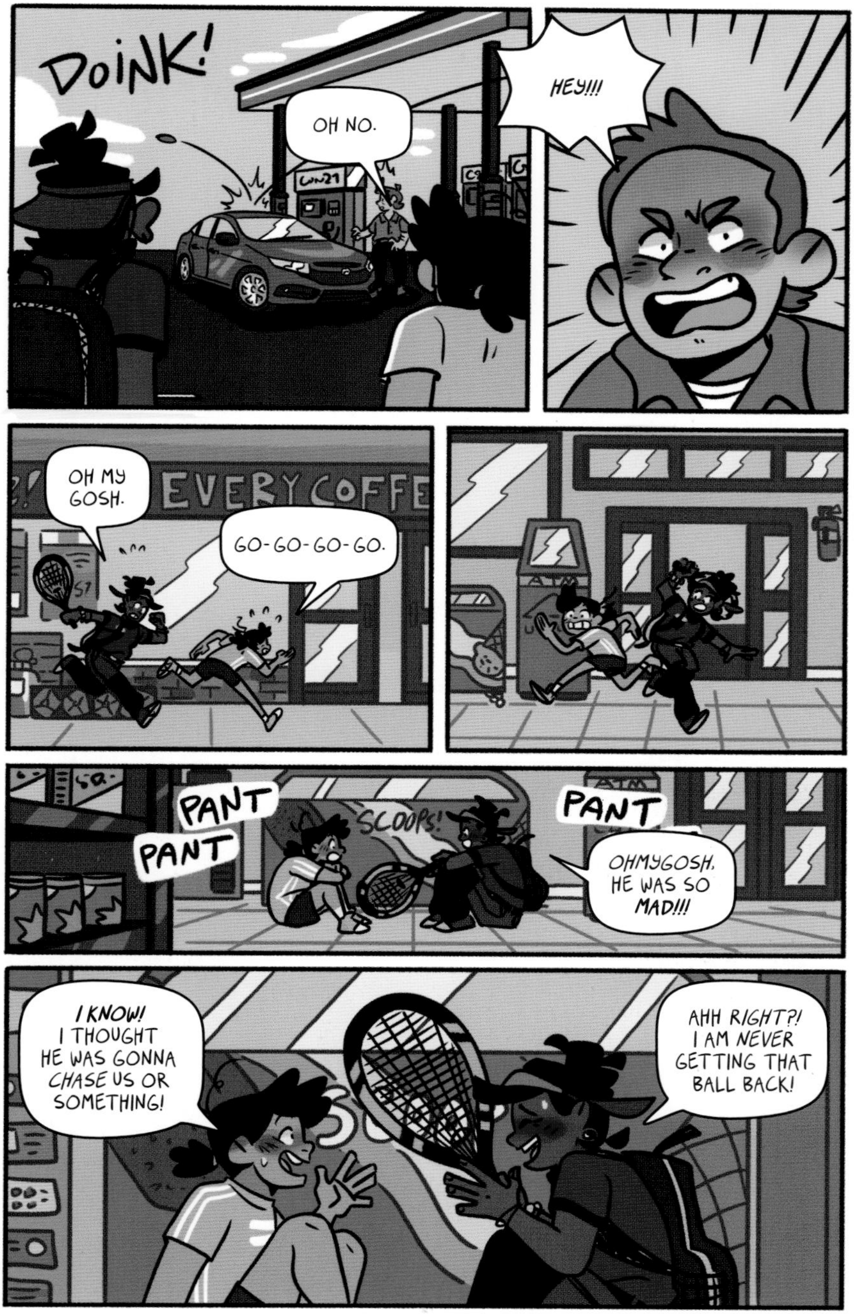
DOINK!
OH NO.
HEY!!!
OH MY GOSH.
EVERY COFFE
GO-GO-GO-GO.
ATM
PANT
PANT
SCOOPS!
PANT
OHMYGOSH, HE WAS SO MAD!!!
I KNOW! I THOUGHT HE WAS GONNA CHASE US OR SOMETHING!
AHH RIGHT?! I AM NEVER GETTING THAT BALL BACK!

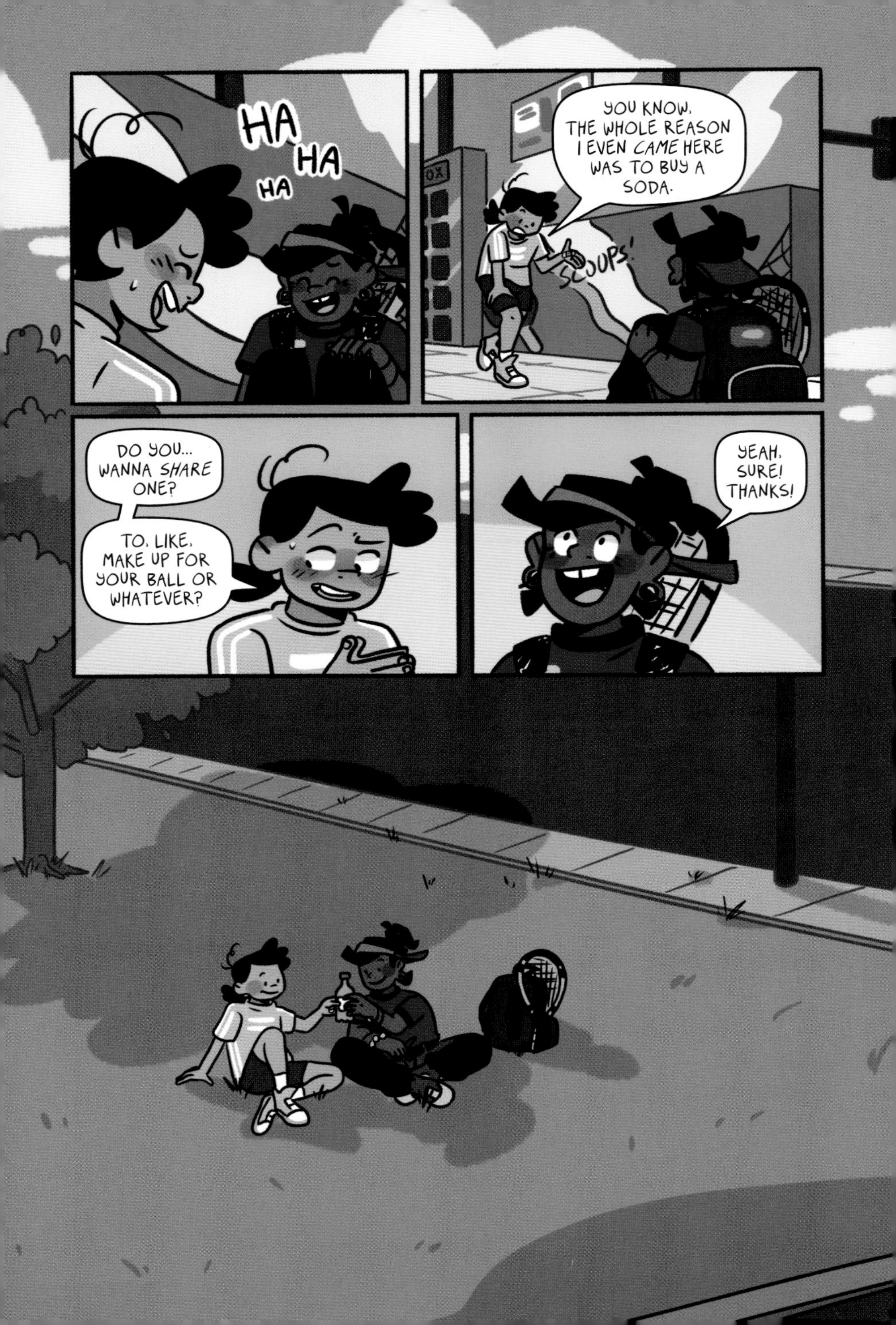
HA HA HA
YOU KNOW, THE WHOLE REASON I EVEN CAME HERE WAS TO BUY A SODA.
SCOOPS!
DO YOU... WANNA SHARE ONE?
TO, LIKE, MAKE UP FOR YOUR BALL OR WHATEVER?
YEAH, SURE! THANKS!

SO, DO YOU GO TO THUNDERCREST? FEEL LIKE I'VE NEVER SEEN YOU BEFORE.

OH. WELL, I JUST MOVED HERE ACTUALLY! BUT THAT'S THE SCHOOL I'M GONNA GO TO!

OH. NICE! WHAT GRADE?

EIGHT!

ME TOO!

BZ^ZT!

OH MAN, I THINK I GOTTA START HEADING HOME. MY MOM WANTS ME BACK FOR DINNER.

UM, I GUESS MAYBE I'LL SEE YOU AT SCHOOL TOMORROW?

FOR SURE!

OKAY! THANKS FOR THE SODA, ROSIE.

YEAH, NO PROBLEM, BLAIR!

Dad's Old teAm

1986 WiN!

RoSie & MoM

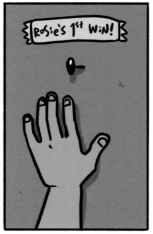

RoSie's 1st WiN!

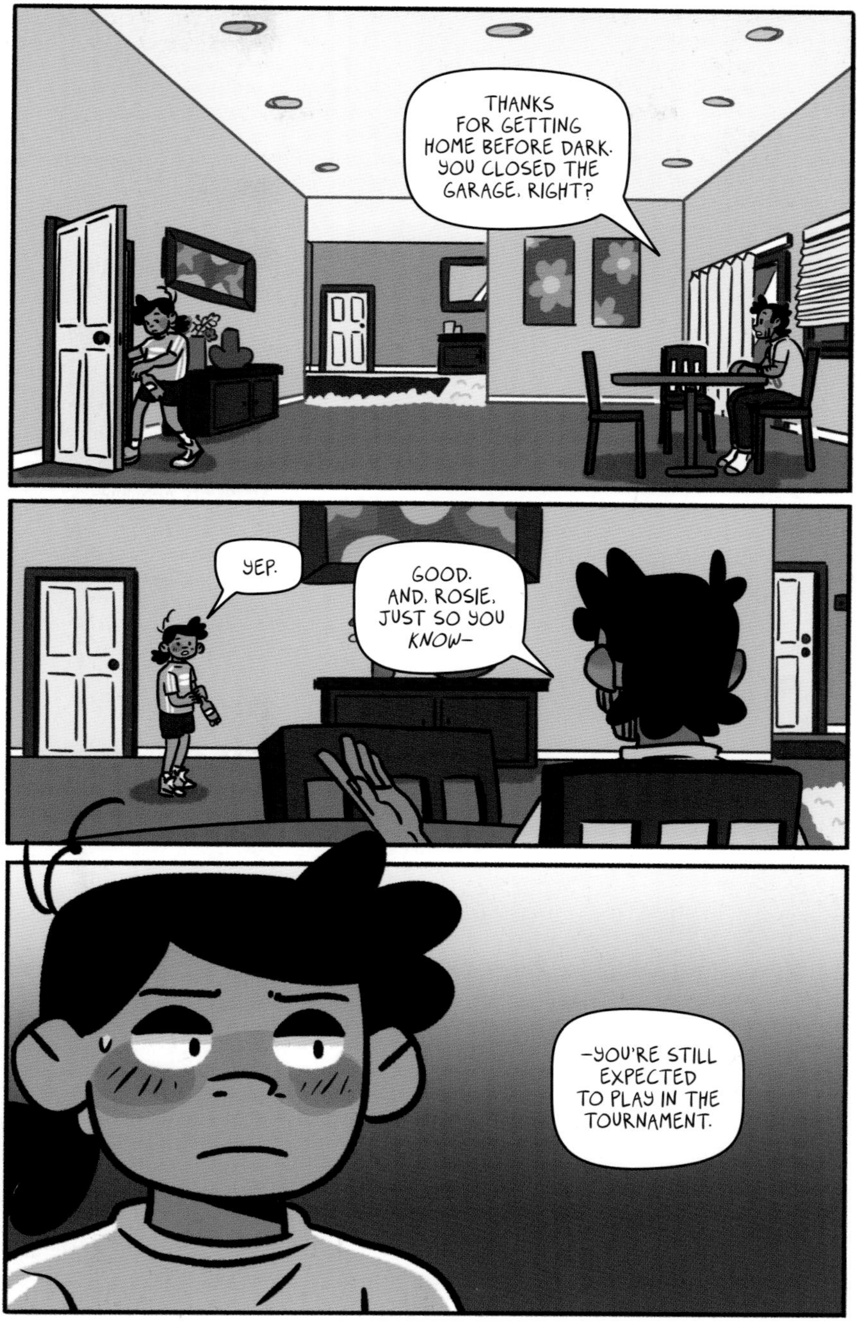
THANKS FOR GETTING HOME BEFORE DARK. YOU CLOSED THE GARAGE, RIGHT?
YEP.
GOOD. AND, ROSIE, JUST SO YOU *KNOW*–
–YOU'RE STILL EXPECTED TO PLAY IN THE TOURNAMENT.

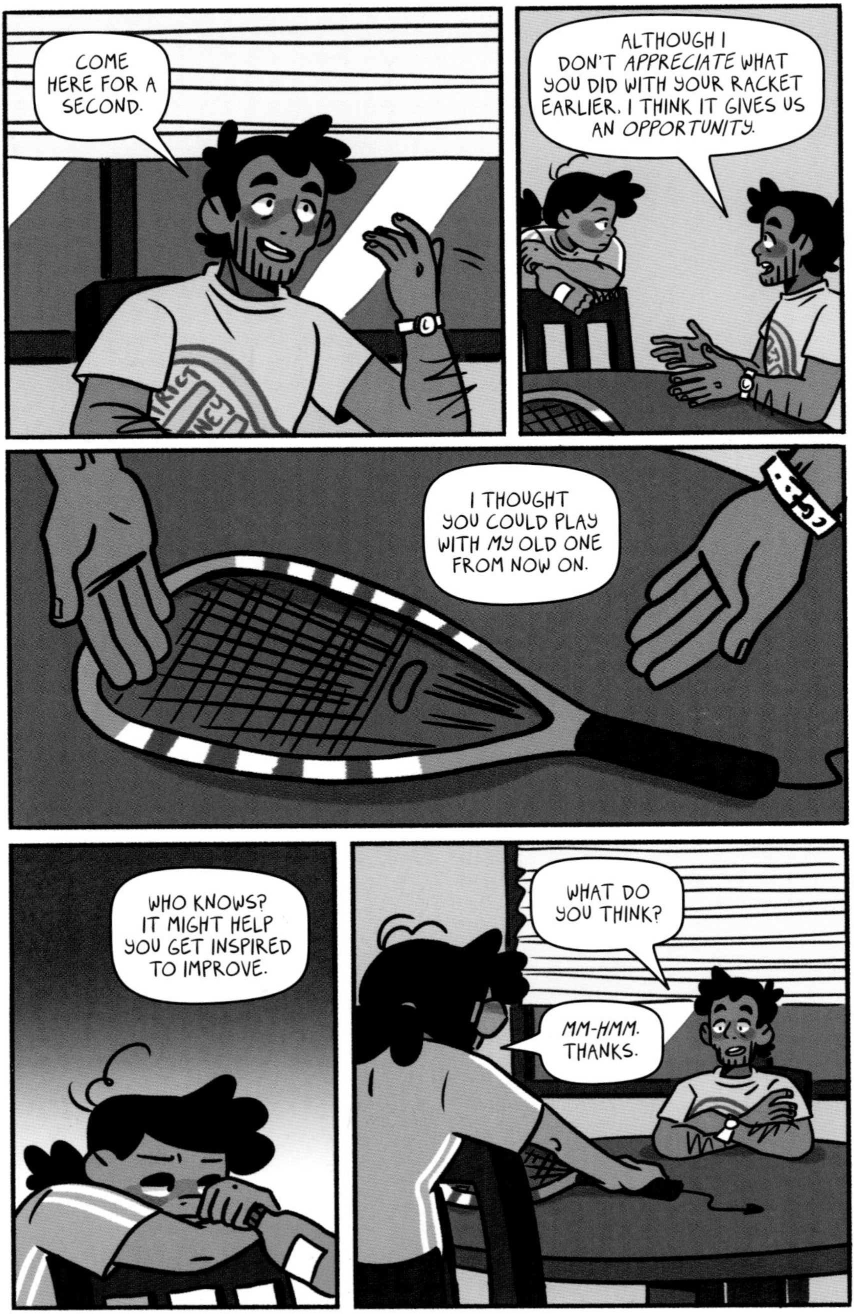
COME HERE FOR A SECOND.
ALTHOUGH I DON'T *APPRECIATE* WHAT YOU DID WITH YOUR RACKET EARLIER, I THINK IT GIVES US AN *OPPORTUNITY*.
I THOUGHT YOU COULD PLAY WITH *MY* OLD ONE FROM NOW ON.
WHO KNOWS? IT MIGHT HELP YOU GET INSPIRED TO IMPROVE.
WHAT DO YOU THINK?
MM-HMM. THANKS.

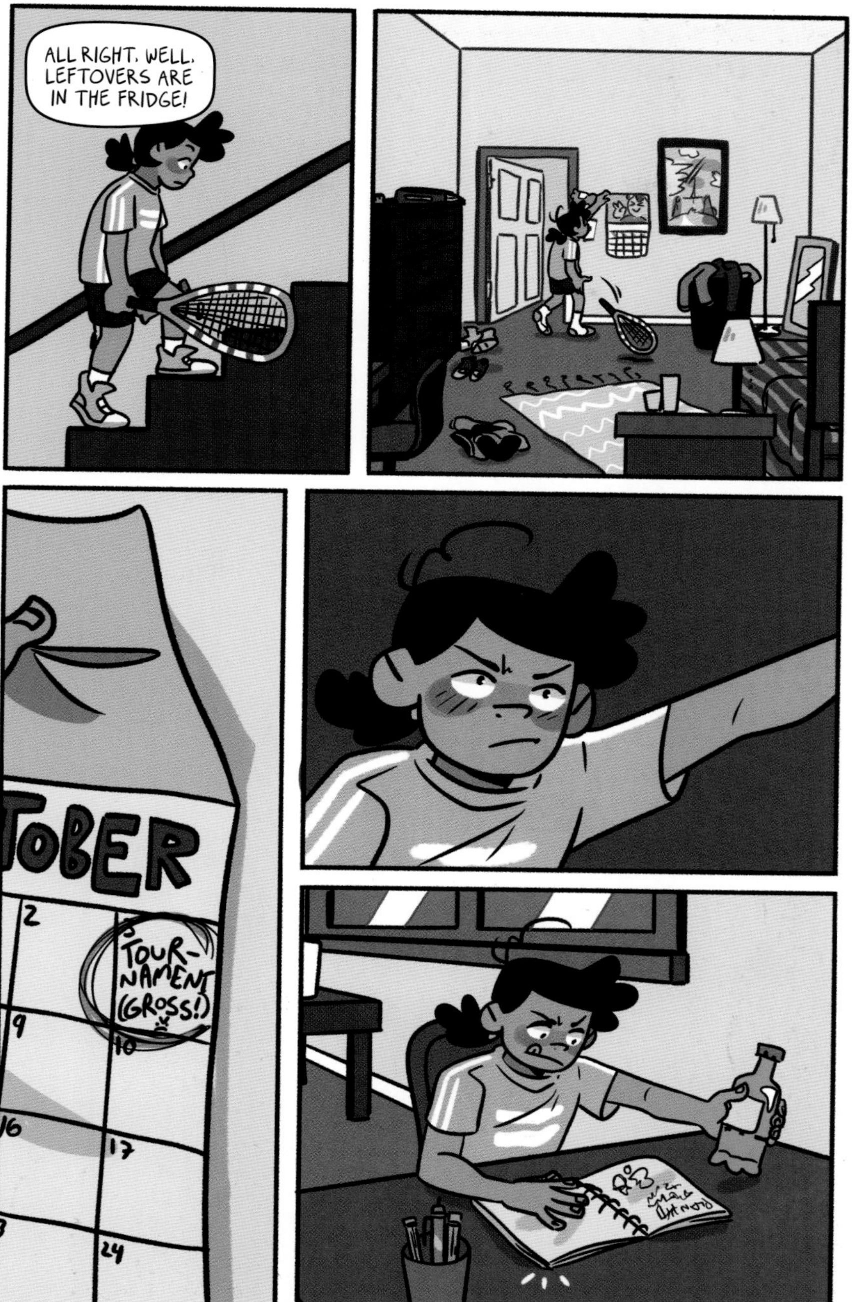
ALL RIGHT. WELL. LEFTOVERS ARE IN THE FRIDGE!
TOBER
2
TOUR-NAMENT (GROSS!)
9
10
16
17
24

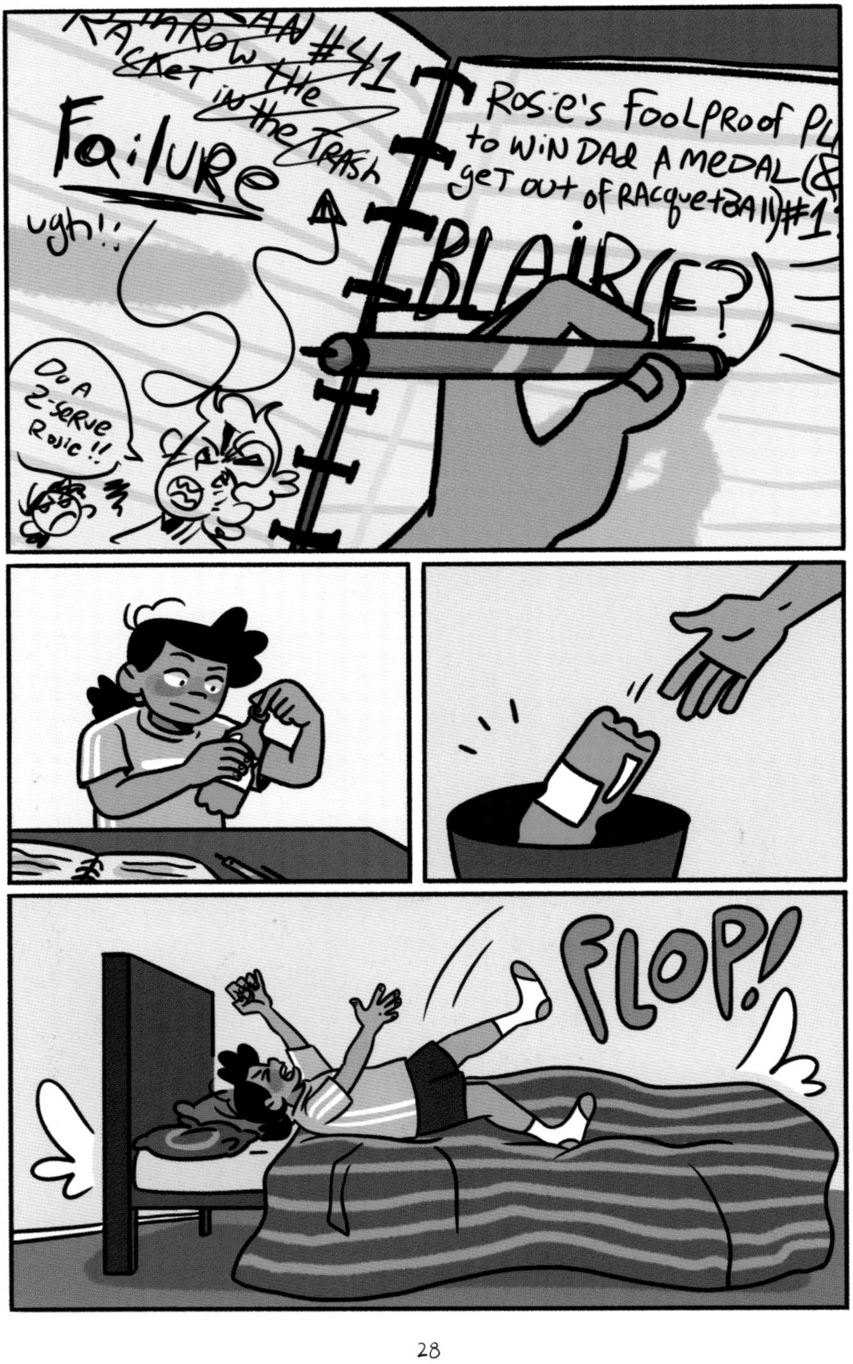

Failure
ugh!!
Do A Z-serve Rosie!!
Rosie's FOOLPROOF PL
to WIN DAD A MEDAL (&
get out of RACQUETBALL) #1
BLAIR(E?)
FLOP!

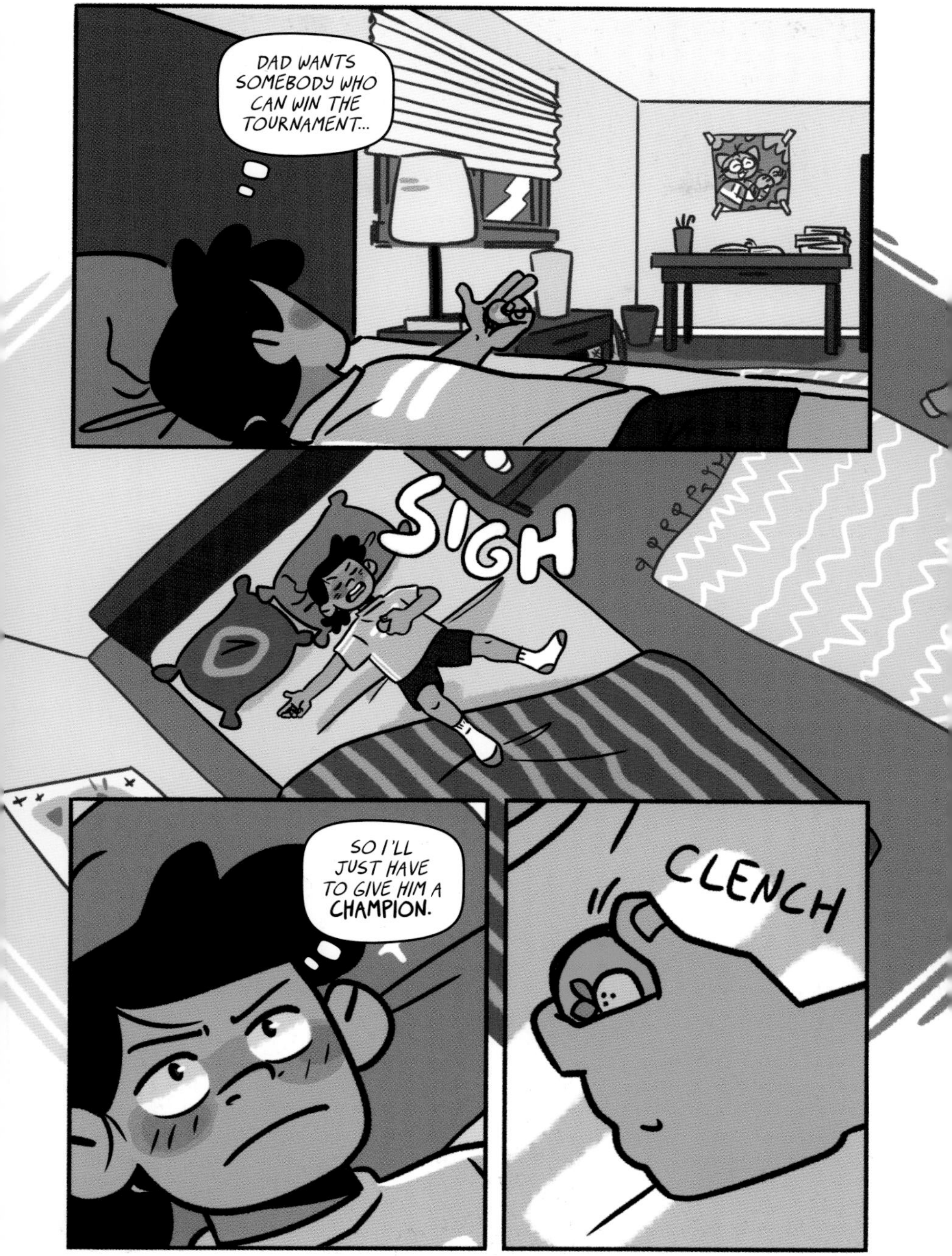
DAD WANTS SOMEBODY WHO CAN WIN THE TOURNAMENT...
SIGH
SO I'LL JUST HAVE TO GIVE HIM A CHAMPION.
CLENCH

CHAPTER 2

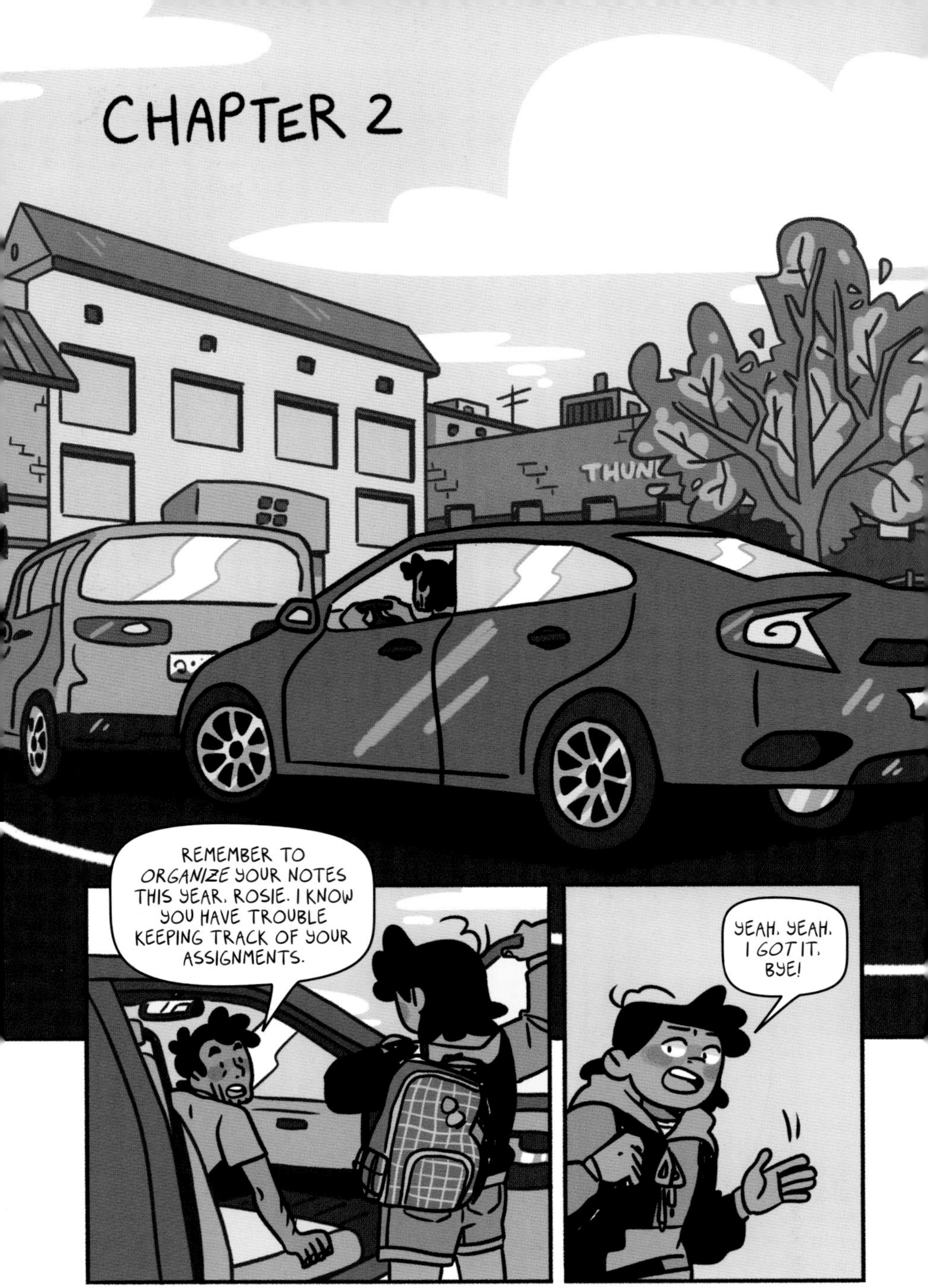
REMEMBER TO *ORGANIZE* YOUR NOTES THIS YEAR, ROSIE. I KNOW YOU HAVE TROUBLE KEEPING TRACK OF YOUR ASSIGNMENTS.
YEAH, YEAH, I *GOT* IT. BYE!

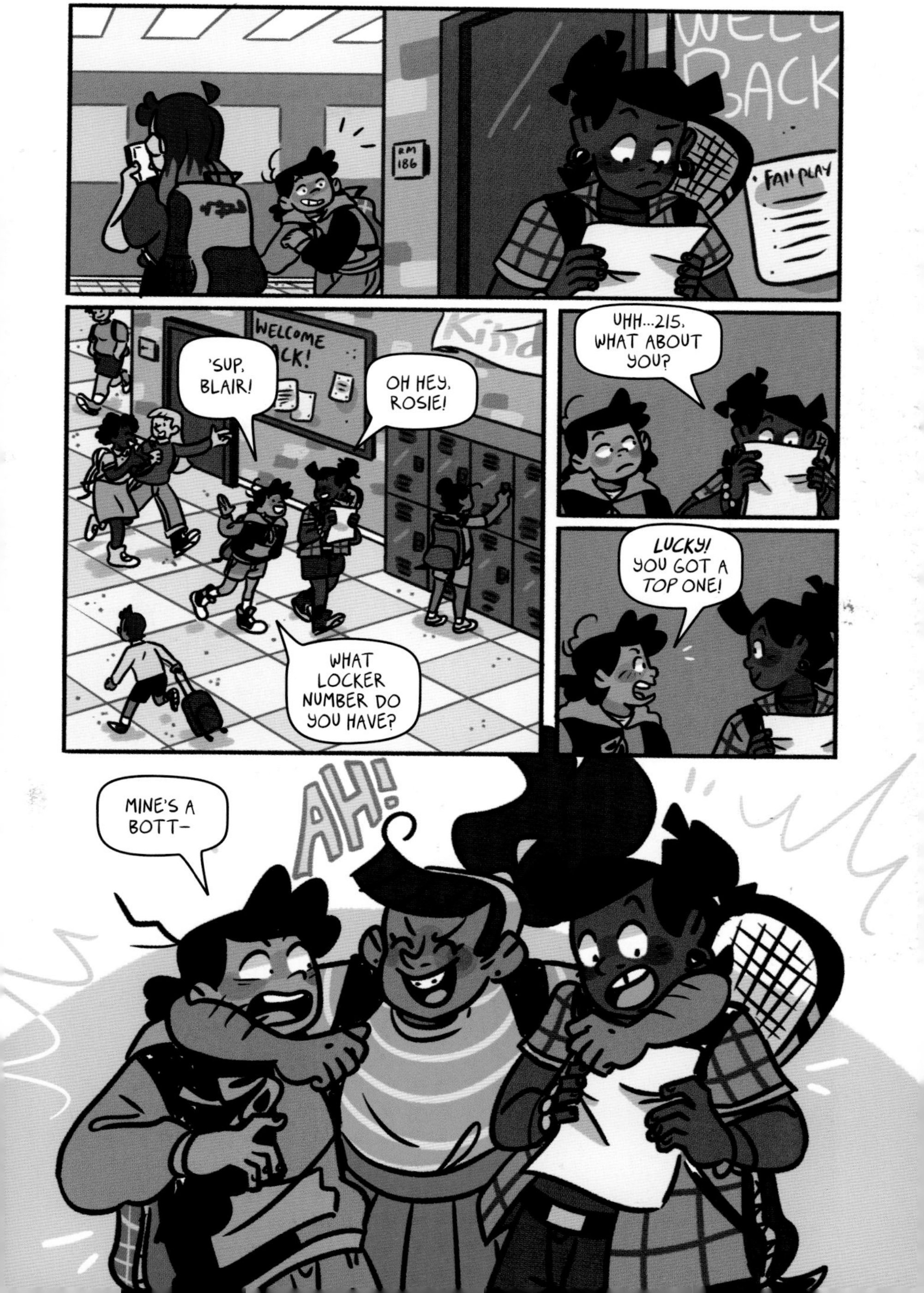

RM 186
WELL
BACK
FAIR PLAY
WELCOME BACK!
'SUP, BLAIR!
OH HEY, ROSIE!
WHAT LOCKER NUMBER DO YOU HAVE?
UHH...215. WHAT ABOUT YOU?
LUCKY! YOU GOT A TOP ONE!
MINE'S A BOTT–
AH!

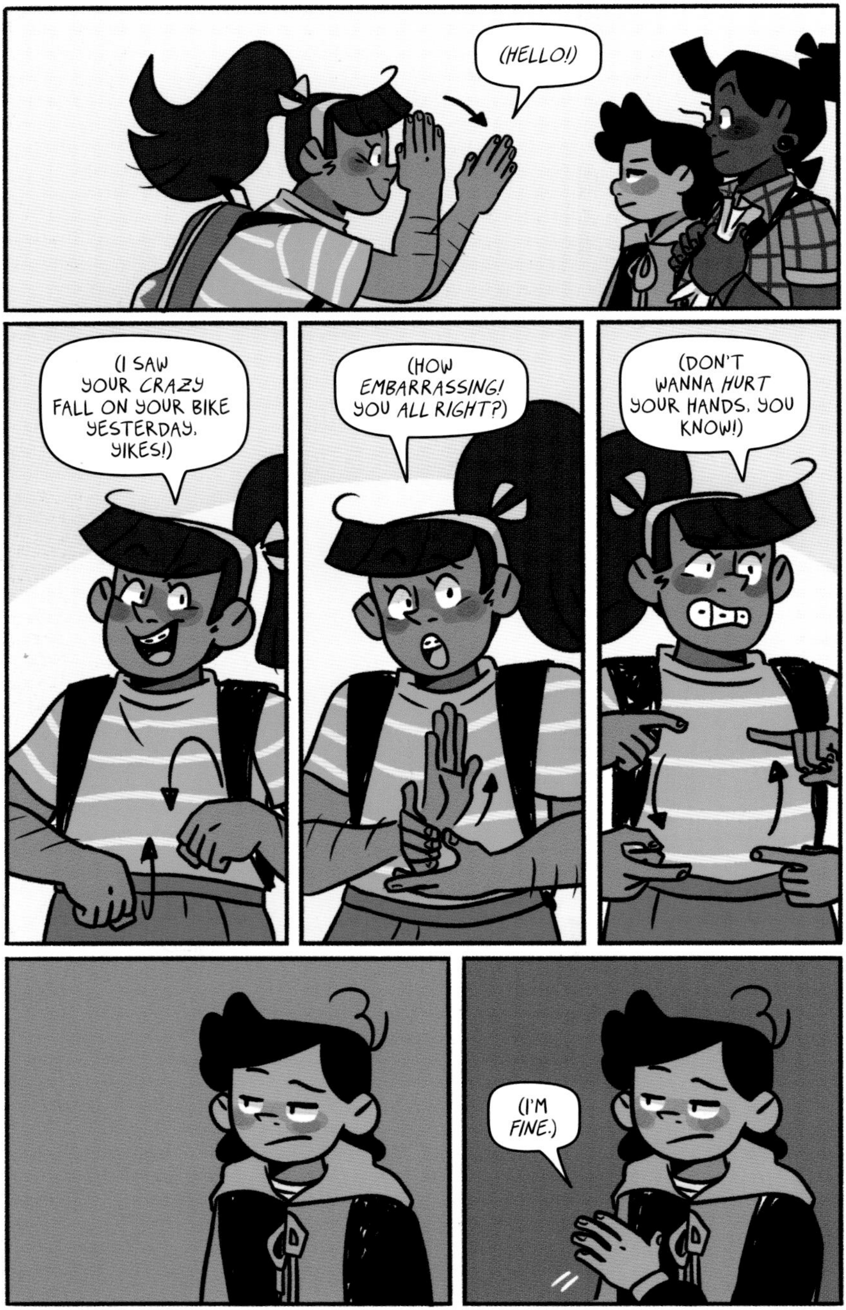
(HELLO!)
(I SAW YOUR CRAZY FALL ON YOUR BIKE YESTERDAY. YIKES!)
(HOW EMBARRASSING! YOU ALL RIGHT?)
(DON'T WANNA HURT YOUR HANDS, YOU KNOW!)
(I'M FINE.)

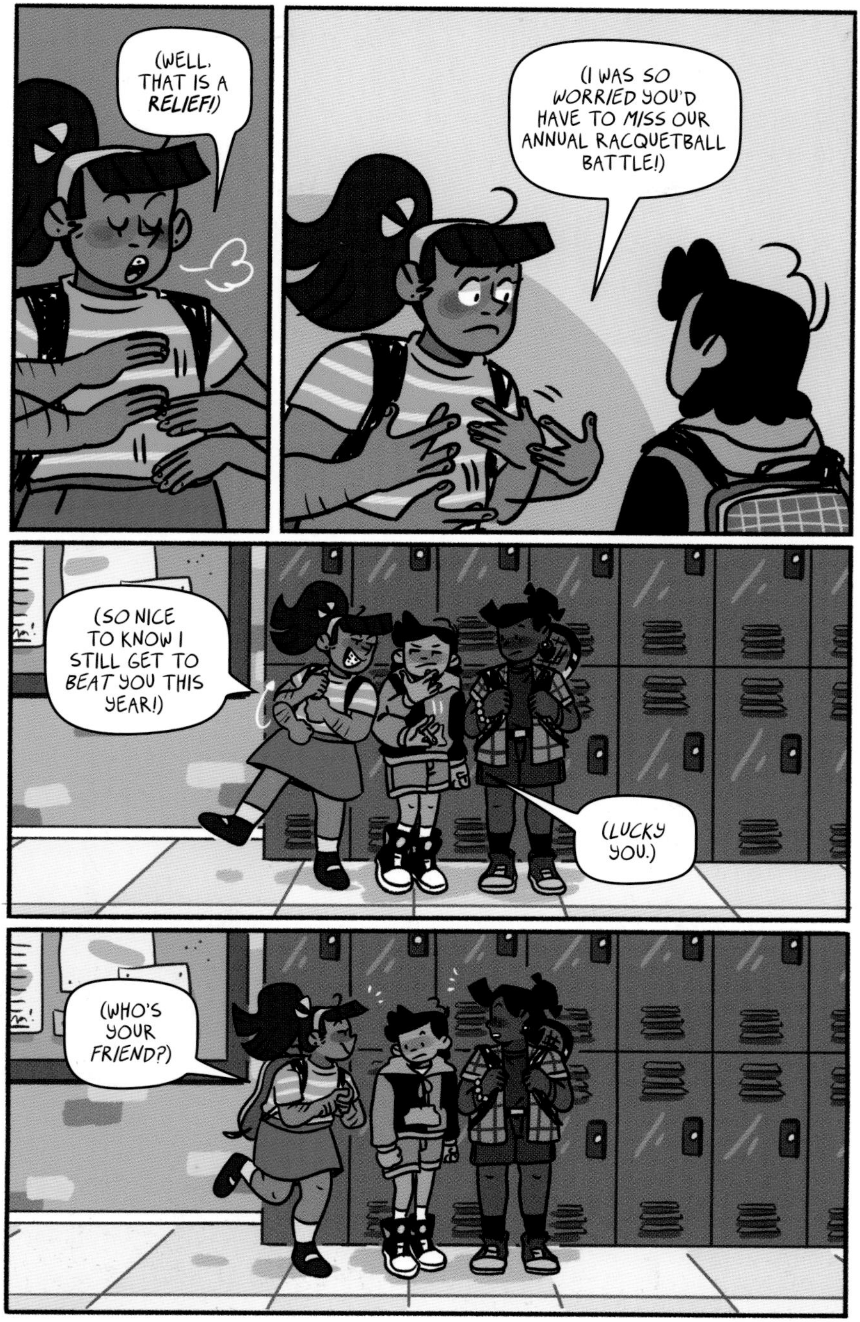
(WELL, THAT IS A RELIEF!)
(I WAS SO WORRIED YOU'D HAVE TO MISS OUR ANNUAL RACQUETBALL BATTLE!)
(SO NICE TO KNOW I STILL GET TO BEAT YOU THIS YEAR!)
(LUCKY YOU.)
(WHO'S YOUR FRIEND?)

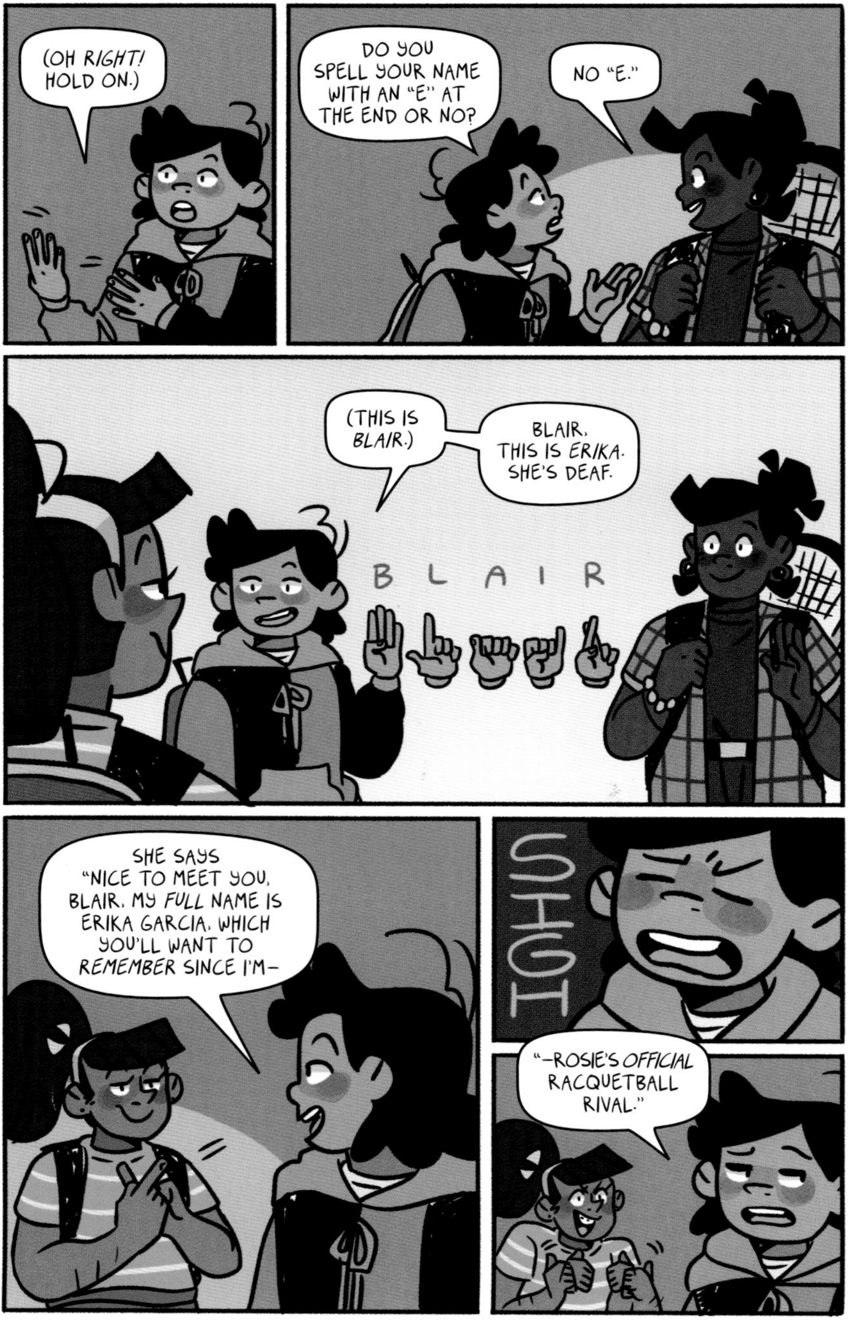

(OH RIGHT! HOLD ON.)
DO YOU SPELL YOUR NAME WITH AN "E" AT THE END OR NO?
NO "E."
(THIS IS BLAIR.)
BLAIR, THIS IS ERIKA. SHE'S DEAF.
B L A I R
SHE SAYS "NICE TO MEET YOU, BLAIR. MY FULL NAME IS ERIKA GARCIA, WHICH YOU'LL WANT TO REMEMBER SINCE I'M—
SIGH
"—ROSIE'S OFFICIAL RACQUETBALL RIVAL."

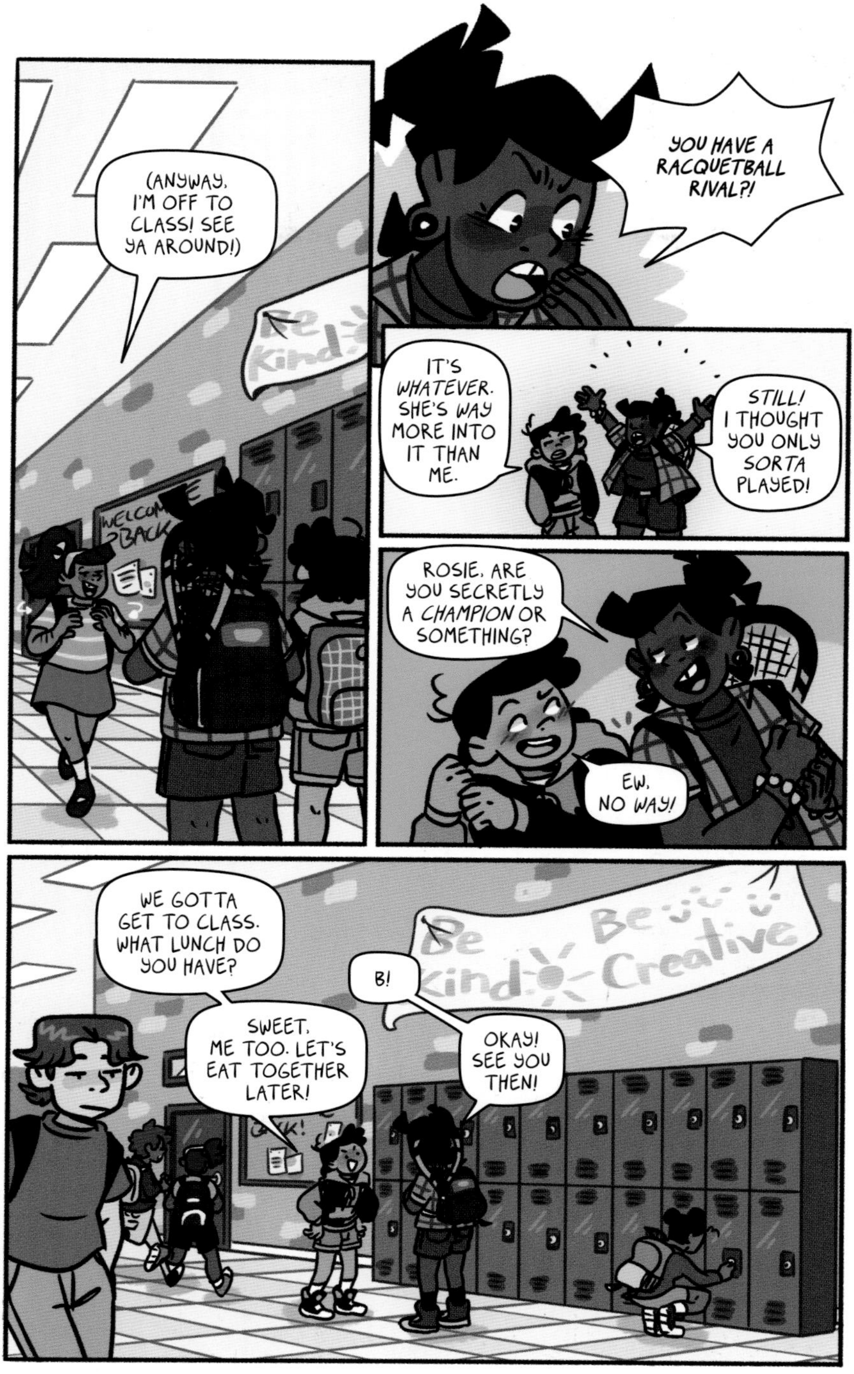
(ANYWAY, I'M OFF TO CLASS! SEE YA AROUND!)
Be Kind
WELCOME BACK
YOU HAVE A RACQUETBALL RIVAL?!
IT'S WHATEVER. SHE'S WAY MORE INTO IT THAN ME.
STILL! I THOUGHT YOU ONLY SORTA PLAYED!
ROSIE, ARE YOU SECRETLY A CHAMPION OR SOMETHING?
EW, NO WAY!
WE GOTTA GET TO CLASS. WHAT LUNCH DO YOU HAVE?
B!
SWEET, ME TOO. LET'S EAT TOGETHER LATER!
OKAY! SEE YOU THEN!
Be Kind Be Creative

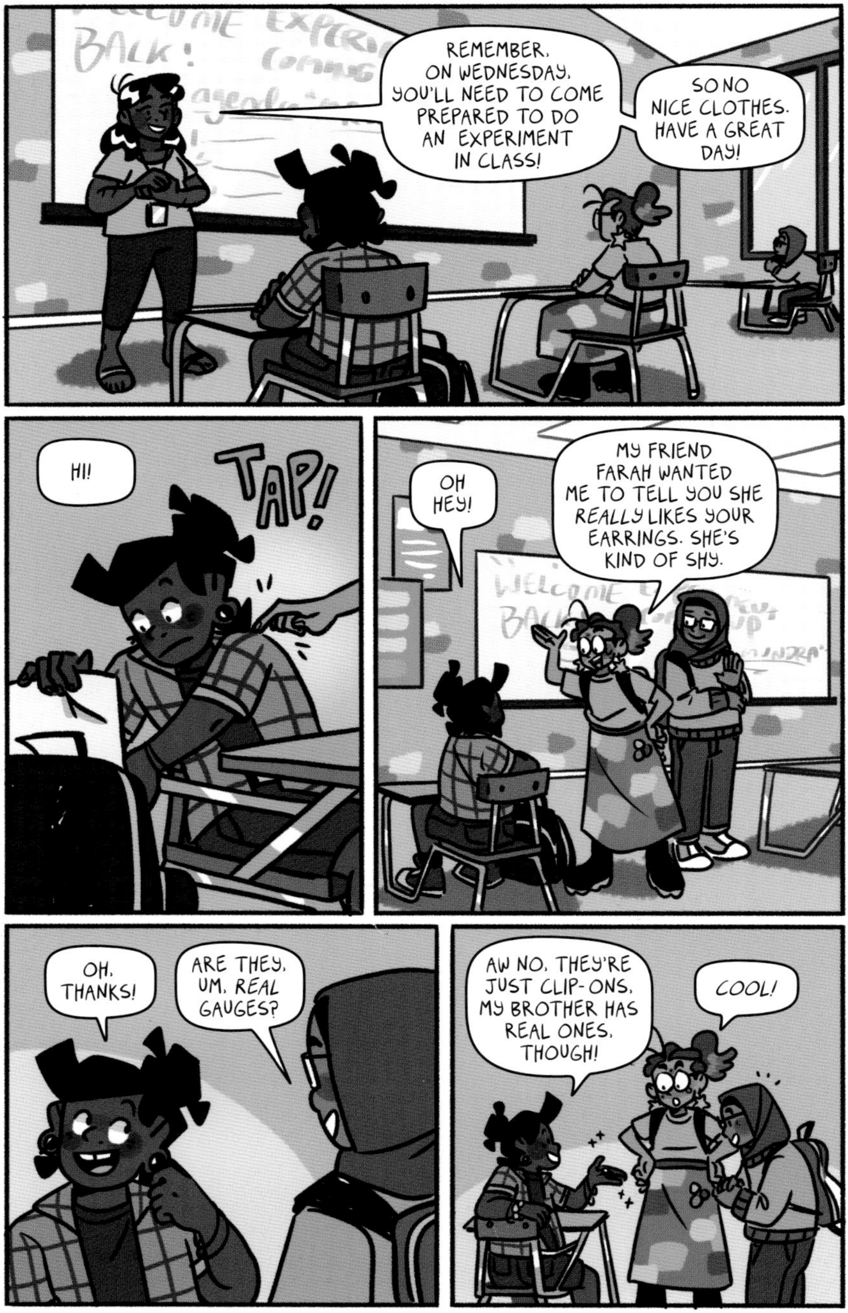
REMEMBER, ON WEDNESDAY, YOU'LL NEED TO COME PREPARED TO DO AN EXPERIMENT IN CLASS!
SO NO NICE CLOTHES. HAVE A GREAT DAY!
HI!
TAP!
OH HEY!
MY FRIEND FARAH WANTED ME TO TELL YOU SHE REALLY LIKES YOUR EARRINGS. SHE'S KIND OF SHY.
OH, THANKS!
ARE THEY, UM, REAL GAUGES?
AW NO, THEY'RE JUST CLIP-ONS, MY BROTHER HAS REAL ONES, THOUGH!
COOL!

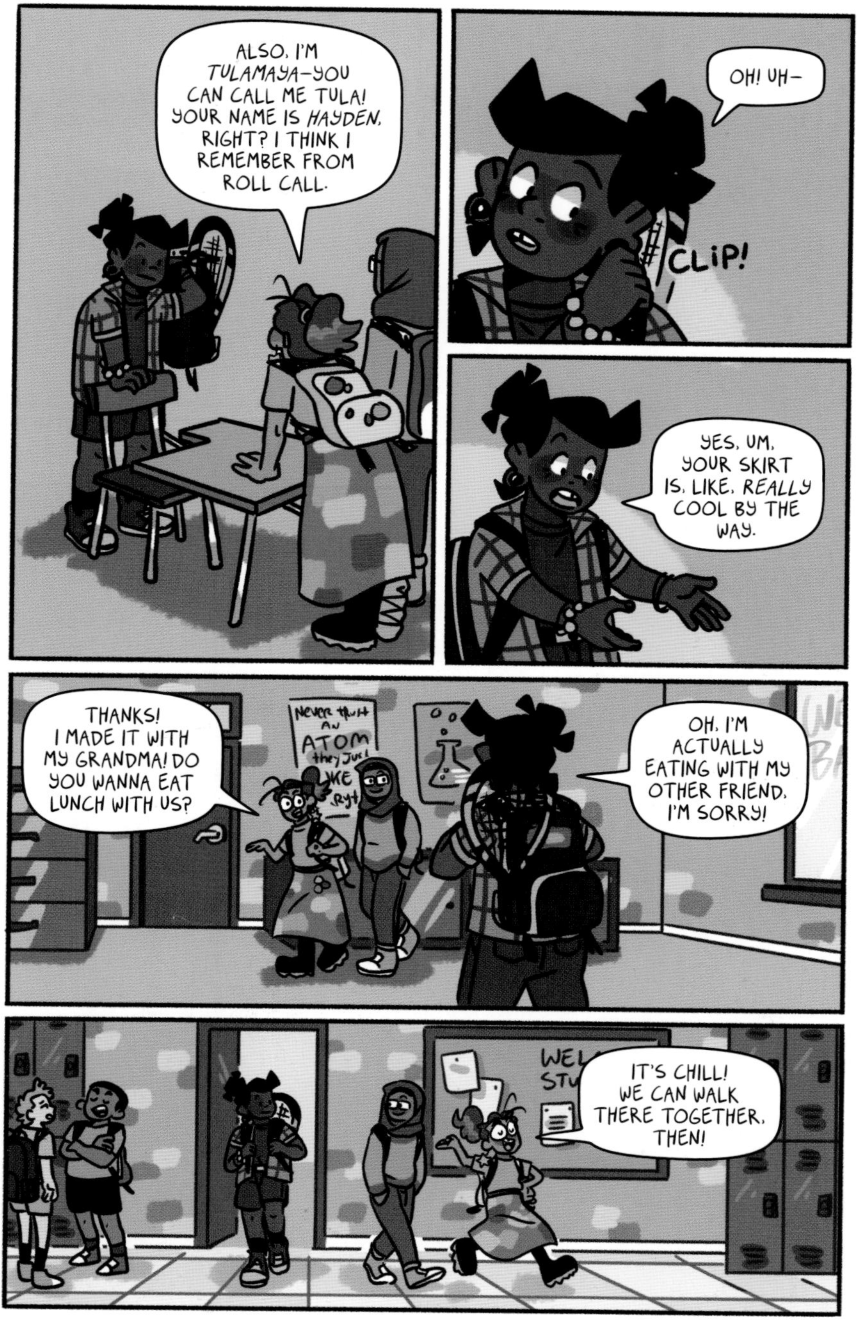
ALSO, I'M TULAMAYA—YOU CAN CALL ME TULA! YOUR NAME IS HAYDEN, RIGHT? I THINK I REMEMBER FROM ROLL CALL.
OH! UH—
CLIP!
YES, UM, YOUR SKIRT IS, LIKE, REALLY COOL BY THE WAY.
THANKS! I MADE IT WITH MY GRANDMA! DO YOU WANNA EAT LUNCH WITH US?
OH, I'M ACTUALLY EATING WITH MY OTHER FRIEND, I'M SORRY!
IT'S CHILL! WE CAN WALK THERE TOGETHER, THEN!

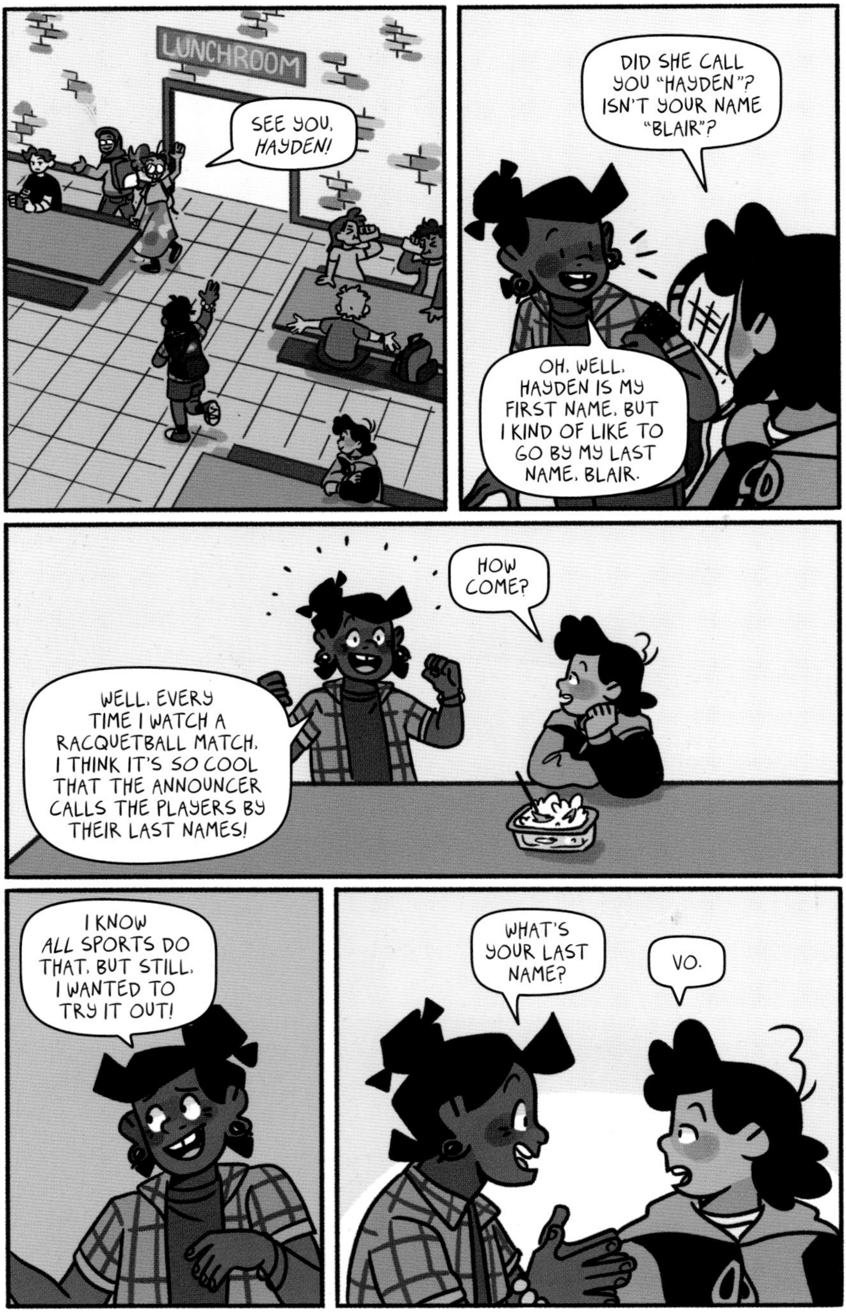
LUNCHROOM
SEE YOU, HAYDEN!
DID SHE CALL YOU "HAYDEN"? ISN'T YOUR NAME "BLAIR"?
OH. WELL. HAYDEN IS MY FIRST NAME, BUT I KIND OF LIKE TO GO BY MY LAST NAME, BLAIR.
HOW COME?
WELL, EVERY TIME I WATCH A RACQUETBALL MATCH, I THINK IT'S SO COOL THAT THE ANNOUNCER CALLS THE PLAYERS BY THEIR LAST NAMES!
I KNOW ALL SPORTS DO THAT, BUT STILL, I WANTED TO TRY IT OUT!
WHAT'S YOUR LAST NAME?
VO.

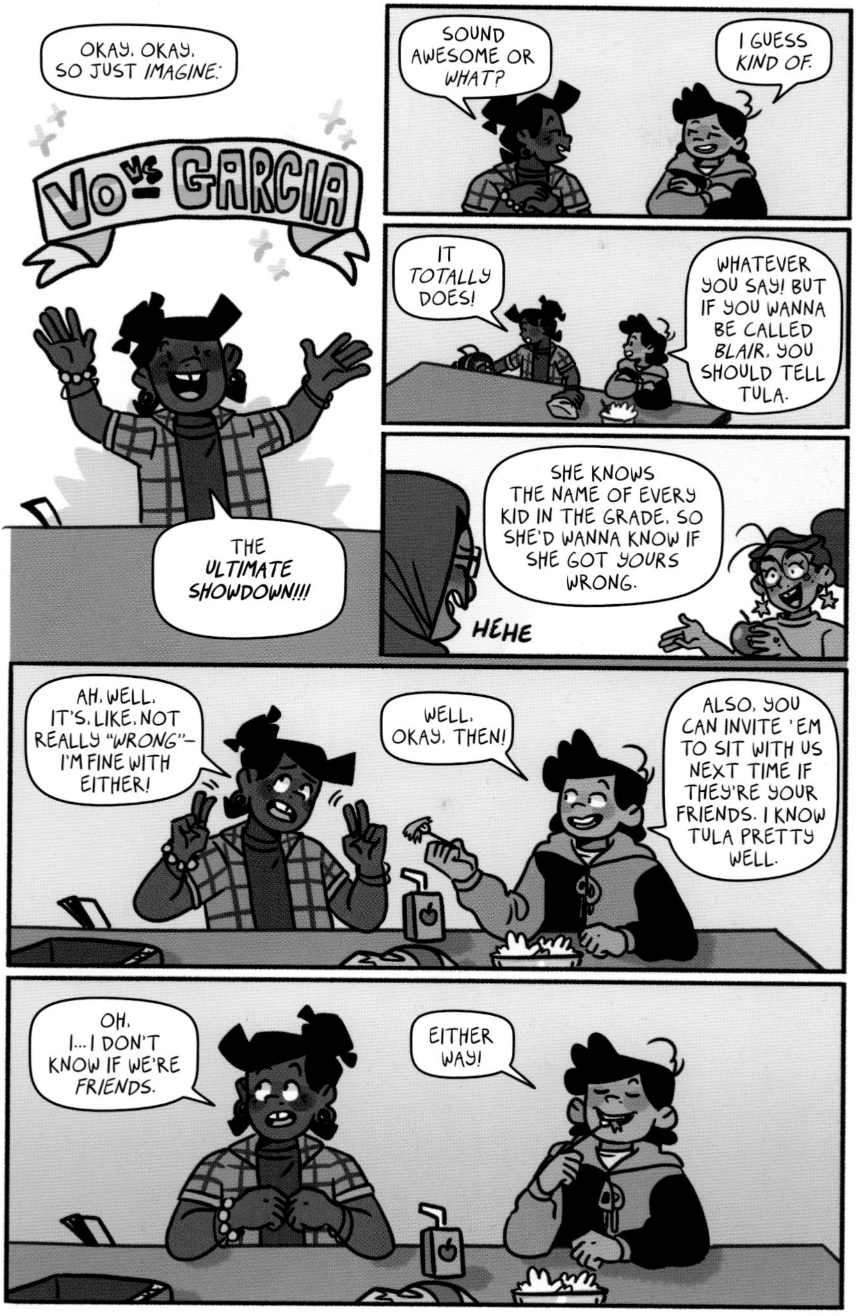
OKAY, OKAY, SO JUST *IMAGINE*:
VO VS GARCIA
THE **ULTIMATE SHOWDOWN!!!**
SOUND AWESOME OR *WHAT*?
I GUESS *KIND OF*.
IT *TOTALLY* DOES!
WHATEVER YOU SAY! BUT IF YOU WANNA BE CALLED *BLAIR*, YOU SHOULD TELL TULA.
SHE KNOWS THE NAME OF EVERY KID IN THE GRADE, SO SHE'D WANNA KNOW IF SHE GOT *YOURS* WRONG.
HEHE
AH, WELL, IT'S, LIKE, NOT REALLY "*WRONG*"— I'M FINE WITH EITHER!
WELL, OKAY, THEN!
ALSO, YOU CAN INVITE 'EM TO SIT WITH US NEXT TIME IF THEY'RE YOUR FRIENDS. I KNOW TULA PRETTY WELL.
OH, I... I DON'T KNOW IF WE'RE *FRIENDS*.
EITHER WAY!

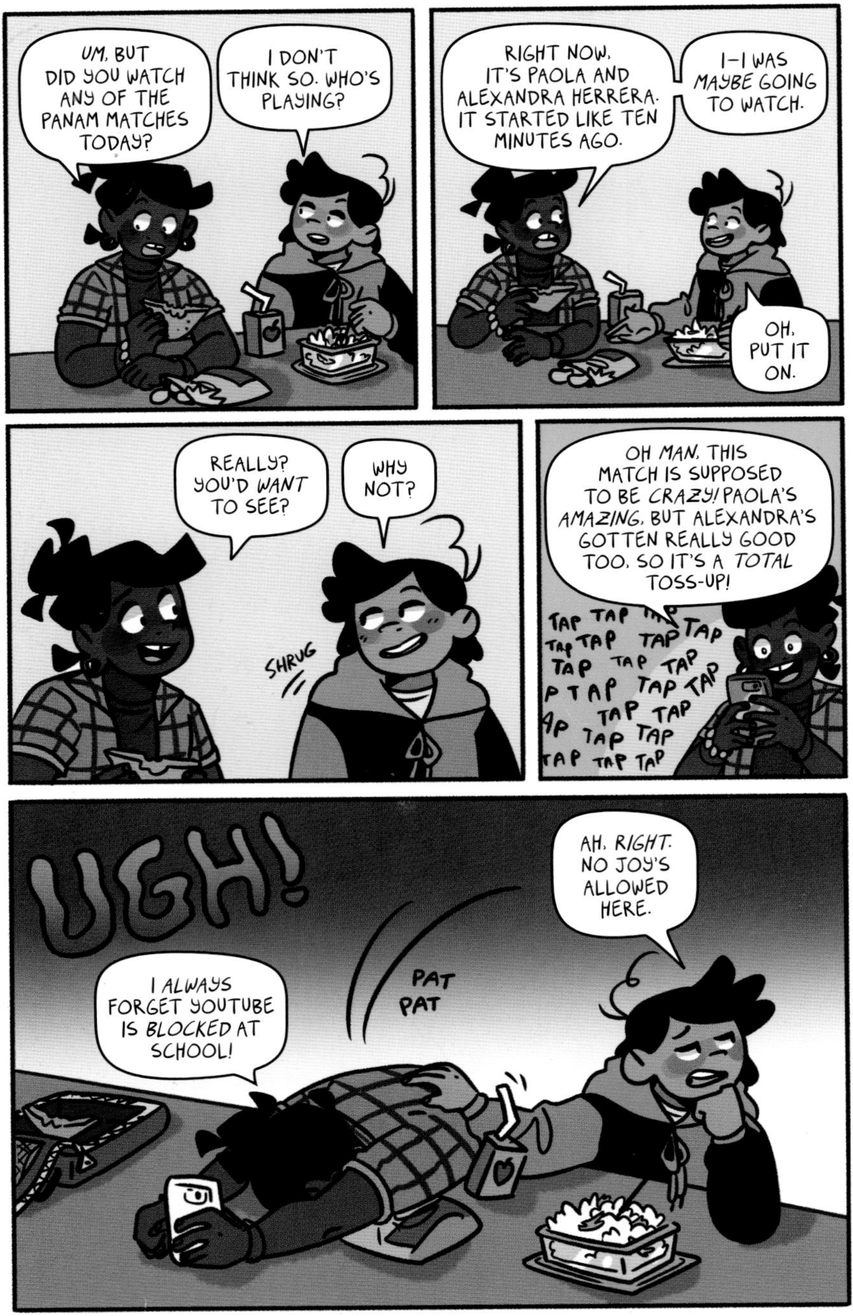
UM, BUT DID YOU WATCH ANY OF THE PANAM MATCHES TODAY?
I DON'T THINK SO. WHO'S PLAYING?
RIGHT NOW, IT'S PAOLA AND ALEXANDRA HERRERA. IT STARTED LIKE TEN MINUTES AGO.
I-I WAS MAYBE GOING TO WATCH.
OH, PUT IT ON.
REALLY? YOU'D WANT TO SEE?
WHY NOT?
SHRUG
OH MAN, THIS MATCH IS SUPPOSED TO BE CRAZY! PAOLA'S AMAZING, BUT ALEXANDRA'S GOTTEN REALLY GOOD TOO, SO IT'S A TOTAL TOSS-UP!
TAP TAP TAP TAP
UGH!
I ALWAYS FORGET YOUTUBE IS BLOCKED AT SCHOOL!
PAT PAT
AH, RIGHT. NO JOY'S ALLOWED HERE.

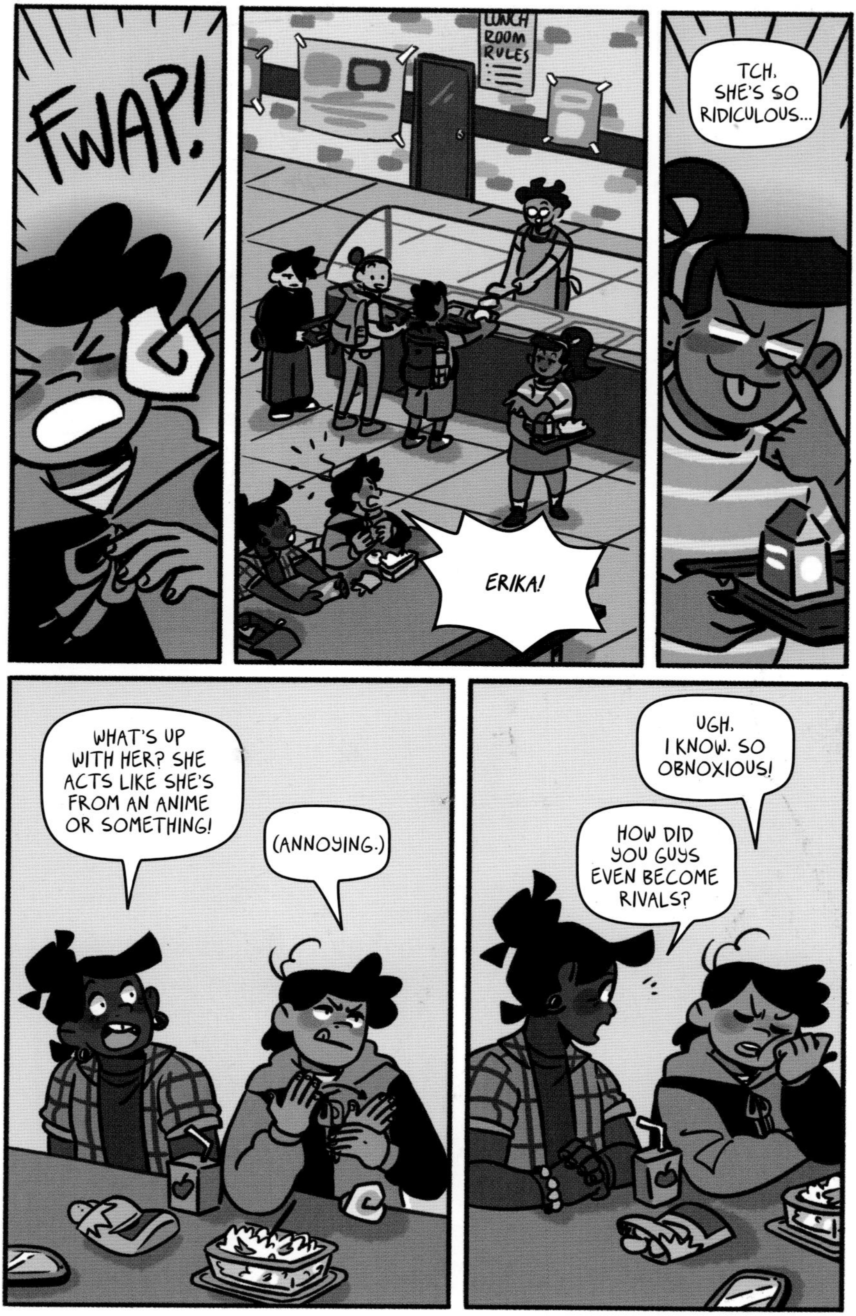
FWAP!
LUNCH ROOM RULES
ERIKA!
TCH. SHE'S SO RIDICULOUS...
WHAT'S UP WITH HER? SHE ACTS LIKE SHE'S FROM AN ANIME OR SOMETHING!
(ANNOYING.)
UGH. I KNOW. SO OBNOXIOUS!
HOW DID YOU GUYS EVEN BECOME RIVALS?

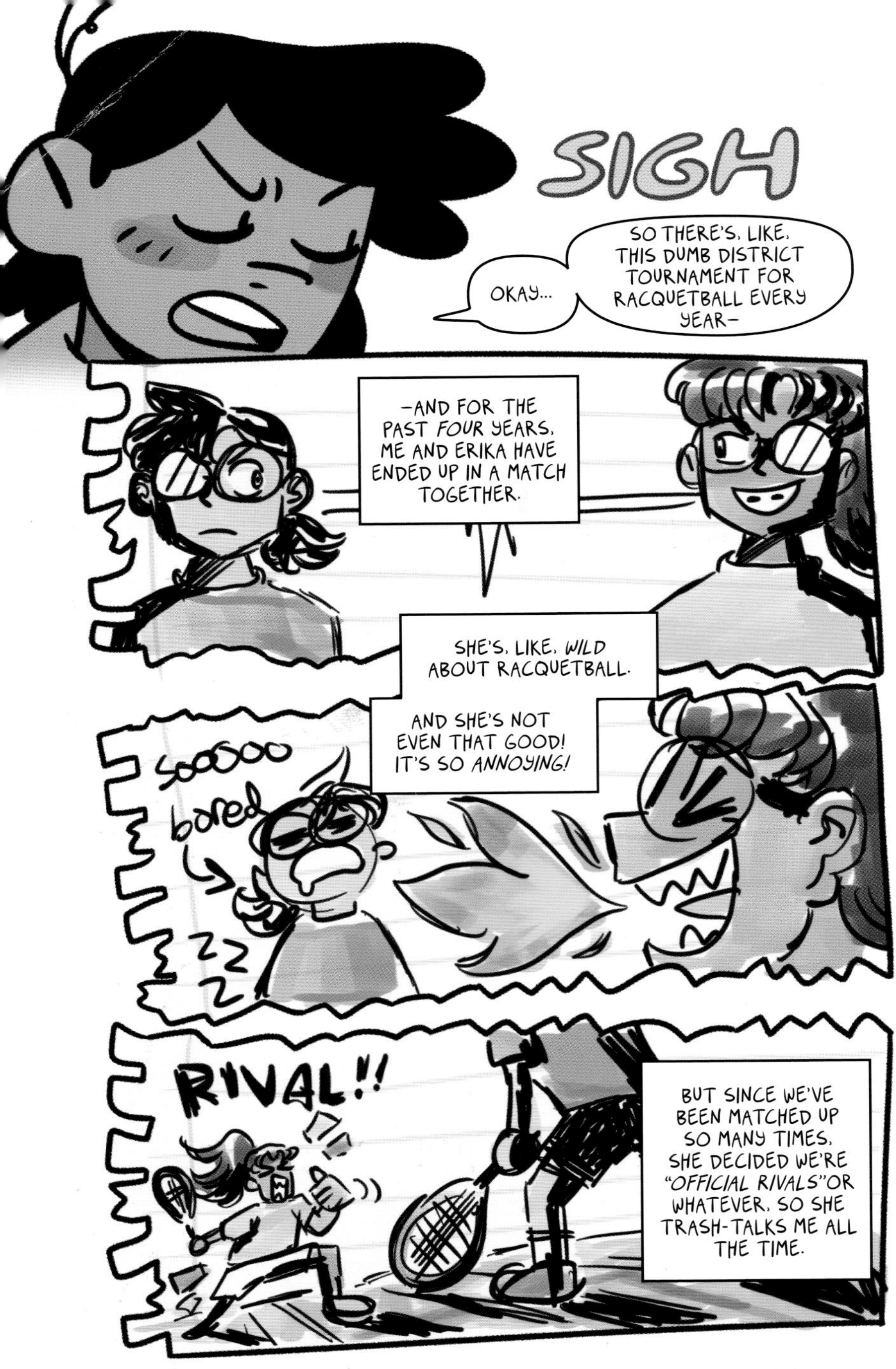
SIGH
OKAY...
SO THERE'S, LIKE, THIS DUMB DISTRICT TOURNAMENT FOR RACQUETBALL EVERY YEAR—
—AND FOR THE PAST *FOUR* YEARS, ME AND ERIKA HAVE ENDED UP IN A MATCH TOGETHER.
SHE'S, LIKE, *WILD* ABOUT RACQUETBALL.
AND SHE'S NOT EVEN THAT GOOD! IT'S SO *ANNOYING!*
soooo bored
Z Z Z
RIVAL!!
BUT SINCE WE'VE BEEN MATCHED UP SO MANY TIMES, SHE DECIDED WE'RE "*OFFICIAL RIVALS*" OR WHATEVER, SO SHE TRASH-TALKS ME ALL THE TIME.

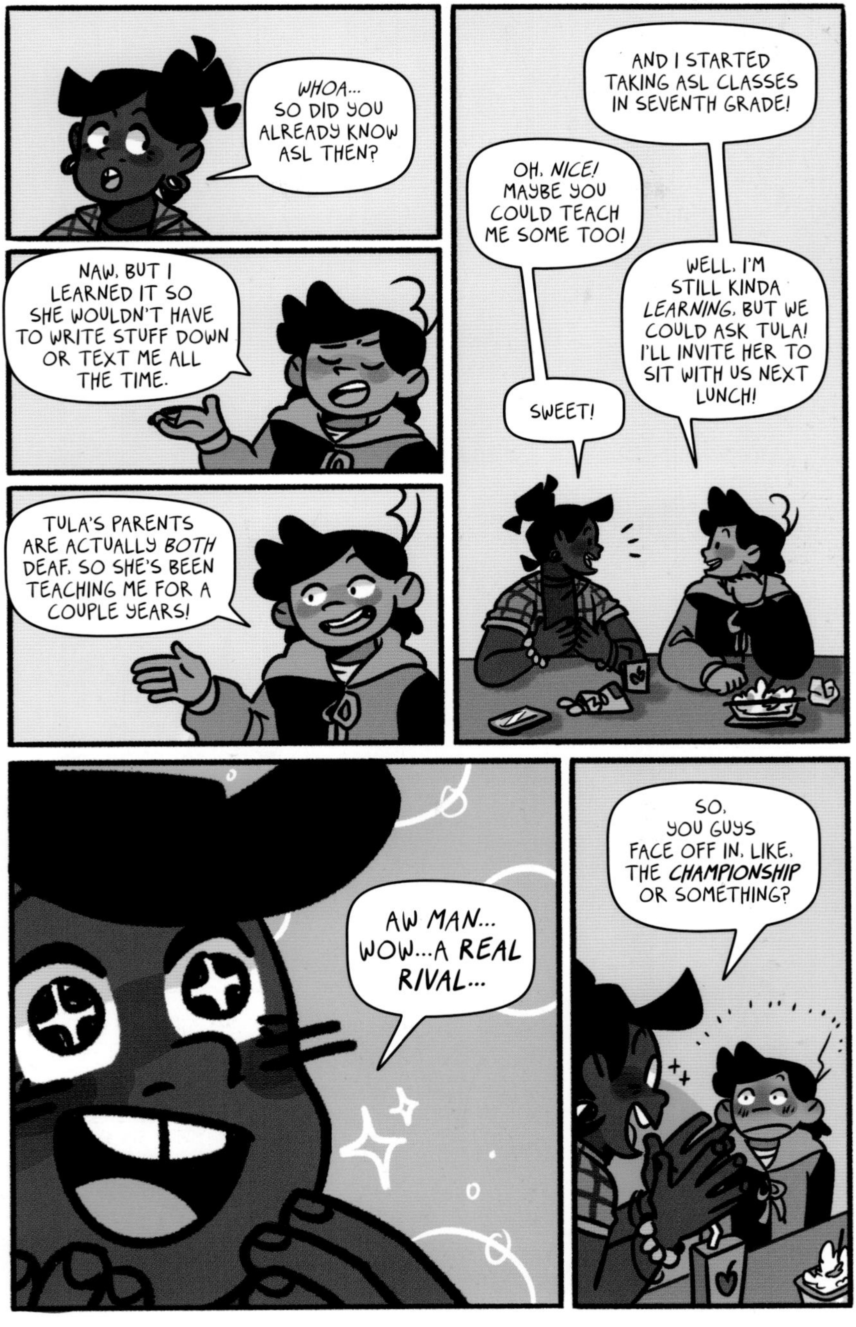
WHOA... SO DID YOU ALREADY KNOW ASL THEN?
NAW, BUT I LEARNED IT SO SHE WOULDN'T HAVE TO WRITE STUFF DOWN OR TEXT ME ALL THE TIME.
TULA'S PARENTS ARE ACTUALLY BOTH DEAF, SO SHE'S BEEN TEACHING ME FOR A COUPLE YEARS!
AND I STARTED TAKING ASL CLASSES IN SEVENTH GRADE!
OH, NICE! MAYBE YOU COULD TEACH ME SOME TOO!
WELL, I'M STILL KINDA LEARNING, BUT WE COULD ASK TULA! I'LL INVITE HER TO SIT WITH US NEXT LUNCH!
SWEET!
AW MAN... WOW...A REAL RIVAL...
SO, YOU GUYS FACE OFF IN, LIKE, THE CHAMPIONSHIP OR SOMETHING?

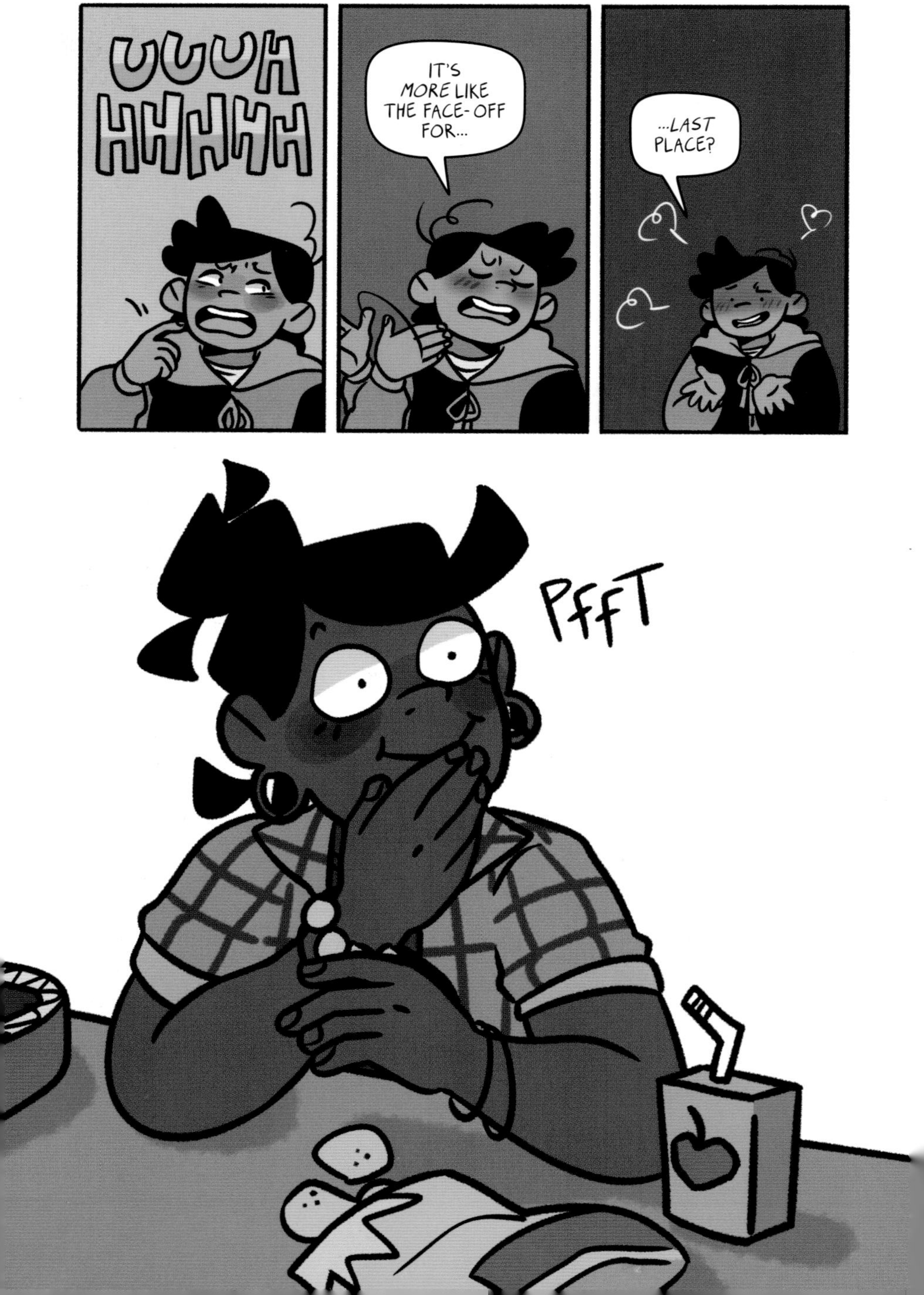
UUUH HHHHH
IT'S MORE LIKE THE FACE-OFF FOR...
...LAST PLACE?
PFFT

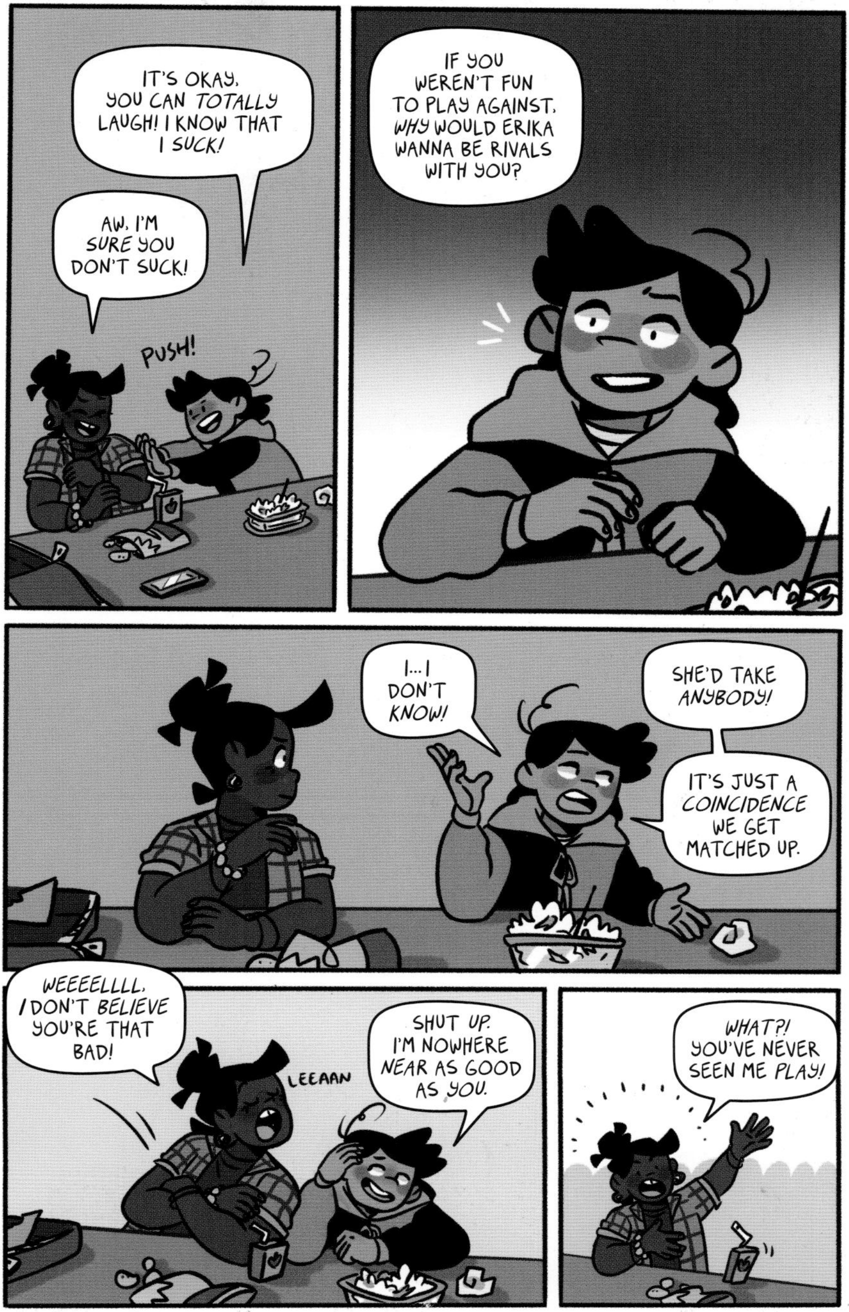
IT'S OKAY. YOU CAN *TOTALLY* LAUGH! I KNOW THAT I *SUCK!*
AW, I'M *SURE* YOU DON'T SUCK!
PUSH!
IF YOU WEREN'T FUN TO PLAY AGAINST, *WHY* WOULD ERIKA WANNA BE RIVALS WITH YOU?
I...I DON'T *KNOW!*
SHE'D TAKE *ANYBODY!*
IT'S JUST A *COINCIDENCE* WE GET MATCHED UP.
WEEEELLLL, I DON'T *BELIEVE* YOU'RE THAT BAD!
LEEAAN
SHUT *UP.* I'M NOWHERE NEAR AS GOOD AS *YOU.*
WHAT?! YOU'VE NEVER SEEN ME *PLAY!*

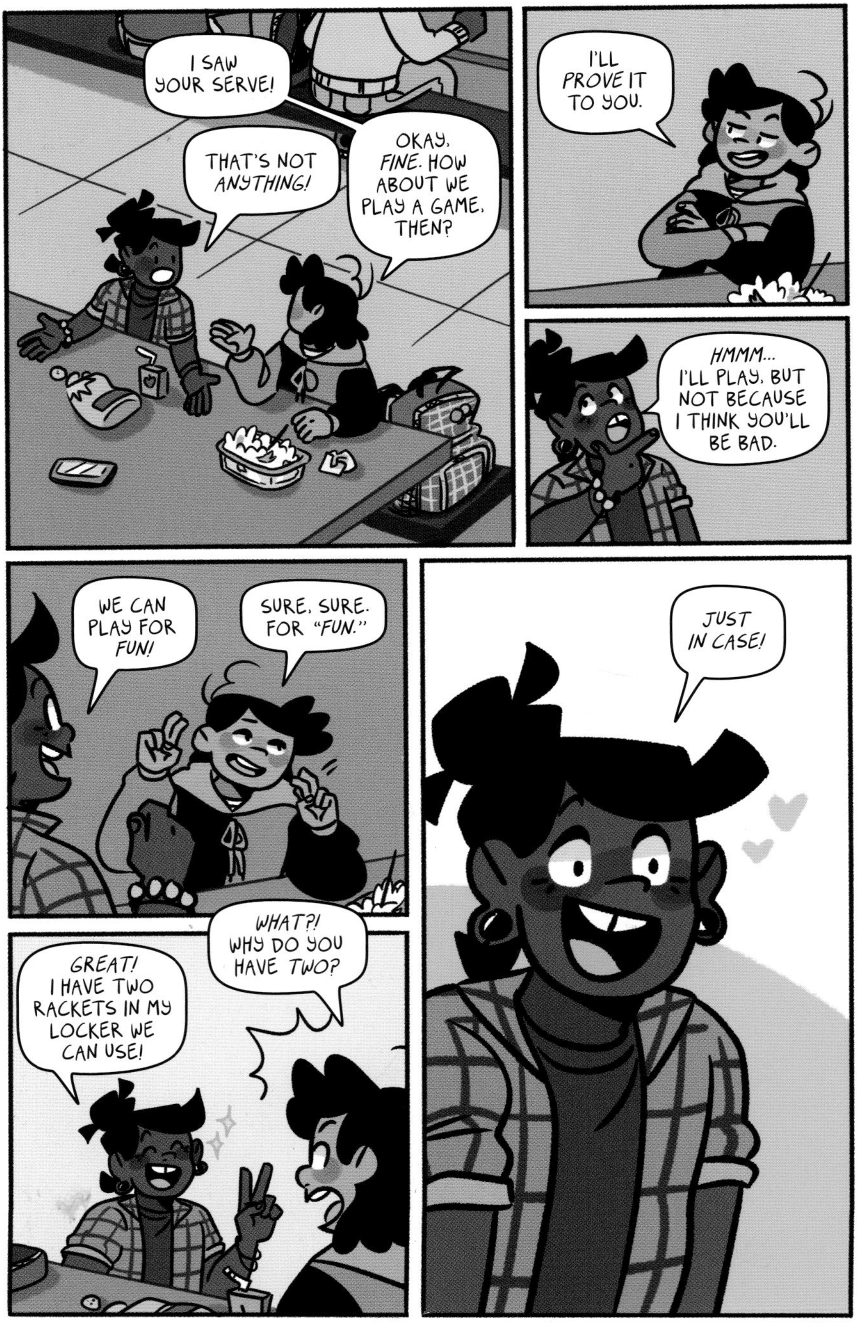
I SAW YOUR SERVE!
THAT'S NOT ANYTHING!
OKAY, FINE. HOW ABOUT WE PLAY A GAME, THEN?
I'LL PROVE IT TO YOU.
HMMM... I'LL PLAY, BUT NOT BECAUSE I THINK YOU'LL BE BAD.
WE CAN PLAY FOR FUN!
SURE, SURE. FOR "FUN."
GREAT! I HAVE TWO RACKETS IN MY LOCKER WE CAN USE!
WHAT?! WHY DO YOU HAVE TWO?
JUST IN CASE!

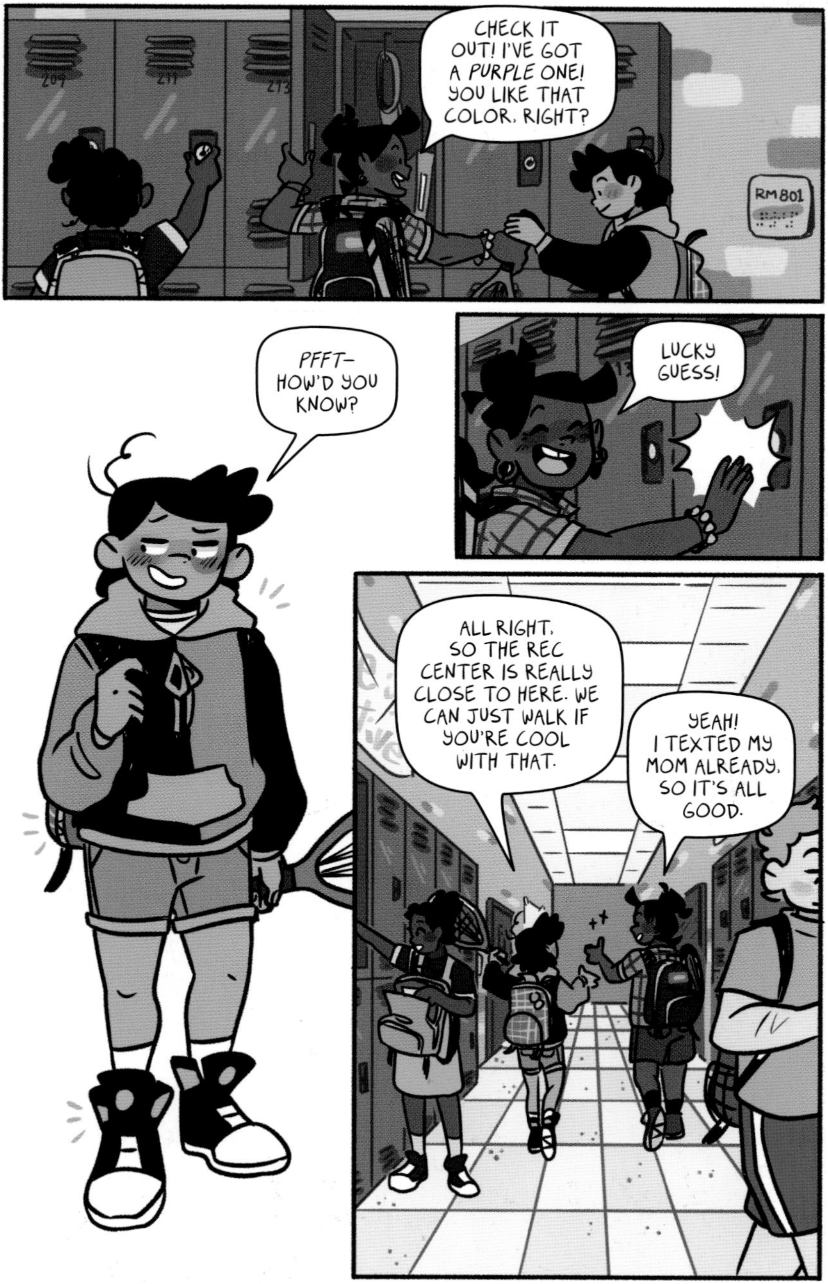
CHECK IT OUT! I'VE GOT A *PURPLE* ONE! YOU LIKE THAT COLOR, RIGHT?
RM 801
PFFT— HOW'D YOU KNOW?
LUCKY GUESS!
ALL RIGHT, SO THE REC CENTER IS REALLY CLOSE TO HERE. WE CAN JUST WALK IF YOU'RE COOL WITH THAT.
YEAH! I TEXTED MY MOM ALREADY, SO IT'S ALL GOOD.

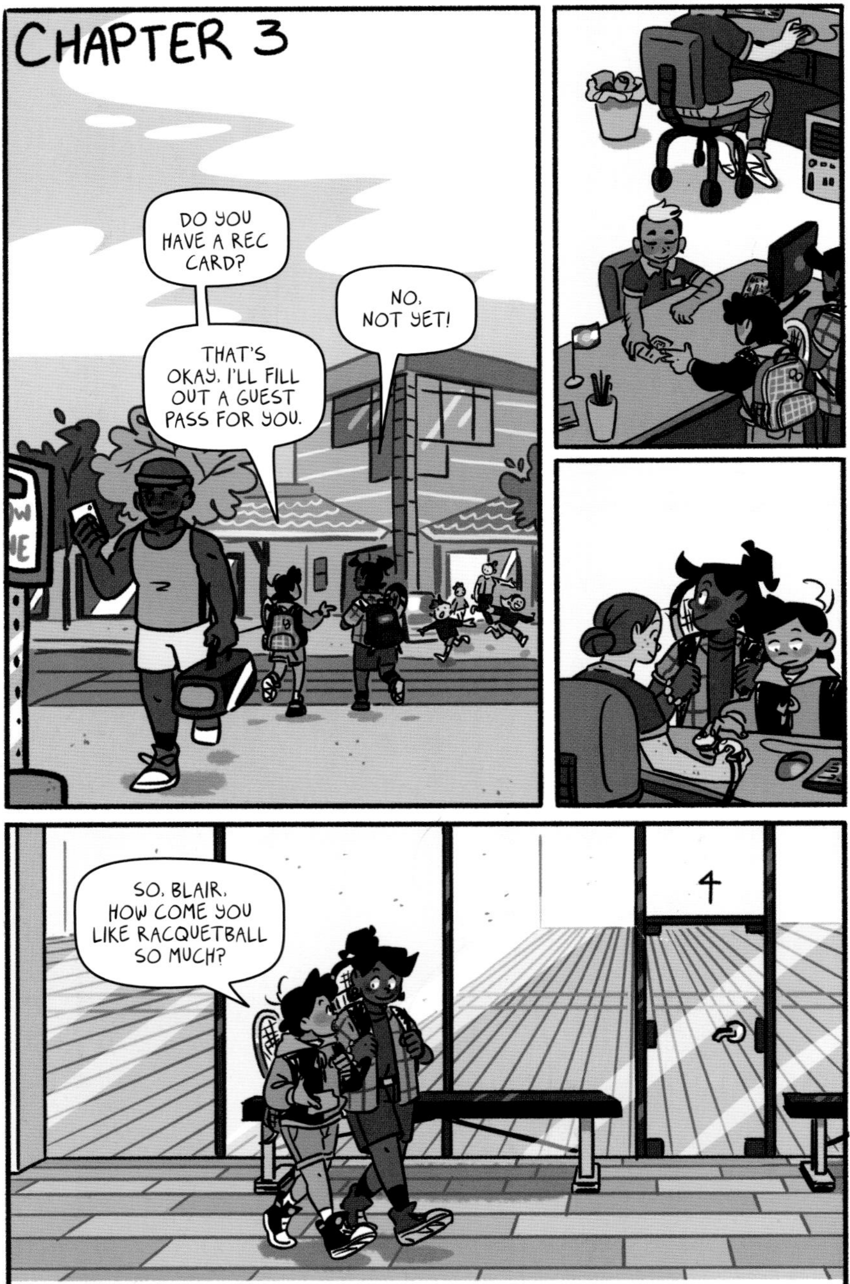
CHAPTER 3
DO YOU HAVE A REC CARD?
NO, NOT YET!
THAT'S OKAY, I'LL FILL OUT A GUEST PASS FOR YOU.
SO, BLAIR, HOW COME YOU LIKE RACQUETBALL SO MUCH?
4

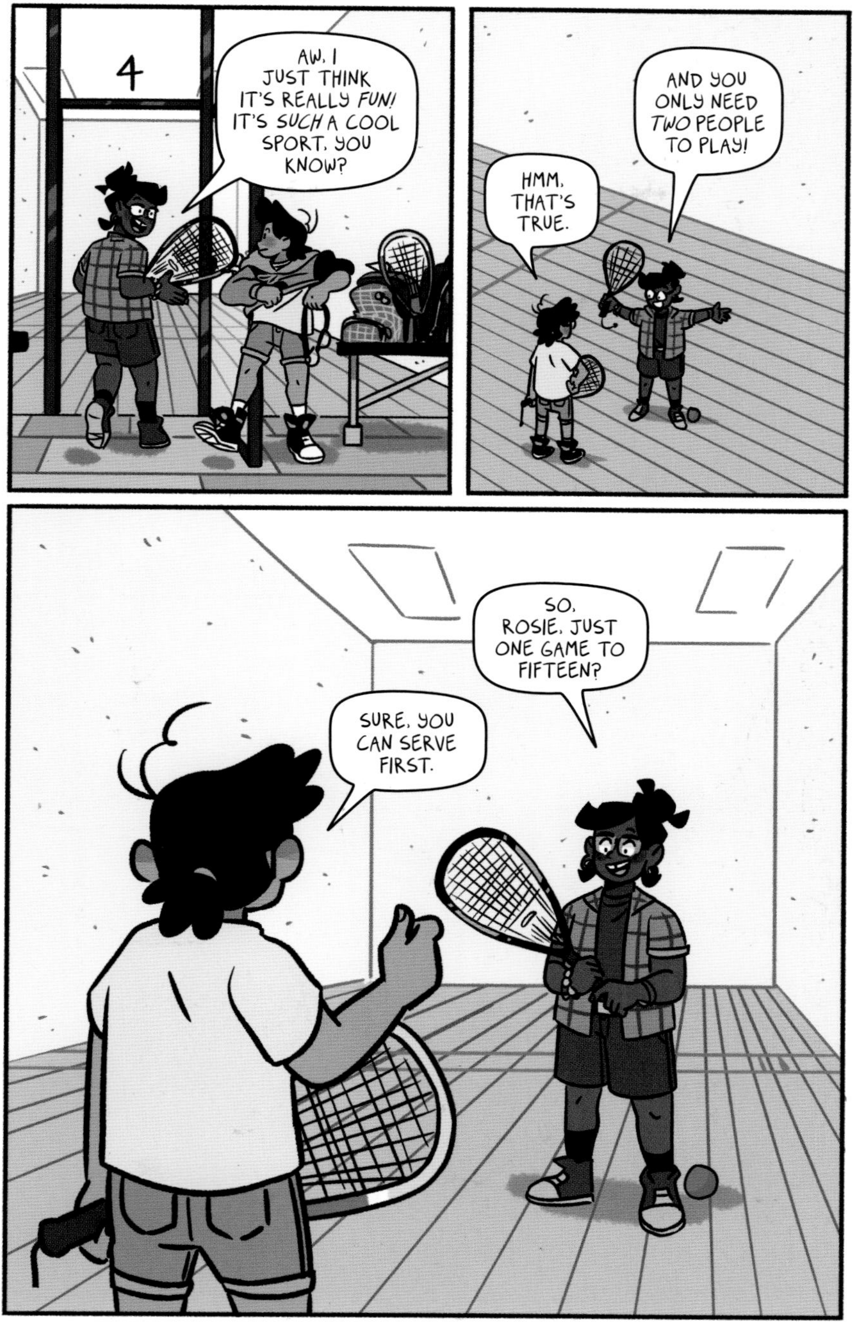
AW, I JUST THINK IT'S REALLY *FUN!* IT'S *SUCH* A COOL SPORT, YOU KNOW?
AND YOU ONLY NEED *TWO* PEOPLE TO PLAY!
HMM. THAT'S TRUE.
SO, ROSIE, JUST ONE GAME TO FIFTEEN?
SURE, YOU CAN SERVE FIRST.

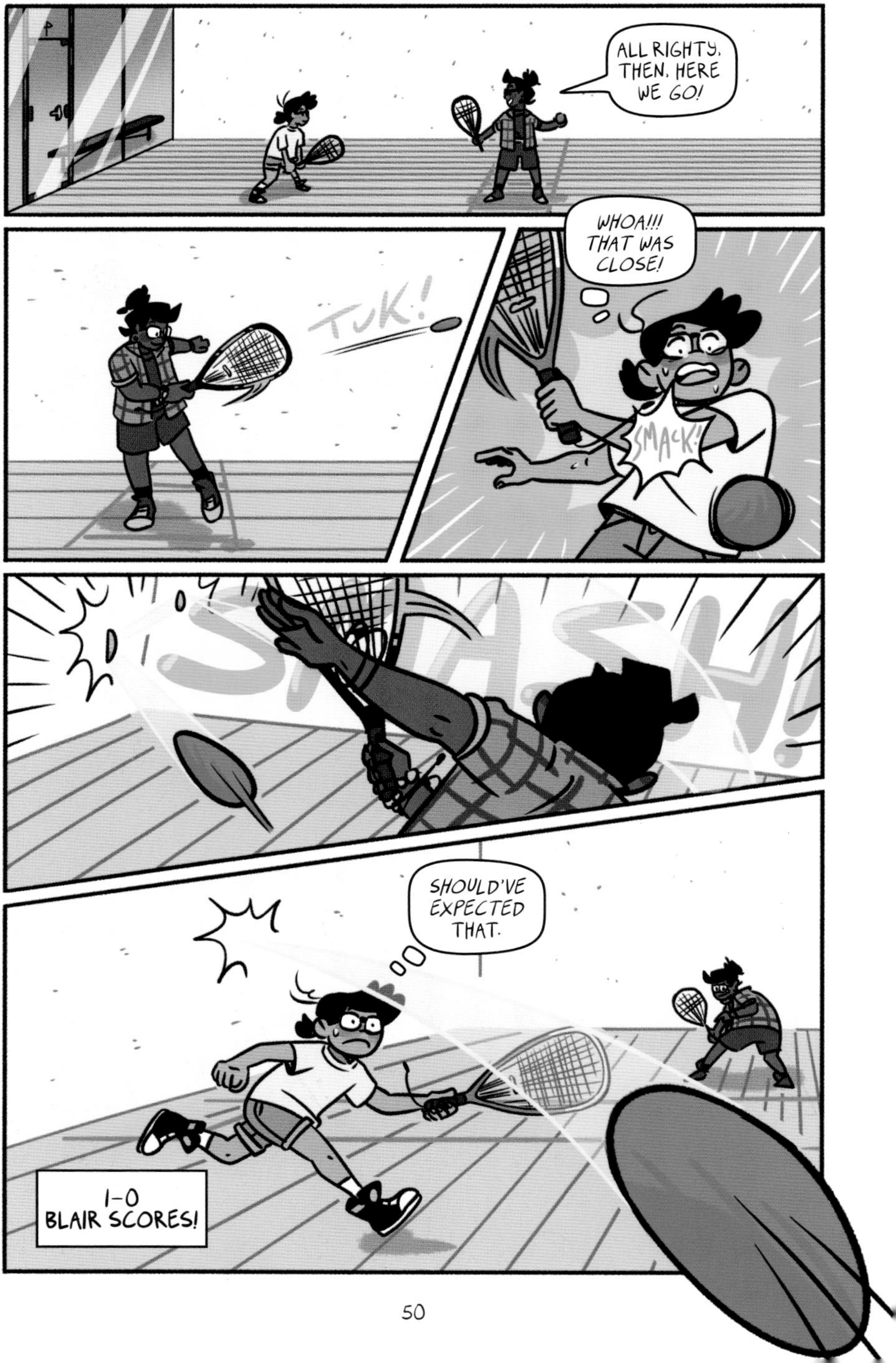
ALL RIGHTY, THEN, HERE WE GO!
TUK!
WHOA!!! THAT WAS CLOSE!
SMACK!
SMASH!
SHOULD'VE EXPECTED THAT.
1–0 BLAIR SCORES!

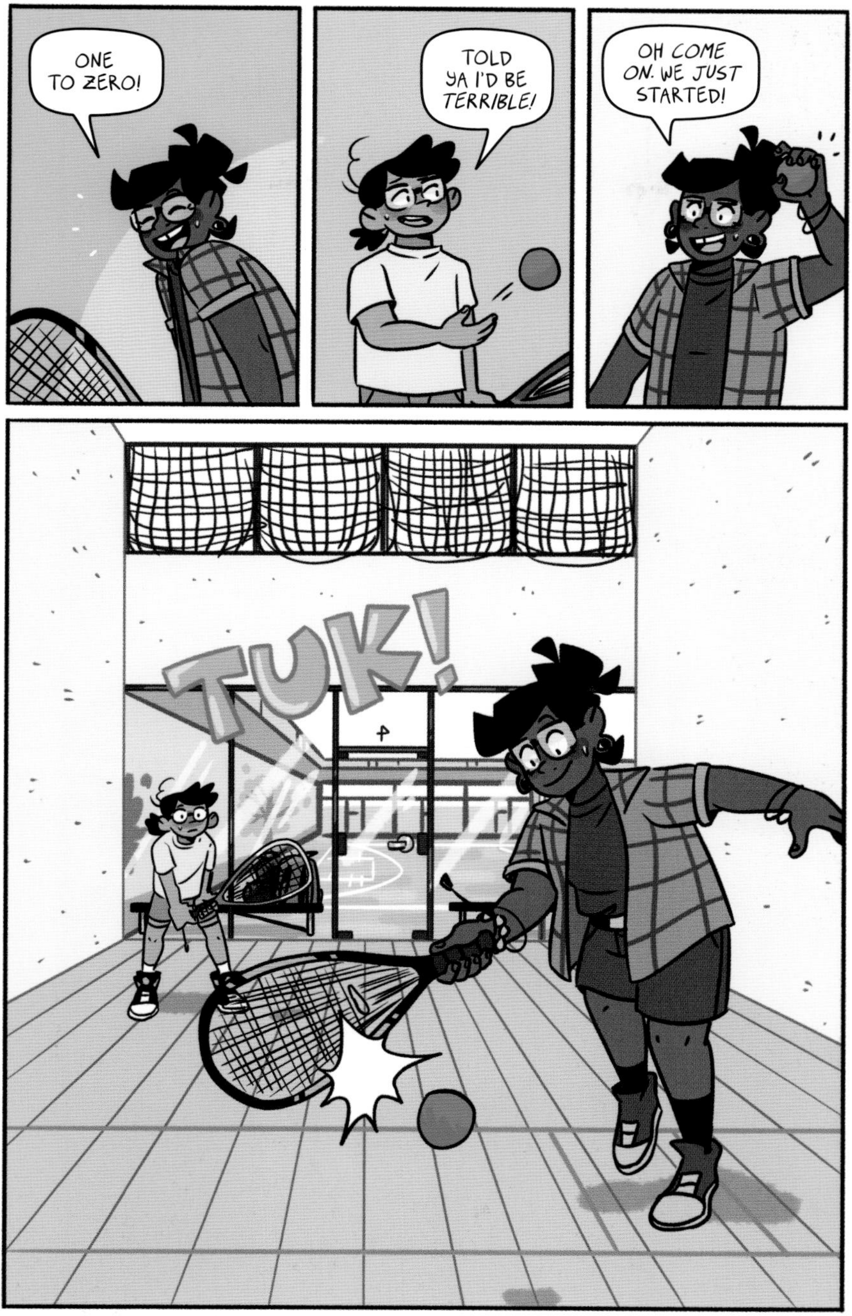
ONE TO ZERO!
TOLD YA I'D BE TERRIBLE!
OH COME ON. WE JUST STARTED!
TUK!

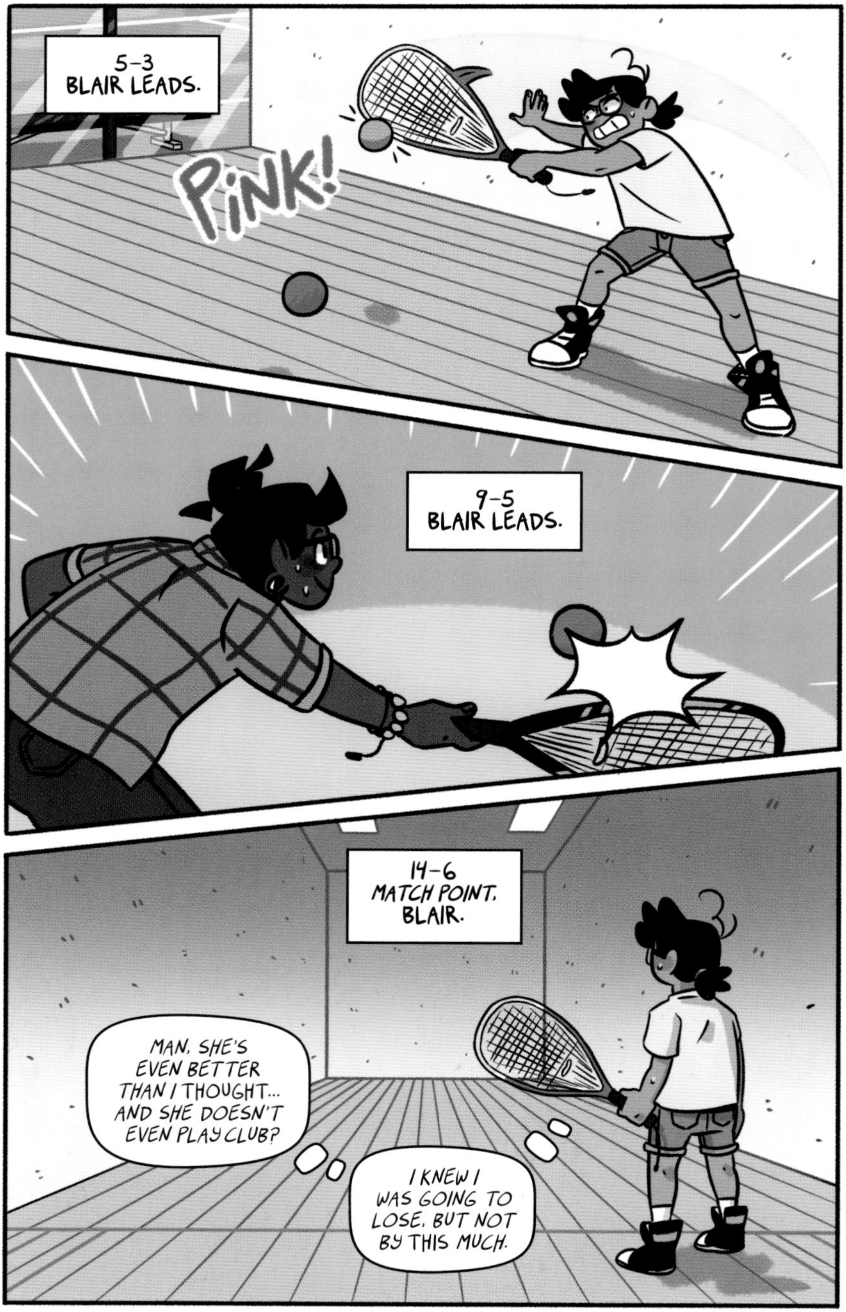
5–3 BLAIR LEADS.
PINK!
9–5 BLAIR LEADS.
14–6 MATCH POINT. BLAIR.
MAN, SHE'S EVEN BETTER THAN I THOUGHT... AND SHE DOESN'T EVEN PLAY CLUB?
I KNEW I WAS GOING TO LOSE, BUT NOT BY THIS MUCH.

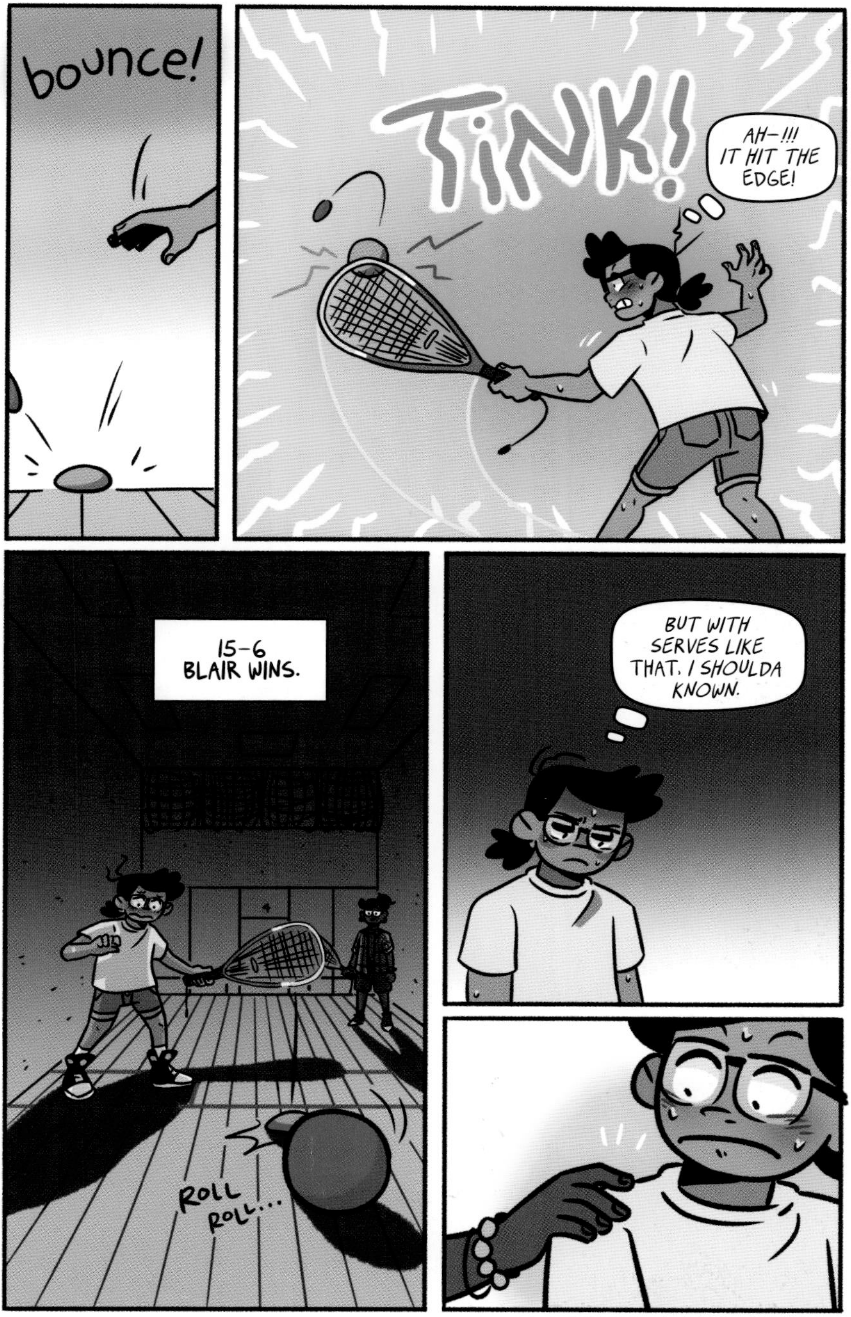
bounce!
TINK!
AH—!!! IT HIT THE EDGE!
15–6 BLAIR WINS.
ROLL ROLL...
BUT WITH SERVES LIKE THAT, I SHOULDA KNOWN.

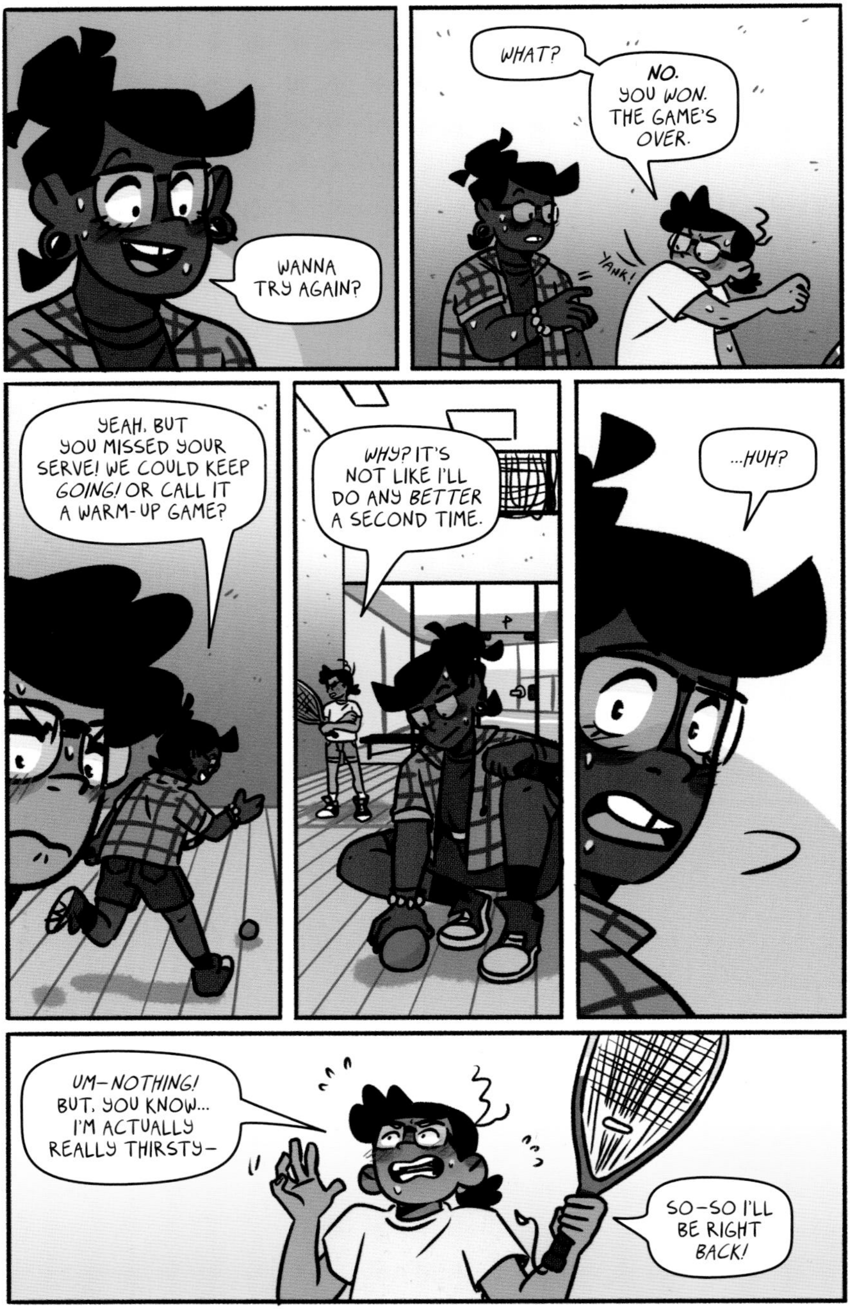
WANNA TRY AGAIN?
WHAT?
NO. YOU WON. THE GAME'S OVER.
YANK!
YEAH, BUT YOU MISSED YOUR SERVE! WE COULD KEEP GOING! OR CALL IT A WARM-UP GAME?
WHY? IT'S NOT LIKE I'LL DO ANY BETTER A SECOND TIME.
...HUH?
UM—NOTHING! BUT, YOU KNOW... I'M ACTUALLY REALLY THIRSTY—
SO—SO I'LL BE RIGHT BACK!

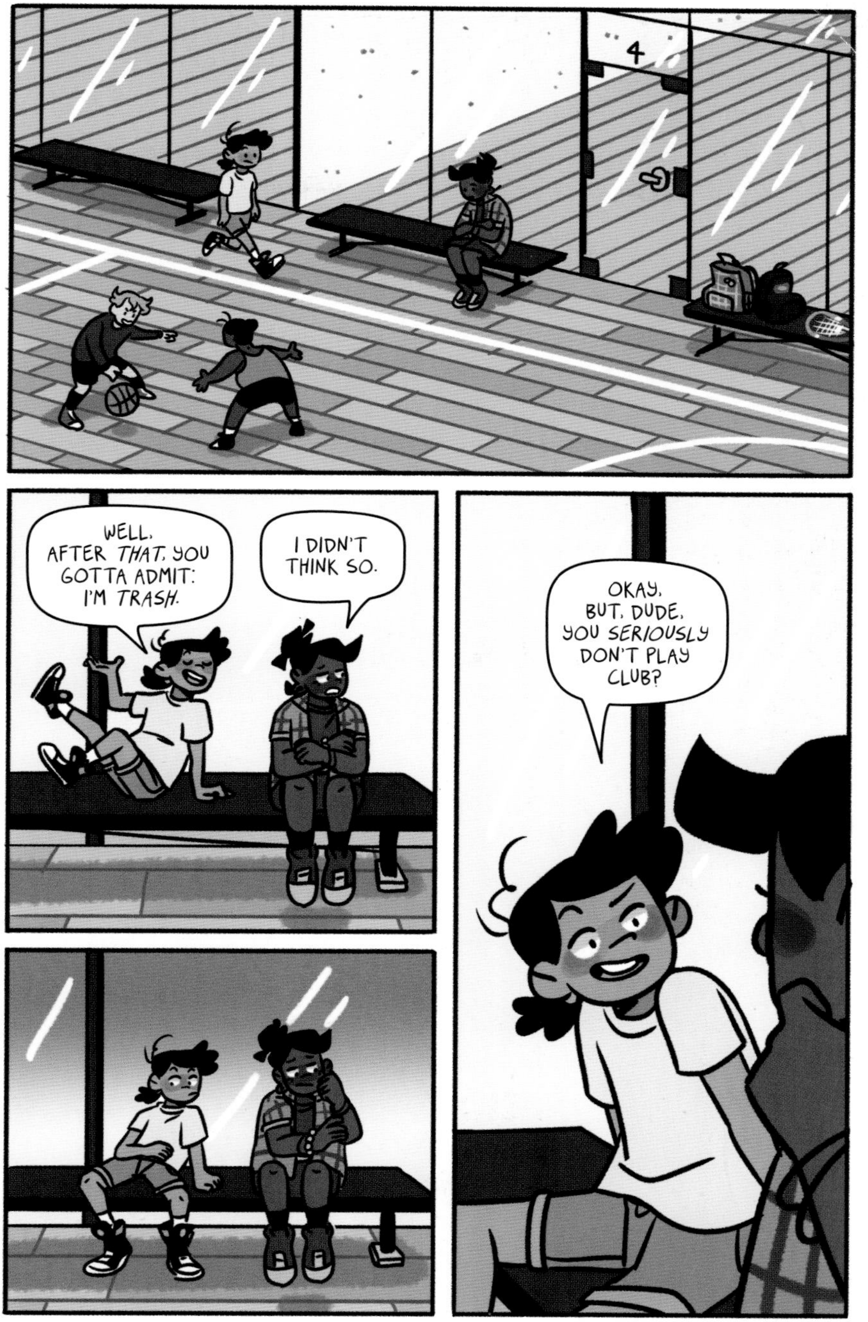
WELL, AFTER THAT, YOU GOTTA ADMIT: I'M TRASH.
I DIDN'T THINK SO.
OKAY, BUT, DUDE, YOU SERIOUSLY DON'T PLAY CLUB?

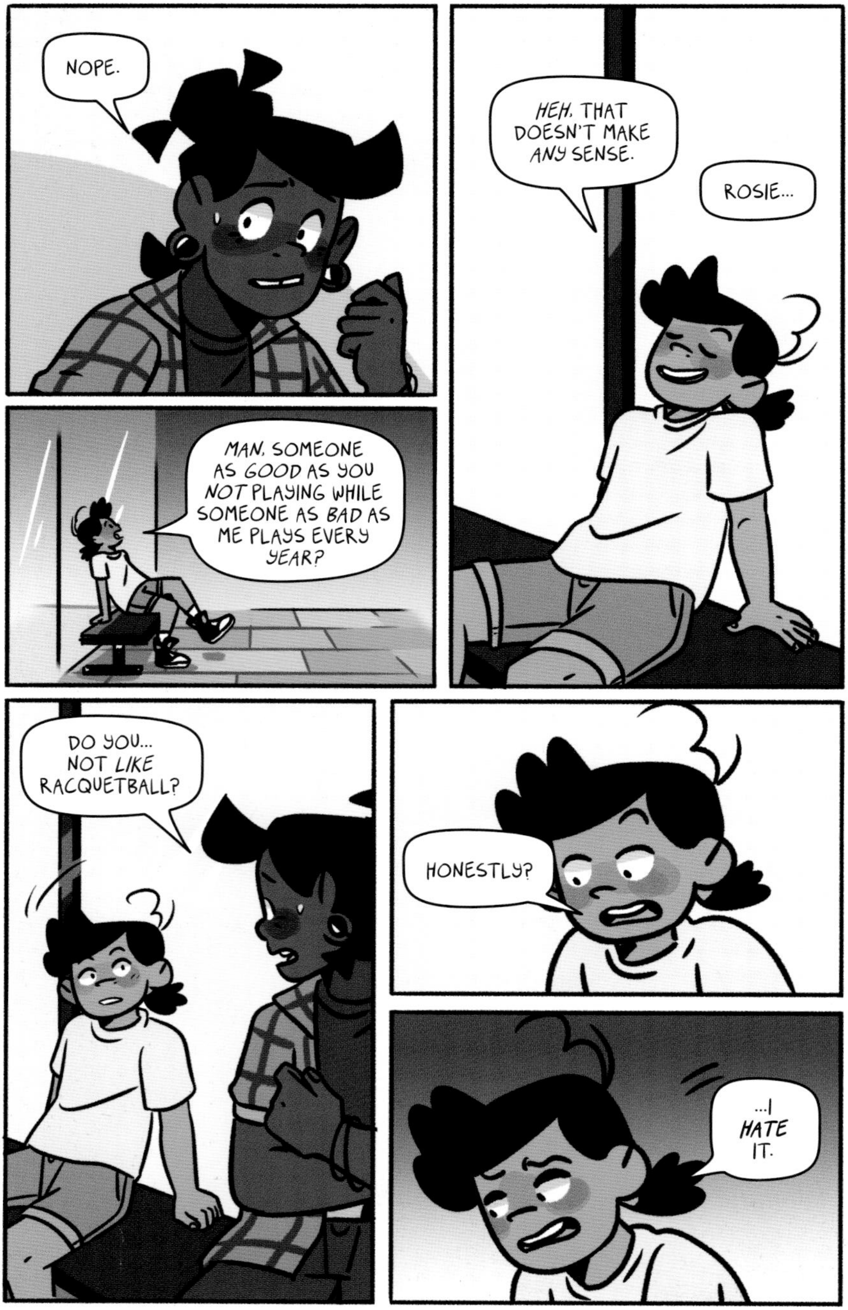
NOPE.
HEH. THAT DOESN'T MAKE ANY SENSE.
ROSIE...
MAN. SOMEONE AS GOOD AS YOU NOT PLAYING WHILE SOMEONE AS BAD AS ME PLAYS EVERY YEAR?
DO YOU... NOT LIKE RACQUETBALL?
HONESTLY?
...I HATE IT.

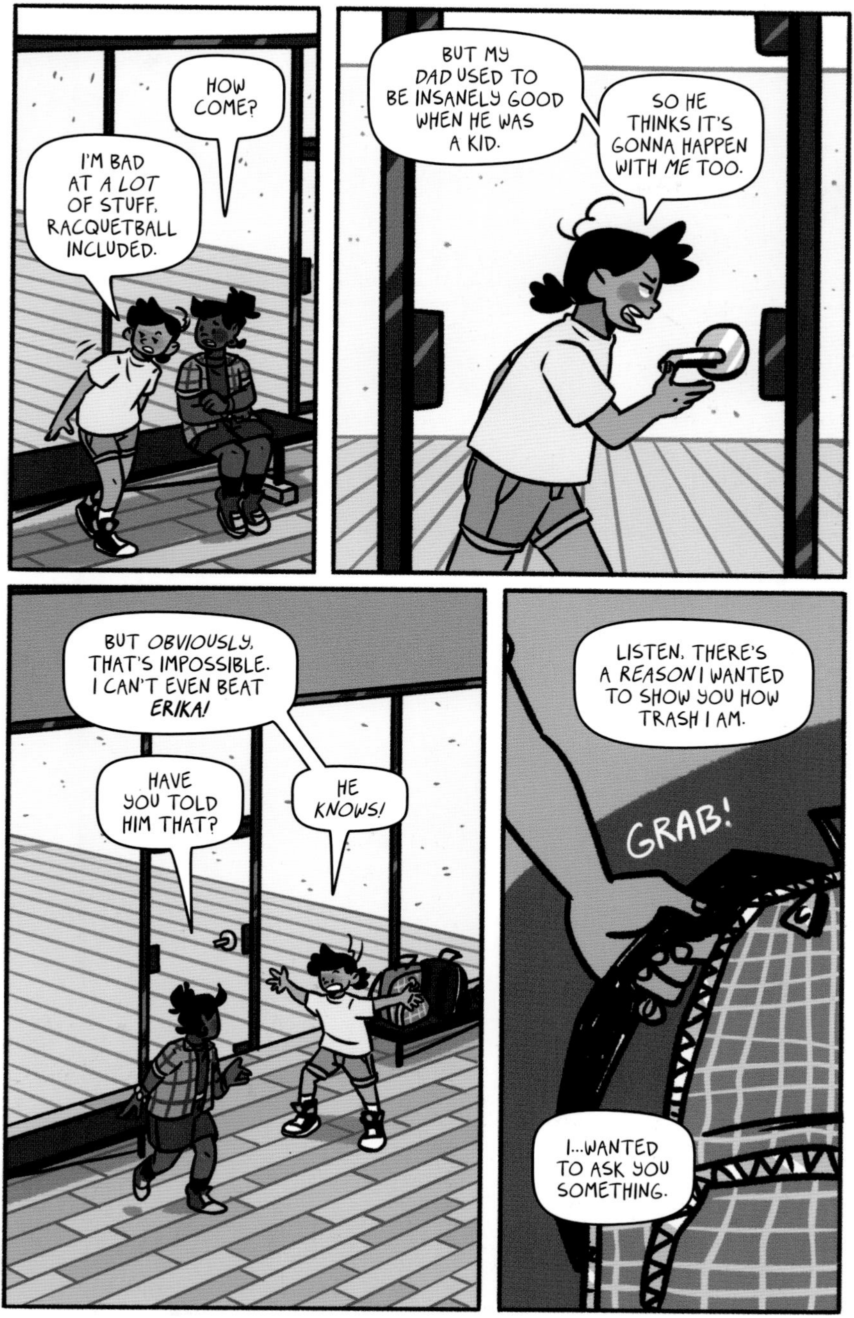
HOW COME?
I'M BAD AT A LOT OF STUFF. RACQUETBALL INCLUDED.
BUT MY DAD USED TO BE INSANELY GOOD WHEN HE WAS A KID.
SO HE THINKS IT'S GONNA HAPPEN WITH ME TOO.
BUT OBVIOUSLY, THAT'S IMPOSSIBLE. I CAN'T EVEN BEAT ERIKA!
HAVE YOU TOLD HIM THAT?
HE KNOWS!
LISTEN. THERE'S A REASON I WANTED TO SHOW YOU HOW TRASH I AM.
GRAB!
I...WANTED TO ASK YOU SOMETHING.

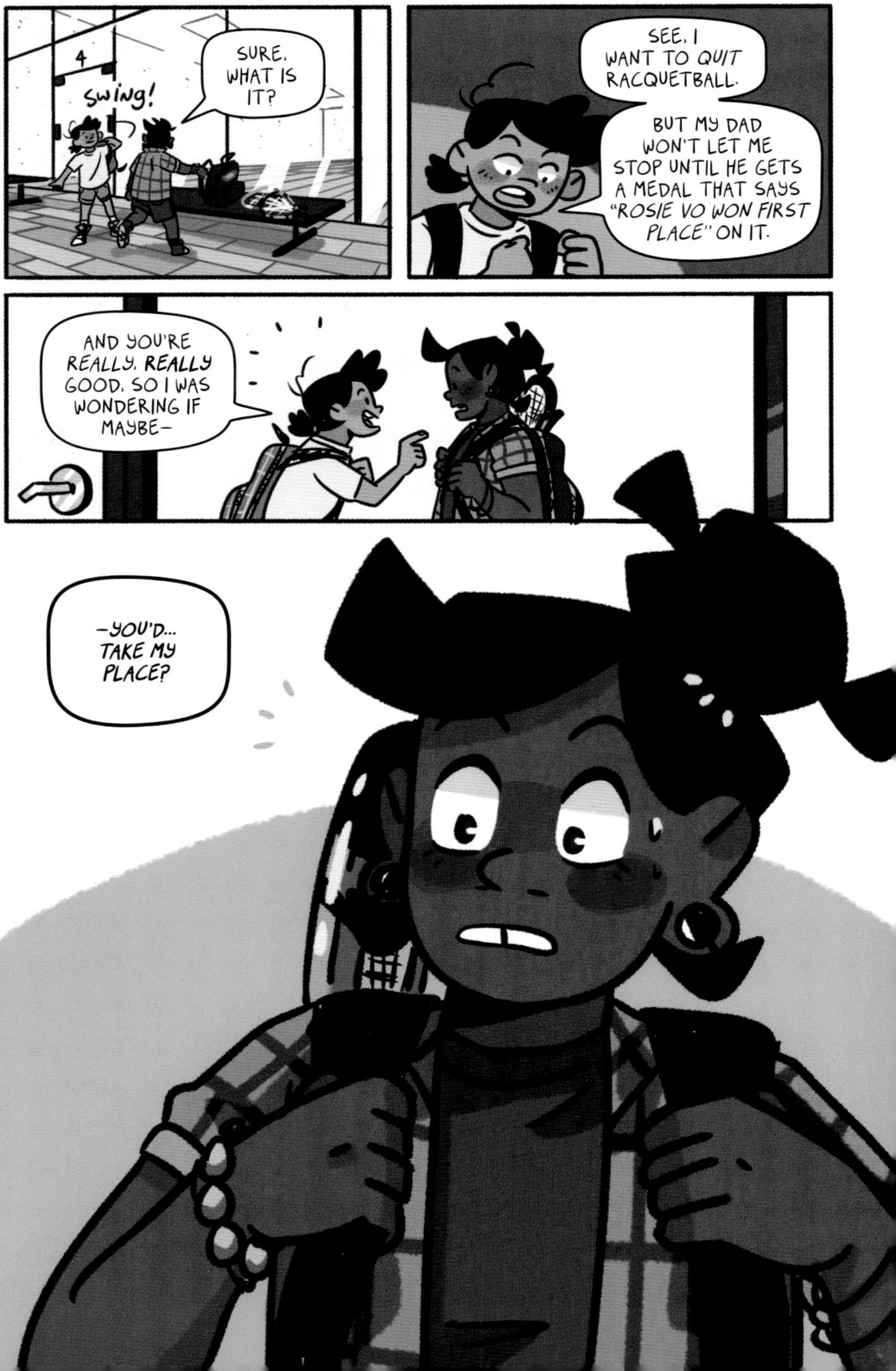

SWING!
SURE. WHAT IS IT?
SEE, I WANT TO *QUIT* RACQUETBALL.
BUT MY DAD WON'T LET ME STOP UNTIL HE GETS A MEDAL THAT SAYS *"ROSIE VO WON FIRST PLACE"* ON IT.
AND YOU'RE REALLY, **REALLY** GOOD. SO I WAS WONDERING IF MAYBE—
—*YOU'D*... TAKE MY PLACE?

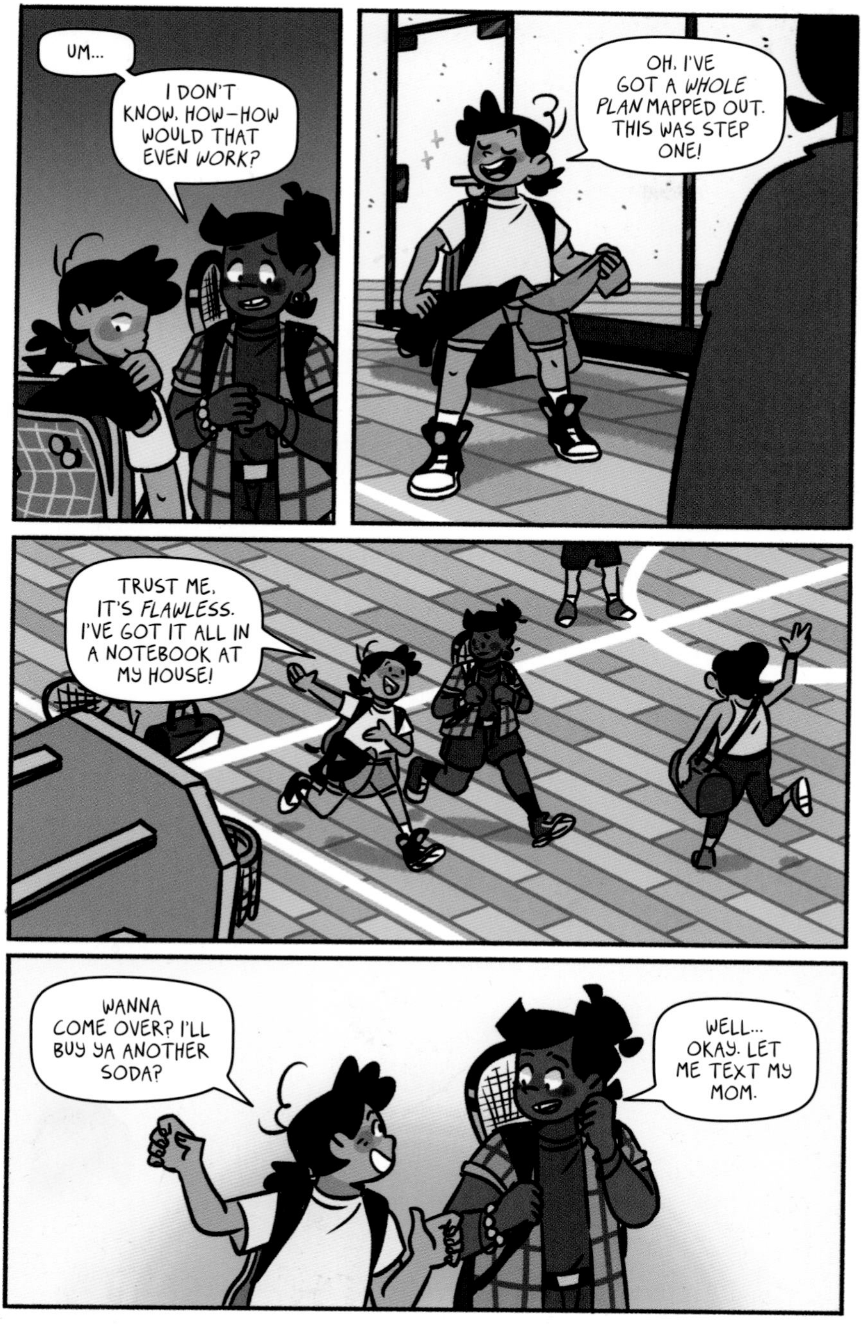
UM...
I DON'T KNOW. HOW–HOW WOULD THAT EVEN WORK?
OH, I'VE GOT A WHOLE PLAN MAPPED OUT. THIS WAS STEP ONE!
TRUST ME, IT'S FLAWLESS. I'VE GOT IT ALL IN A NOTEBOOK AT MY HOUSE!
WANNA COME OVER? I'LL BUY YA ANOTHER SODA?
WELL... OKAY. LET ME TEXT MY MOM.

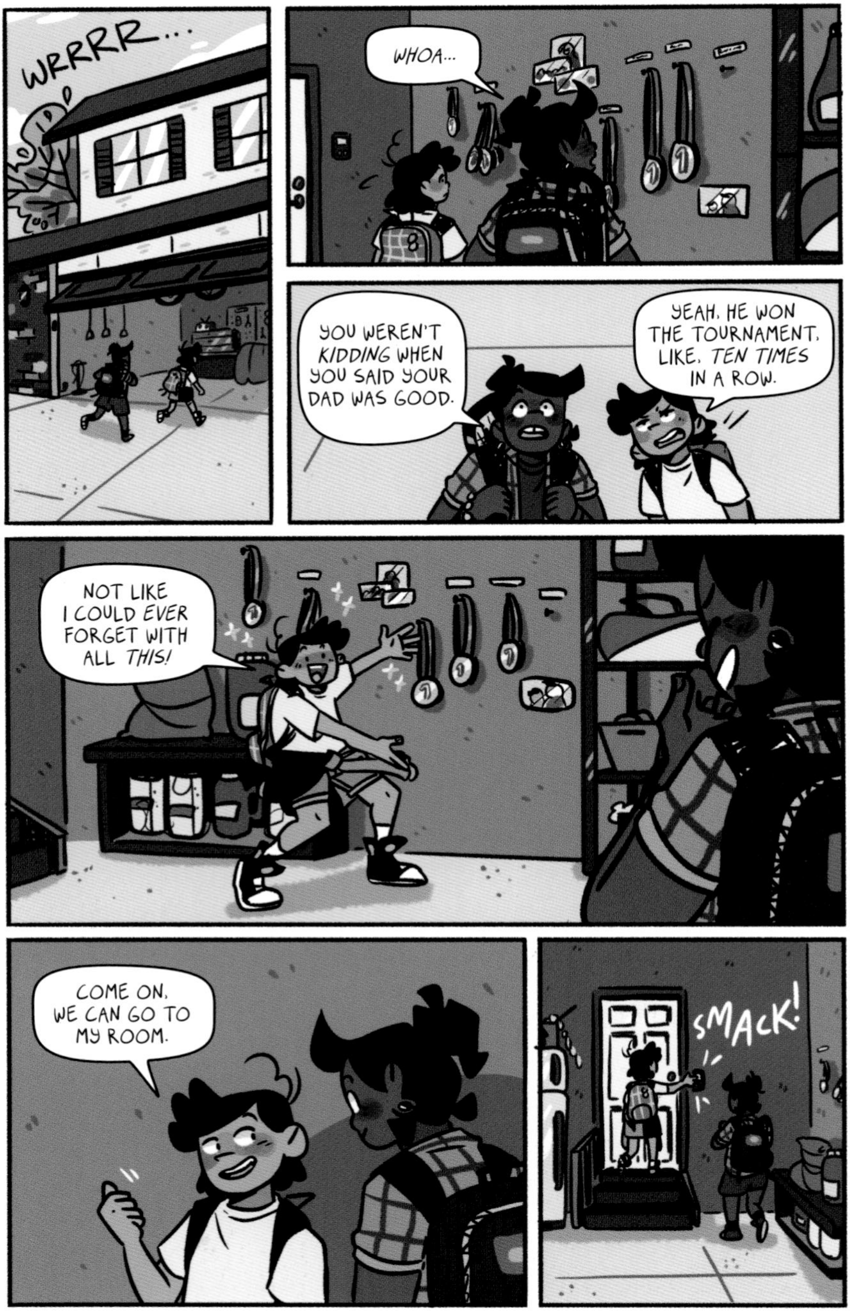
WRRRR...
WHOA...
YOU WEREN'T *KIDDING* WHEN YOU SAID YOUR DAD WAS GOOD.
YEAH, HE WON THE TOURNAMENT, LIKE, *TEN TIMES* IN A ROW.
NOT LIKE I COULD EVER FORGET WITH ALL *THIS!*
COME ON, WE CAN GO TO MY ROOM.
SMACK!

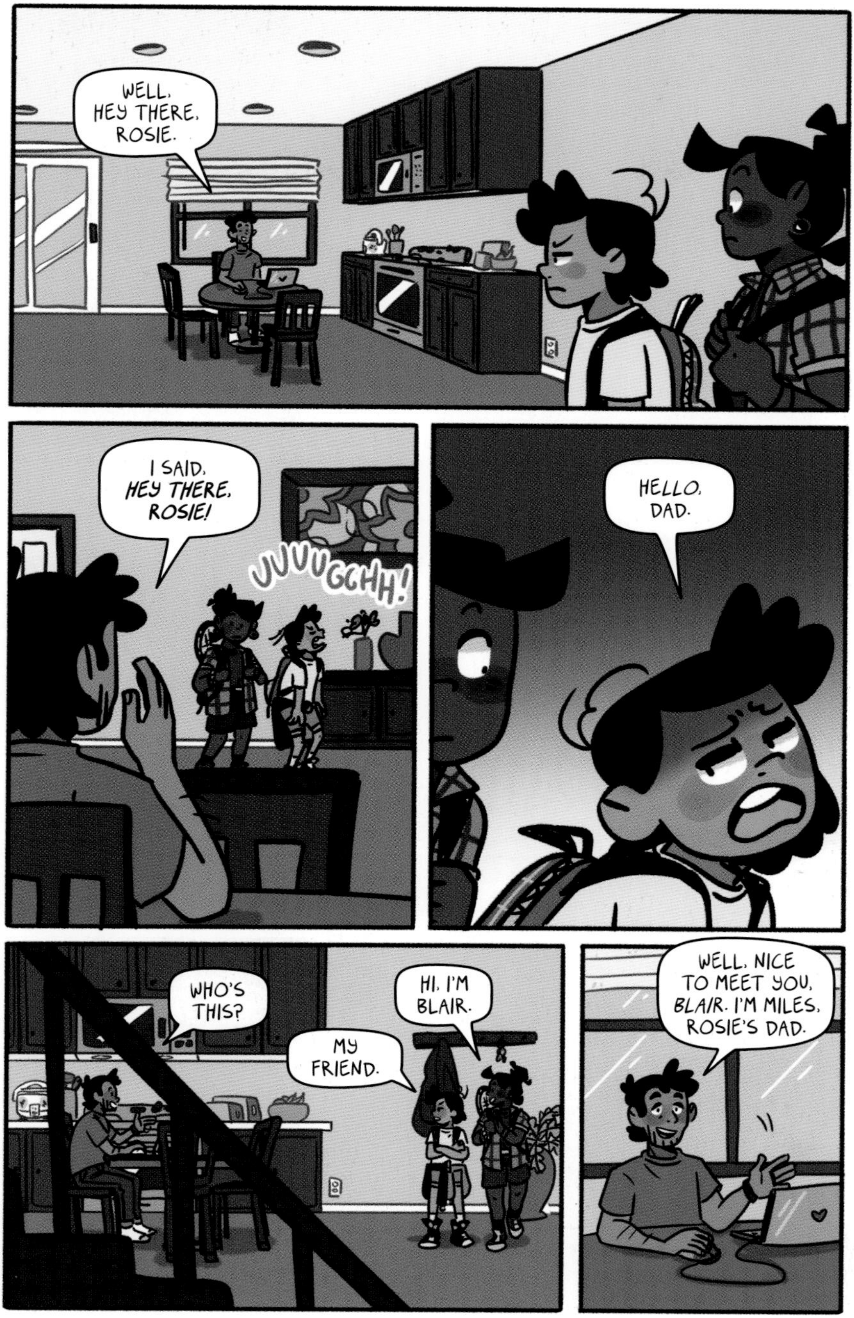
WELL, HEY THERE, ROSIE.
I SAID, *HEY THERE, ROSIE!*
UUUUGGHH!
HELLO, DAD.
WHO'S THIS?
MY FRIEND.
HI, I'M BLAIR.
WELL, NICE TO MEET YOU, *BLAIR*. I'M MILES, ROSIE'S DAD.

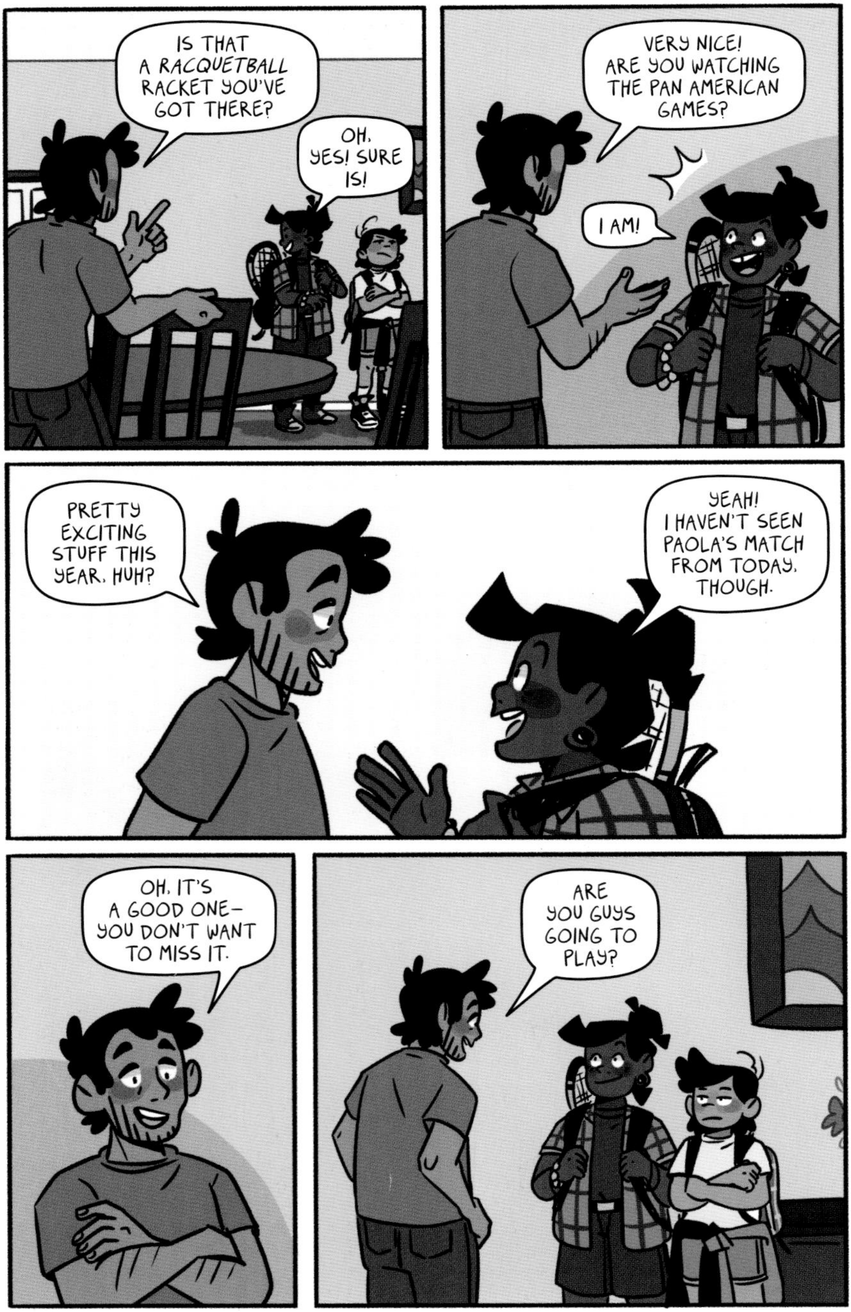
IS THAT A RACQUETBALL RACKET YOU'VE GOT THERE?
OH, YES! SURE IS!
VERY NICE! ARE YOU WATCHING THE PAN AMERICAN GAMES?
I AM!
PRETTY EXCITING STUFF THIS YEAR, HUH?
YEAH! I HAVEN'T SEEN PAOLA'S MATCH FROM TODAY, THOUGH.
OH, IT'S A GOOD ONE— YOU DON'T WANT TO MISS IT.
ARE YOU GUYS GOING TO PLAY?

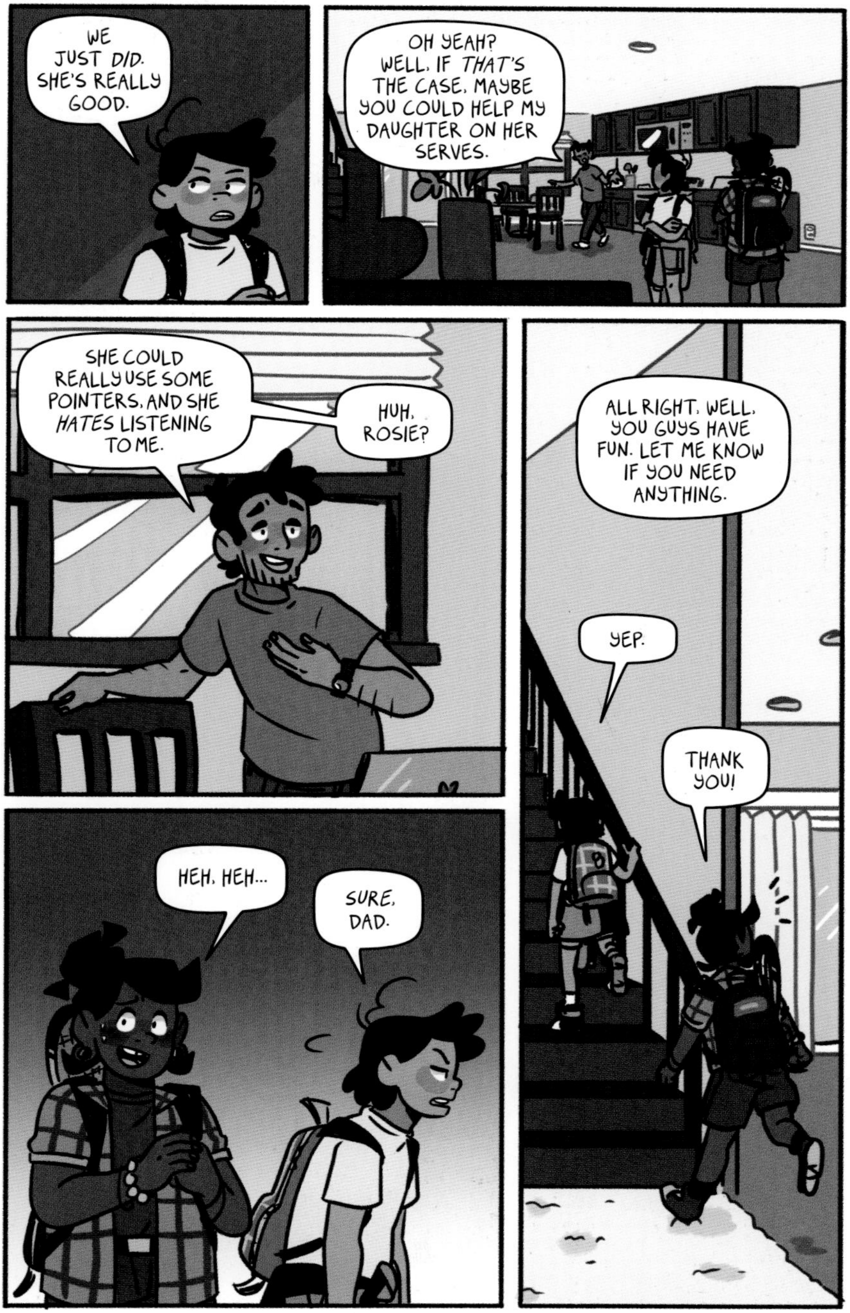
WE JUST *DID*. SHE'S REALLY GOOD.
OH YEAH? WELL, IF *THAT'S* THE CASE, MAYBE YOU COULD HELP MY DAUGHTER ON HER SERVES.
SHE COULD REALLY USE SOME POINTERS, AND SHE *HATES* LISTENING TO ME.
HUH, ROSIE?
HEH, HEH...
SURE, DAD.
ALL RIGHT, WELL, YOU GUYS HAVE FUN. LET ME KNOW IF YOU NEED ANYTHING.
YEP.
THANK YOU!

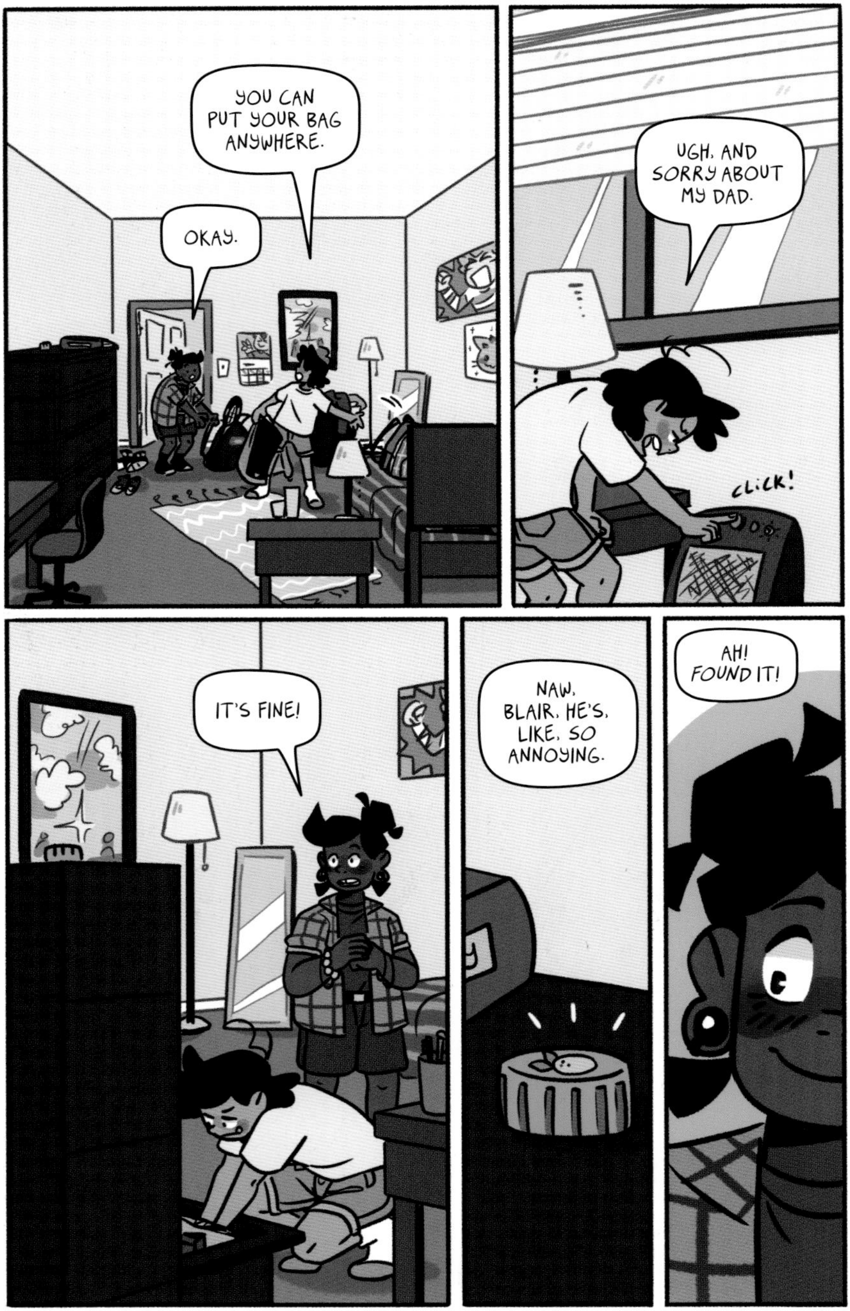
YOU CAN PUT YOUR BAG ANYWHERE.
OKAY.
UGH, AND SORRY ABOUT MY DAD.
CLICK!
IT'S FINE!
NAW, BLAIR, HE'S, LIKE, SO ANNOYING.
AH! FOUND IT!

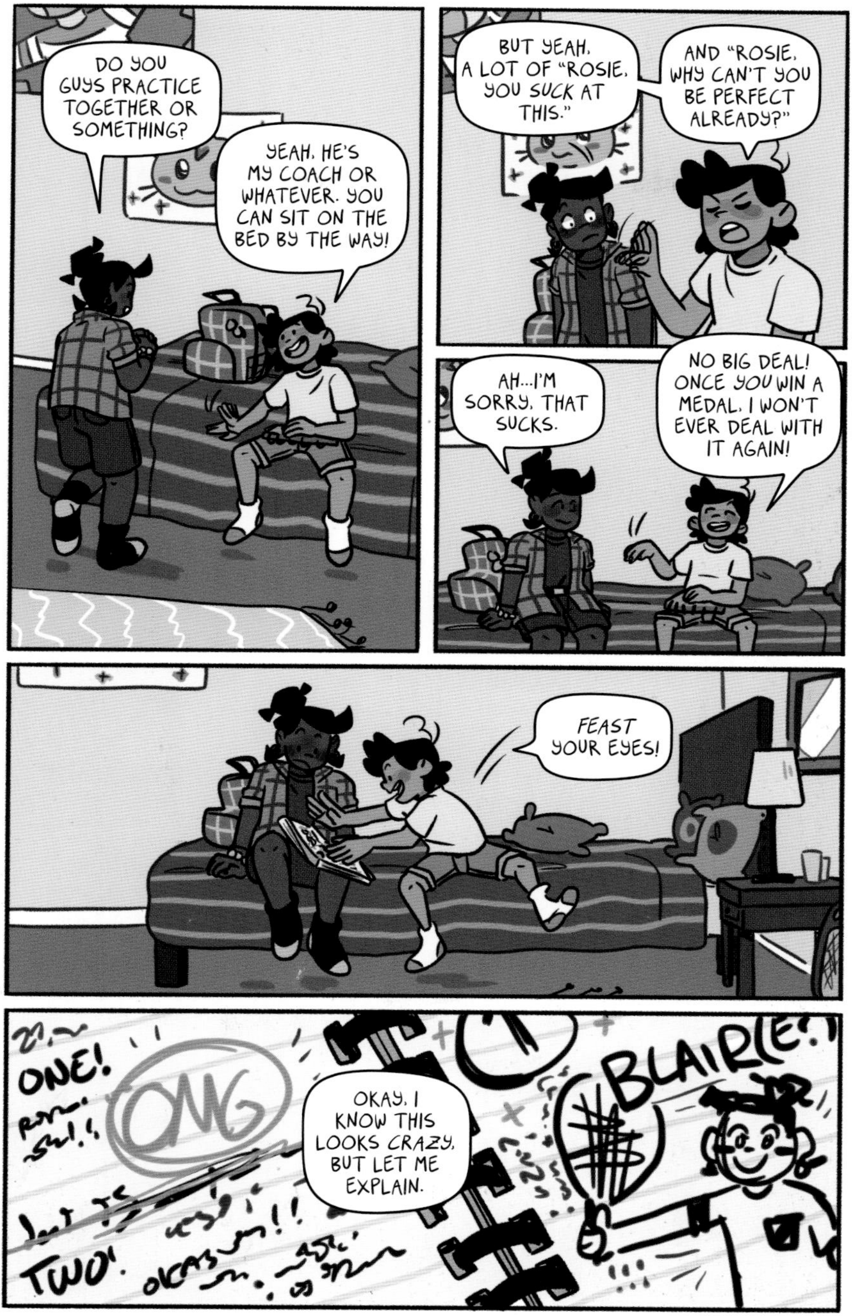
DO YOU GUYS PRACTICE TOGETHER OR SOMETHING?
YEAH, HE'S MY COACH OR WHATEVER. YOU CAN SIT ON THE BED BY THE WAY!
BUT YEAH, A LOT OF "ROSIE, YOU SUCK AT THIS."
AND "ROSIE, WHY CAN'T YOU BE PERFECT ALREADY?"
AH...I'M SORRY, THAT SUCKS.
NO BIG DEAL! ONCE YOU WIN A MEDAL, I WON'T EVER DEAL WITH IT AGAIN!
FEAST YOUR EYES!
ONE!
OMG
TWO!
BLAIR
OKAY, I KNOW THIS LOOKS CRAZY, BUT LET ME EXPLAIN.

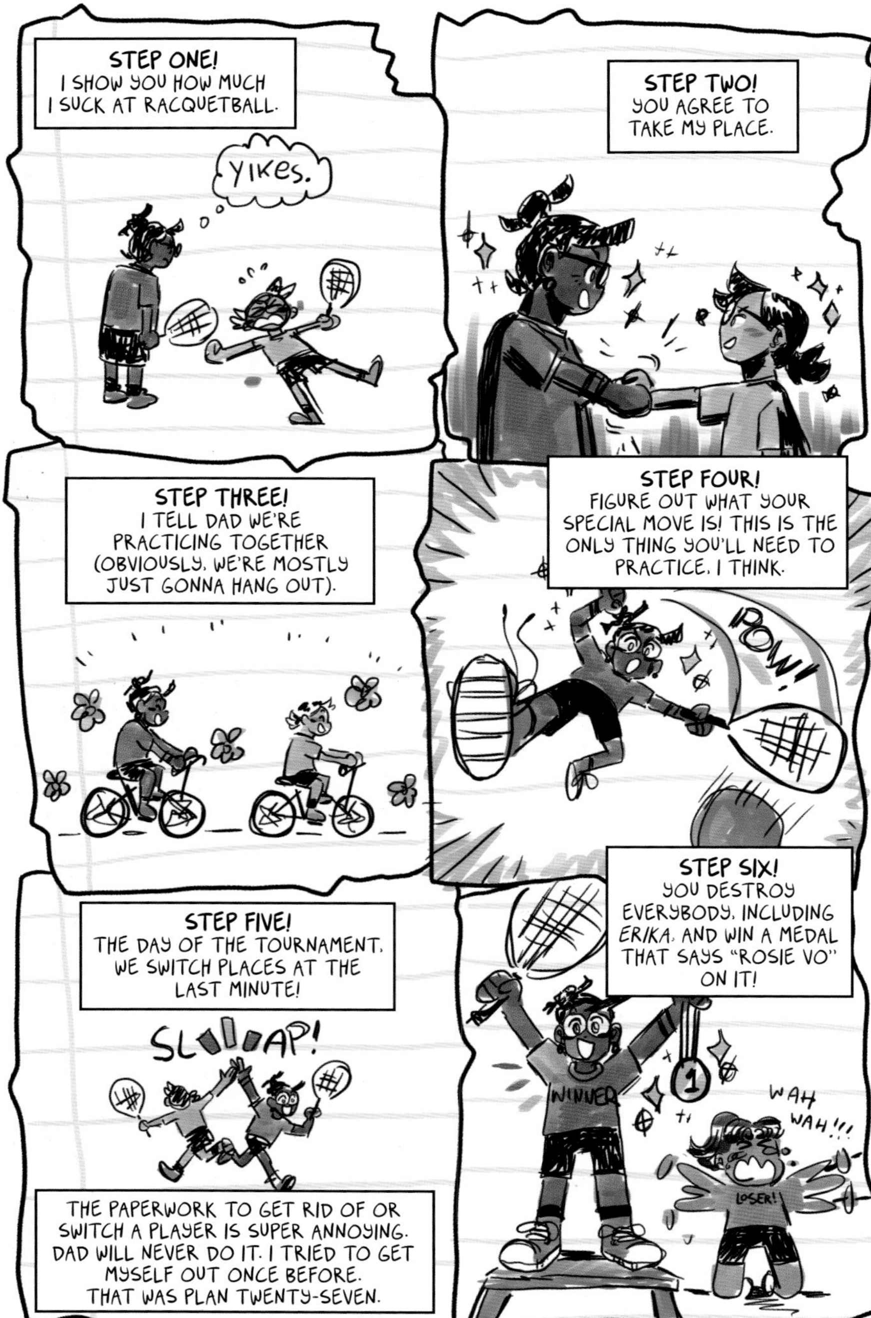

STEP ONE!
I SHOW YOU HOW MUCH I SUCK AT RACQUETBALL.
YIKES.
STEP TWO!
YOU AGREE TO TAKE MY PLACE.
STEP THREE!
I TELL DAD WE'RE PRACTICING TOGETHER (OBVIOUSLY, WE'RE MOSTLY JUST GONNA HANG OUT).
STEP FOUR!
FIGURE OUT WHAT YOUR SPECIAL MOVE IS! THIS IS THE ONLY THING YOU'LL NEED TO PRACTICE, I THINK.
POW!
STEP FIVE!
THE DAY OF THE TOURNAMENT, WE SWITCH PLACES AT THE LAST MINUTE!
SLAP!
THE PAPERWORK TO GET RID OF OR SWITCH A PLAYER IS SUPER ANNOYING. DAD WILL NEVER DO IT. I TRIED TO GET MYSELF OUT ONCE BEFORE. THAT WAS PLAN TWENTY-SEVEN.
STEP SIX!
YOU DESTROY EVERYBODY, INCLUDING ERIKA, AND WIN A MEDAL THAT SAYS "ROSIE VO" ON IT!
WINNER
1
WAH WAH!!!
LOSER!

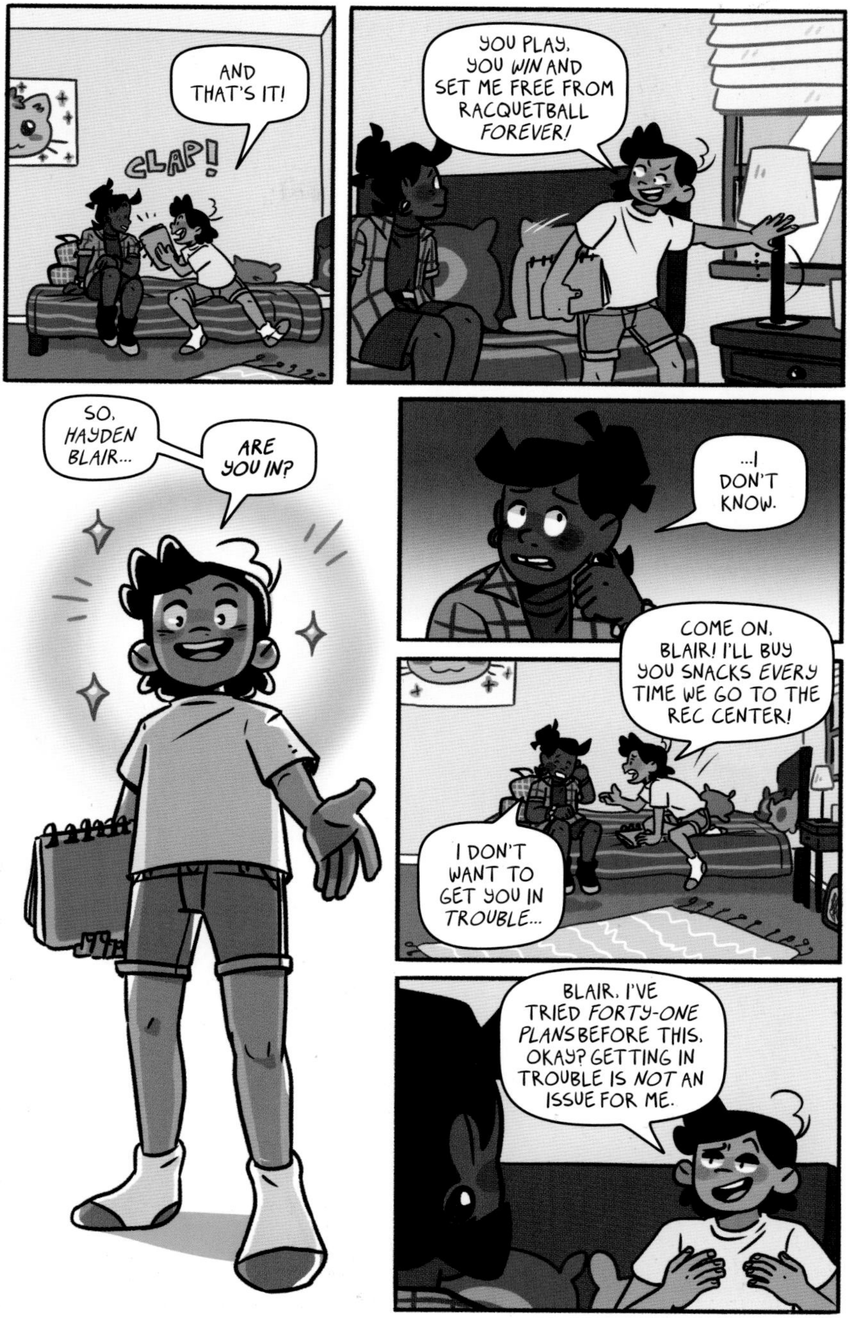
AND THAT'S IT!
CLAP!
YOU PLAY, YOU WIN AND SET ME FREE FROM RACQUETBALL FOREVER!
SO, HAYDEN BLAIR...
ARE YOU IN?
...I DON'T KNOW.
COME ON, BLAIR! I'LL BUY YOU SNACKS EVERY TIME WE GO TO THE REC CENTER!
I DON'T WANT TO GET YOU IN TROUBLE...
BLAIR, I'VE TRIED FORTY-ONE PLANS BEFORE THIS, OKAY? GETTING IN TROUBLE IS NOT AN ISSUE FOR ME.

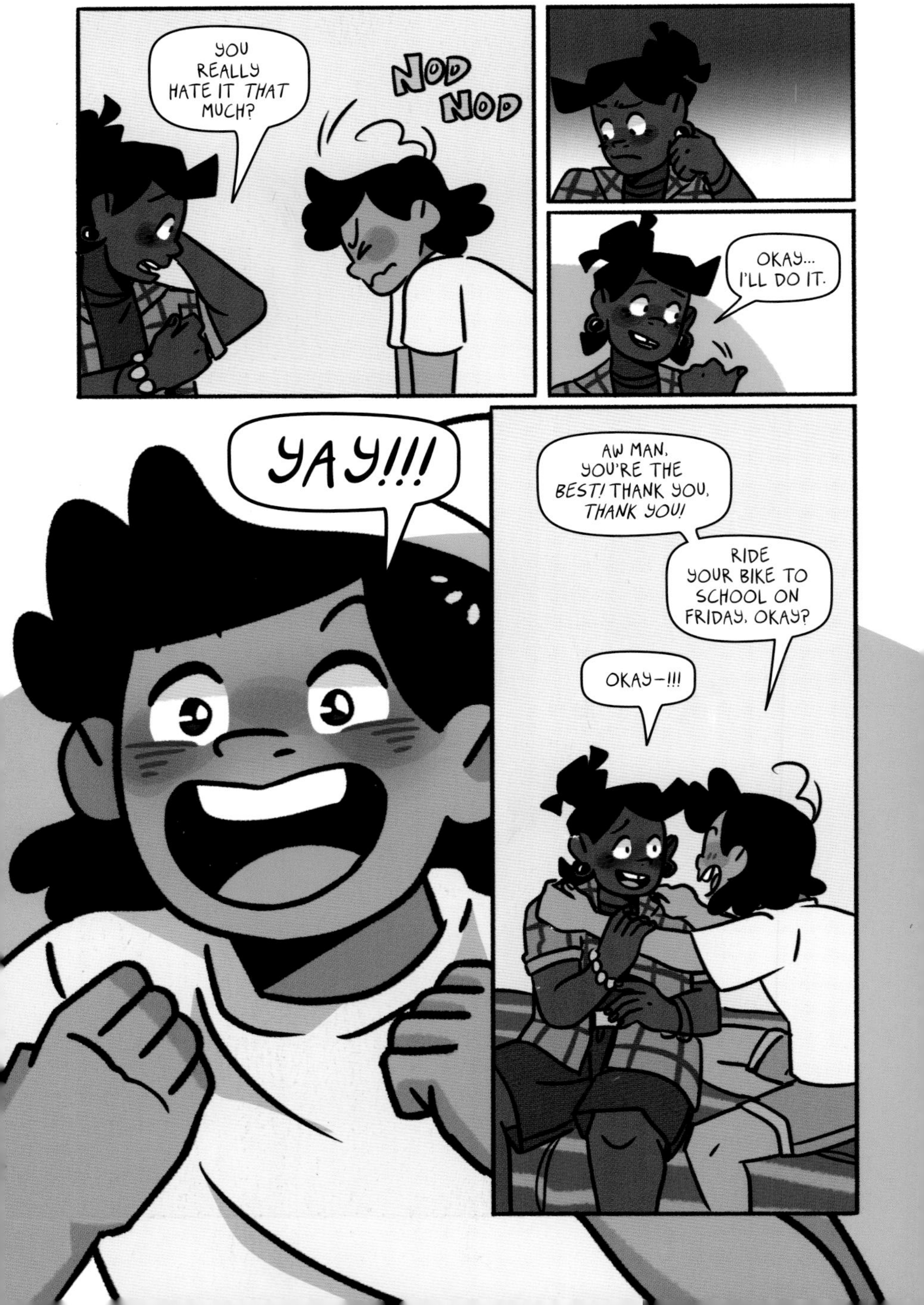
YOU REALLY HATE IT THAT MUCH?
NOD NOD
OKAY... I'LL DO IT.
YAY!!!
AW MAN, YOU'RE THE BEST! THANK YOU, THANK YOU!
RIDE YOUR BIKE TO SCHOOL ON FRIDAY, OKAY?
OKAY–!!!

CHAPTER 4

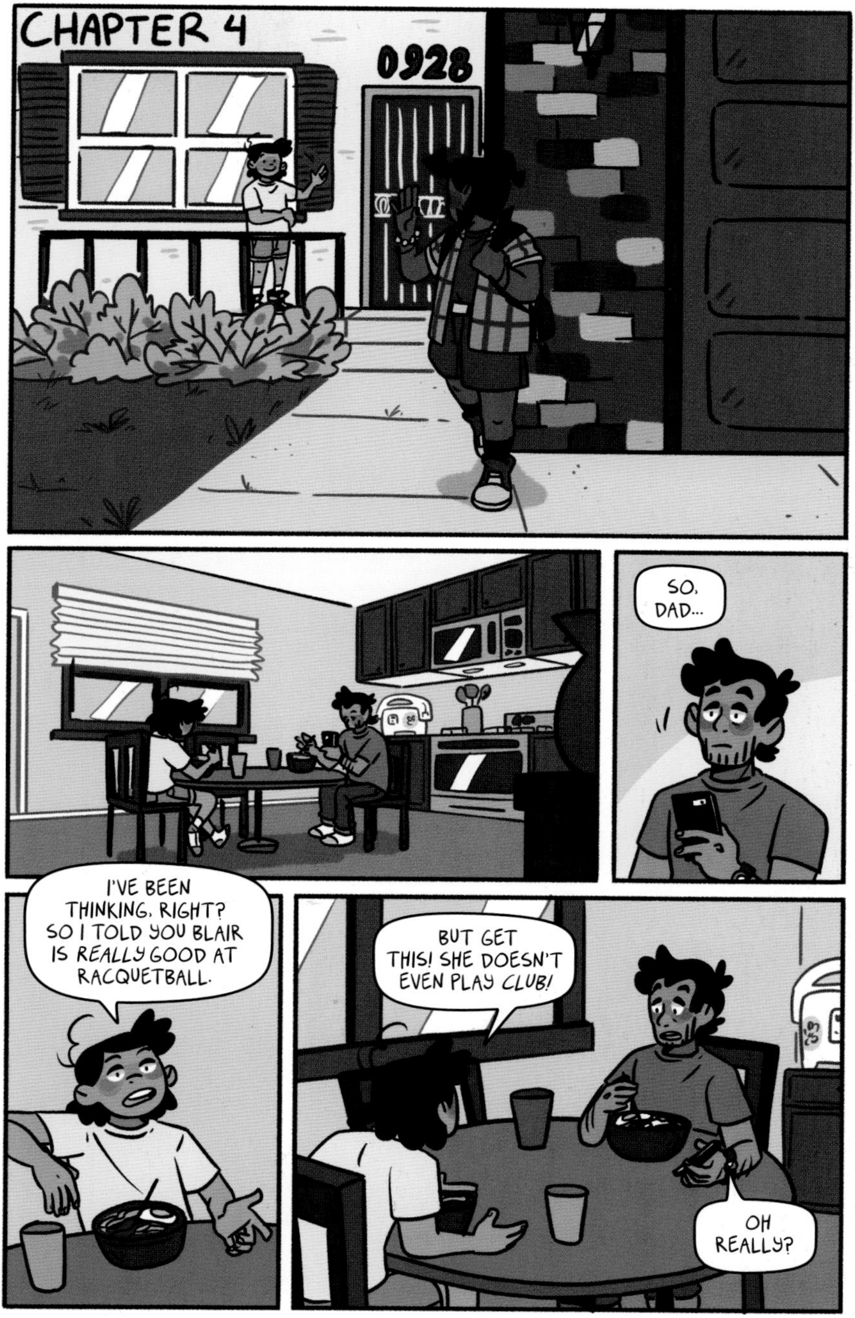
CHAPTER 4
0928
SO, DAD...
I'VE BEEN THINKING, RIGHT? SO I TOLD YOU BLAIR IS *REALLY* GOOD AT RACQUETBALL.
BUT GET THIS! SHE DOESN'T EVEN PLAY *CLUB*!
OH REALLY?

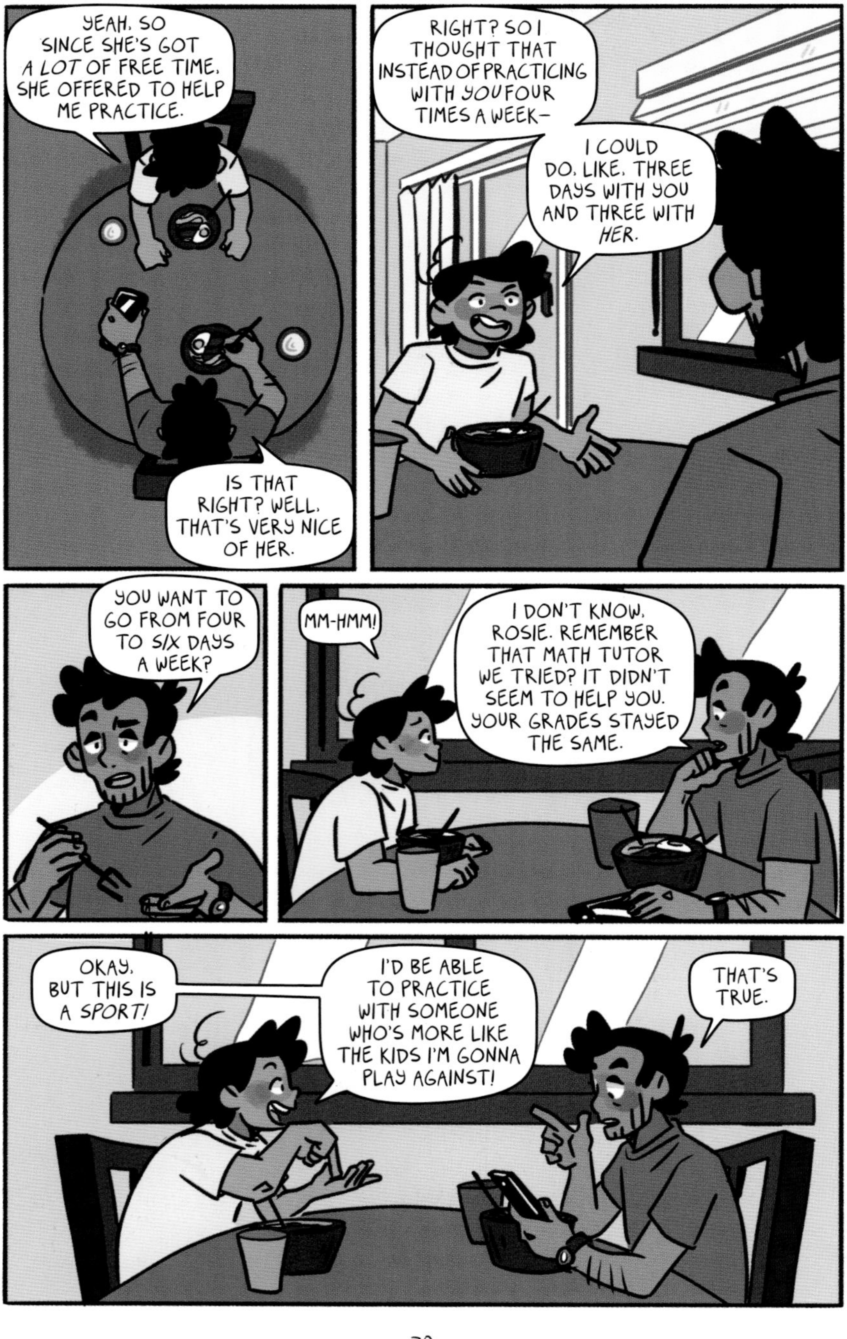
YEAH, SO SINCE SHE'S GOT A *LOT* OF FREE TIME, SHE OFFERED TO HELP ME PRACTICE.
IS THAT RIGHT? WELL, THAT'S VERY NICE OF HER.
RIGHT? SO I THOUGHT THAT INSTEAD OF PRACTICING WITH *YOU* FOUR TIMES A WEEK—
I COULD DO, LIKE, THREE DAYS WITH YOU AND THREE WITH *HER*.
YOU WANT TO GO FROM FOUR TO *SIX* DAYS A WEEK?
MM-HMM!
I DON'T KNOW, ROSIE. REMEMBER THAT MATH TUTOR WE TRIED? IT DIDN'T SEEM TO HELP YOU. YOUR GRADES STAYED THE SAME.
OKAY, BUT THIS IS A *SPORT*!
I'D BE ABLE TO PRACTICE WITH SOMEONE WHO'S MORE LIKE THE KIDS I'M GONNA PLAY AGAINST!
THAT'S TRUE.

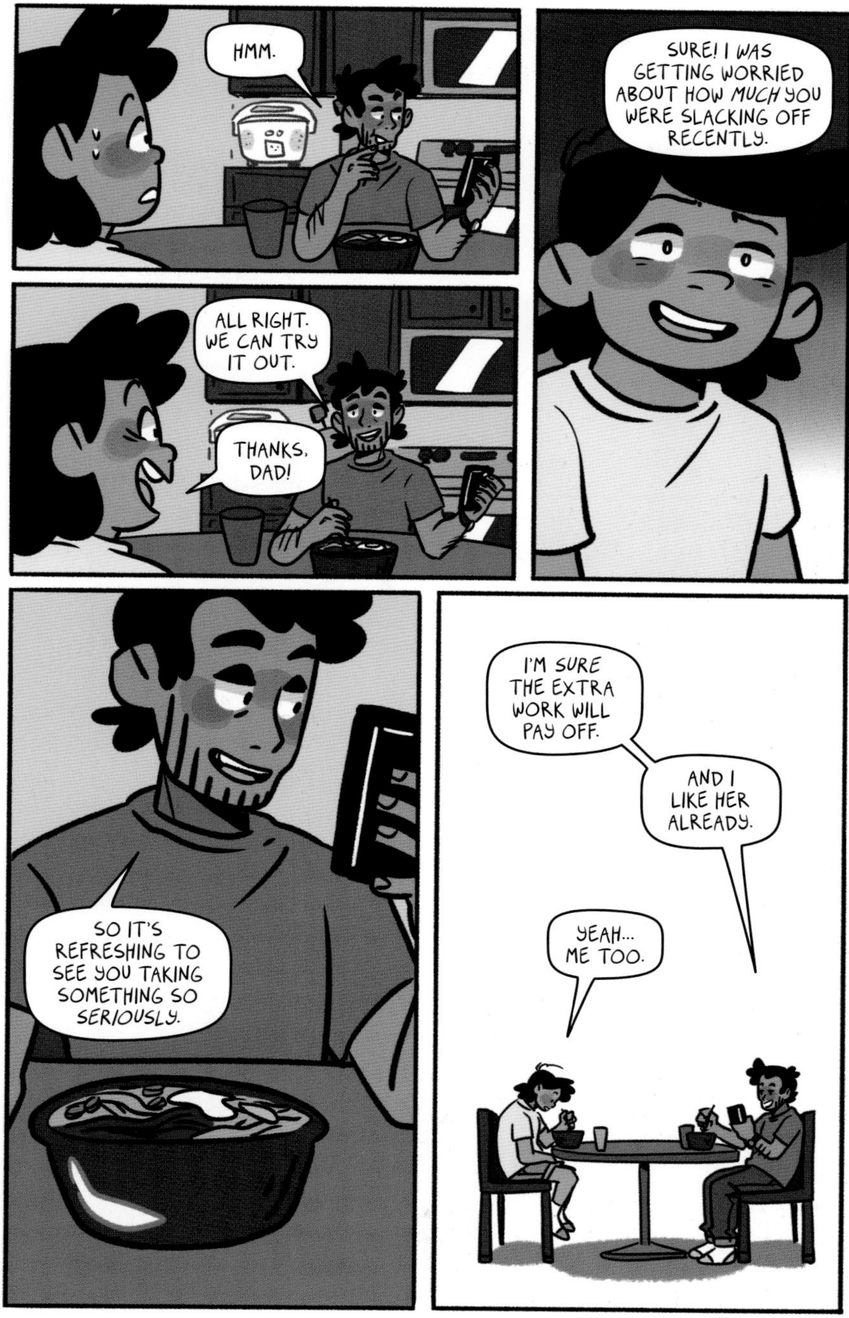
HMM.
SURE! I WAS GETTING WORRIED ABOUT HOW *MUCH* YOU WERE SLACKING OFF RECENTLY.
ALL RIGHT. WE CAN TRY IT OUT.
THANKS, DAD!
SO IT'S REFRESHING TO SEE YOU TAKING SOMETHING SO *SERIOUSLY*.
I'M SURE THE EXTRA WORK WILL PAY OFF.
AND I LIKE HER ALREADY.
YEAH... ME TOO.

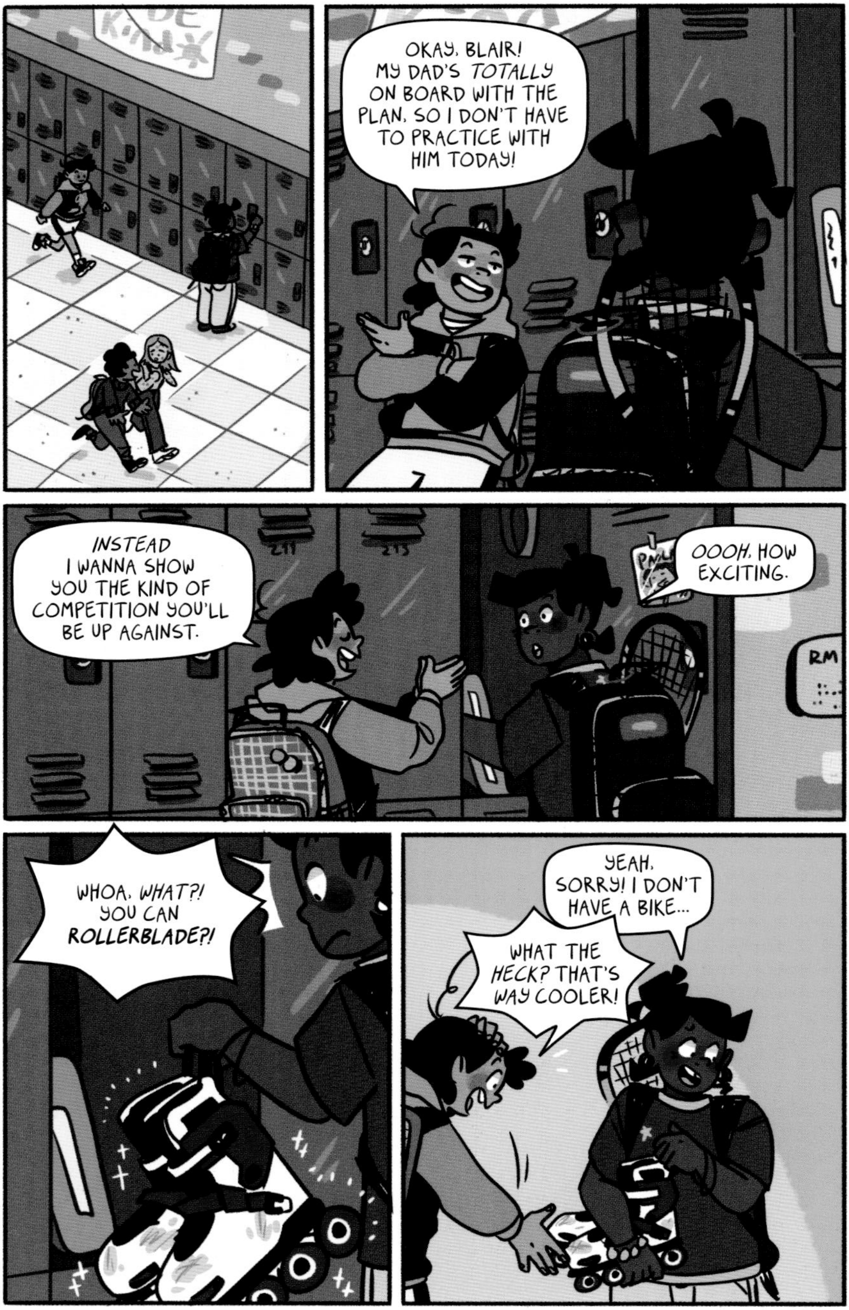
OKAY, BLAIR! MY DAD'S *TOTALLY* ON BOARD WITH THE PLAN, SO I DON'T HAVE TO PRACTICE WITH HIM TODAY!
INSTEAD I WANNA SHOW YOU THE KIND OF COMPETITION YOU'LL BE UP AGAINST.
OOOH, HOW EXCITING.
WHOA, *WHAT?!* YOU CAN **ROLLERBLADE?!**
YEAH, SORRY! I DON'T HAVE A BIKE...
WHAT THE *HECK?* THAT'S *WAY* COOLER!

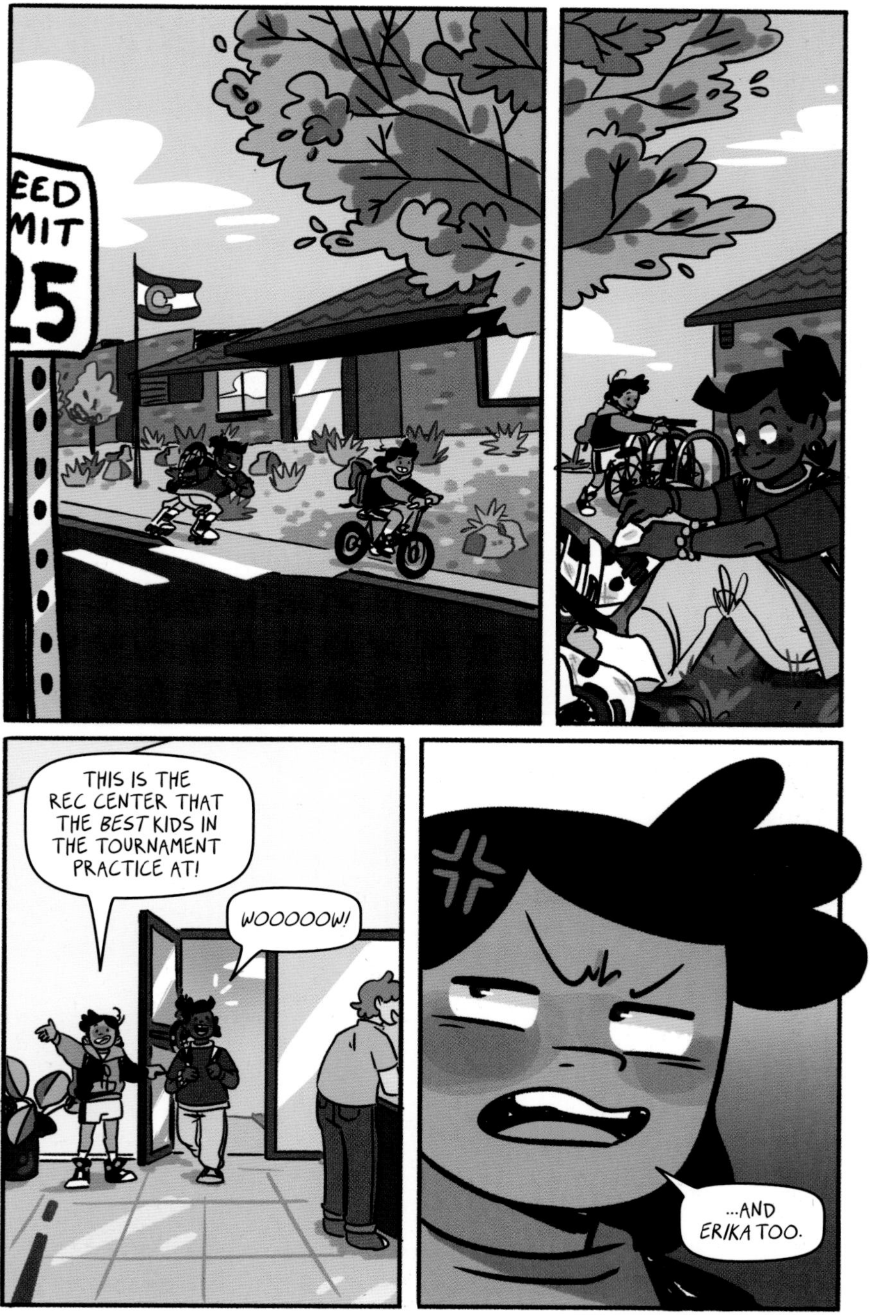
EED
MIT
25
THIS IS THE REC CENTER THAT THE *BEST* KIDS IN THE TOURNAMENT PRACTICE AT!
WOOOOOW!
...AND ERIKA TOO.

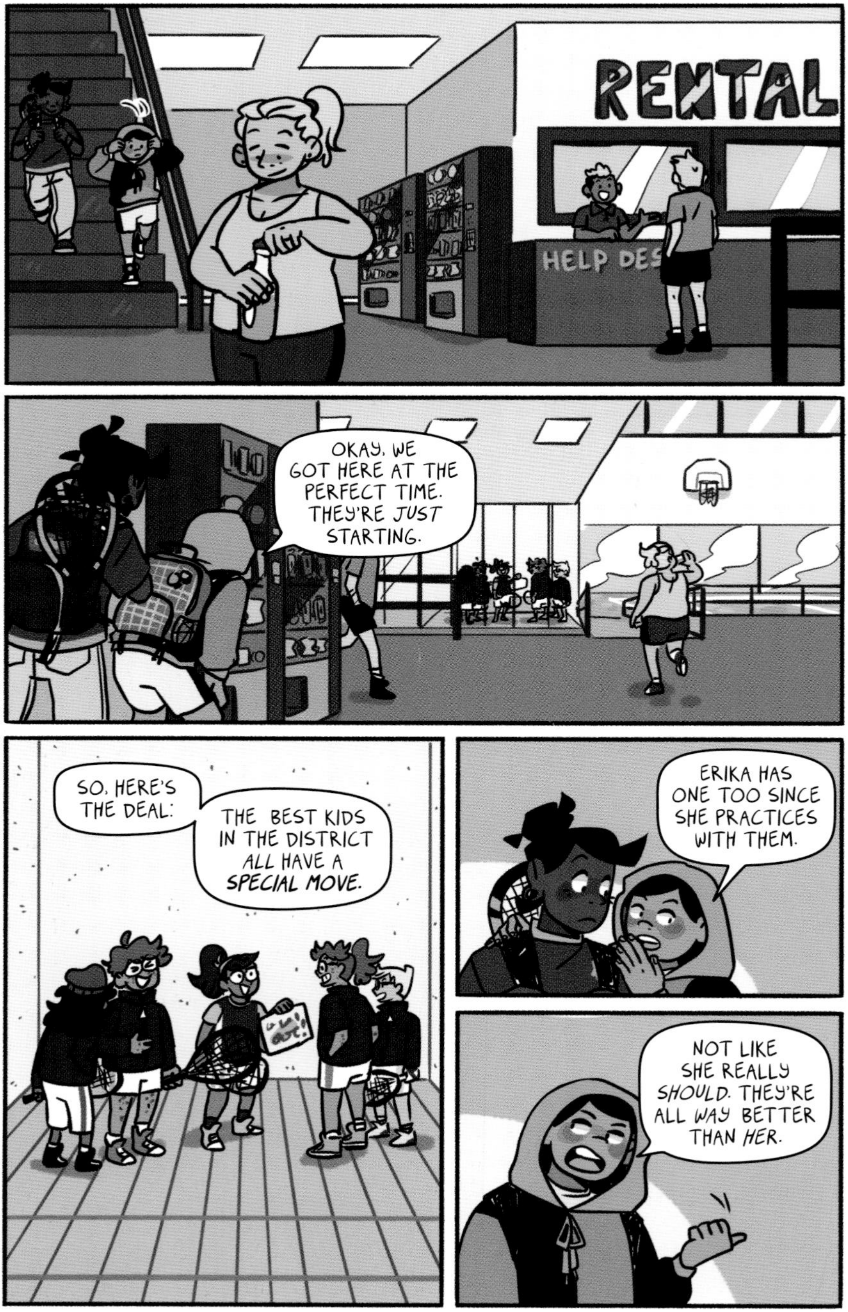
RENTAL
HELP DES
OKAY, WE GOT HERE AT THE PERFECT TIME. THEY'RE JUST STARTING.
SO, HERE'S THE DEAL:
THE BEST KIDS IN THE DISTRICT ALL HAVE A SPECIAL MOVE.
ERIKA HAS ONE TOO SINCE SHE PRACTICES WITH THEM.
NOT LIKE SHE REALLY SHOULD. THEY'RE ALL WAY BETTER THAN HER.

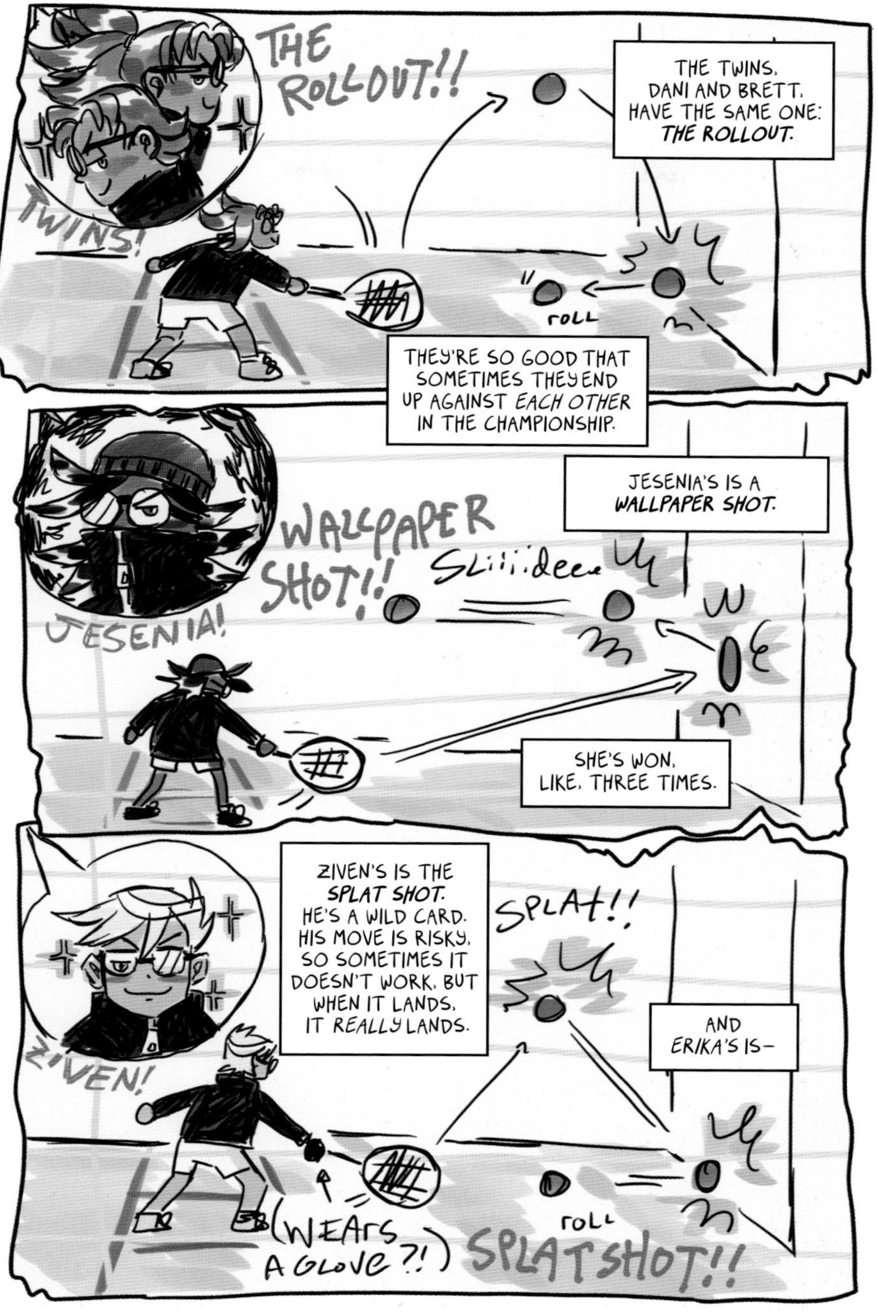
THE ROLLOUT!!
TWINS!
THE TWINS, DANI AND BRETT, HAVE THE SAME ONE: *THE ROLLOUT*.
ROLL
THEY'RE SO GOOD THAT SOMETIMES THEY END UP AGAINST *EACH OTHER* IN THE CHAMPIONSHIP.
WALLPAPER SHOT!!
JESENIA!
JESENIA'S IS A *WALLPAPER SHOT*.
SLIIIIdeee
SHE'S WON, LIKE, THREE TIMES.
ZIVEN'S IS THE *SPLAT SHOT*. HE'S A WILD CARD. HIS MOVE IS RISKY, SO SOMETIMES IT DOESN'T WORK, BUT WHEN IT LANDS, IT *REALLY* LANDS.
SPLAT!!
ZIVEN!
AND ERIKA'S IS—
(WEARS A GLOVE?!)
ROLL
SPLAT SHOT!!

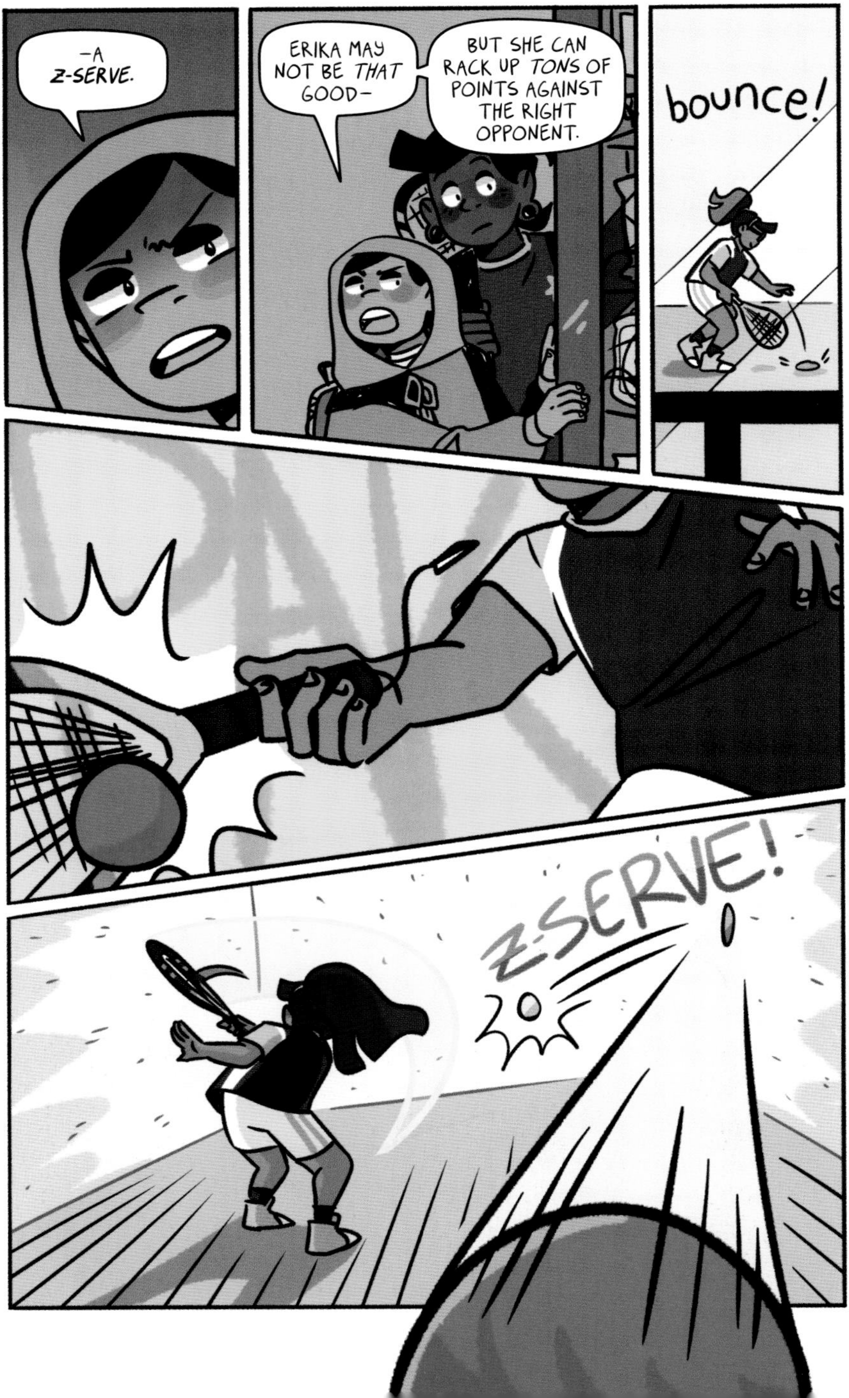
-A Z-SERVE.
ERIKA MAY NOT BE THAT GOOD-
BUT SHE CAN RACK UP TONS OF POINTS AGAINST THE RIGHT OPPONENT.
bounce!
PAW
Z-SERVE!

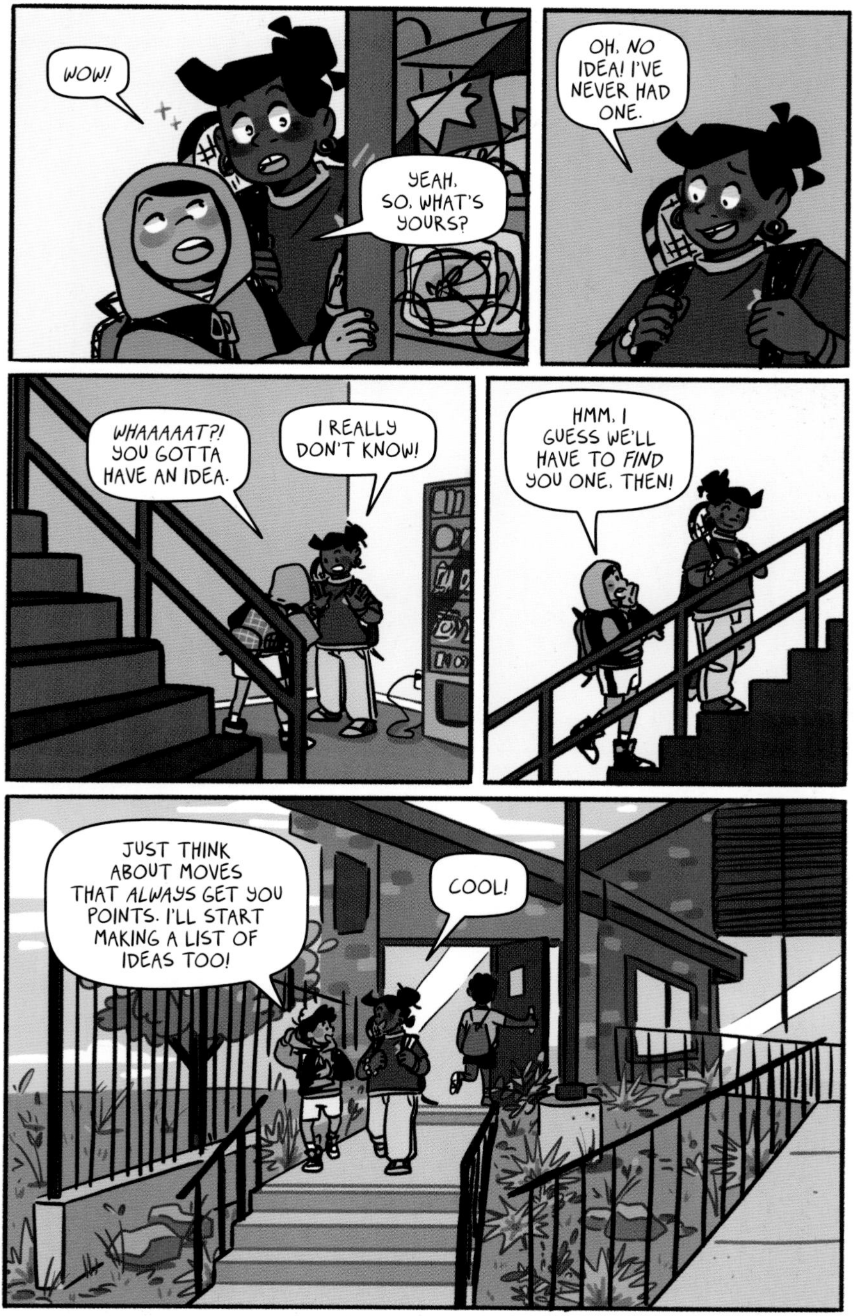
WOW!
YEAH, SO, WHAT'S YOURS?
OH, NO IDEA! I'VE NEVER HAD ONE.
WHAAAAAT?! YOU GOTTA HAVE AN IDEA.
I REALLY DON'T KNOW!
HMM, I GUESS WE'LL HAVE TO FIND YOU ONE, THEN!
JUST THINK ABOUT MOVES THAT ALWAYS GET YOU POINTS. I'LL START MAKING A LIST OF IDEAS TOO!
COOL!

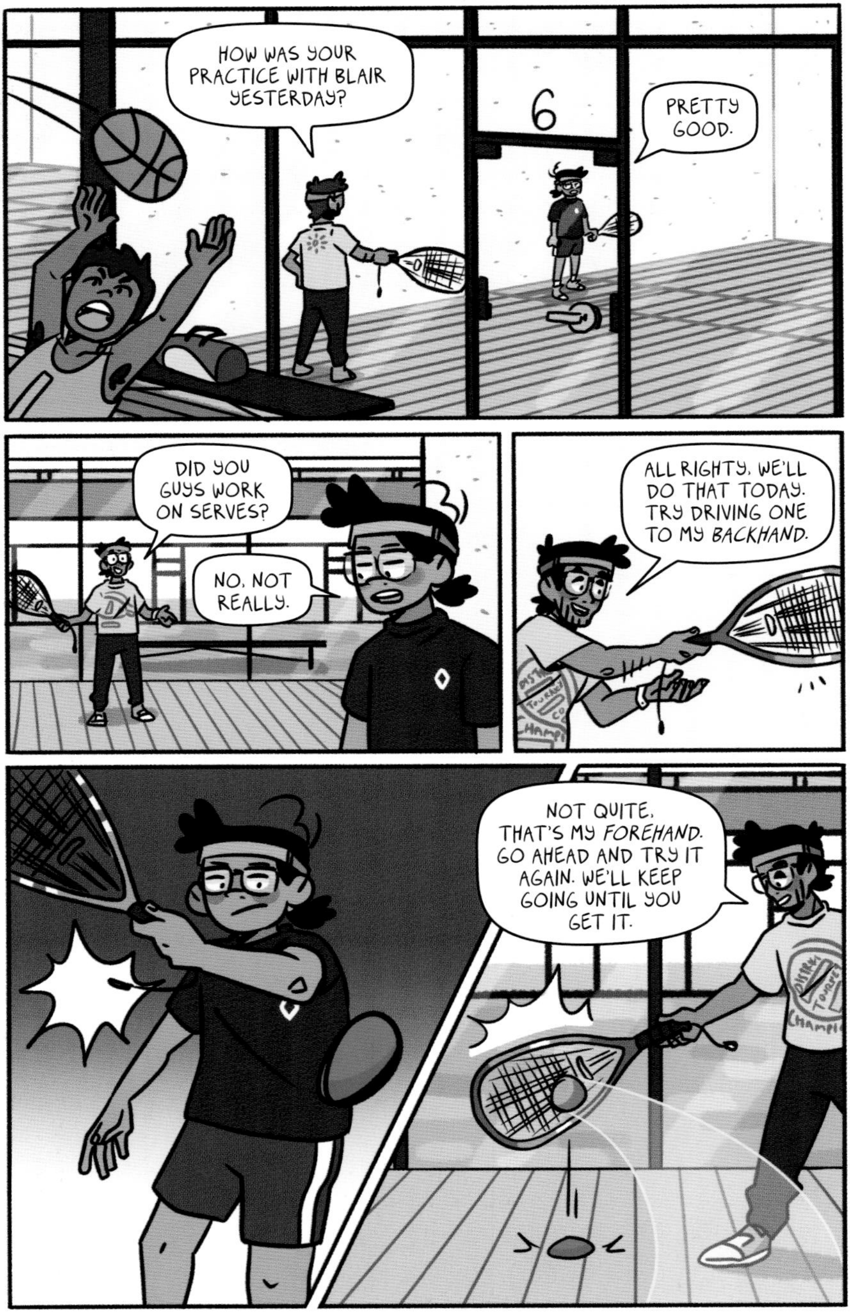
HOW WAS YOUR PRACTICE WITH BLAIR YESTERDAY?
6
PRETTY GOOD.
DID YOU GUYS WORK ON SERVES?
NO, NOT REALLY.
ALL RIGHTY, WE'LL DO THAT TODAY. TRY DRIVING ONE TO MY *BACKHAND*.
NOT QUITE, THAT'S MY *FOREHAND*. GO AHEAD AND TRY IT AGAIN. WE'LL KEEP GOING UNTIL YOU GET IT.

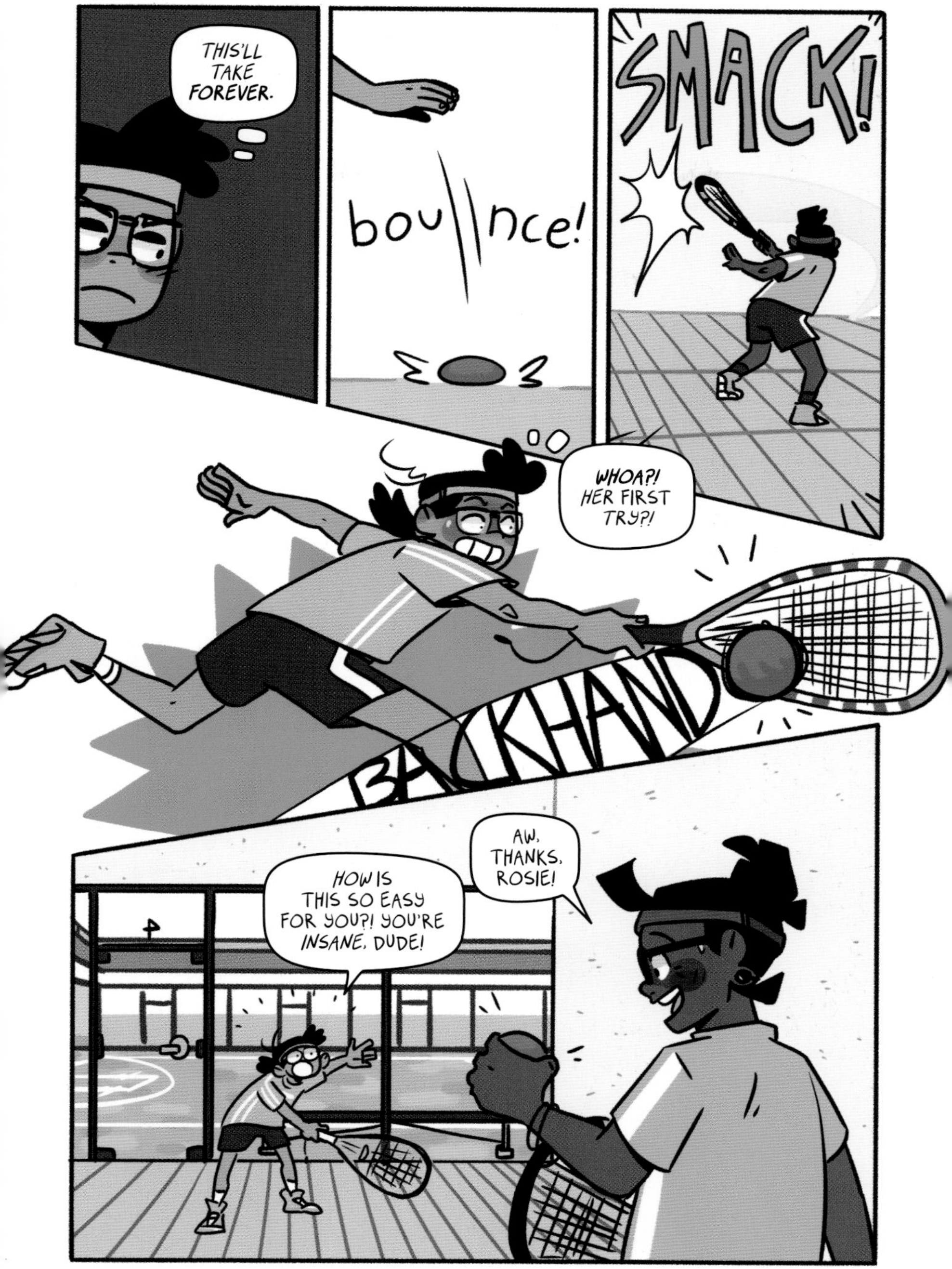
THIS'LL TAKE FOREVER.
bou||nce!
SMACK!
WHOA?! HER FIRST TRY?!
BACKHAND
HOW IS THIS SO EASY FOR YOU?! YOU'RE INSANE, DUDE!
AW, THANKS, ROSIE!

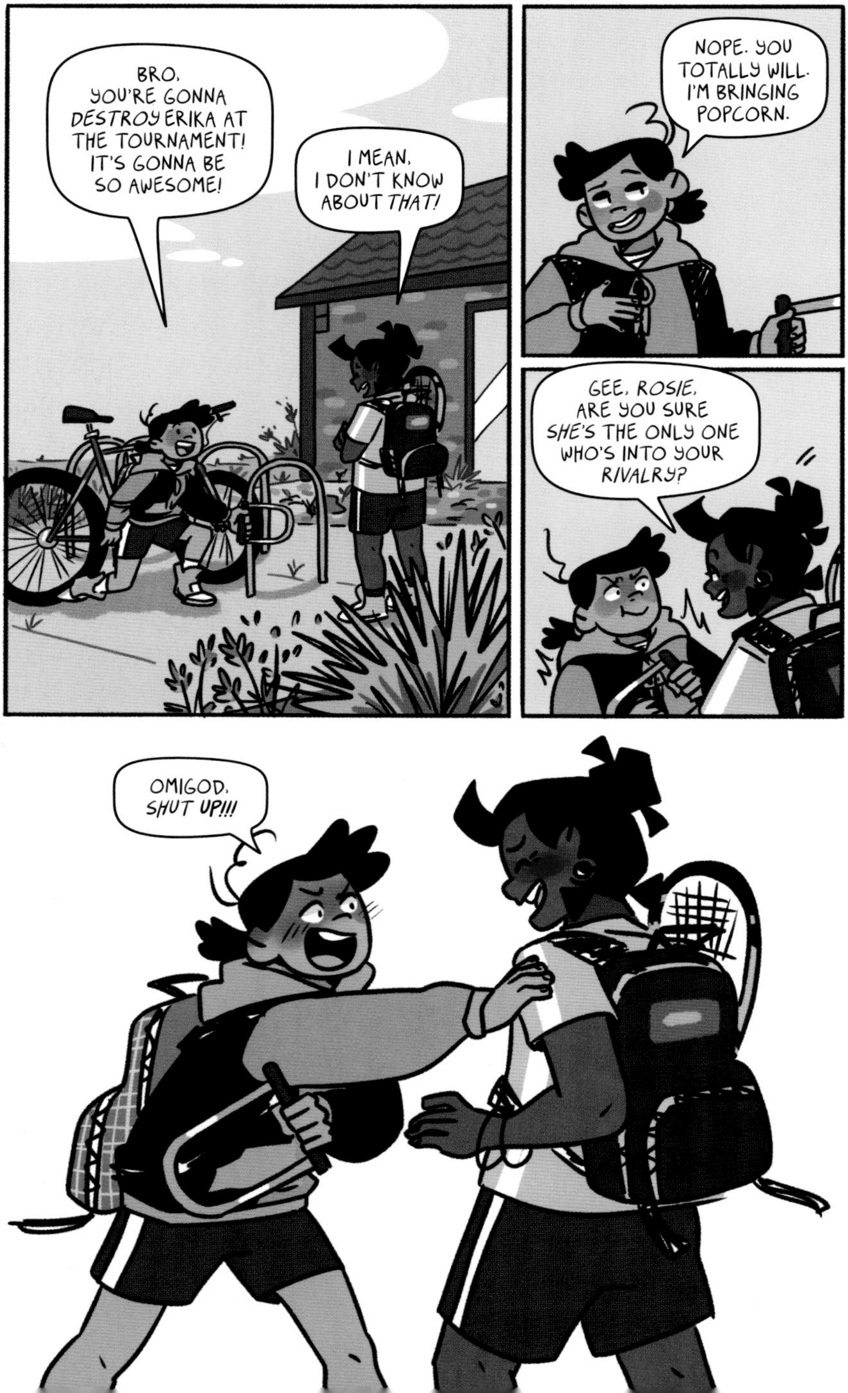
BRO, YOU'RE GONNA DESTROY ERIKA AT THE TOURNAMENT! IT'S GONNA BE SO AWESOME!
I MEAN, I DON'T KNOW ABOUT THAT!
NOPE. YOU TOTALLY WILL. I'M BRINGING POPCORN.
GEE, ROSIE, ARE YOU SURE SHE'S THE ONLY ONE WHO'S INTO YOUR RIVALRY?
OMIGOD. SHUT UP!!!

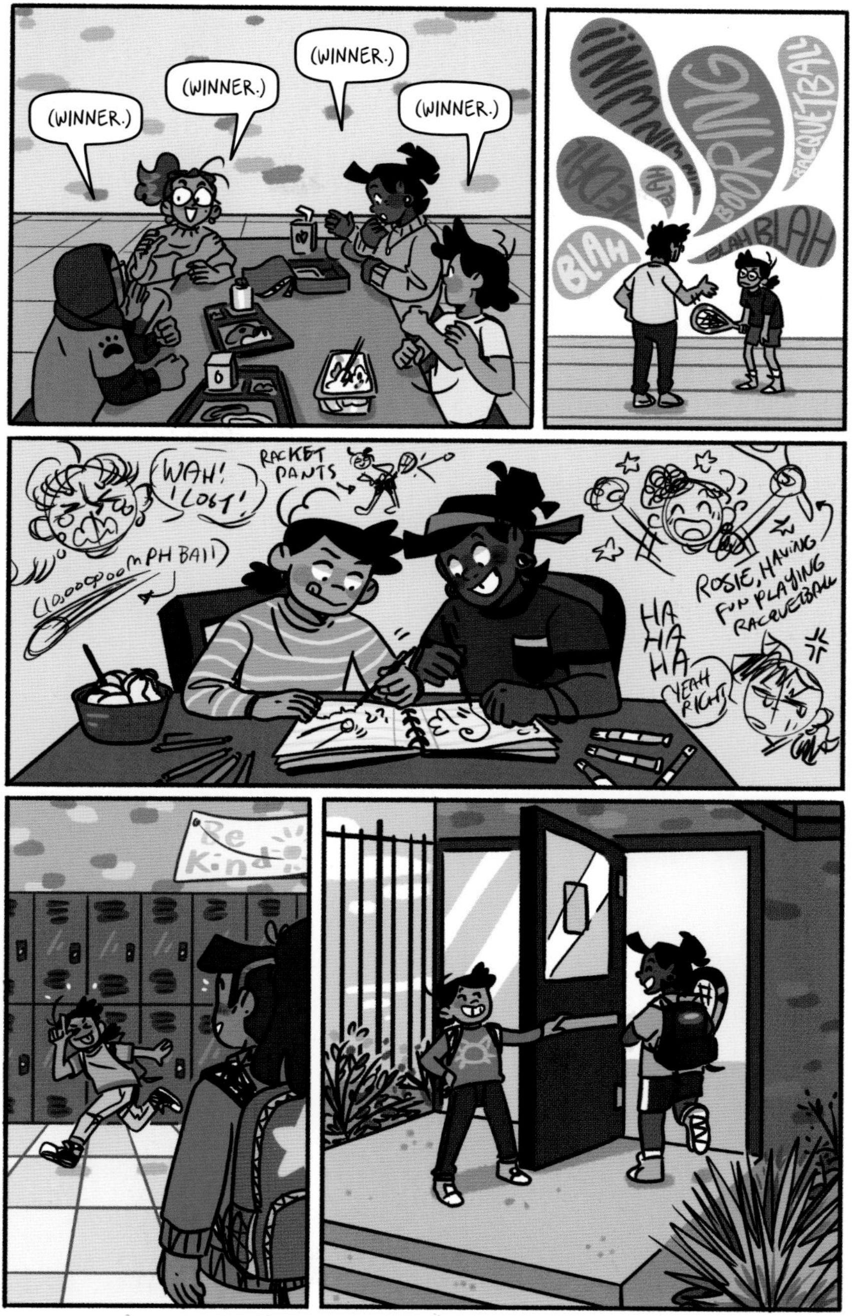
(WINNER.)
(WINNER.)
(WINNER.)
(WINNER.)
WINNING!
BORING
RACQUETBALL
BLAH
BLAH BLAH BLAH
WAH! I LOST!
RACKET PANTS
(10,000,000 MPH BALL)
ROSIE, HAVING FUN PLAYING RACQUETBALL
HA HA HA
YEAH RIGHT
Be Kind

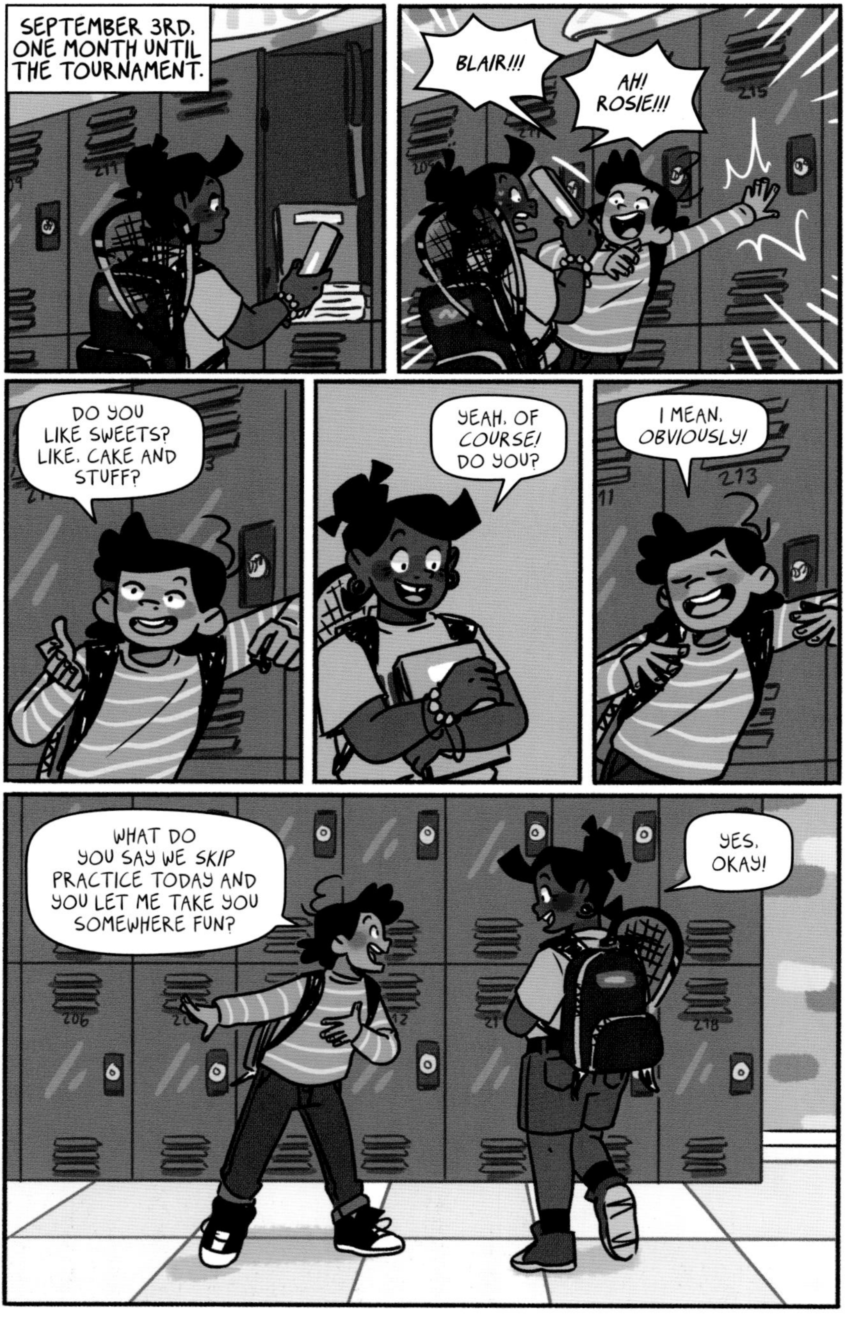
SEPTEMBER 3RD. ONE MONTH UNTIL THE TOURNAMENT.
BLAIR!!!
AH! ROSIE!!!
DO YOU LIKE SWEETS? LIKE, CAKE AND STUFF?
YEAH, OF COURSE! DO YOU?
I MEAN, OBVIOUSLY!
WHAT DO YOU SAY WE SKIP PRACTICE TODAY AND YOU LET ME TAKE YOU SOMEWHERE FUN?
YES, OKAY!

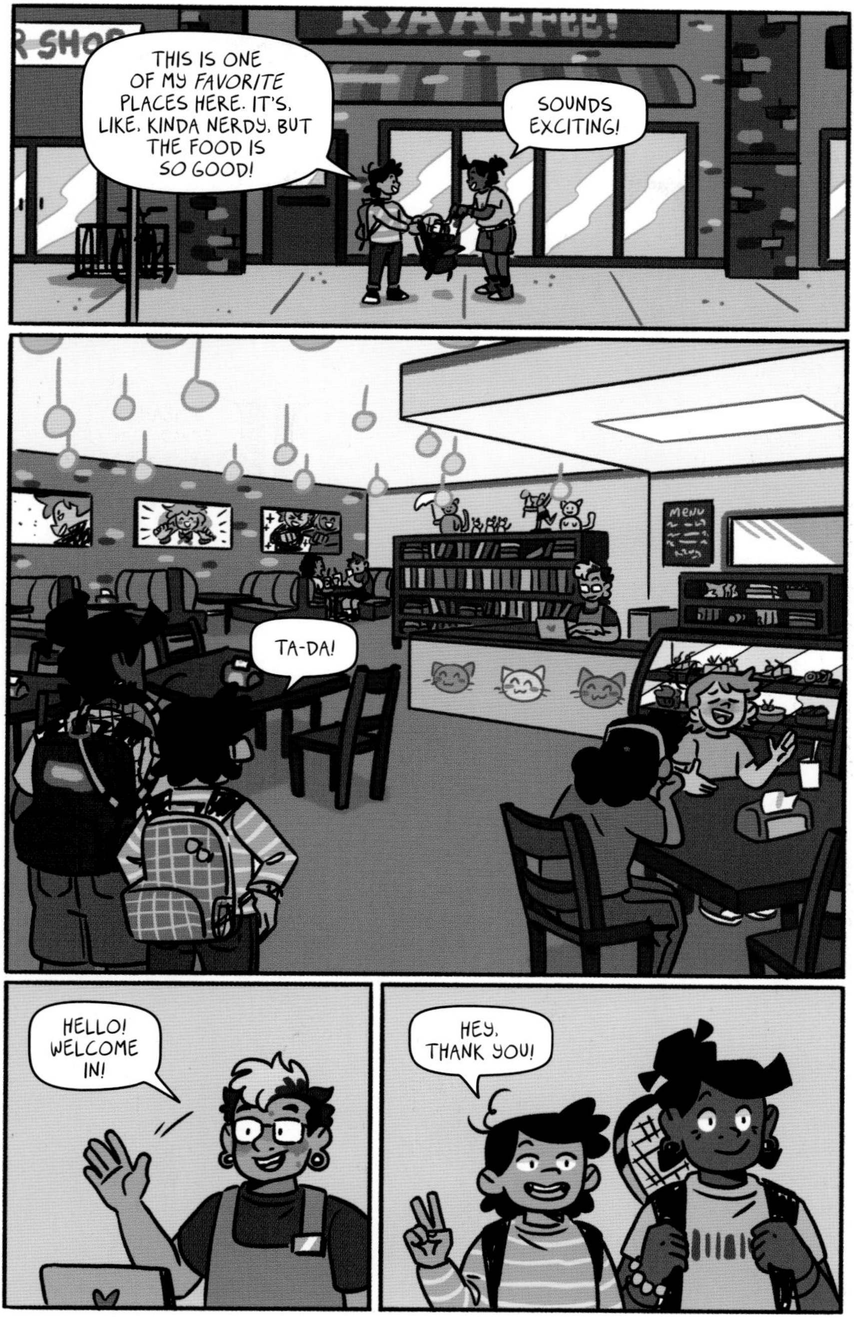
THIS IS ONE OF MY *FAVORITE* PLACES HERE. IT'S, LIKE, KINDA NERDY, BUT THE FOOD IS SO GOOD!
SOUNDS EXCITING!
TA-DA!
HELLO! WELCOME IN!
HEY, THANK YOU!

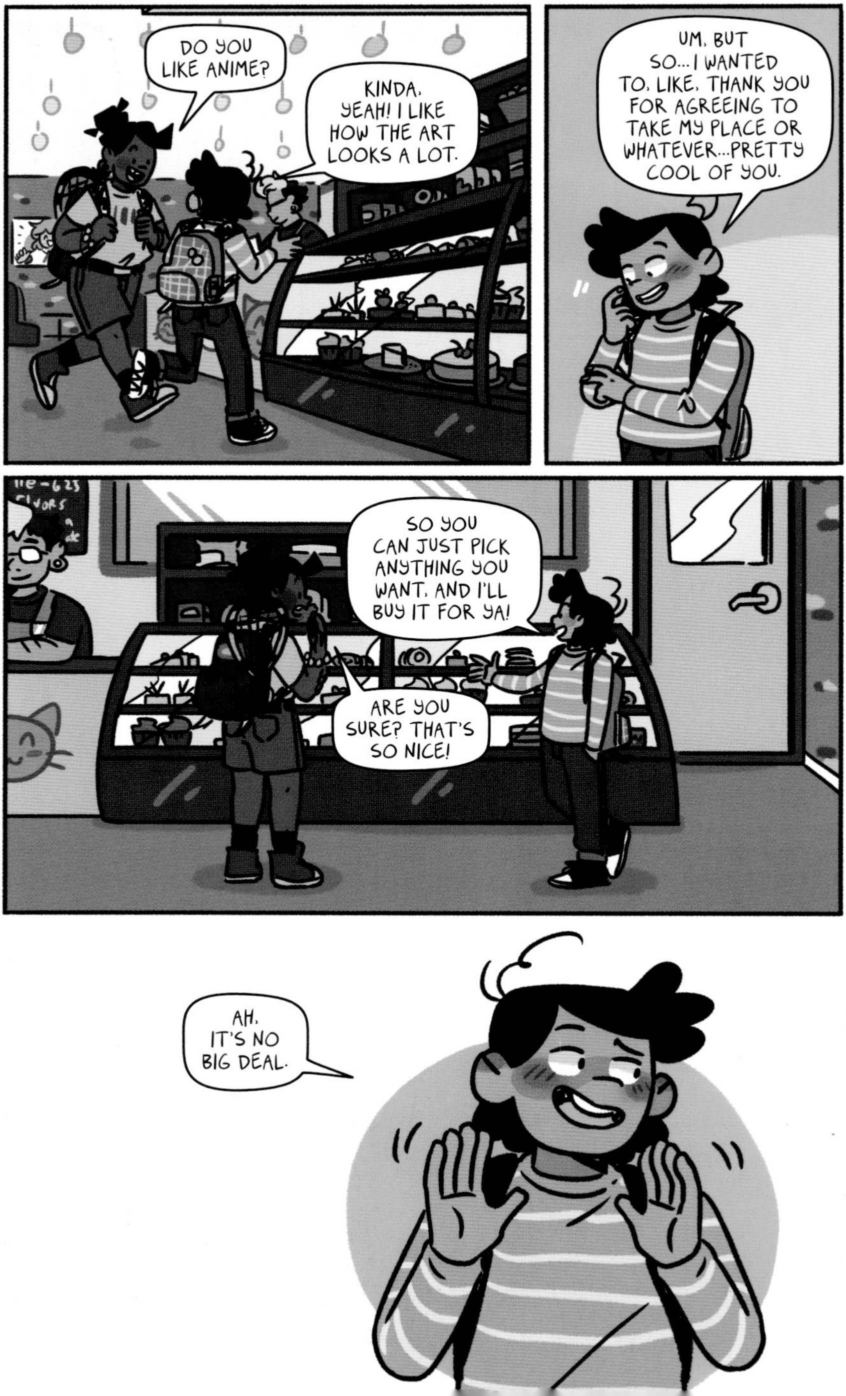
DO YOU LIKE ANIME?
KINDA, YEAH! I LIKE HOW THE ART LOOKS A LOT.
UM, BUT SO... I WANTED TO, LIKE, THANK YOU FOR AGREEING TO TAKE MY PLACE OR WHATEVER... PRETTY COOL OF YOU.
SO YOU CAN JUST PICK ANYTHING YOU WANT, AND I'LL BUY IT FOR YA!
ARE YOU SURE? THAT'S SO NICE!
AH, IT'S NO BIG DEAL.

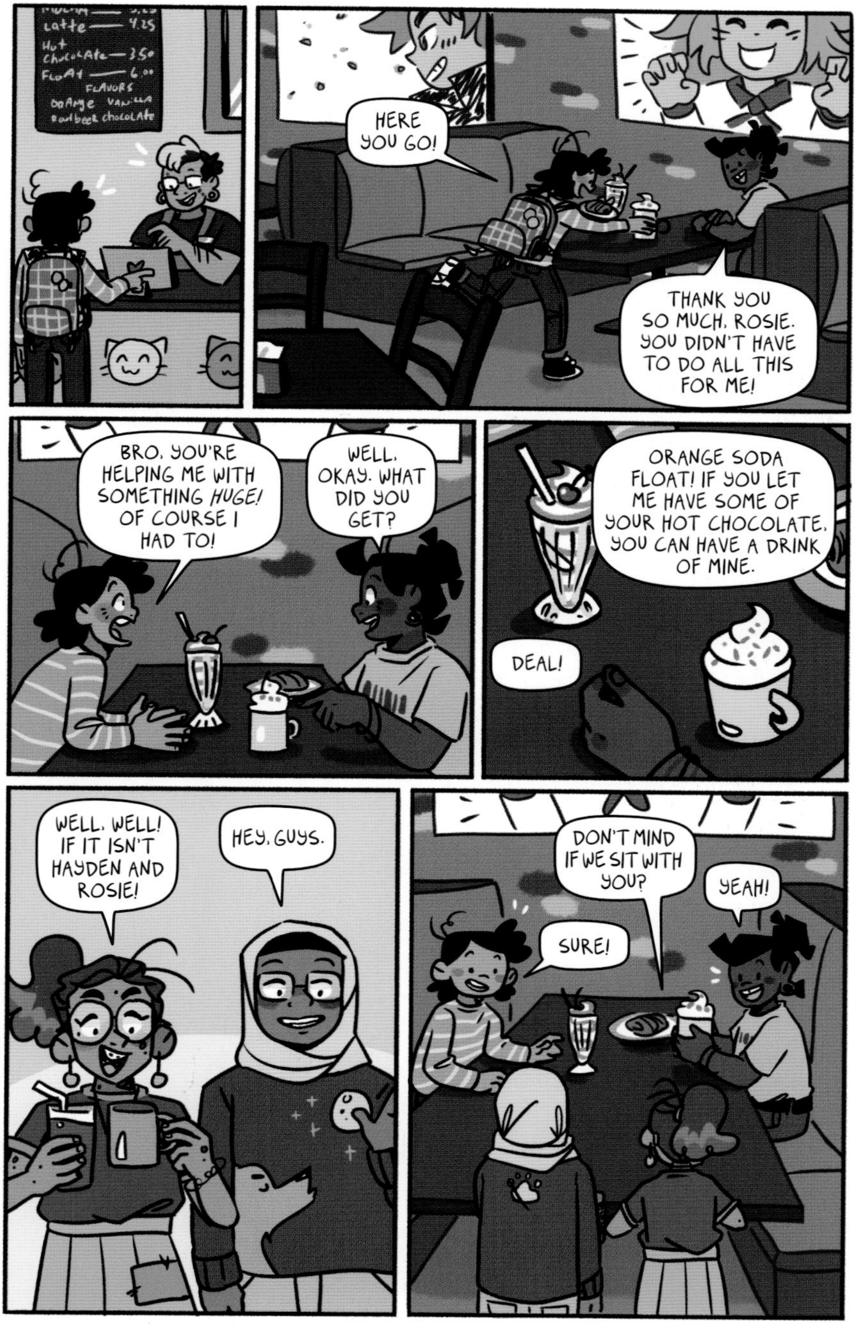
Latte — 4.25
Hot Chocolate — 3.50
Float — 6.00
FLAVOURS
orange vanilla
rootbeer chocolate
HERE YOU GO!
THANK YOU SO MUCH, ROSIE. YOU DIDN'T HAVE TO DO ALL THIS FOR ME!
BRO, YOU'RE HELPING ME WITH SOMETHING *HUGE!* OF COURSE I HAD TO!
WELL, OKAY. WHAT DID YOU GET?
ORANGE SODA FLOAT! IF YOU LET ME HAVE SOME OF YOUR HOT CHOCOLATE, YOU CAN HAVE A DRINK OF MINE.
DEAL!
WELL, WELL! IF IT ISN'T HAYDEN AND ROSIE!
HEY, GUYS.
DON'T MIND IF WE SIT WITH YOU?
SURE!
YEAH!

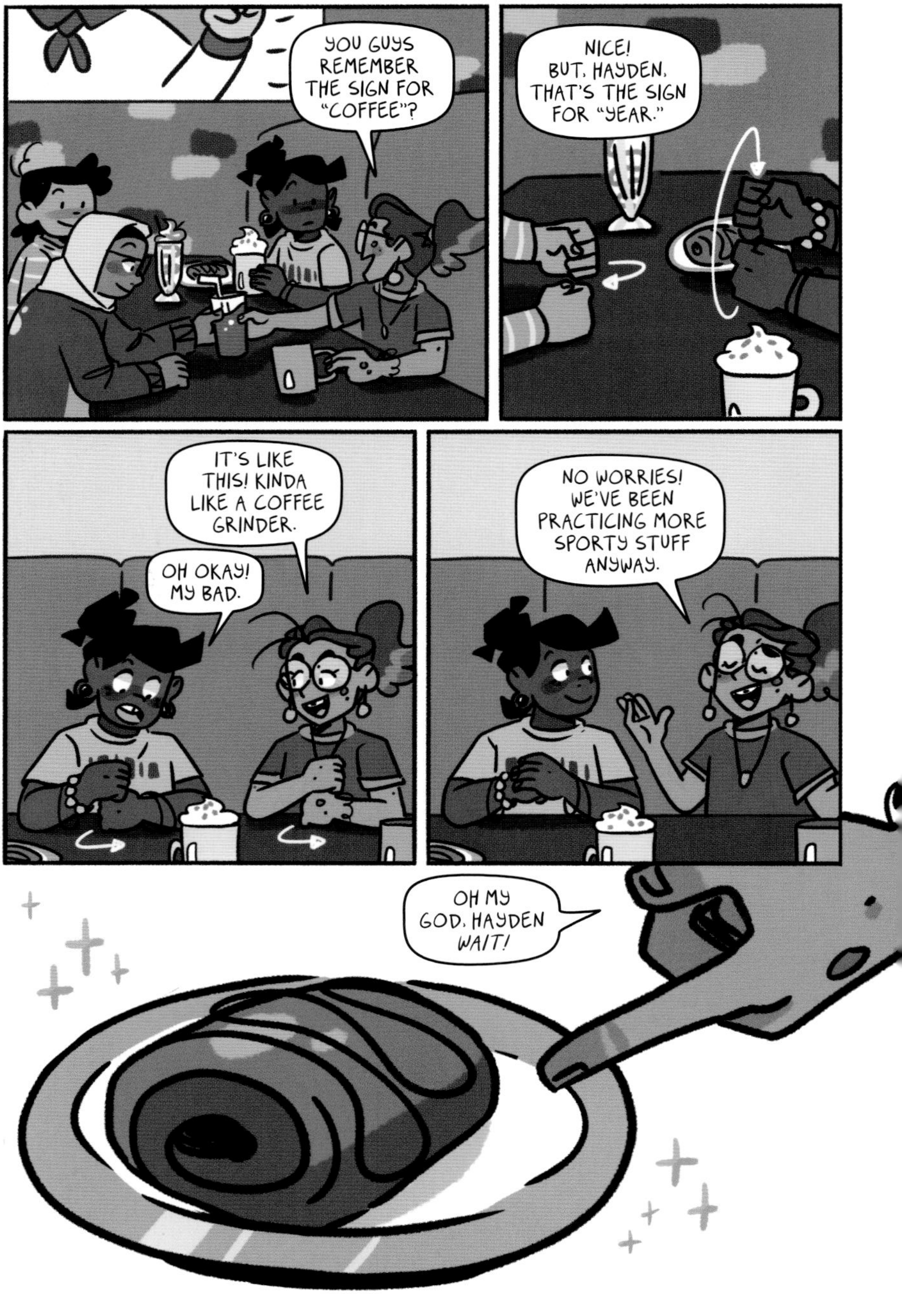
YOU GUYS REMEMBER THE SIGN FOR "COFFEE"?
NICE! BUT, HAYDEN, THAT'S THE SIGN FOR "YEAR."
IT'S LIKE THIS! KINDA LIKE A COFFEE GRINDER.
OH OKAY! MY BAD.
NO WORRIES! WE'VE BEEN PRACTICING MORE SPORTY STUFF ANYWAY.
OH MY GOD, HAYDEN WAIT!

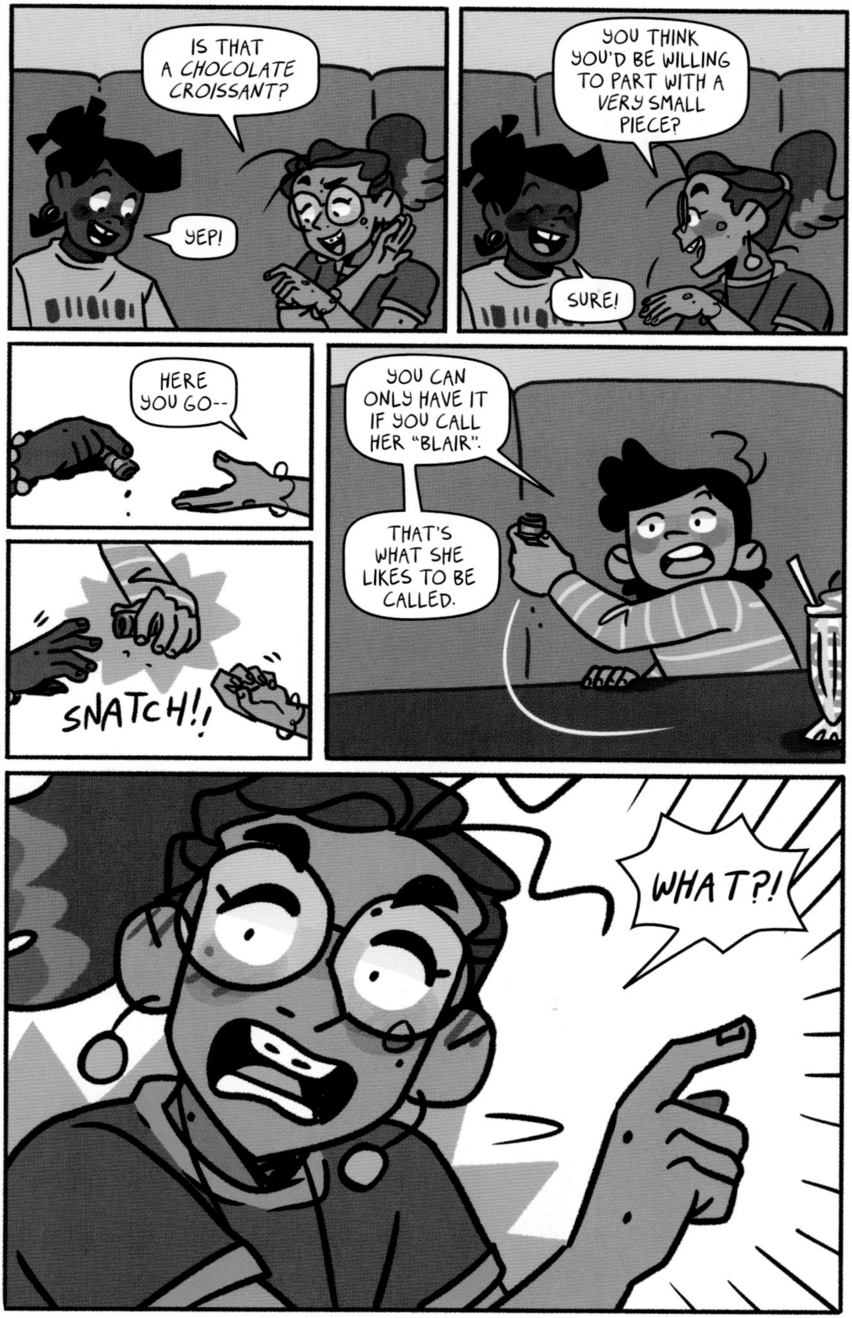
IS THAT A *CHOCOLATE* CROISSANT?
YEP!
YOU THINK YOU'D BE WILLING TO PART WITH A *VERY* SMALL PIECE?
SURE!
HERE YOU GO--
SNATCH!!
YOU CAN ONLY HAVE IT IF YOU CALL HER "BLAIR".
THAT'S WHAT SHE LIKES TO BE CALLED.
WHAT?!

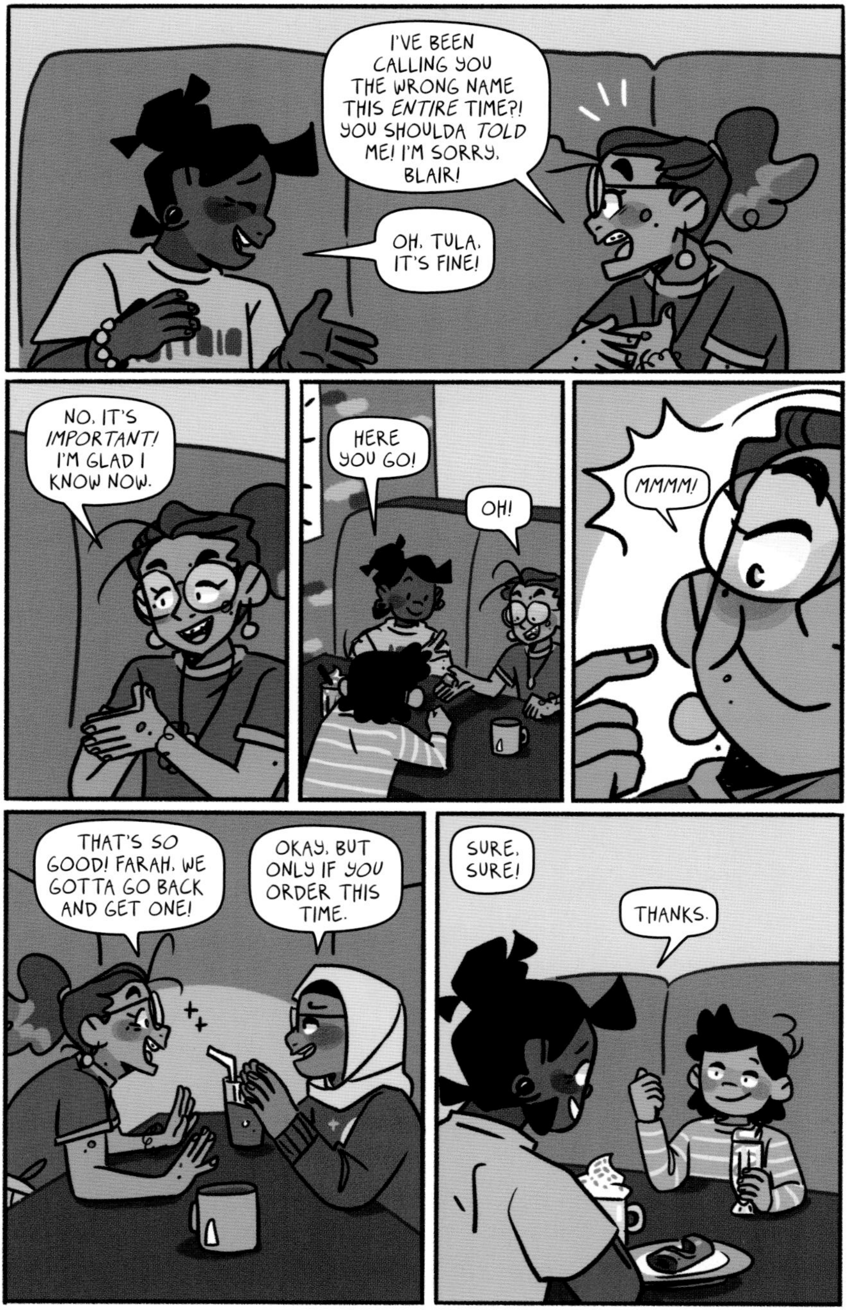
I'VE BEEN CALLING YOU THE WRONG NAME THIS *ENTIRE* TIME?! YOU SHOULDA *TOLD* ME! I'M SORRY, BLAIR!
OH, TULA, IT'S FINE!
NO, IT'S *IMPORTANT!* I'M GLAD I KNOW NOW.
HERE YOU GO!
OH!
MMMM!
THAT'S SO GOOD! FARAH, WE GOTTA GO BACK AND GET ONE!
OKAY, BUT ONLY IF *YOU* ORDER THIS TIME.
SURE, SURE!
THANKS.

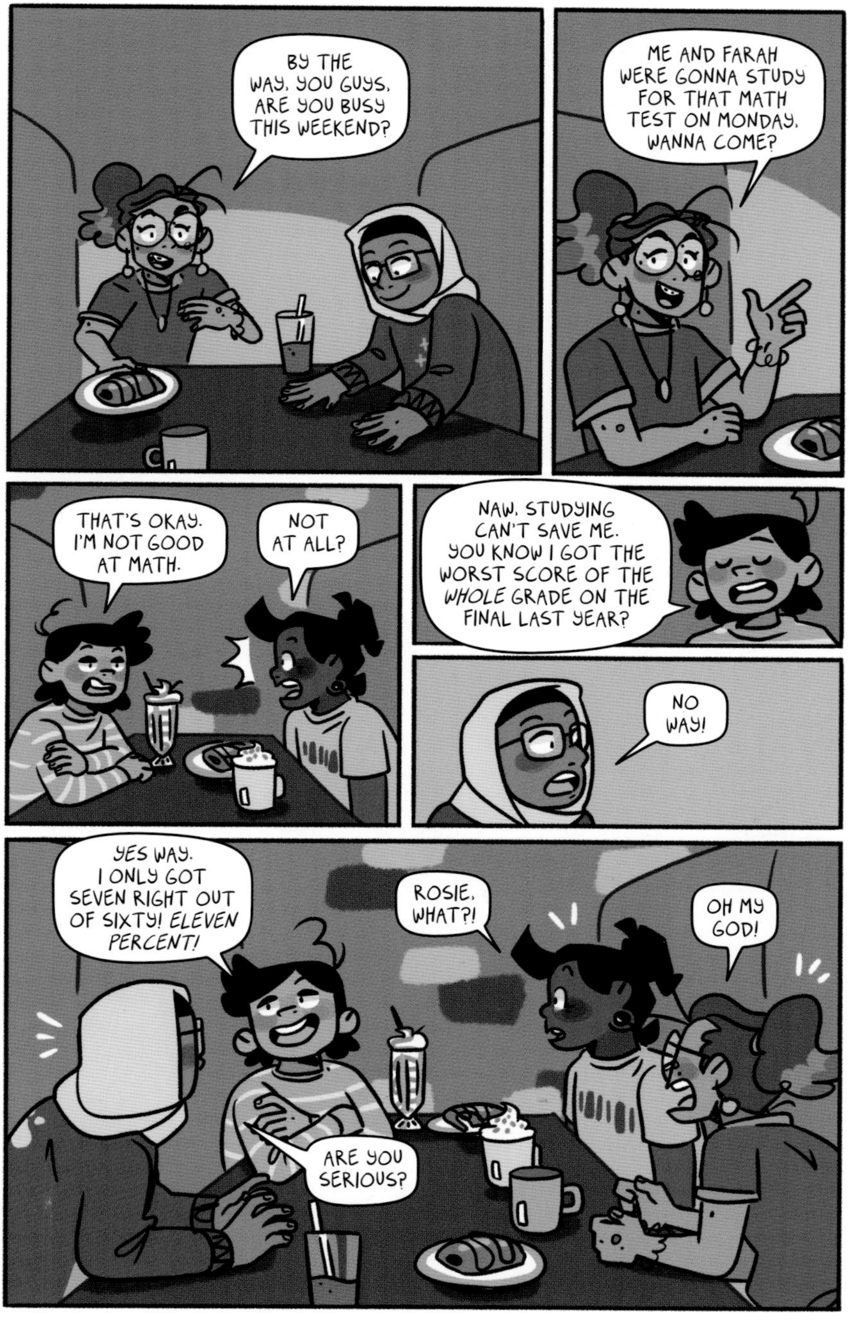
BY THE WAY, YOU GUYS, ARE YOU BUSY THIS WEEKEND?
ME AND FARAH WERE GONNA STUDY FOR THAT MATH TEST ON MONDAY. WANNA COME?
THAT'S OKAY. I'M NOT GOOD AT MATH.
NOT AT ALL?
NAW, STUDYING CAN'T SAVE ME. YOU KNOW I GOT THE WORST SCORE OF THE *WHOLE* GRADE ON THE FINAL LAST YEAR?
NO WAY!
YES WAY. I ONLY GOT SEVEN RIGHT OUT OF SIXTY! ELEVEN PERCENT!
ROSIE, WHAT?!
OH MY GOD!
ARE YOU SERIOUS?

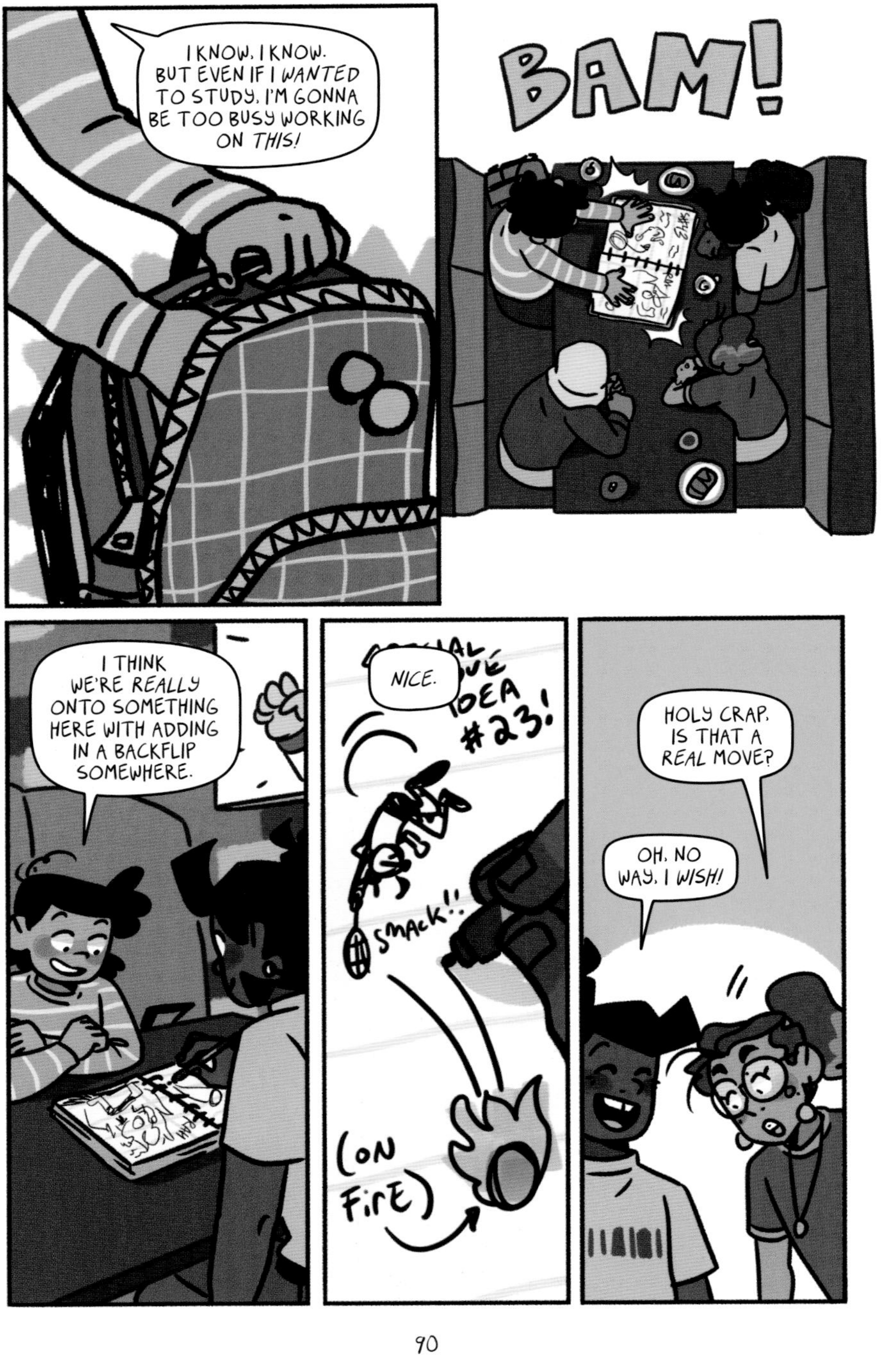
I KNOW, I KNOW. BUT EVEN IF I *WANTED* TO STUDY, I'M GONNA BE TOO BUSY WORKING ON *THIS!*
BAM!
I THINK WE'RE *REALLY* ONTO SOMETHING HERE WITH ADDING IN A BACKFLIP SOMEWHERE.
NICE.
IDEA #23!
SMACK!!
(ON FIRE)
HOLY CRAP, IS THAT A *REAL* MOVE?
OH, NO WAY, I *WISH!*

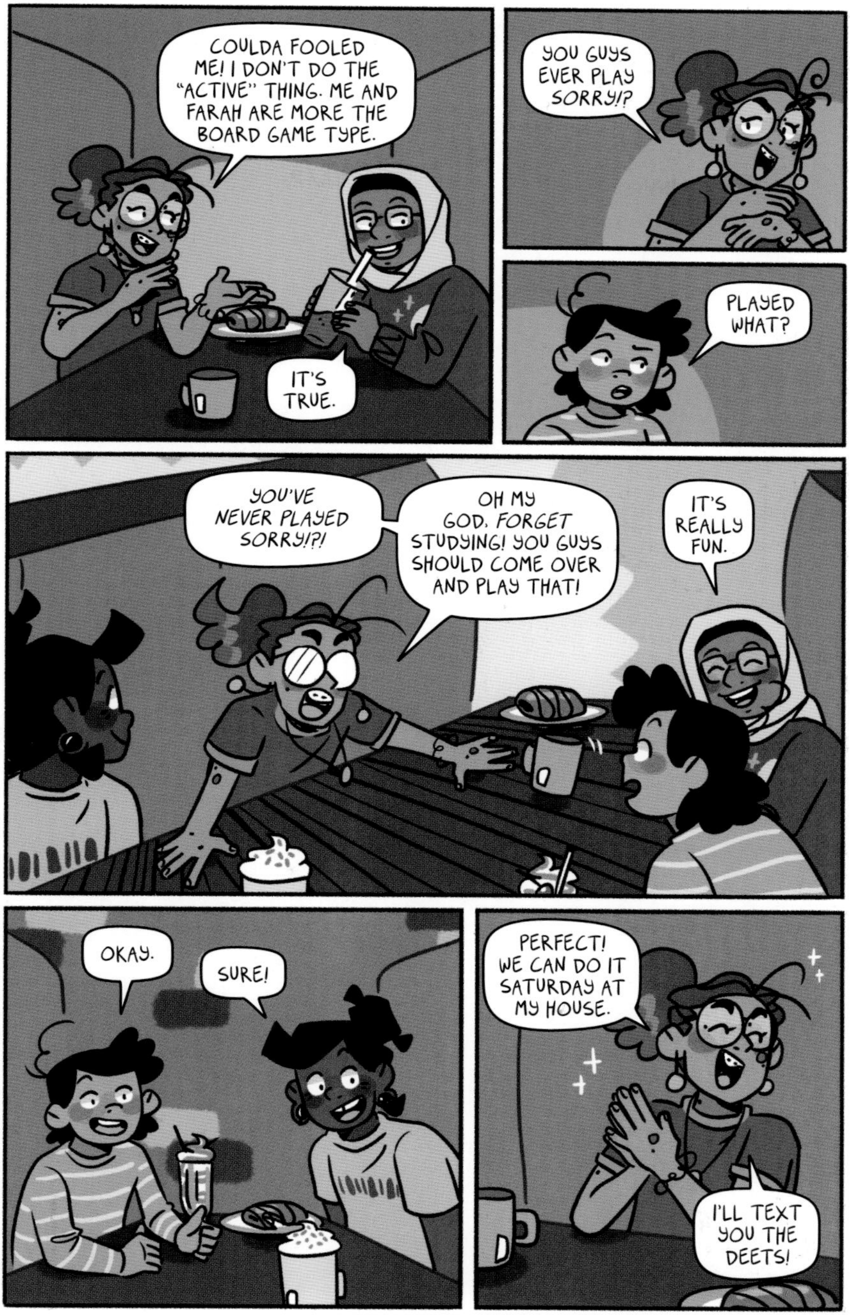
COULDA FOOLED ME! I DON'T DO THE "ACTIVE" THING. ME AND FARAH ARE MORE THE BOARD GAME TYPE.
IT'S TRUE.
YOU GUYS EVER PLAY SORRY!?
PLAYED WHAT?
YOU'VE NEVER PLAYED SORRY!?!
OH MY GOD, FORGET STUDYING! YOU GUYS SHOULD COME OVER AND PLAY THAT!
IT'S REALLY FUN.
OKAY.
SURE!
PERFECT! WE CAN DO IT SATURDAY AT MY HOUSE.
I'LL TEXT YOU THE DEETS!

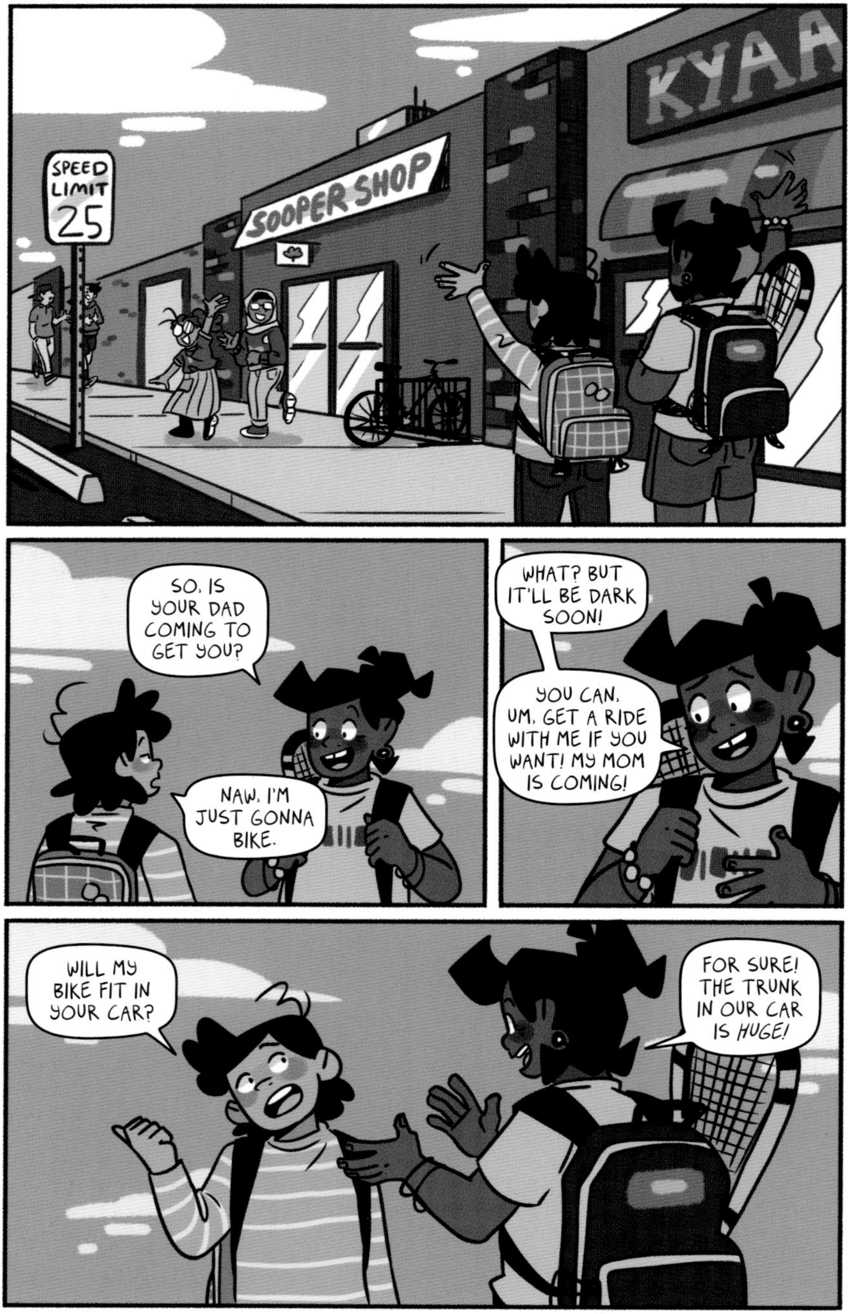
SPEED LIMIT 25
SOOPER SHOP
KYAA
SO, IS YOUR DAD COMING TO GET YOU?
NAW, I'M JUST GONNA BIKE.
WHAT? BUT IT'LL BE DARK SOON!
YOU CAN, UM, GET A RIDE WITH ME IF YOU WANT! MY MOM IS COMING!
WILL MY BIKE FIT IN YOUR CAR?
FOR SURE! THE TRUNK IN OUR CAR IS *HUGE!*

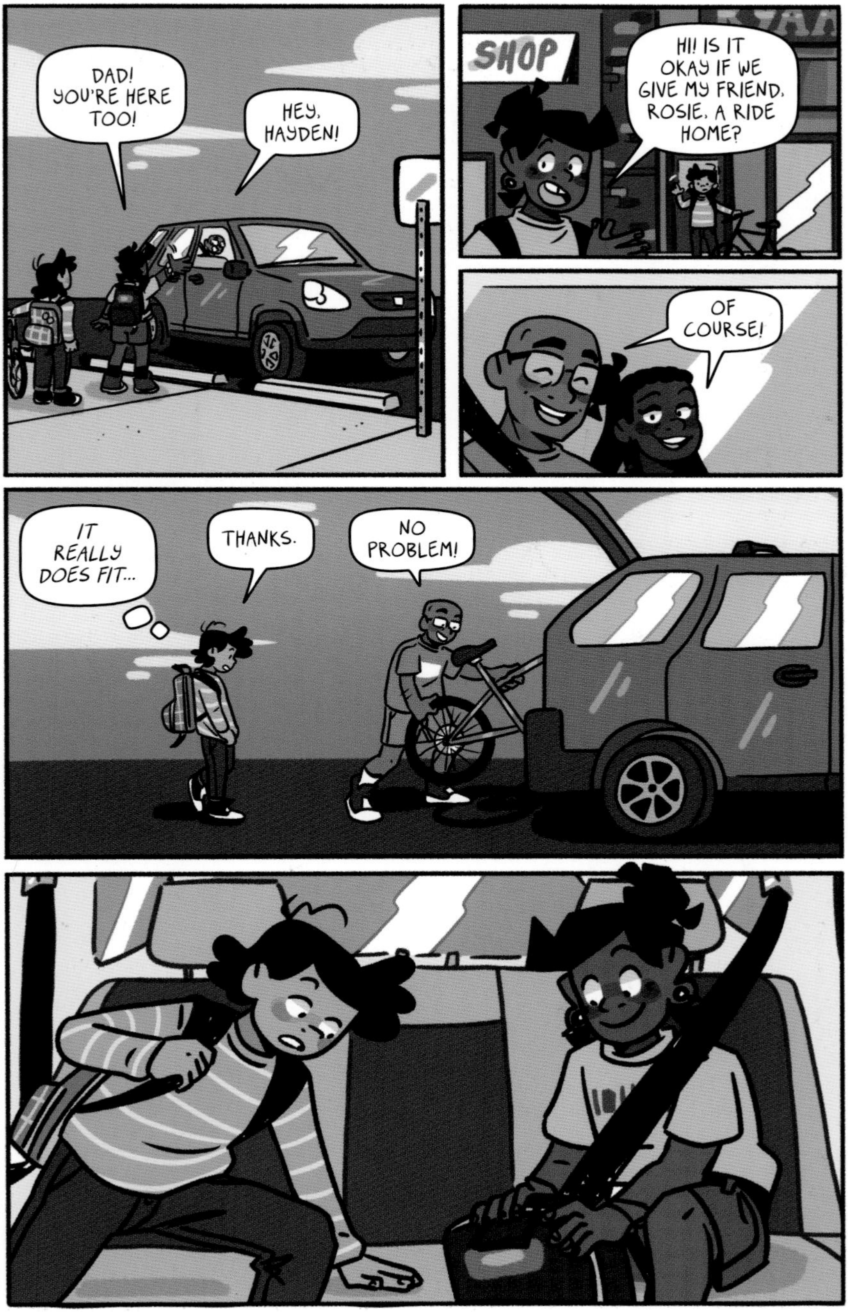
DAD! YOU'RE HERE TOO!
HEY, HAYDEN!
SHOP
HI! IS IT OKAY IF WE GIVE MY FRIEND, ROSIE, A RIDE HOME?
OF COURSE!
IT REALLY DOES FIT...
THANKS.
NO PROBLEM!

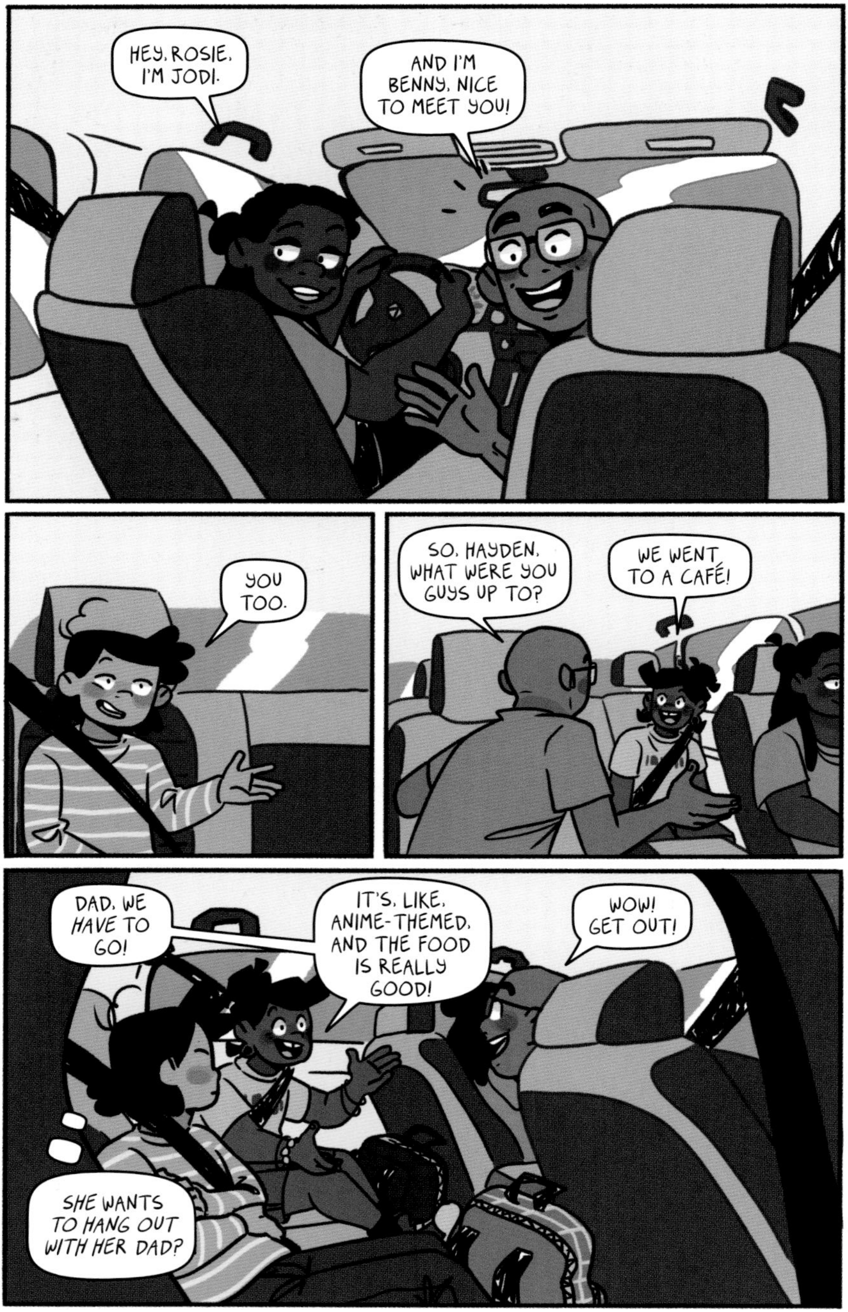
HEY, ROSIE, I'M JODI.
AND I'M BENNY, NICE TO MEET YOU!
YOU TOO.
SO, HAYDEN, WHAT WERE YOU GUYS UP TO?
WE WENT TO A CAFÉ!
DAD, WE HAVE TO GO!
IT'S, LIKE, ANIME-THEMED, AND THE FOOD IS REALLY GOOD!
WOW! GET OUT!
SHE WANTS TO HANG OUT WITH HER DAD?

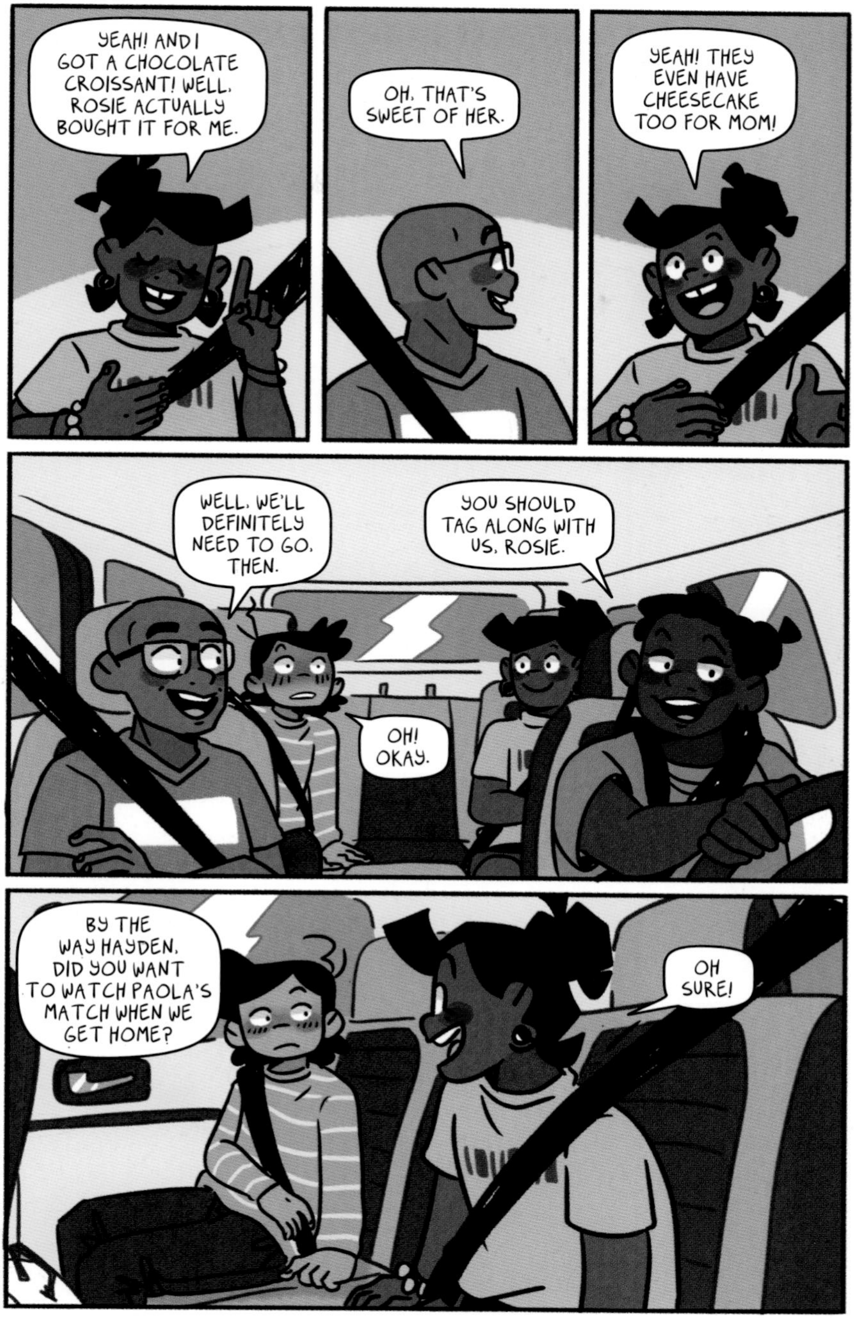
YEAH! AND I GOT A CHOCOLATE CROISSANT! WELL, ROSIE ACTUALLY BOUGHT IT FOR ME.
OH, THAT'S SWEET OF HER.
YEAH! THEY EVEN HAVE CHEESECAKE TOO FOR MOM!
WELL, WE'LL DEFINITELY NEED TO GO, THEN.
YOU SHOULD TAG ALONG WITH US, ROSIE.
OH! OKAY.
BY THE WAY HAYDEN, DID YOU WANT TO WATCH PAOLA'S MATCH WHEN WE GET HOME?
OH SURE!

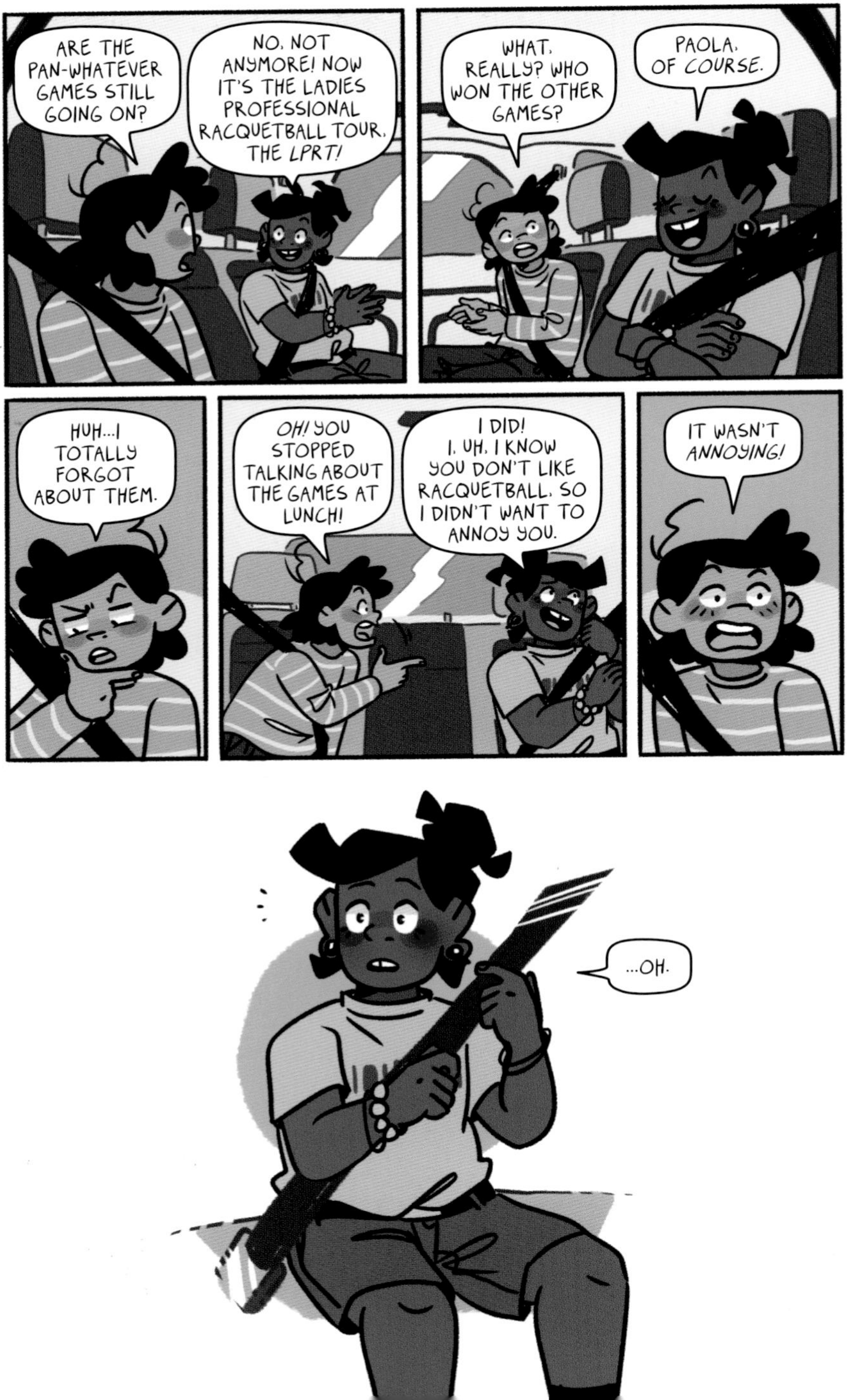
ARE THE PAN-WHATEVER GAMES STILL GOING ON?
NO, NOT ANYMORE! NOW IT'S THE LADIES PROFESSIONAL RACQUETBALL TOUR, THE *LPRT!*
WHAT, REALLY? WHO WON THE OTHER GAMES?
PAOLA, OF *COURSE.*
HUH...I TOTALLY FORGOT ABOUT THEM.
OH! YOU STOPPED TALKING ABOUT THE GAMES AT LUNCH!
I DID! I, UH, I KNOW YOU DON'T LIKE RACQUETBALL, SO I DIDN'T WANT TO ANNOY YOU.
IT WASN'T *ANNOYING!*
...OH.

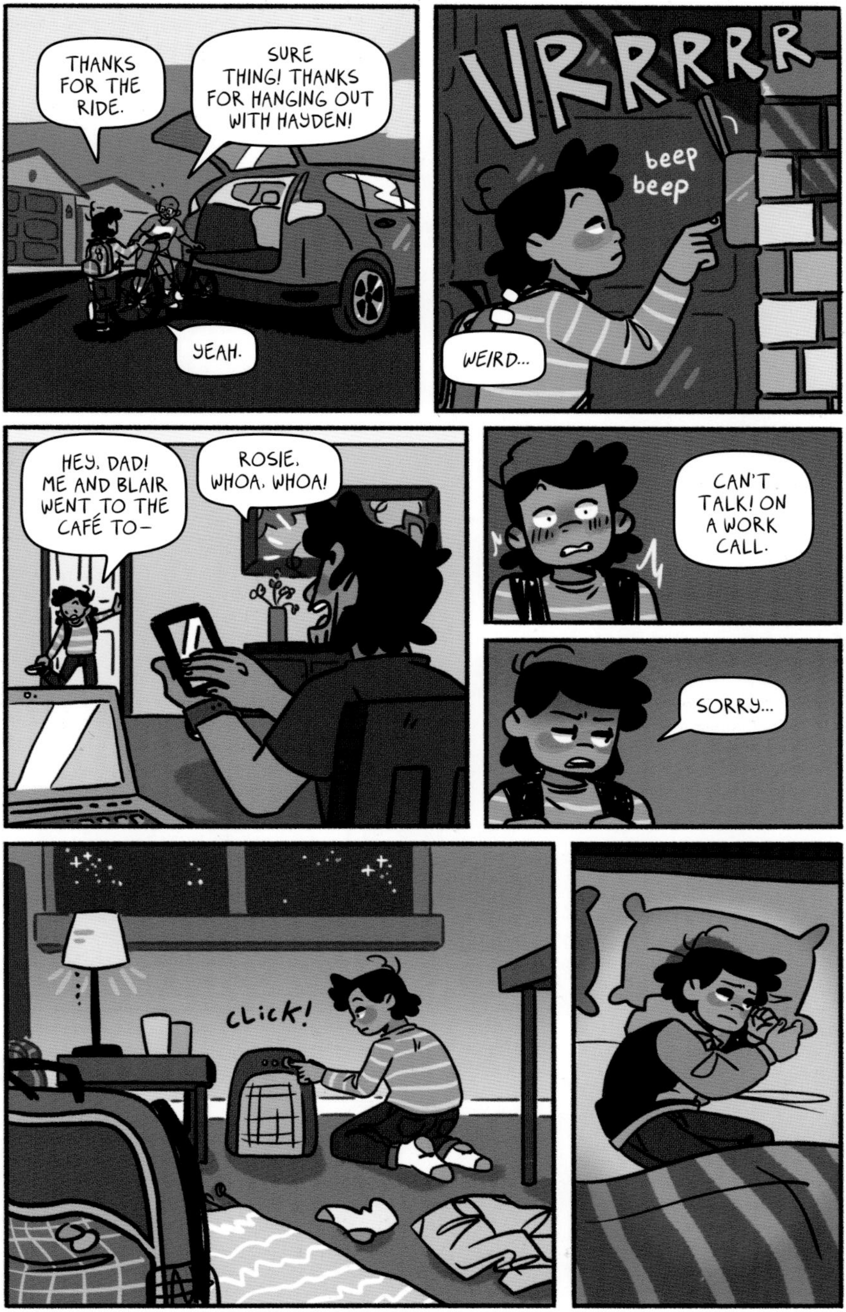
THANKS FOR THE RIDE.
SURE THING! THANKS FOR HANGING OUT WITH HAYDEN!
YEAH.
VRRRRR
beep beep
WEIRD...
HEY, DAD! ME AND BLAIR WENT TO THE CAFÉ TO—
ROSIE, WHOA, WHOA!
CAN'T TALK! ON A WORK CALL.
SORRY...
CLICK!

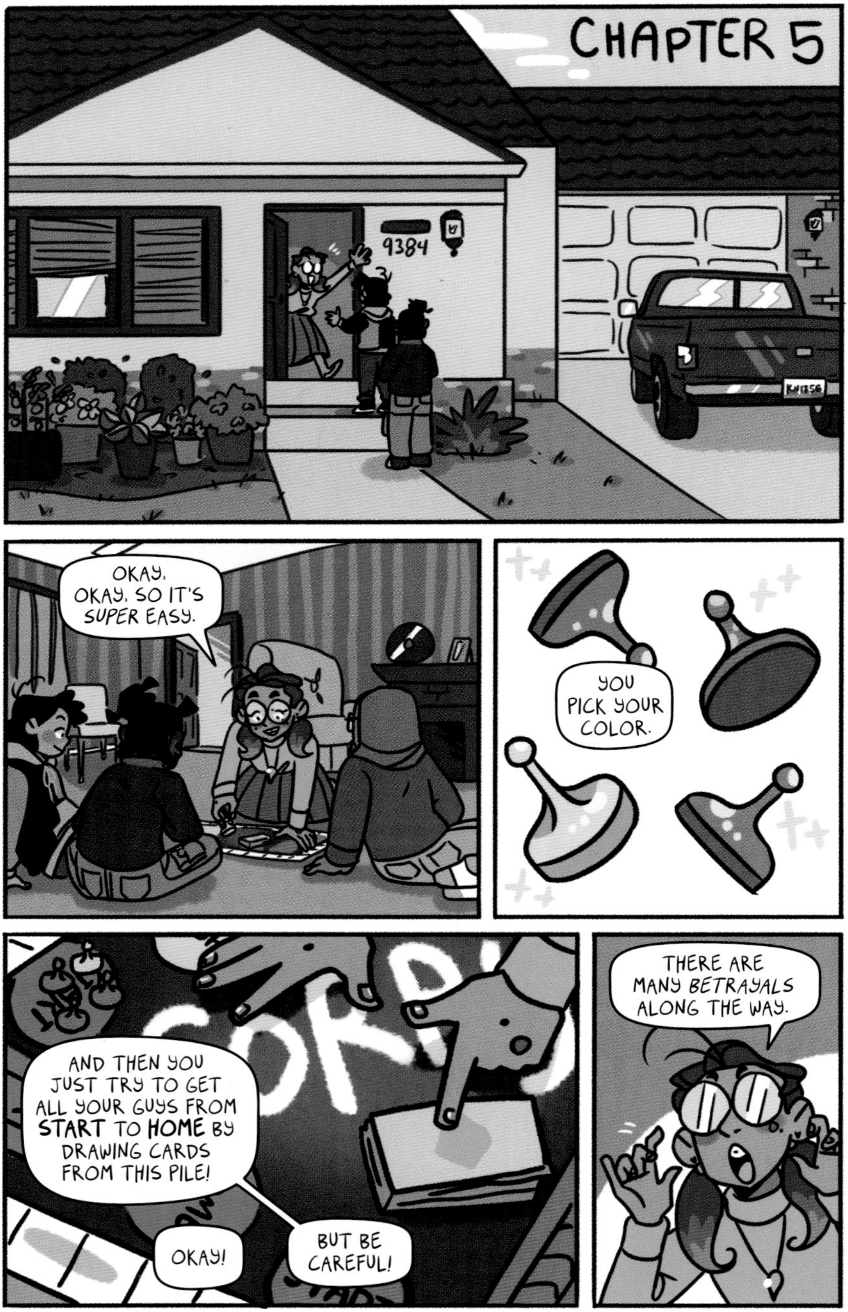
CHAPTER 5
9384
OKAY, OKAY, SO IT'S SUPER EASY.
YOU PICK YOUR COLOR.
AND THEN YOU JUST TRY TO GET ALL YOUR GUYS FROM **START** TO **HOME** BY DRAWING CARDS FROM THIS PILE!
OKAY!
BUT BE CAREFUL!
THERE ARE MANY BETRAYALS ALONG THE WAY.

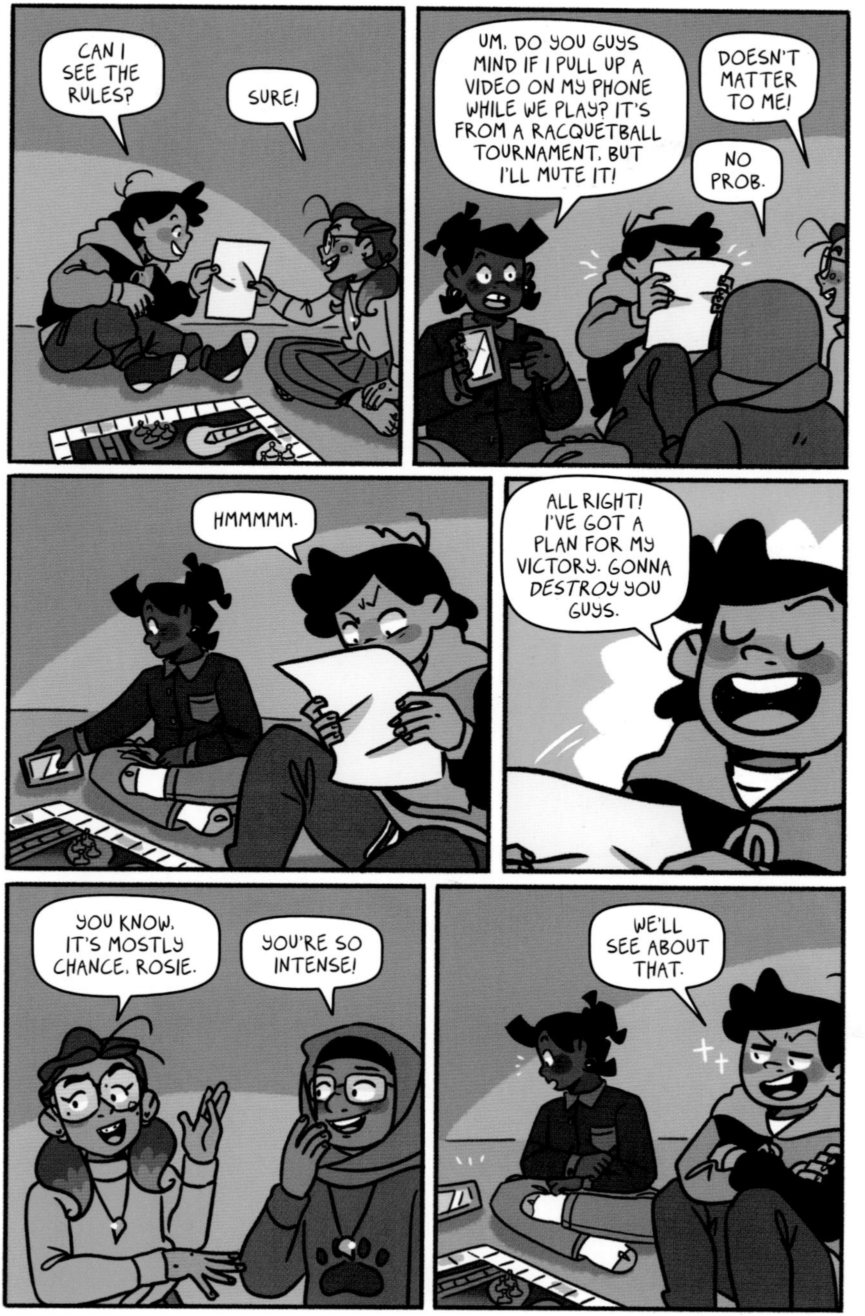
CAN I SEE THE RULES?
SURE!
UM, DO YOU GUYS MIND IF I PULL UP A VIDEO ON MY PHONE WHILE WE PLAY? IT'S FROM A RACQUETBALL TOURNAMENT, BUT I'LL MUTE IT!
DOESN'T MATTER TO ME!
NO PROB.
HMMMMM.
ALL RIGHT! I'VE GOT A PLAN FOR MY VICTORY. GONNA DESTROY YOU GUYS.
YOU KNOW, IT'S MOSTLY CHANCE, ROSIE.
YOU'RE SO INTENSE!
WE'LL SEE ABOUT THAT.

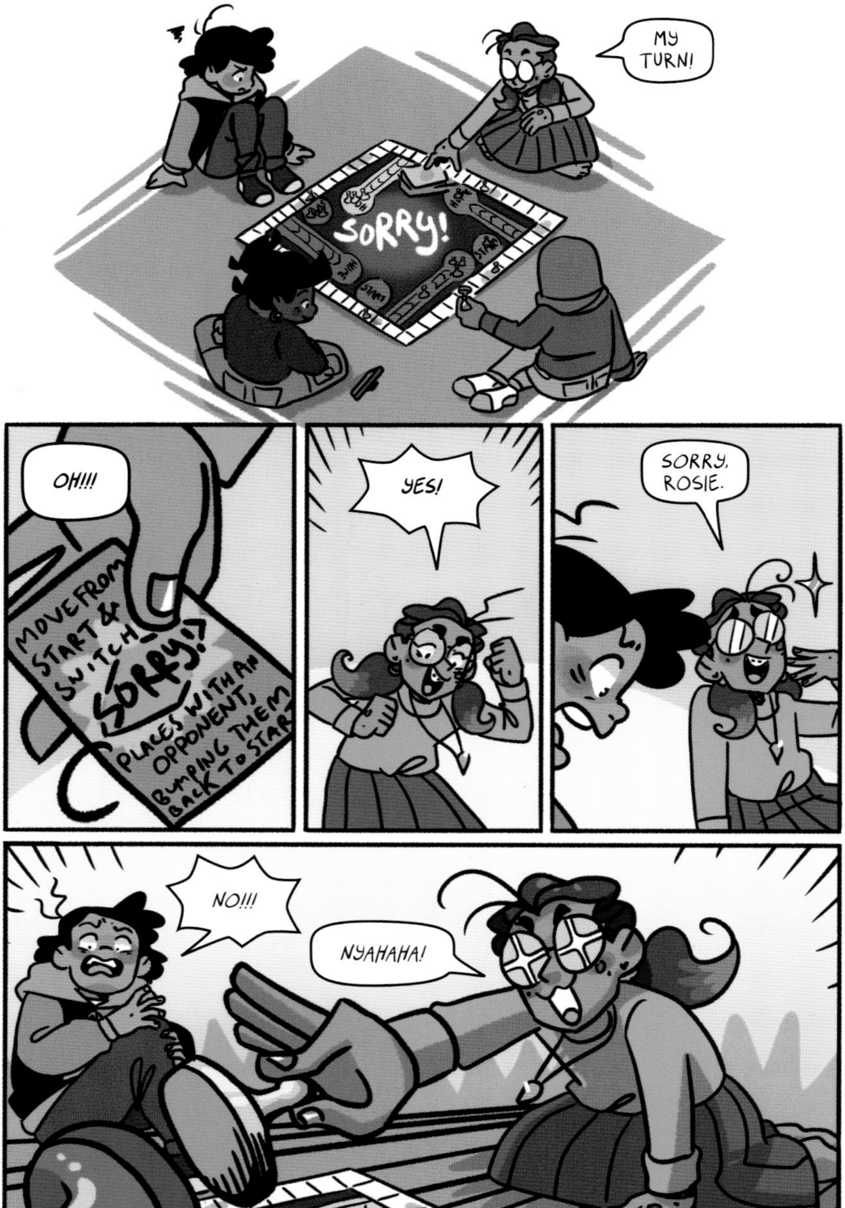
MY TURN!
SORRY!
START
HOME
OH!!!
MOVE FROM START & SWITCH
SORRY!
PLACES WITH AN OPPONENT, BUMPING THEM BACK TO START
YES!
SORRY, ROSIE.
NO!!!
NYAHAHA!
START

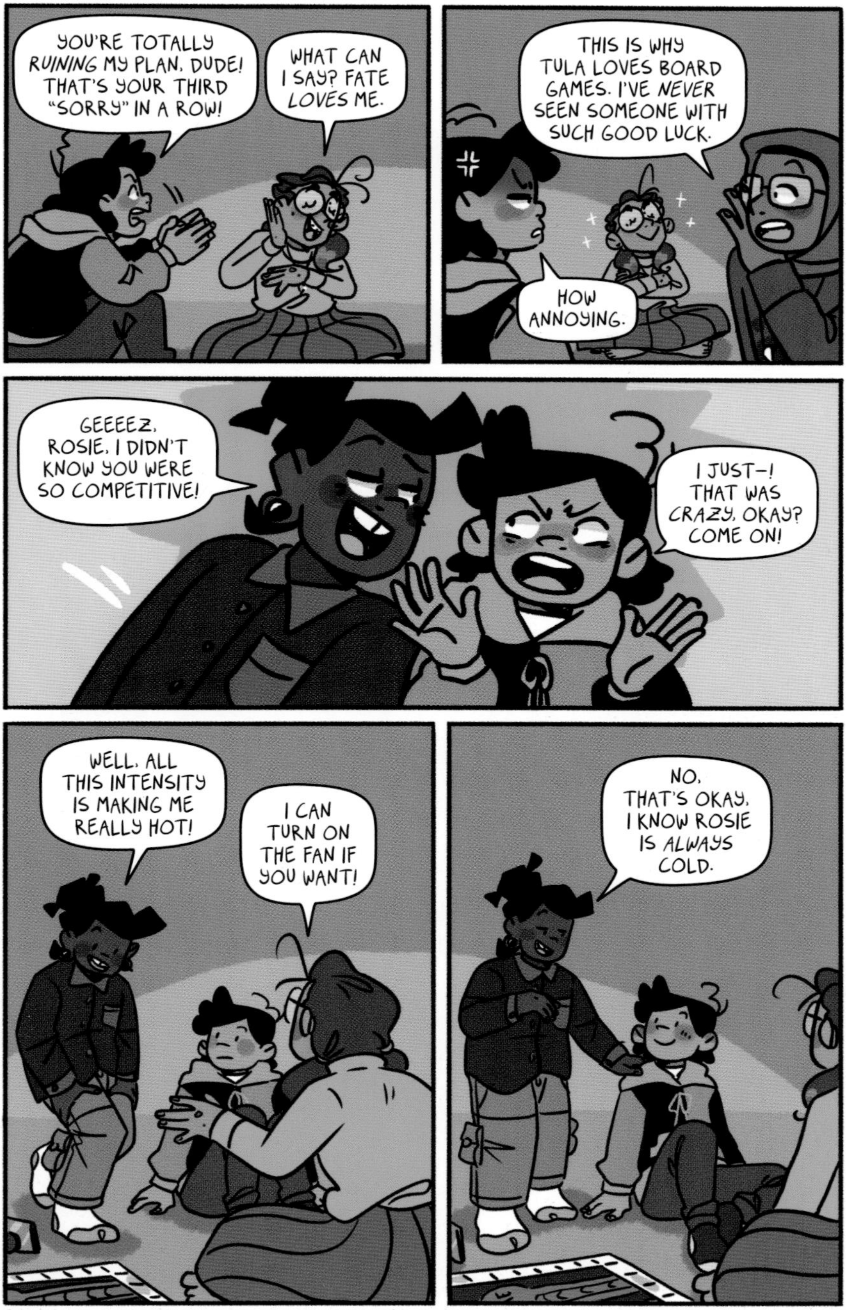
YOU'RE TOTALLY RUINING MY PLAN, DUDE! THAT'S YOUR THIRD "SORRY" IN A ROW!
WHAT CAN I SAY? FATE LOVES ME.
THIS IS WHY TULA LOVES BOARD GAMES. I'VE NEVER SEEN SOMEONE WITH SUCH GOOD LUCK.
HOW ANNOYING.
GEEEEZ, ROSIE, I DIDN'T KNOW YOU WERE SO COMPETITIVE!
I JUST—! THAT WAS CRAZY, OKAY? COME ON!
WELL, ALL THIS INTENSITY IS MAKING ME REALLY HOT!
I CAN TURN ON THE FAN IF YOU WANT!
NO, THAT'S OKAY. I KNOW ROSIE IS ALWAYS COLD.

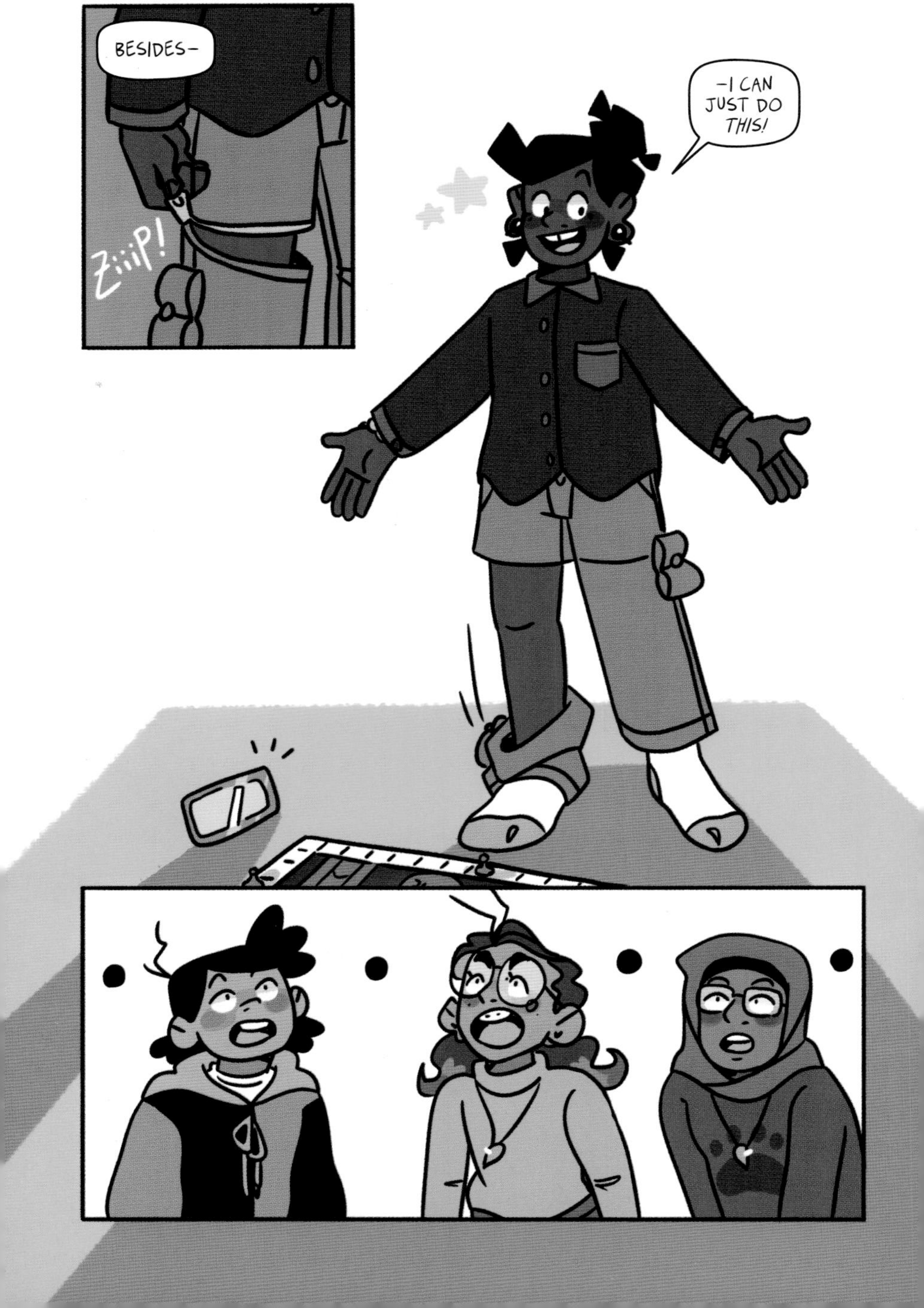
BESIDES—
ZiiiP!
—I CAN JUST DO THIS!

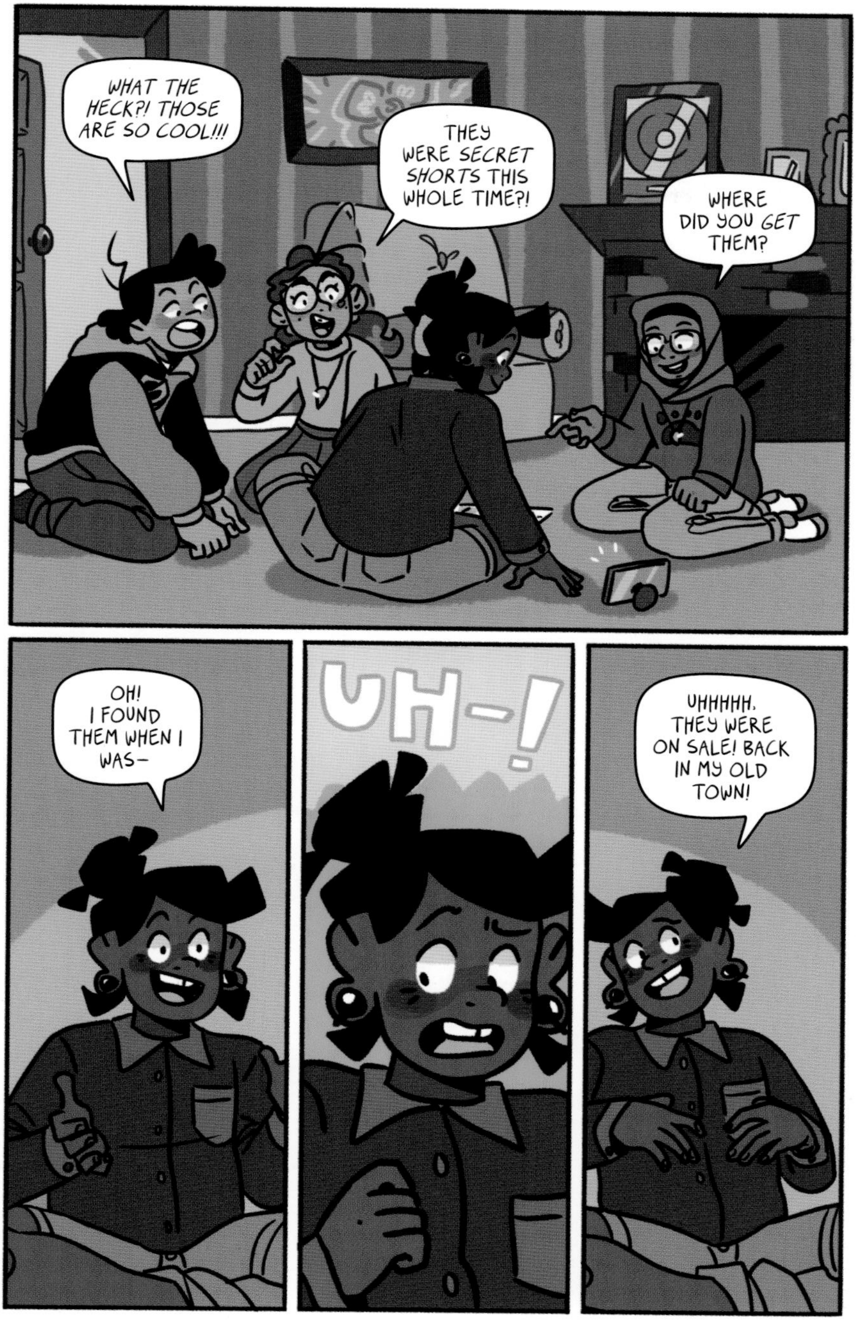
WHAT THE HECK?! THOSE ARE SO COOL!!!
THEY WERE SECRET SHORTS THIS WHOLE TIME?!
WHERE DID YOU GET THEM?
OH! I FOUND THEM WHEN I WAS—
UH—!
UHHHHH, THEY WERE ON SALE! BACK IN MY OLD TOWN!

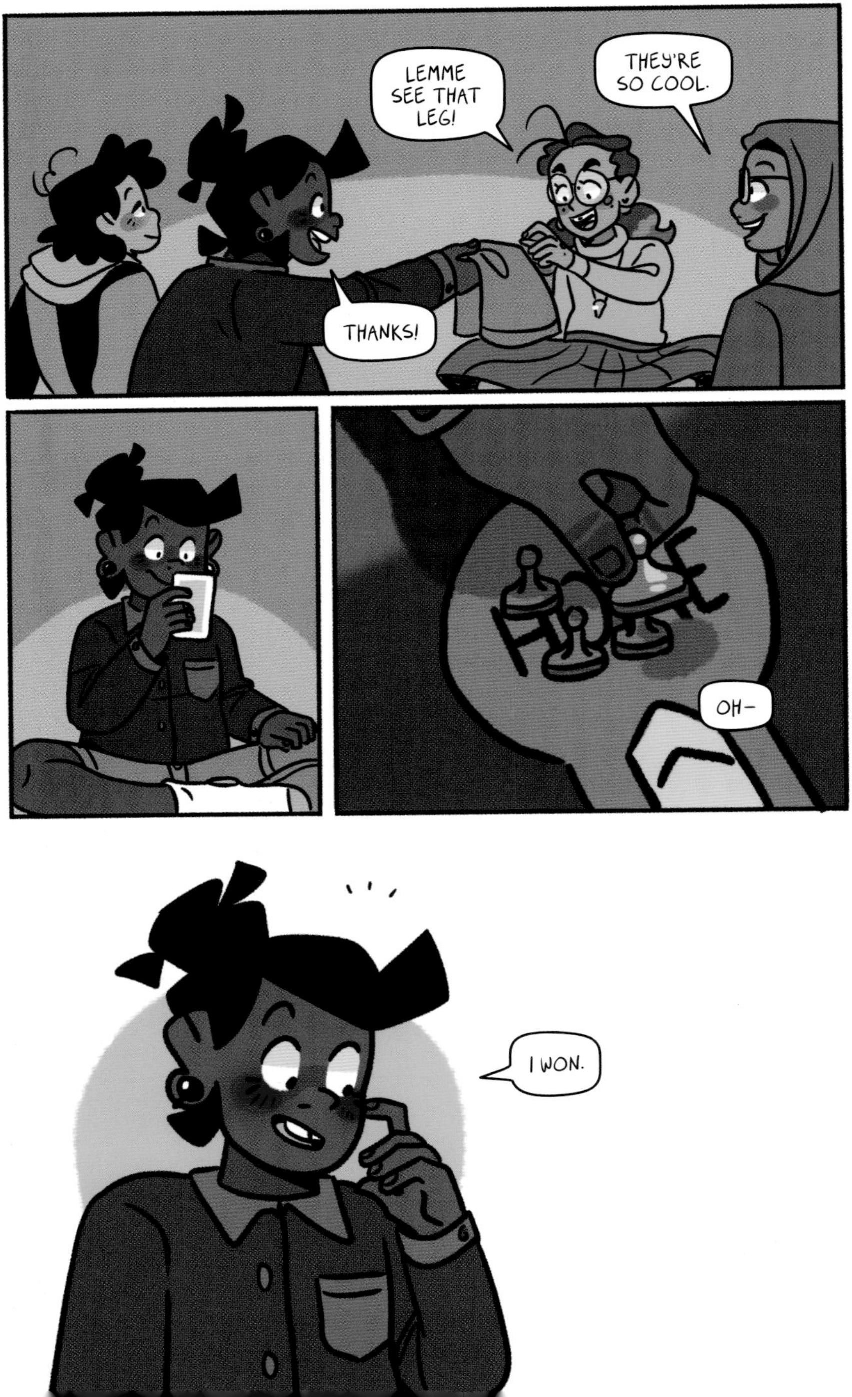
LEMME SEE THAT LEG!
THEY'RE SO COOL.
THANKS!
OH–
I WON.

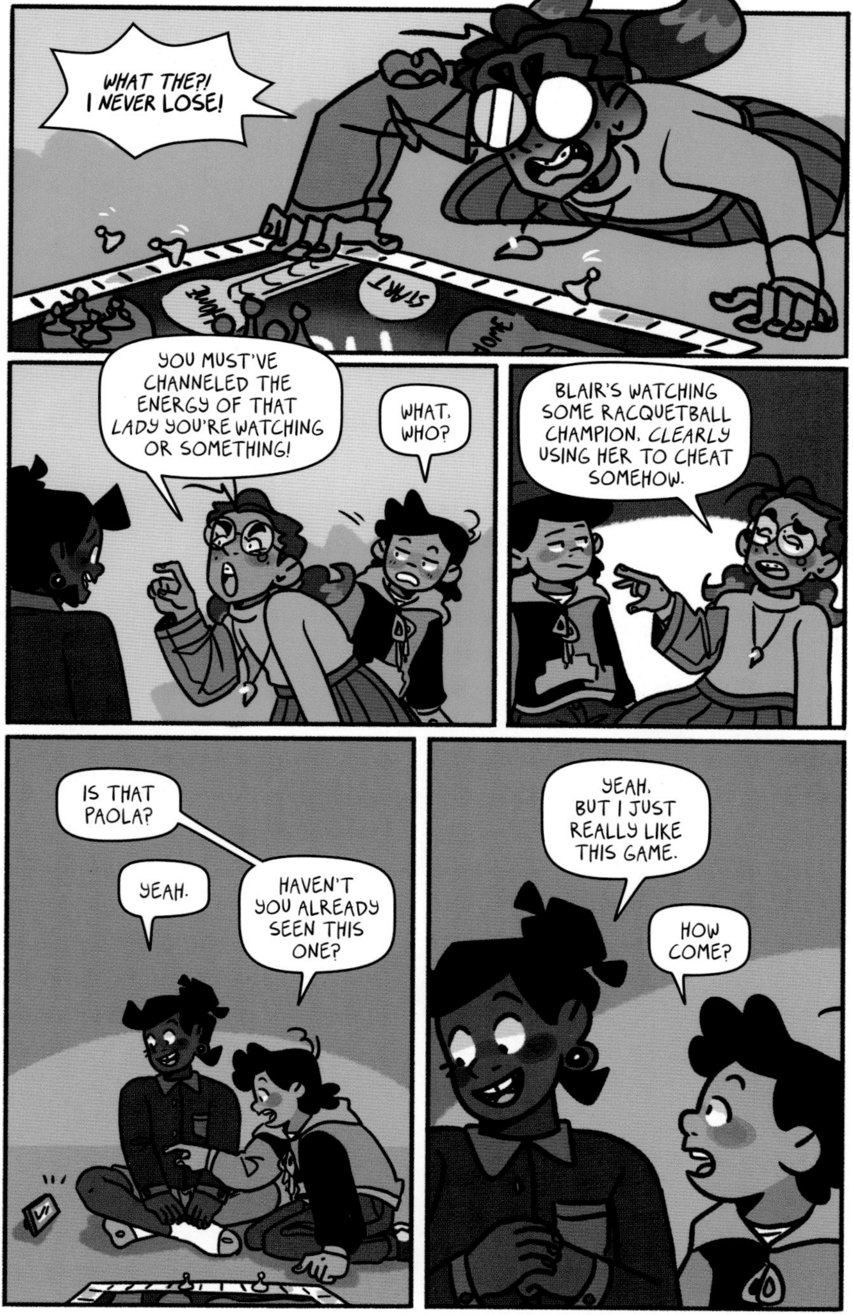
WHAT THE?! I NEVER LOSE!
YOU MUST'VE CHANNELED THE ENERGY OF THAT LADY YOU'RE WATCHING OR SOMETHING!
WHAT, WHO?
BLAIR'S WATCHING SOME RACQUETBALL CHAMPION, CLEARLY USING HER TO CHEAT SOMEHOW.
IS THAT PAOLA?
YEAH.
HAVEN'T YOU ALREADY SEEN THIS ONE?
YEAH, BUT I JUST REALLY LIKE THIS GAME.
HOW COME?

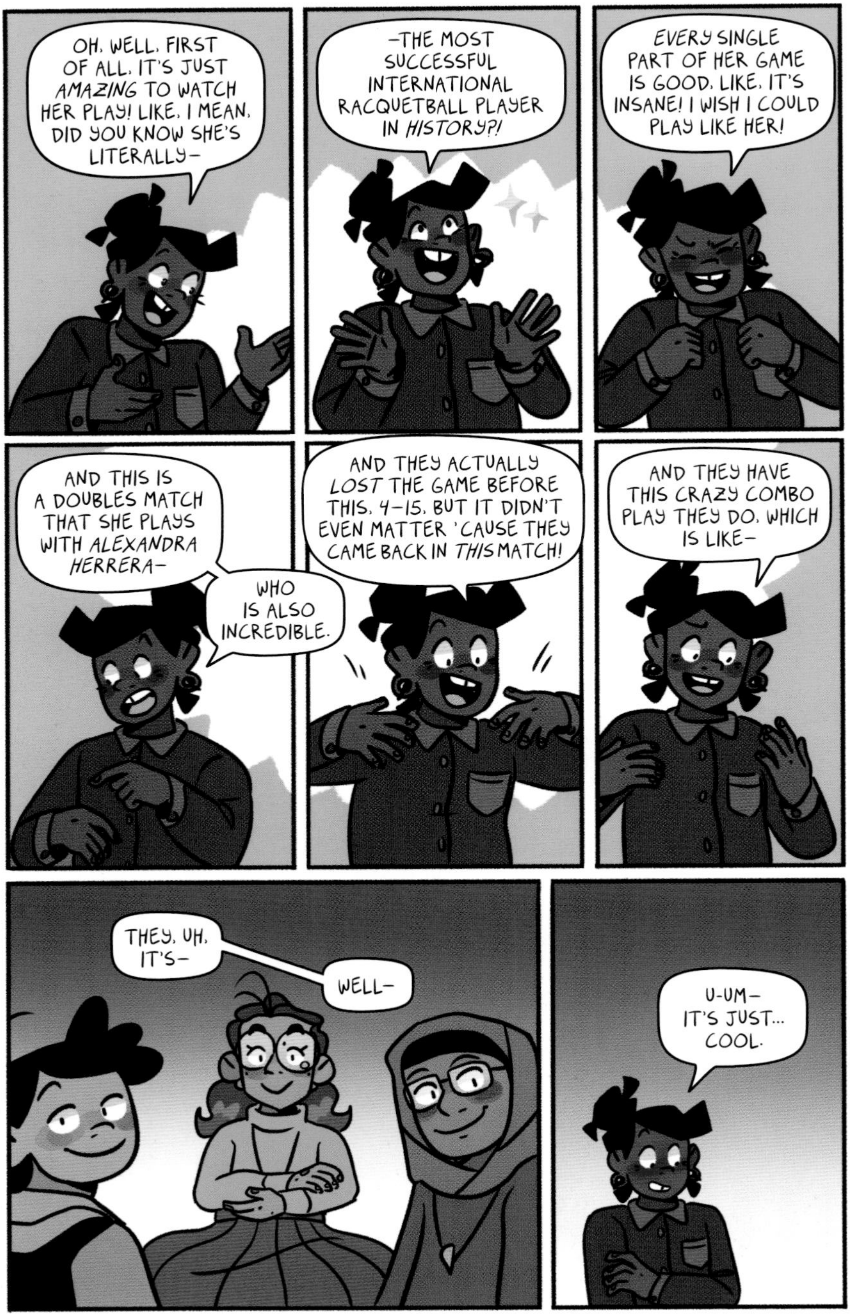
OH, WELL, FIRST OF ALL, IT'S JUST AMAZING TO WATCH HER PLAY! LIKE, I MEAN, DID YOU KNOW SHE'S LITERALLY–
–THE MOST SUCCESSFUL INTERNATIONAL RACQUETBALL PLAYER IN HISTORY?!
EVERY SINGLE PART OF HER GAME IS GOOD, LIKE, IT'S INSANE! I WISH I COULD PLAY LIKE HER!
AND THIS IS A DOUBLES MATCH THAT SHE PLAYS WITH ALEXANDRA HERRERA–
WHO IS ALSO INCREDIBLE.
AND THEY ACTUALLY LOST THE GAME BEFORE THIS, 4–15, BUT IT DIDN'T EVEN MATTER 'CAUSE THEY CAME BACK IN THIS MATCH!
AND THEY HAVE THIS CRAZY COMBO PLAY THEY DO, WHICH IS LIKE–
THEY, UH, IT'S–
WELL–
U-UM– IT'S JUST... COOL.

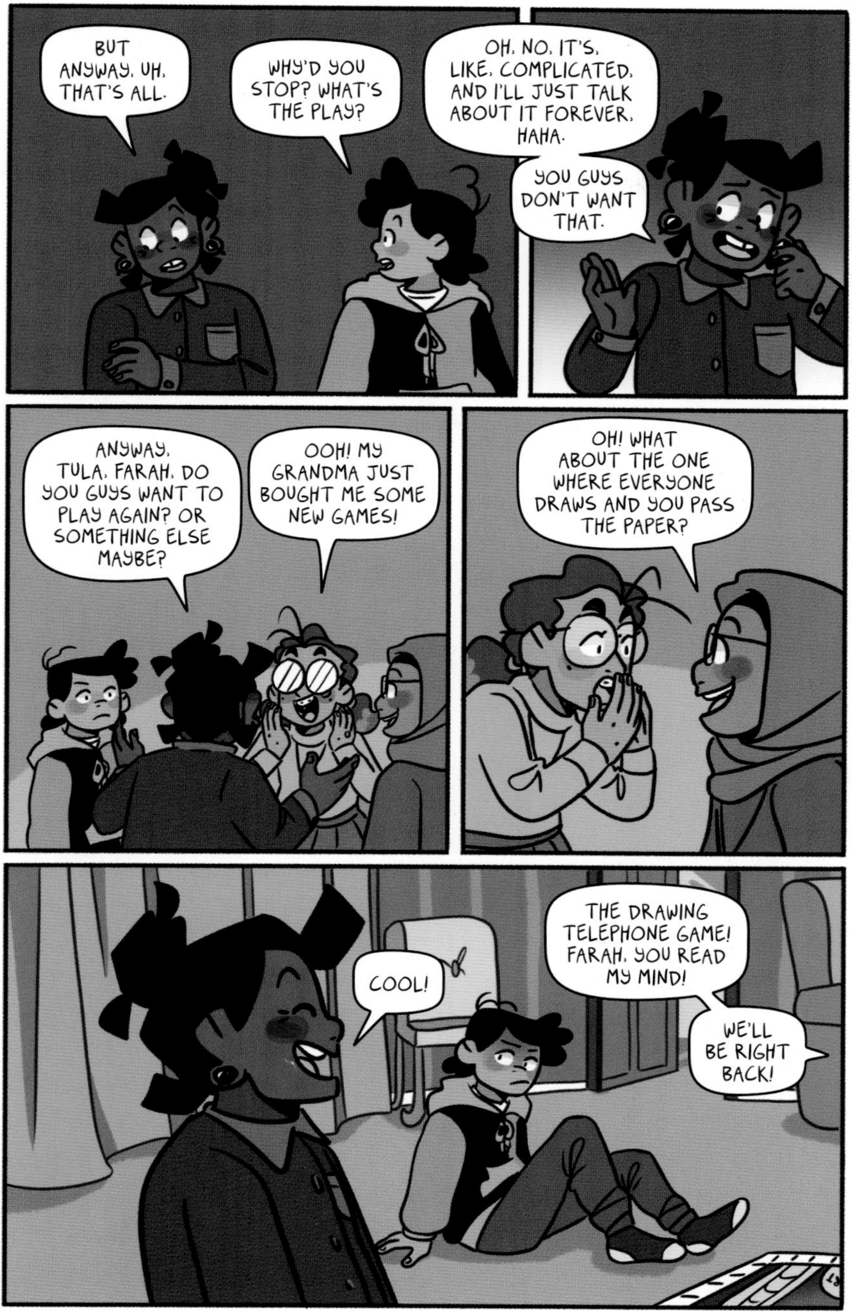
BUT ANYWAY, UH, THAT'S ALL.
WHY'D YOU STOP? WHAT'S THE PLAY?
OH, NO, IT'S, LIKE, COMPLICATED, AND I'LL JUST TALK ABOUT IT FOREVER, HAHA.
YOU GUYS DON'T WANT THAT.
ANYWAY, TULA, FARAH, DO YOU GUYS WANT TO PLAY AGAIN? OR SOMETHING ELSE MAYBE?
OOH! MY GRANDMA JUST BOUGHT ME SOME NEW GAMES!
OH! WHAT ABOUT THE ONE WHERE EVERYONE DRAWS AND YOU PASS THE PAPER?
COOL!
THE DRAWING TELEPHONE GAME! FARAH, YOU READ MY MIND!
WE'LL BE RIGHT BACK!

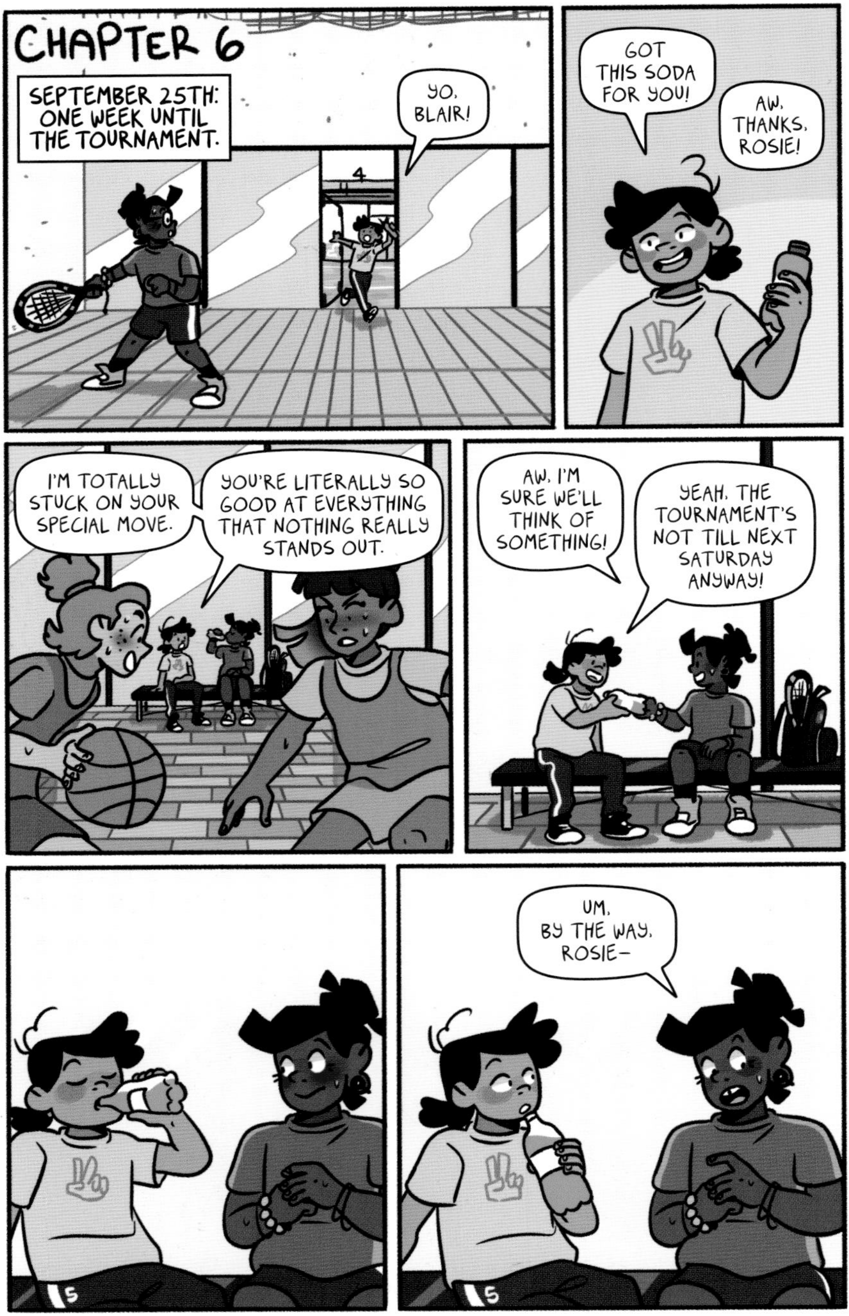

CHAPTER 6
SEPTEMBER 25TH: ONE WEEK UNTIL THE TOURNAMENT.
YO, BLAIR!
4
GOT THIS SODA FOR YOU!
AW, THANKS, ROSIE!
I'M TOTALLY STUCK ON YOUR SPECIAL MOVE.
YOU'RE LITERALLY SO GOOD AT EVERYTHING THAT NOTHING REALLY STANDS OUT.
AW, I'M SURE WE'LL THINK OF SOMETHING!
YEAH, THE TOURNAMENT'S NOT TILL NEXT SATURDAY ANYWAY!
UM, BY THE WAY, ROSIE–

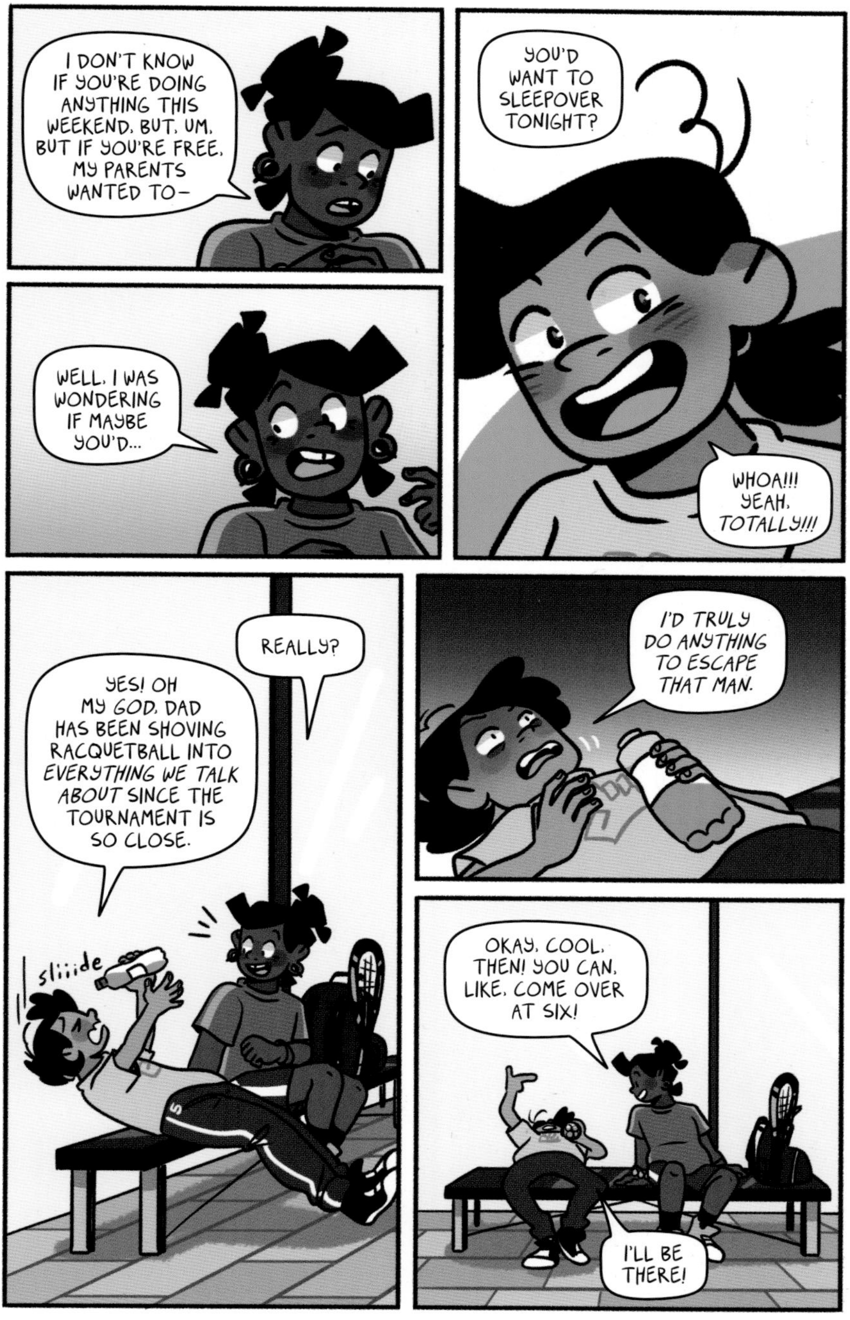
I DON'T KNOW IF YOU'RE DOING ANYTHING THIS WEEKEND, BUT, UM, BUT IF YOU'RE FREE, MY PARENTS WANTED TO—
WELL, I WAS WONDERING IF MAYBE YOU'D...
YOU'D WANT TO SLEEPOVER TONIGHT?
WHOA!!! YEAH, TOTALLY!!!
REALLY?
YES! OH MY GOD, DAD HAS BEEN SHOVING RACQUETBALL INTO EVERYTHING WE TALK ABOUT SINCE THE TOURNAMENT IS SO CLOSE.
sliiide
I'D TRULY DO ANYTHING TO ESCAPE THAT MAN.
OKAY, COOL, THEN! YOU CAN, LIKE, COME OVER AT SIX!
I'LL BE THERE!

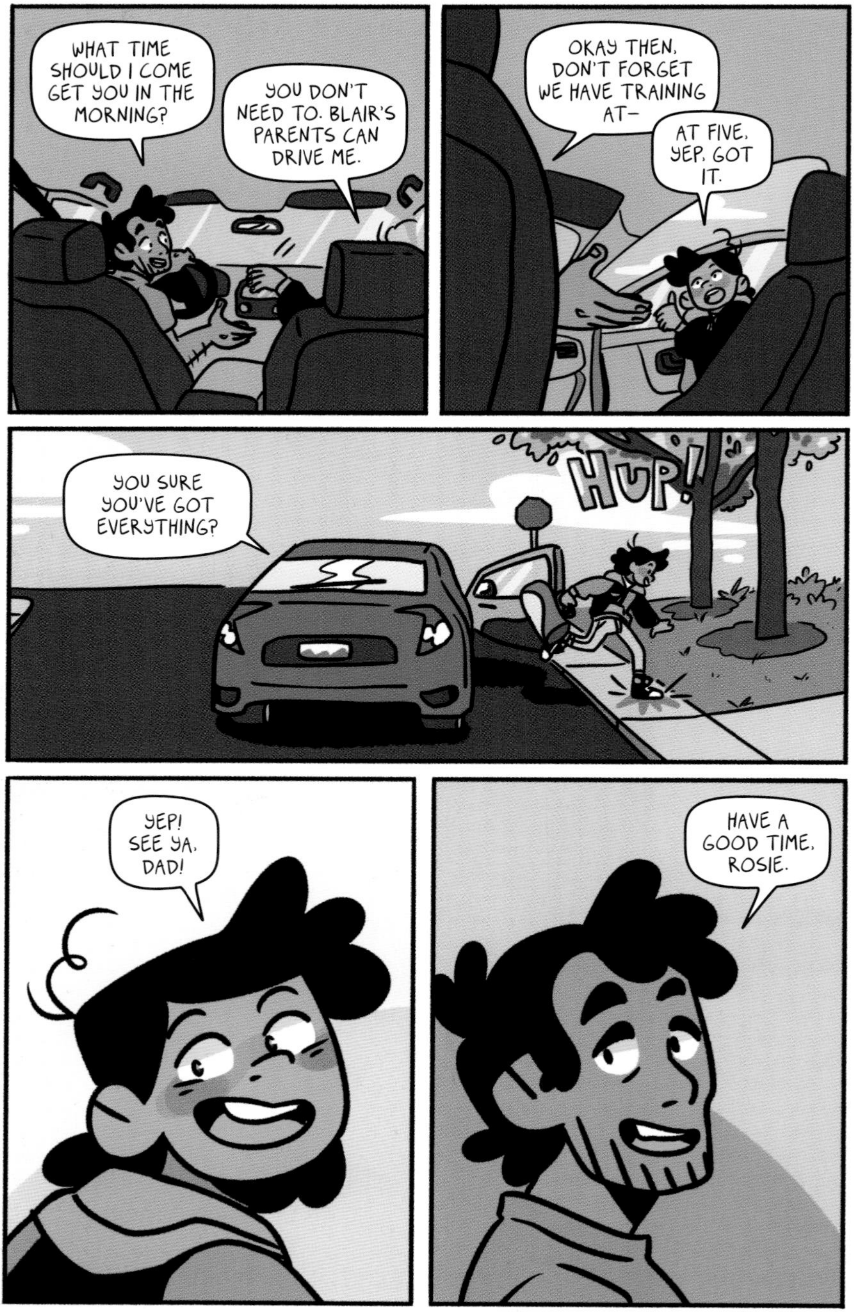
WHAT TIME SHOULD I COME GET YOU IN THE MORNING?
YOU DON'T NEED TO. BLAIR'S PARENTS CAN DRIVE ME.
OKAY THEN, DON'T FORGET WE HAVE TRAINING AT–
AT FIVE, YEP. GOT IT.
YOU SURE YOU'VE GOT EVERYTHING?
HUP!
YEP! SEE YA, DAD!
HAVE A GOOD TIME, ROSIE.

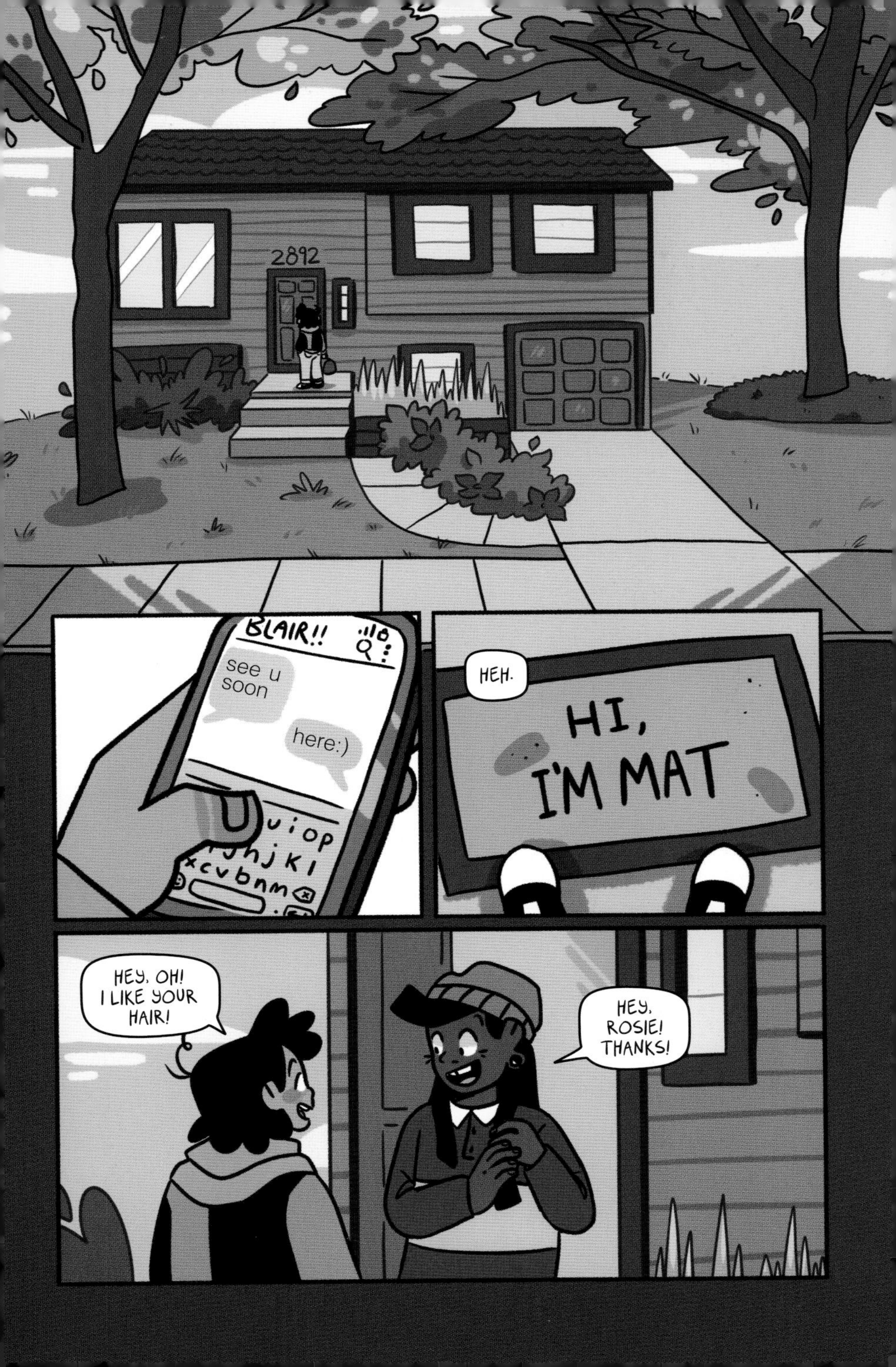
2892
BLAIR!!
see u soon
here:)
HEH.
HI, I'M MAT
HEY, OH! I LIKE YOUR HAIR!
HEY, ROSIE! THANKS!

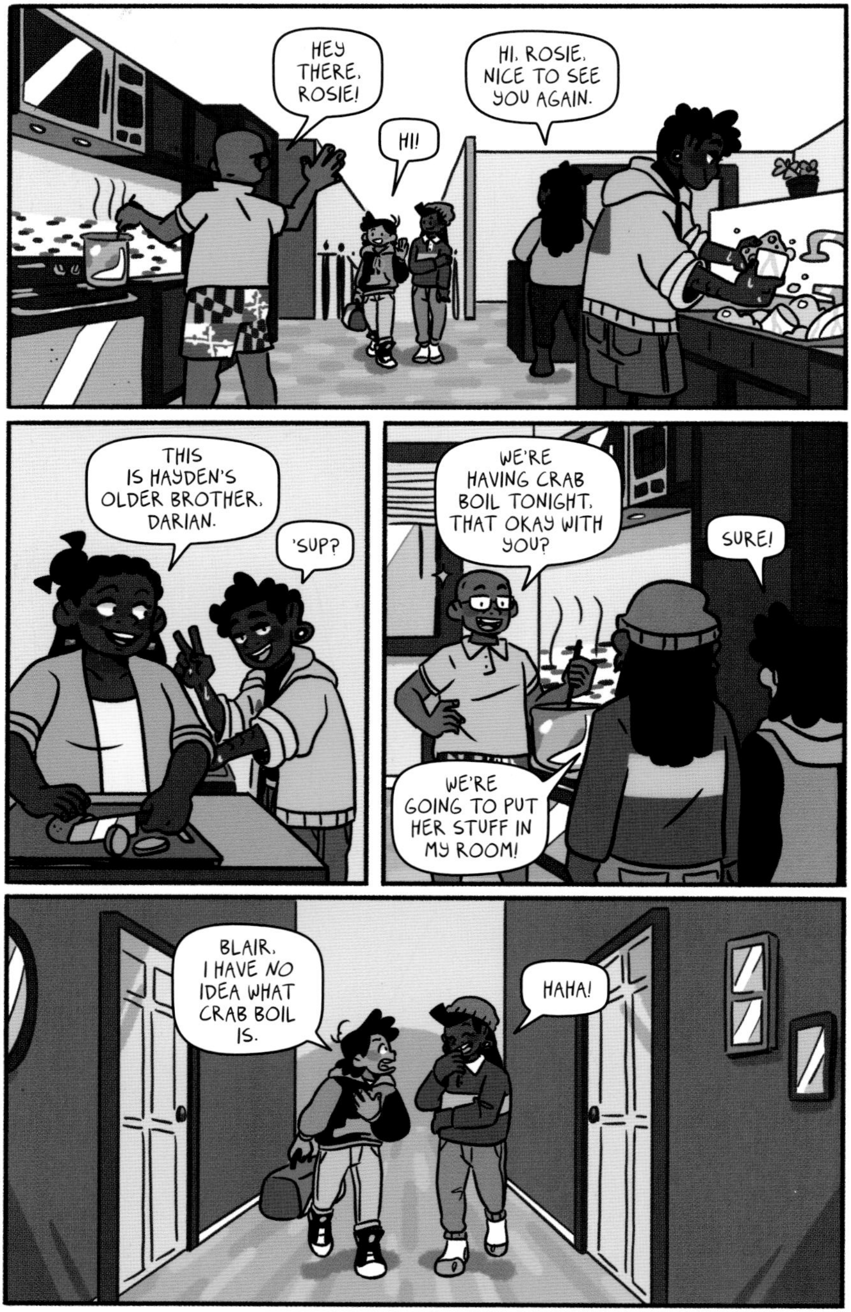
HEY THERE, ROSIE!
HI!
HI, ROSIE, NICE TO SEE YOU AGAIN.
THIS IS HAYDEN'S OLDER BROTHER, DARIAN.
'SUP?
WE'RE HAVING CRAB BOIL TONIGHT, THAT OKAY WITH YOU?
SURE!
WE'RE GOING TO PUT HER STUFF IN MY ROOM!
BLAIR, I HAVE NO IDEA WHAT CRAB BOIL IS.
HAHA!

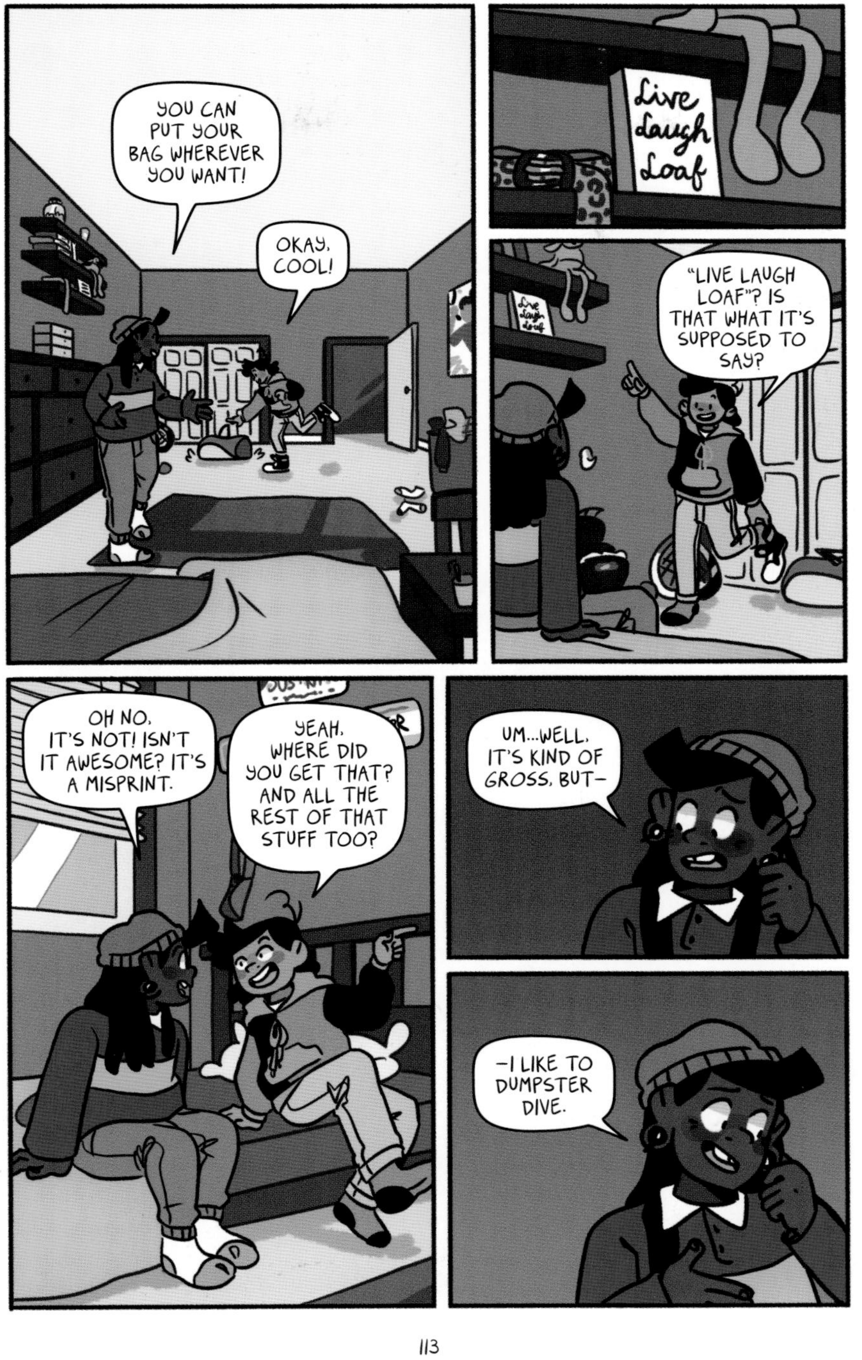
YOU CAN PUT YOUR BAG WHEREVER YOU WANT!
OKAY, COOL!
Live Laugh Loaf
"LIVE LAUGH LOAF"? IS THAT WHAT IT'S SUPPOSED TO SAY?
OH NO, IT'S NOT! ISN'T IT AWESOME? IT'S A MISPRINT.
YEAH, WHERE DID YOU GET THAT? AND ALL THE REST OF THAT STUFF TOO?
UM...WELL, IT'S KIND OF GROSS, BUT–
–I LIKE TO DUMPSTER DIVE.

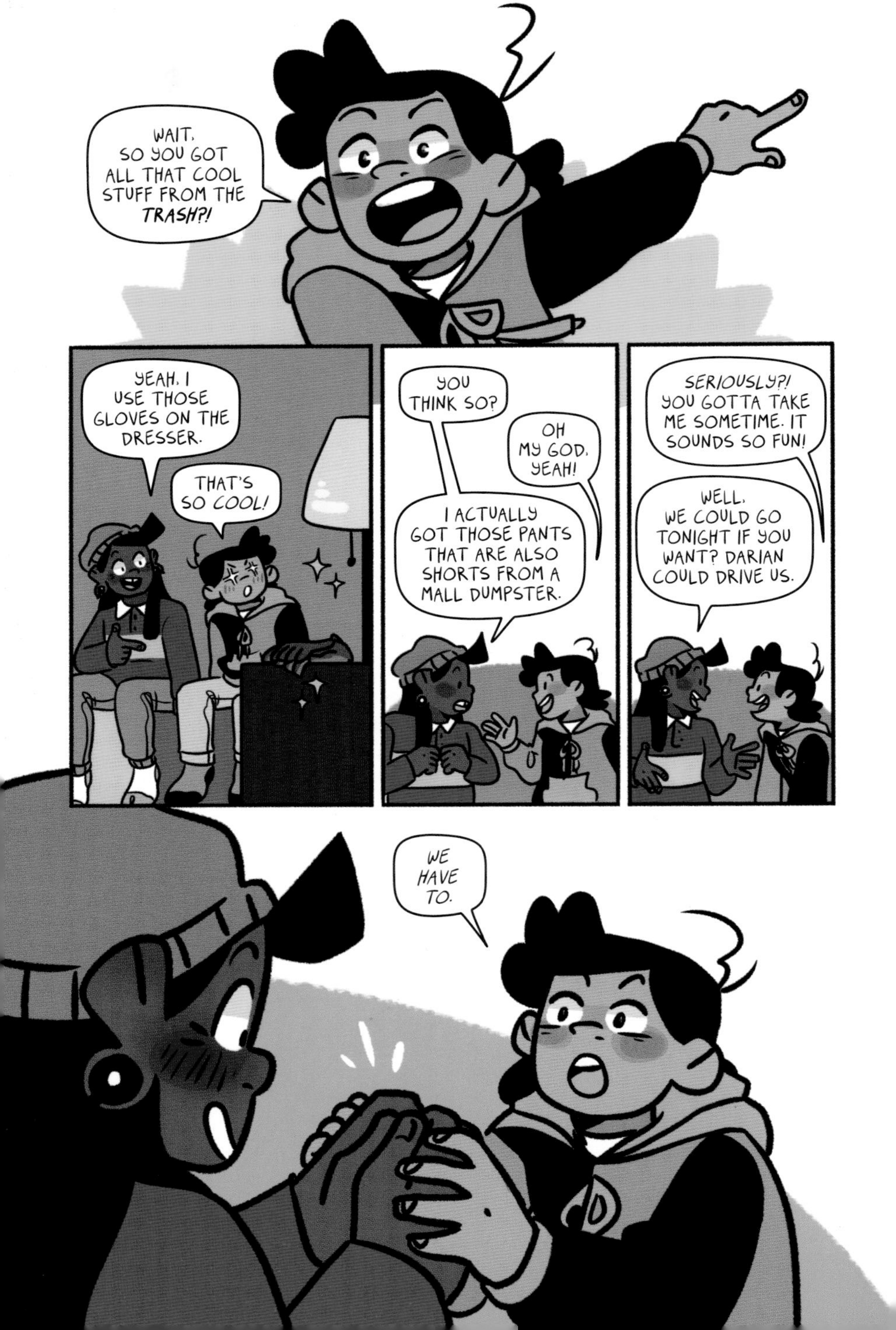
WAIT. SO YOU GOT ALL THAT COOL STUFF FROM THE *TRASH?!*
YEAH, I USE THOSE GLOVES ON THE DRESSER.
THAT'S SO *COOL!*
YOU THINK SO?
OH MY GOD, YEAH!
I ACTUALLY GOT THOSE PANTS THAT ARE ALSO SHORTS FROM A MALL DUMPSTER.
SERIOUSLY?! YOU GOTTA TAKE ME SOMETIME. IT SOUNDS SO FUN!
WELL, WE COULD GO TONIGHT IF YOU WANT? DARIAN COULD DRIVE US.
WE HAVE TO.

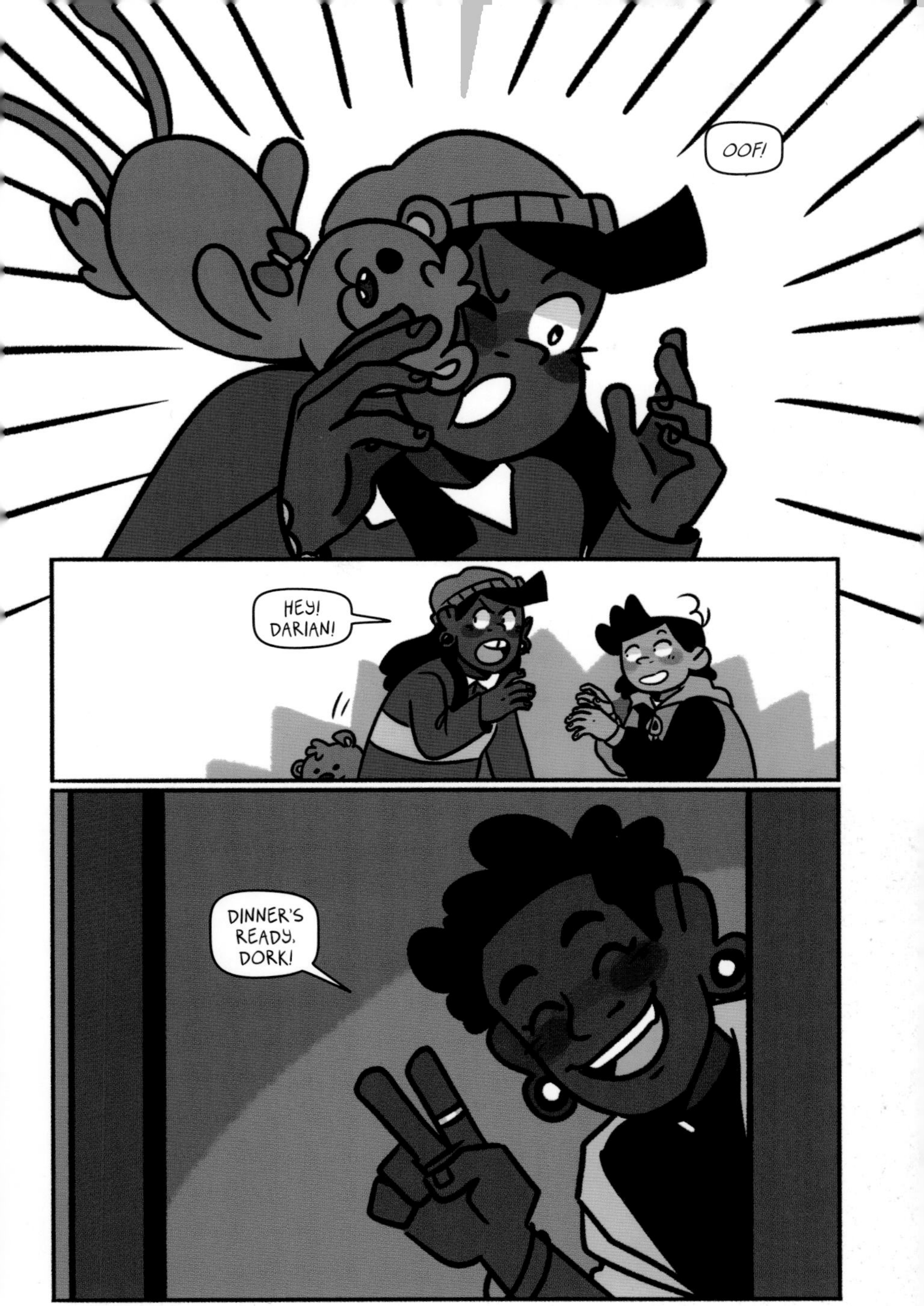
OOF!
HEY! DARIAN!
DINNER'S READY, DORK!

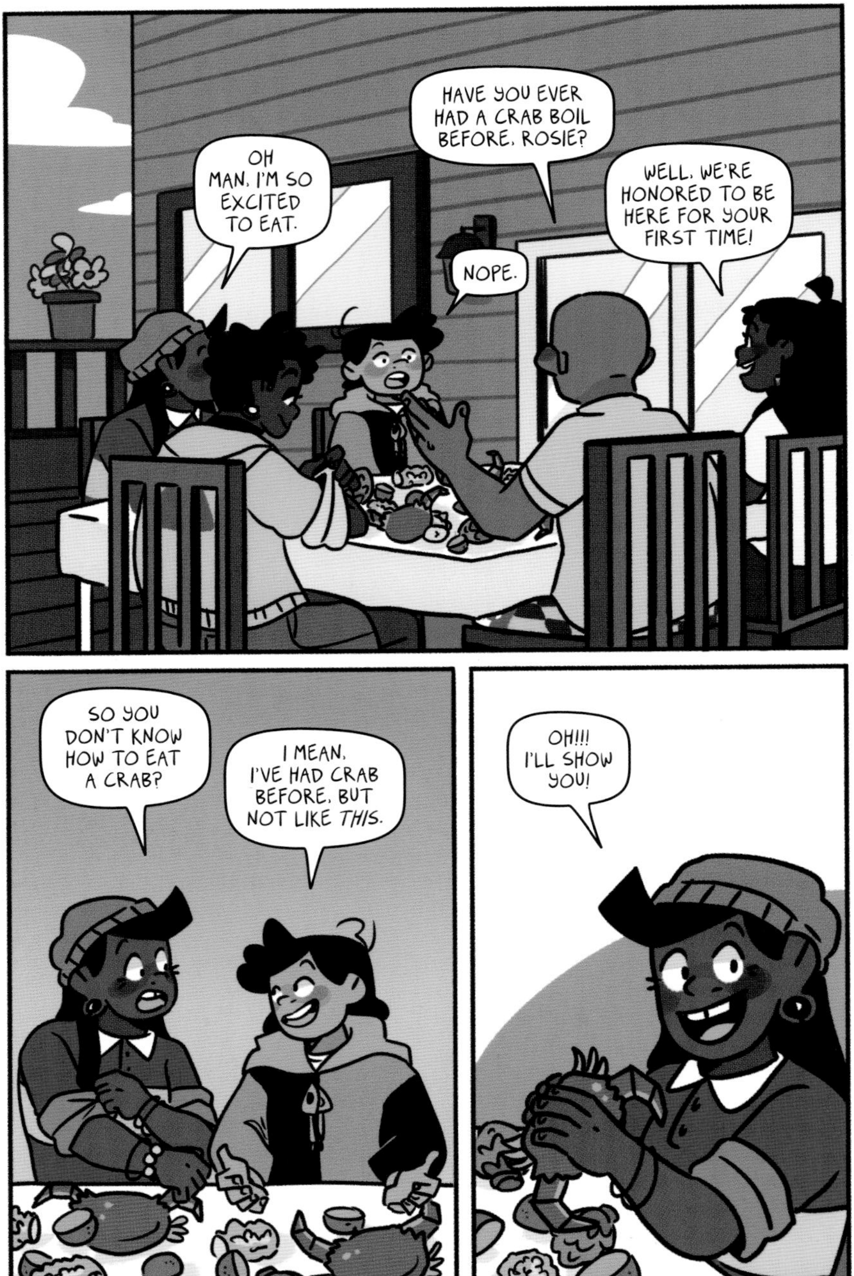
OH MAN, I'M SO EXCITED TO EAT.
HAVE YOU EVER HAD A CRAB BOIL BEFORE, ROSIE?
NOPE.
WELL, WE'RE HONORED TO BE HERE FOR YOUR FIRST TIME!
SO YOU DON'T KNOW HOW TO EAT A CRAB?
I MEAN, I'VE HAD CRAB BEFORE, BUT NOT LIKE *THIS*.
OH!!! I'LL SHOW YOU!

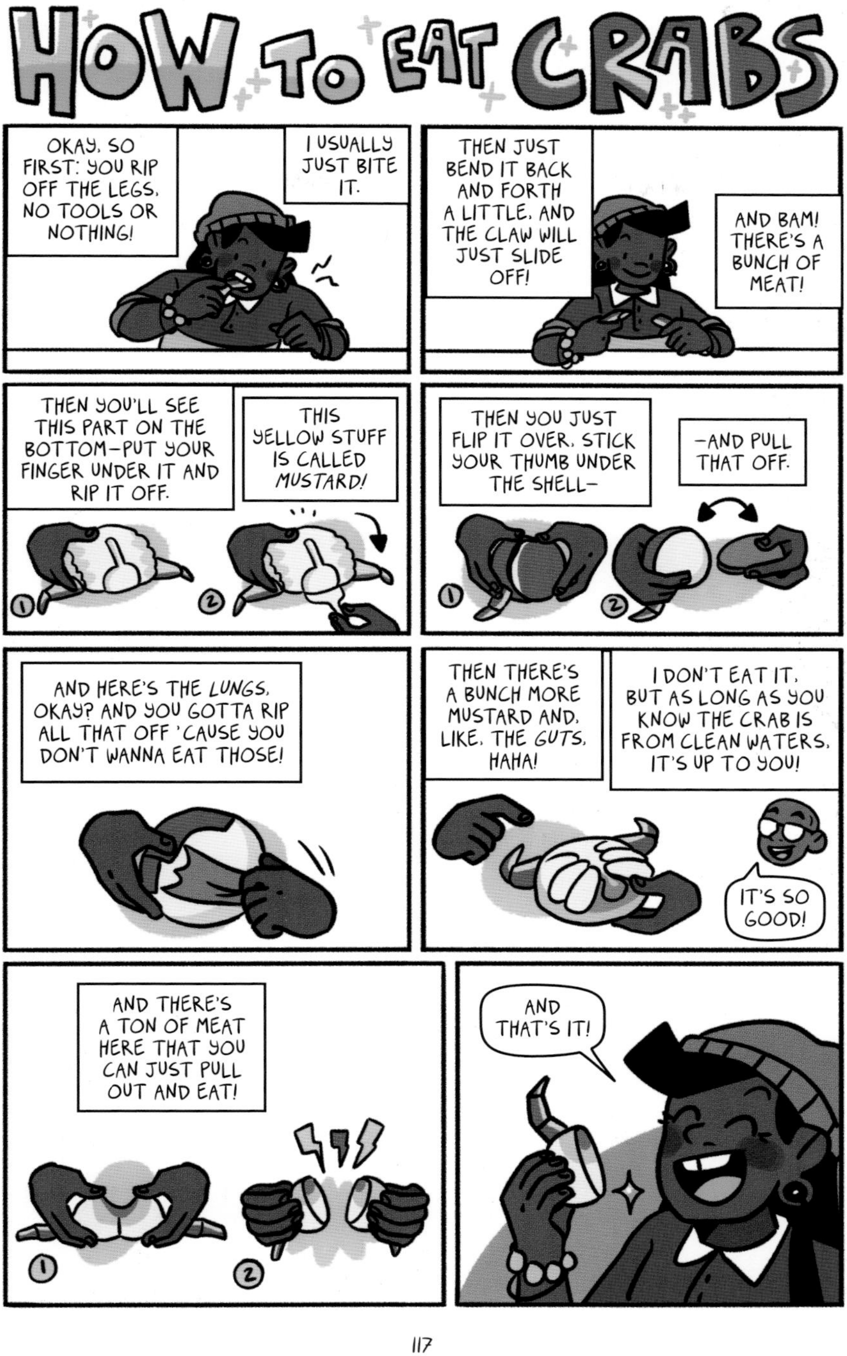
HOW TO EAT CRABS
OKAY, SO FIRST: YOU RIP OFF THE LEGS, NO TOOLS OR NOTHING!
I USUALLY JUST BITE IT.
THEN JUST BEND IT BACK AND FORTH A LITTLE, AND THE CLAW WILL JUST SLIDE OFF!
AND BAM! THERE'S A BUNCH OF MEAT!
THEN YOU'LL SEE THIS PART ON THE BOTTOM—PUT YOUR FINGER UNDER IT AND RIP IT OFF.
THIS YELLOW STUFF IS CALLED *MUSTARD!*
1
2
THEN YOU JUST FLIP IT OVER, STICK YOUR THUMB UNDER THE SHELL—
—AND PULL THAT OFF.
1
2
AND HERE'S THE *LUNGS*, OKAY? AND YOU GOTTA RIP ALL THAT OFF 'CAUSE YOU DON'T WANNA EAT THOSE!
THEN THERE'S A BUNCH MORE MUSTARD AND, LIKE, THE *GUTS*, HAHA!
I DON'T EAT IT, BUT AS LONG AS YOU KNOW THE CRAB IS FROM CLEAN WATERS, IT'S UP TO YOU!
IT'S SO GOOD!
AND THERE'S A TON OF MEAT HERE THAT YOU CAN JUST PULL OUT AND EAT!
1
2
AND THAT'S IT!

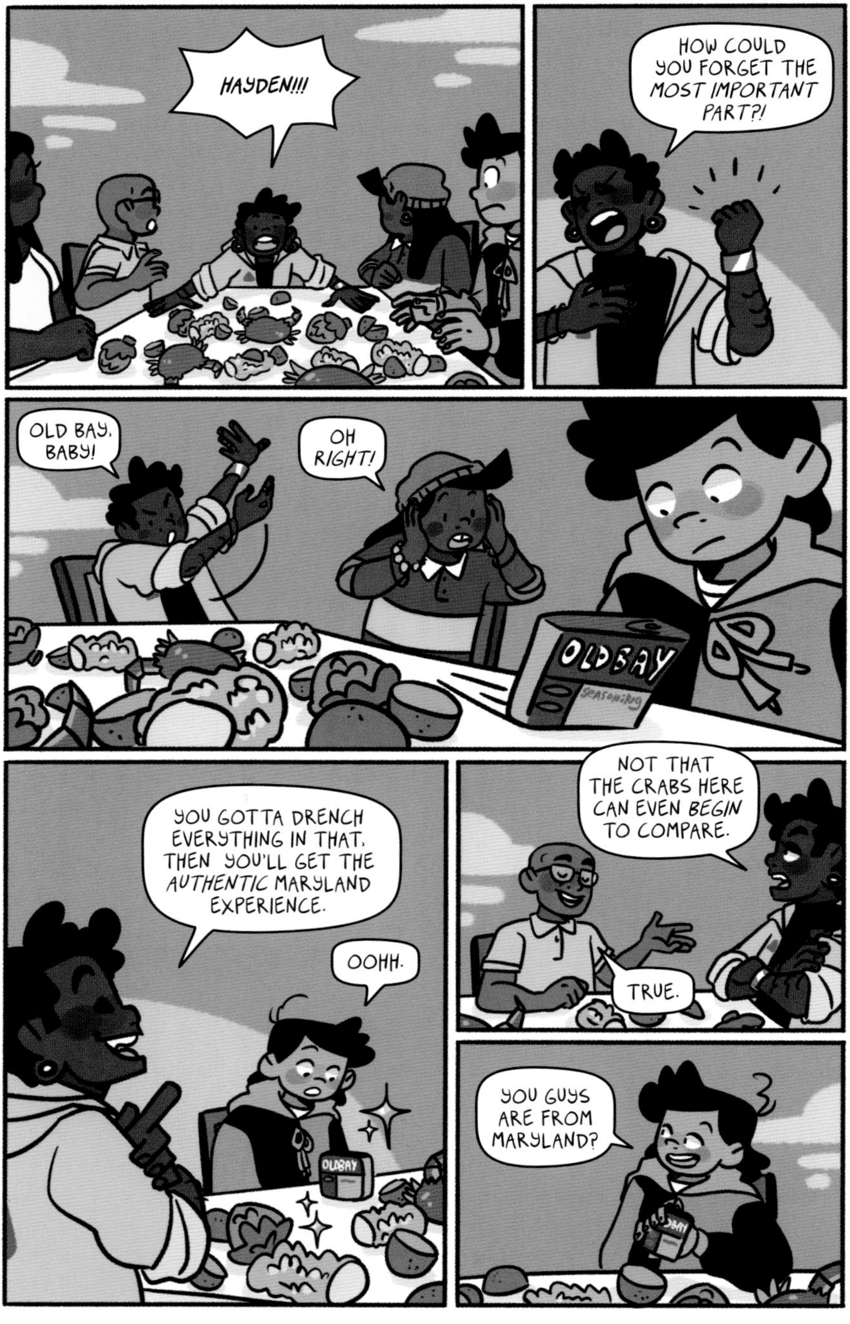
HAYDEN!!!
HOW COULD YOU FORGET THE MOST IMPORTANT PART?!
OLD BAY, BABY!
OH RIGHT!
OLDBAY
seasoning
YOU GOTTA DRENCH EVERYTHING IN THAT, THEN YOU'LL GET THE AUTHENTIC MARYLAND EXPERIENCE.
OOHH.
OLDBAY
NOT THAT THE CRABS HERE CAN EVEN BEGIN TO COMPARE.
TRUE.
YOU GUYS ARE FROM MARYLAND?

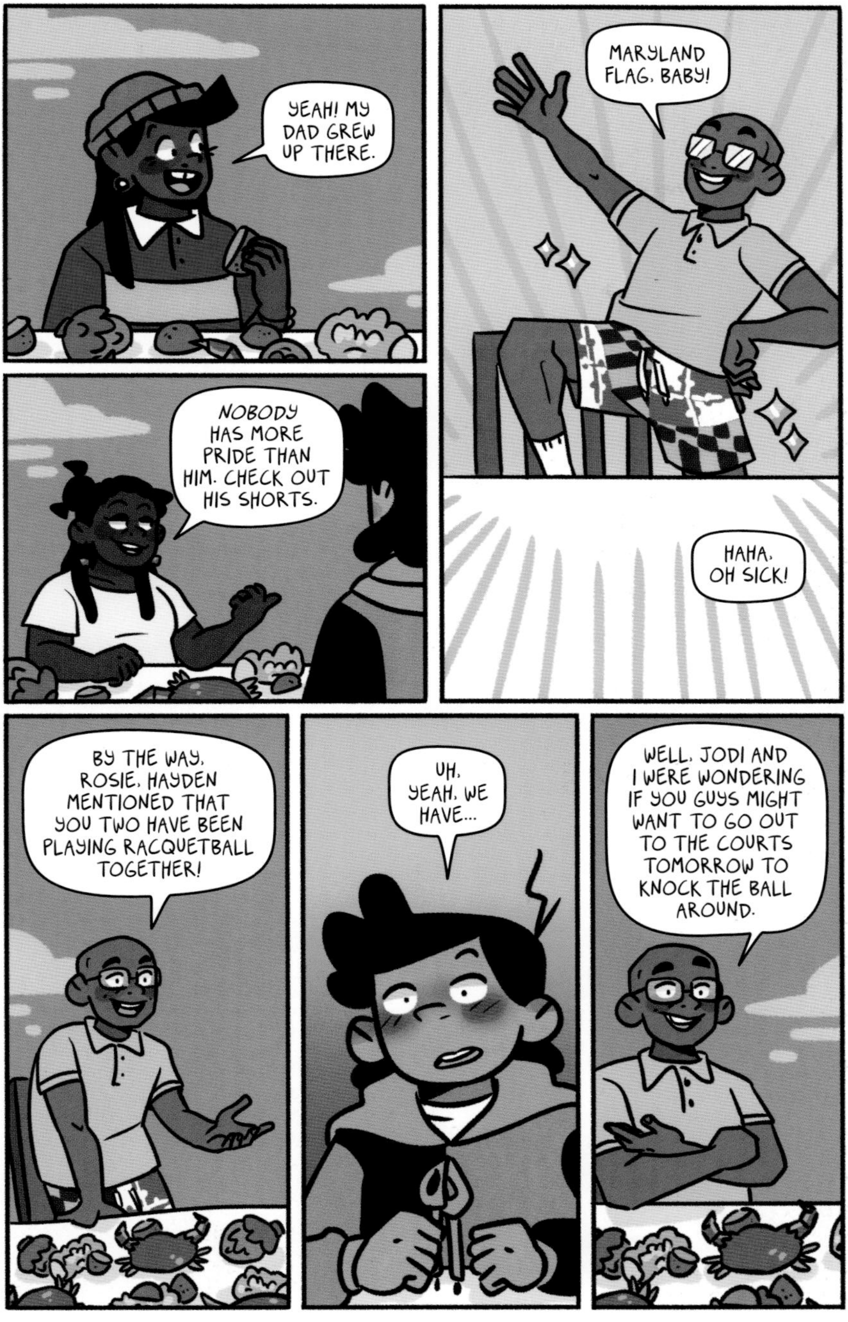
YEAH! MY DAD GREW UP THERE.
MARYLAND FLAG, BABY!
NOBODY HAS MORE PRIDE THAN HIM. CHECK OUT HIS SHORTS.
HAHA, OH SICK!
BY THE WAY, ROSIE, HAYDEN MENTIONED THAT YOU TWO HAVE BEEN PLAYING RACQUETBALL TOGETHER!
UH, YEAH, WE HAVE...
WELL, JODI AND I WERE WONDERING IF YOU GUYS MIGHT WANT TO GO OUT TO THE COURTS TOMORROW TO KNOCK THE BALL AROUND.

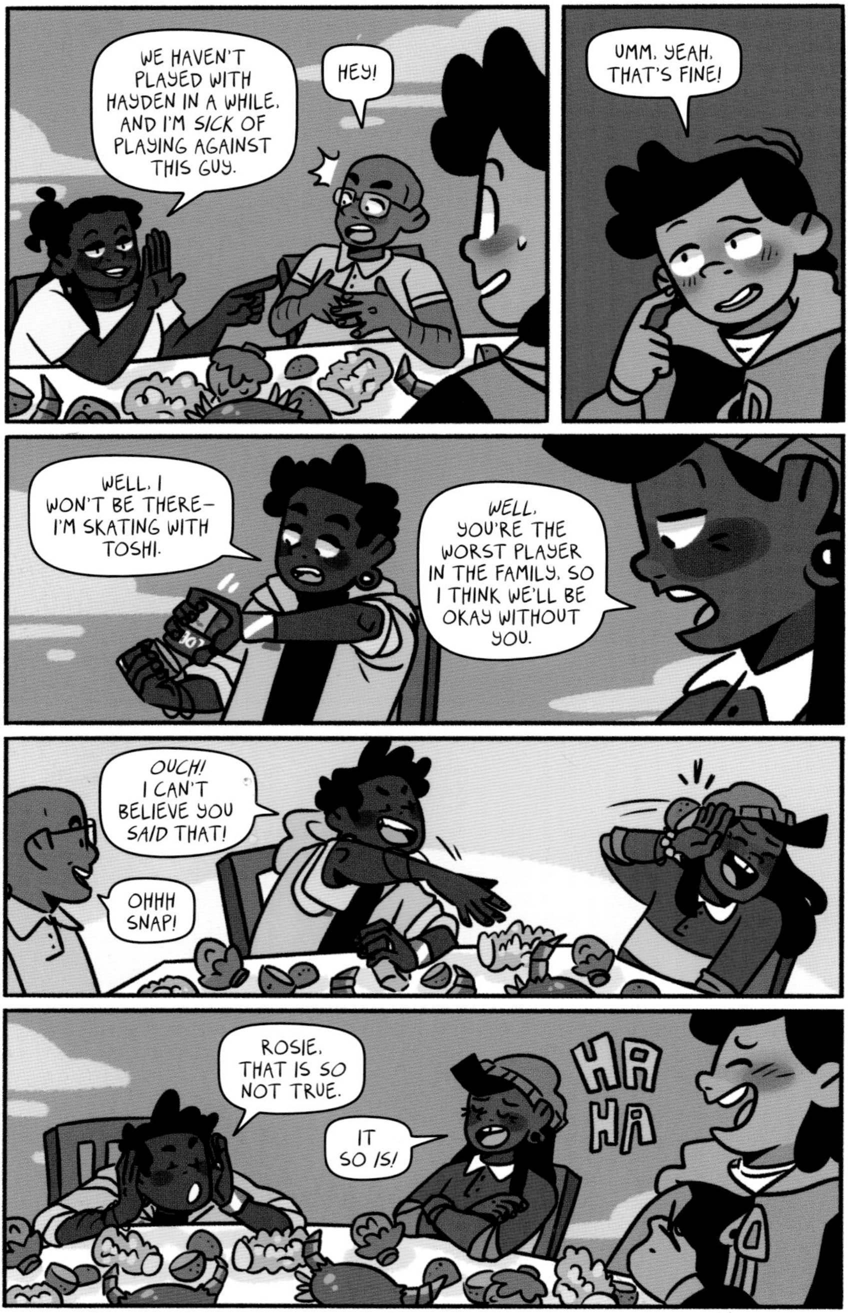
WE HAVEN'T PLAYED WITH HAYDEN IN A WHILE, AND I'M SICK OF PLAYING AGAINST THIS GUY.
HEY!
UMM, YEAH, THAT'S FINE!
WELL, I WON'T BE THERE— I'M SKATING WITH TOSHI.
WELL, YOU'RE THE WORST PLAYER IN THE FAMILY, SO I THINK WE'LL BE OKAY WITHOUT YOU.
OUCH! I CAN'T BELIEVE YOU SAID THAT!
OHHH SNAP!
ROSIE, THAT IS SO NOT TRUE.
IT SO IS!
HA HA

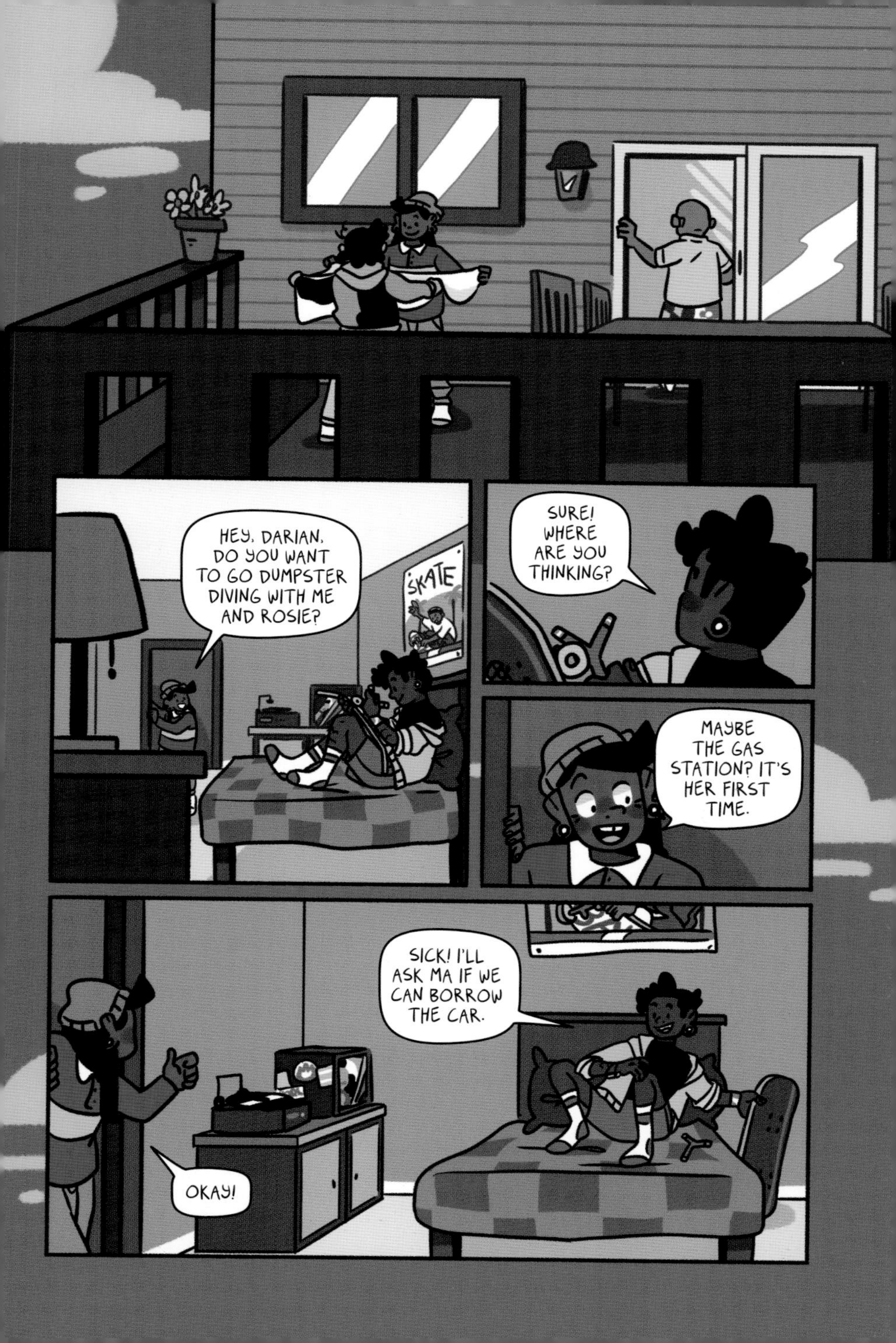
SKATE
HEY, DARIAN, DO YOU WANT TO GO DUMPSTER DIVING WITH ME AND ROSIE?
SURE! WHERE ARE YOU THINKING?
MAYBE THE GAS STATION? IT'S HER FIRST TIME.
SICK! I'LL ASK MA IF WE CAN BORROW THE CAR.
OKAY!

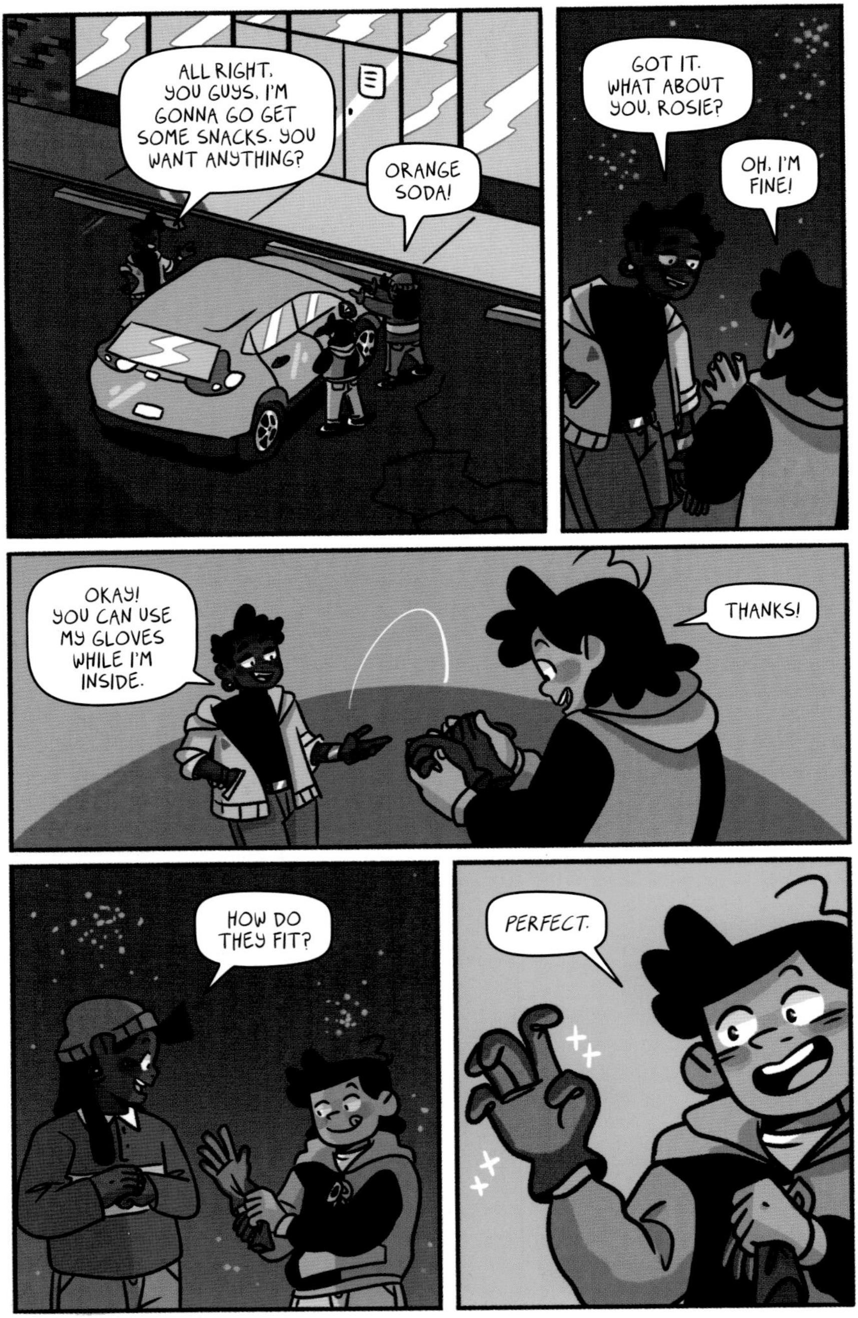
ALL RIGHT, YOU GUYS, I'M GONNA GO GET SOME SNACKS. YOU WANT ANYTHING?
ORANGE SODA!
GOT IT. WHAT ABOUT YOU, ROSIE?
OH, I'M FINE!
OKAY! YOU CAN USE MY GLOVES WHILE I'M INSIDE.
THANKS!
HOW DO THEY FIT?
PERFECT.

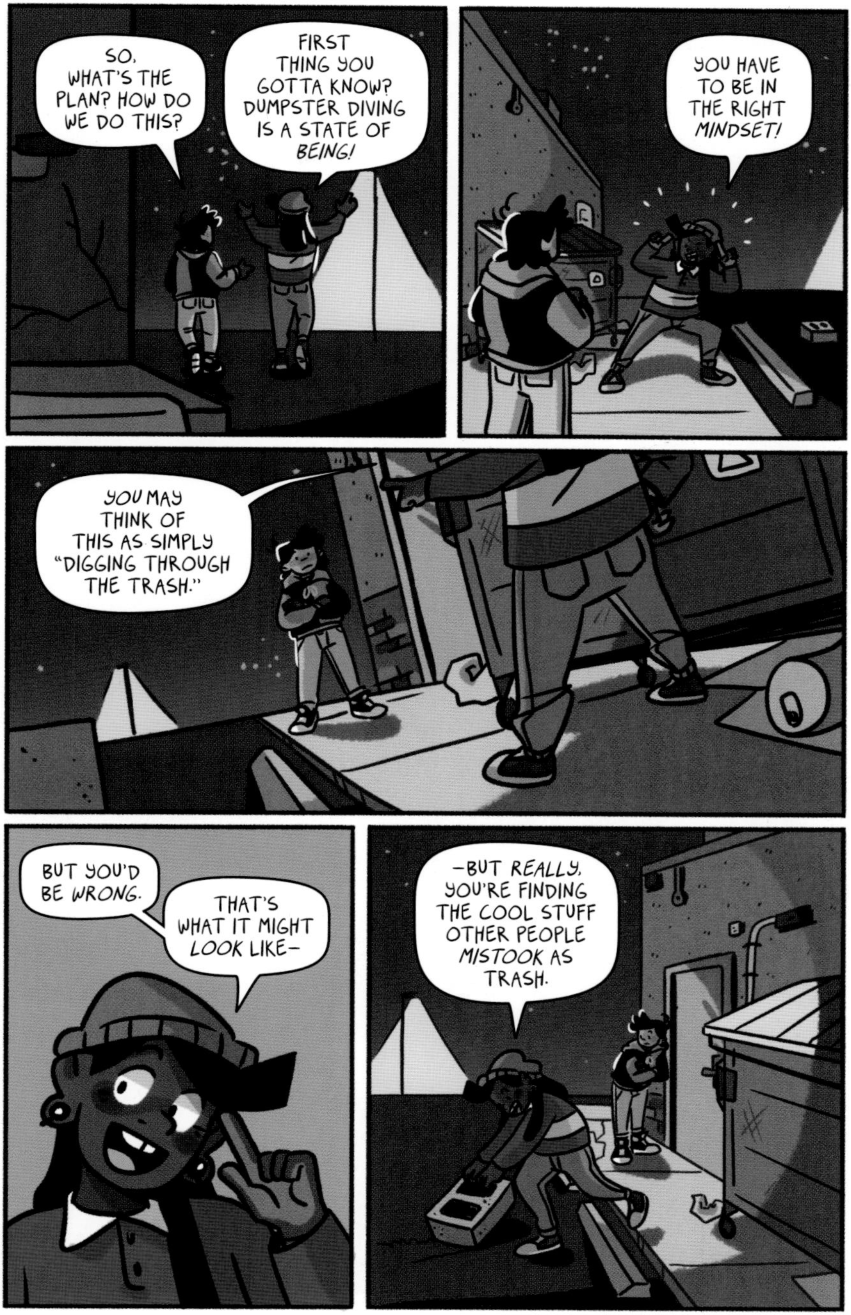
SO, WHAT'S THE PLAN? HOW DO WE DO THIS?
FIRST THING YOU GOTTA KNOW? DUMPSTER DIVING IS A STATE OF *BEING!*
YOU HAVE TO BE IN THE RIGHT *MINDSET!*
YOU MAY THINK OF THIS AS SIMPLY "DIGGING THROUGH THE TRASH."
BUT YOU'D BE *WRONG.*
THAT'S WHAT IT MIGHT *LOOK* LIKE—
—BUT *REALLY,* YOU'RE FINDING THE COOL STUFF OTHER PEOPLE *MISTOOK* AS TRASH.

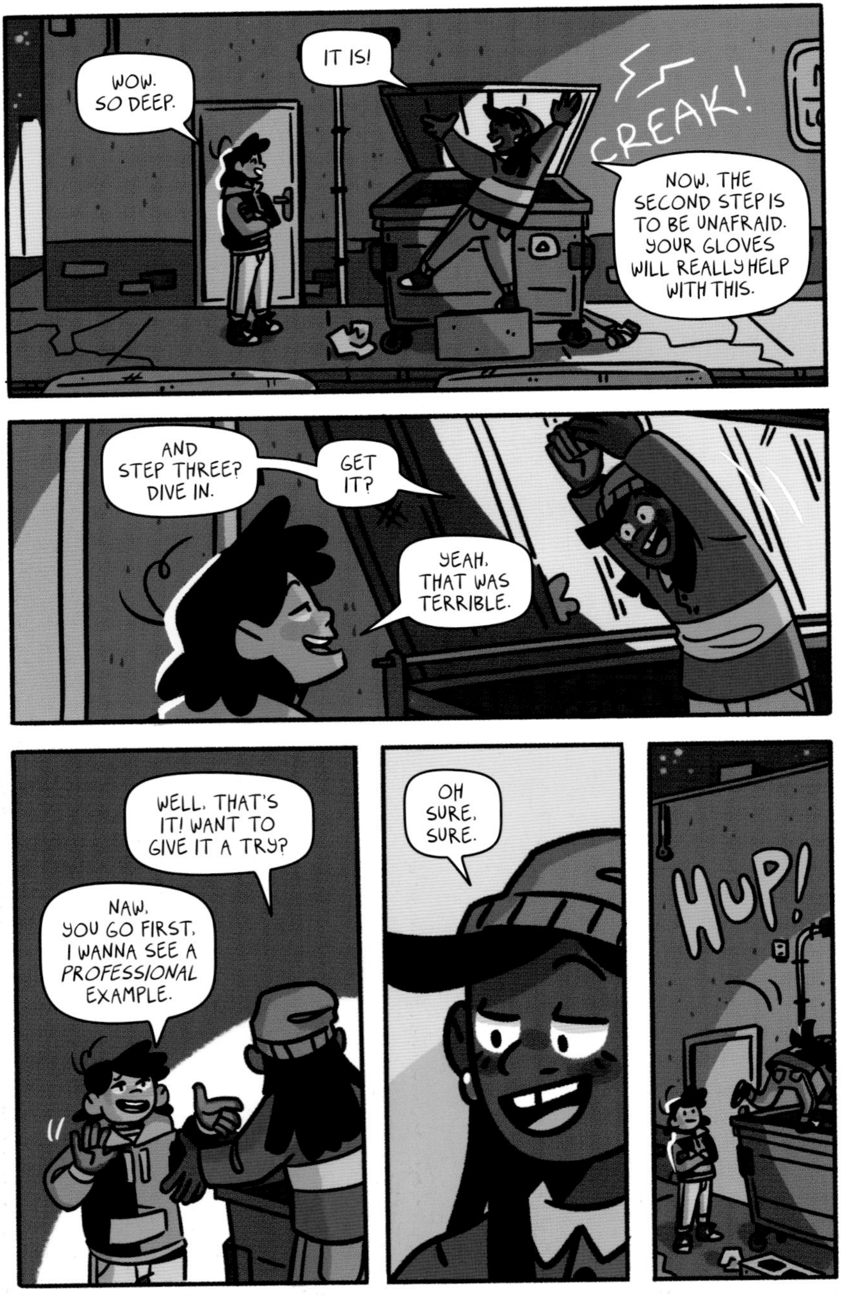
WOW. SO DEEP.
IT IS!
CREAK!
NOW, THE SECOND STEP IS TO BE UNAFRAID. YOUR GLOVES WILL REALLY HELP WITH THIS.
AND STEP THREE? DIVE IN.
GET IT?
YEAH, THAT WAS TERRIBLE.
WELL, THAT'S IT! WANT TO GIVE IT A TRY?
NAW, YOU GO FIRST. I WANNA SEE A *PROFESSIONAL* EXAMPLE.
OH SURE, SURE.
HUP!

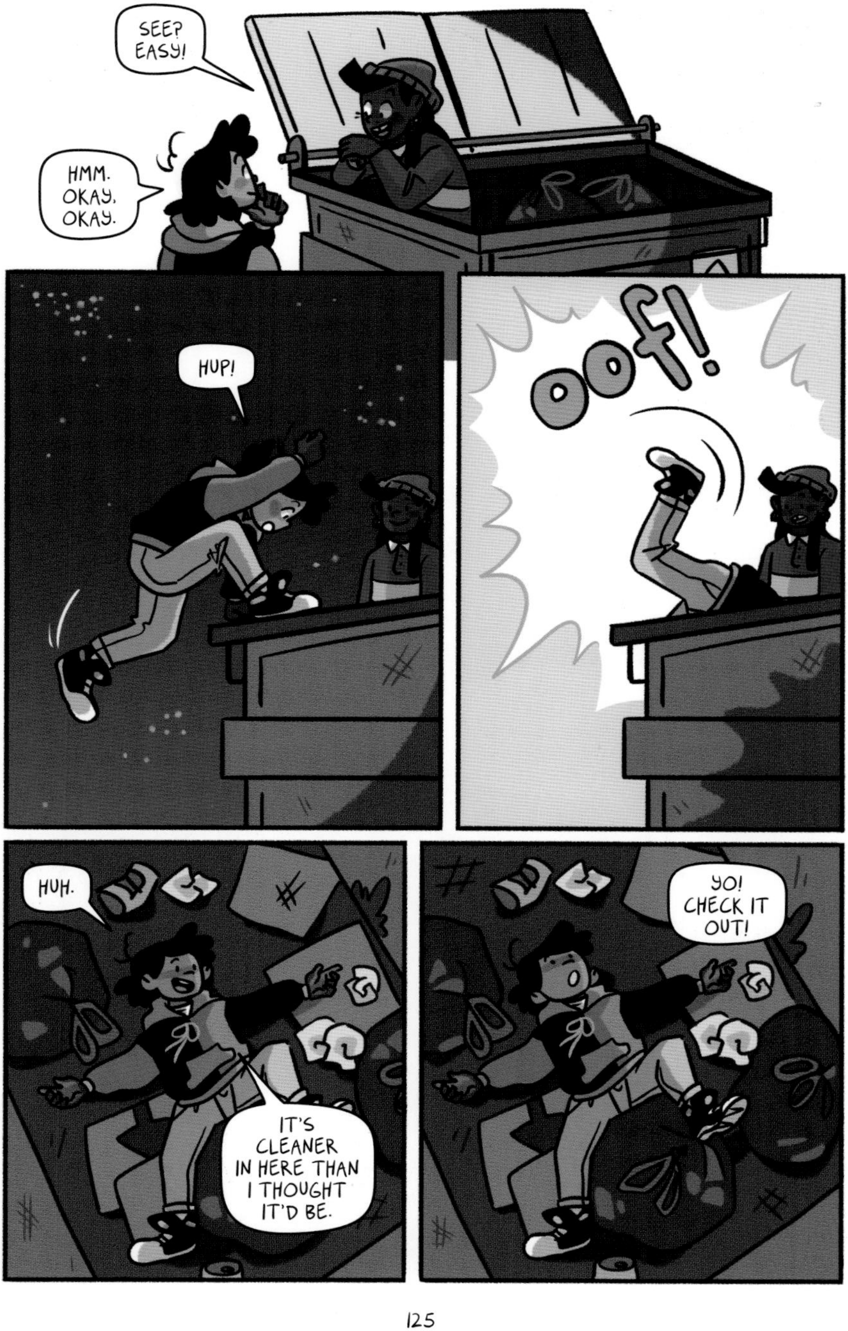
SEE? EASY!
HMM. OKAY, OKAY.
HUP!
OOF!
HUH.
IT'S CLEANER IN HERE THAN I THOUGHT IT'D BE.
YO! CHECK IT OUT!

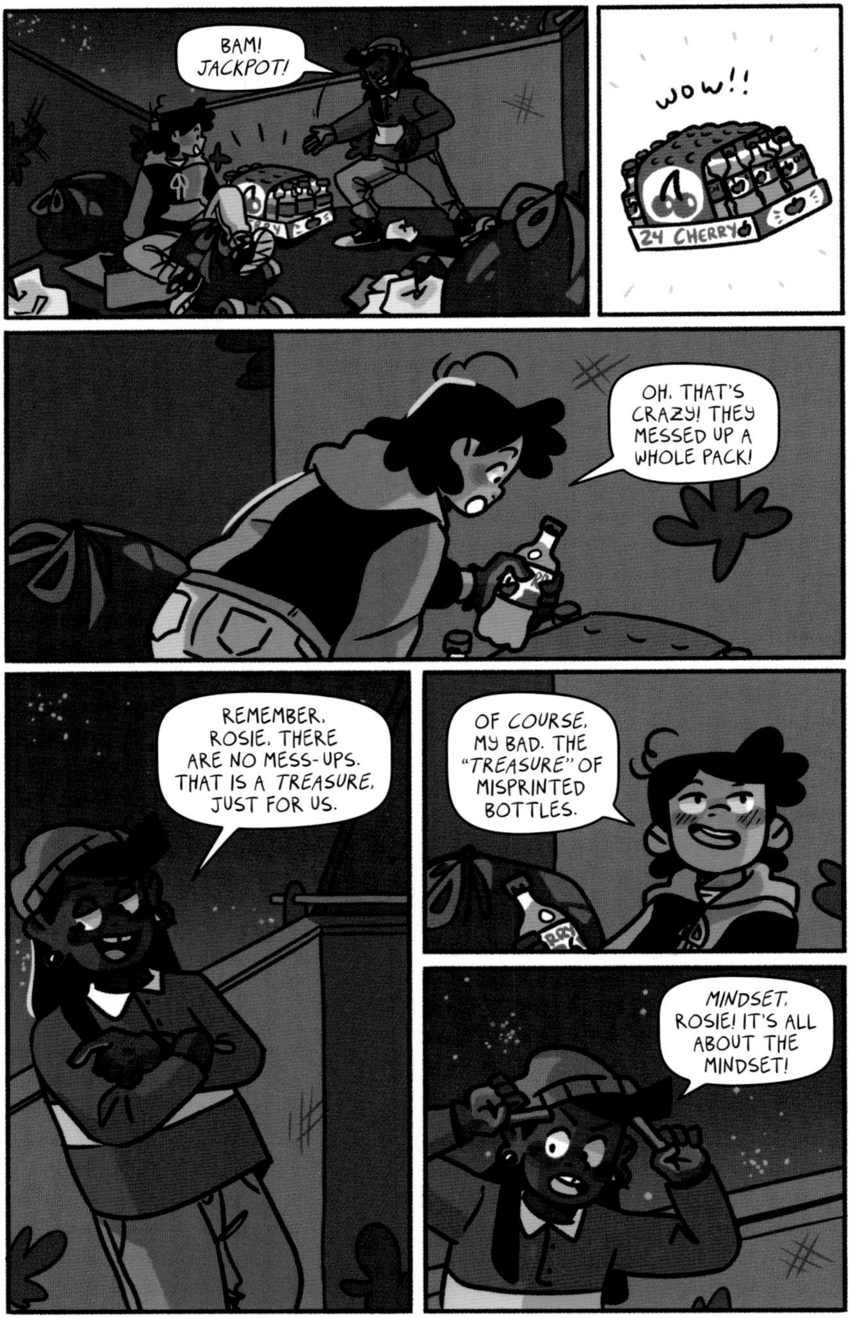
BAM! JACKPOT!
WOW!!
24 CHERRY
OH, THAT'S CRAZY! THEY MESSED UP A WHOLE PACK!
REMEMBER, ROSIE, THERE ARE NO MESS-UPS. THAT IS A *TREASURE*, JUST FOR US.
OF COURSE, MY BAD. THE "*TREASURE*" OF MISPRINTED BOTTLES.
MINDSET, ROSIE! IT'S ALL ABOUT THE MINDSET!

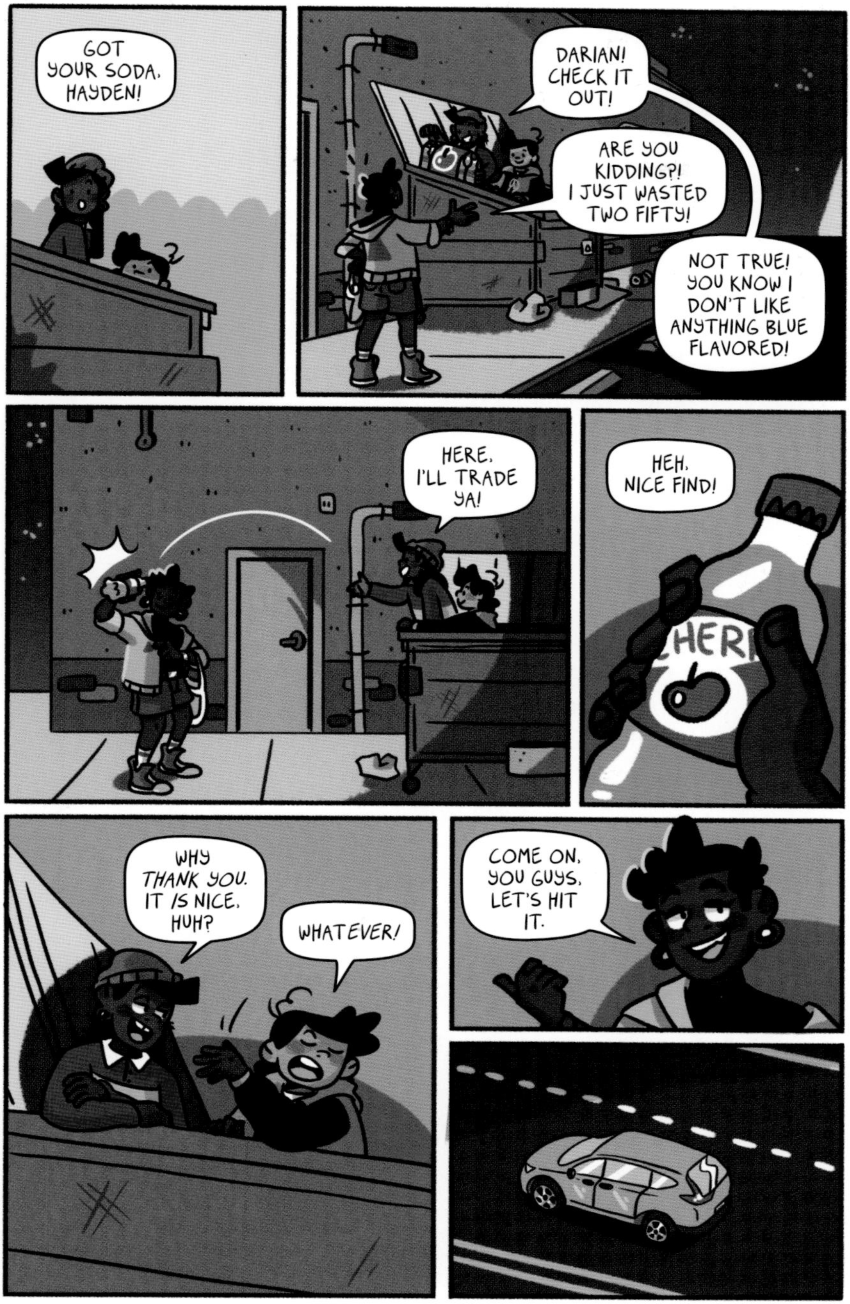
GOT YOUR SODA, HAYDEN!
DARIAN! CHECK IT OUT!
ARE YOU KIDDING?! I JUST WASTED TWO FIFTY!
NOT TRUE! YOU KNOW I DON'T LIKE ANYTHING BLUE FLAVORED!
HERE, I'LL TRADE YA!
HEH, NICE FIND!
CHERI
WHY THANK YOU. IT IS NICE, HUH?
WHATEVER!
COME ON, YOU GUYS, LET'S HIT IT.

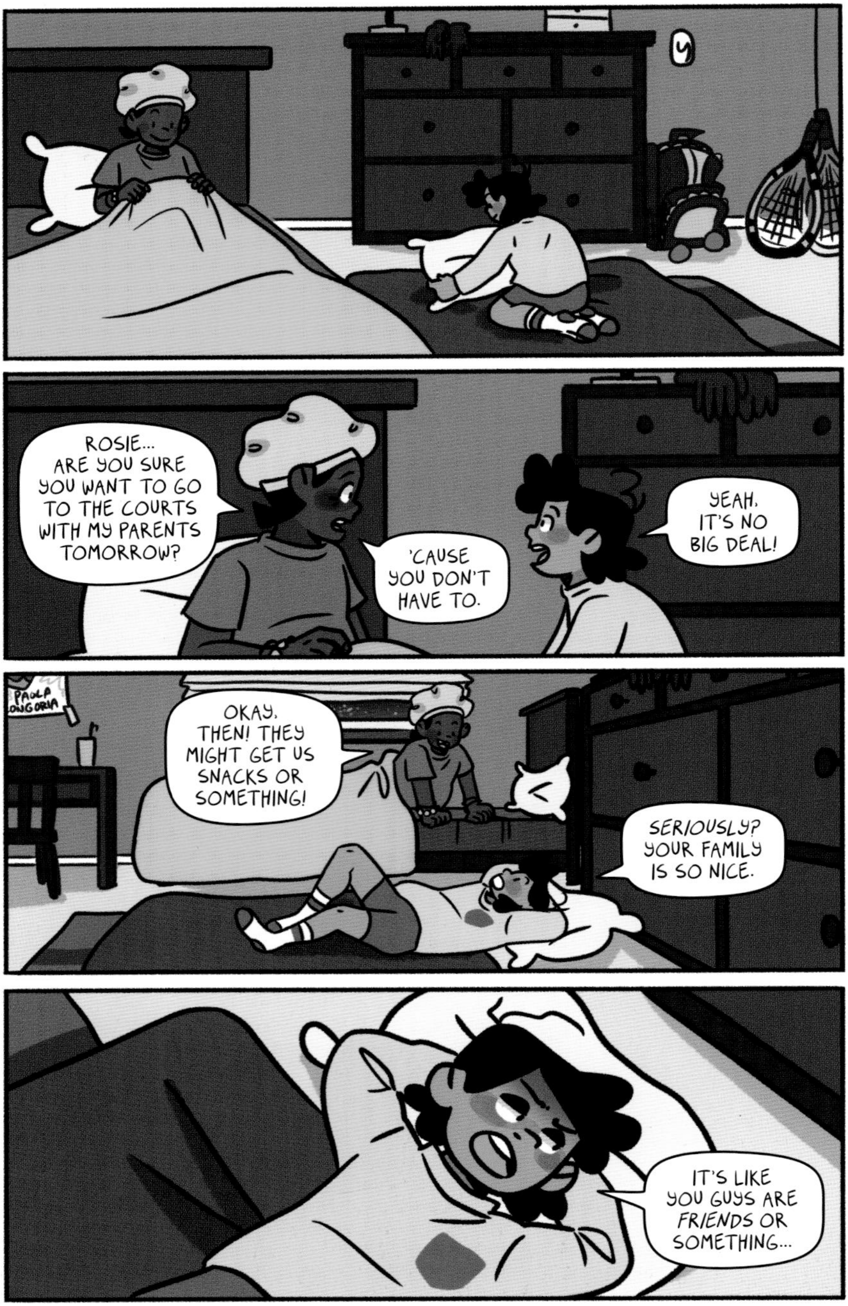
PAOLA LONGORIA
ROSIE... ARE YOU SURE YOU WANT TO GO TO THE COURTS WITH MY PARENTS TOMORROW?
'CAUSE YOU DON'T HAVE TO.
YEAH. IT'S NO BIG DEAL!
OKAY, THEN! THEY MIGHT GET US SNACKS OR SOMETHING!
SERIOUSLY? YOUR FAMILY IS SO NICE.
IT'S LIKE YOU GUYS ARE *FRIENDS* OR SOMETHING...

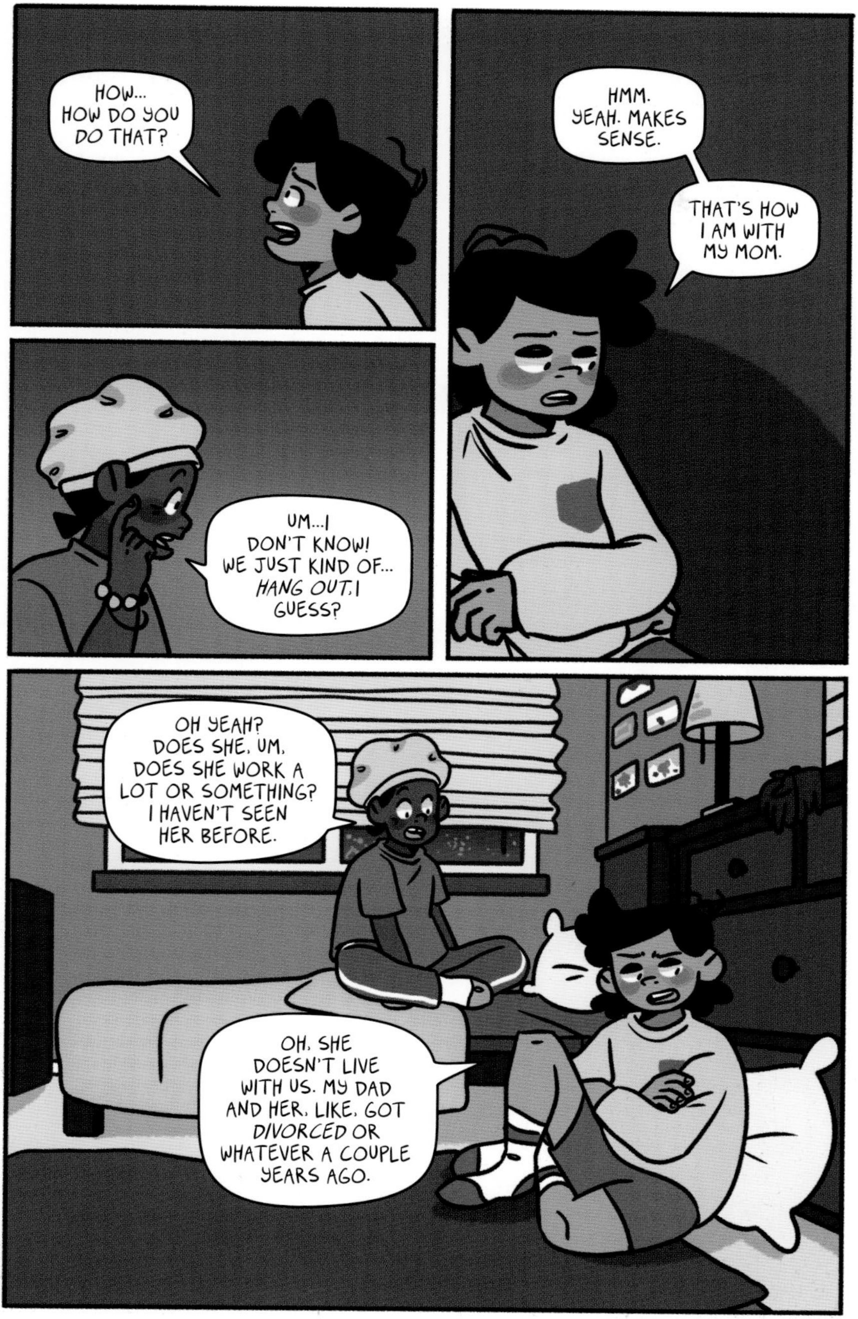
HOW... HOW DO YOU DO THAT?
UM...I DON'T KNOW! WE JUST KIND OF... *HANG OUT*, I GUESS?
HMM. YEAH. MAKES SENSE.
THAT'S HOW I AM WITH MY MOM.
OH YEAH? DOES SHE, UM, DOES SHE WORK A LOT OR SOMETHING? I HAVEN'T SEEN HER BEFORE.
OH, SHE DOESN'T LIVE WITH US. MY DAD AND HER, LIKE, GOT *DIVORCED* OR WHATEVER A COUPLE YEARS AGO.

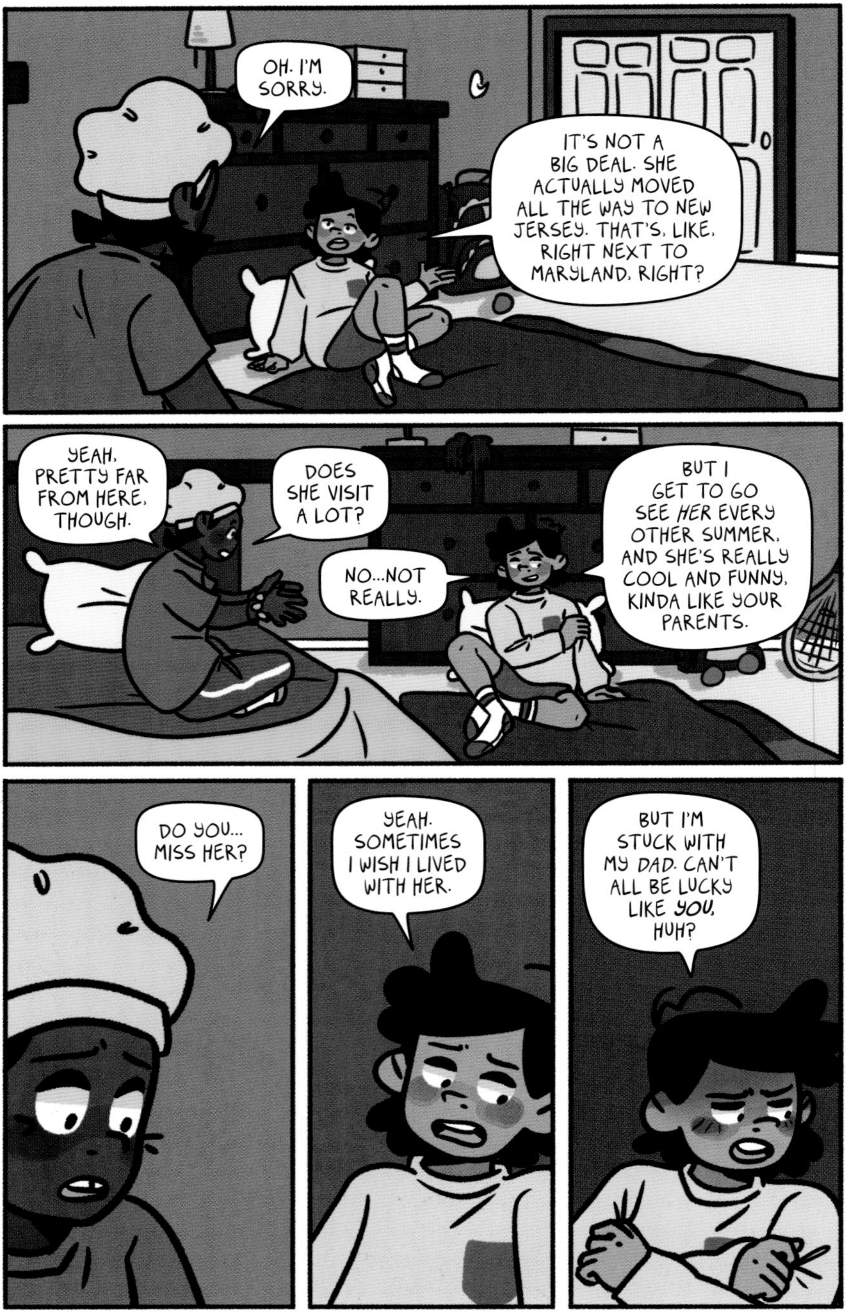
OH. I'M SORRY.
IT'S NOT A BIG DEAL. SHE ACTUALLY MOVED ALL THE WAY TO NEW JERSEY. THAT'S, LIKE, RIGHT NEXT TO MARYLAND, RIGHT?
YEAH, PRETTY FAR FROM HERE, THOUGH.
DOES SHE VISIT A LOT?
NO...NOT REALLY.
BUT I GET TO GO SEE HER EVERY OTHER SUMMER, AND SHE'S REALLY COOL AND FUNNY, KINDA LIKE YOUR PARENTS.
DO YOU... MISS HER?
YEAH. SOMETIMES I WISH I LIVED WITH HER.
BUT I'M STUCK WITH MY DAD. CAN'T ALL BE LUCKY LIKE YOU, HUH?

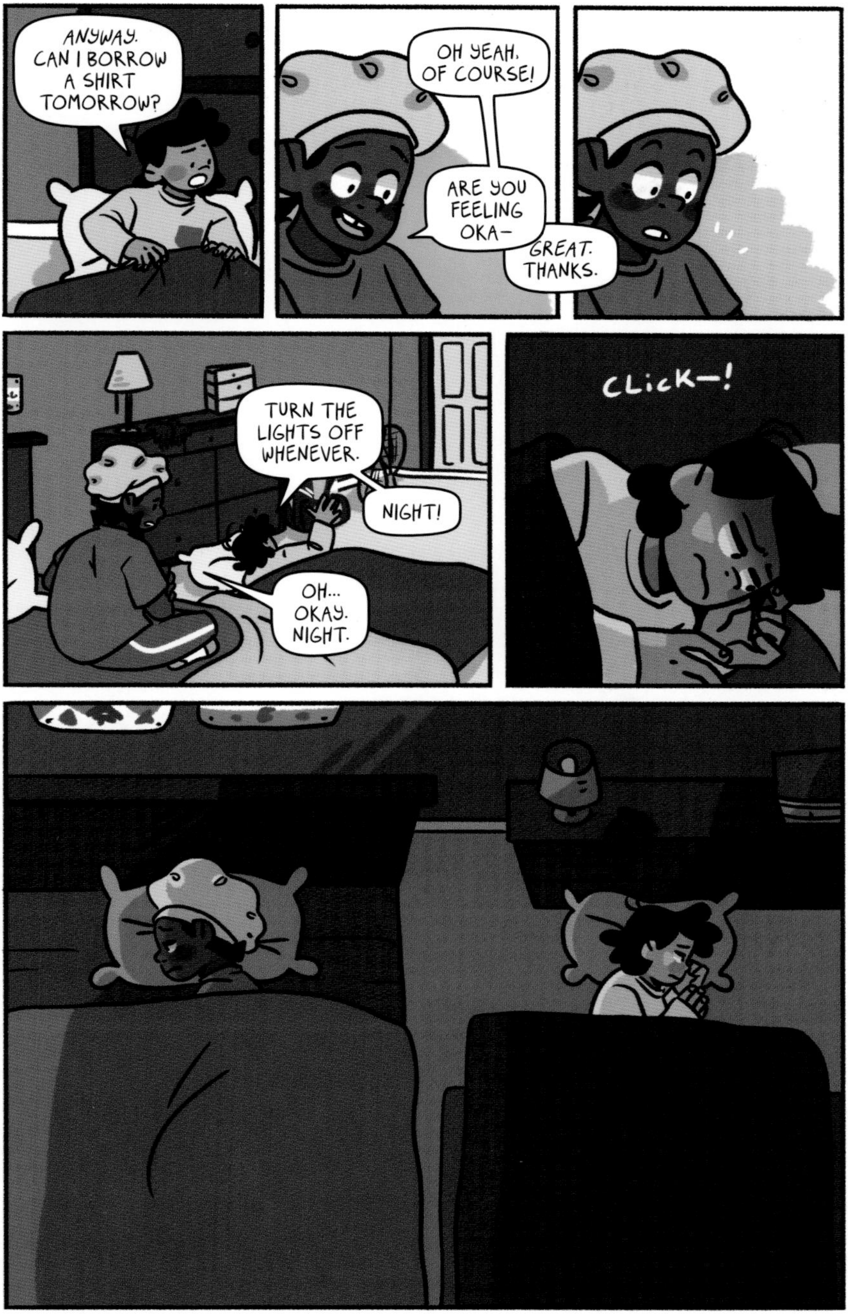
ANYWAY. CAN I BORROW A SHIRT TOMORROW?
OH YEAH, OF COURSE!
ARE YOU FEELING OKA—
GREAT. THANKS.
TURN THE LIGHTS OFF WHENEVER.
NIGHT!
OH... OKAY. NIGHT.
CLICK—!

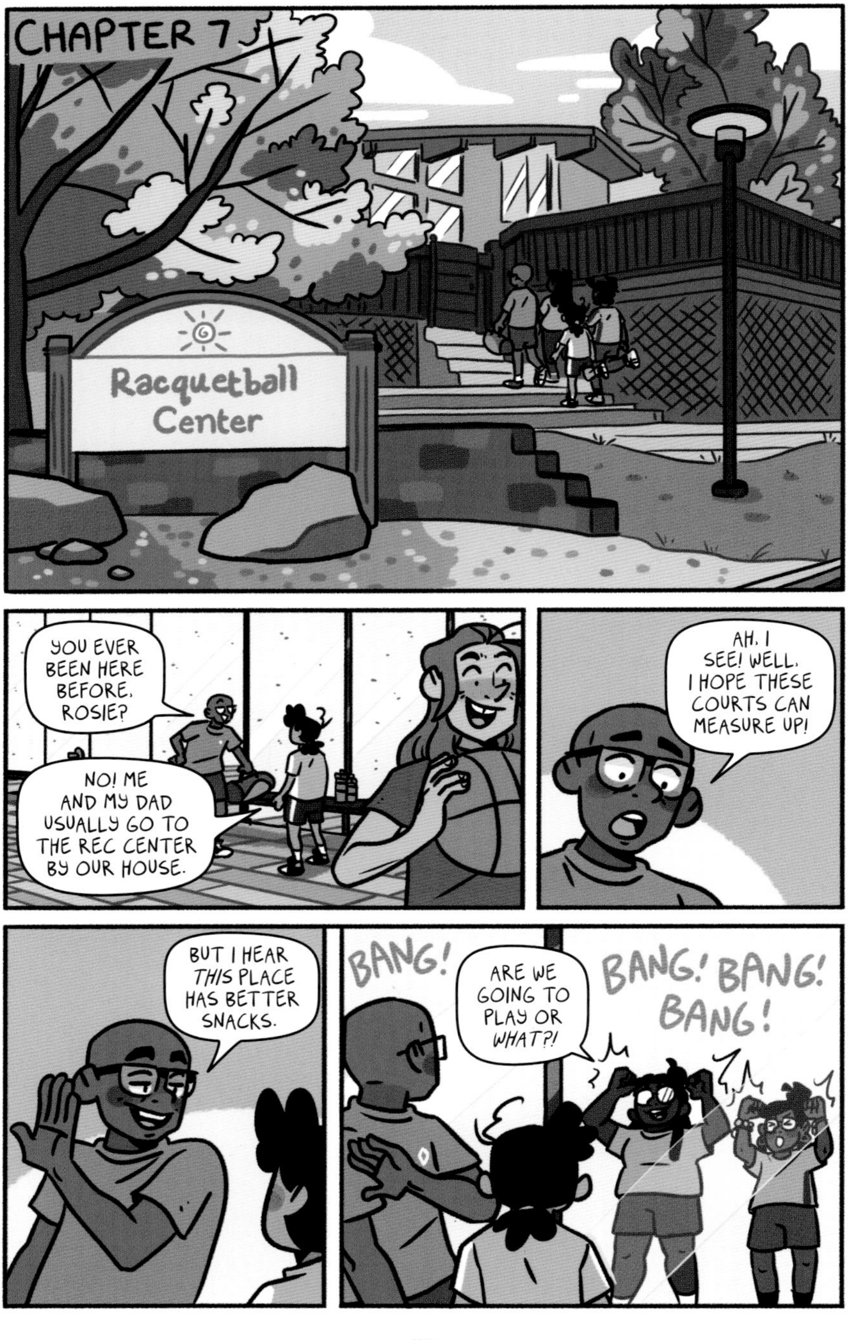
CHAPTER 7
Racquetball Center
YOU EVER BEEN HERE BEFORE, ROSIE?
NO! ME AND MY DAD USUALLY GO TO THE REC CENTER BY OUR HOUSE.
AH, I SEE! WELL, I HOPE THESE COURTS CAN MEASURE UP!
BUT I HEAR *THIS* PLACE HAS BETTER SNACKS.
BANG!
ARE WE GOING TO PLAY OR *WHAT?!*
BANG! BANG!
BANG!

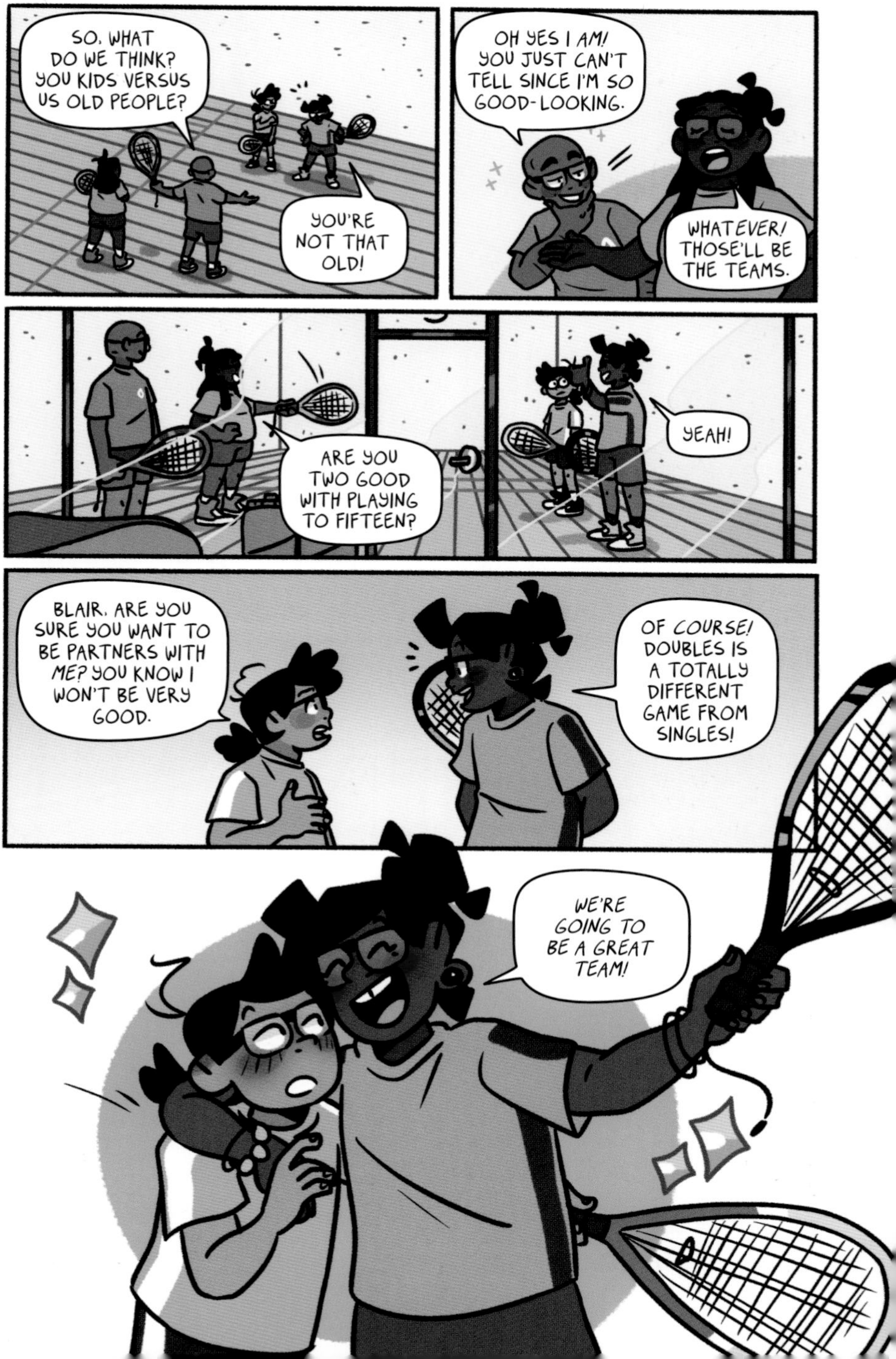
SO, WHAT DO WE THINK? YOU KIDS VERSUS US OLD PEOPLE?
YOU'RE NOT THAT OLD!
OH YES I AM! YOU JUST CAN'T TELL SINCE I'M SO GOOD-LOOKING.
WHATEVER! THOSE'LL BE THE TEAMS.
ARE YOU TWO GOOD WITH PLAYING TO FIFTEEN?
YEAH!
BLAIR, ARE YOU SURE YOU WANT TO BE PARTNERS WITH ME? YOU KNOW I WON'T BE VERY GOOD.
OF COURSE! DOUBLES IS A TOTALLY DIFFERENT GAME FROM SINGLES!
WE'RE GOING TO BE A GREAT TEAM!

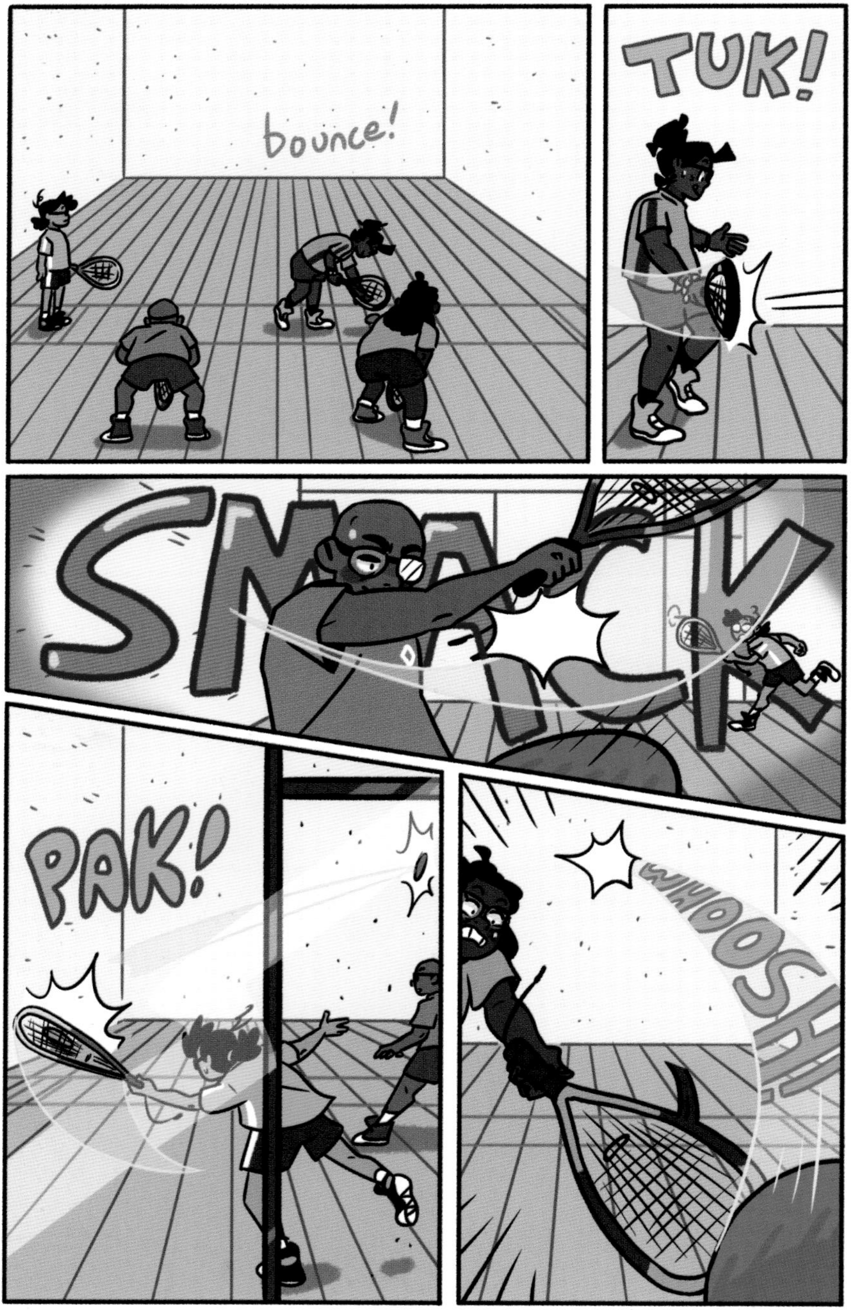
bounce!
TUK!
SMACK
PAK!
WHOOSH!

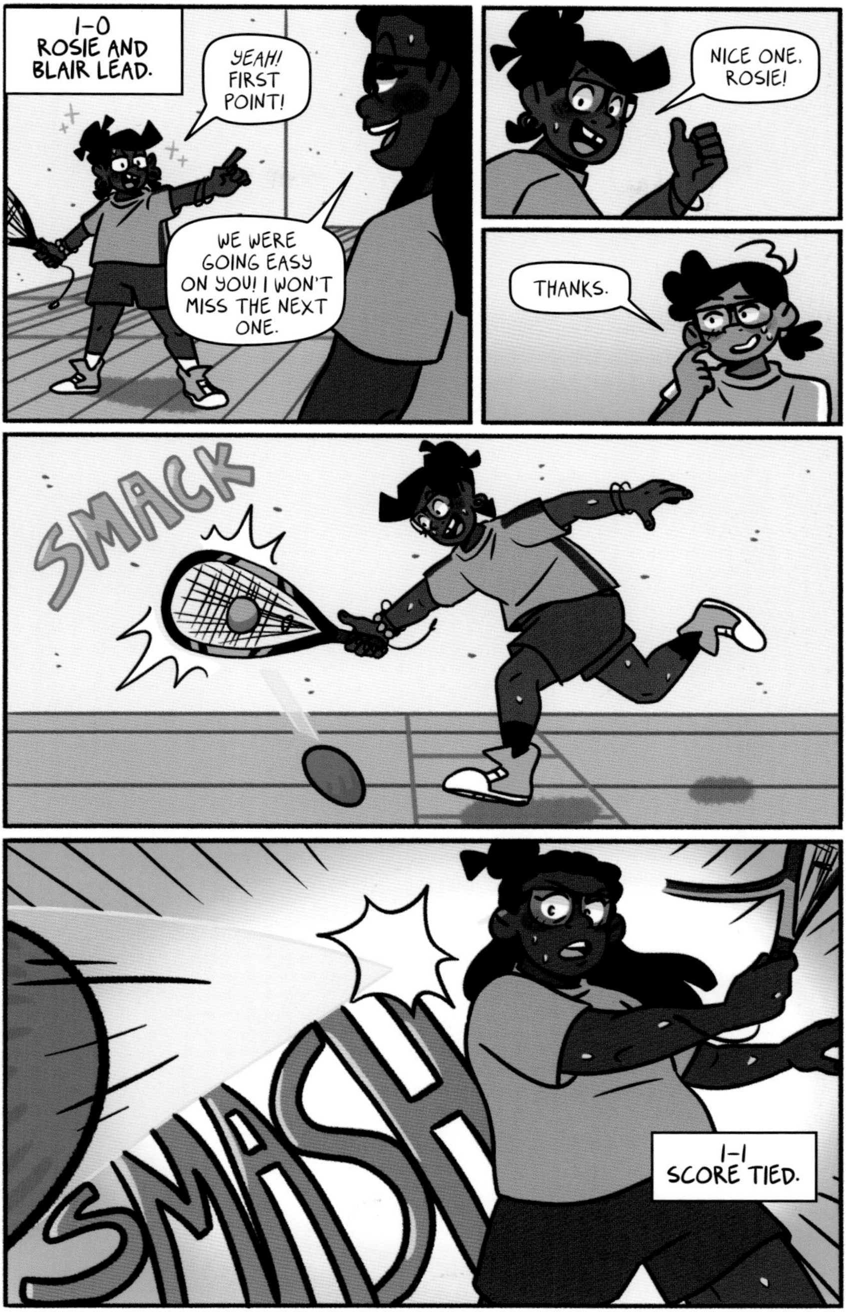
1–0
ROSIE AND BLAIR LEAD.
YEAH! FIRST POINT!
WE WERE GOING EASY ON YOU! I WON'T MISS THE NEXT ONE.
NICE ONE, ROSIE!
THANKS.
SMACK
SMASH
1–1
SCORE TIED.

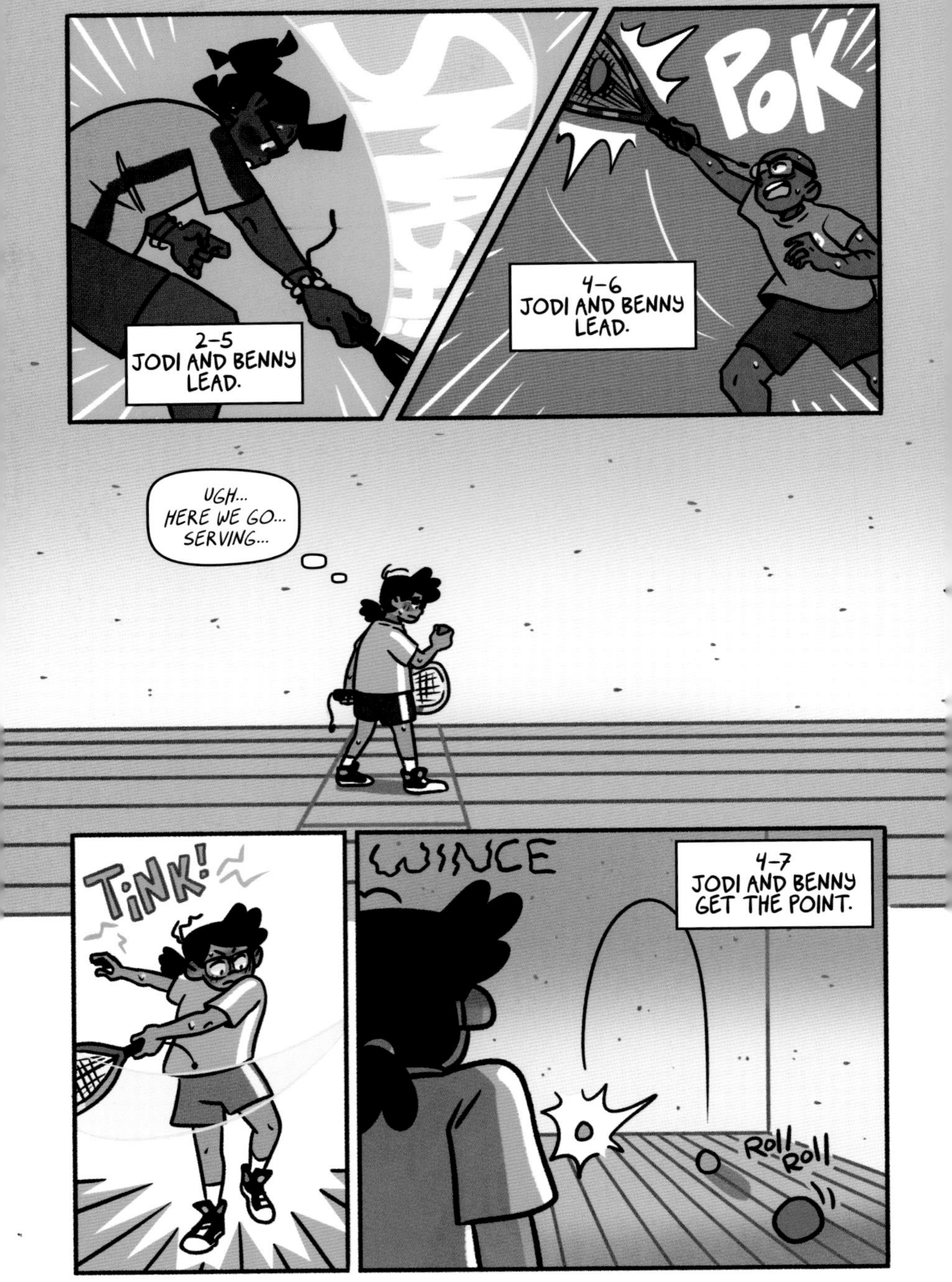
SMASH
2–5
JODI AND BENNY
LEAD.
POK
4–6
JODI AND BENNY
LEAD.
UGH...
HERE WE GO...
SERVING...
TINK!
WINCE
4–7
JODI AND BENNY
GET THE POINT.
ROLL
ROLL

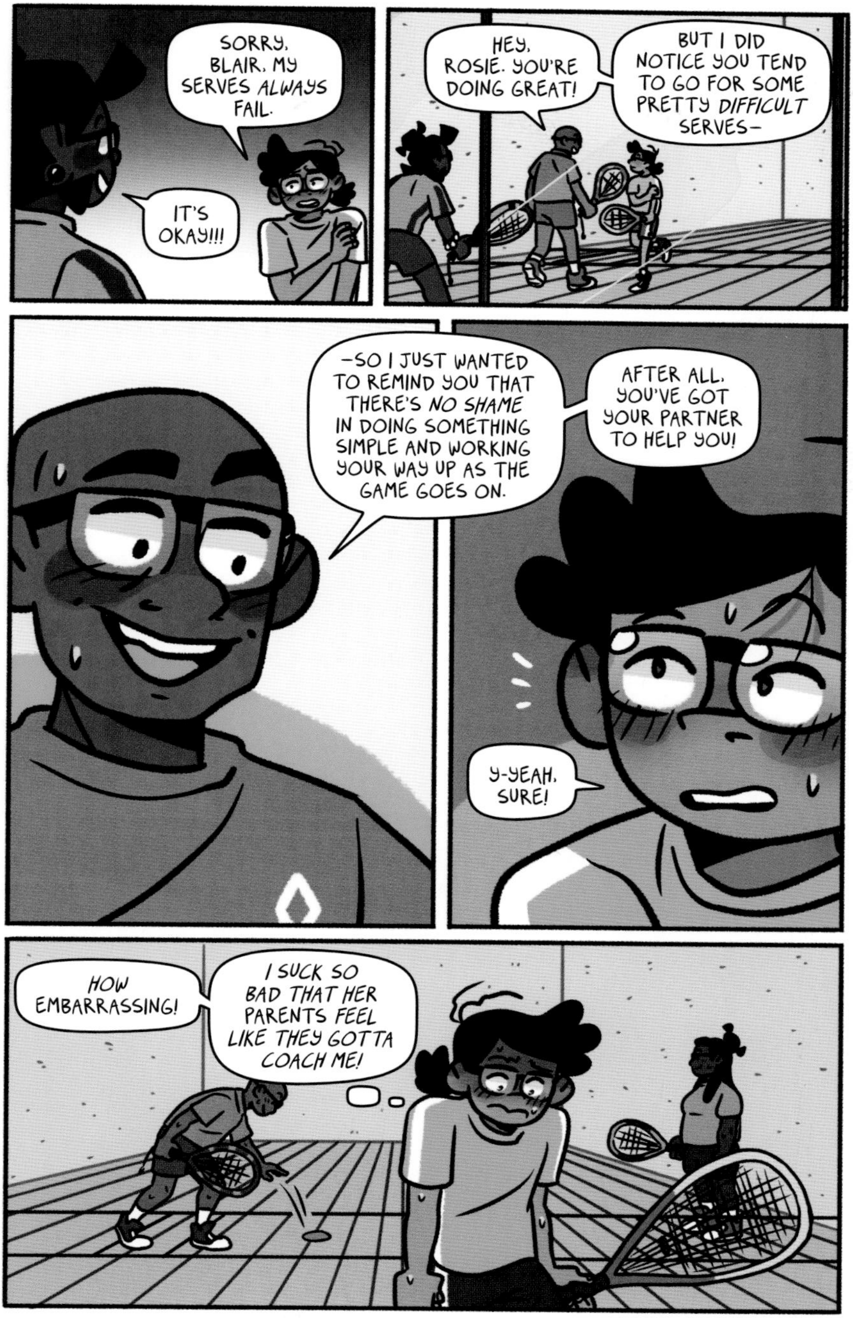
SORRY, BLAIR, MY SERVES ALWAYS FAIL.
IT'S OKAY!!!
HEY, ROSIE. YOU'RE DOING GREAT!
BUT I DID NOTICE YOU TEND TO GO FOR SOME PRETTY DIFFICULT SERVES—
—SO I JUST WANTED TO REMIND YOU THAT THERE'S NO SHAME IN DOING SOMETHING SIMPLE AND WORKING YOUR WAY UP AS THE GAME GOES ON.
AFTER ALL, YOU'VE GOT YOUR PARTNER TO HELP YOU!
Y-YEAH, SURE!
HOW EMBARRASSING!
I SUCK SO BAD THAT HER PARENTS FEEL LIKE THEY GOTTA COACH ME!

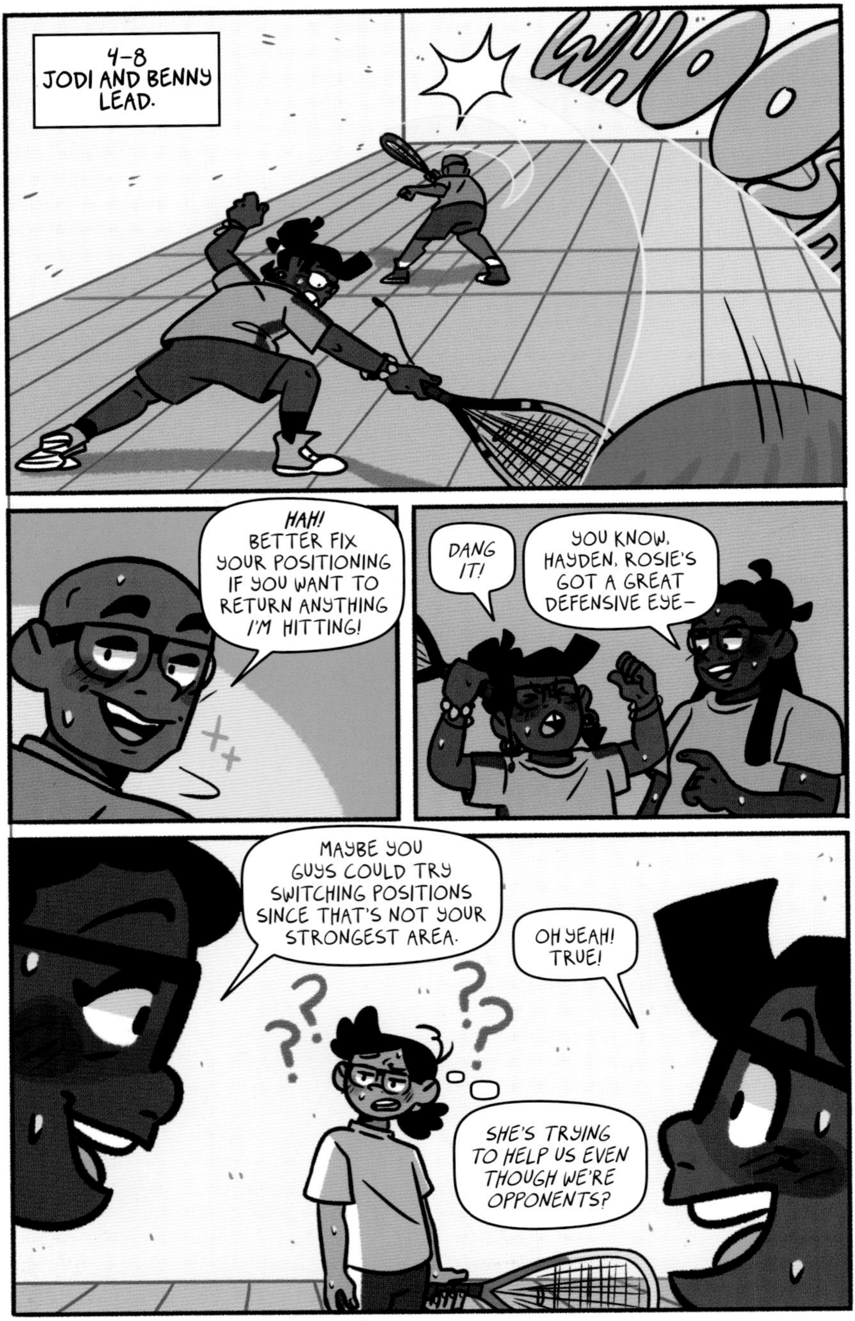
4–8
JODI AND BENNY LEAD.
WHOOSH
HAH! BETTER FIX YOUR POSITIONING IF YOU WANT TO RETURN ANYTHING I'M HITTING!
DANG IT!
YOU KNOW, HAYDEN, ROSIE'S GOT A GREAT DEFENSIVE EYE—
MAYBE YOU GUYS COULD TRY SWITCHING POSITIONS SINCE THAT'S NOT YOUR STRONGEST AREA.
OH YEAH! TRUE!
SHE'S TRYING TO HELP US EVEN THOUGH WE'RE OPPONENTS?

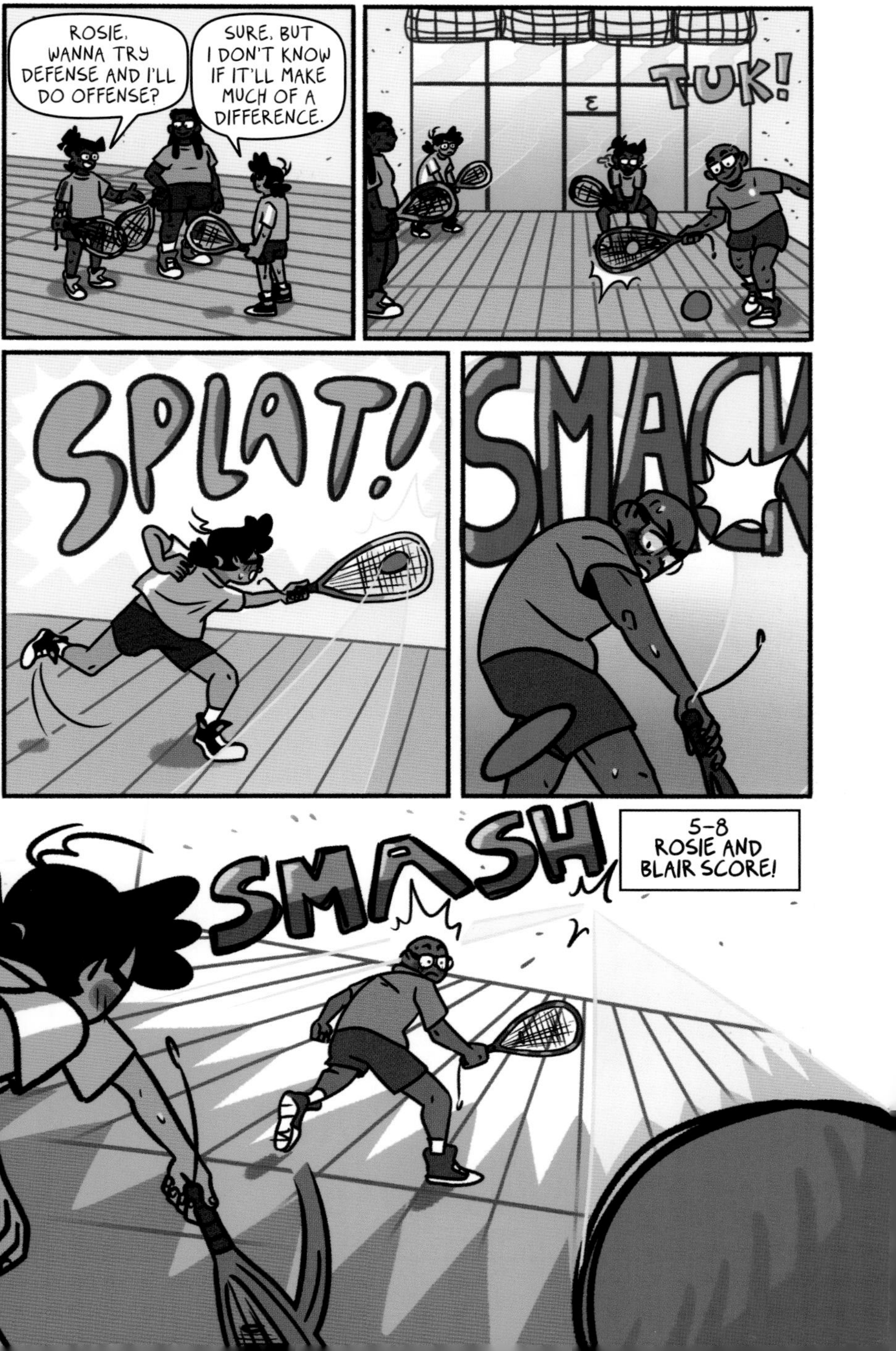
ROSIE, WANNA TRY DEFENSE AND I'LL DO OFFENSE?
SURE, BUT I DON'T KNOW IF IT'LL MAKE MUCH OF A DIFFERENCE.
TUK!
SPLAT!
SMACK
SMASH
5–8 ROSIE AND BLAIR SCORE!

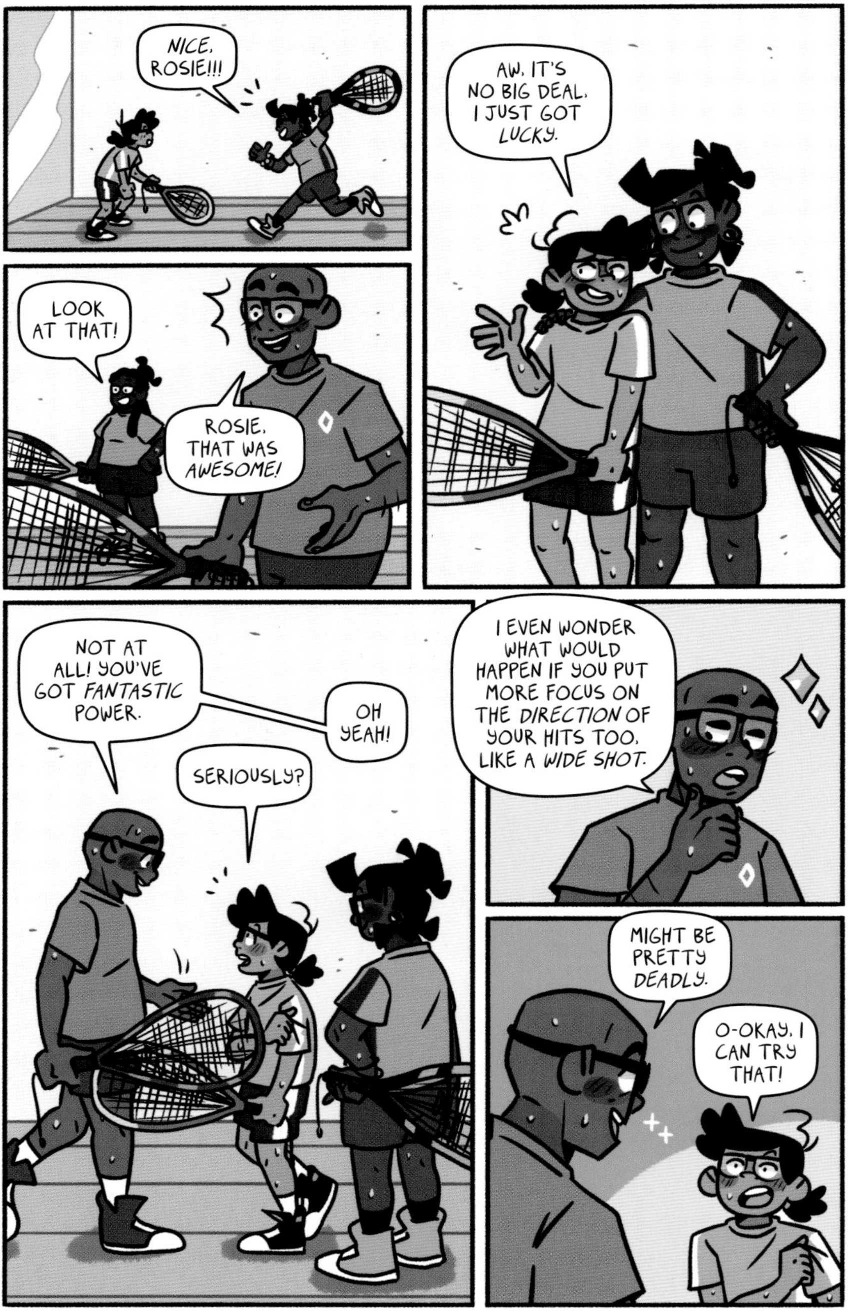
NICE, ROSIE!!!
AW, IT'S NO BIG DEAL. I JUST GOT *LUCKY*.
LOOK AT THAT!
ROSIE, THAT WAS *AWESOME!*
NOT AT ALL! YOU'VE GOT *FANTASTIC* POWER.
OH YEAH!
SERIOUSLY?
I EVEN WONDER WHAT WOULD HAPPEN IF YOU PUT MORE FOCUS ON THE *DIRECTION* OF YOUR HITS TOO, LIKE A *WIDE SHOT*.
MIGHT BE PRETTY *DEADLY*.
O-OKAY, I CAN TRY THAT!

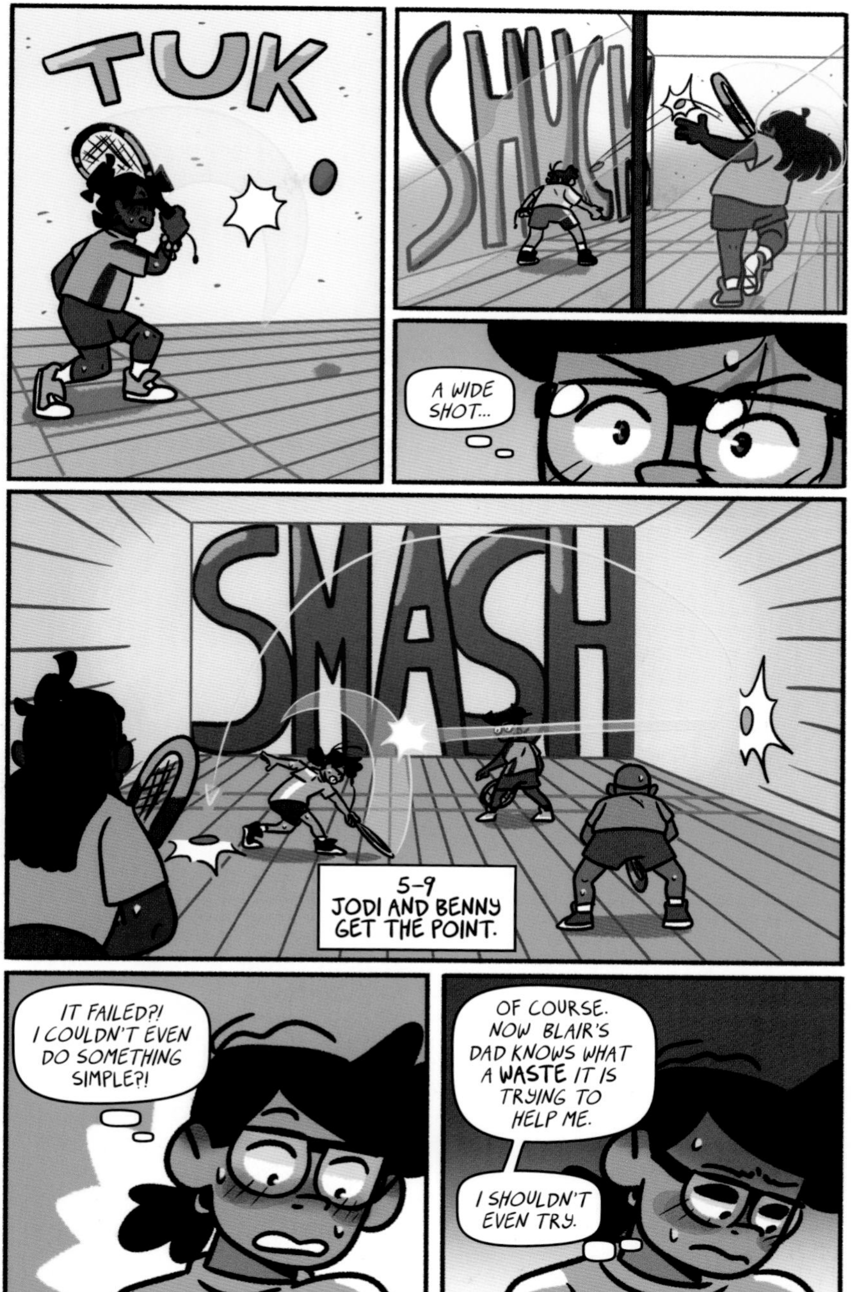
TUK
SHUCK
A WIDE SHOT...
SMASH
5-9
JODI AND BENNY GET THE POINT.
IT FAILED?! I COULDN'T EVEN DO SOMETHING SIMPLE?!
OF COURSE. NOW BLAIR'S DAD KNOWS WHAT A **WASTE** IT IS TRYING TO HELP ME.
I SHOULDN'T EVEN TRY.

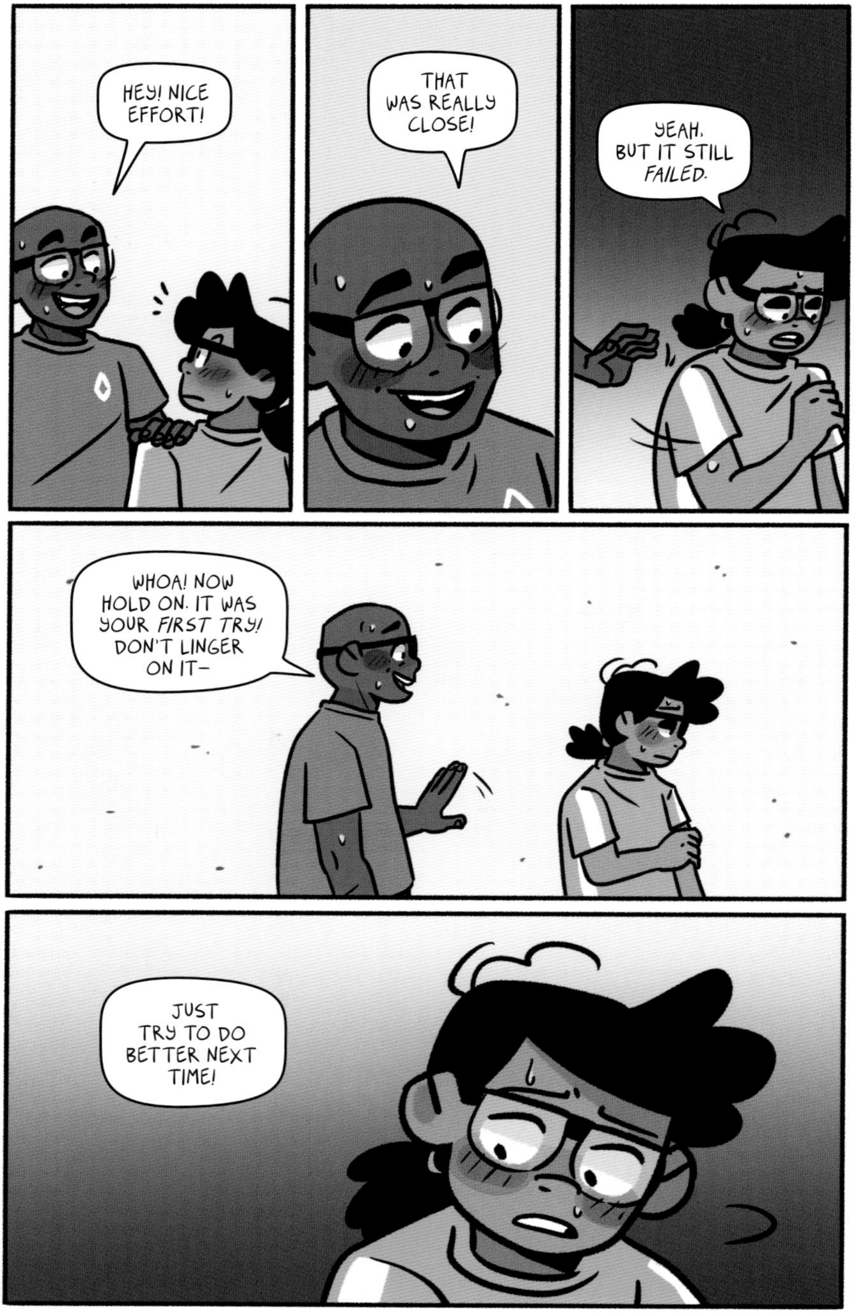
HEY! NICE EFFORT!
THAT WAS REALLY CLOSE!
YEAH, BUT IT STILL *FAILED*.
WHOA! NOW HOLD ON. IT WAS YOUR *FIRST TRY!* DON'T LINGER ON IT–
JUST TRY TO DO BETTER NEXT TIME!

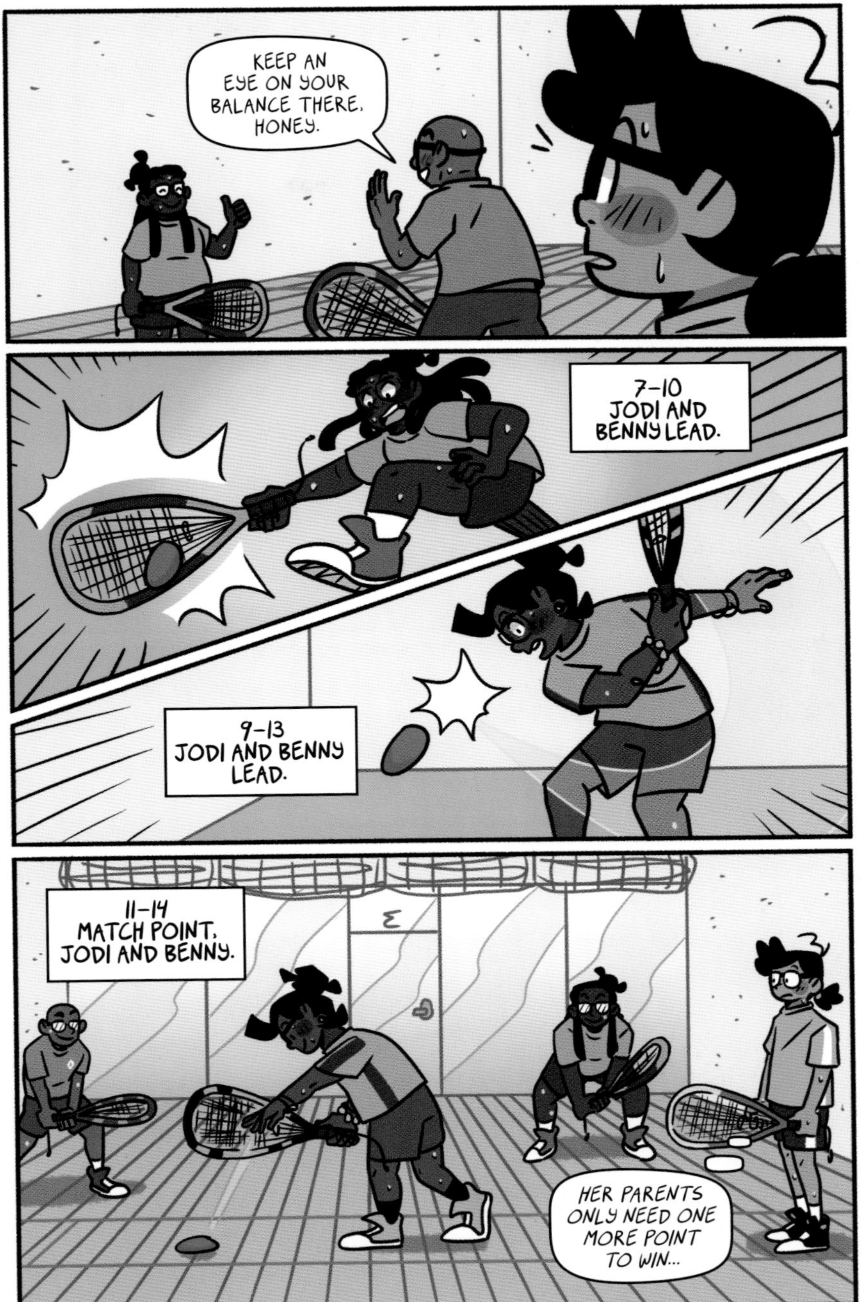
KEEP AN EYE ON YOUR BALANCE THERE, HONEY.
7–10 JODI AND BENNY LEAD.
9–13 JODI AND BENNY LEAD.
11–14 MATCH POINT, JODI AND BENNY.
HER PARENTS ONLY NEED ONE MORE POINT TO WIN...

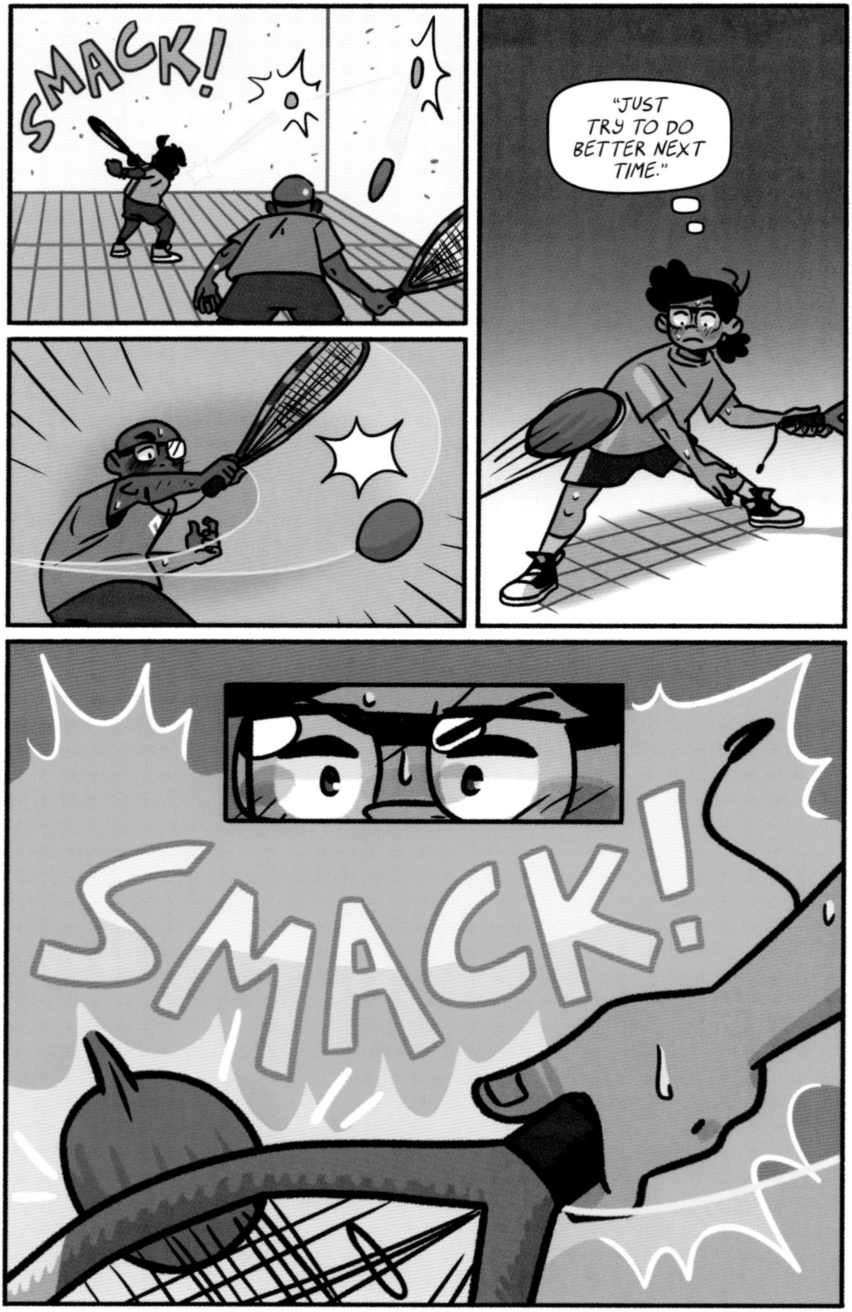
SMACK!
"JUST TRY TO DO BETTER NEXT TIME."
SMACK!

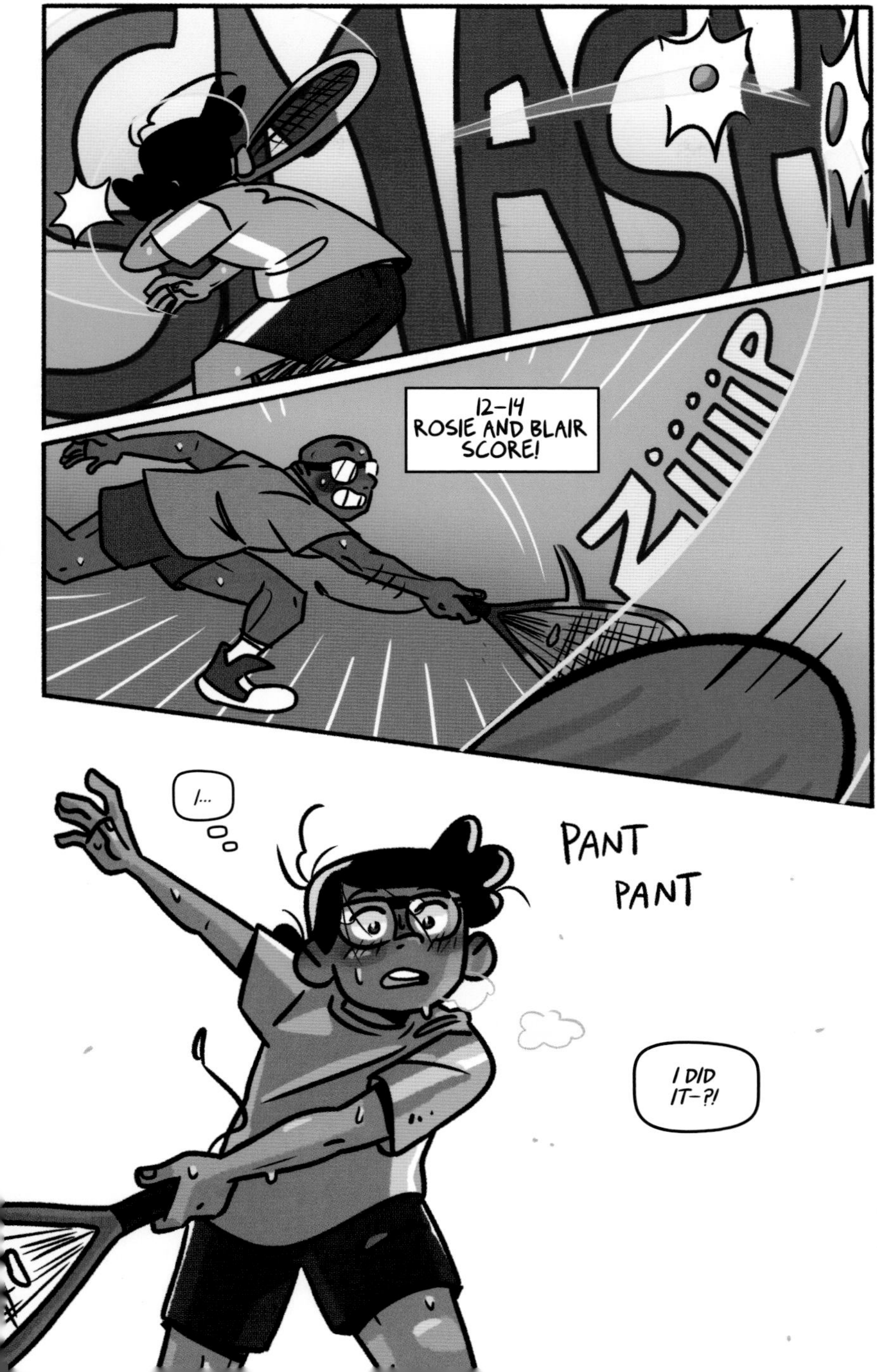
SMASH
ZIIIIP
12–14
ROSIE AND BLAIR
SCORE!
I...
PANT
PANT
I DID
IT–?!

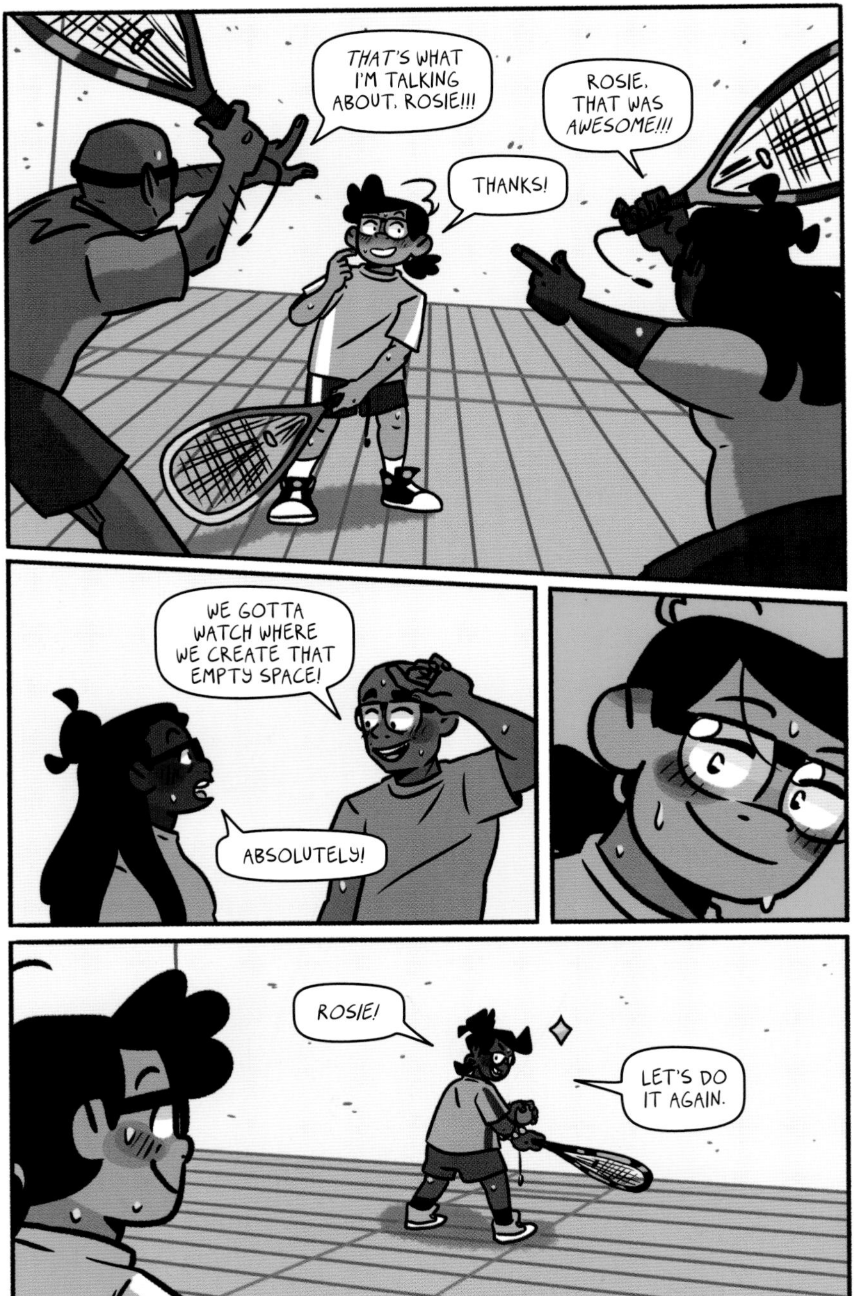
THAT'S WHAT I'M TALKING ABOUT, ROSIE!!!
ROSIE, THAT WAS AWESOME!!!
THANKS!
WE GOTTA WATCH WHERE WE CREATE THAT EMPTY SPACE!
ABSOLUTELY!
ROSIE!
LET'S DO IT AGAIN.

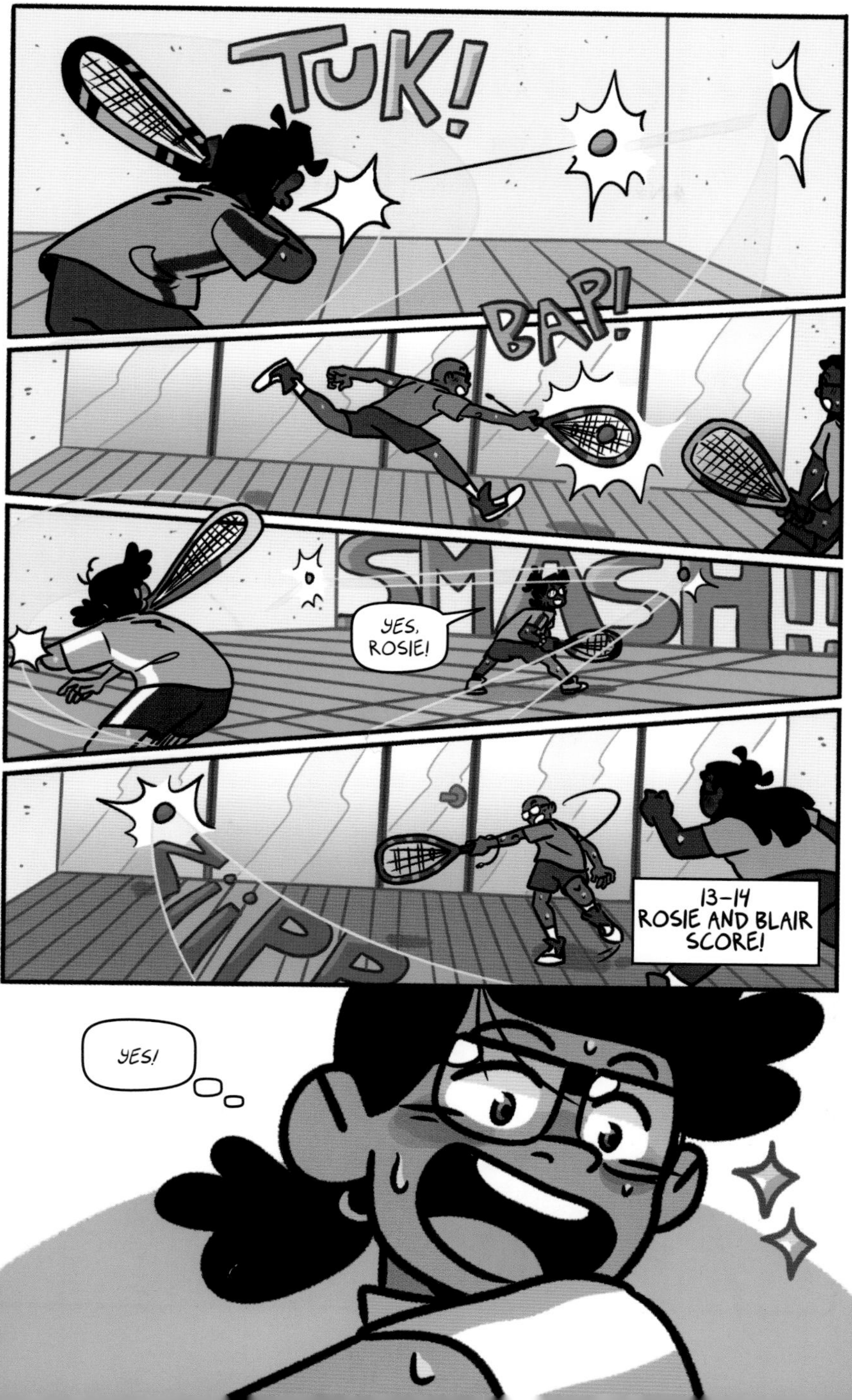
TUK!
BAP!
SMASH!
YES, ROSIE!
ZWIPP
13–14
ROSIE AND BLAIR SCORE!
YES!

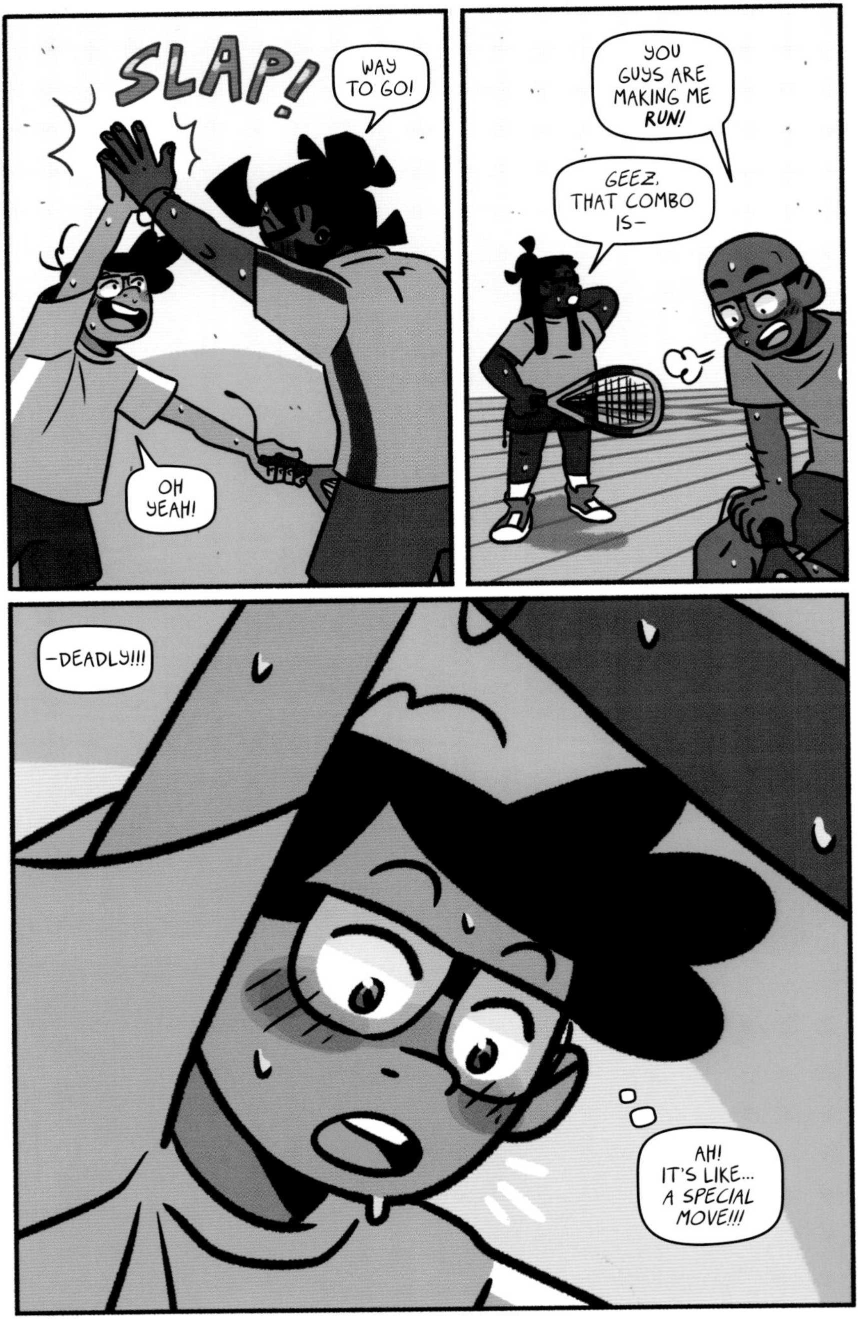
SLAP!
WAY TO GO!
OH YEAH!
YOU GUYS ARE MAKING ME RUN!
GEEZ, THAT COMBO IS—
—DEADLY!!!
AH! IT'S LIKE... A SPECIAL MOVE!!!

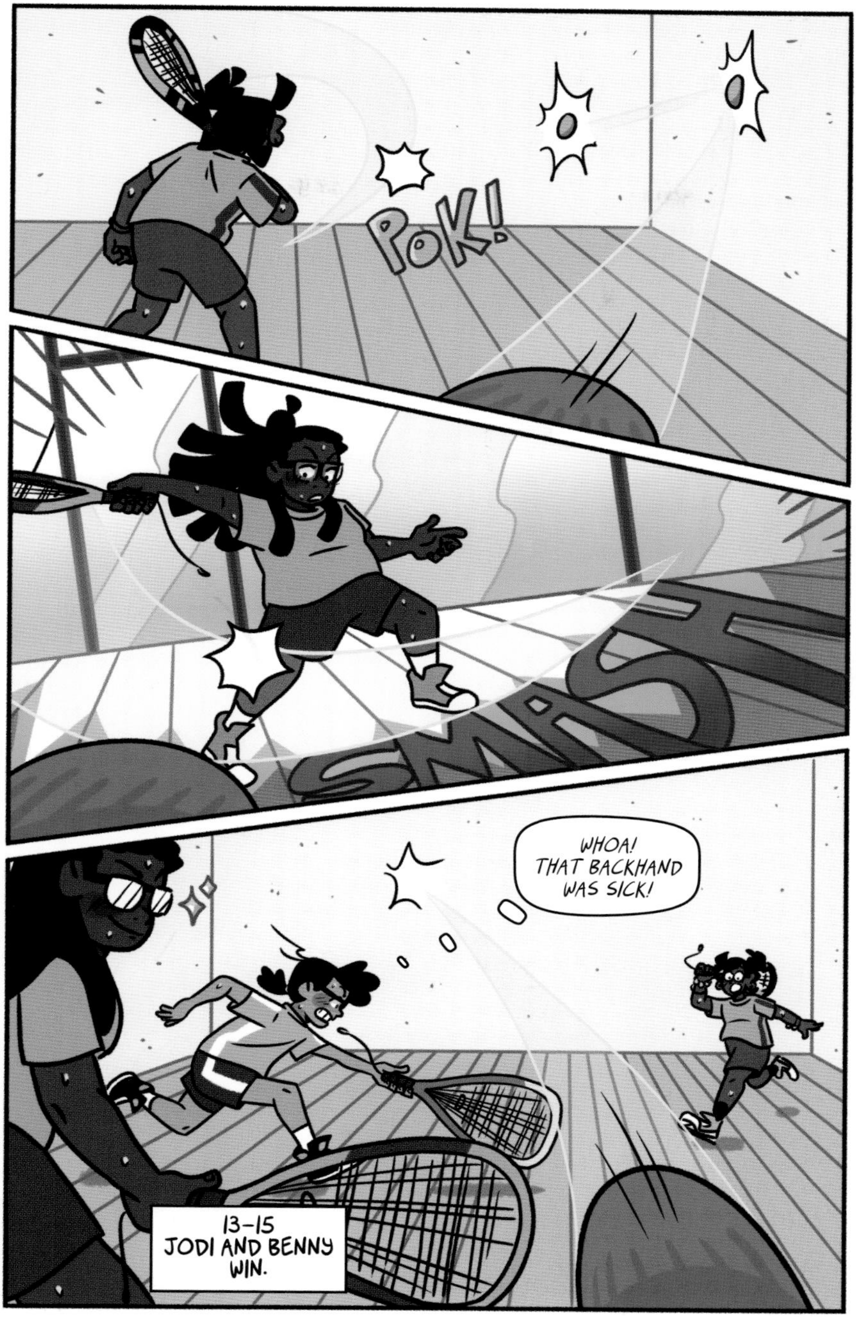
POK!
SMASH
WHOA! THAT BACKHAND WAS SICK!
13–15
JODI AND BENNY WIN.

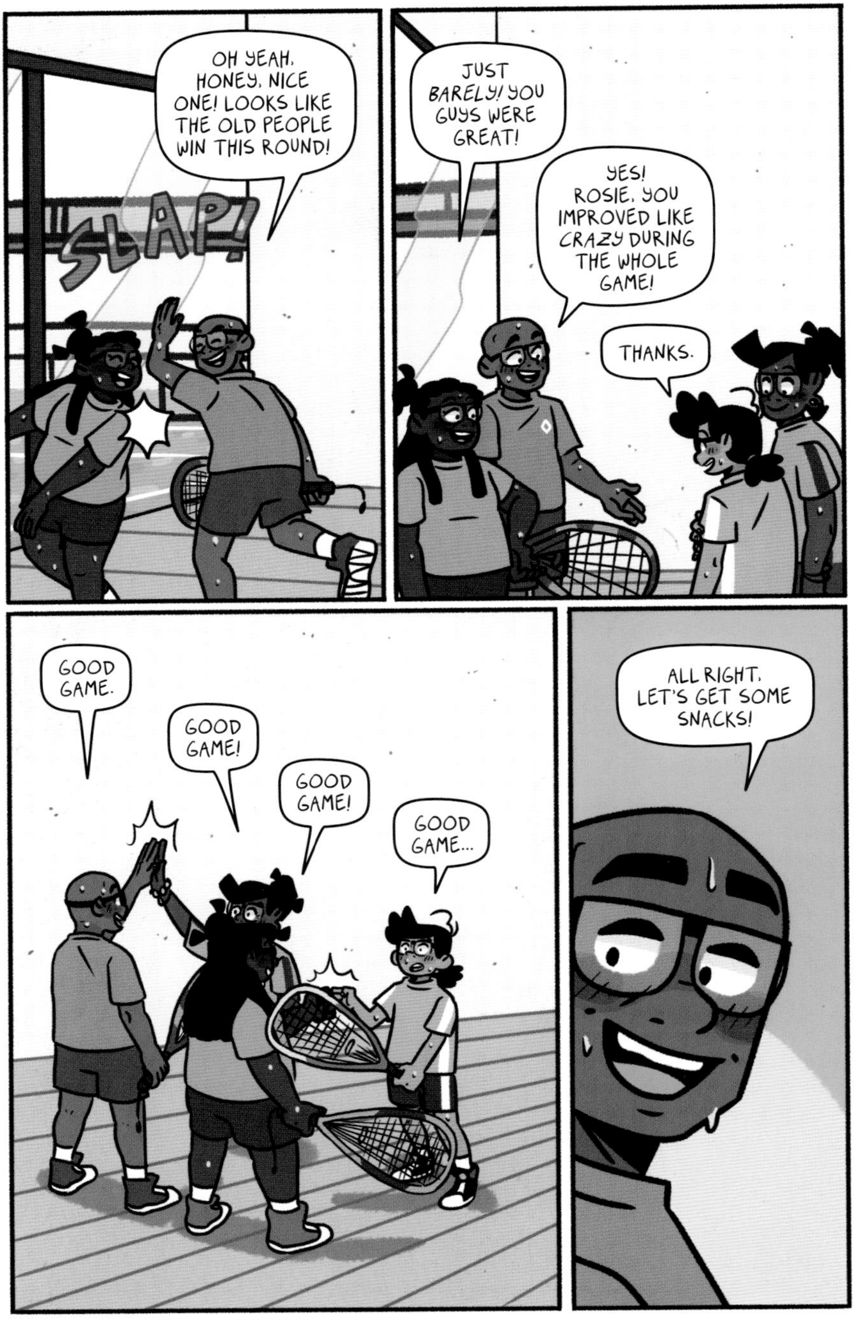
OH YEAH, HONEY, NICE ONE! LOOKS LIKE THE OLD PEOPLE WIN THIS ROUND!
SLAP!
JUST BARELY! YOU GUYS WERE GREAT!
YES! ROSIE, YOU IMPROVED LIKE CRAZY DURING THE WHOLE GAME!
THANKS.
GOOD GAME.
GOOD GAME!
GOOD GAME!
GOOD GAME...
ALL RIGHT, LET'S GET SOME SNACKS!

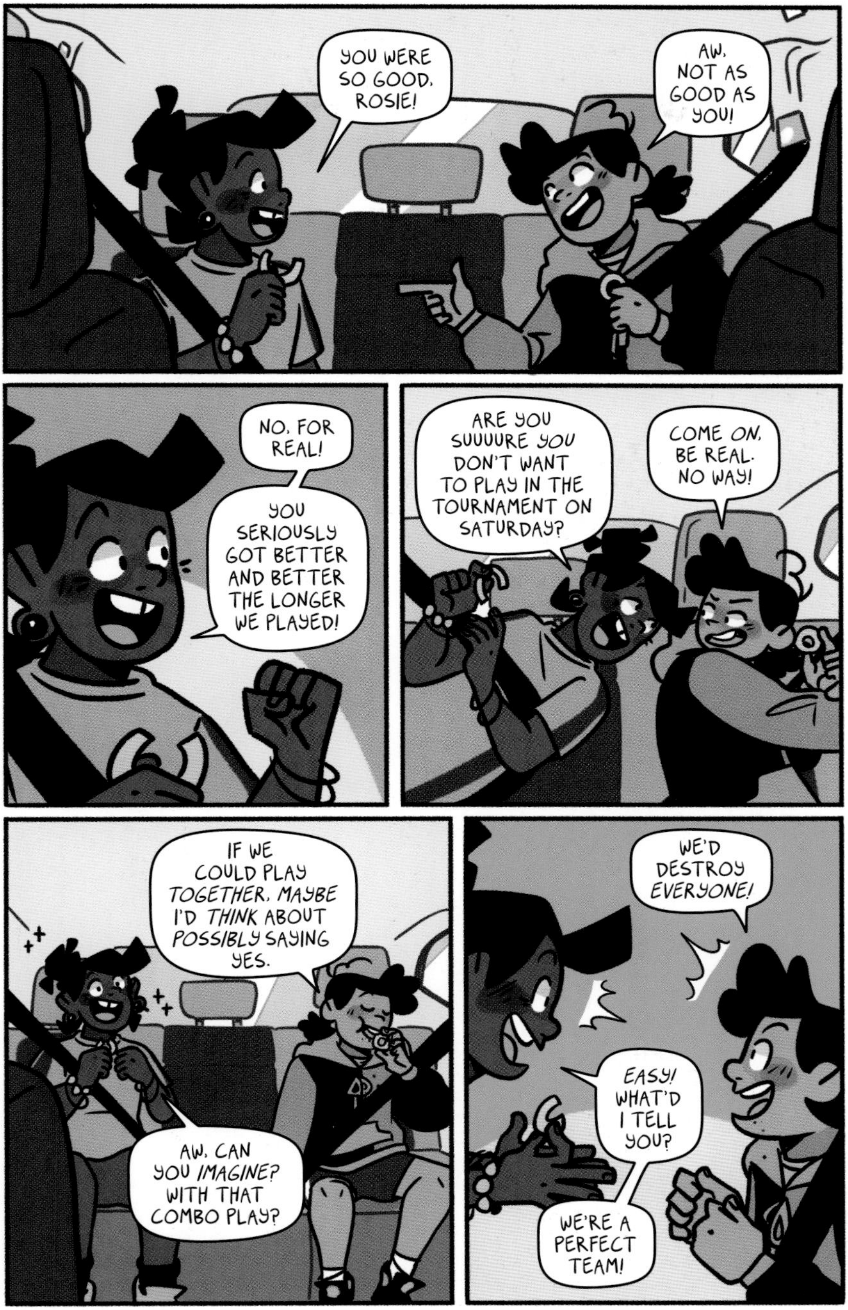
YOU WERE SO GOOD, ROSIE!
AW, NOT AS GOOD AS YOU!
NO, FOR REAL!
YOU SERIOUSLY GOT BETTER AND BETTER THE LONGER WE PLAYED!
ARE YOU SUUUURE YOU DON'T WANT TO PLAY IN THE TOURNAMENT ON SATURDAY?
COME ON, BE REAL. NO WAY!
IF WE COULD PLAY TOGETHER, MAYBE I'D THINK ABOUT POSSIBLY SAYING YES.
AW, CAN YOU IMAGINE? WITH THAT COMBO PLAY?
WE'D DESTROY EVERYONE!
EASY! WHAT'D I TELL YOU?
WE'RE A PERFECT TEAM!

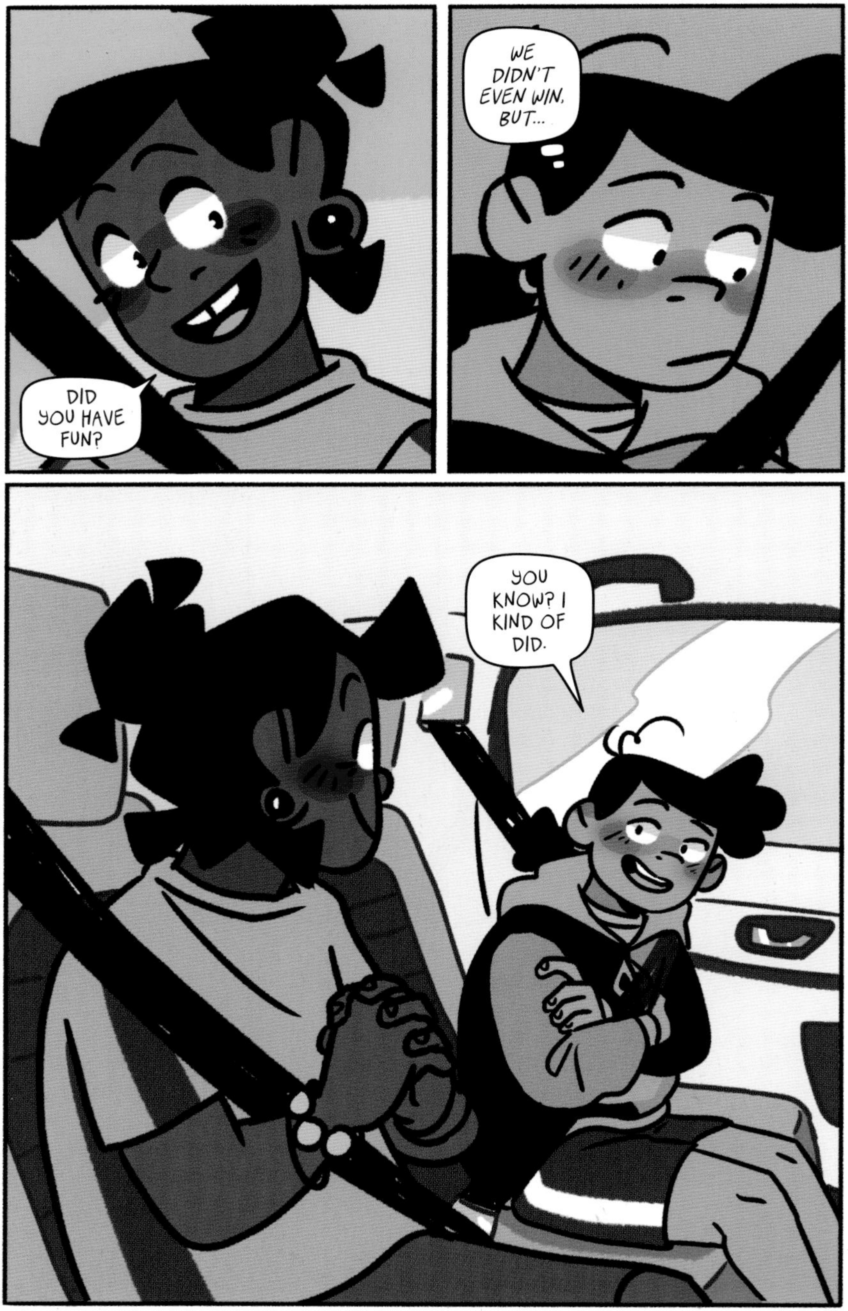
DID YOU HAVE FUN?
WE DIDN'T EVEN WIN, BUT...
YOU KNOW? I KIND OF DID.

CHAPTER 8

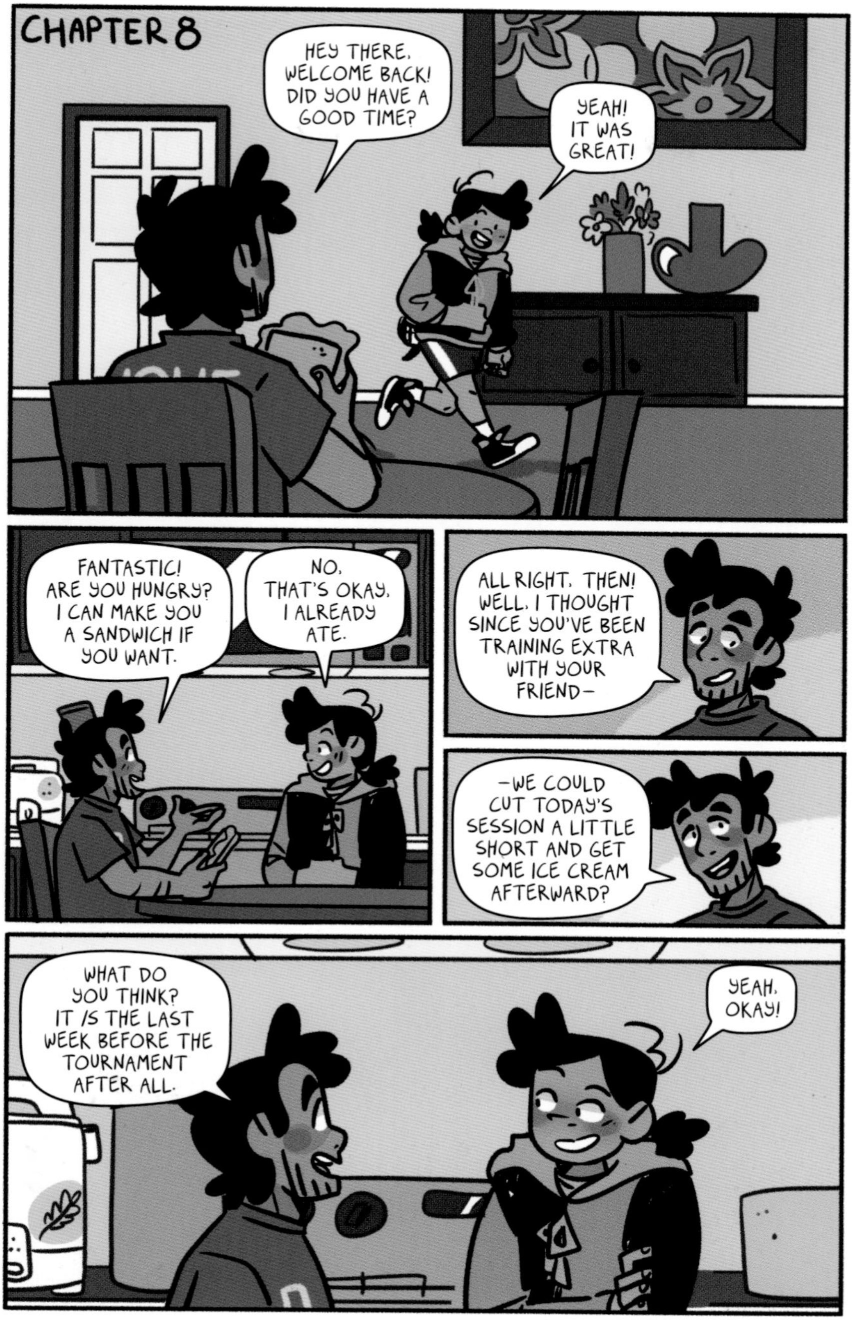
HEY THERE. WELCOME BACK! DID YOU HAVE A GOOD TIME?
YEAH! IT WAS GREAT!
FANTASTIC! ARE YOU HUNGRY? I CAN MAKE YOU A SANDWICH IF YOU WANT.
NO. THAT'S OKAY. I ALREADY ATE.
ALL RIGHT. THEN! WELL, I THOUGHT SINCE YOU'VE BEEN TRAINING EXTRA WITH YOUR FRIEND—
—WE COULD CUT TODAY'S SESSION A LITTLE SHORT AND GET SOME ICE CREAM AFTERWARD?
WHAT DO YOU THINK? IT IS THE LAST WEEK BEFORE THE TOURNAMENT AFTER ALL.
YEAH. OKAY!

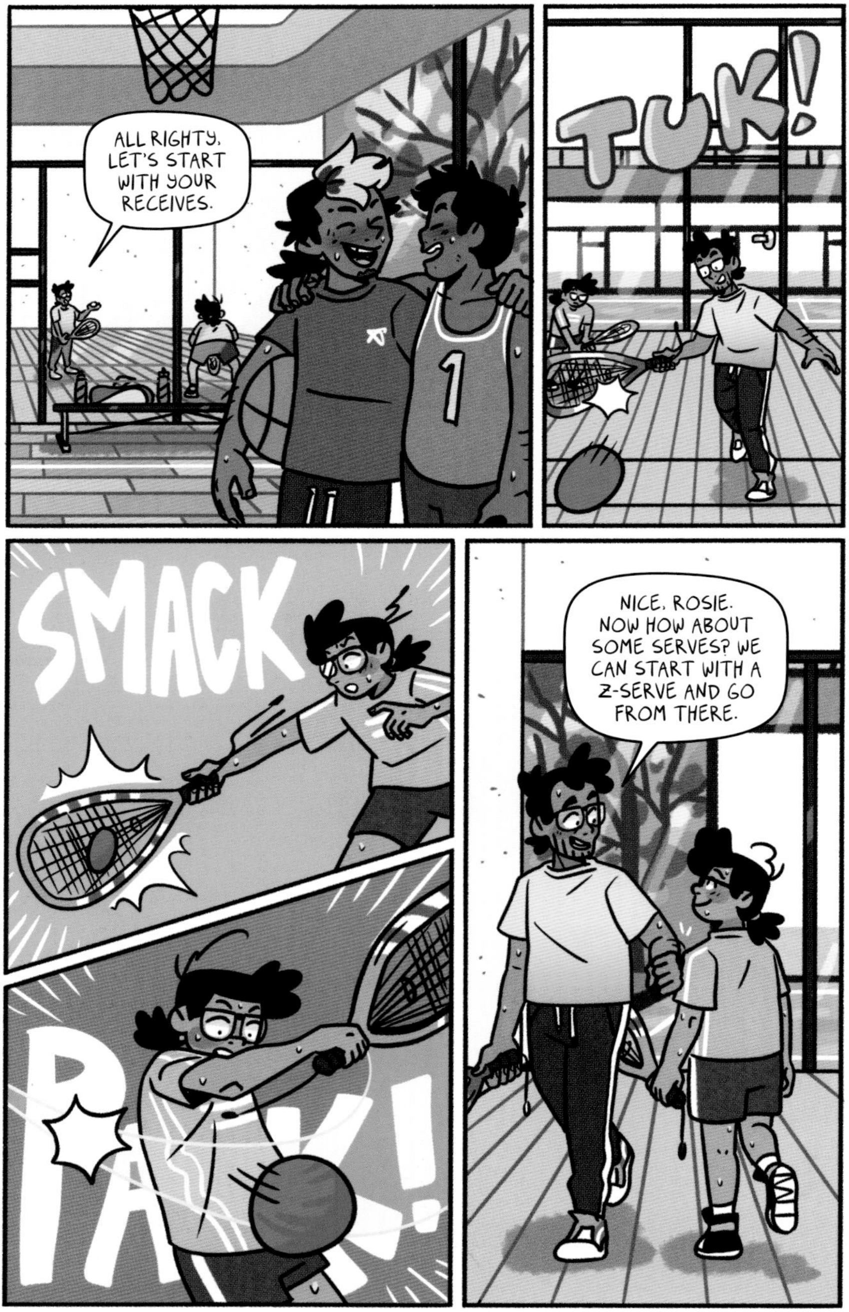
ALL RIGHTY, LET'S START WITH YOUR RECEIVES.
TUK!
SMACK
PAK!
NICE, ROSIE. NOW HOW ABOUT SOME SERVES? WE CAN START WITH A Z-SERVE AND GO FROM THERE.

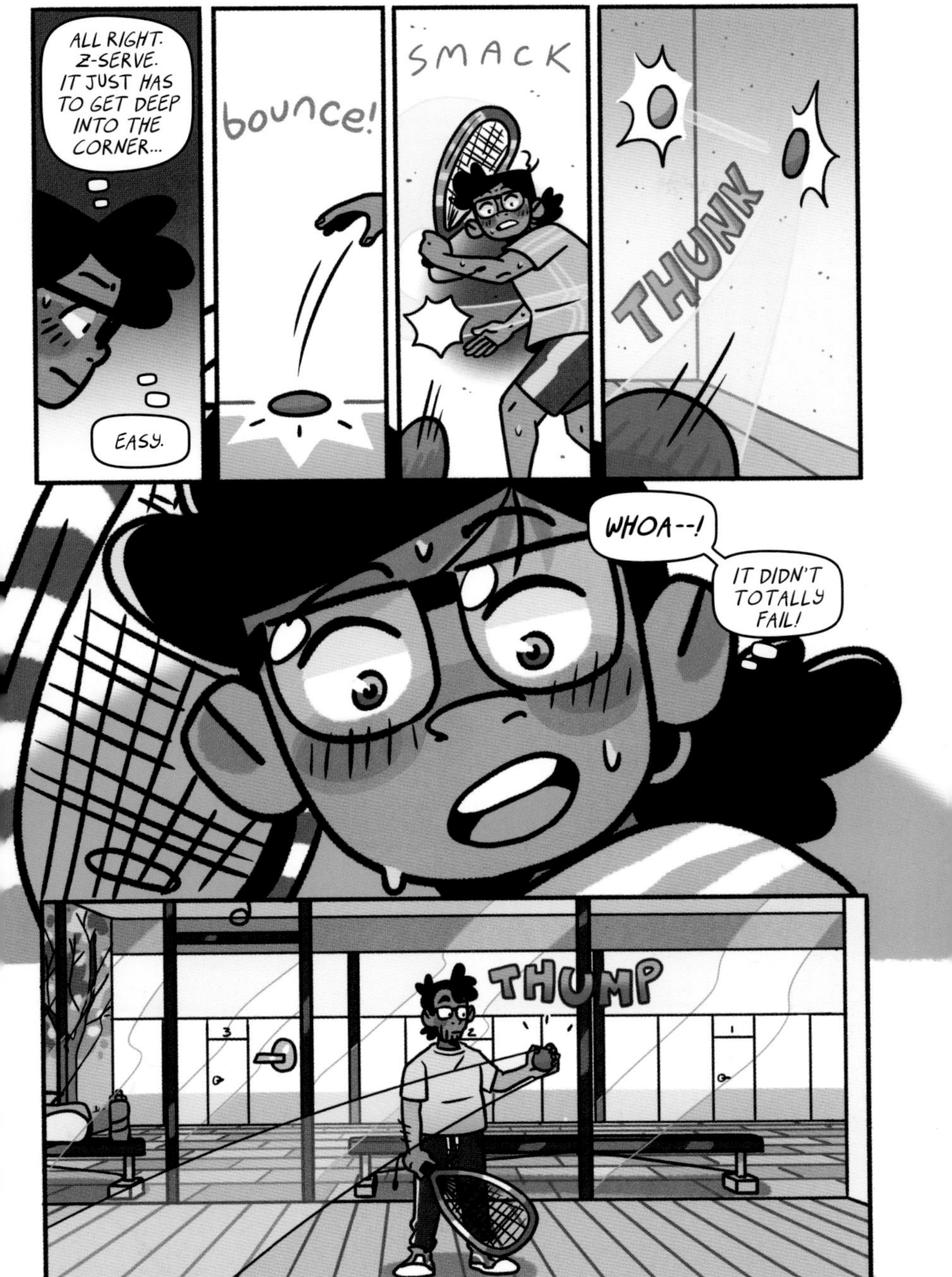
ALL RIGHT. Z-SERVE. IT JUST HAS TO GET DEEP INTO THE CORNER...
EASY.
bounce!
SMACK
THUNK
WHOA--!
IT DIDN'T TOTALLY FAIL!
THUMP

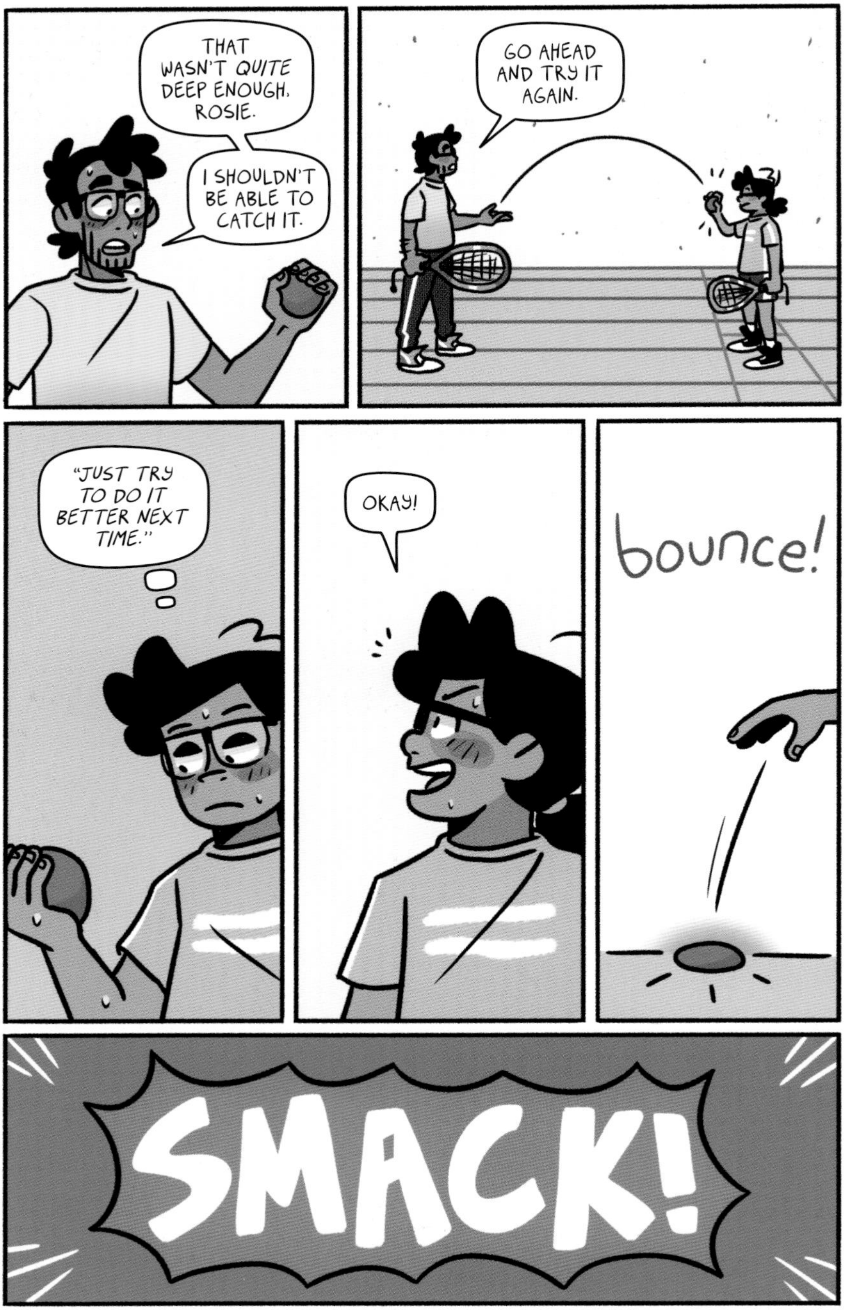
THAT WASN'T QUITE DEEP ENOUGH, ROSIE.
I SHOULDN'T BE ABLE TO CATCH IT.
GO AHEAD AND TRY IT AGAIN.
"JUST TRY TO DO IT BETTER NEXT TIME."
OKAY!
bounce!
SMACK!

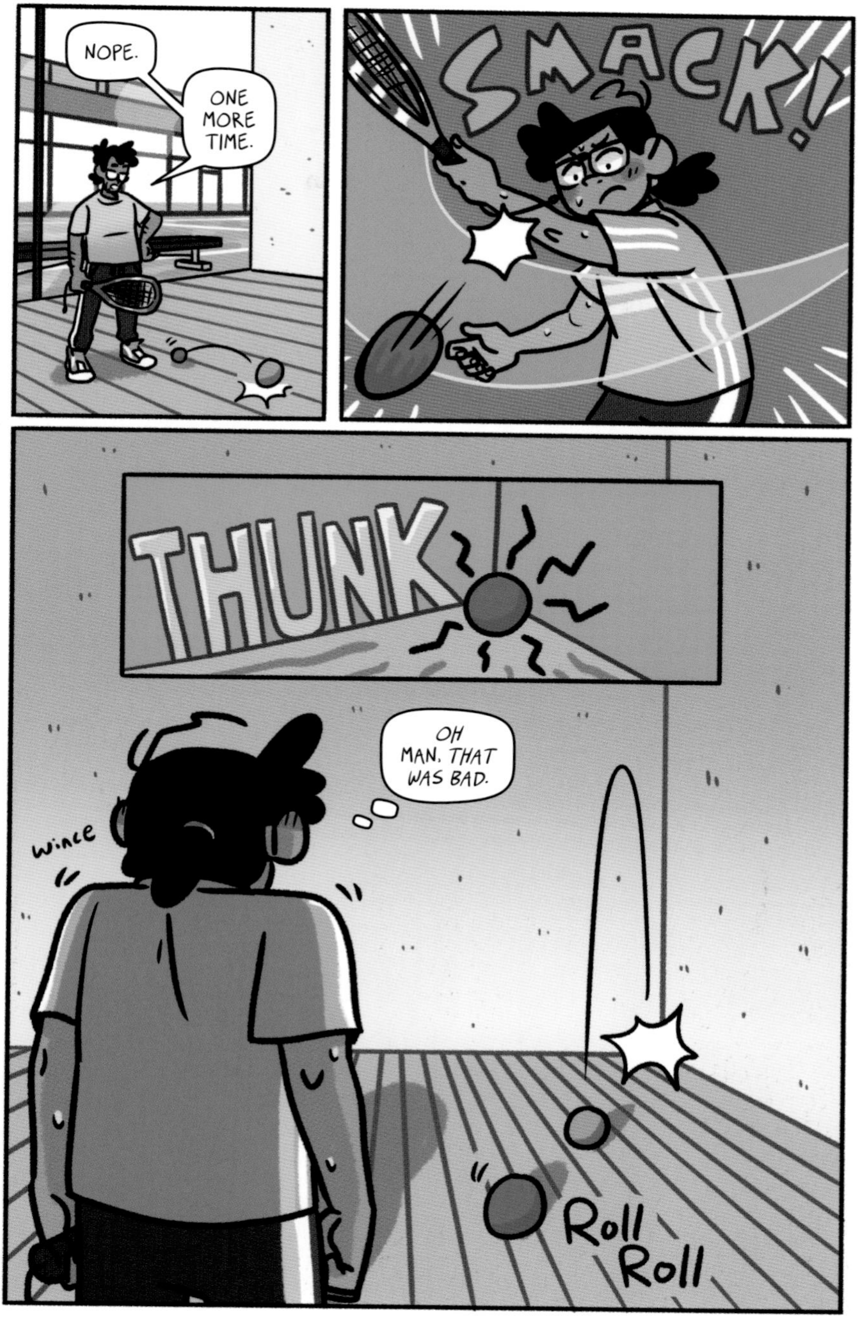
NOPE.
ONE MORE TIME.
SMACK!
THUNK
OH MAN, THAT WAS BAD.
wince
Roll Roll

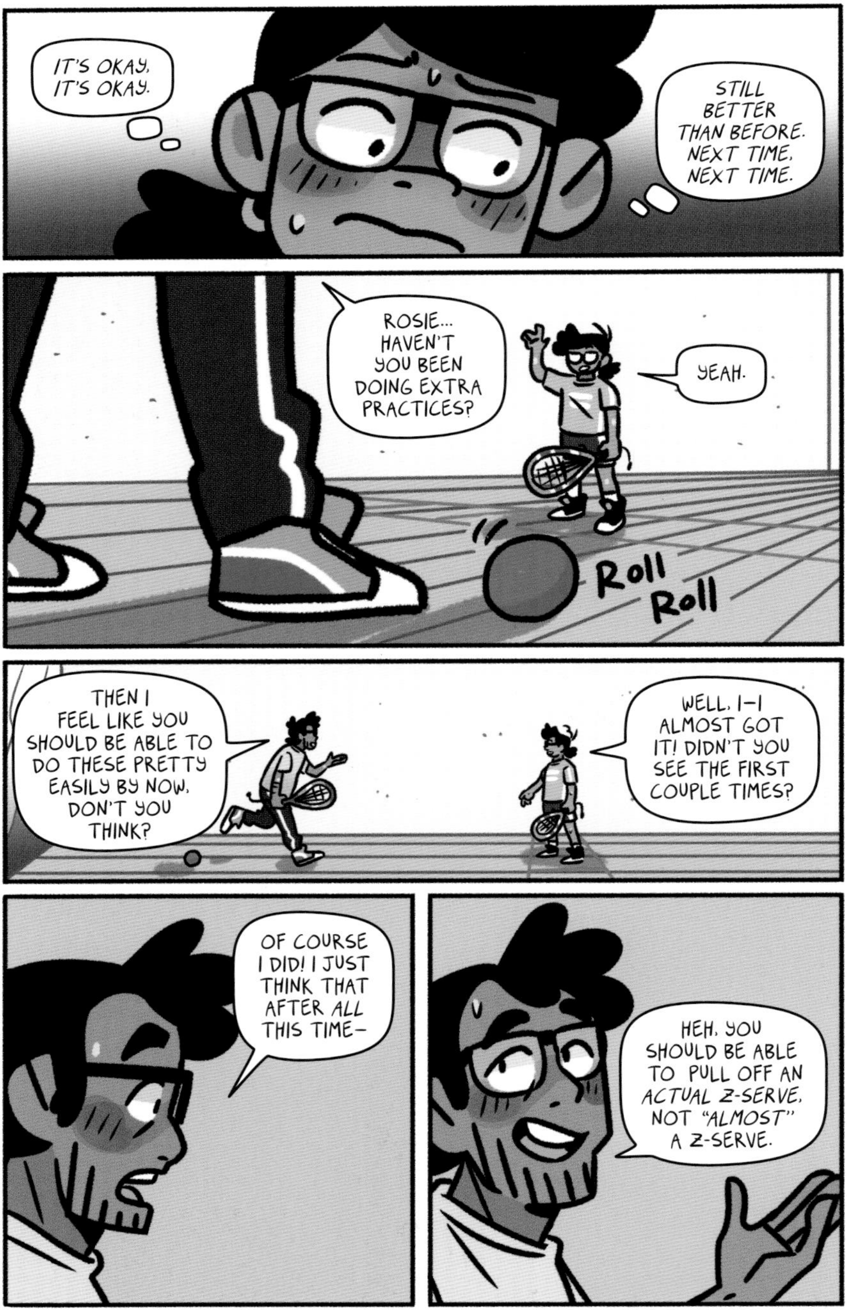
IT'S OKAY, IT'S OKAY.
STILL BETTER THAN BEFORE. NEXT TIME, NEXT TIME.
ROSIE... HAVEN'T YOU BEEN DOING EXTRA PRACTICES?
YEAH.
Roll Roll
THEN I FEEL LIKE YOU SHOULD BE ABLE TO DO THESE PRETTY EASILY BY NOW, DON'T YOU THINK?
WELL, I-I ALMOST GOT IT! DIDN'T YOU SEE THE FIRST COUPLE TIMES?
OF COURSE I DID! I JUST THINK THAT AFTER ALL THIS TIME–
HEH, YOU SHOULD BE ABLE TO PULL OFF AN ACTUAL Z-SERVE, NOT "ALMOST" A Z-SERVE.

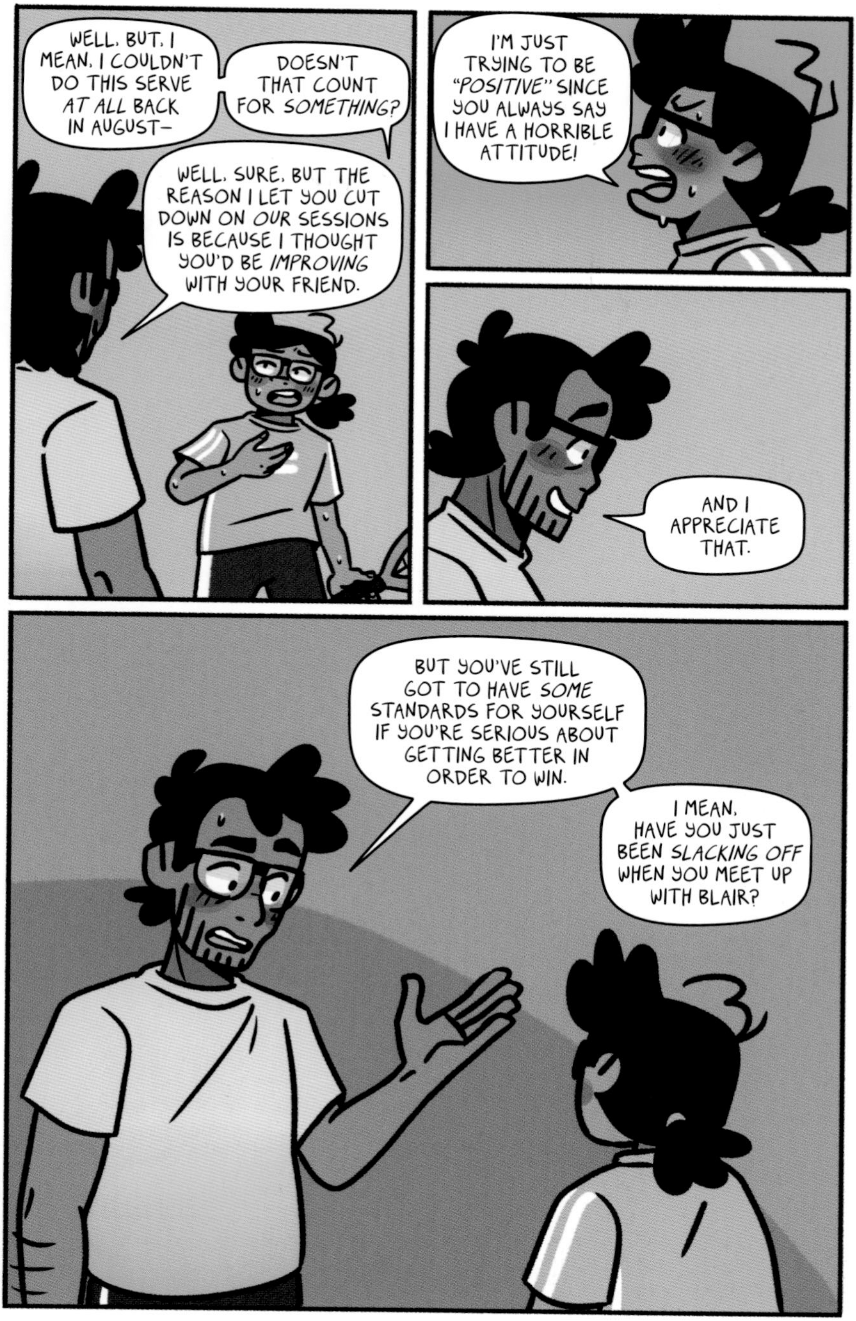
WELL, BUT, I MEAN, I COULDN'T DO THIS SERVE *AT ALL* BACK IN AUGUST—
DOESN'T THAT COUNT FOR *SOMETHING?*
WELL, SURE, BUT THE REASON I LET YOU CUT DOWN ON *OUR* SESSIONS IS BECAUSE I THOUGHT YOU'D BE *IMPROVING* WITH YOUR FRIEND.
I'M JUST TRYING TO BE *"POSITIVE"* SINCE YOU ALWAYS SAY I HAVE A HORRIBLE ATTITUDE!
AND I APPRECIATE THAT.
BUT YOU'VE STILL GOT TO HAVE *SOME* STANDARDS FOR YOURSELF IF YOU'RE SERIOUS ABOUT GETTING BETTER IN ORDER TO WIN.
I MEAN, HAVE YOU JUST BEEN *SLACKING OFF* WHEN YOU MEET UP WITH BLAIR?

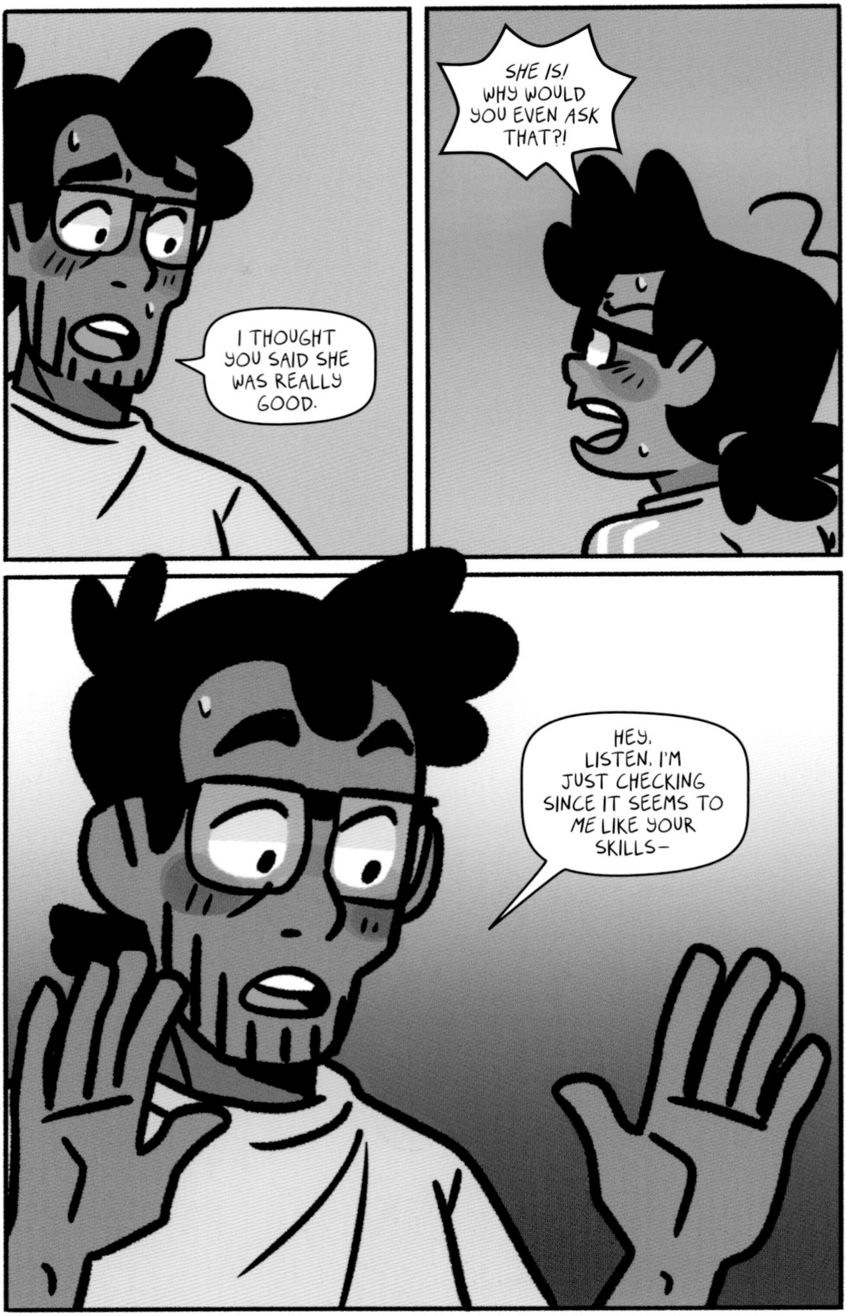
I THOUGHT YOU SAID SHE WAS REALLY GOOD.
SHE IS! WHY WOULD YOU EVEN ASK THAT?!
HEY, LISTEN, I'M JUST CHECKING SINCE IT SEEMS TO ME LIKE YOUR SKILLS–

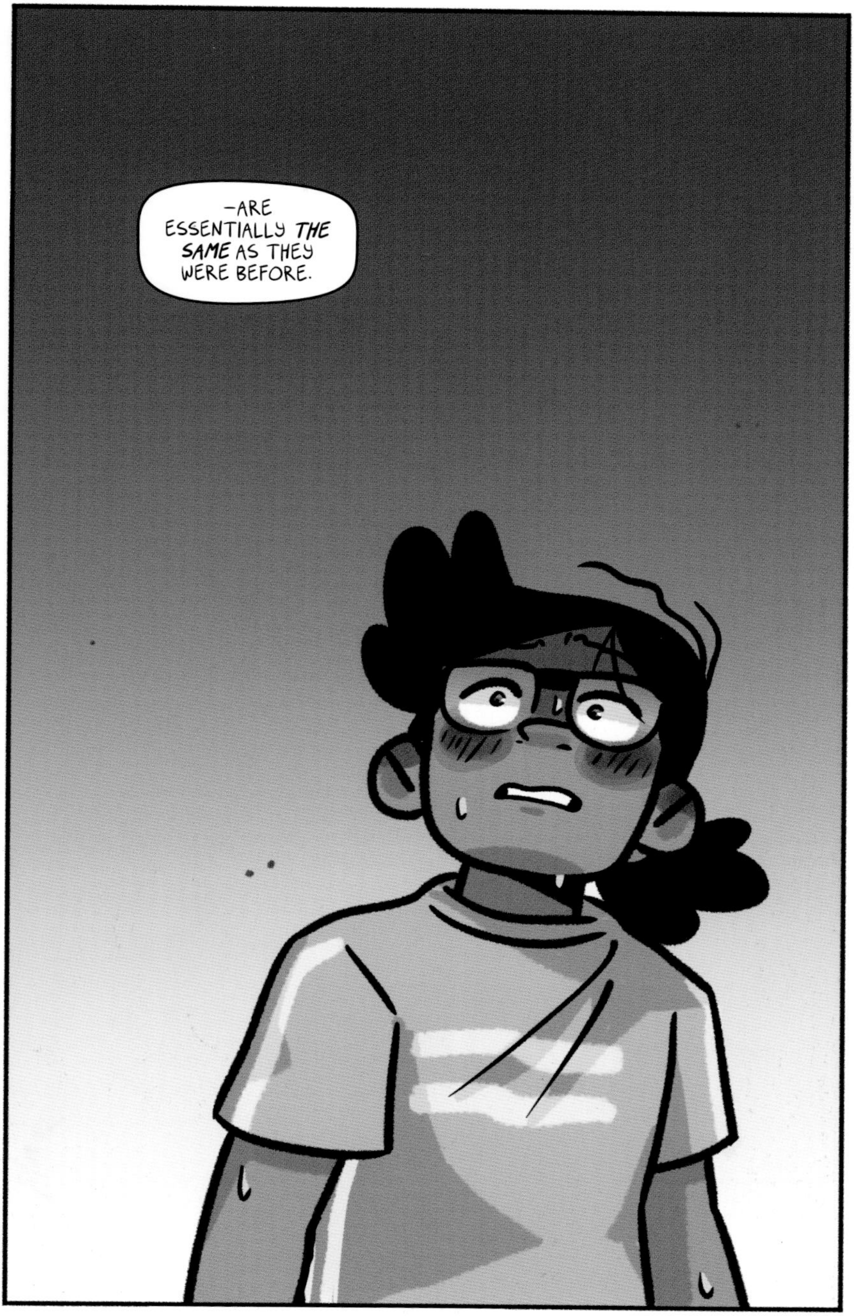
—ARE ESSENTIALLY *THE SAME* AS THEY WERE BEFORE.

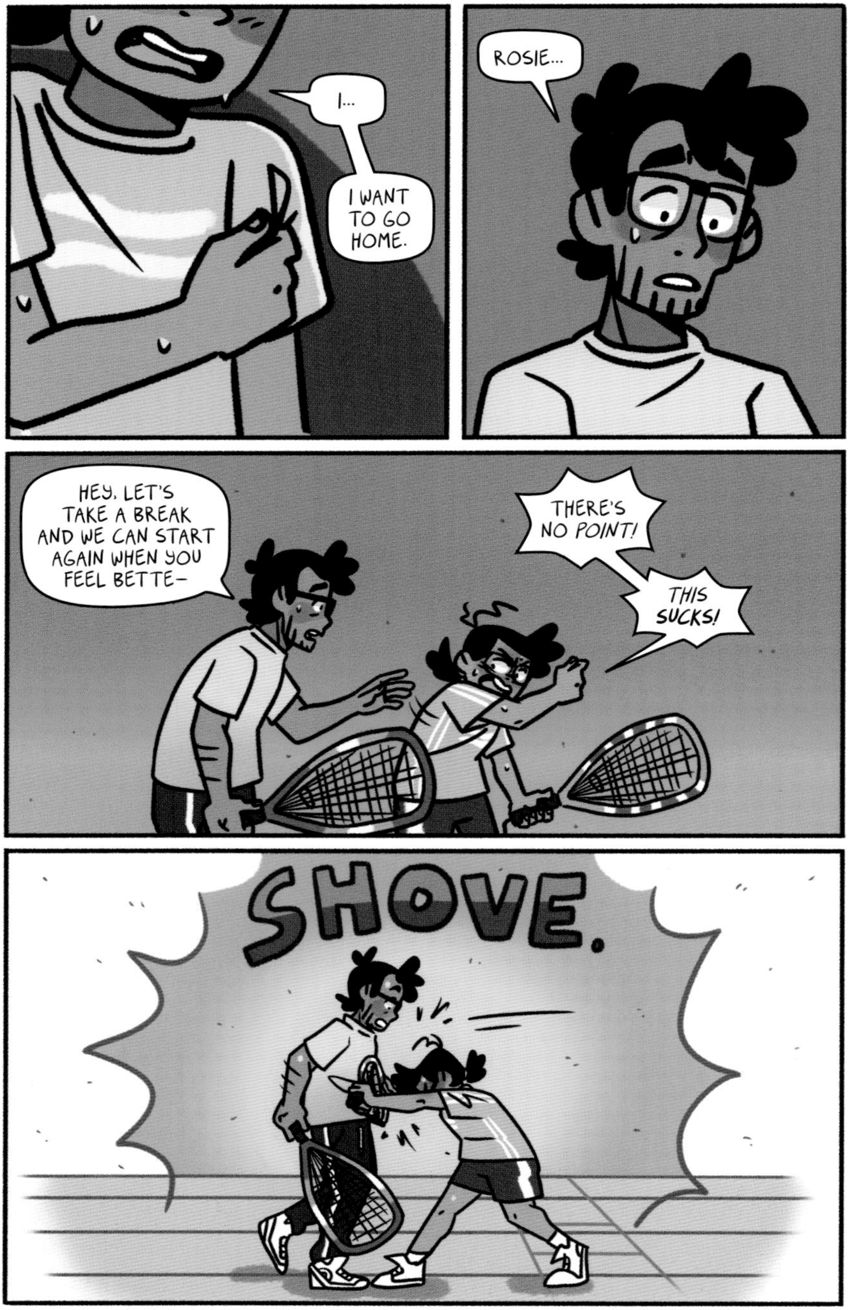
I...
I WANT TO GO HOME.
ROSIE...
HEY, LET'S TAKE A BREAK AND WE CAN START AGAIN WHEN YOU FEEL BETTE–
THERE'S NO POINT!
THIS SUCKS!
SHOVE.

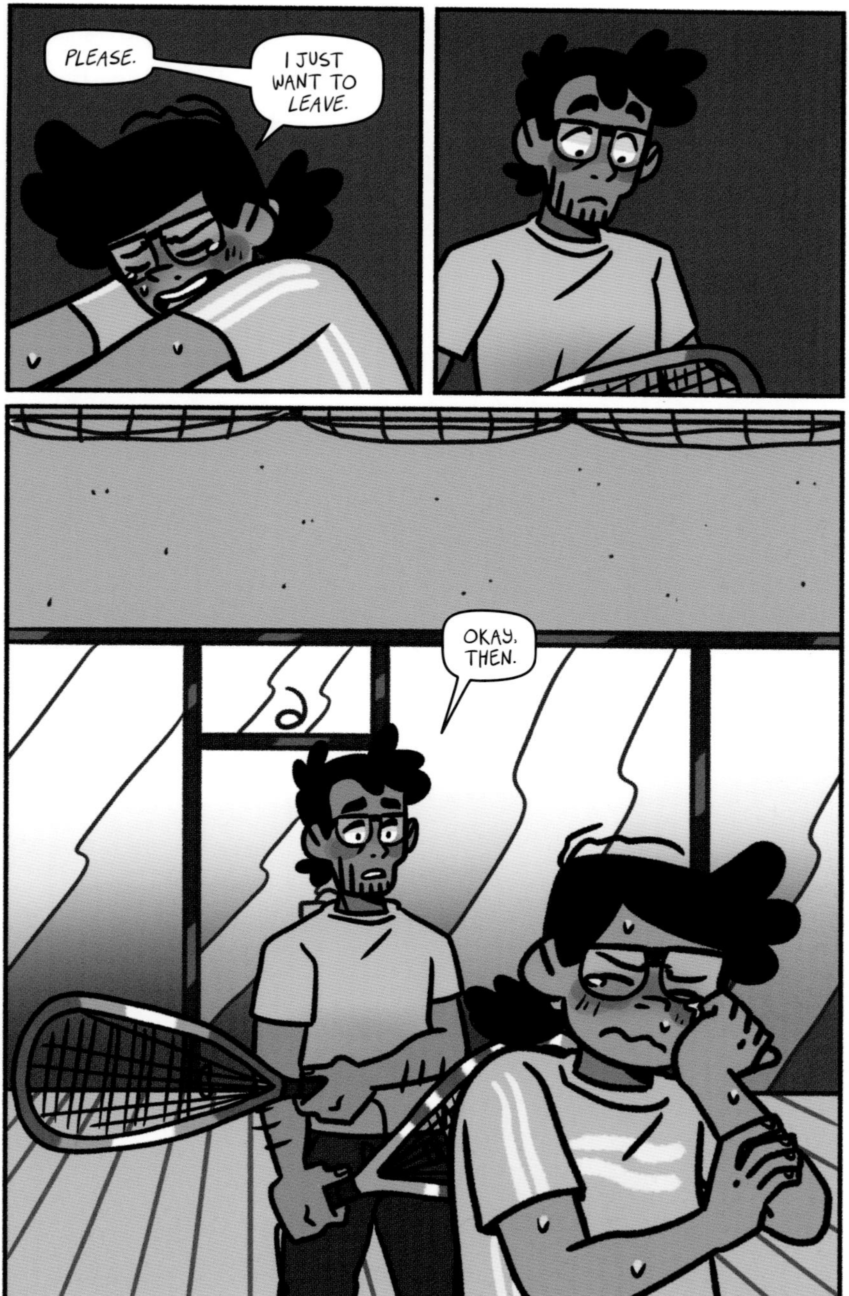
PLEASE.
I JUST WANT TO LEAVE.
OKAY, THEN.

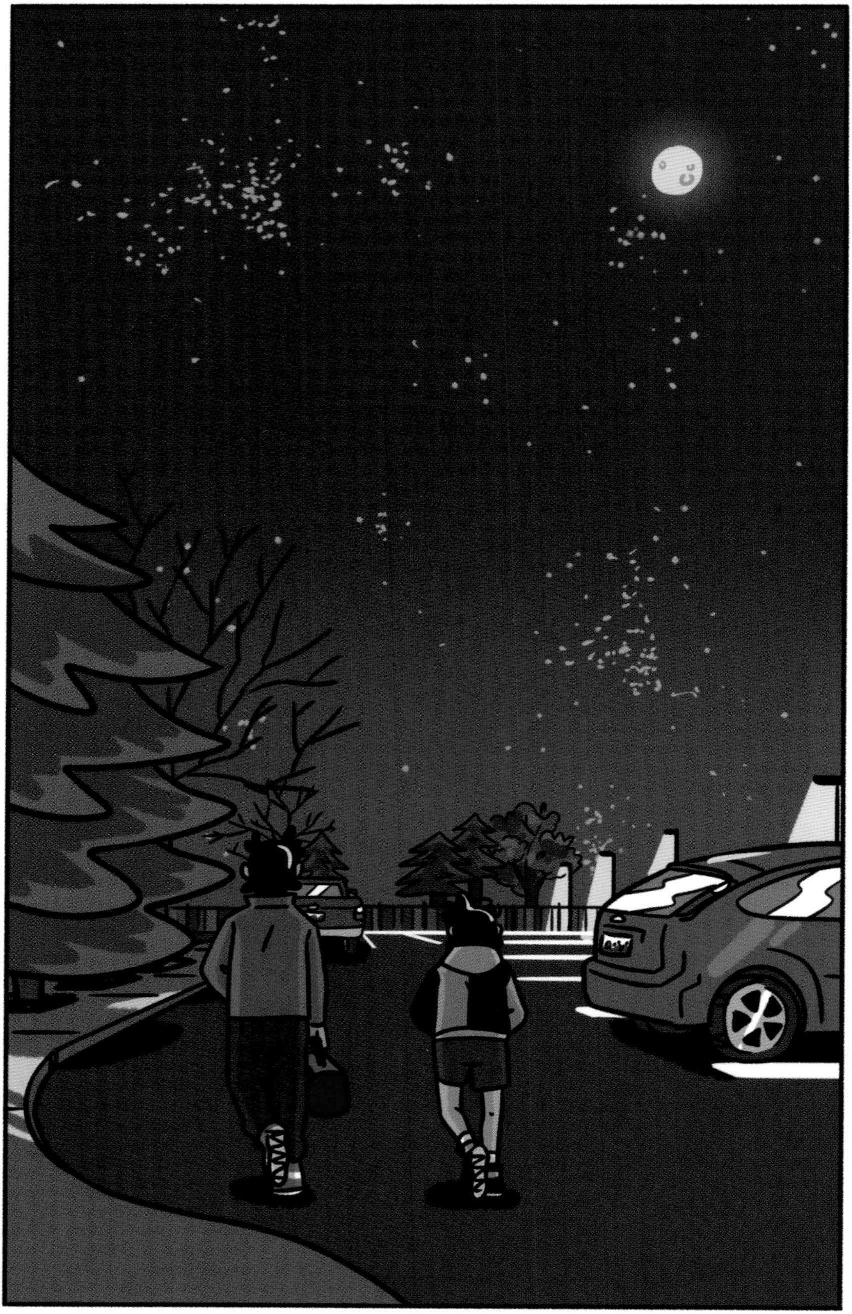

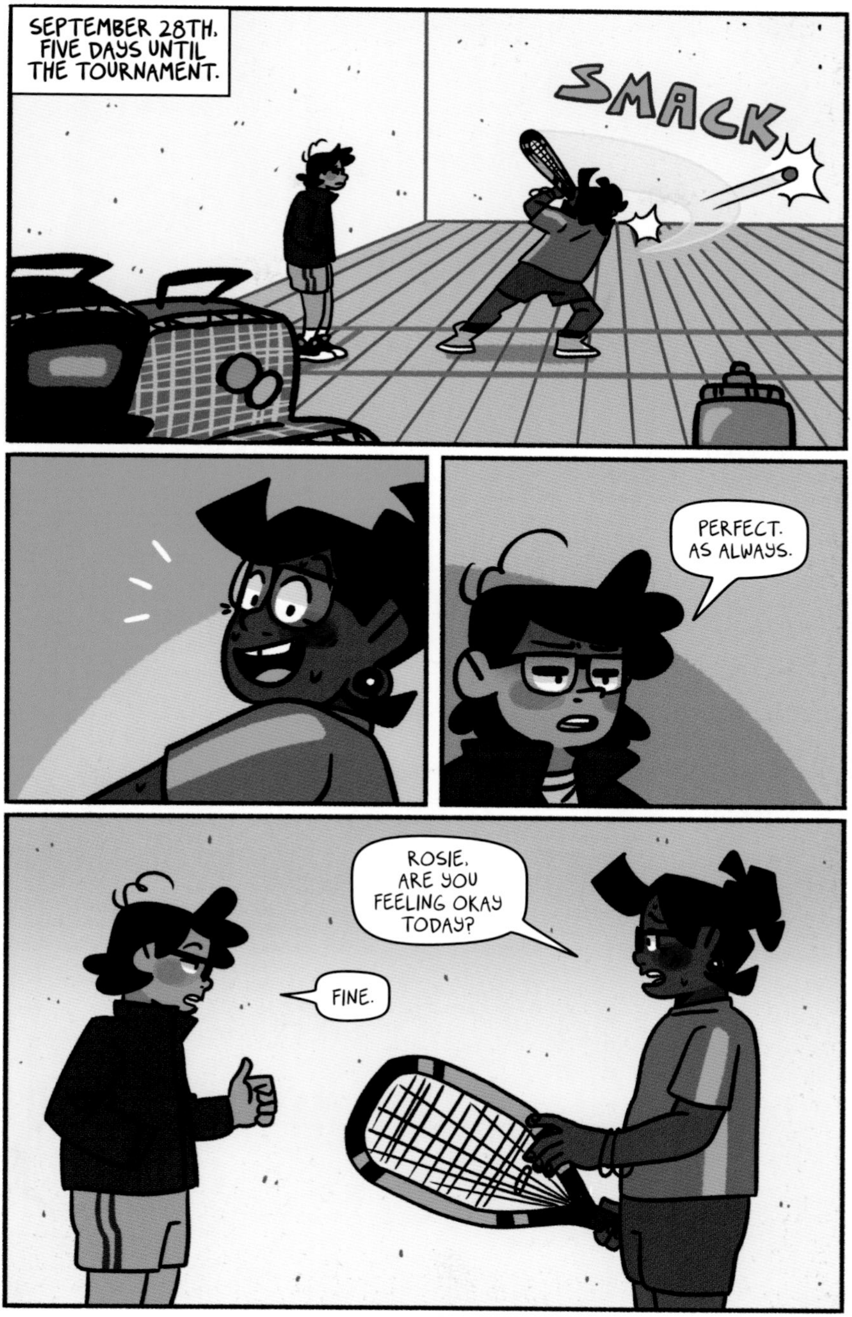
SEPTEMBER 28TH. FIVE DAYS UNTIL THE TOURNAMENT.
SMACK
PERFECT. AS ALWAYS.
ROSIE, ARE YOU FEELING OKAY TODAY?
FINE.

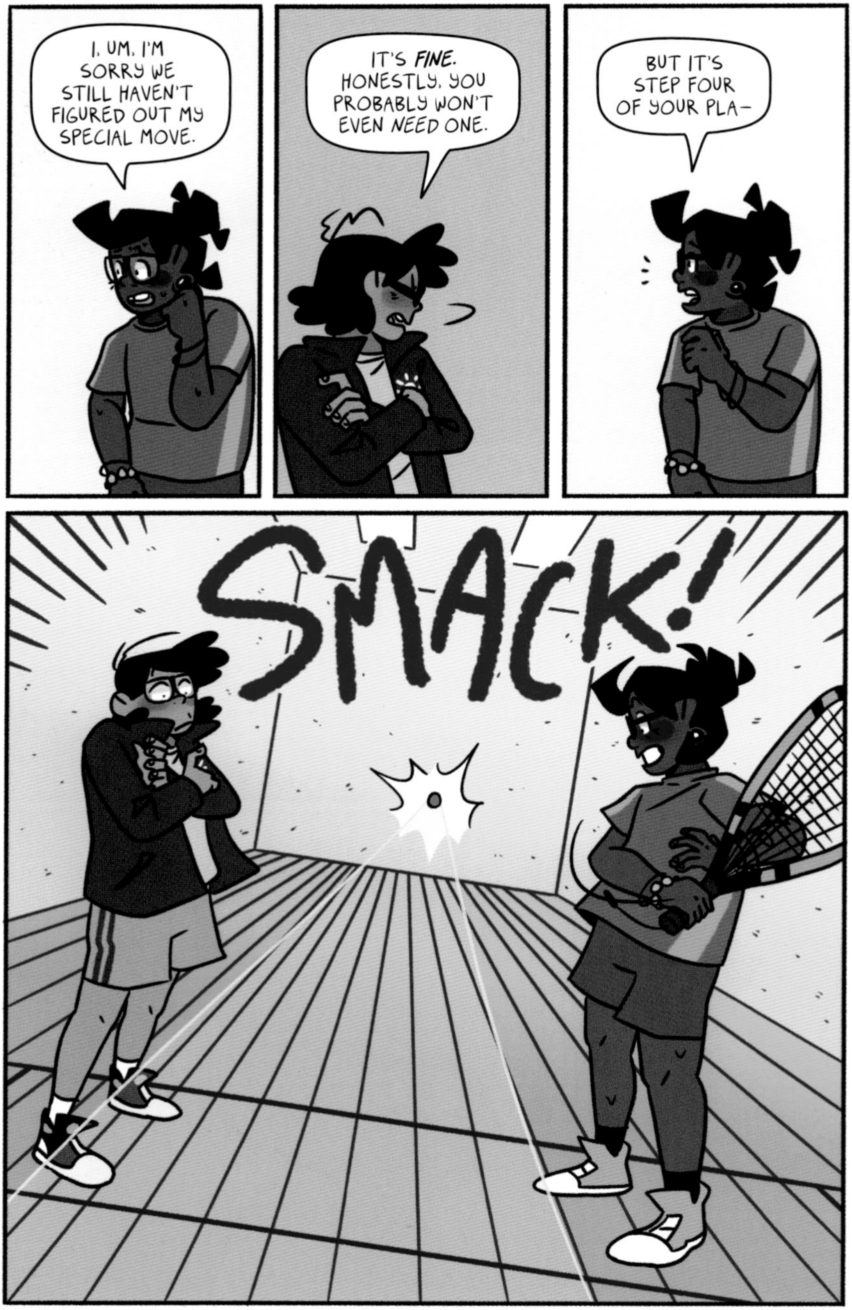
I, UM, I'M SORRY WE STILL HAVEN'T FIGURED OUT MY SPECIAL MOVE.
IT'S *FINE*. HONESTLY, YOU PROBABLY WON'T EVEN *NEED* ONE.
BUT IT'S STEP FOUR OF YOUR PLA—
SMACK!

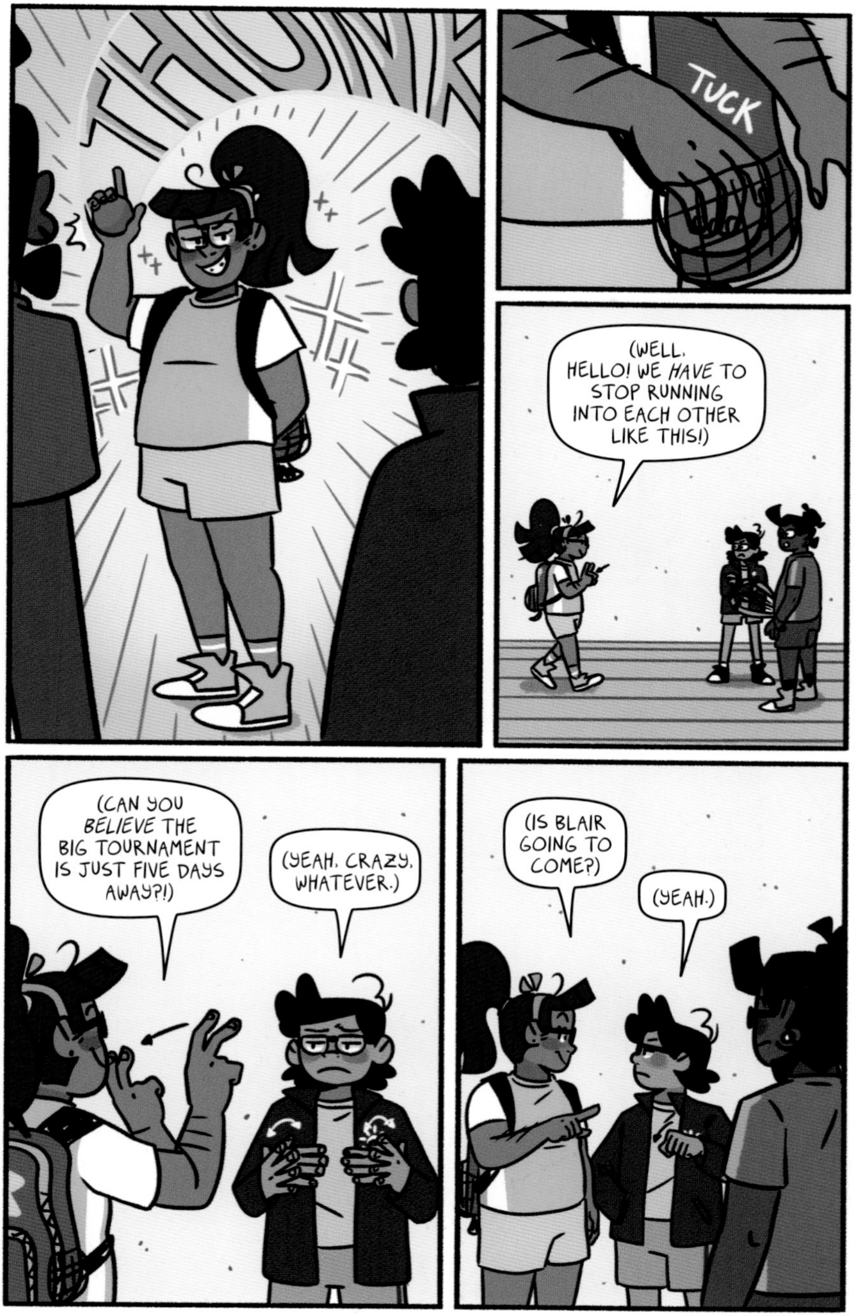
THUNK
TUCK
(WELL, HELLO! WE *HAVE* TO STOP RUNNING INTO EACH OTHER LIKE THIS!)
(CAN YOU *BELIEVE* THE BIG TOURNAMENT IS JUST FIVE DAYS AWAY?!)
(YEAH, CRAZY, WHATEVER.)
(IS BLAIR GOING TO COME?)
(YEAH.)

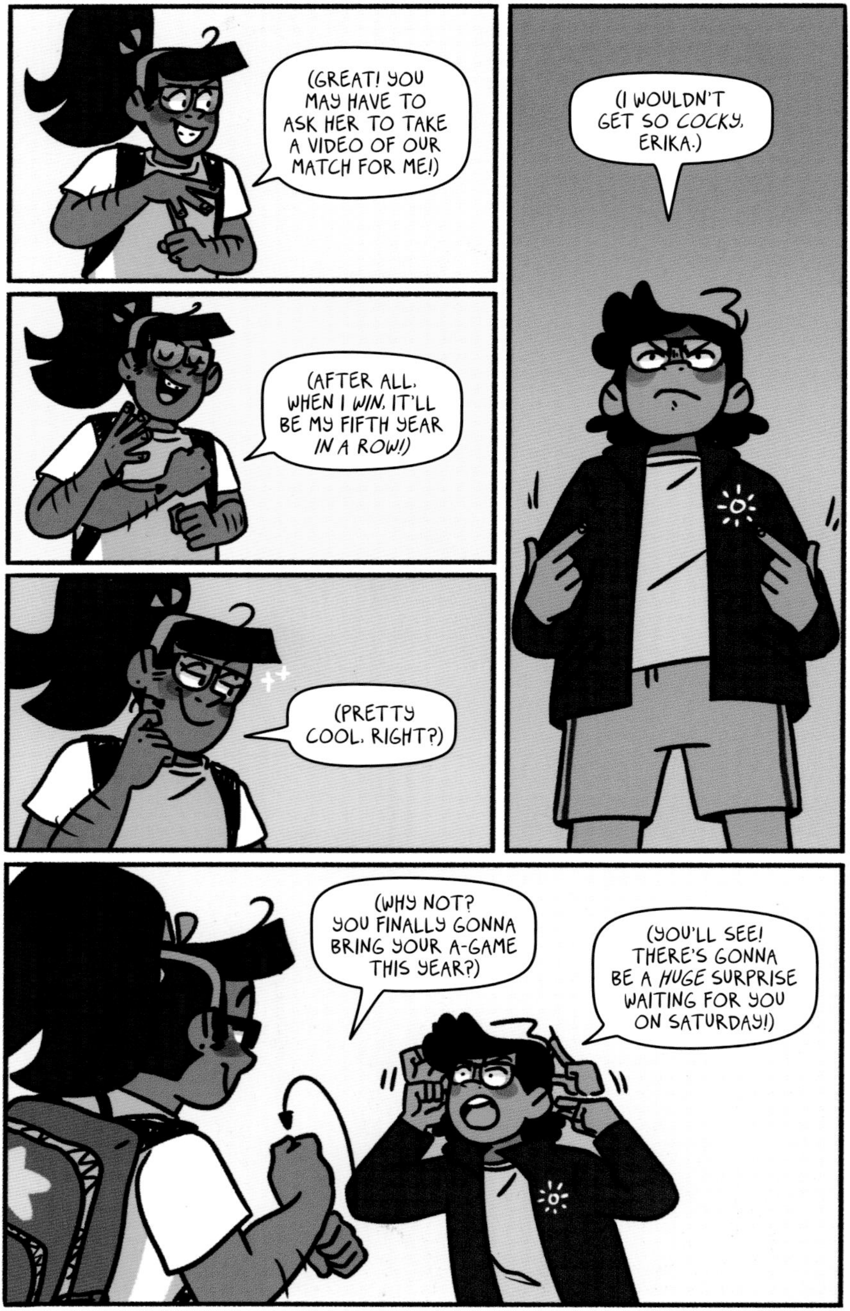
(GREAT! YOU MAY HAVE TO ASK HER TO TAKE A VIDEO OF OUR MATCH FOR ME!)
(AFTER ALL, WHEN I *WIN*, IT'LL BE MY FIFTH YEAR *IN A ROW!*)
(PRETTY COOL, RIGHT?)
(I WOULDN'T GET SO *COCKY*, ERIKA.)
(WHY NOT? YOU FINALLY GONNA BRING YOUR A-GAME THIS YEAR?)
(YOU'LL SEE! THERE'S GONNA BE A *HUGE* SURPRISE WAITING FOR YOU ON SATURDAY!)

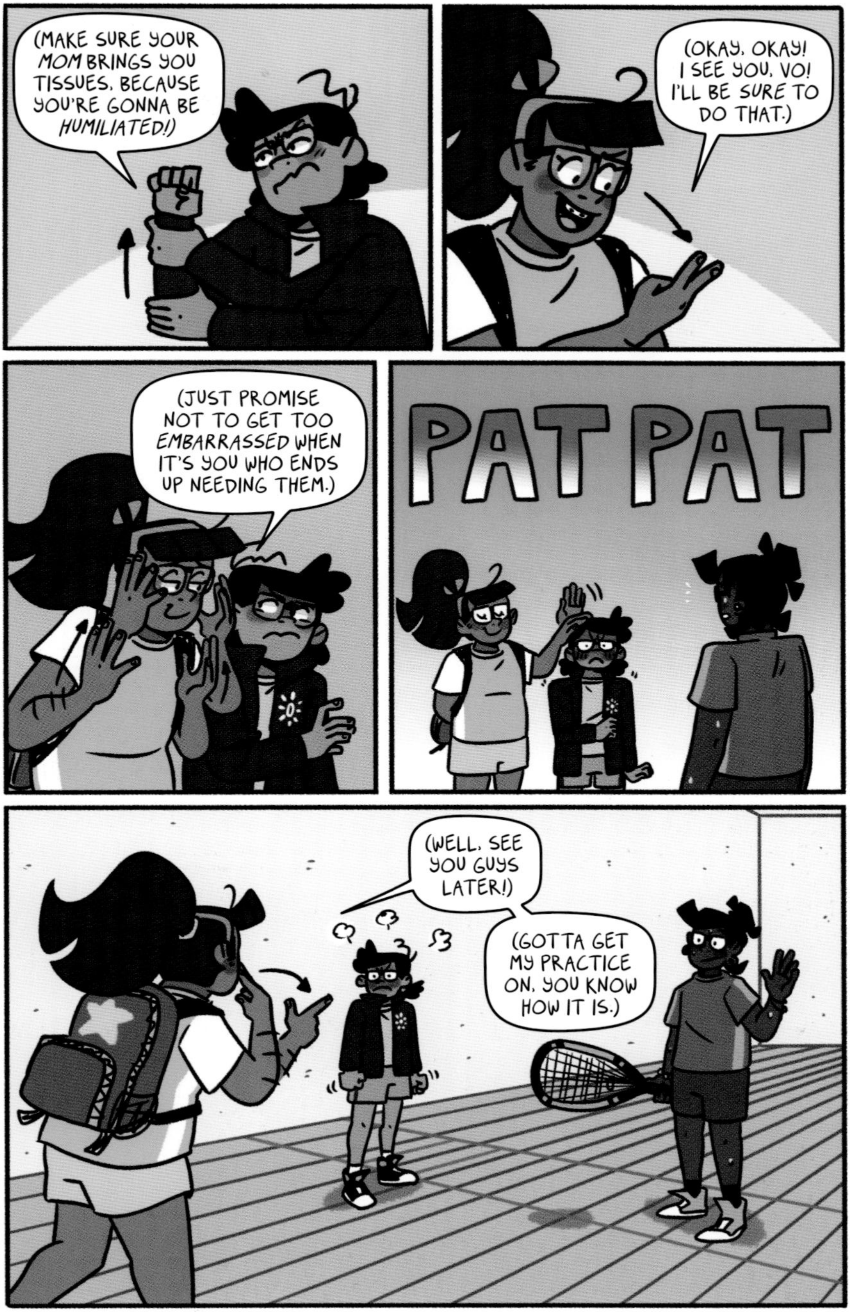
(MAKE SURE YOUR MOM BRINGS YOU TISSUES, BECAUSE YOU'RE GONNA BE HUMILIATED!)
(OKAY, OKAY! I SEE YOU, VO! I'LL BE SURE TO DO THAT.)
(JUST PROMISE NOT TO GET TOO EMBARRASSED WHEN IT'S YOU WHO ENDS UP NEEDING THEM.)
PAT PAT
(WELL, SEE YOU GUYS LATER!)
(GOTTA GET MY PRACTICE ON, YOU KNOW HOW IT IS.)

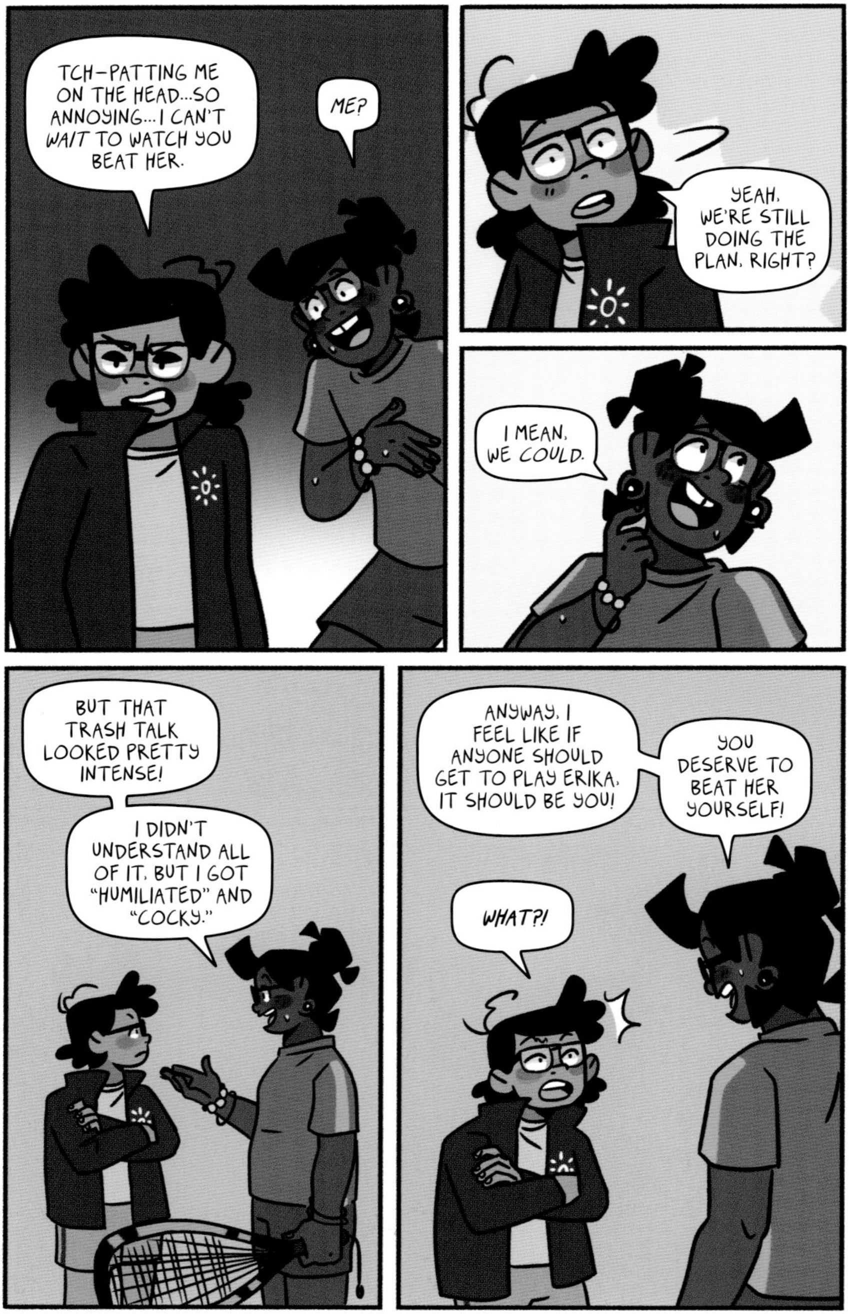
TCH—PATTING ME ON THE HEAD...SO ANNOYING...I CAN'T WAIT TO WATCH YOU BEAT HER.
ME?
YEAH, WE'RE STILL DOING THE PLAN, RIGHT?
I MEAN, WE COULD.
BUT THAT TRASH TALK LOOKED PRETTY INTENSE!
I DIDN'T UNDERSTAND ALL OF IT, BUT I GOT "HUMILIATED" AND "COCKY."
ANYWAY, I FEEL LIKE IF ANYONE SHOULD GET TO PLAY ERIKA, IT SHOULD BE YOU!
YOU DESERVE TO BEAT HER YOURSELF!
WHAT?!

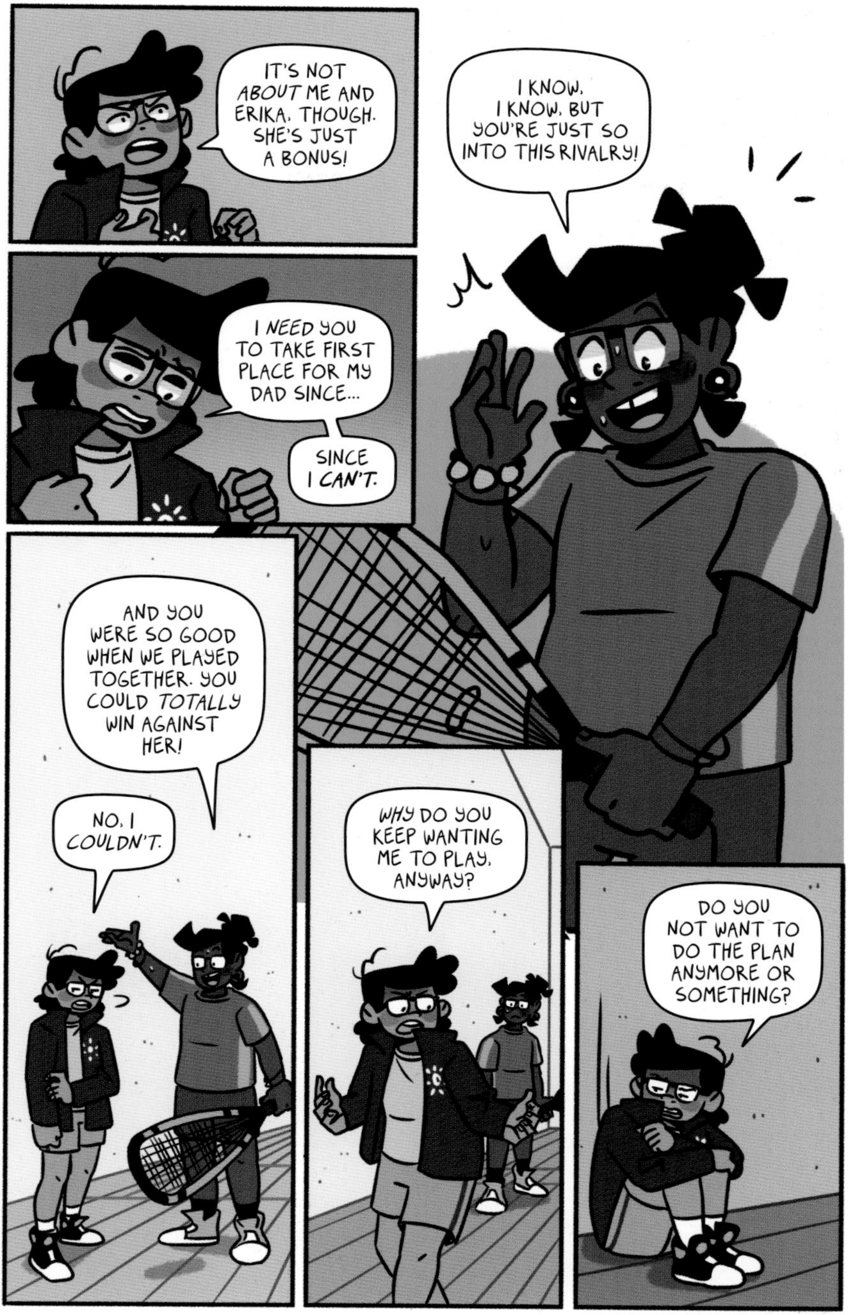
IT'S NOT *ABOUT* ME AND ERIKA, THOUGH. SHE'S JUST A BONUS!
I KNOW, I KNOW, BUT YOU'RE JUST SO INTO THIS RIVALRY!
I *NEED* YOU TO TAKE FIRST PLACE FOR MY DAD SINCE...
SINCE I *CAN'T*.
AND YOU WERE SO GOOD WHEN WE PLAYED TOGETHER. YOU COULD *TOTALLY* WIN AGAINST HER!
NO, I COULDN'T.
WHY DO YOU KEEP WANTING ME TO PLAY, ANYWAY?
DO YOU NOT WANT TO DO THE PLAN ANYMORE OR SOMETHING?

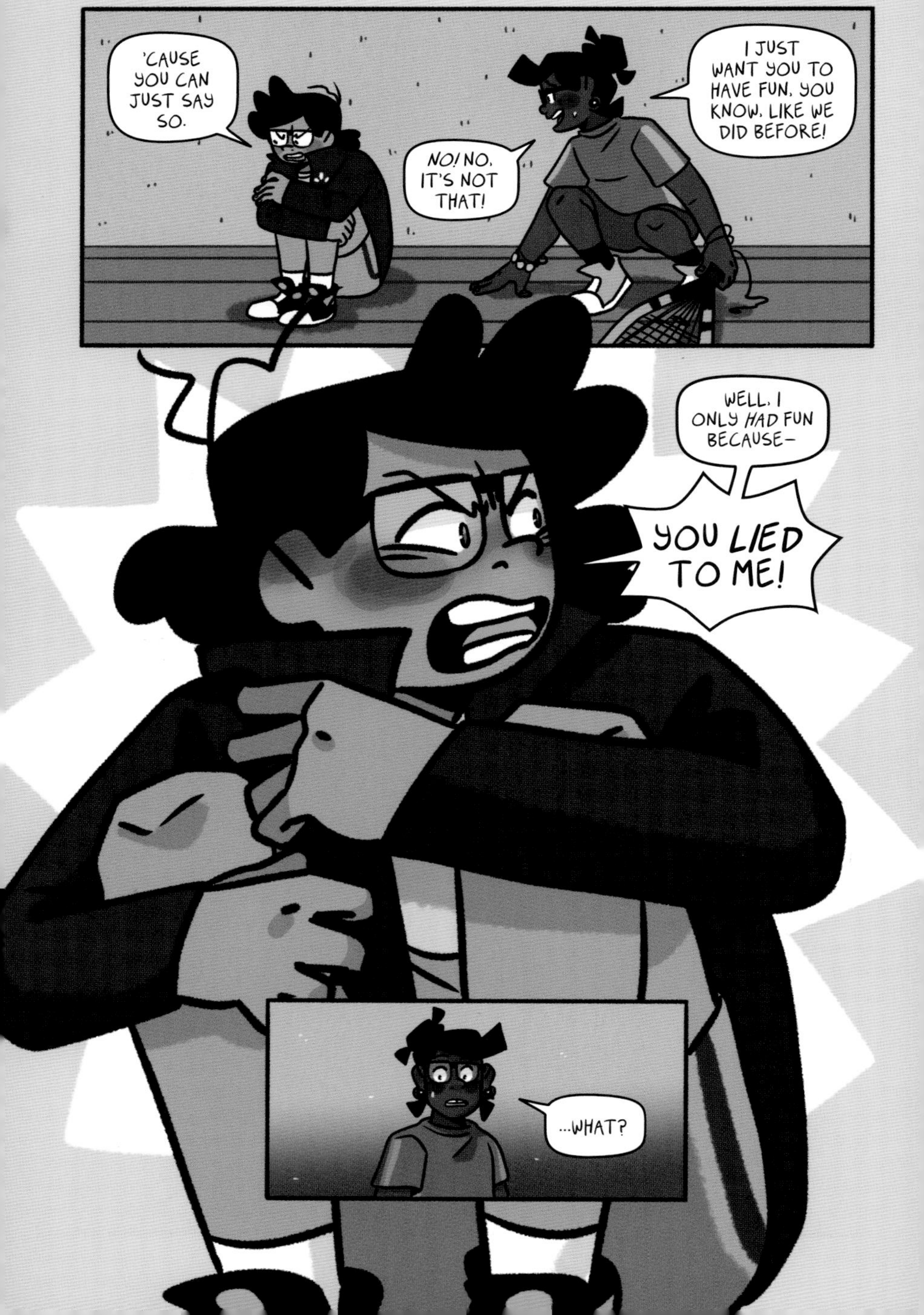
'CAUSE YOU CAN JUST SAY SO.
NO! NO, IT'S NOT THAT!
I JUST WANT YOU TO HAVE FUN, YOU KNOW, LIKE WE DID BEFORE!
WELL, I ONLY HAD FUN BECAUSE–
YOU LIED TO ME!
...WHAT?

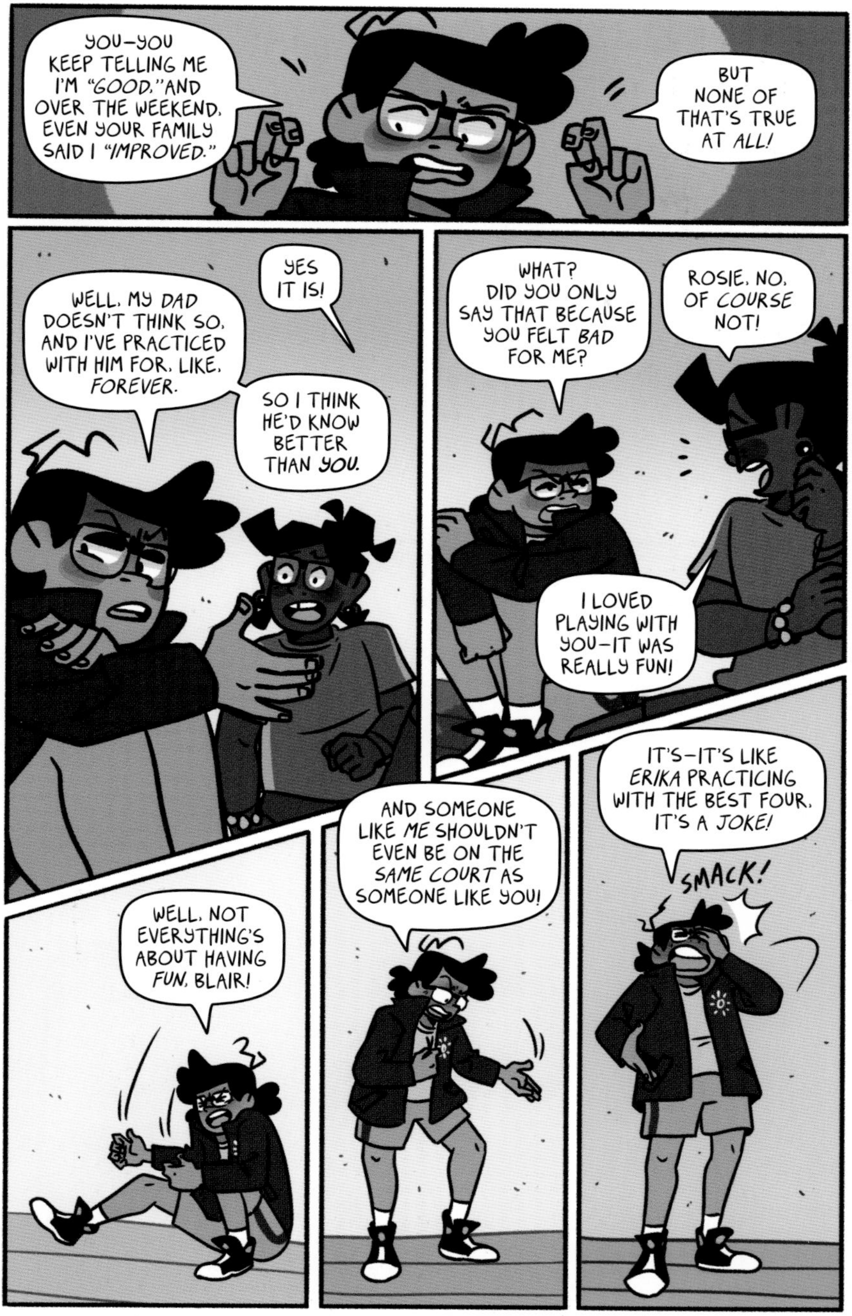
YOU—YOU KEEP TELLING ME I'M "GOOD," AND OVER THE WEEKEND, EVEN YOUR FAMILY SAID I "IMPROVED."
BUT NONE OF THAT'S TRUE AT ALL!
WELL, MY DAD DOESN'T THINK SO, AND I'VE PRACTICED WITH HIM FOR, LIKE, FOREVER.
YES IT IS!
SO I THINK HE'D KNOW BETTER THAN YOU.
WHAT? DID YOU ONLY SAY THAT BECAUSE YOU FELT BAD FOR ME?
ROSIE, NO, OF COURSE NOT!
I LOVED PLAYING WITH YOU—IT WAS REALLY FUN!
WELL, NOT EVERYTHING'S ABOUT HAVING FUN, BLAIR!
AND SOMEONE LIKE ME SHOULDN'T EVEN BE ON THE SAME COURT AS SOMEONE LIKE YOU!
IT'S—IT'S LIKE ERIKA PRACTICING WITH THE BEST FOUR, IT'S A JOKE!
SMACK!

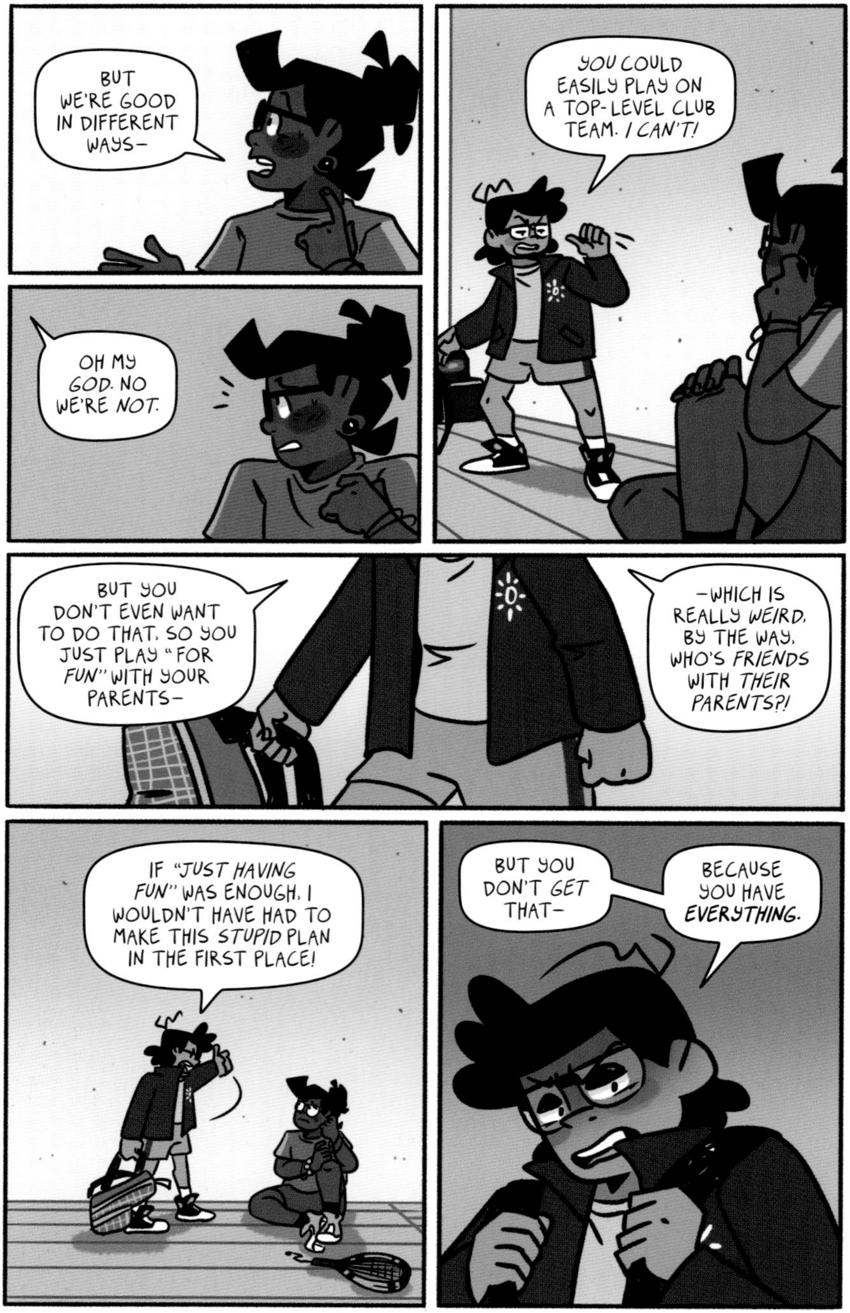
BUT WE'RE GOOD IN DIFFERENT WAYS—
YOU COULD EASILY PLAY ON A TOP-LEVEL CLUB TEAM. *I CAN'T!*
OH MY GOD. NO WE'RE *NOT.*
BUT YOU DON'T EVEN WANT TO DO THAT. SO YOU JUST PLAY "FOR *FUN*" WITH YOUR PARENTS—
—WHICH IS REALLY *WEIRD*, BY THE WAY. WHO'S *FRIENDS* WITH *THEIR* PARENTS?!
IF "*JUST HAVING FUN*" WAS ENOUGH, I WOULDN'T HAVE HAD TO MAKE THIS *STUPID* PLAN IN THE FIRST PLACE!
BUT YOU DON'T *GET* THAT—
BECAUSE YOU HAVE **EVERYTHING.**

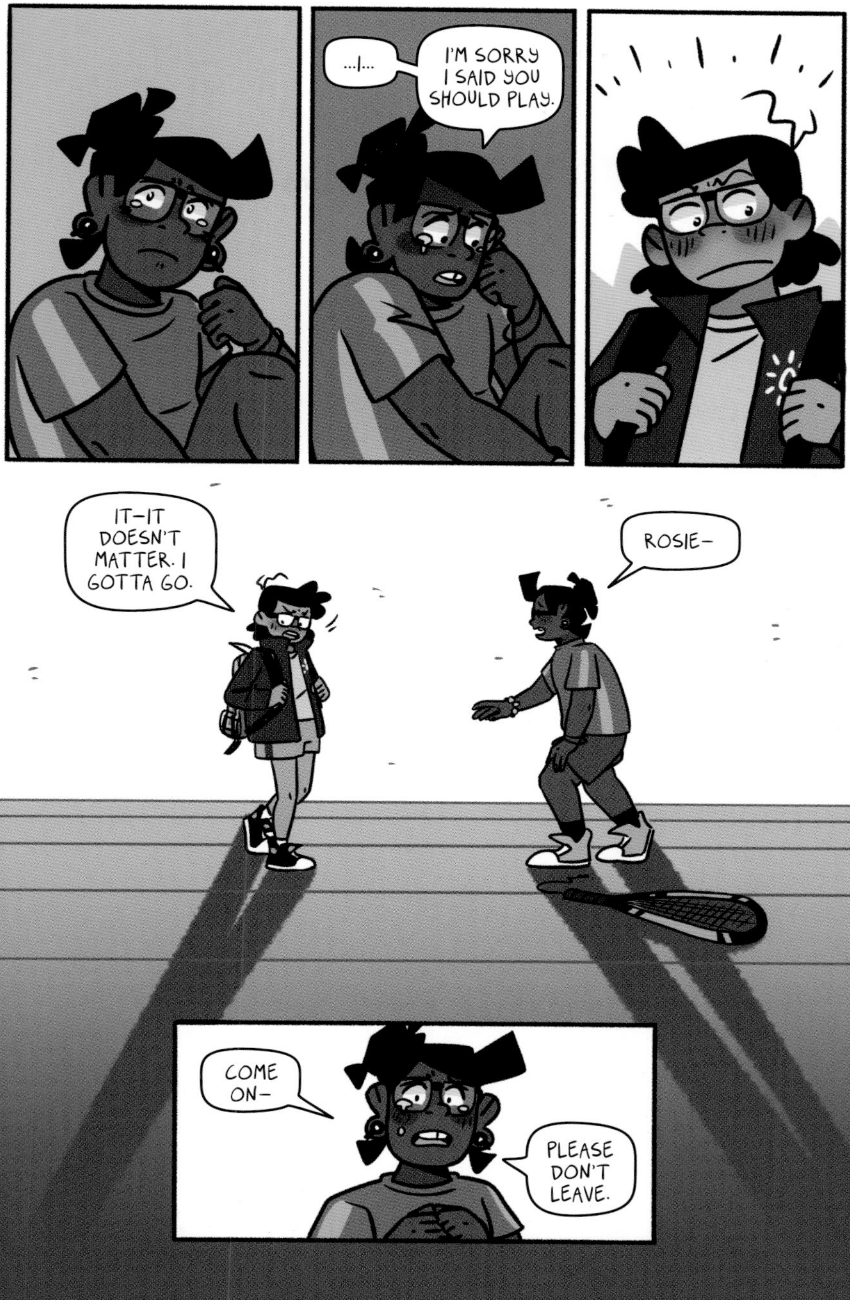
...I...
I'M SORRY I SAID YOU SHOULD PLAY.
IT—IT DOESN'T MATTER. I GOTTA GO.
ROSIE—
COME ON—
PLEASE DON'T LEAVE.

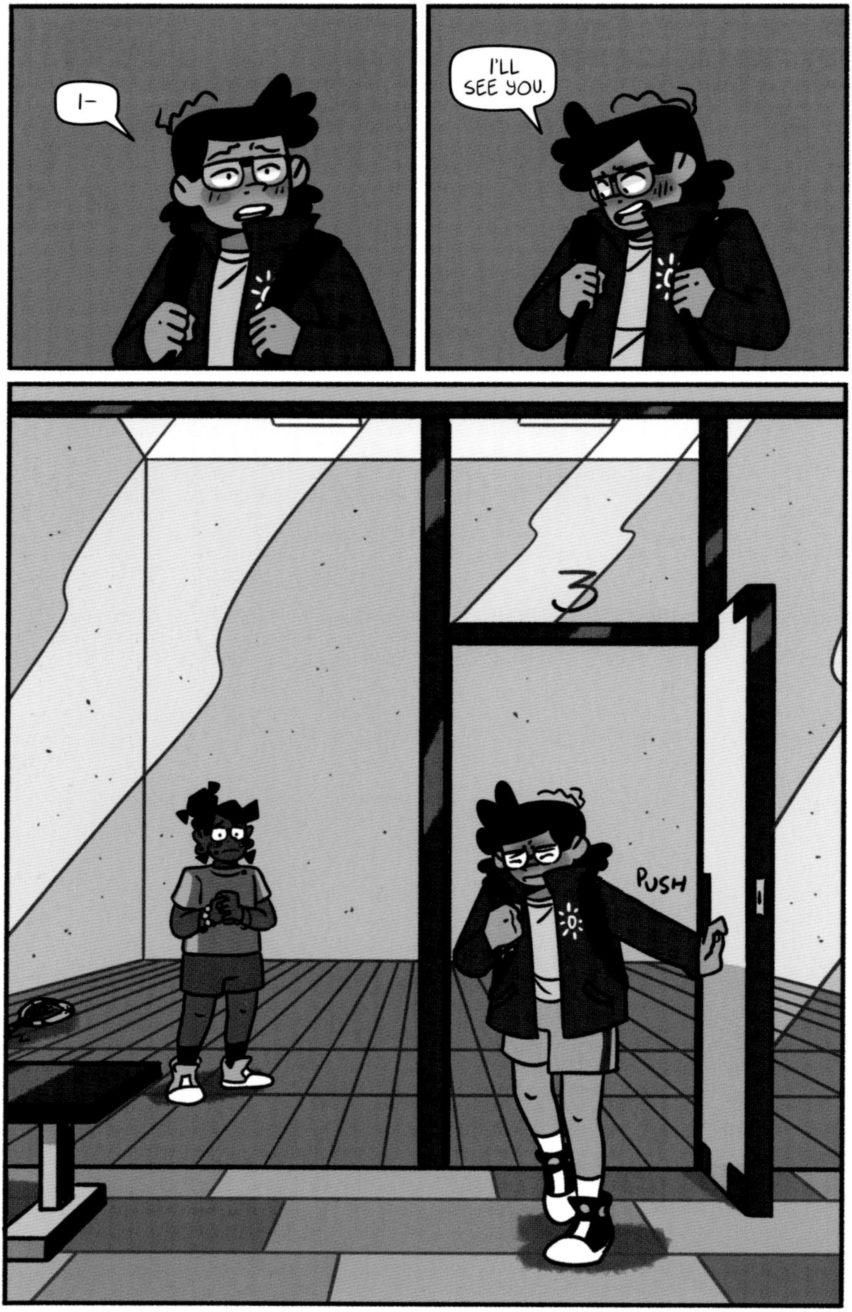
I–
I'LL SEE YOU.
3
PUSH

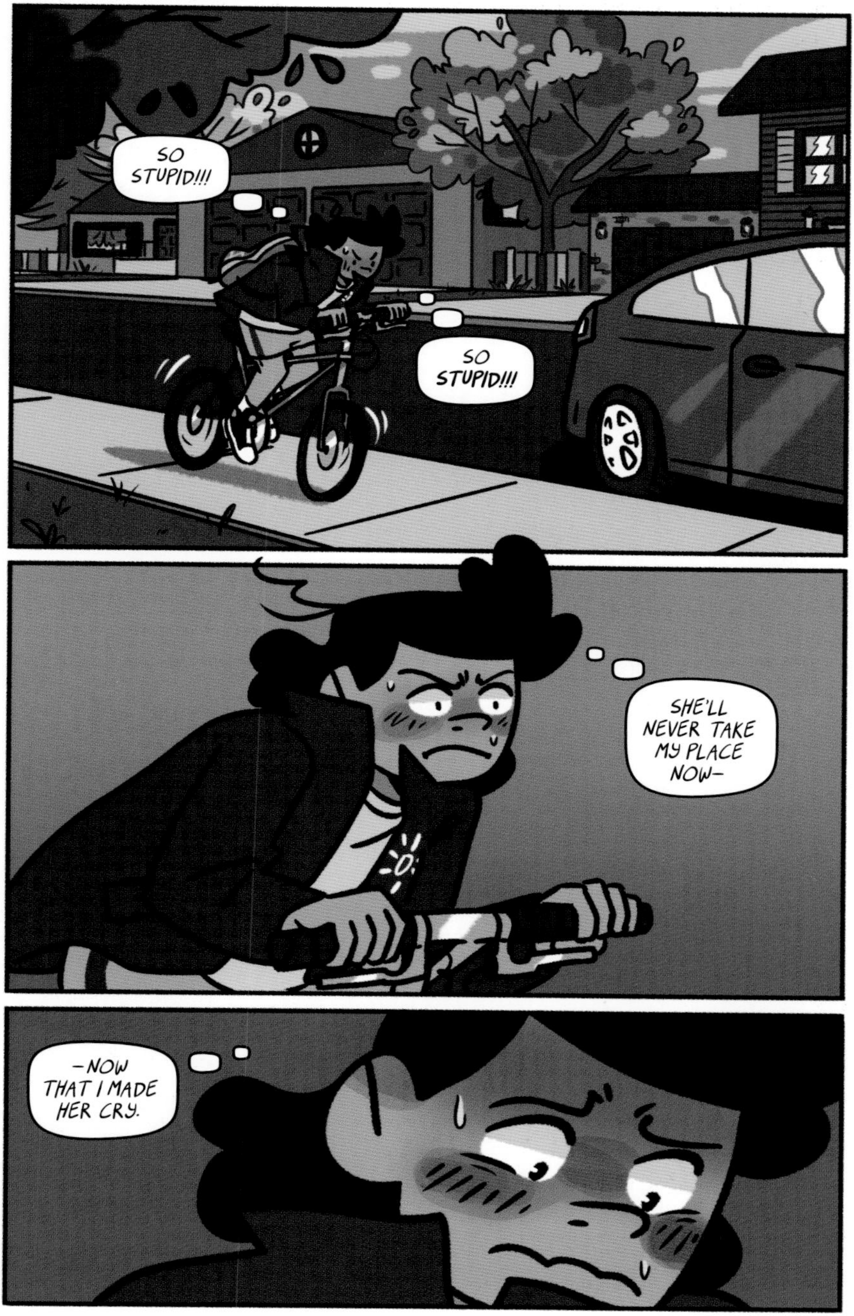
SO STUPID!!!
SO STUPID!!!
SHE'LL NEVER TAKE MY PLACE NOW—
—NOW THAT I MADE HER CRY.

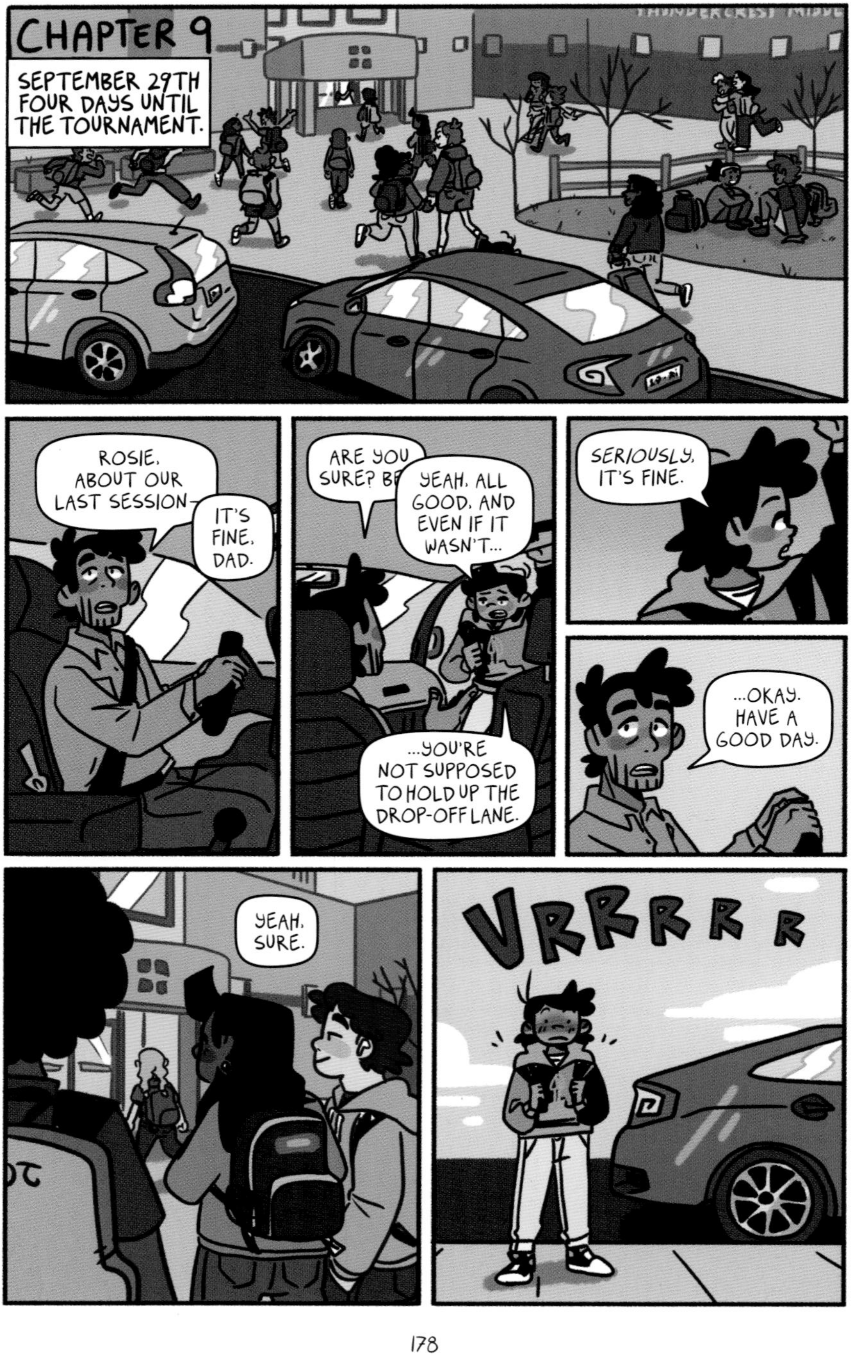
CHAPTER 9
SEPTEMBER 29TH FOUR DAYS UNTIL THE TOURNAMENT.
THUNDERCREST MIDDL
ROSIE, ABOUT OUR LAST SESSION—
IT'S FINE, DAD.
ARE YOU SURE? BE
YEAH, ALL GOOD. AND EVEN IF IT WASN'T...
...YOU'RE NOT SUPPOSED TO HOLD UP THE DROP-OFF LANE.
SERIOUSLY, IT'S FINE.
...OKAY. HAVE A GOOD DAY.
YEAH, SURE.
VRRRRR

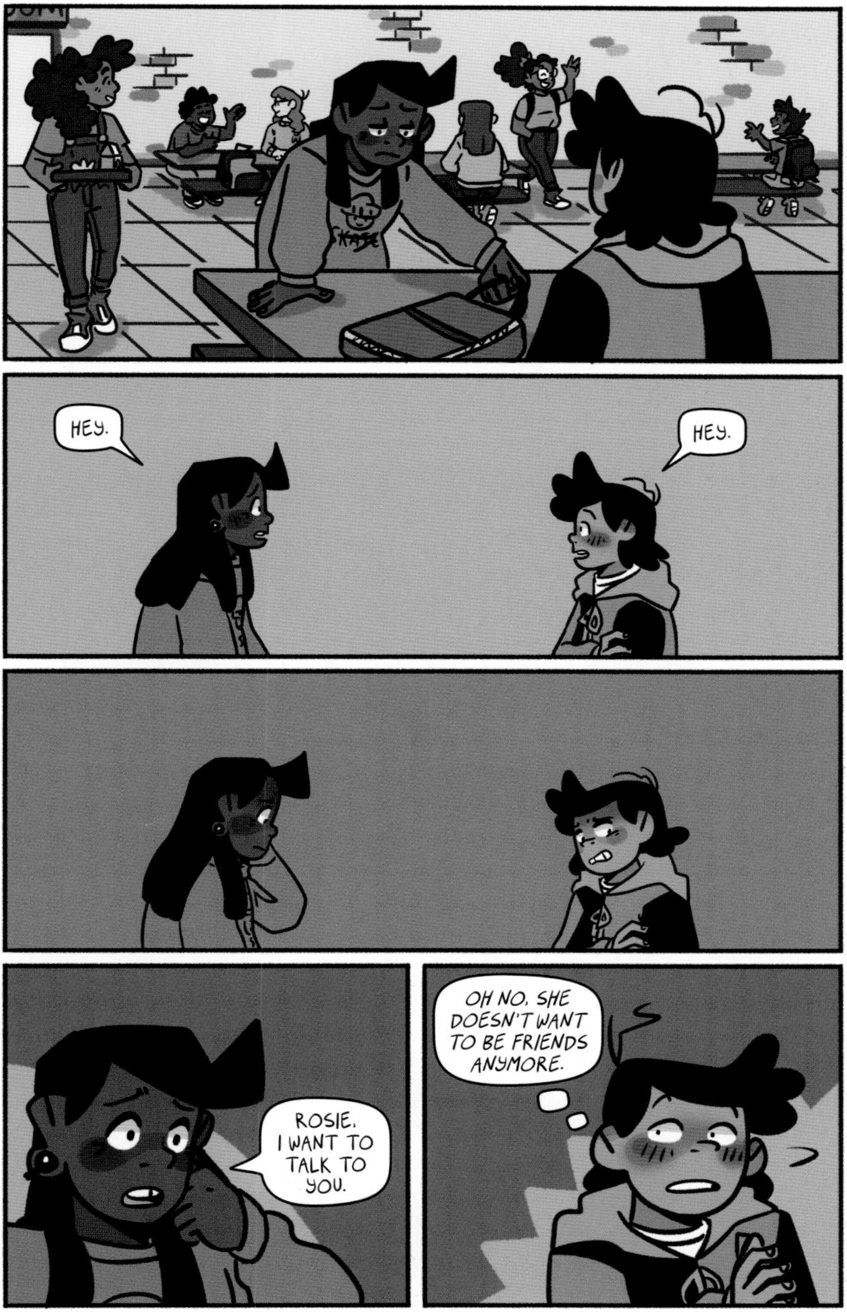
HEY.
HEY.
ROSIE, I WANT TO TALK TO YOU.
OH NO, SHE DOESN'T WANT TO BE FRIENDS ANYMORE.

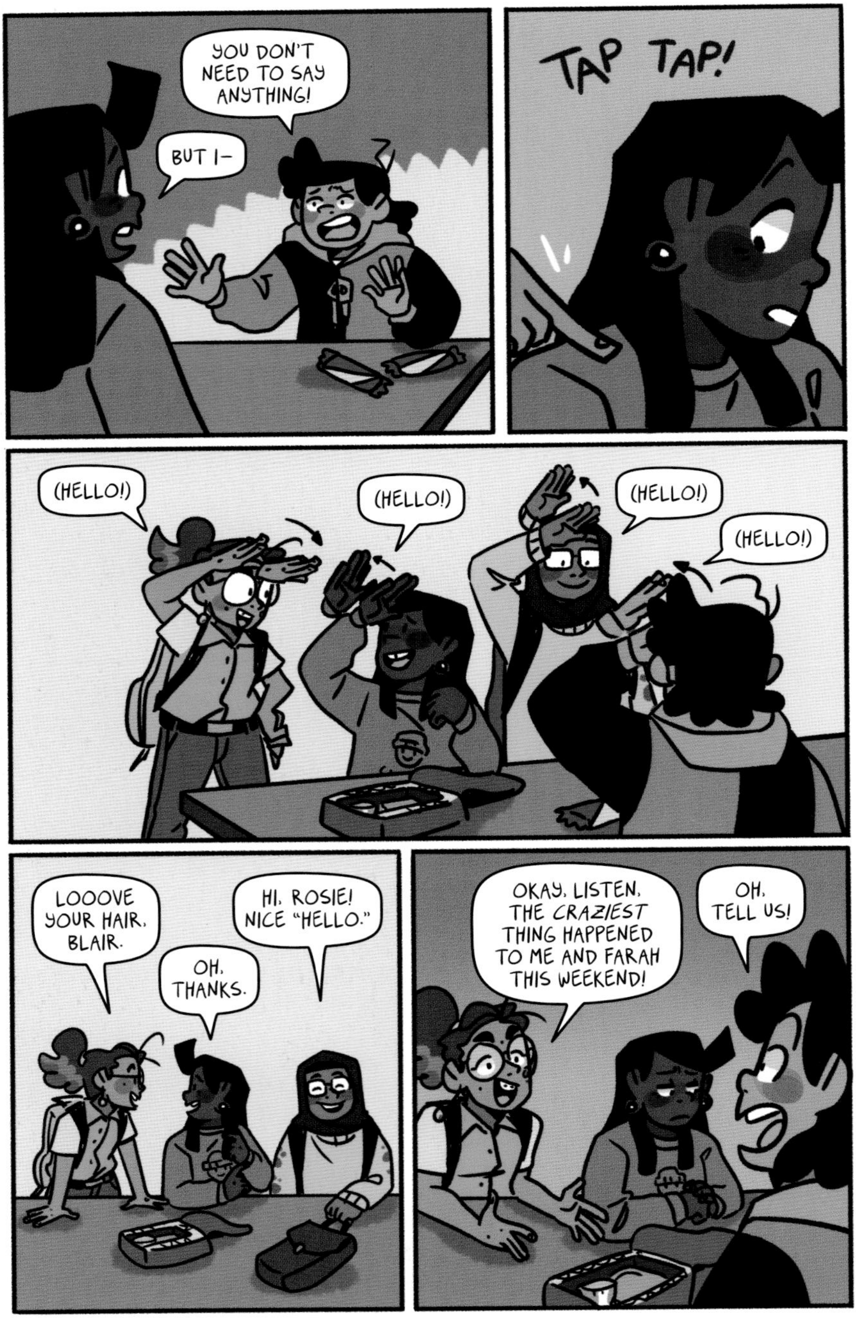
YOU DON'T NEED TO SAY ANYTHING!
BUT I—
TAP TAP!
(HELLO!)
(HELLO!)
(HELLO!)
(HELLO!)
LOOOVE YOUR HAIR, BLAIR.
OH, THANKS.
HI, ROSIE! NICE "HELLO."
OKAY, LISTEN, THE *CRAZIEST* THING HAPPENED TO ME AND FARAH THIS WEEKEND!
OH, TELL US!

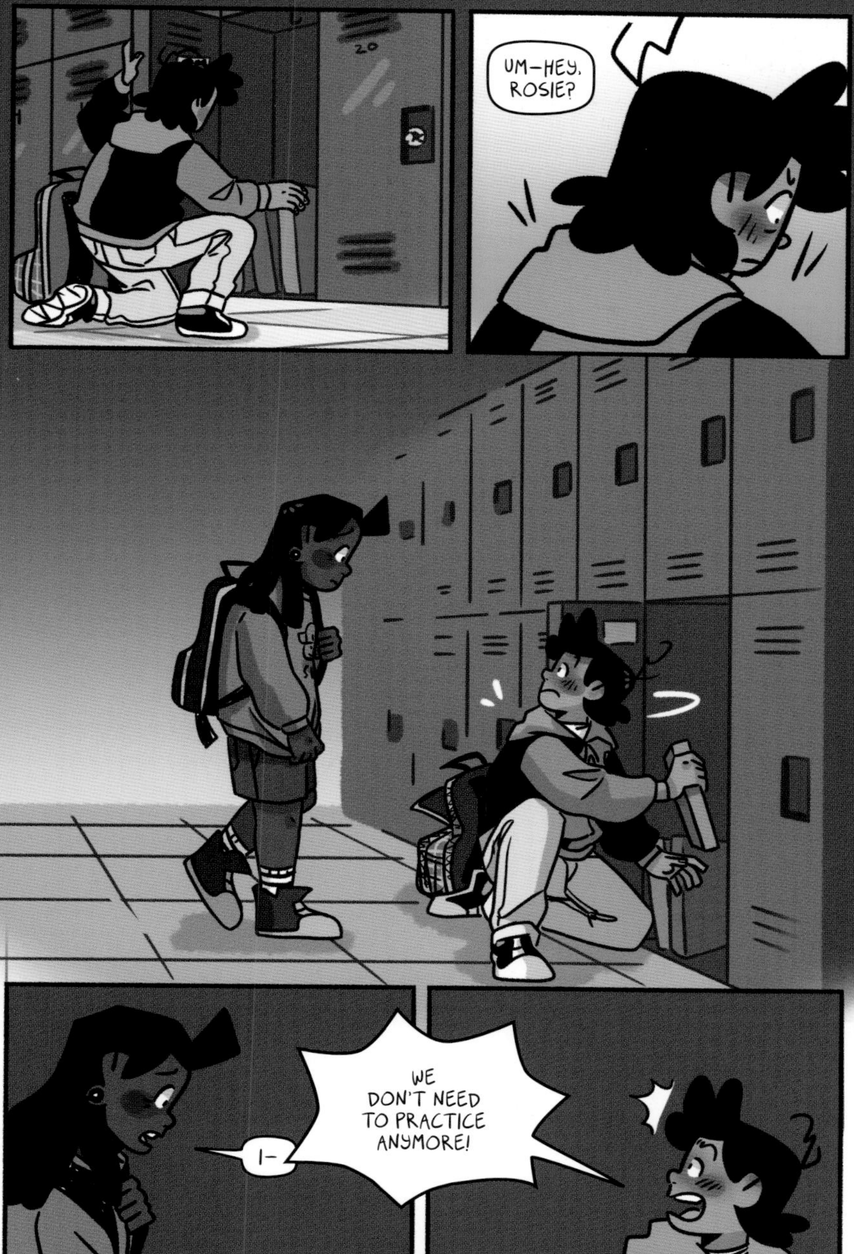
UM—HEY, ROSIE?
I—
WE DON'T NEED TO PRACTICE ANYMORE!

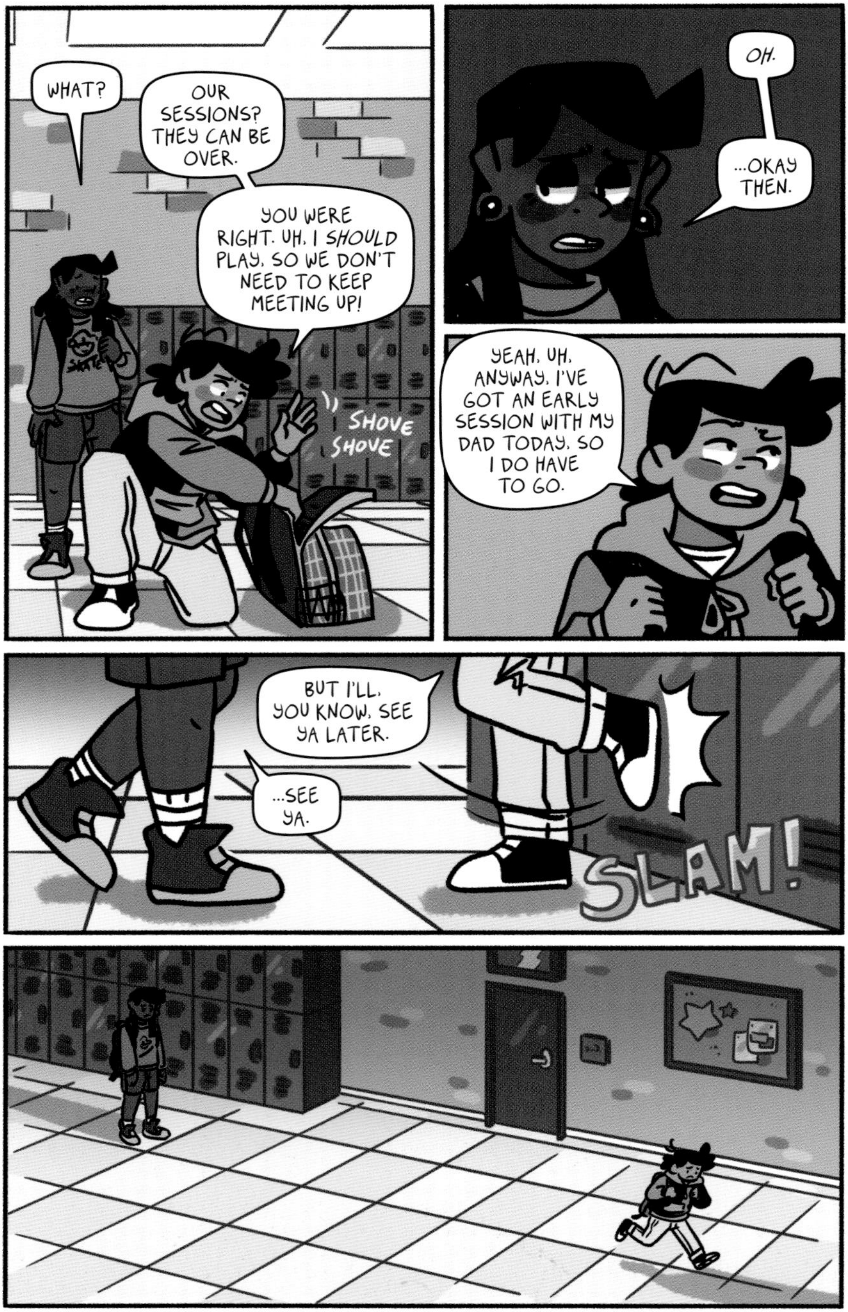
WHAT?
OUR SESSIONS? THEY CAN BE OVER.
YOU WERE RIGHT. UH, I *SHOULD* PLAY, SO WE DON'T NEED TO KEEP MEETING UP!
SHOVE SHOVE
OH.
...OKAY THEN.
YEAH, UH, ANYWAY, I'VE GOT AN EARLY SESSION WITH MY DAD TODAY, SO I DO HAVE TO GO.
BUT I'LL, YOU KNOW, SEE YA LATER.
...SEE YA.
SLAM!

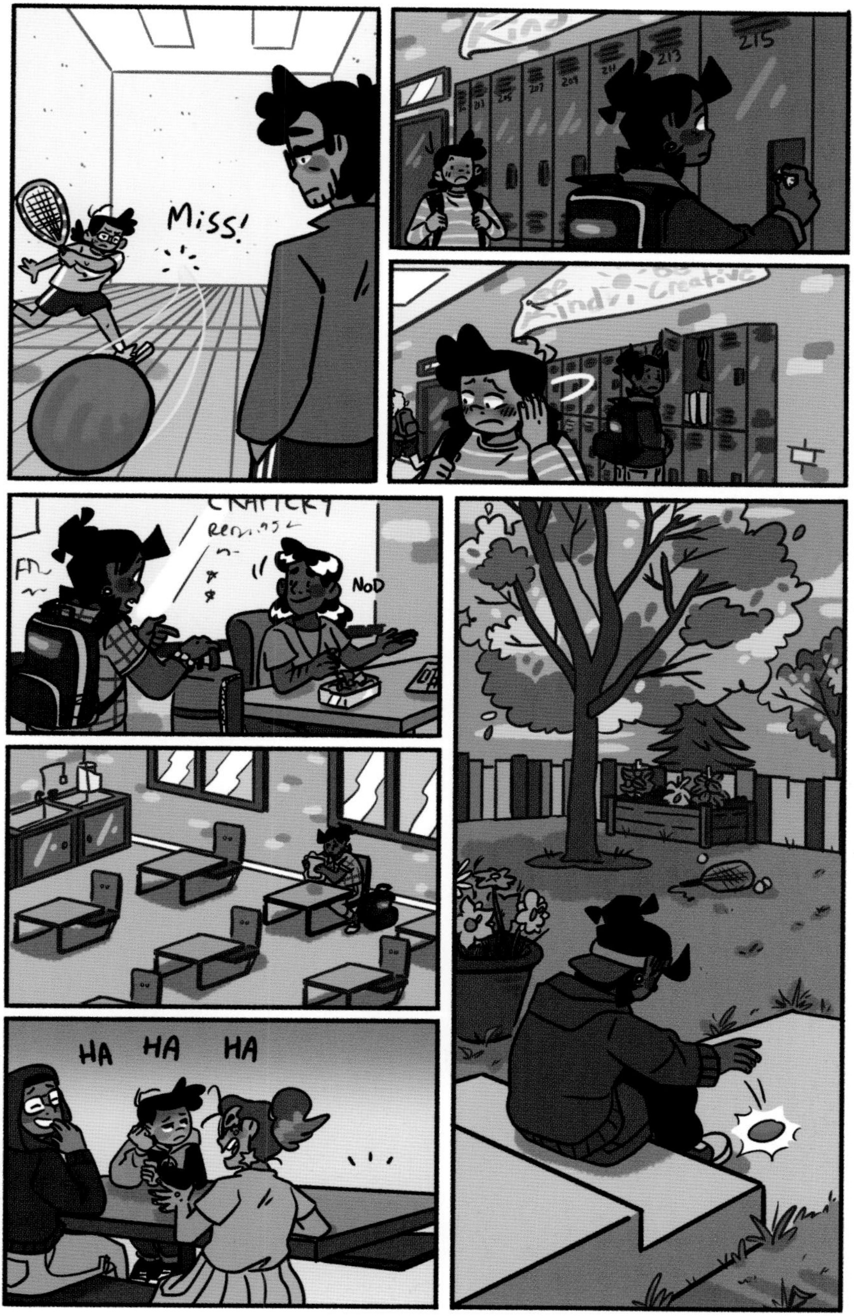
MISS!
215
Be Kind Be Creative
NOD
HA HA HA

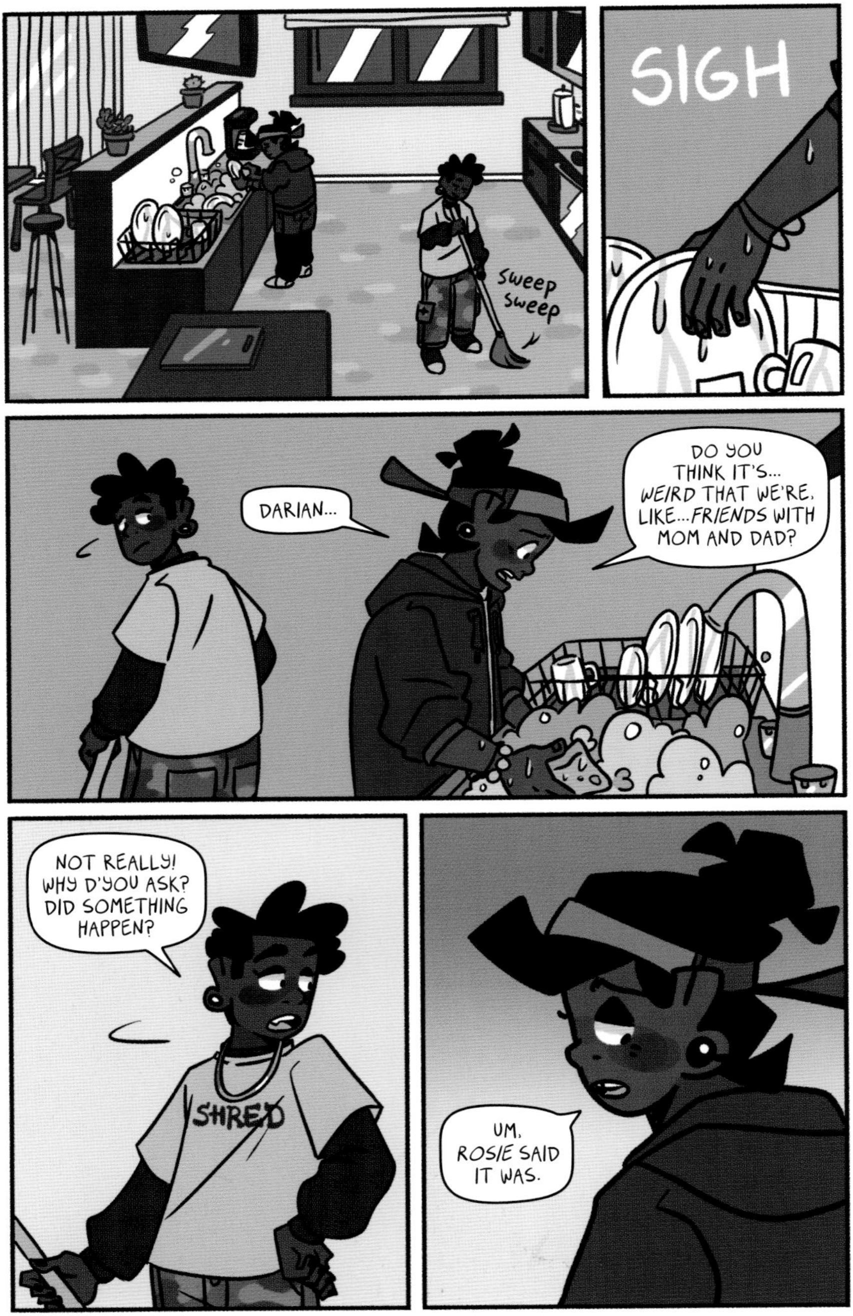
Sweep sweep
SIGH
DARIAN...
DO YOU THINK IT'S... WEIRD THAT WE'RE, LIKE... FRIENDS WITH MOM AND DAD?
NOT REALLY! WHY D'YOU ASK? DID SOMETHING HAPPEN?
SHRED
UM, ROSIE SAID IT WAS.

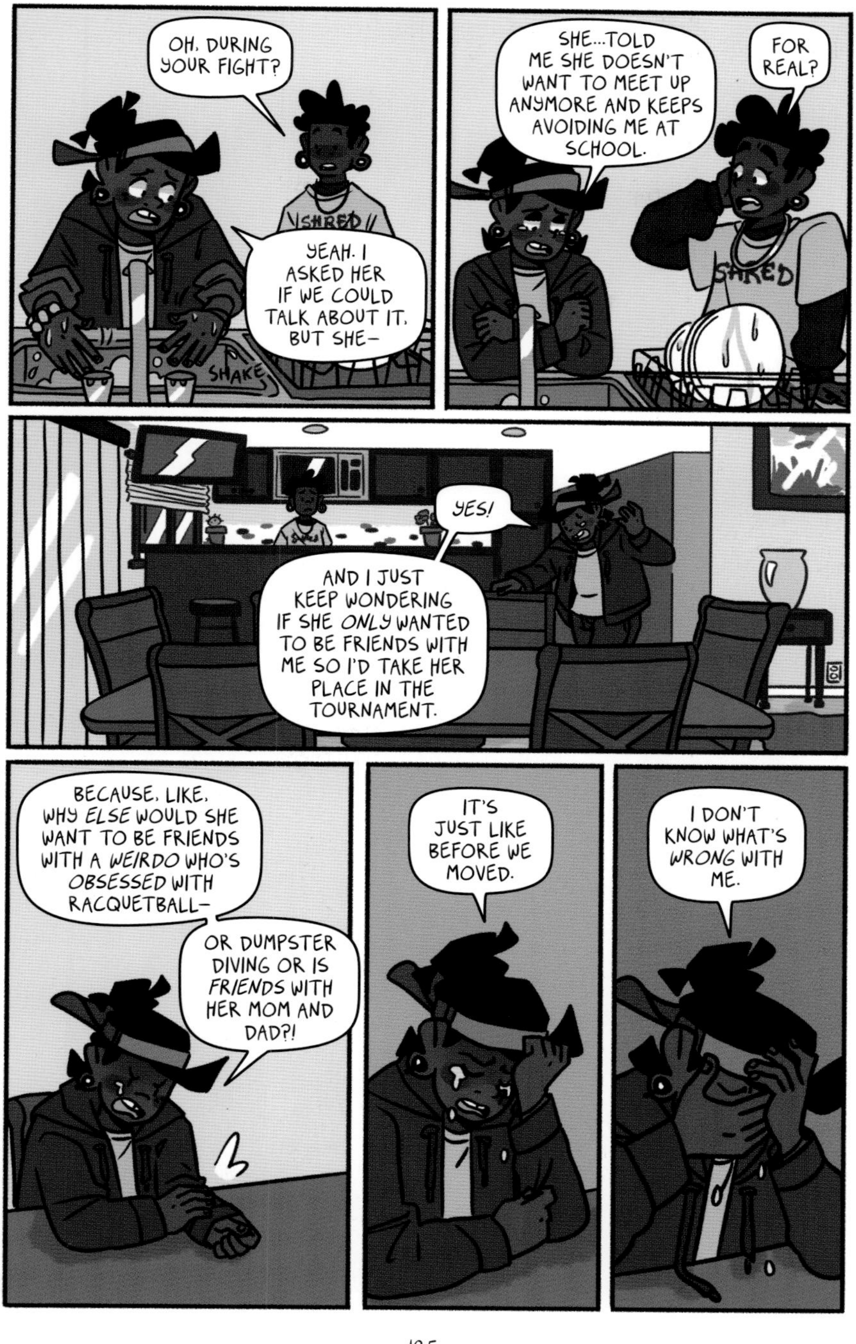
OH, DURING YOUR FIGHT?
SHRED
YEAH. I ASKED HER IF WE COULD TALK ABOUT IT, BUT SHE–
SHAKE
SHE...TOLD ME SHE DOESN'T WANT TO MEET UP ANYMORE AND KEEPS AVOIDING ME AT SCHOOL.
FOR REAL?
SHRED
YES!
AND I JUST KEEP WONDERING IF SHE *ONLY* WANTED TO BE FRIENDS WITH ME SO I'D TAKE HER PLACE IN THE TOURNAMENT.
BECAUSE, LIKE, WHY *ELSE* WOULD SHE WANT TO BE FRIENDS WITH A *WEIRDO* WHO'S *OBSESSED* WITH RACQUETBALL–
OR DUMPSTER DIVING OR IS *FRIENDS* WITH HER MOM AND DAD?!
IT'S JUST LIKE BEFORE WE MOVED.
I DON'T KNOW WHAT'S *WRONG* WITH ME.

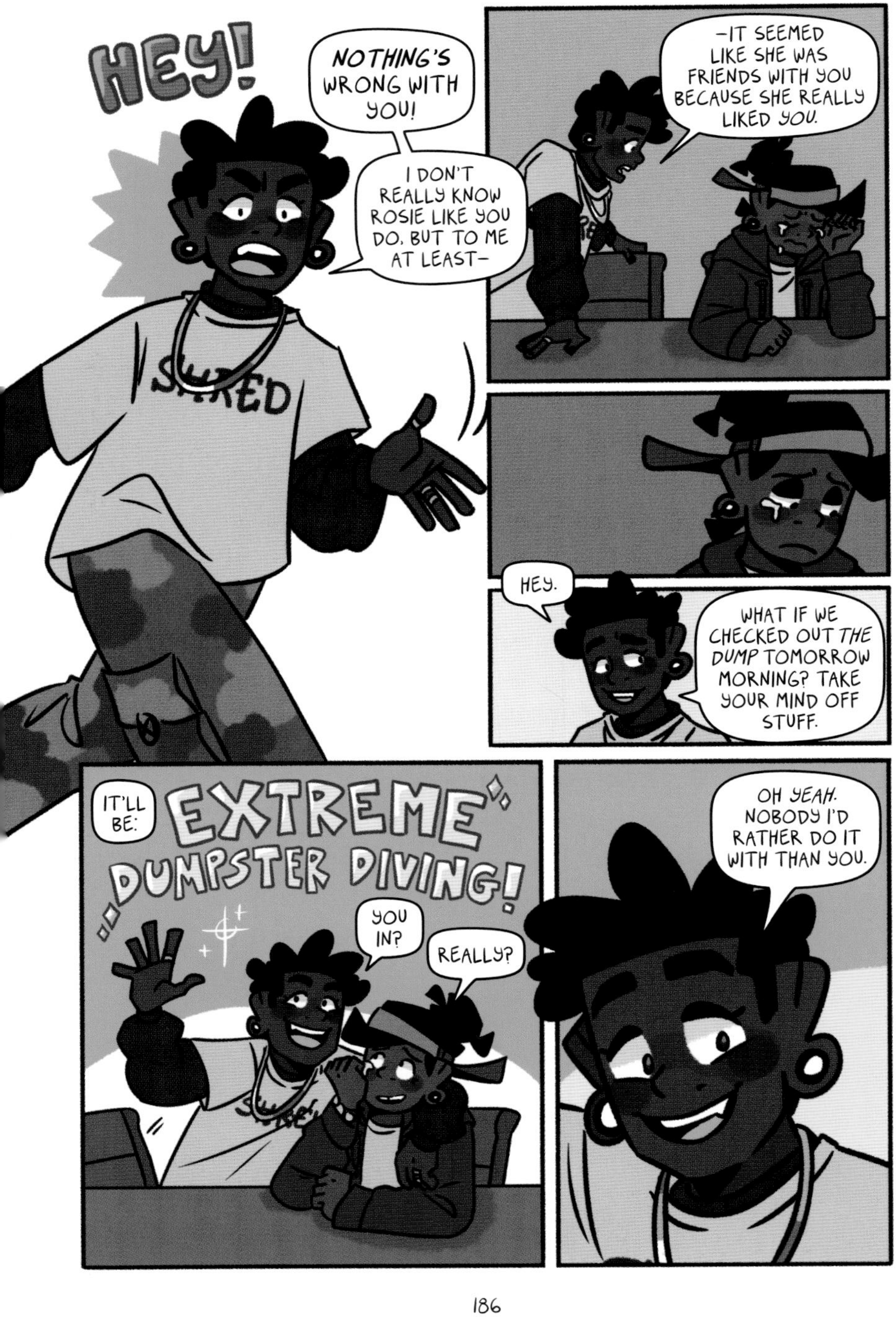
HEY!
NOTHING'S WRONG WITH YOU!
I DON'T REALLY KNOW ROSIE LIKE YOU DO, BUT TO ME AT LEAST–
SHRED
–IT SEEMED LIKE SHE WAS FRIENDS WITH YOU BECAUSE SHE REALLY LIKED YOU.
HEY.
WHAT IF WE CHECKED OUT THE DUMP TOMORROW MORNING? TAKE YOUR MIND OFF STUFF.
IT'LL BE:
EXTREME DUMPSTER DIVING!
YOU IN?
REALLY?
OH YEAH. NOBODY I'D RATHER DO IT WITH THAN YOU.

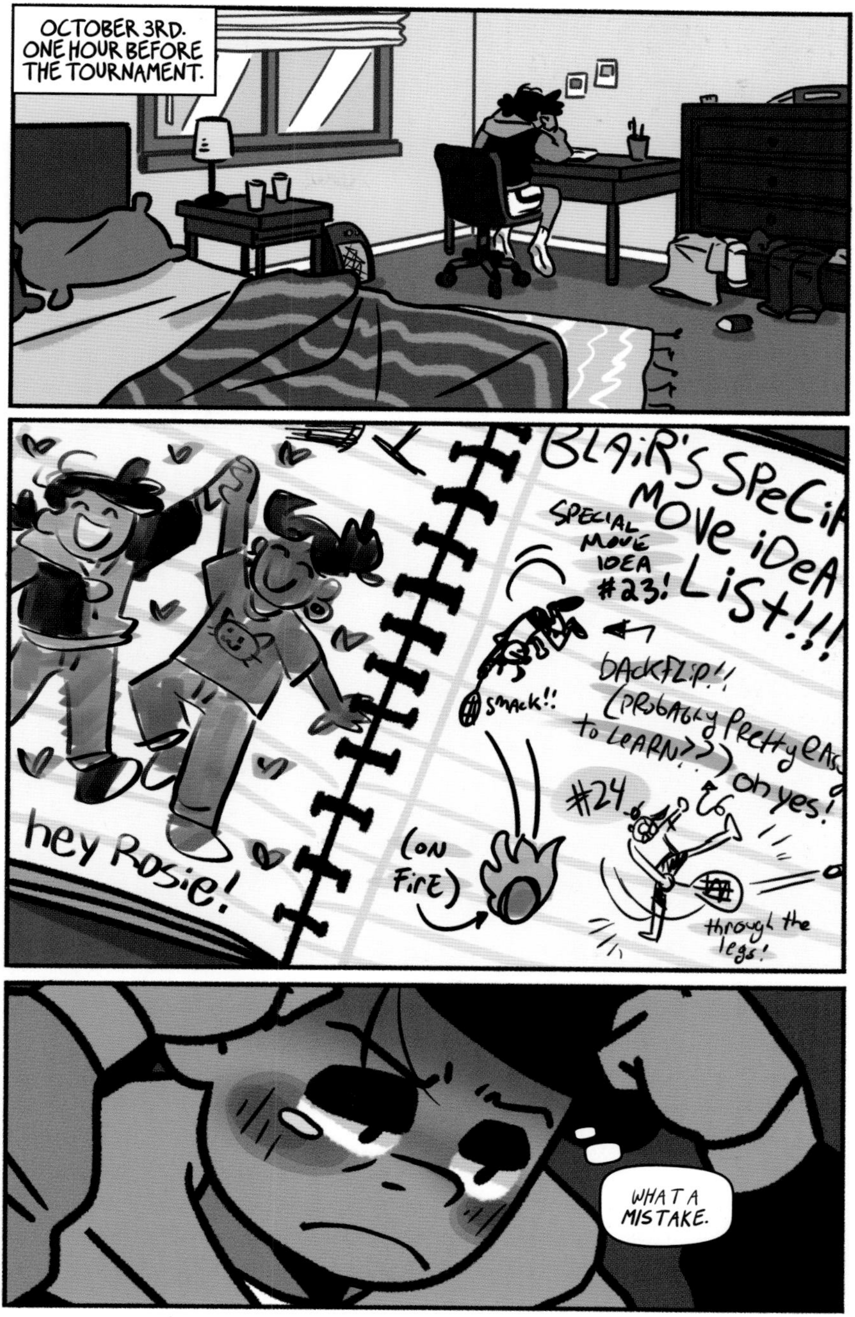
OCTOBER 3RD. ONE HOUR BEFORE THE TOURNAMENT.
hey Rosie!
BLAiR'S SPeCiA MOVE iDeA LiST!!!
SPECiAL MOVE iDEA #23!
BACKFLiP!! (PRoBABLY PReTTY eASY to LeARN??) oh yes!
SMACK!!
(ON FiRE)
#24
through the legs!
WHAT A MISTAKE.

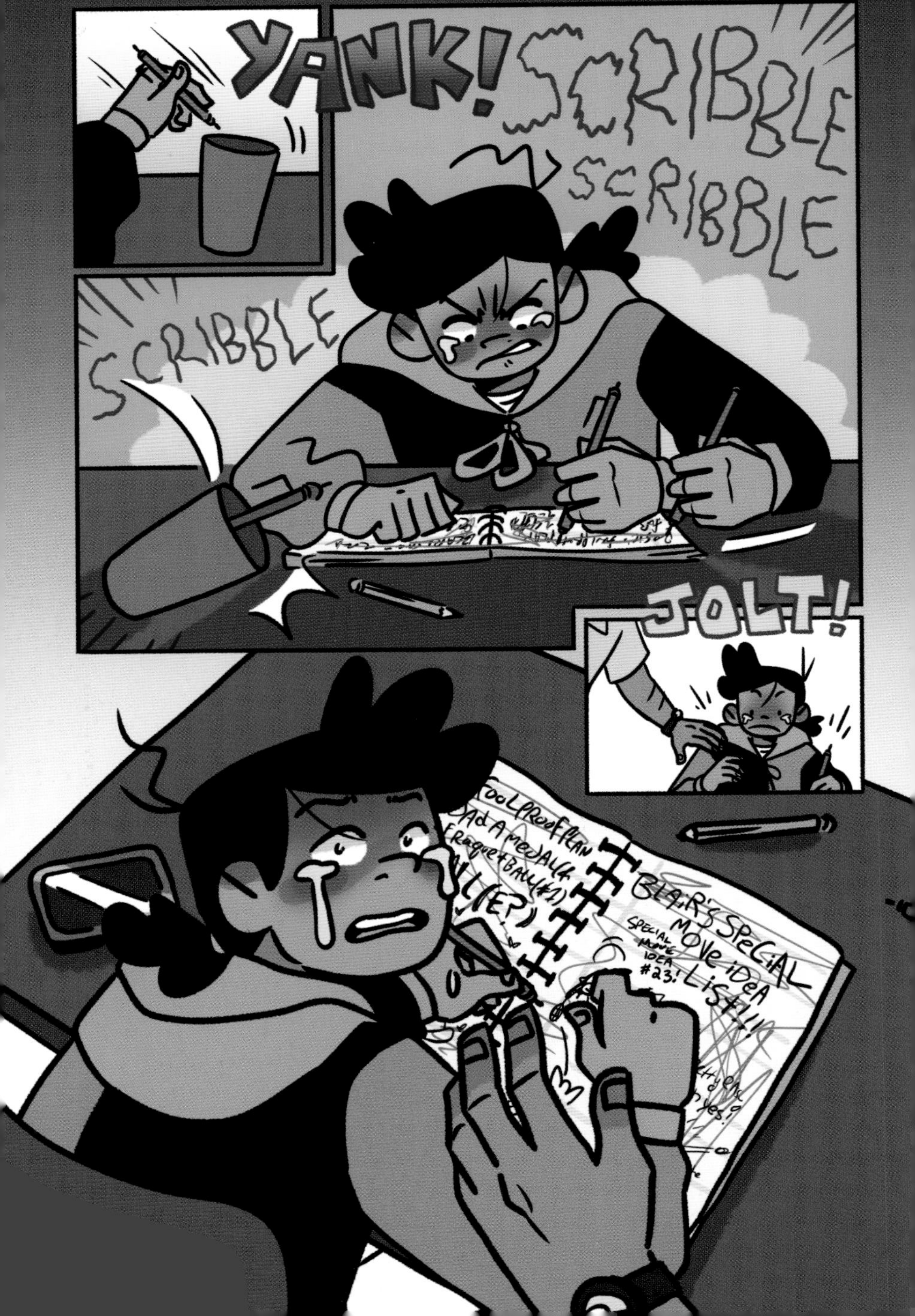
YANK!
SCRIBBLE
SCRIBBLE
SCRIBBLE
JOLT!
FOOLPROOF PLAN
BLAIR'S SPECIAL MOVE IDEA LIST!!!
SPECIAL MOVE IDEA #23!

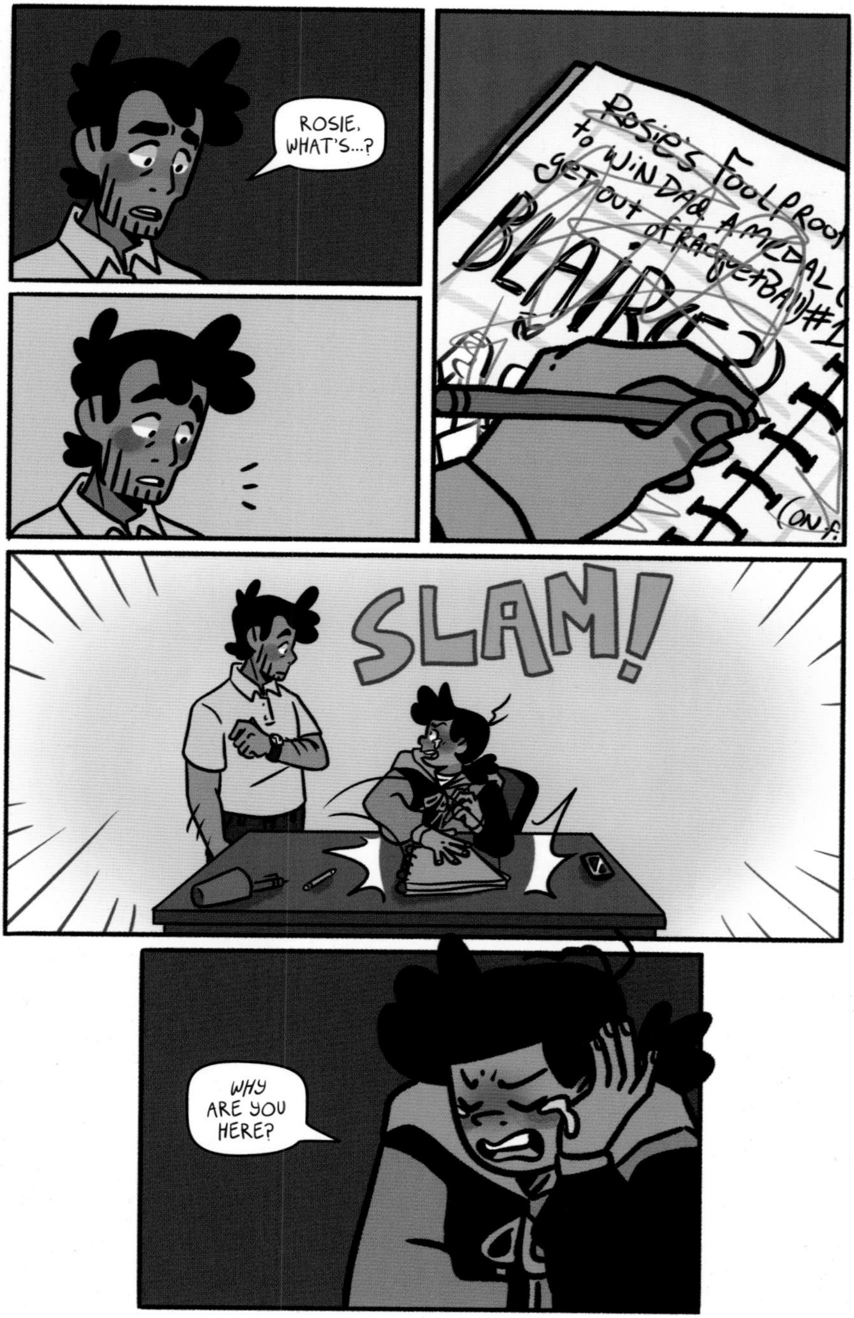
ROSIE, WHAT'S...?
Rosie's
to WIN DAD A MEDAL
get out of RACQUETBALL
SLAM!
WHY ARE YOU HERE?

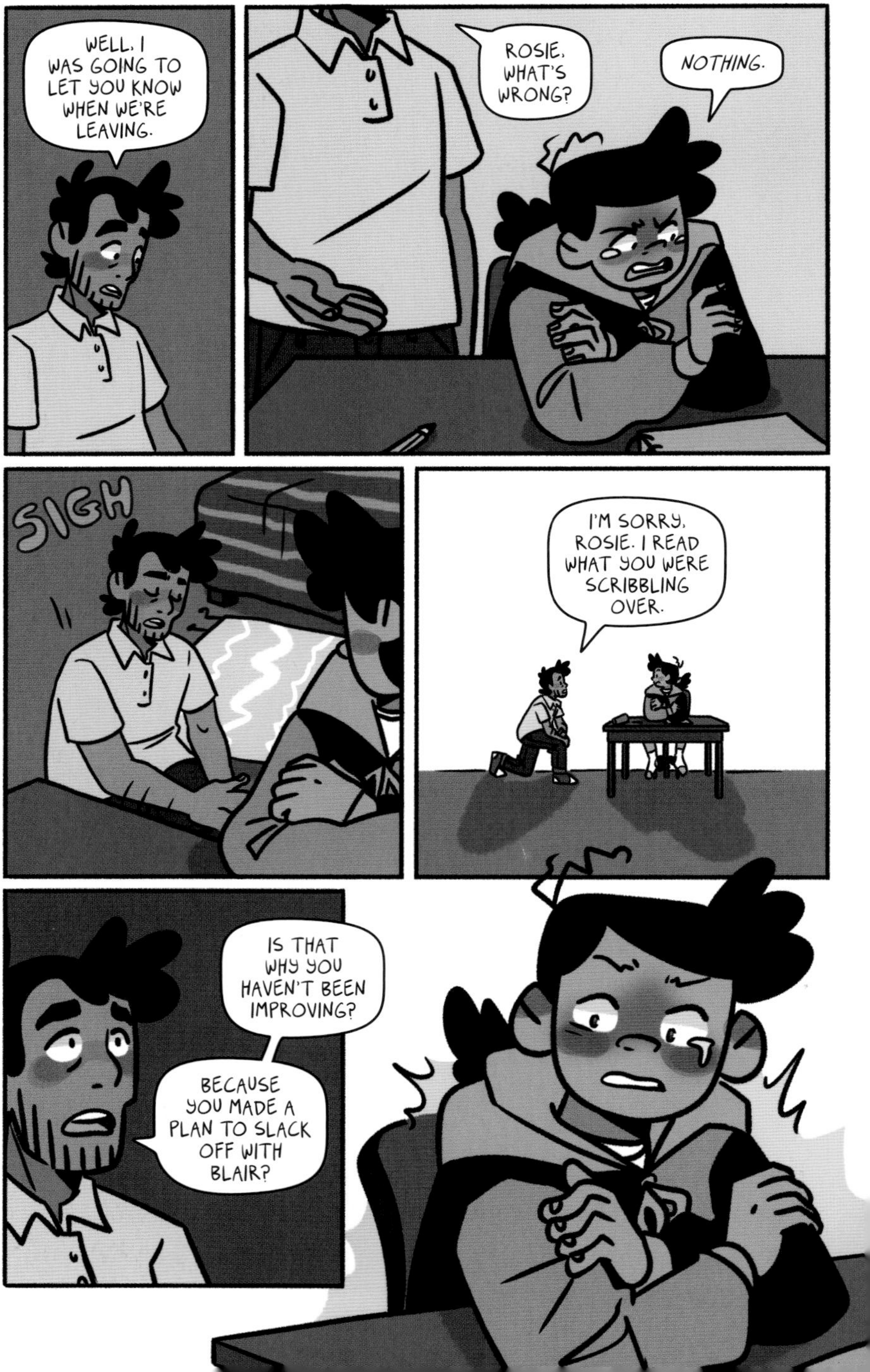
WELL, I WAS GOING TO LET YOU KNOW WHEN WE'RE LEAVING.
ROSIE, WHAT'S WRONG?
NOTHING.
SIGH
I'M SORRY, ROSIE. I READ WHAT YOU WERE SCRIBBLING OVER.
IS THAT WHY YOU HAVEN'T BEEN IMPROVING?
BECAUSE YOU MADE A PLAN TO SLACK OFF WITH BLAIR?

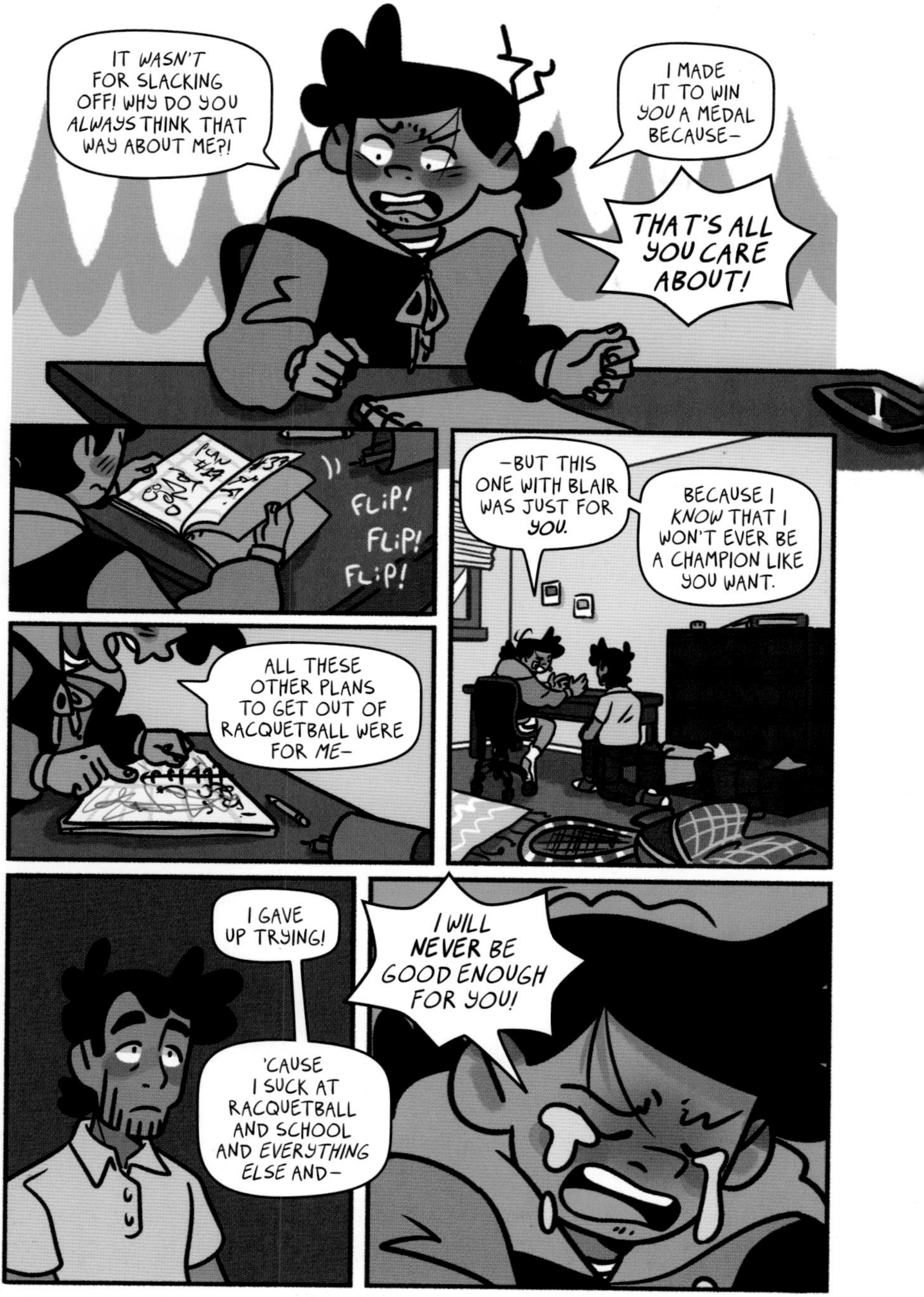
IT WASN'T FOR SLACKING OFF! WHY DO YOU ALWAYS THINK THAT WAY ABOUT ME?!
I MADE IT TO WIN YOU A MEDAL BECAUSE—
THAT'S ALL YOU CARE ABOUT!
FLIP!
FLIP!
FLIP!
—BUT THIS ONE WITH BLAIR WAS JUST FOR YOU.
BECAUSE I KNOW THAT I WON'T EVER BE A CHAMPION LIKE YOU WANT.
ALL THESE OTHER PLANS TO GET OUT OF RACQUETBALL WERE FOR ME—
I GAVE UP TRYING!
'CAUSE I SUCK AT RACQUETBALL AND SCHOOL AND EVERYTHING ELSE AND—
I WILL NEVER BE GOOD ENOUGH FOR YOU!

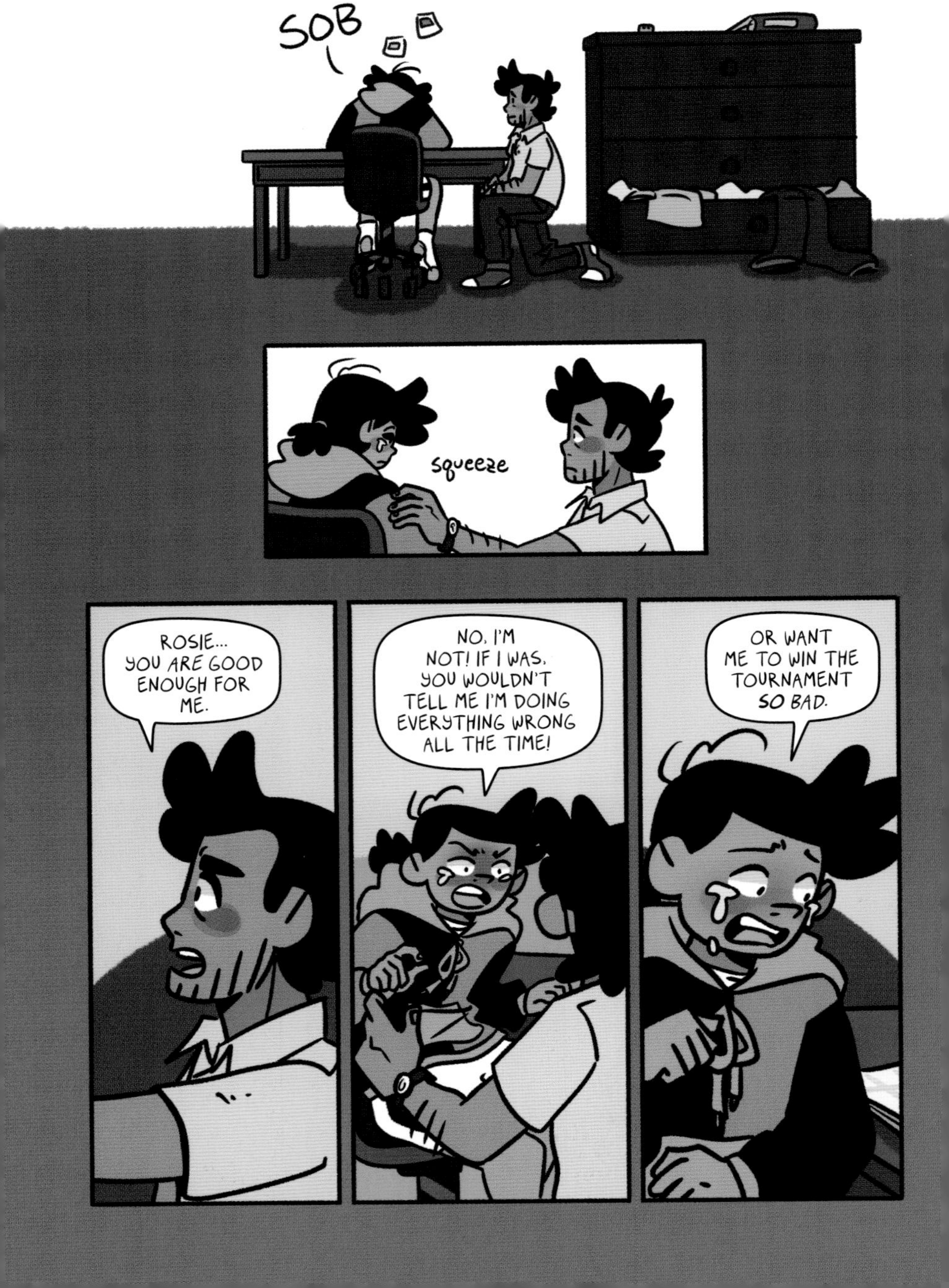
SOB
squeeze
ROSIE... YOU ARE GOOD ENOUGH FOR ME.
NO, I'M NOT! IF I WAS, YOU WOULDN'T TELL ME I'M DOING EVERYTHING WRONG ALL THE TIME!
OR WANT ME TO WIN THE TOURNAMENT SO BAD.

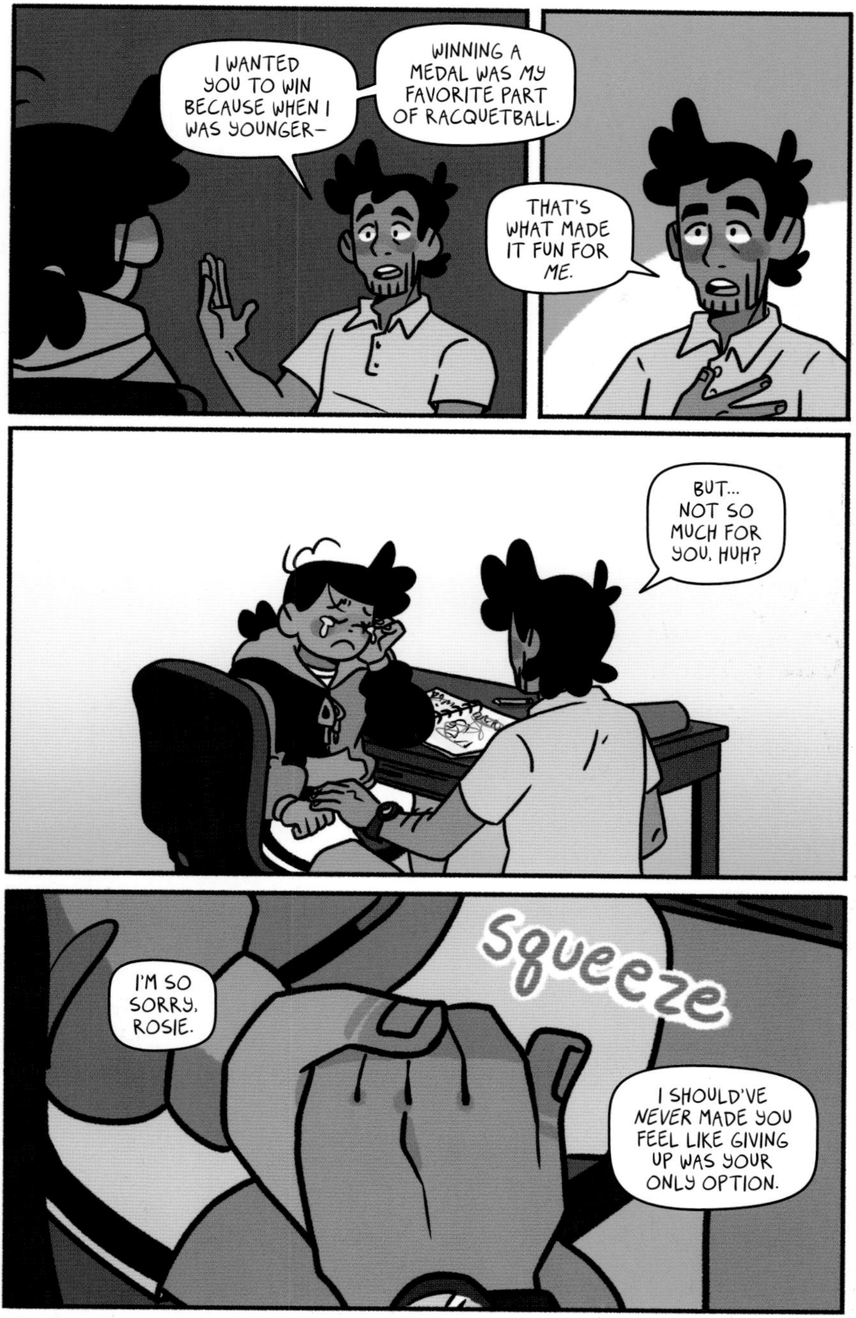
I WANTED YOU TO WIN BECAUSE WHEN I WAS YOUNGER—
WINNING A MEDAL WAS MY FAVORITE PART OF RACQUETBALL.
THAT'S WHAT MADE IT FUN FOR ME.
BUT... NOT SO MUCH FOR YOU, HUH?
SQUEEZE
I'M SO SORRY, ROSIE.
I SHOULD'VE NEVER MADE YOU FEEL LIKE GIVING UP WAS YOUR ONLY OPTION.

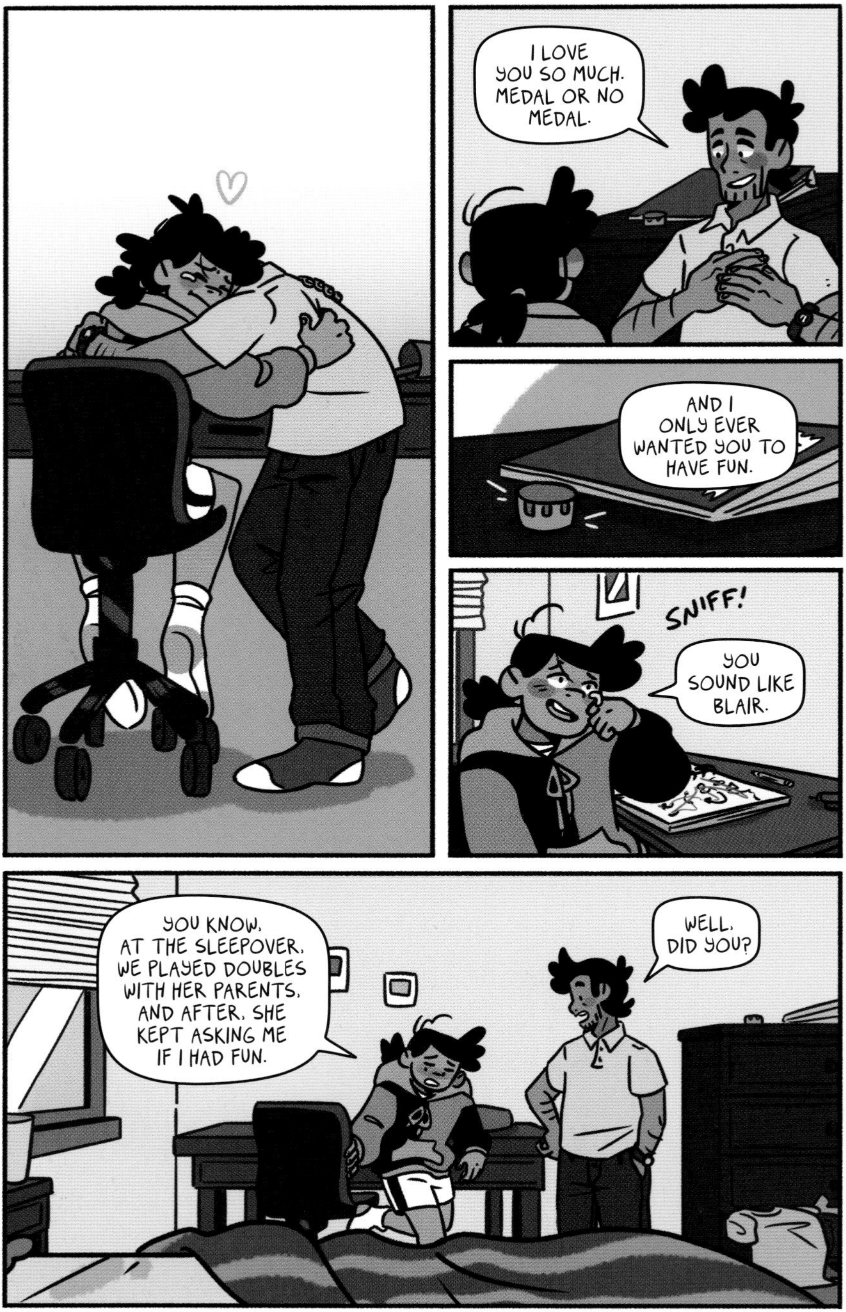
I LOVE YOU SO MUCH. MEDAL OR NO MEDAL.
AND I ONLY EVER WANTED YOU TO HAVE FUN.
SNIFF!
YOU SOUND LIKE BLAIR.
YOU KNOW, AT THE SLEEPOVER, WE PLAYED DOUBLES WITH HER PARENTS, AND AFTER, SHE KEPT ASKING ME IF I HAD FUN.
WELL, DID YOU?

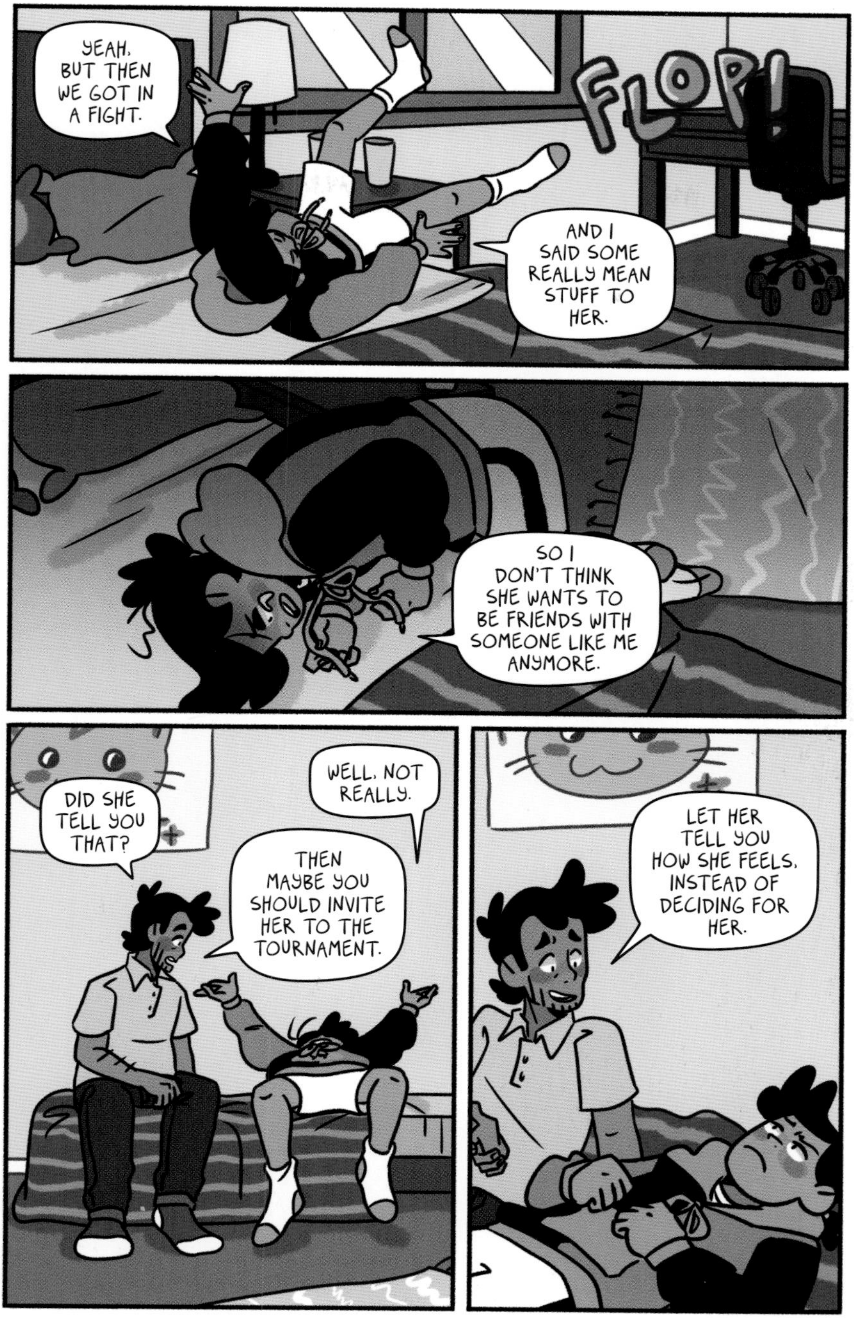
YEAH, BUT THEN WE GOT IN A FIGHT.
FLOP!
AND I SAID SOME REALLY MEAN STUFF TO HER.
SO I DON'T THINK SHE WANTS TO BE FRIENDS WITH SOMEONE LIKE ME ANYMORE.
DID SHE TELL YOU THAT?
WELL, NOT REALLY.
THEN MAYBE YOU SHOULD INVITE HER TO THE TOURNAMENT.
LET HER TELL YOU HOW SHE FEELS, INSTEAD OF DECIDING FOR HER.

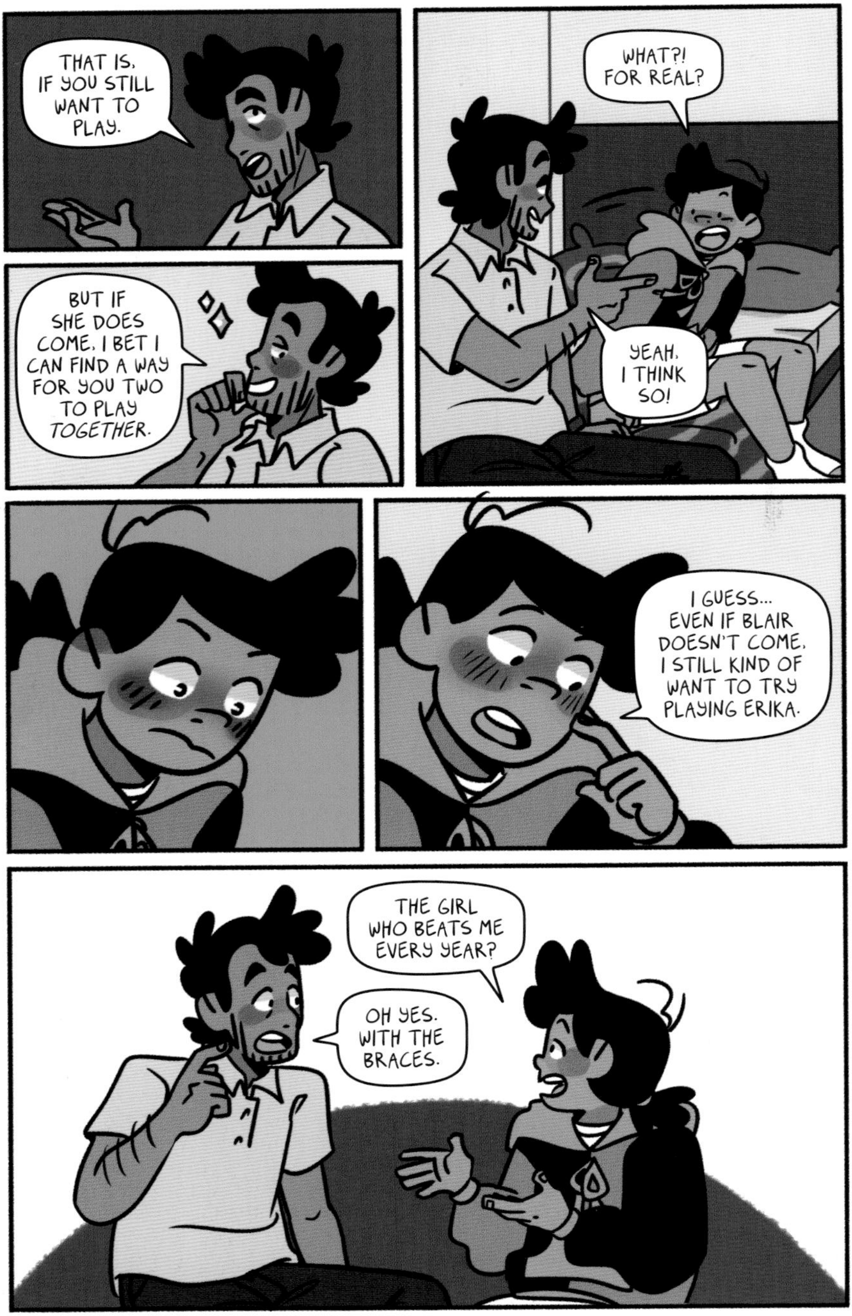

THAT IS, IF YOU STILL WANT TO PLAY.
WHAT?! FOR REAL?
BUT IF SHE DOES COME, I BET I CAN FIND A WAY FOR YOU TWO TO PLAY *TOGETHER*.
YEAH, I THINK SO!
I GUESS... EVEN IF BLAIR DOESN'T COME, I STILL KIND OF WANT TO TRY PLAYING ERIKA.
THE GIRL WHO BEATS ME EVERY YEAR?
OH YES. WITH THE BRACES.

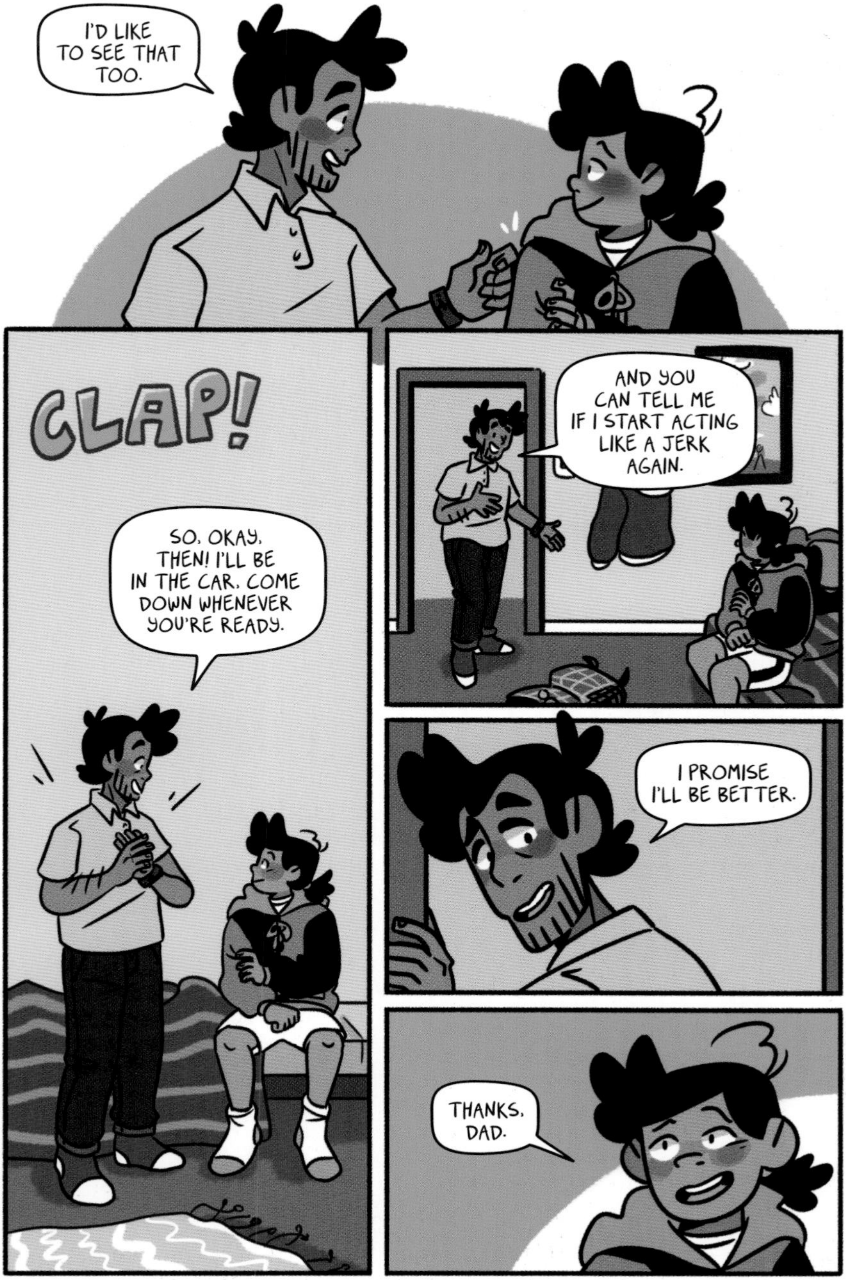
I'D LIKE TO SEE THAT TOO.
CLAP!
SO, OKAY, THEN! I'LL BE IN THE CAR. COME DOWN WHENEVER YOU'RE READY.
AND YOU CAN TELL ME IF I START ACTING LIKE A JERK AGAIN.
I PROMISE I'LL BE BETTER.
THANKS, DAD.

BLAIR!!

blair i kno ive been a jerk this week n i gotta say a lotta stuff to u but im about to leave for the tournament

if u can pls come early, ur fam is totally invited too

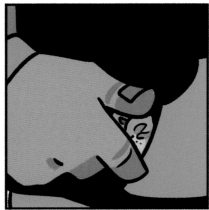

CHAPTER 10

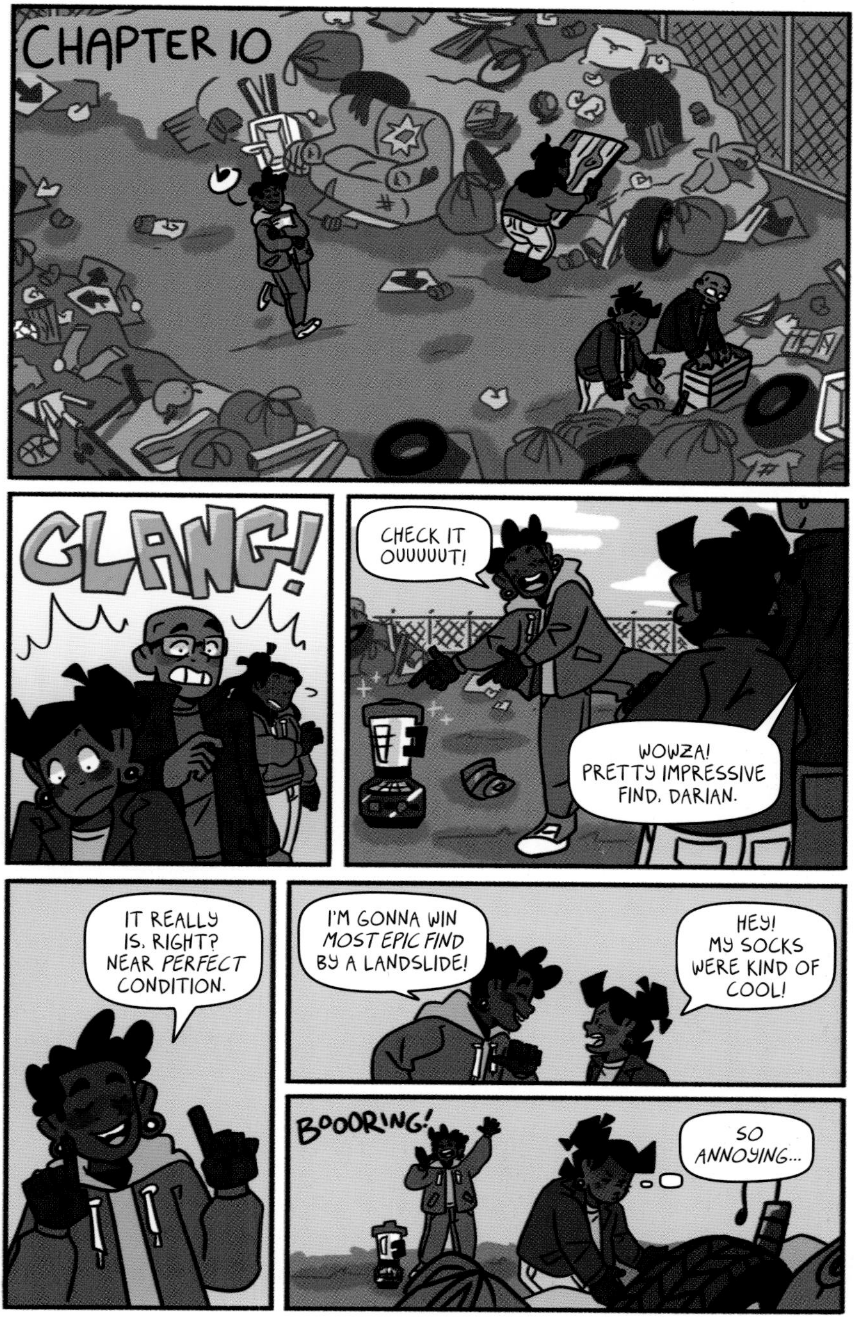
CLANG!
CHECK IT OUUUUUT!
WOWZA! PRETTY IMPRESSIVE FIND, DARIAN.
IT REALLY IS, RIGHT? NEAR PERFECT CONDITION.
I'M GONNA WIN MOST EPIC FIND BY A LANDSLIDE!
HEY! MY SOCKS WERE KIND OF COOL!
BOOORING!
SO ANNOYING...

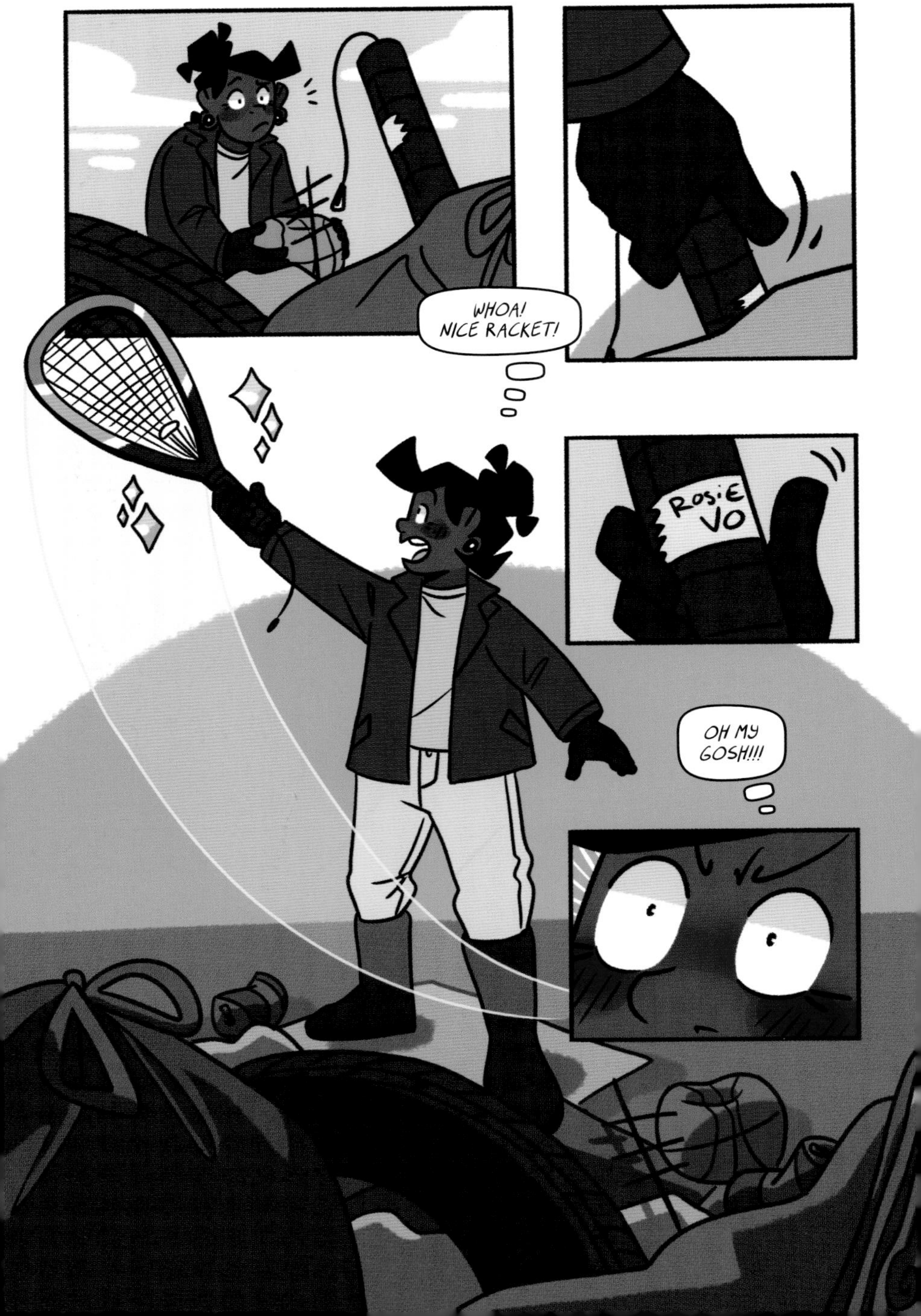
WHOA!
NICE RACKET!
ROSIE
VO
OH MY
GOSH!!!

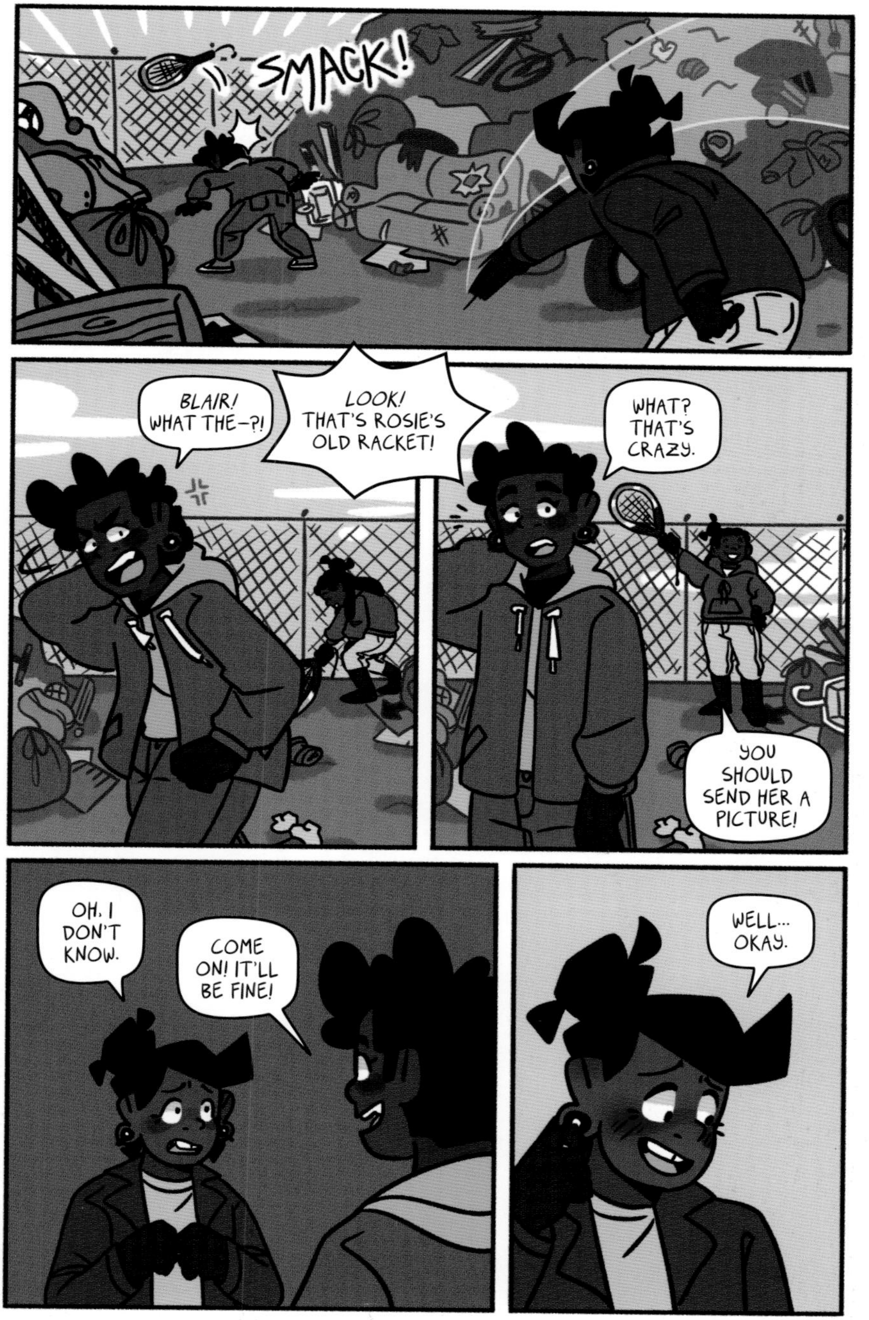
SMACK!
BLAIR! WHAT THE–?!
LOOK! THAT'S ROSIE'S OLD RACKET!
WHAT? THAT'S CRAZY.
YOU SHOULD SEND HER A PICTURE!
OH, I DON'T KNOW.
COME ON! IT'LL BE FINE!
WELL... OKAY.

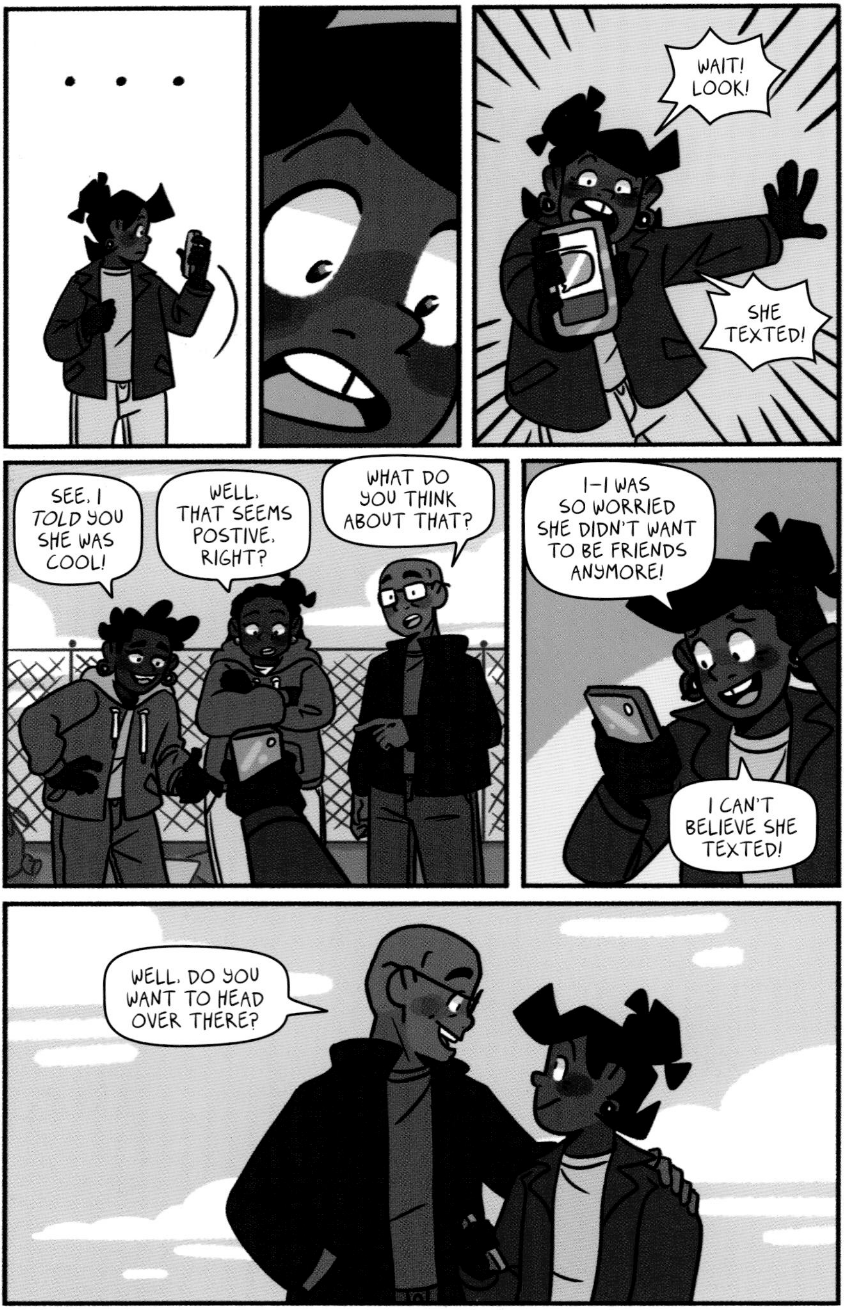
. . .
WAIT! LOOK!
SHE TEXTED!
SEE, I TOLD YOU SHE WAS COOL!
WELL, THAT SEEMS POSTIVE, RIGHT?
WHAT DO YOU THINK ABOUT THAT?
I-I WAS SO WORRIED SHE DIDN'T WANT TO BE FRIENDS ANYMORE!
I CAN'T BELIEVE SHE TEXTED!
WELL, DO YOU WANT TO HEAD OVER THERE?

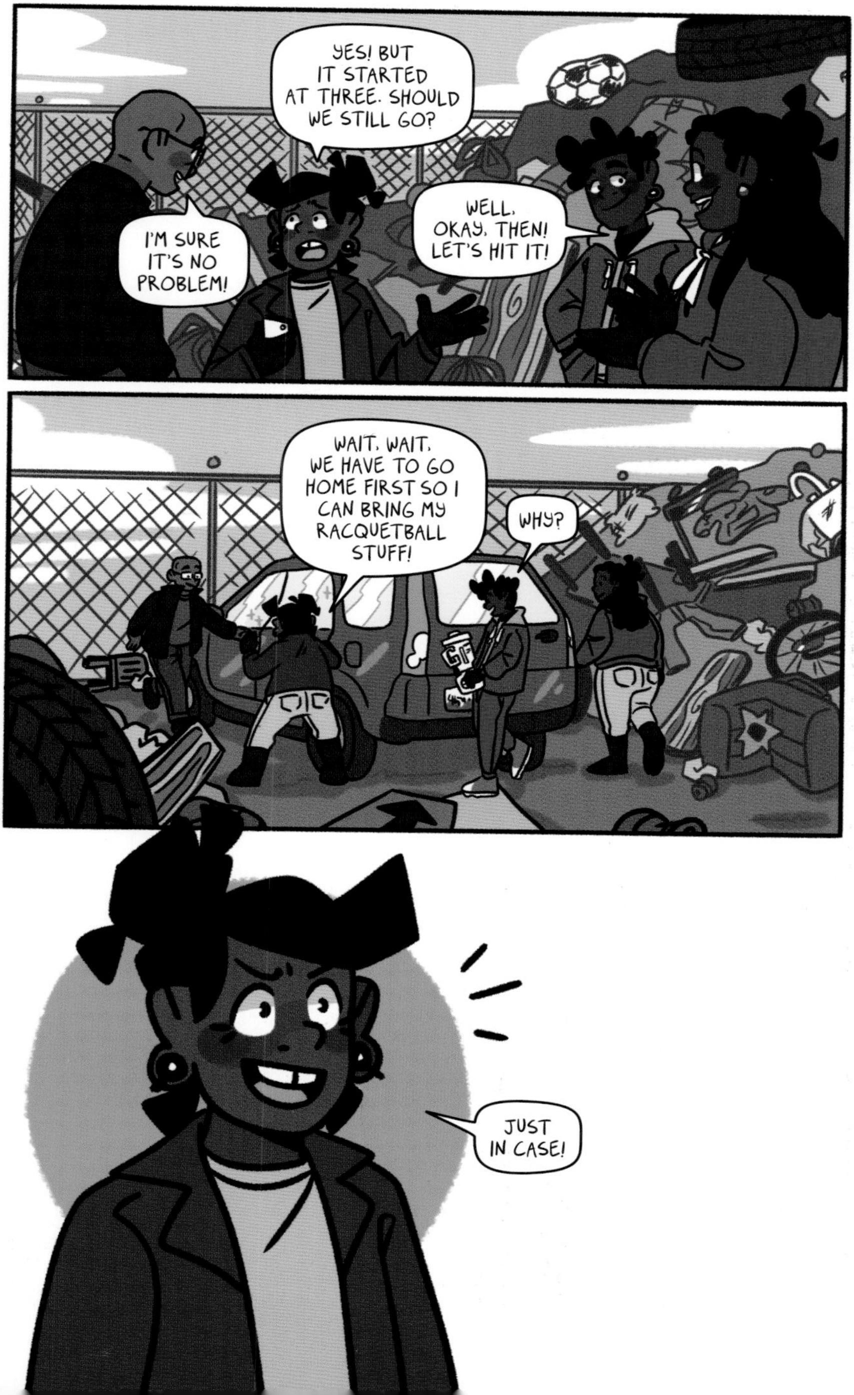
YES! BUT IT STARTED AT THREE. SHOULD WE STILL GO?
I'M SURE IT'S NO PROBLEM!
WELL, OKAY, THEN! LET'S HIT IT!
WAIT, WAIT, WE HAVE TO GO HOME FIRST SO I CAN BRING MY RACQUETBALL STUFF!
WHY?
JUST IN CASE!

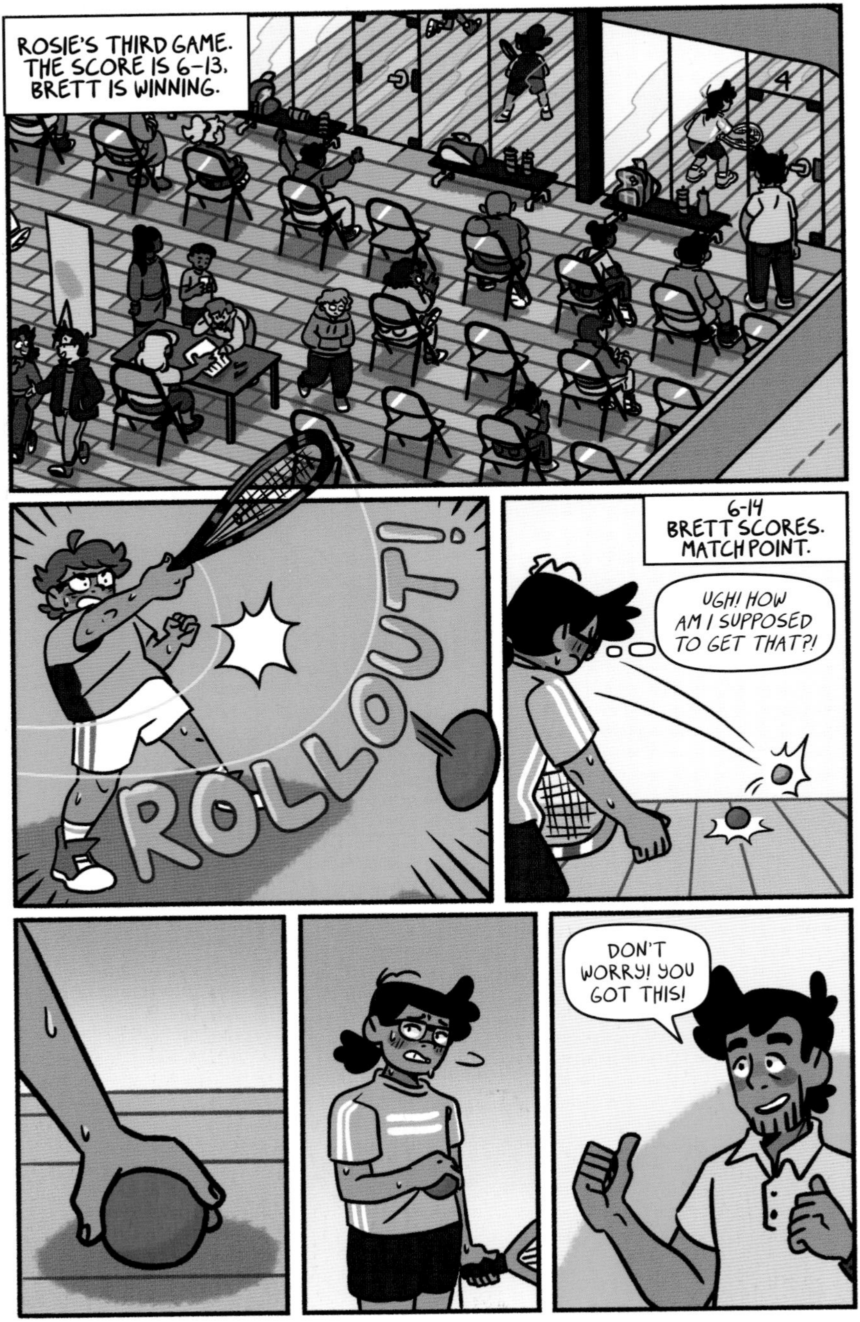
ROSIE'S THIRD GAME. THE SCORE IS 6–13. BRETT IS WINNING.
4
ROLLOUT!
6-14 BRETT SCORES. MATCH POINT.
UGH! HOW AM I SUPPOSED TO GET THAT?!
DON'T WORRY! YOU GOT THIS!

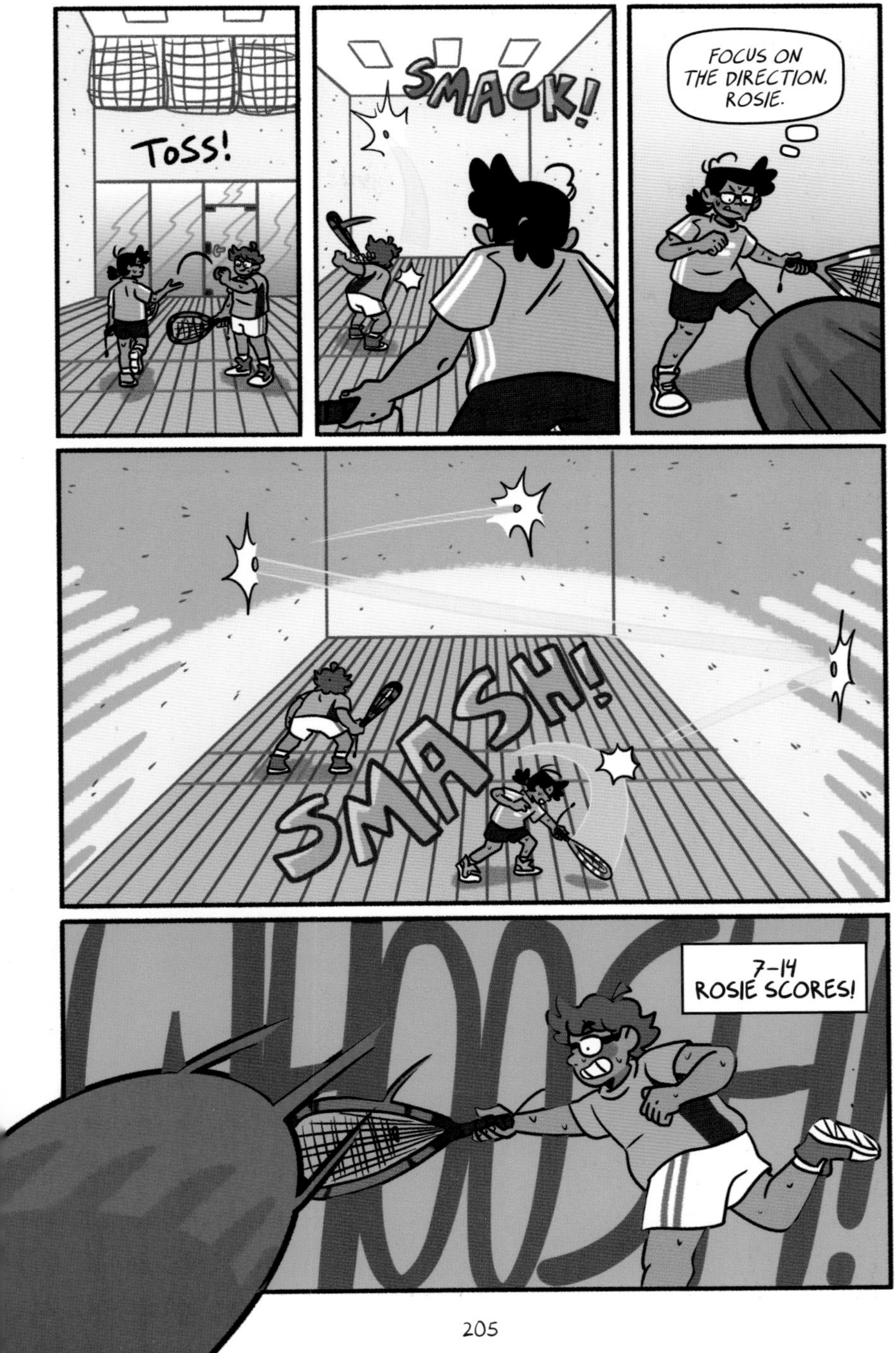
TOSS!
SMACK!
FOCUS ON THE DIRECTION, ROSIE.
SMASH!
7–14
ROSIE SCORES!

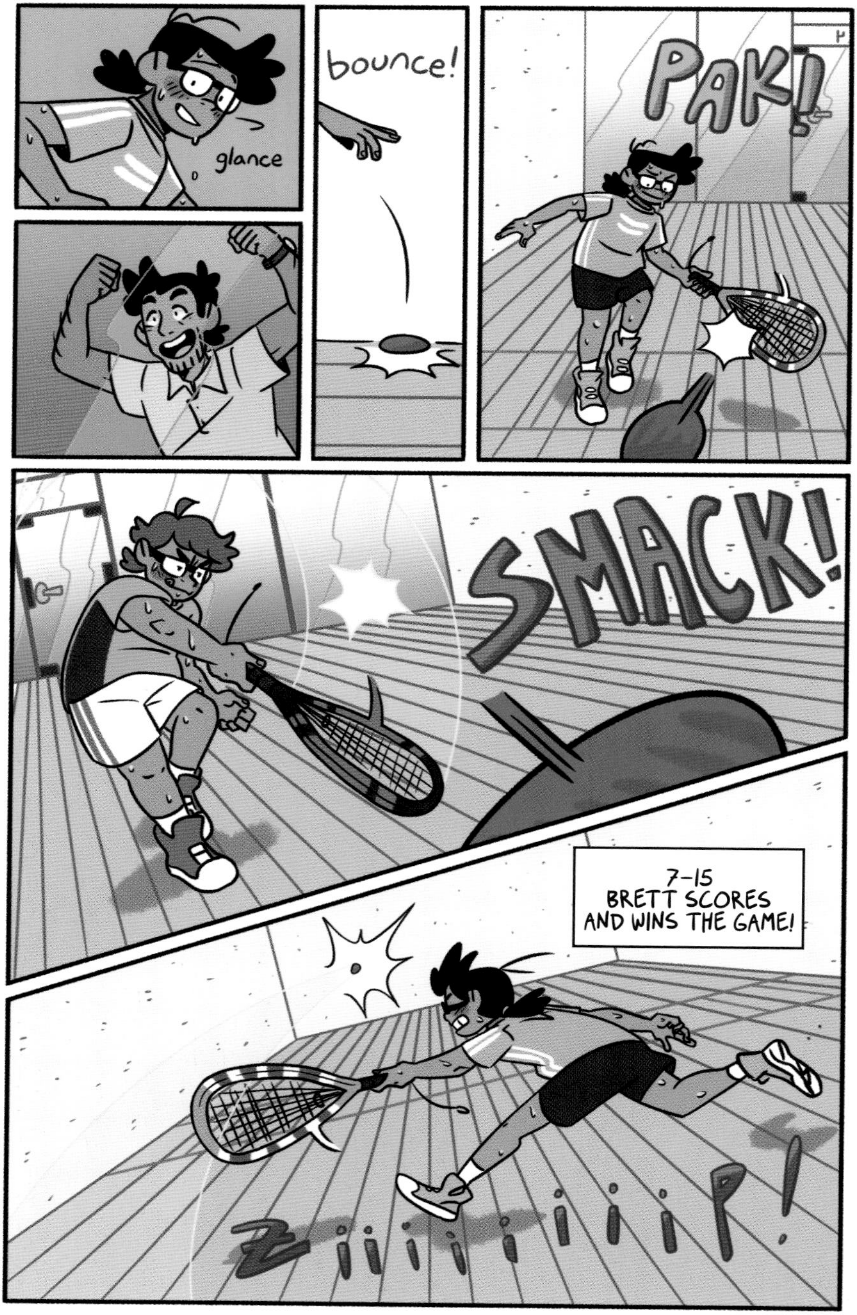
glance
bounce!
PAK!
SMACK!
7–15
BRETT SCORES
AND WINS THE GAME!
ZIIIIIIIP!

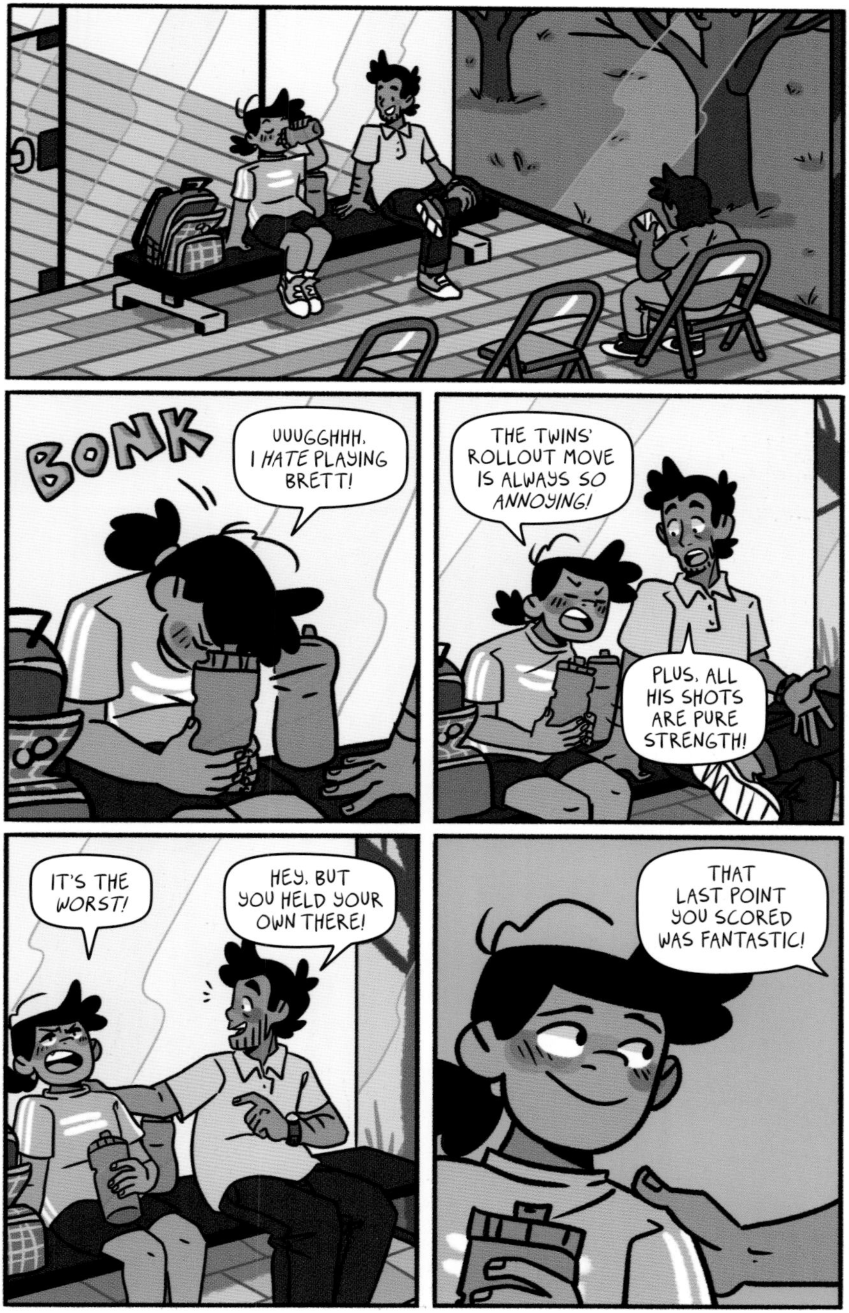
BONK
UUUGGHHH, I HATE PLAYING BRETT!
THE TWINS' ROLLOUT MOVE IS ALWAYS SO ANNOYING!
PLUS, ALL HIS SHOTS ARE PURE STRENGTH!
IT'S THE WORST!
HEY, BUT YOU HELD YOUR OWN THERE!
THAT LAST POINT YOU SCORED WAS FANTASTIC!

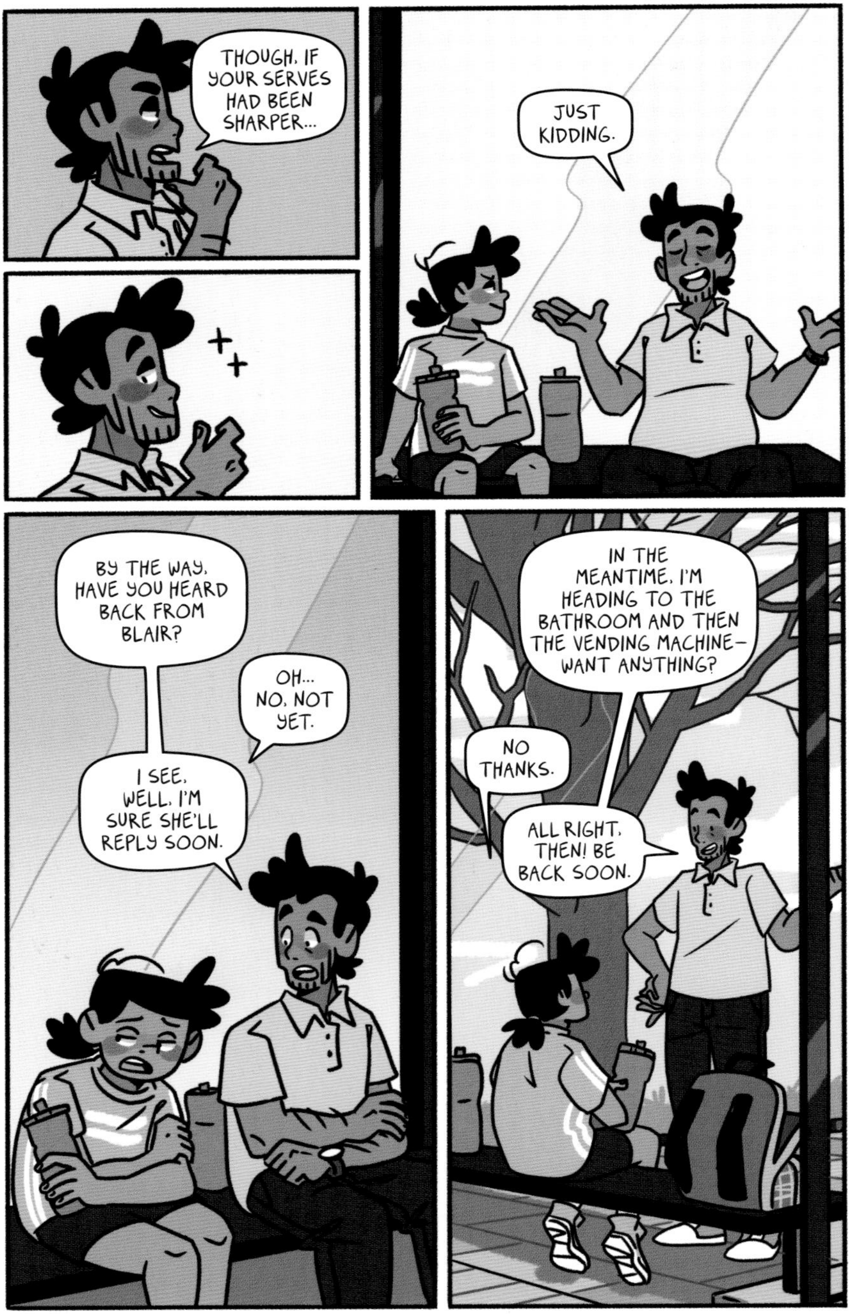
THOUGH, IF YOUR SERVES HAD BEEN SHARPER...
JUST KIDDING.
BY THE WAY, HAVE YOU HEARD BACK FROM BLAIR?
OH... NO, NOT YET.
I SEE. WELL, I'M SURE SHE'LL REPLY SOON.
IN THE MEANTIME, I'M HEADING TO THE BATHROOM AND THEN THE VENDING MACHINE— WANT ANYTHING?
NO THANKS.
ALL RIGHT, THEN! BE BACK SOON.

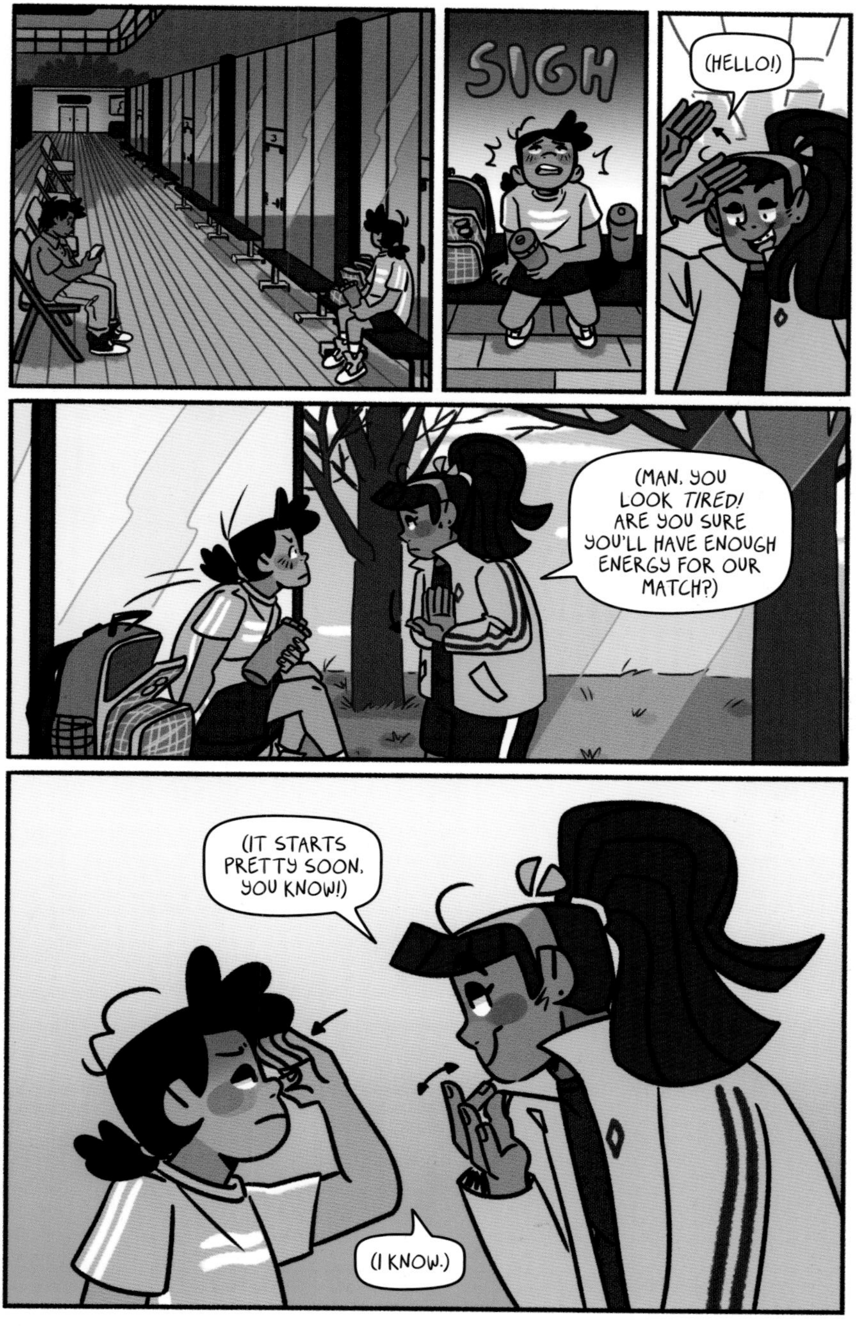
SIGH
(HELLO!)
(MAN, YOU LOOK TIRED! ARE YOU SURE YOU'LL HAVE ENOUGH ENERGY FOR OUR MATCH?)
(IT STARTS PRETTY SOON, YOU KNOW!)
(I KNOW.)

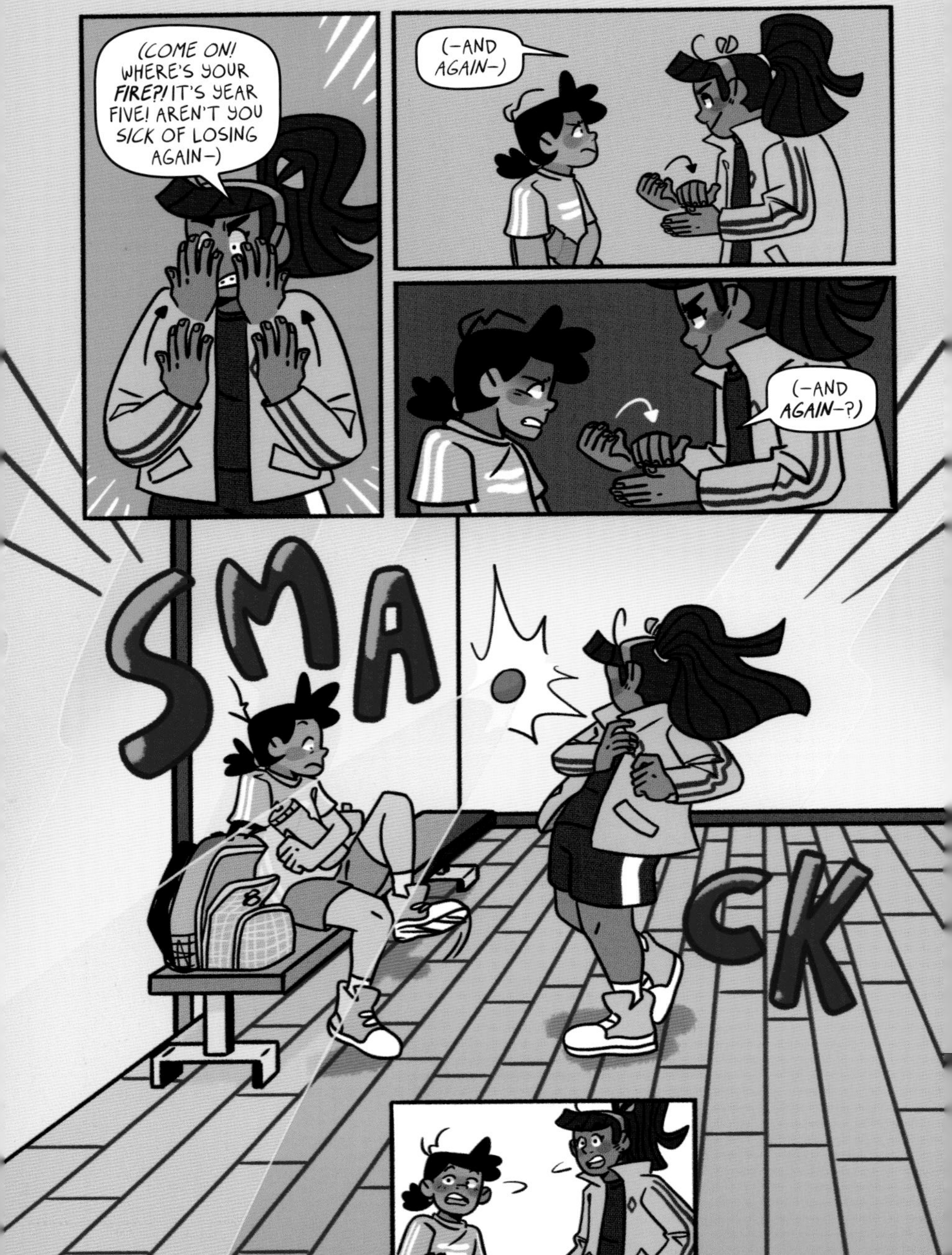
(COME ON! WHERE'S YOUR FIRE?! IT'S YEAR FIVE! AREN'T YOU SICK OF LOSING AGAIN–)
(–AND AGAIN–)
(–AND AGAIN–?)
SMACK

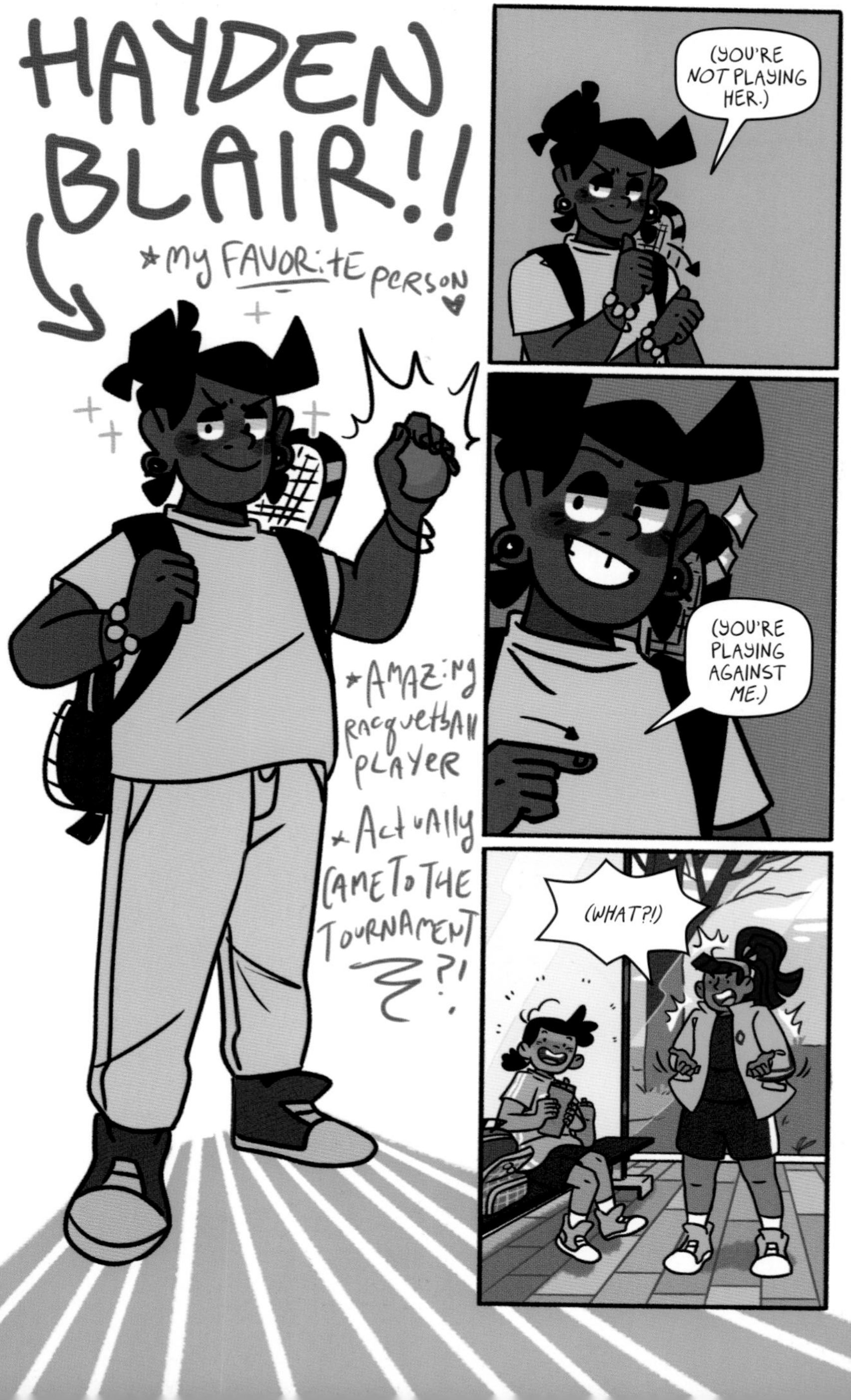
HAYDEN BLAIR!!
* my FAVORite person
* AMAZing racquetball player
* Actually CAME To THE TOURNAMENT ?!
(YOU'RE NOT PLAYING HER.)
(YOU'RE PLAYING AGAINST ME.)
(WHAT?!)

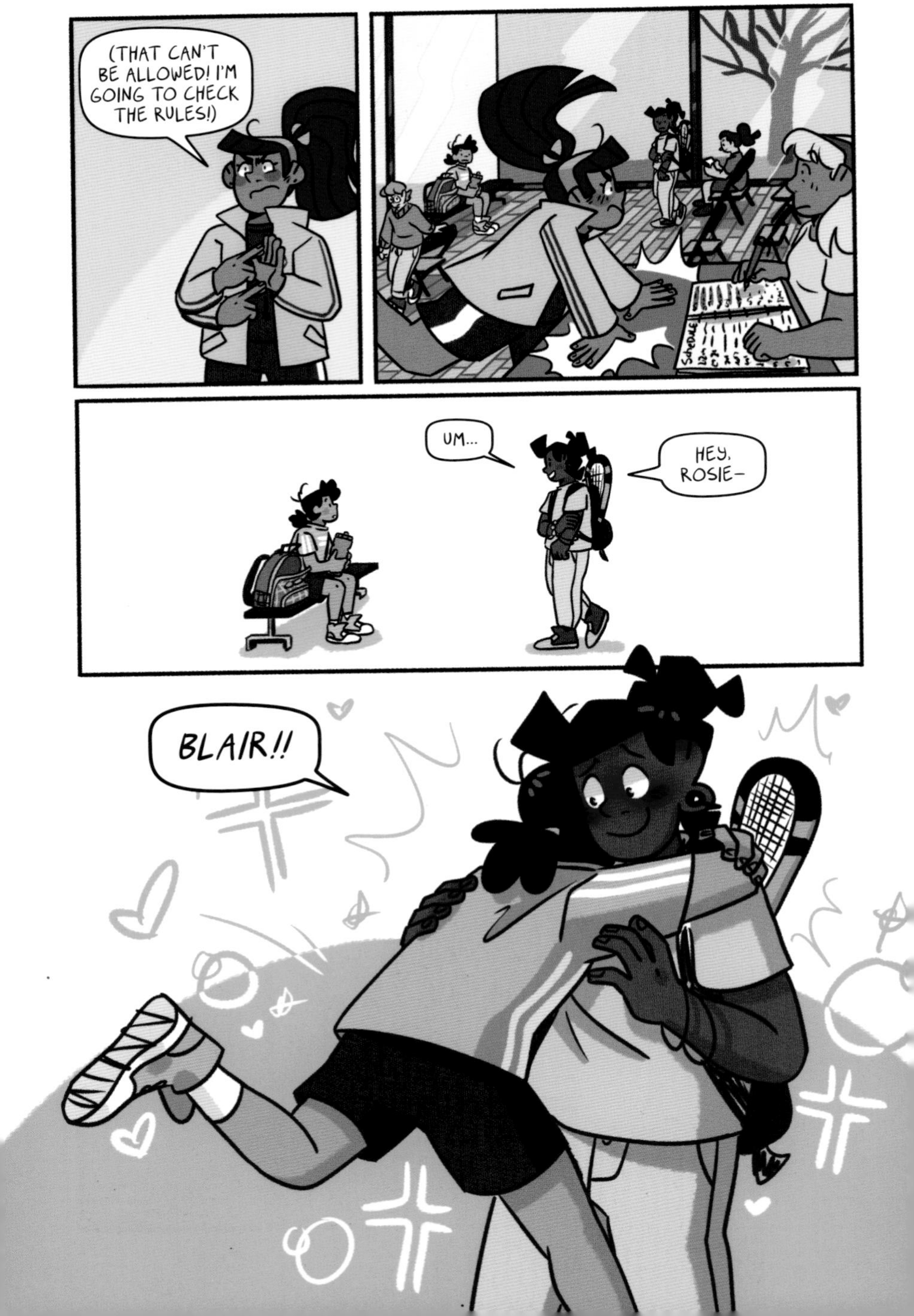
(THAT CAN'T BE ALLOWED! I'M GOING TO CHECK THE RULES!)
HEY, ROSIE—
UM...
BLAIR!!

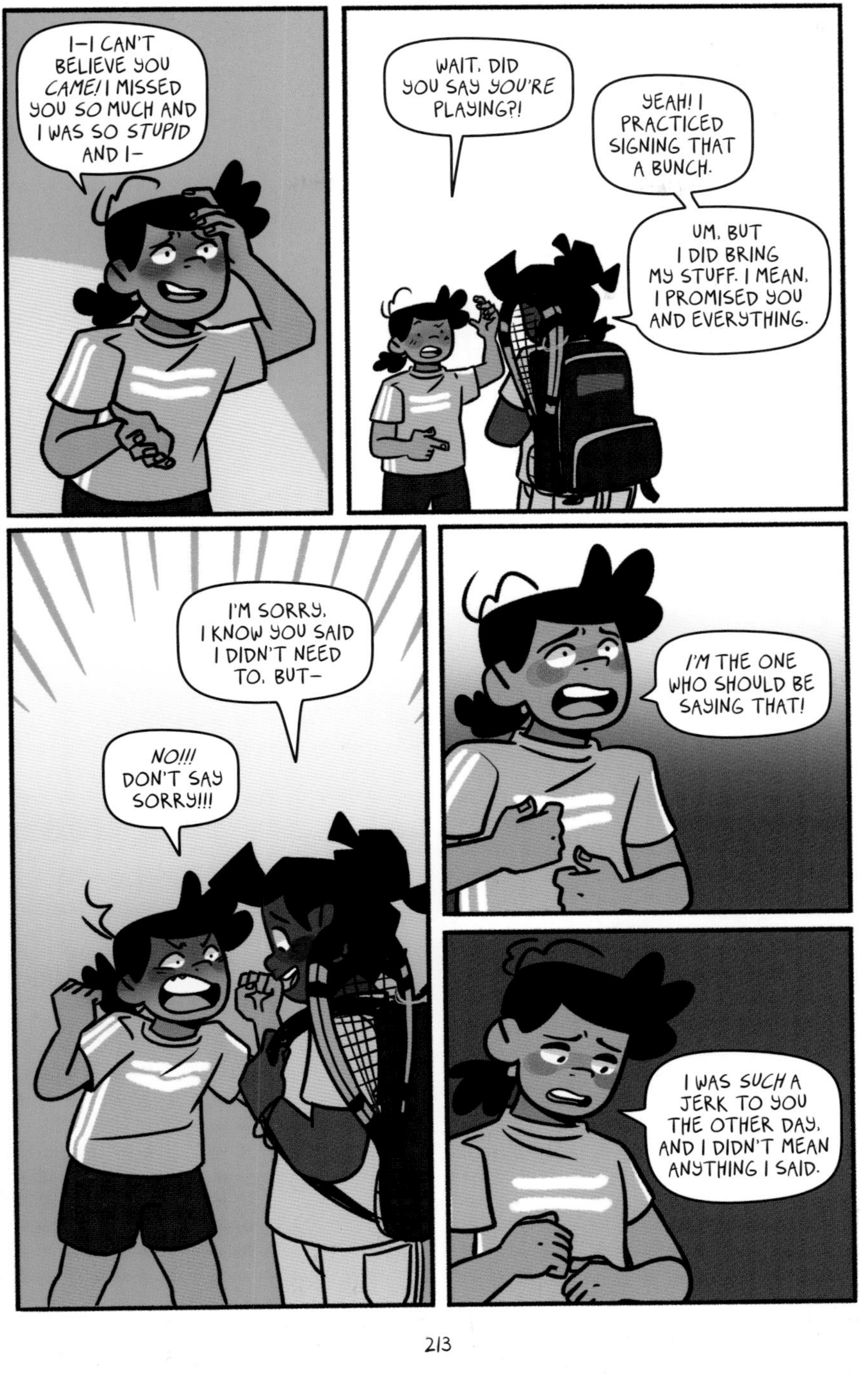
I-I CAN'T BELIEVE YOU CAME! I MISSED YOU SO MUCH AND I WAS SO STUPID AND I-
WAIT. DID YOU SAY YOU'RE PLAYING?!
YEAH! I PRACTICED SIGNING THAT A BUNCH.
UM. BUT I DID BRING MY STUFF. I MEAN. I PROMISED YOU AND EVERYTHING.
I'M SORRY. I KNOW YOU SAID I DIDN'T NEED TO. BUT-
NO!!! DON'T SAY SORRY!!!
I'M THE ONE WHO SHOULD BE SAYING THAT!
I WAS SUCH A JERK TO YOU THE OTHER DAY. AND I DIDN'T MEAN ANYTHING I SAID.

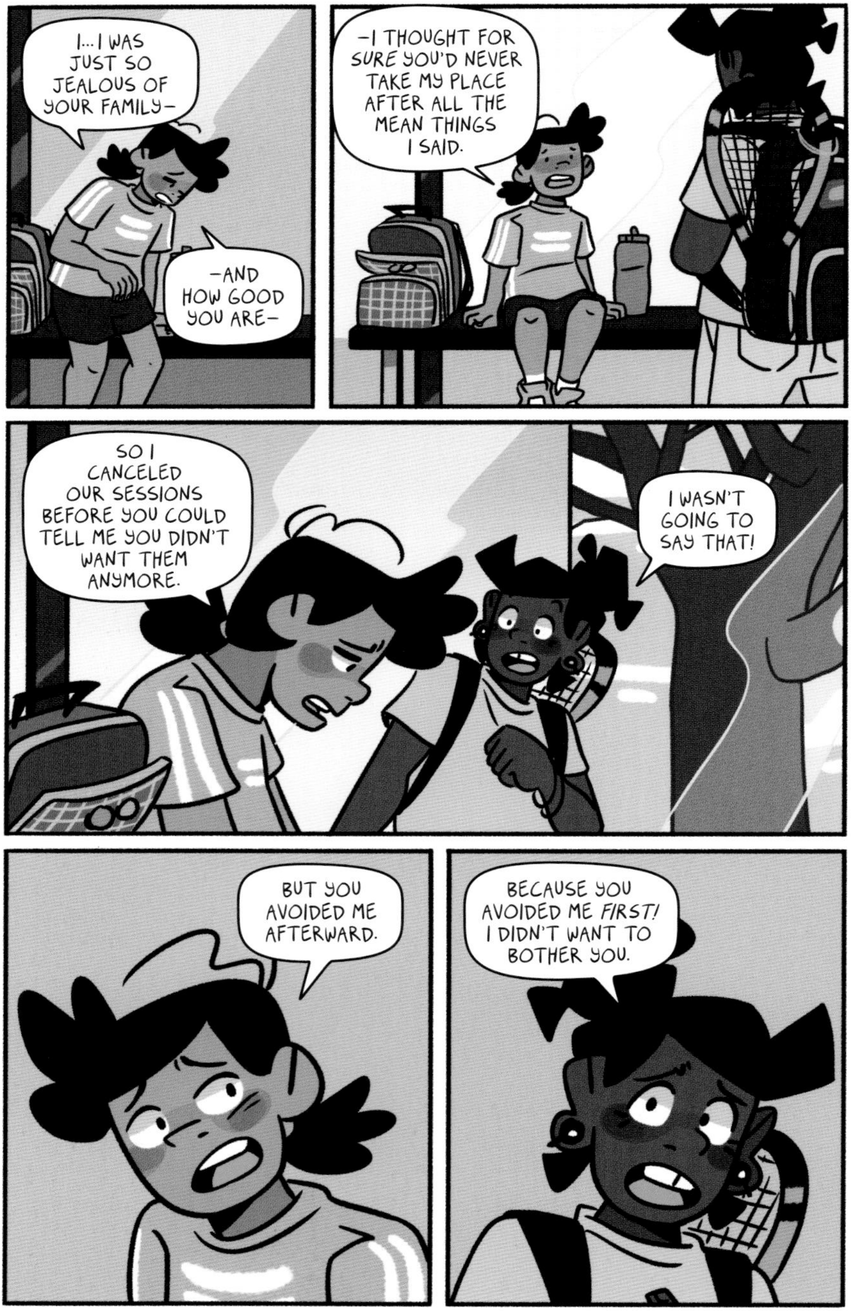
I...I WAS JUST SO JEALOUS OF YOUR FAMILY—
—AND HOW GOOD YOU ARE—
—I THOUGHT FOR SURE YOU'D NEVER TAKE MY PLACE AFTER ALL THE MEAN THINGS I SAID.
SO I CANCELED OUR SESSIONS BEFORE YOU COULD TELL ME YOU DIDN'T WANT THEM ANYMORE.
I WASN'T GOING TO SAY THAT!
BUT YOU AVOIDED ME AFTERWARD.
BECAUSE YOU AVOIDED ME *FIRST!* I DIDN'T WANT TO BOTHER YOU.

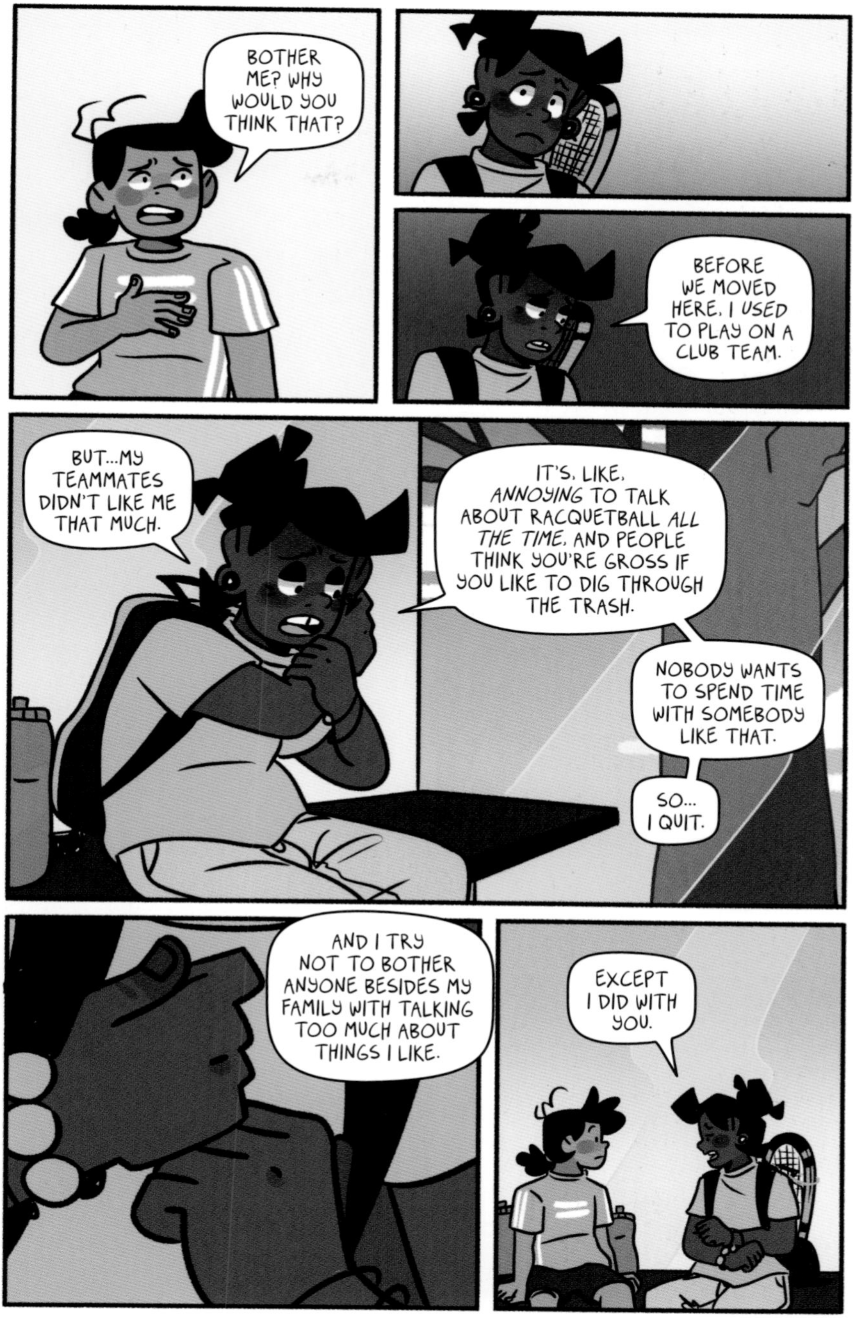
BOTHER ME? WHY WOULD YOU THINK THAT?
BEFORE WE MOVED HERE, I USED TO PLAY ON A CLUB TEAM.
BUT...MY TEAMMATES DIDN'T LIKE ME THAT MUCH.
IT'S, LIKE, *ANNOYING* TO TALK ABOUT RACQUETBALL *ALL THE TIME*, AND PEOPLE THINK YOU'RE GROSS IF YOU LIKE TO DIG THROUGH THE TRASH.
NOBODY WANTS TO SPEND TIME WITH SOMEBODY LIKE THAT.
SO... I QUIT.
AND I TRY NOT TO BOTHER ANYONE BESIDES MY FAMILY WITH TALKING TOO MUCH ABOUT THINGS I LIKE.
EXCEPT I DID WITH YOU.

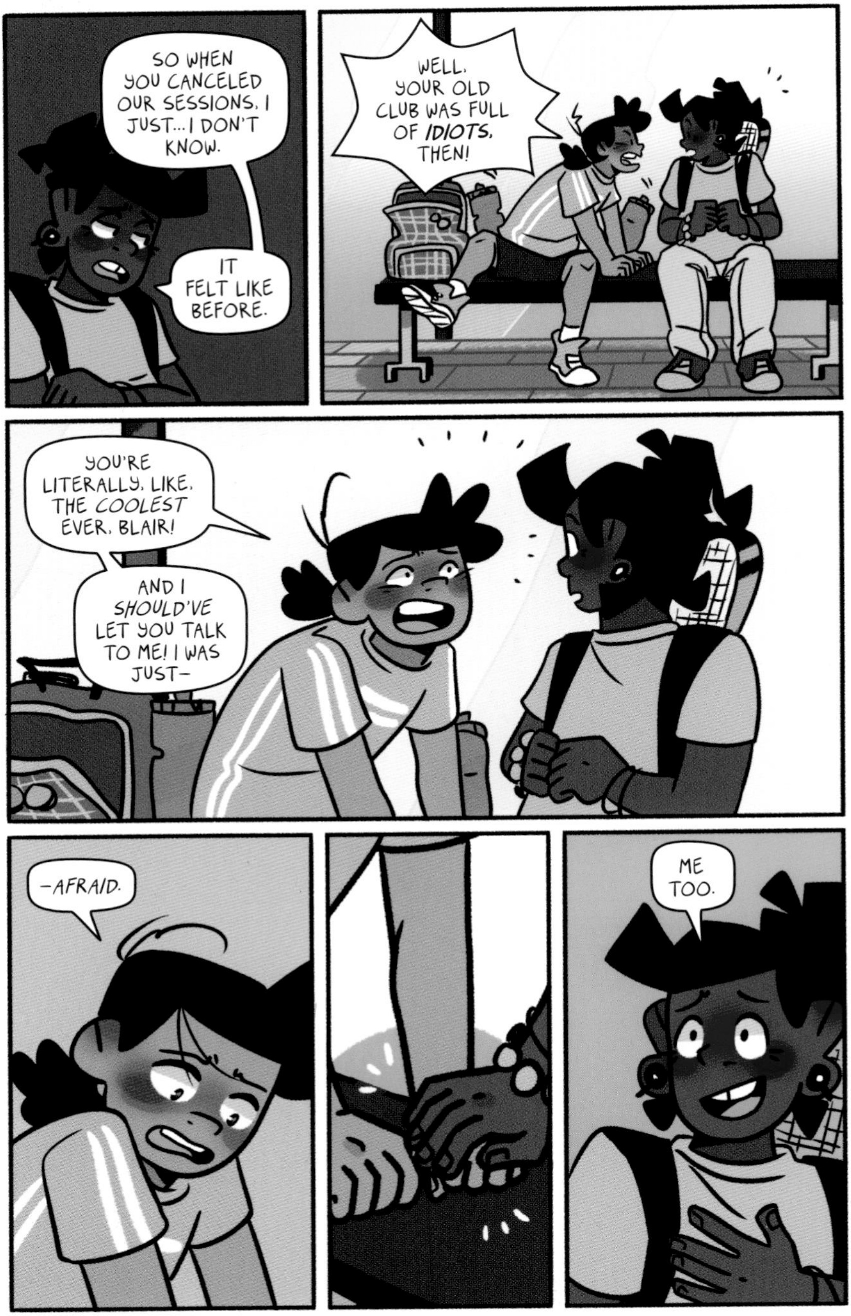
SO WHEN YOU CANCELED OUR SESSIONS, I JUST...I DON'T KNOW.
IT FELT LIKE BEFORE.
WELL, YOUR OLD CLUB WAS FULL OF *IDIOTS*, THEN!
YOU'RE LITERALLY, LIKE, THE *COOLEST* EVER, BLAIR!
AND I *SHOULD'VE* LET YOU TALK TO ME! I WAS JUST—
—*AFRAID*.
ME TOO.

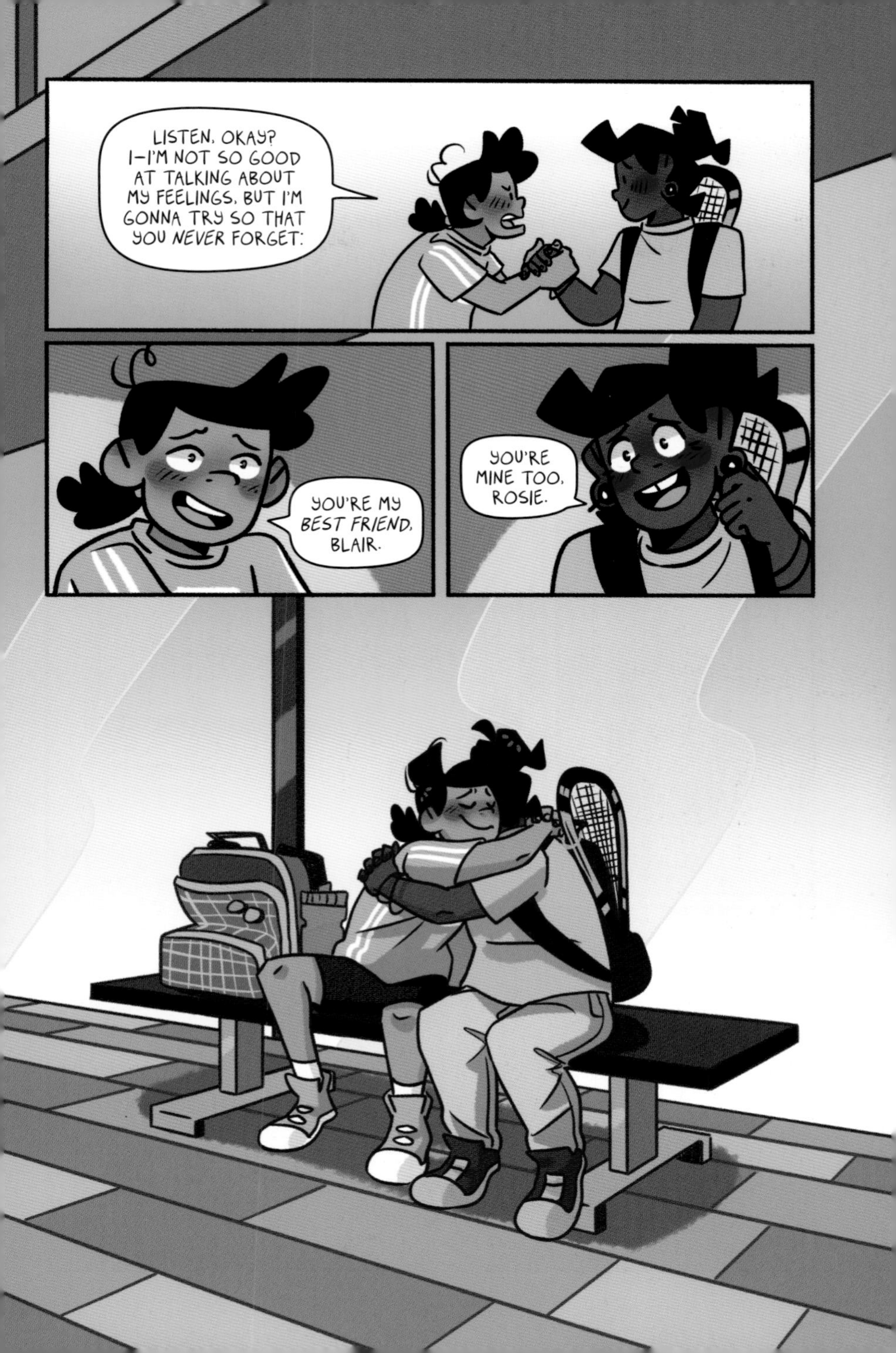
LISTEN, OKAY? I—I'M NOT SO GOOD AT TALKING ABOUT MY FEELINGS, BUT I'M GONNA TRY SO THAT YOU *NEVER* FORGET:
YOU'RE MY *BEST FRIEND*, BLAIR.
YOU'RE MINE TOO, ROSIE.

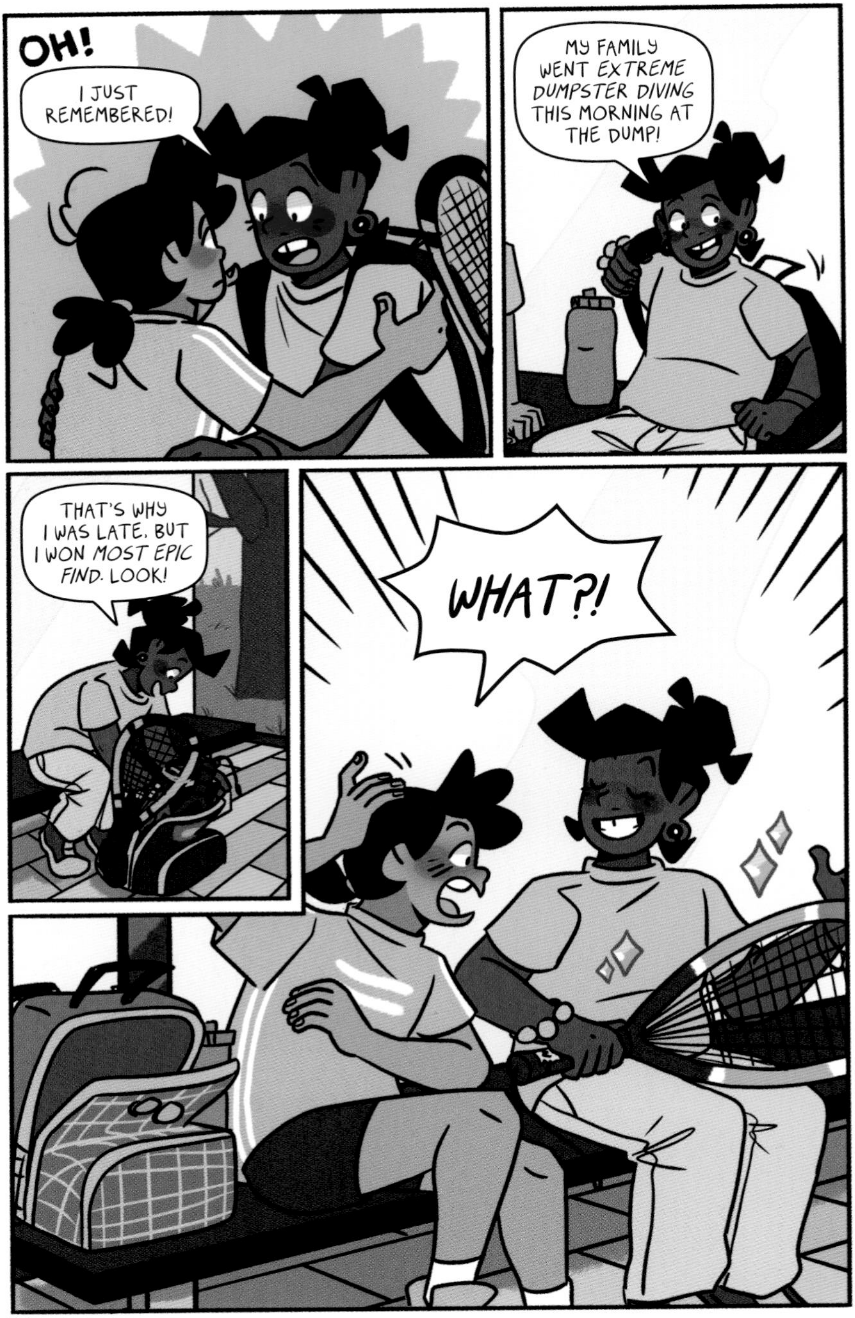
OH!
I JUST REMEMBERED!
MY FAMILY WENT EXTREME DUMPSTER DIVING THIS MORNING AT THE DUMP!
THAT'S WHY I WAS LATE, BUT I WON MOST EPIC FIND. LOOK!
WHAT?!

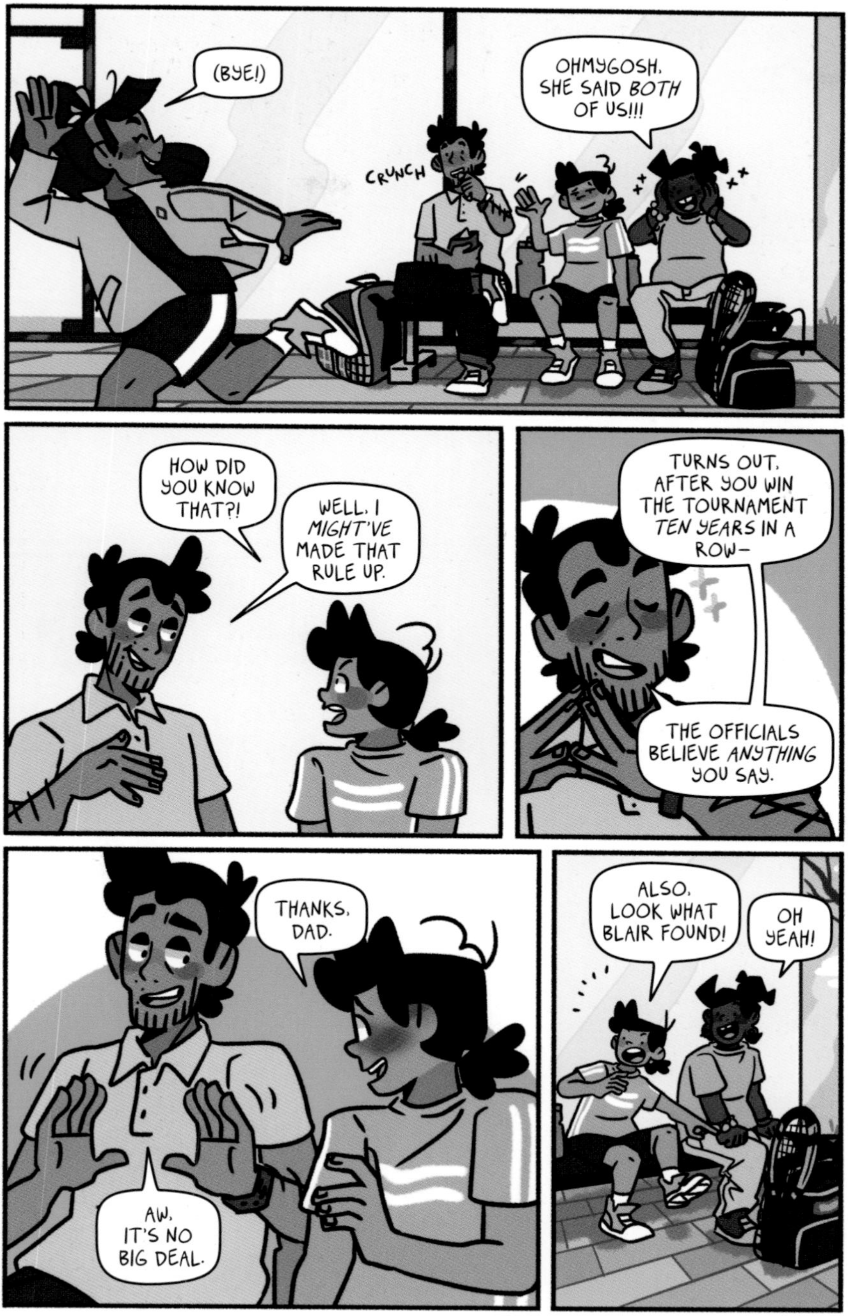
(BYE!)
OHMYGOSH, SHE SAID BOTH OF US!!!
CRUNCH
HOW DID YOU KNOW THAT?!
WELL, I MIGHT'VE MADE THAT RULE UP.
TURNS OUT, AFTER YOU WIN THE TOURNAMENT TEN YEARS IN A ROW—
THE OFFICIALS BELIEVE ANYTHING YOU SAY.
THANKS, DAD.
AW, IT'S NO BIG DEAL.
ALSO, LOOK WHAT BLAIR FOUND!
OH YEAH!

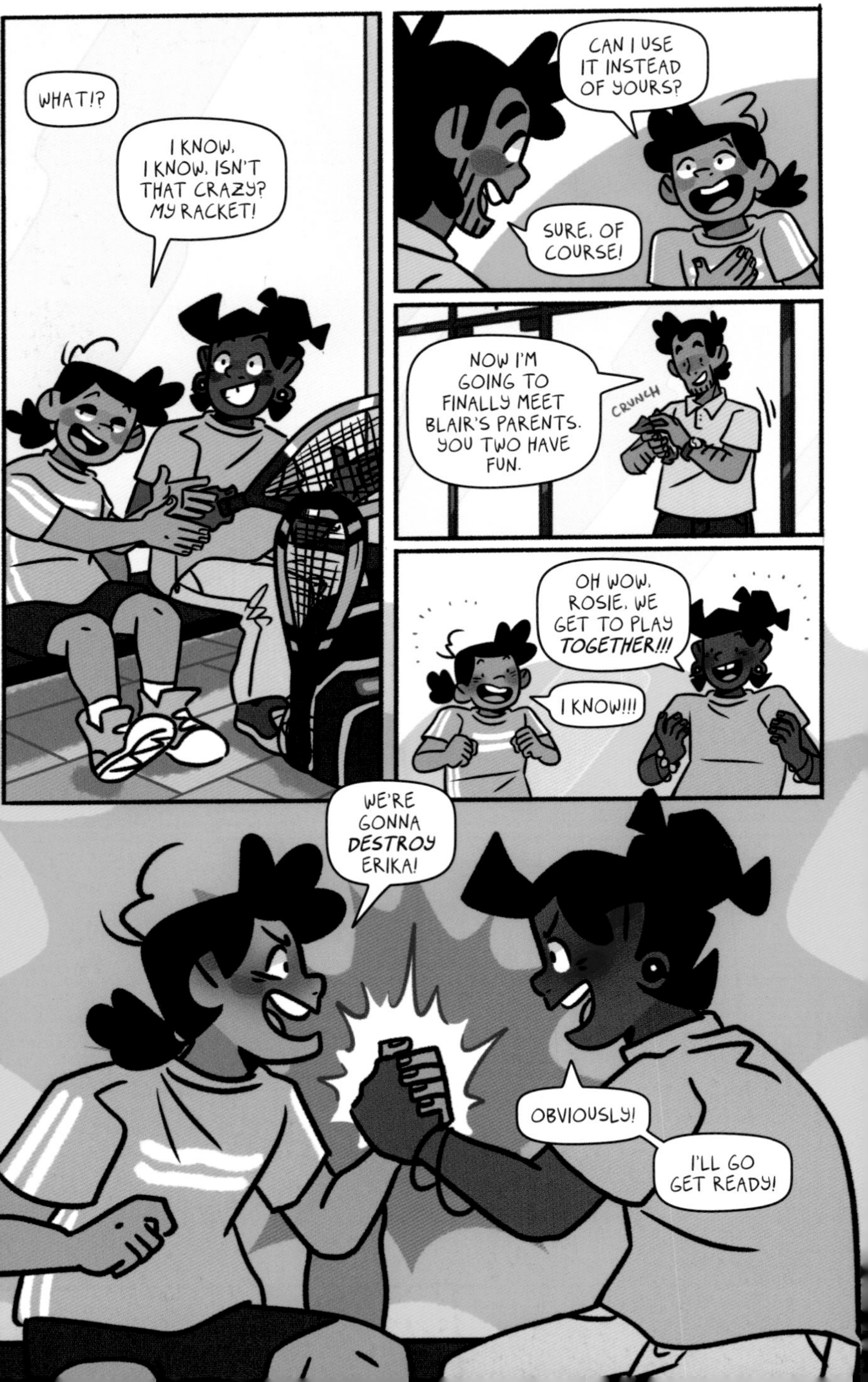
WHAT!?
I KNOW, I KNOW, ISN'T THAT CRAZY? MY RACKET!
CAN I USE IT INSTEAD OF YOURS?
SURE, OF COURSE!
NOW I'M GOING TO FINALLY MEET BLAIR'S PARENTS. YOU TWO HAVE FUN.
CRUNCH
OH WOW, ROSIE, WE GET TO PLAY TOGETHER!!!
I KNOW!!!
WE'RE GONNA DESTROY ERIKA!
OBVIOUSLY!
I'LL GO GET READY!

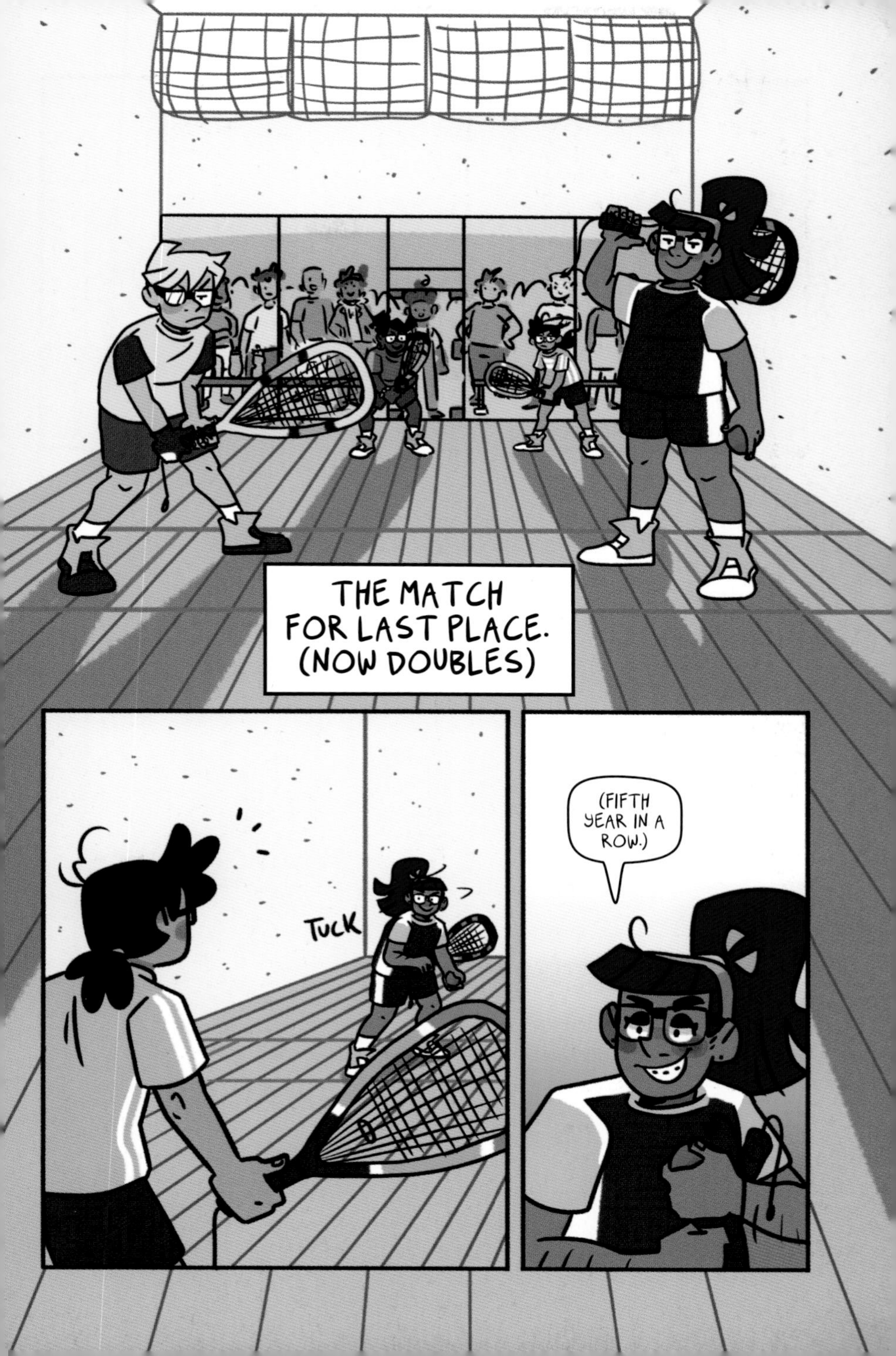
THE MATCH
FOR LAST PLACE.
(NOW DOUBLES)
TUCK
(FIFTH
YEAR IN A
ROW.)

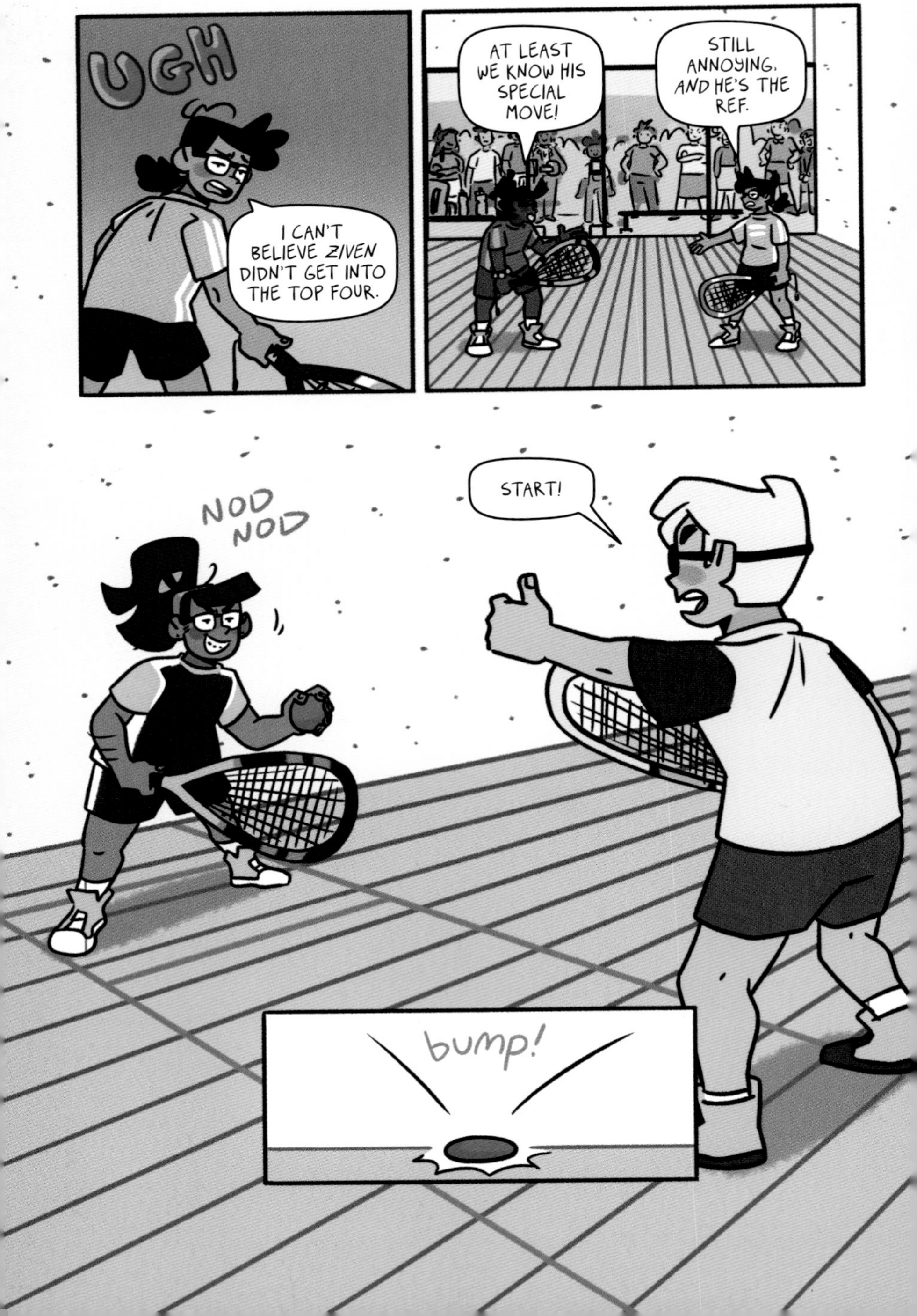
UGH
I CAN'T BELIEVE ZIVEN DIDN'T GET INTO THE TOP FOUR.
AT LEAST WE KNOW HIS SPECIAL MOVE!
STILL ANNOYING. AND HE'S THE REF.
NOD NOD
START!
bump!

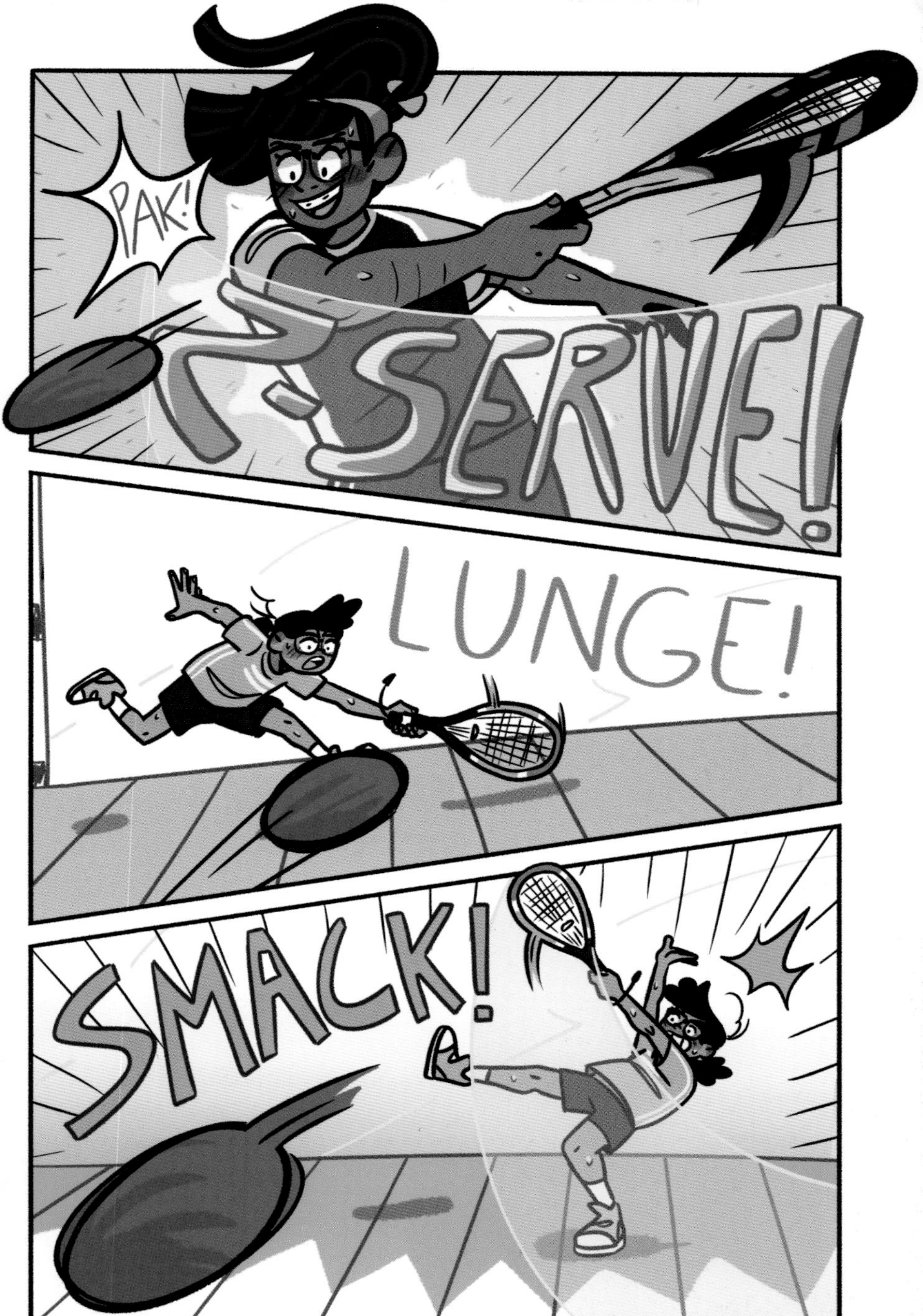
PAK!
SERVE!
LUNGE!
SMACK!

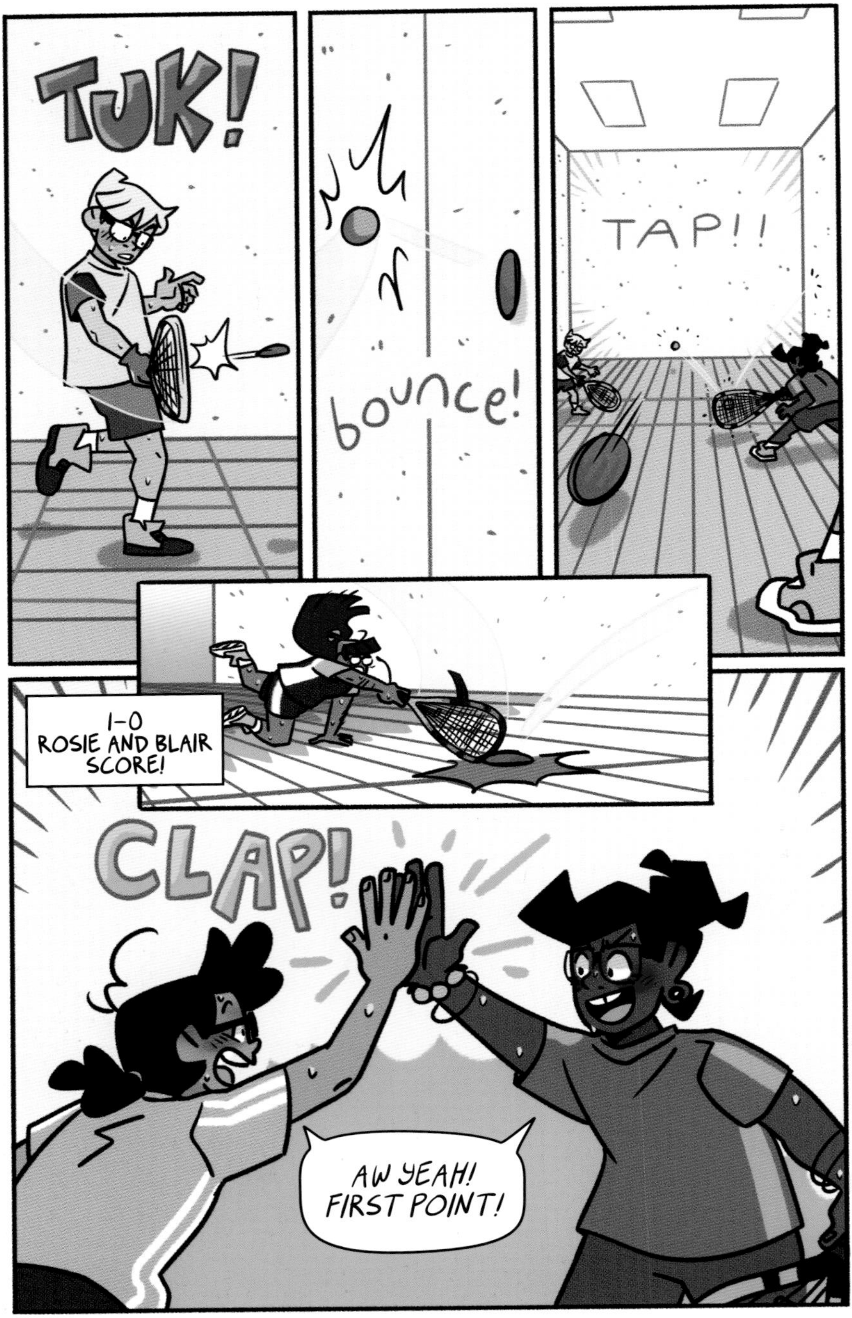
TUK!
bounce!
TAP!!
1-0
ROSIE AND BLAIR
SCORE!
CLAP!
AW YEAH!
FIRST POINT!

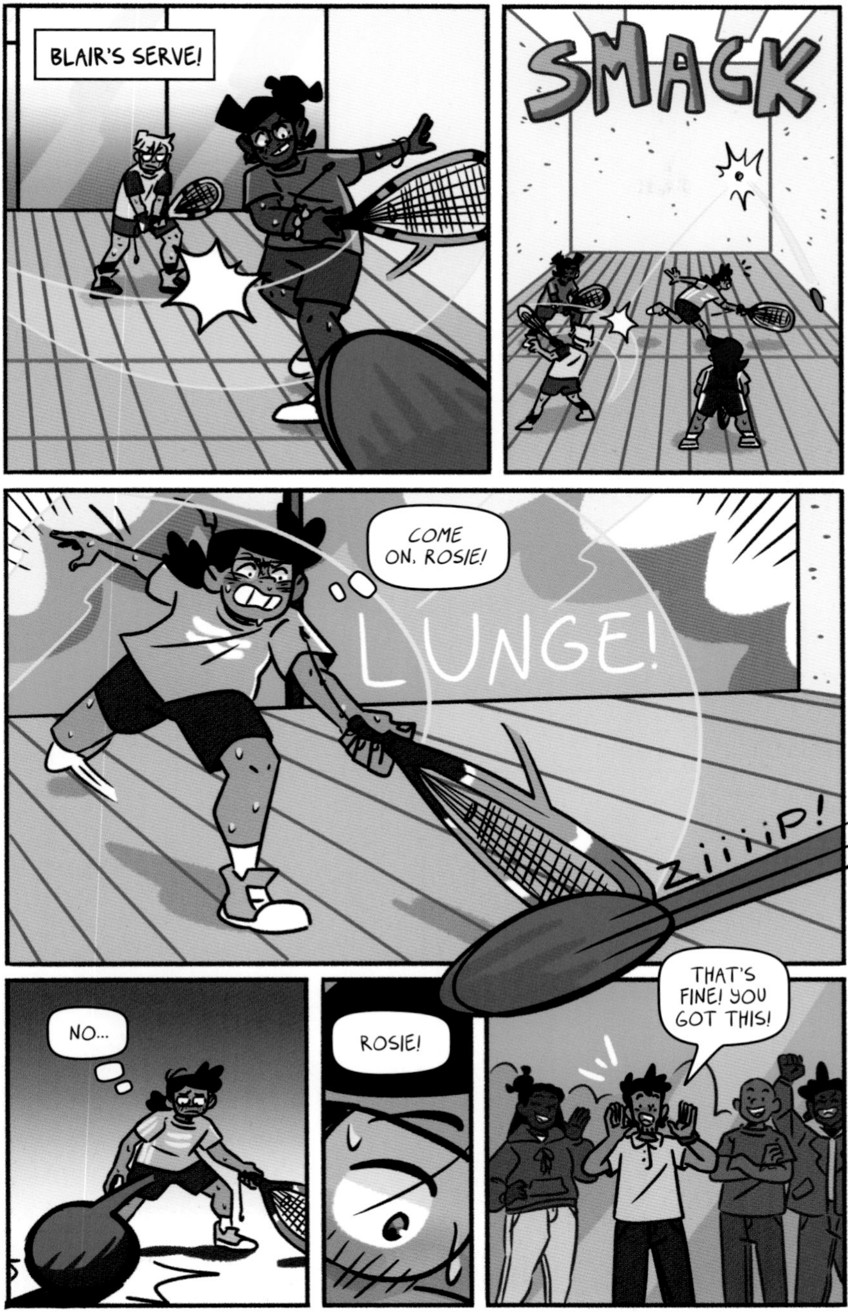
BLAIR'S SERVE!
SMACK
COME ON, ROSIE!
LUNGE!
ZIIIIP!
NO...
ROSIE!
THAT'S FINE! YOU GOT THIS!

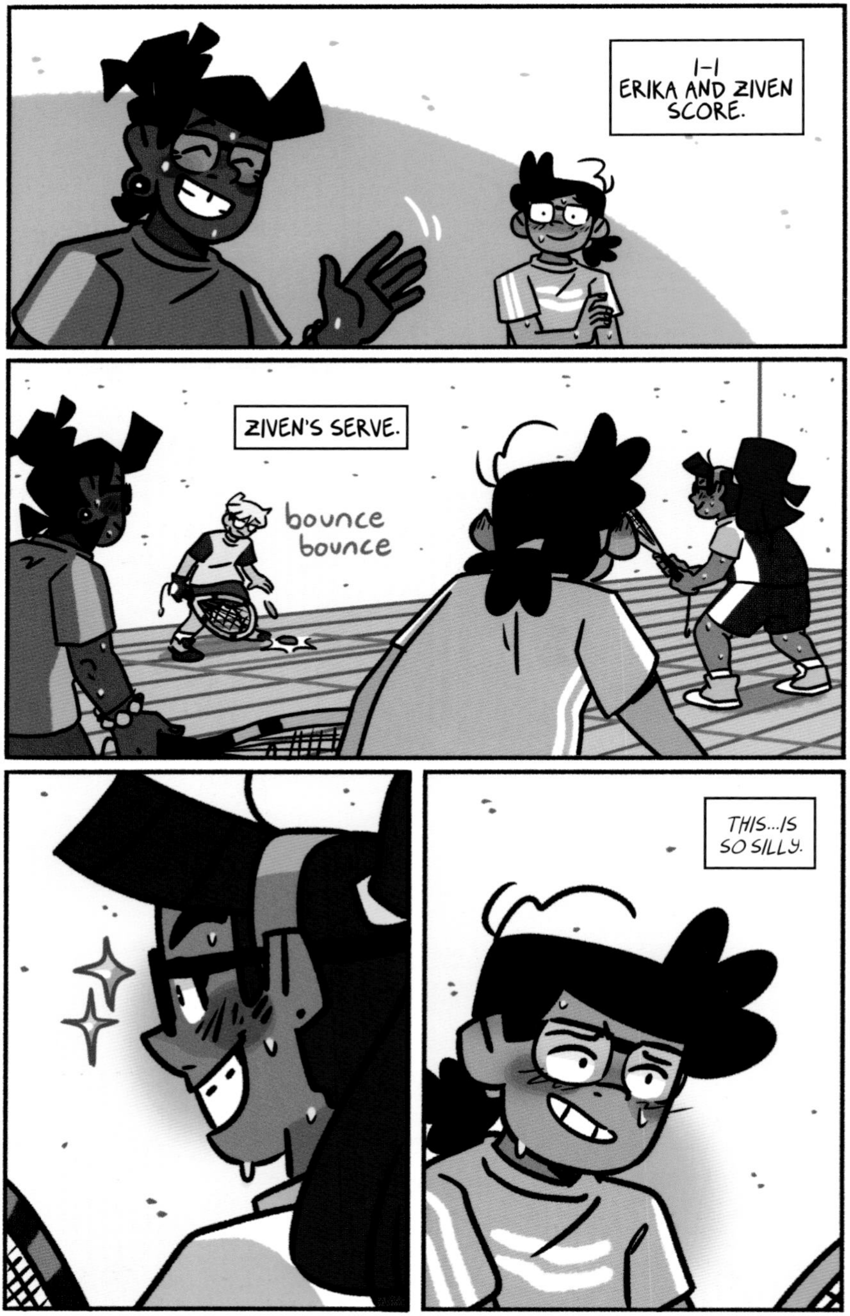

1-1
ERIKA AND ZIVEN SCORE.
ZIVEN'S SERVE.
bounce
bounce
THIS...IS SO SILLY.

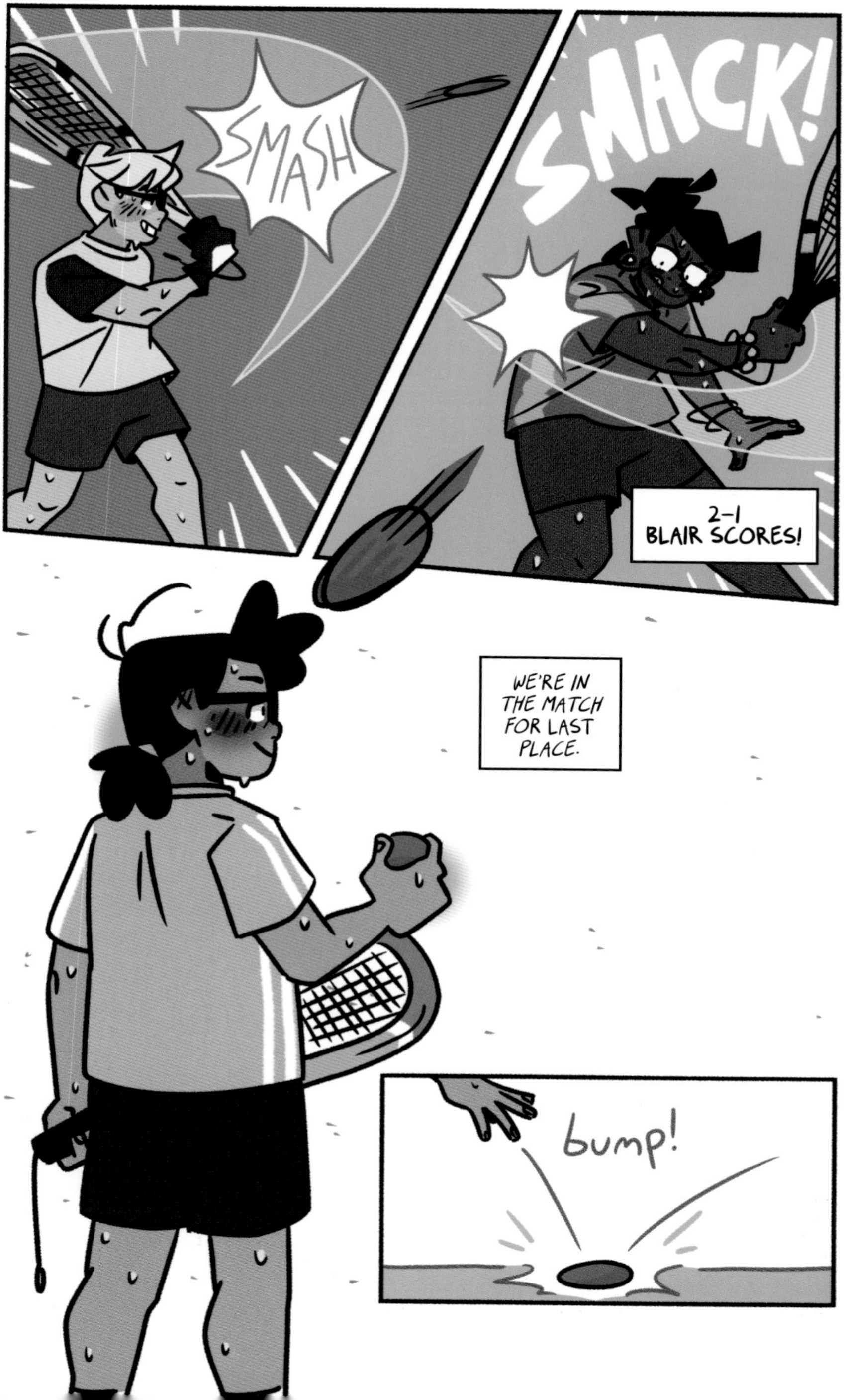
SMASH
SMACK!
2–1
BLAIR SCORES!
WE'RE IN THE MATCH FOR LAST PLACE.
bump!

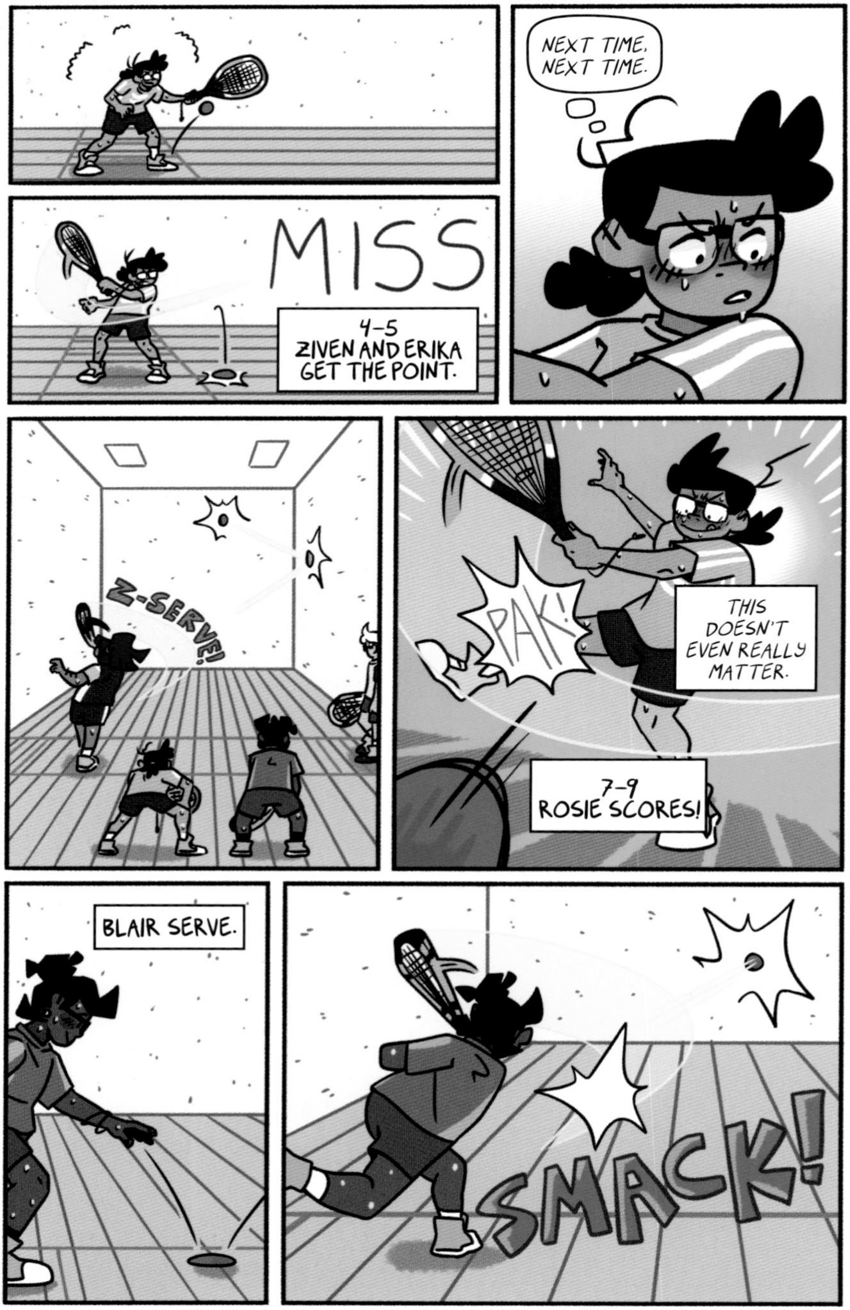
NEXT TIME, NEXT TIME.
MISS
4-5
ZIVEN AND ERIKA GET THE POINT.
Z-SERVE!
PAK!
THIS DOESN'T EVEN REALLY MATTER.
7-9
ROSIE SCORES!
BLAIR SERVE.
SMACK!

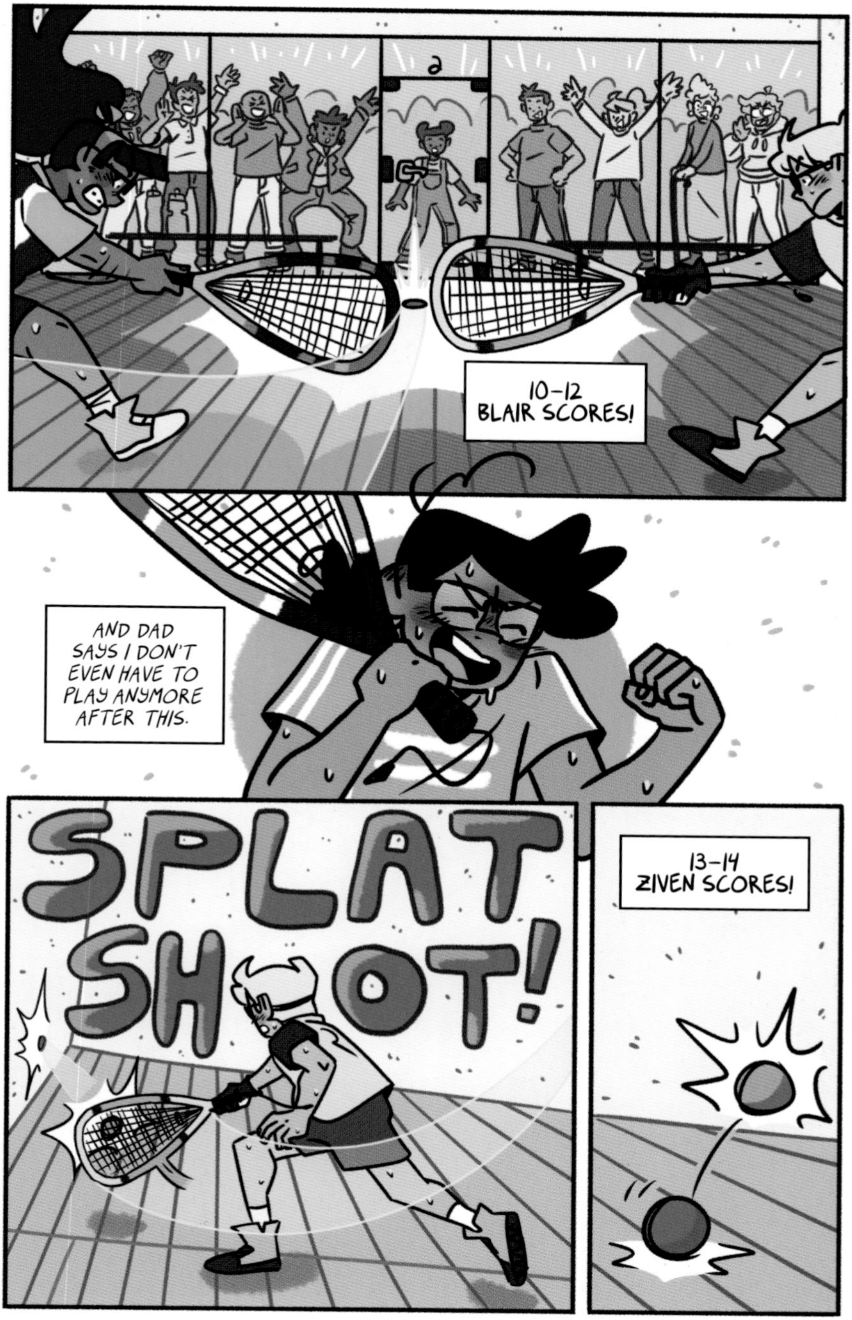
10–12
BLAIR SCORES!
AND DAD SAYS I DON'T EVEN HAVE TO PLAY ANYMORE AFTER THIS.
SPLAT SHOT!
13–14
ZIVEN SCORES!

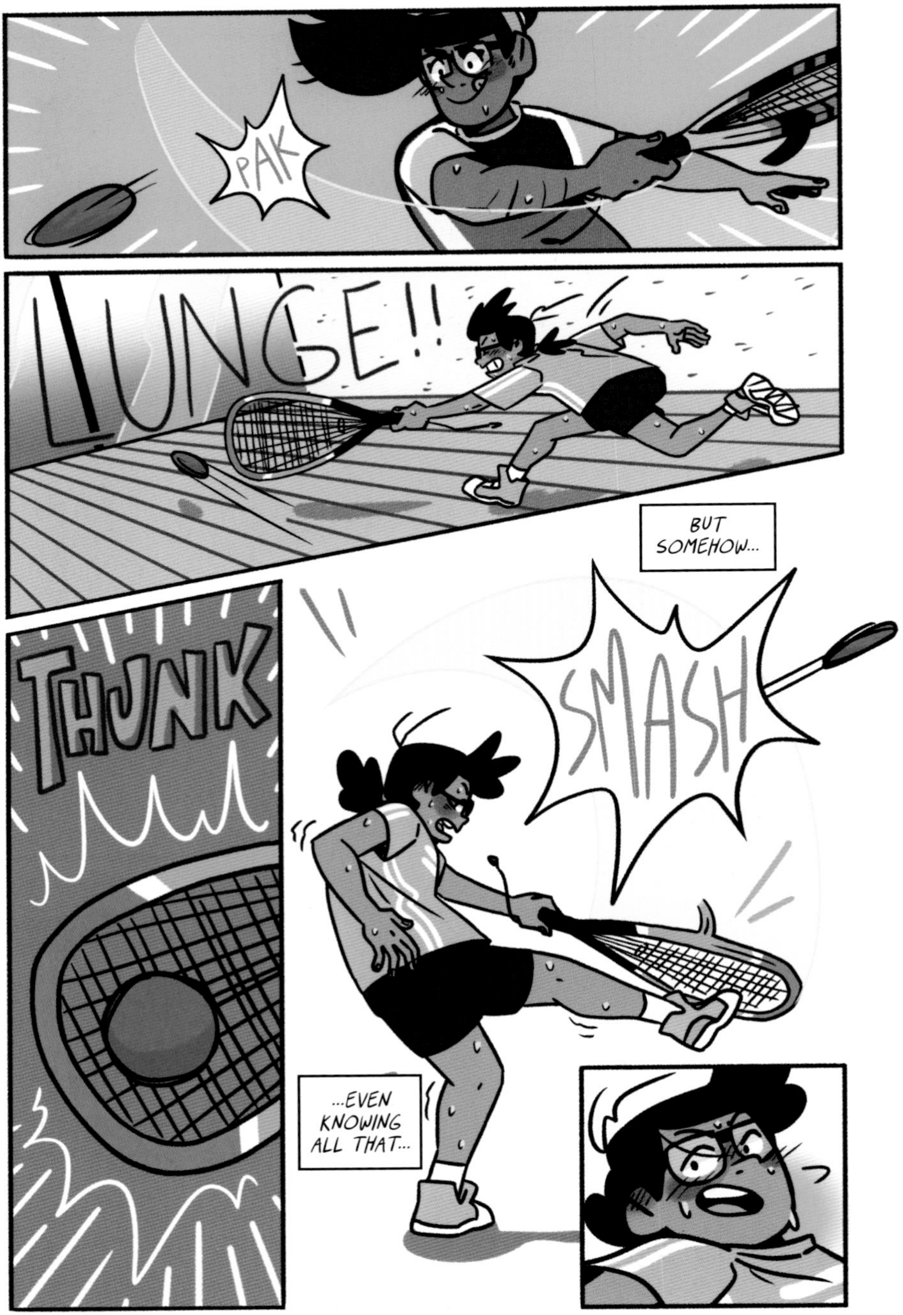
PAK
LUNGE!!
BUT SOMEHOW...
THUNK
SMASH
...EVEN KNOWING ALL THAT...

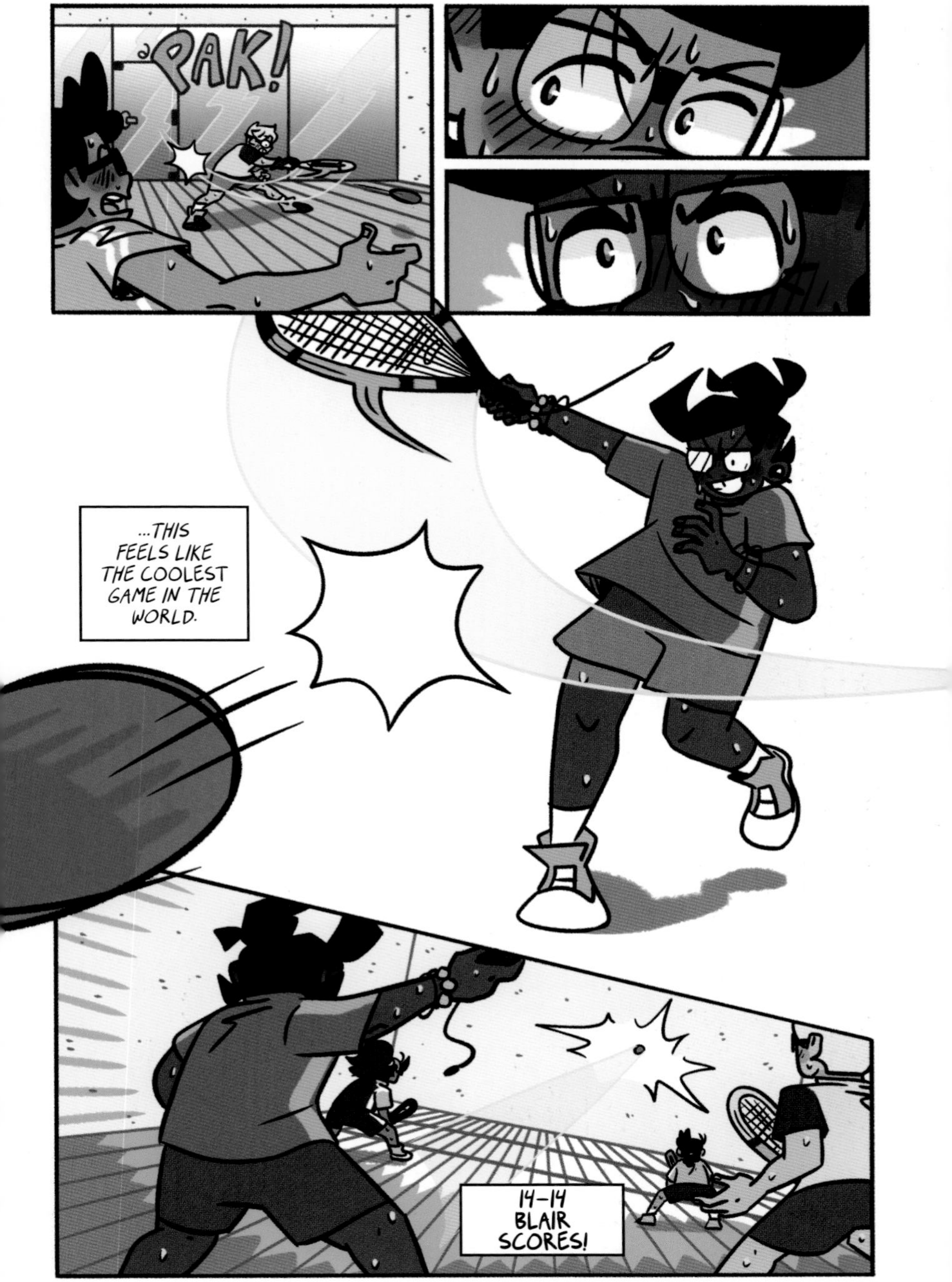
PAK!
...THIS FEELS LIKE THE COOLEST GAME IN THE WORLD.
14–14 BLAIR SCORES!

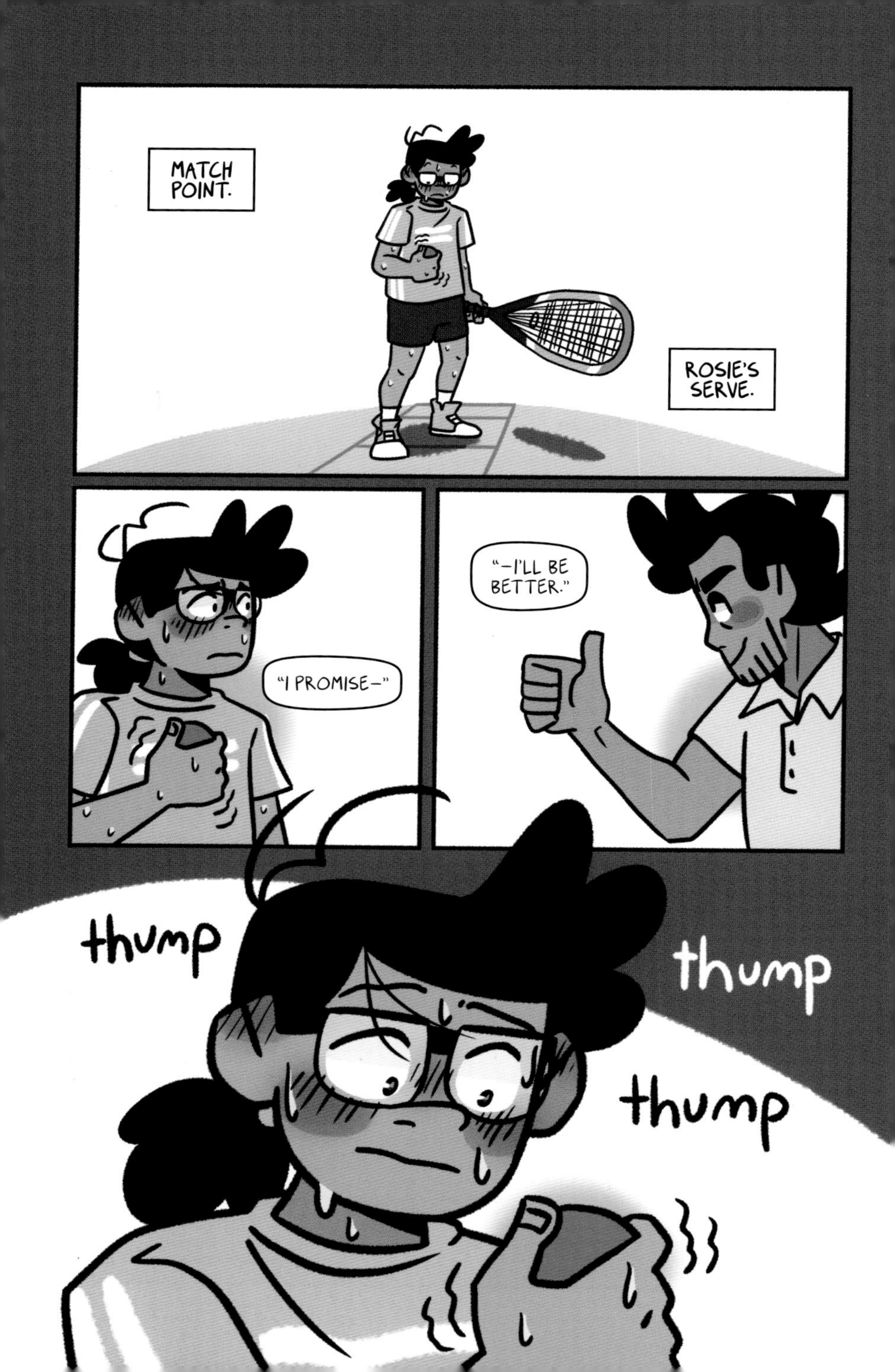
MATCH POINT.
ROSIE'S SERVE.
"I PROMISE—"
"—I'LL BE BETTER."
thump
thump
thump

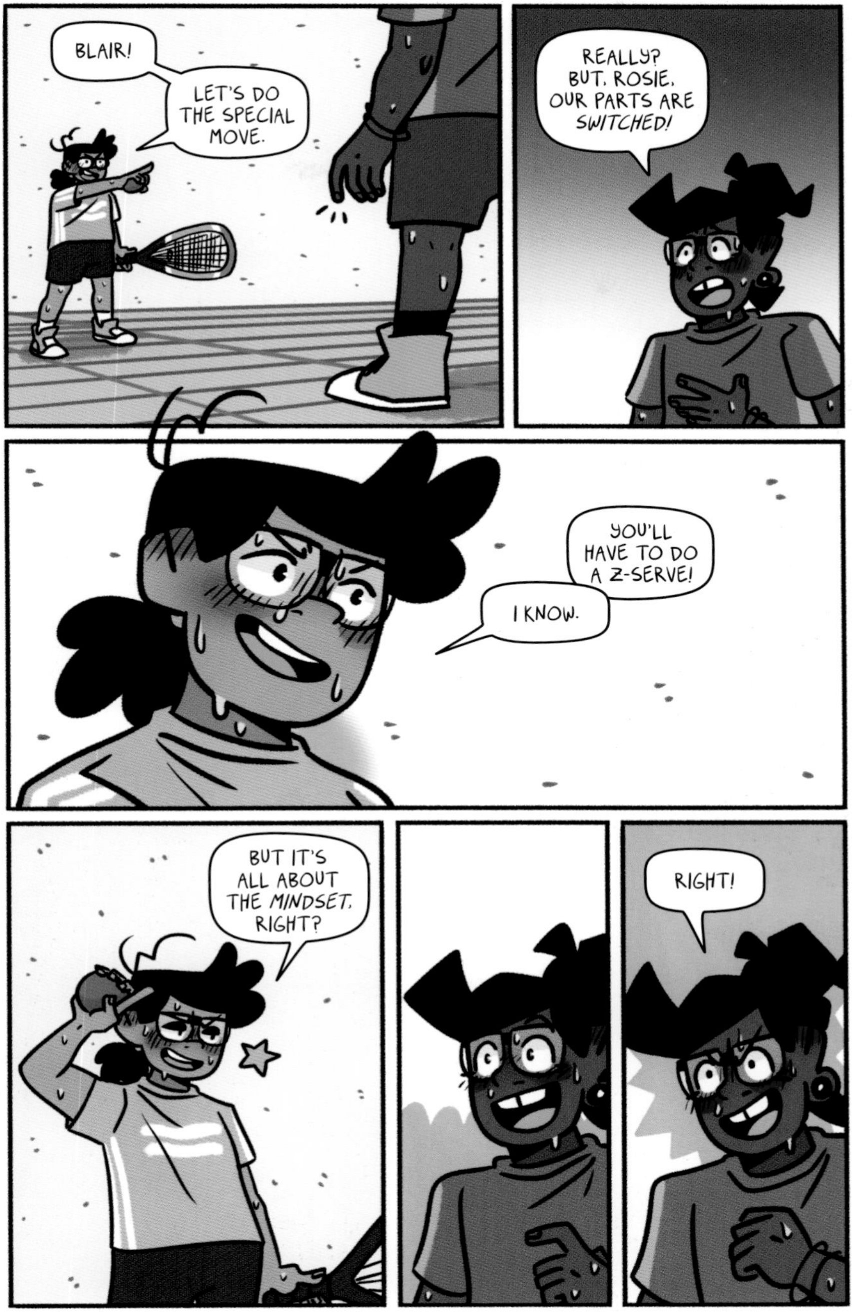
BLAIR!
LET'S DO THE SPECIAL MOVE.
REALLY? BUT, ROSIE, OUR PARTS ARE *SWITCHED!*
YOU'LL HAVE TO DO A Z-SERVE!
I KNOW.
BUT IT'S ALL ABOUT THE *MINDSET*, RIGHT?
RIGHT!

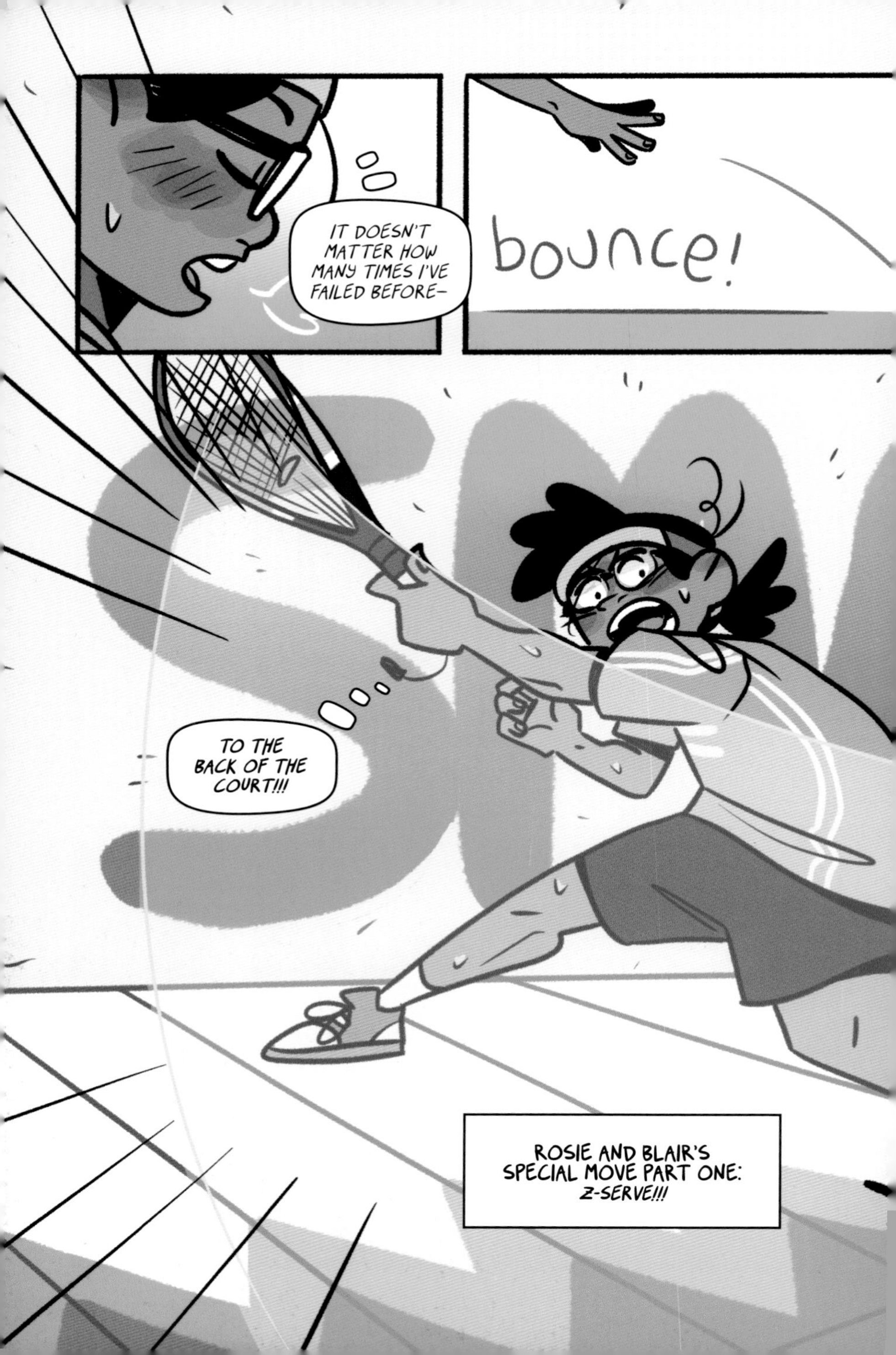
IT DOESN'T MATTER HOW MANY TIMES I'VE FAILED BEFORE–
bounce!
TO THE BACK OF THE COURT!!!
ROSIE AND BLAIR'S SPECIAL MOVE PART ONE: Z-SERVE!!!

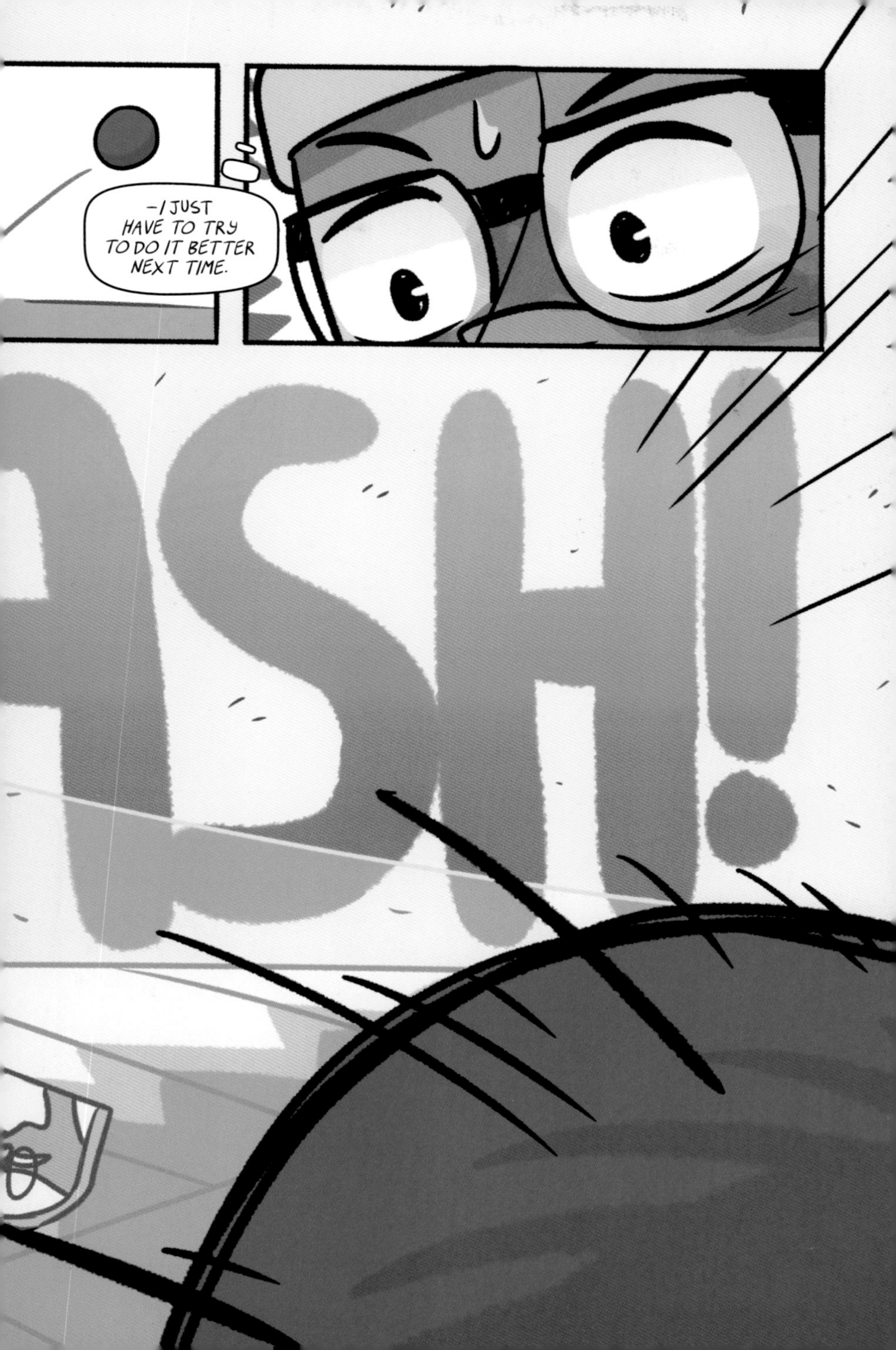
—I JUST HAVE TO TRY TO DO IT BETTER NEXT TIME.
SH!

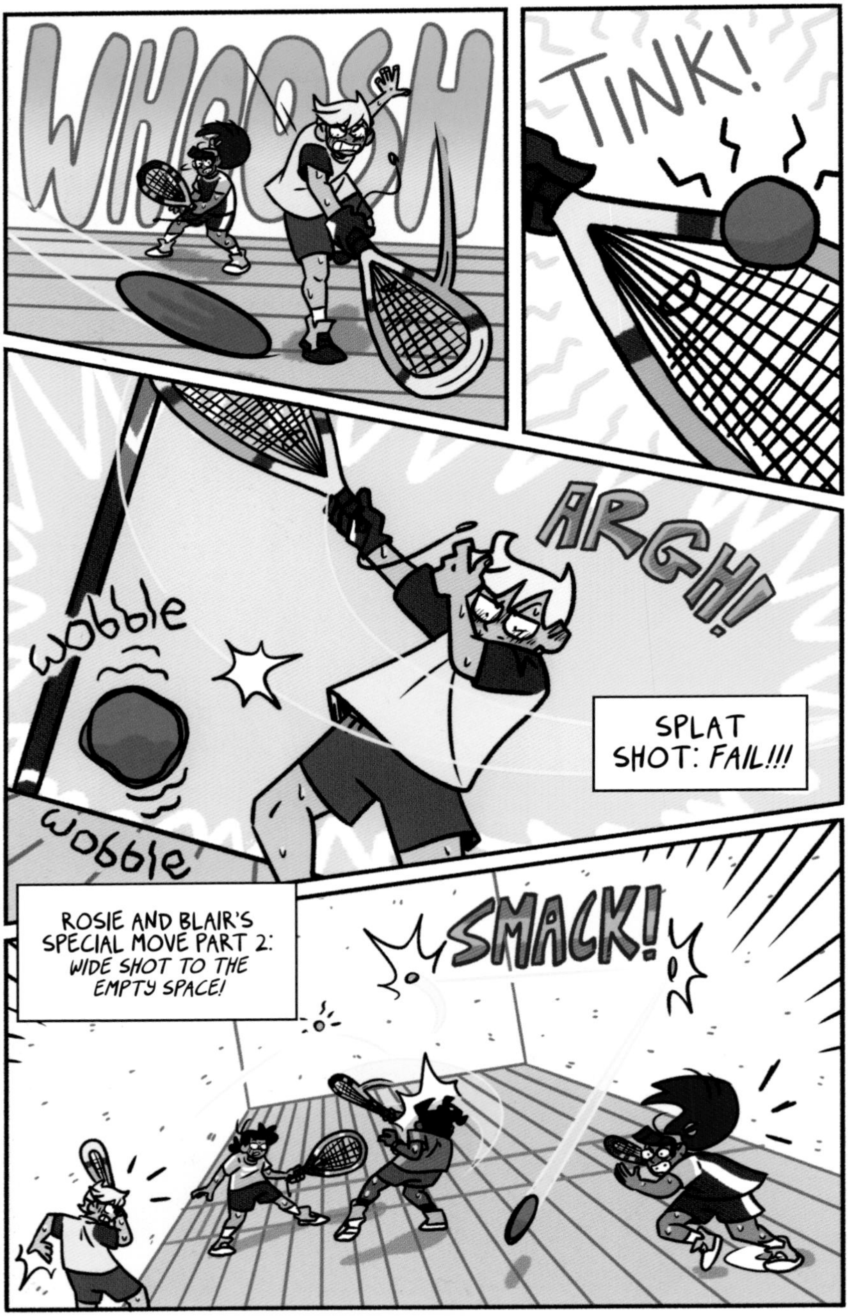
WHOOSH
TINK!
ARGH!
wobble
wobble
SPLAT SHOT: *FAIL!!!*
ROSIE AND BLAIR'S SPECIAL MOVE PART 2: *WIDE SHOT TO THE EMPTY SPACE!*
SMACK!

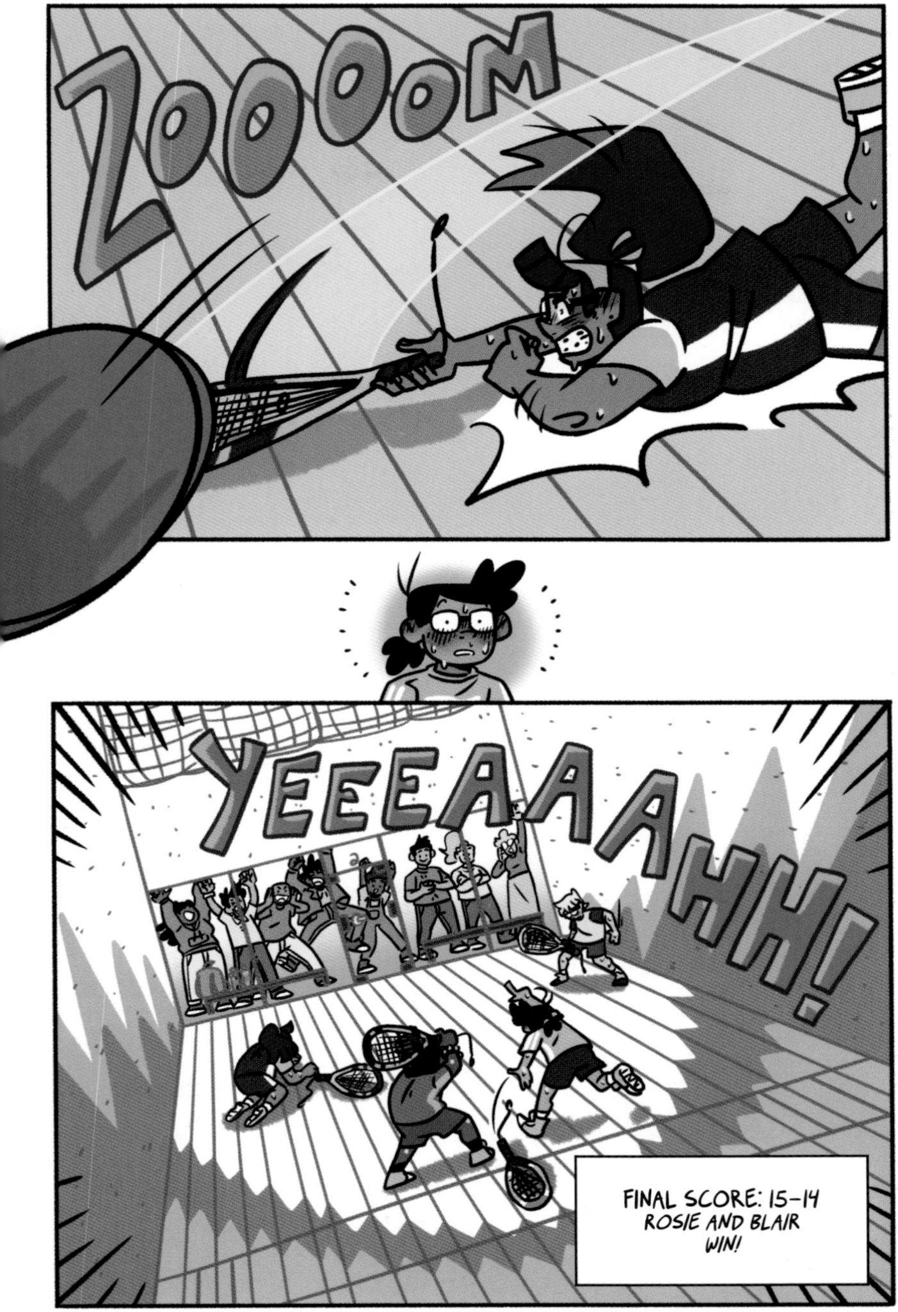
ZOOOOM
YEEEAAAAHH!
FINAL SCORE: 15-14
ROSIE AND BLAIR
WIN!

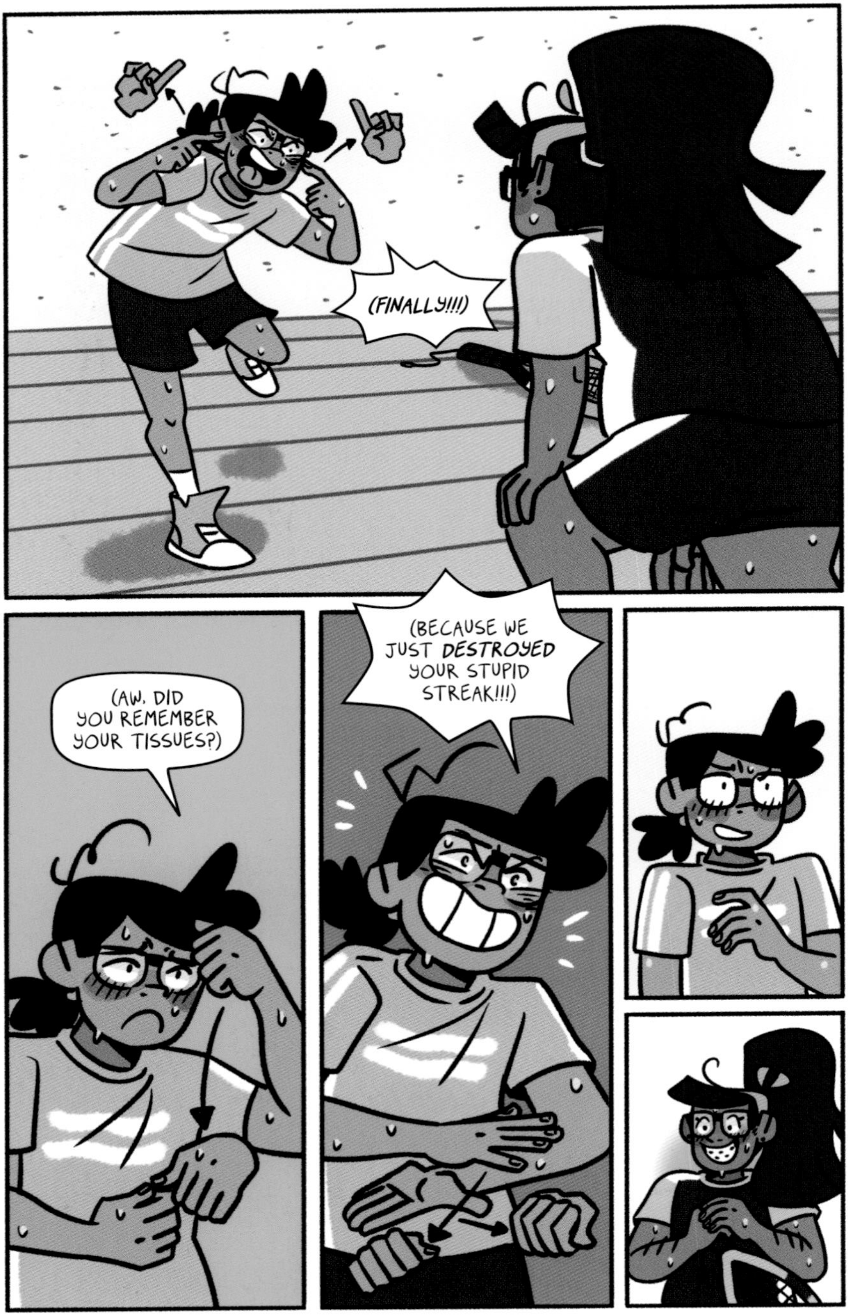
(FINALLY!!!)
(AW, DID YOU REMEMBER YOUR TISSUES?)
(BECAUSE WE JUST **DESTROYED** YOUR STUPID STREAK!!!)

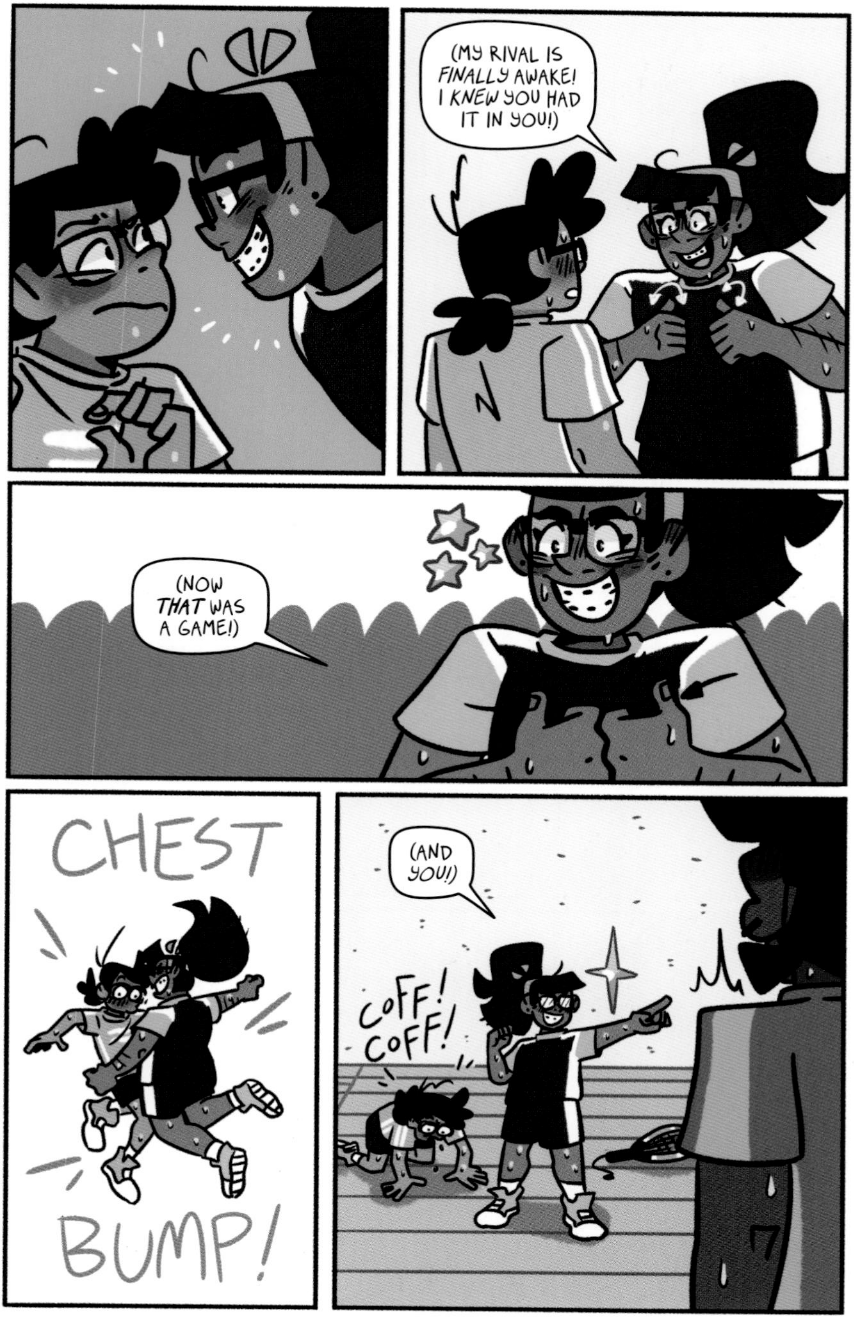

(MY RIVAL IS FINALLY AWAKE! I KNEW YOU HAD IT IN YOU!)
(NOW THAT WAS A GAME!)
CHEST
BUMP!
(AND YOU!)
COFF! COFF!

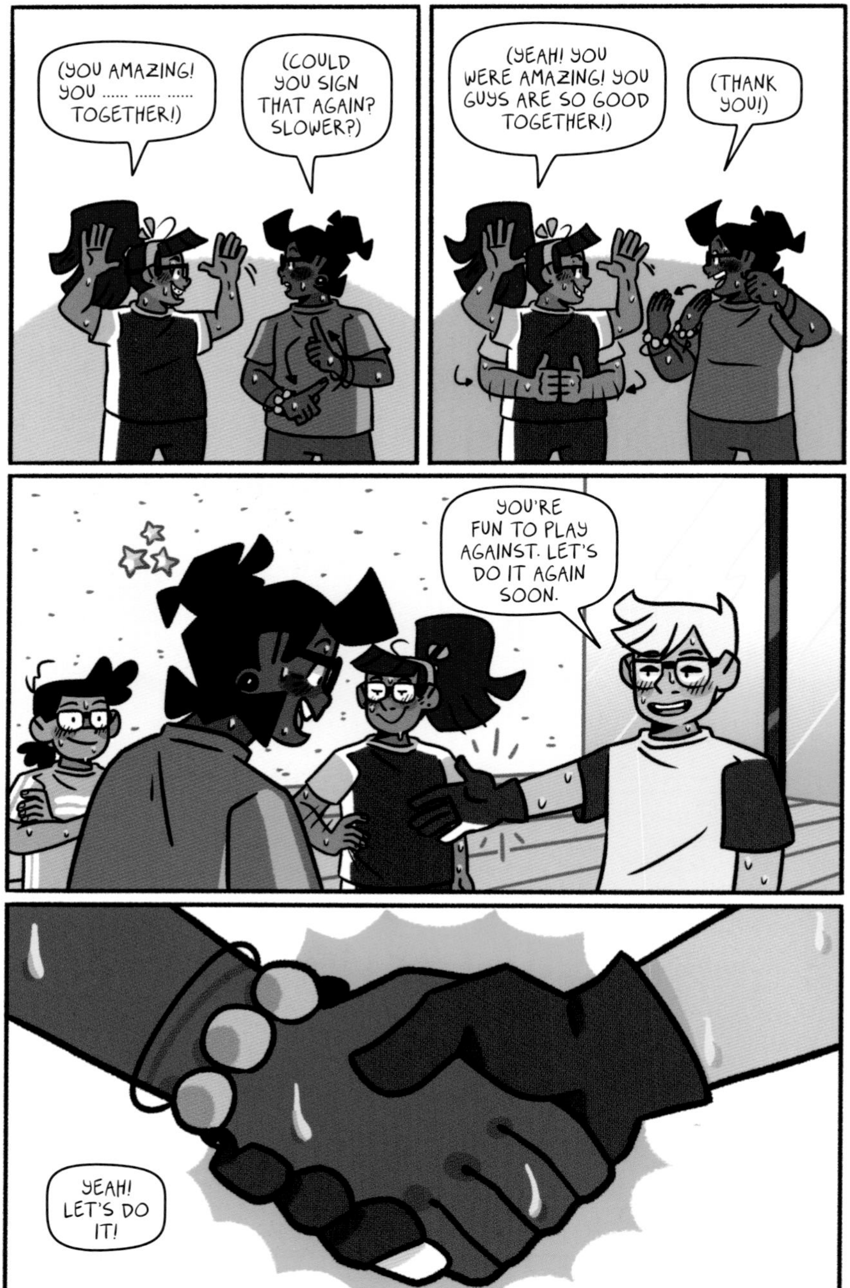
(YOU AMAZING! YOU .... TOGETHER!)
(COULD YOU SIGN THAT AGAIN? SLOWER?)
(YEAH! YOU WERE AMAZING! YOU GUYS ARE SO GOOD TOGETHER!)
(THANK YOU!)
YOU'RE FUN TO PLAY AGAINST. LET'S DO IT AGAIN SOON.
YEAH! LET'S DO IT!

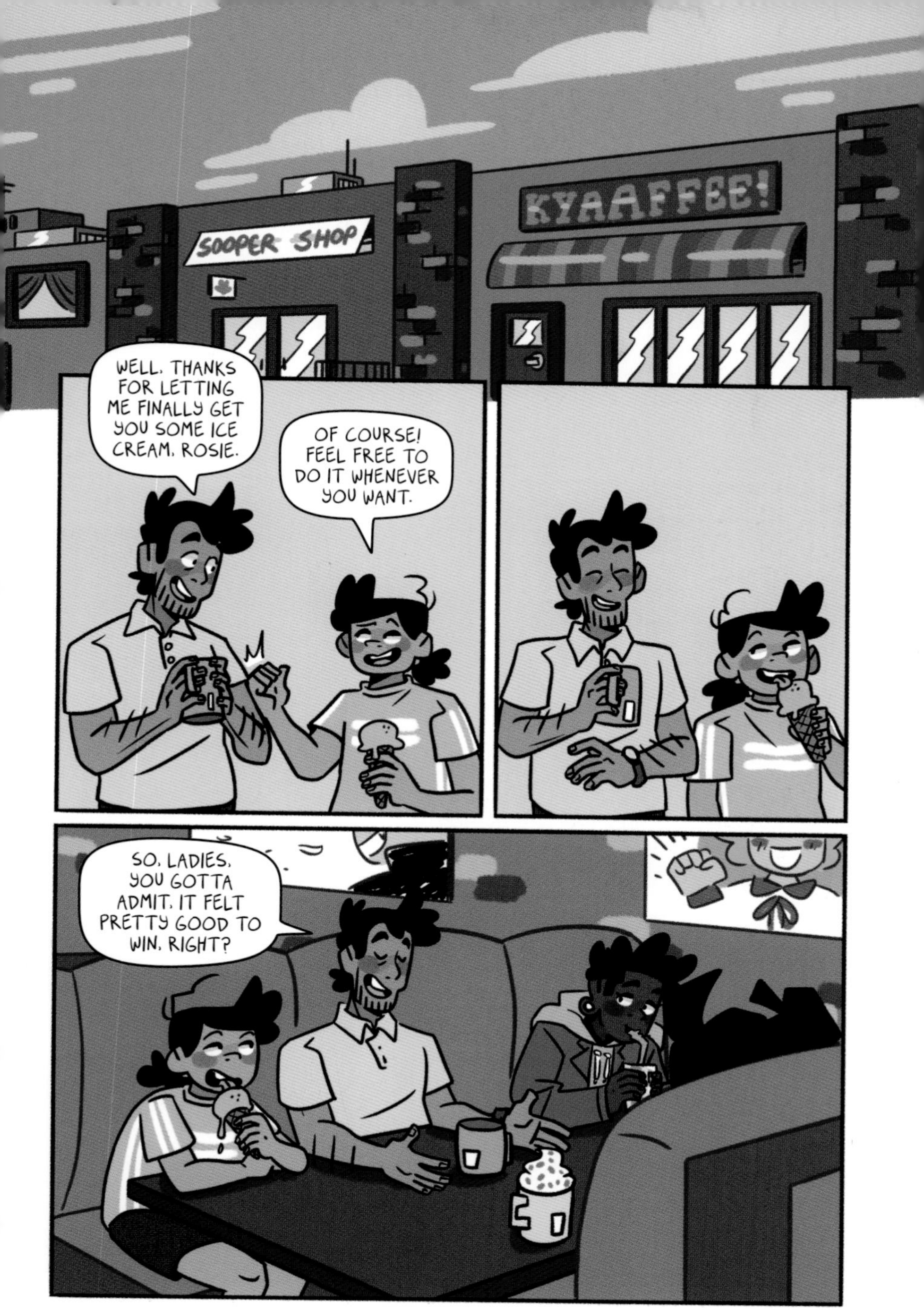

SOOPER SHOP
KYAAFFEE!
WELL. THANKS FOR LETTING ME FINALLY GET YOU SOME ICE CREAM, ROSIE.
OF COURSE! FEEL FREE TO DO IT WHENEVER YOU WANT.
SO, LADIES, YOU GOTTA ADMIT, IT FELT PRETTY GOOD TO WIN, RIGHT?

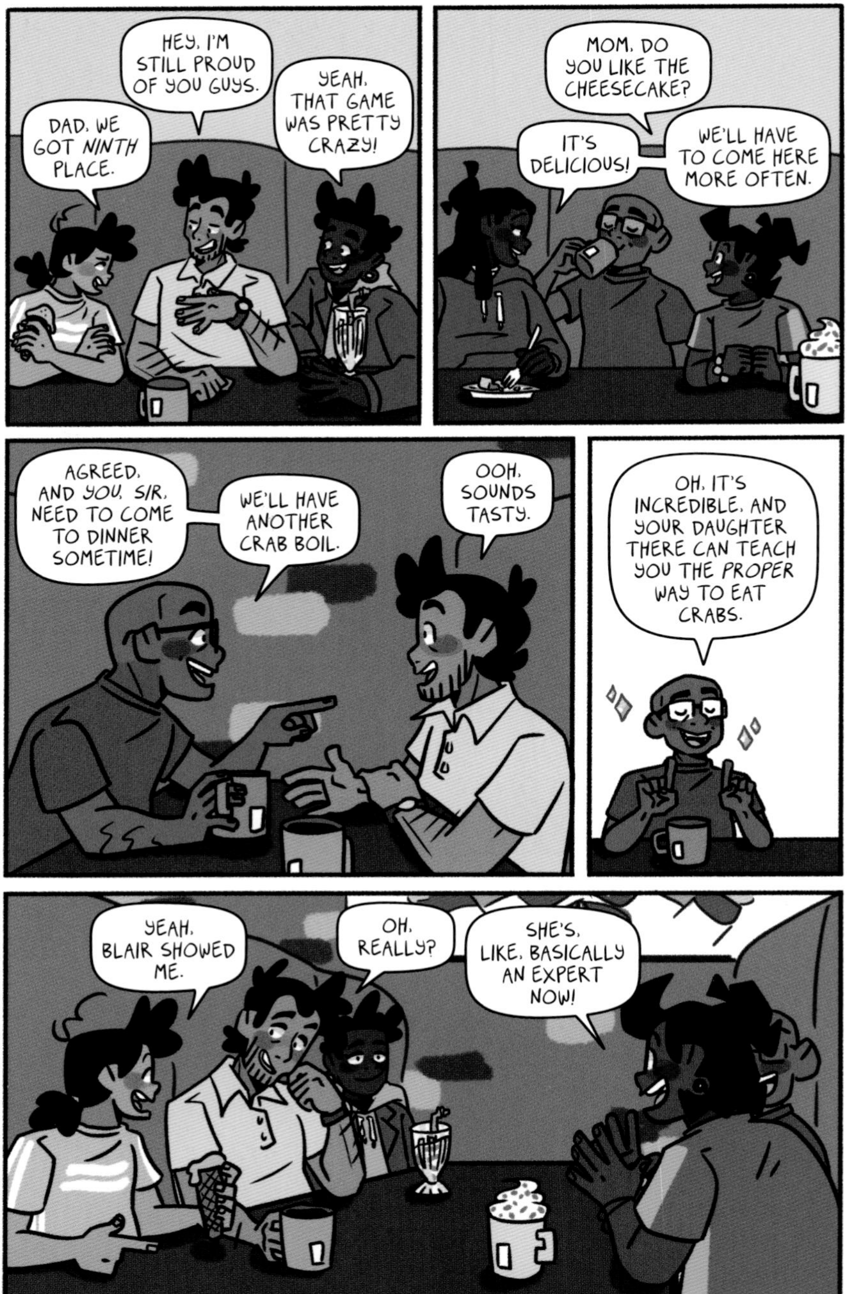
DAD, WE GOT *NINTH* PLACE.
HEY, I'M STILL PROUD OF YOU GUYS.
YEAH, THAT GAME WAS PRETTY CRAZY!
MOM, DO YOU LIKE THE CHEESECAKE?
IT'S DELICIOUS!
WE'LL HAVE TO COME HERE MORE OFTEN.
AGREED, AND *YOU, SIR,* NEED TO COME TO DINNER SOMETIME!
WE'LL HAVE ANOTHER CRAB BOIL.
OOH, SOUNDS TASTY.
OH, IT'S INCREDIBLE, AND YOUR DAUGHTER THERE CAN TEACH YOU THE *PROPER* WAY TO EAT CRABS.
YEAH, BLAIR SHOWED ME.
OH, REALLY?
SHE'S, LIKE, BASICALLY AN EXPERT NOW!

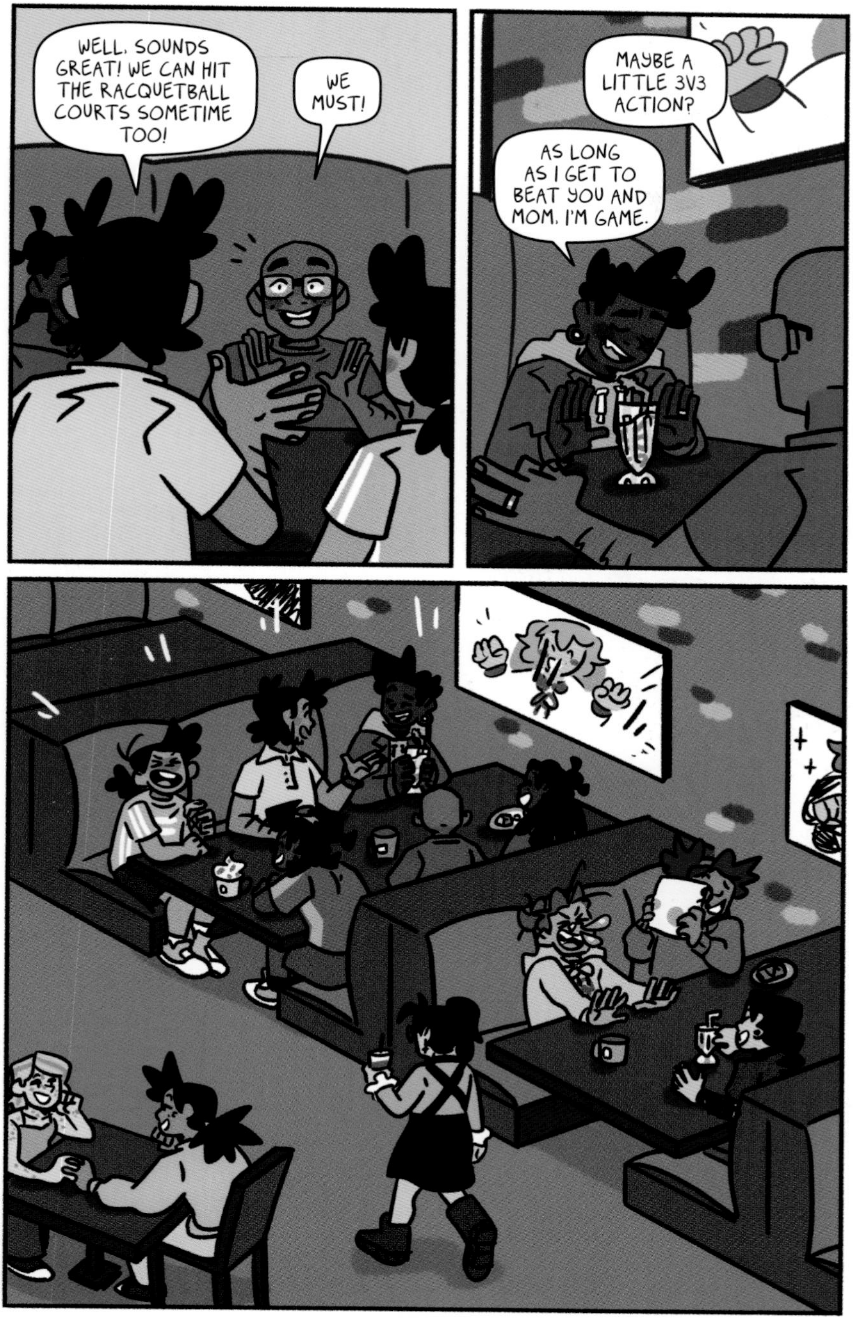
WELL, SOUNDS GREAT! WE CAN HIT THE RACQUETBALL COURTS SOMETIME TOO!
WE MUST!
MAYBE A LITTLE 3V3 ACTION?
AS LONG AS I GET TO BEAT YOU AND MOM, I'M GAME.

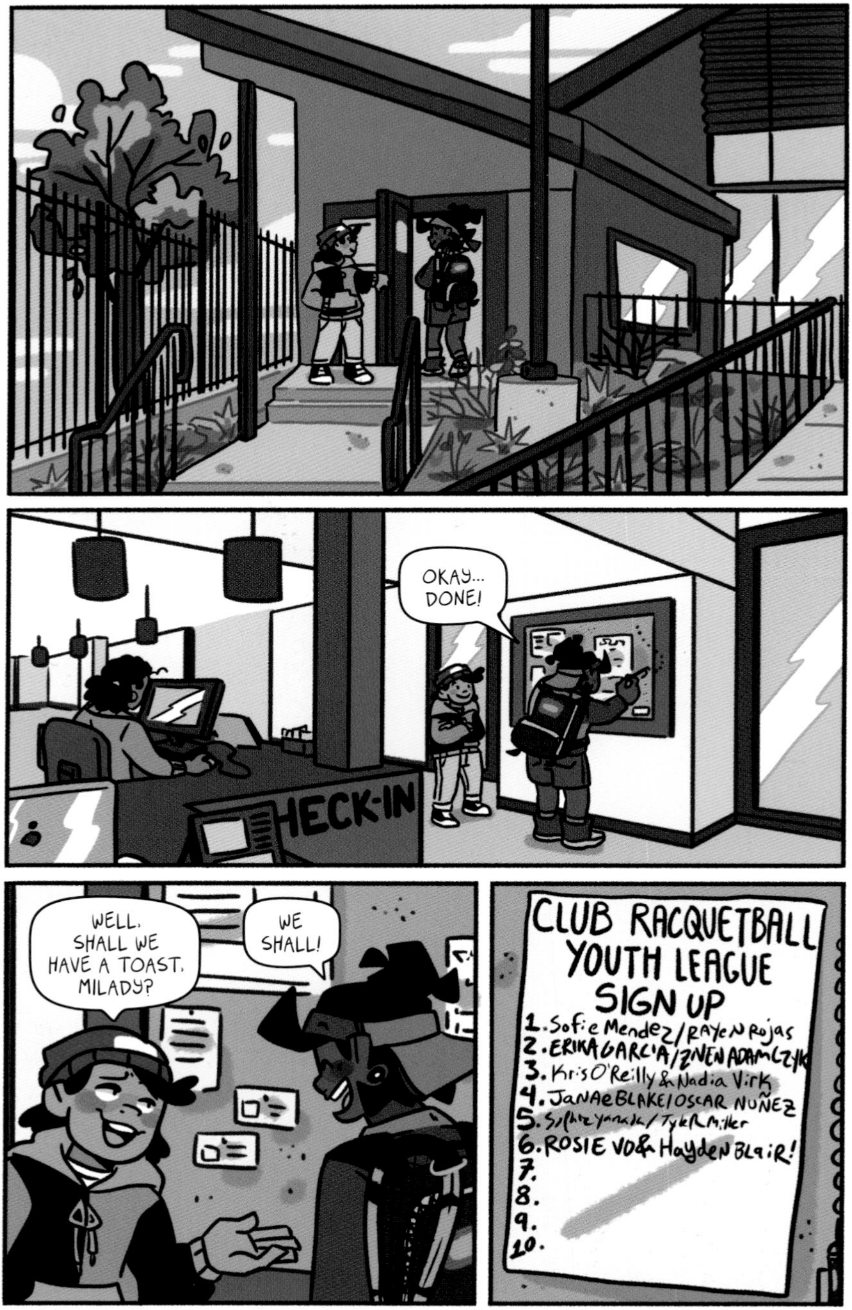
OKAY... DONE!
HECK-IN
WELL, SHALL WE HAVE A TOAST, MILADY?
WE SHALL!
CLUB RACQUETBALL YOUTH LEAGUE SIGN UP
1. Sofie Mendez / Rayen Rojas
2. ERIKA GARCIA / ZNEN ADAMCZYK
3. Kris O'Reilly & Nadia Virk
4. Janae BLAKE / OSCAR NUÑEZ
5. / Tyler Miller
6. ROSIE VO & Hayden Blair!
7.
8.
9.
10.

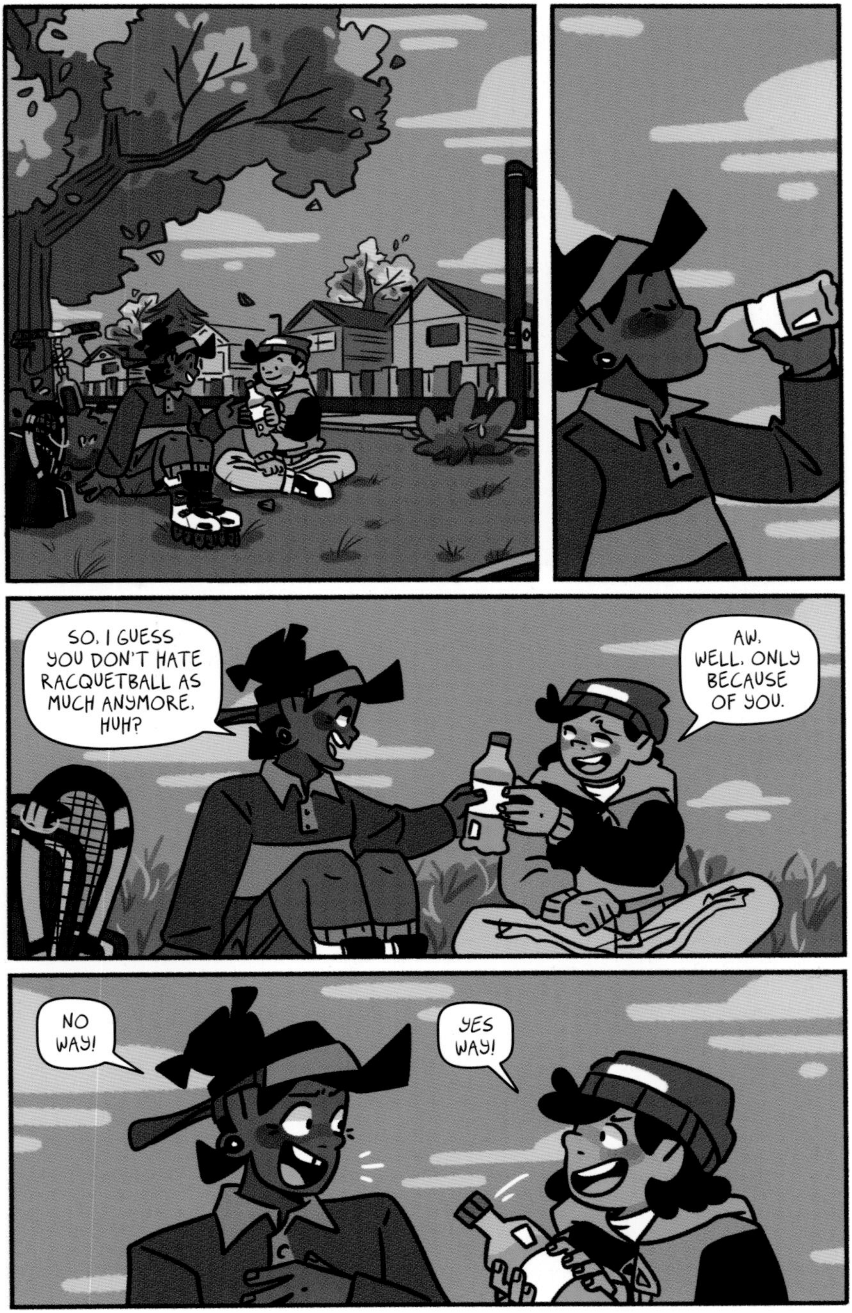
SO, I GUESS YOU DON'T HATE RACQUETBALL AS MUCH ANYMORE, HUH?
AW, WELL, ONLY BECAUSE OF YOU.
NO WAY!
YES WAY!

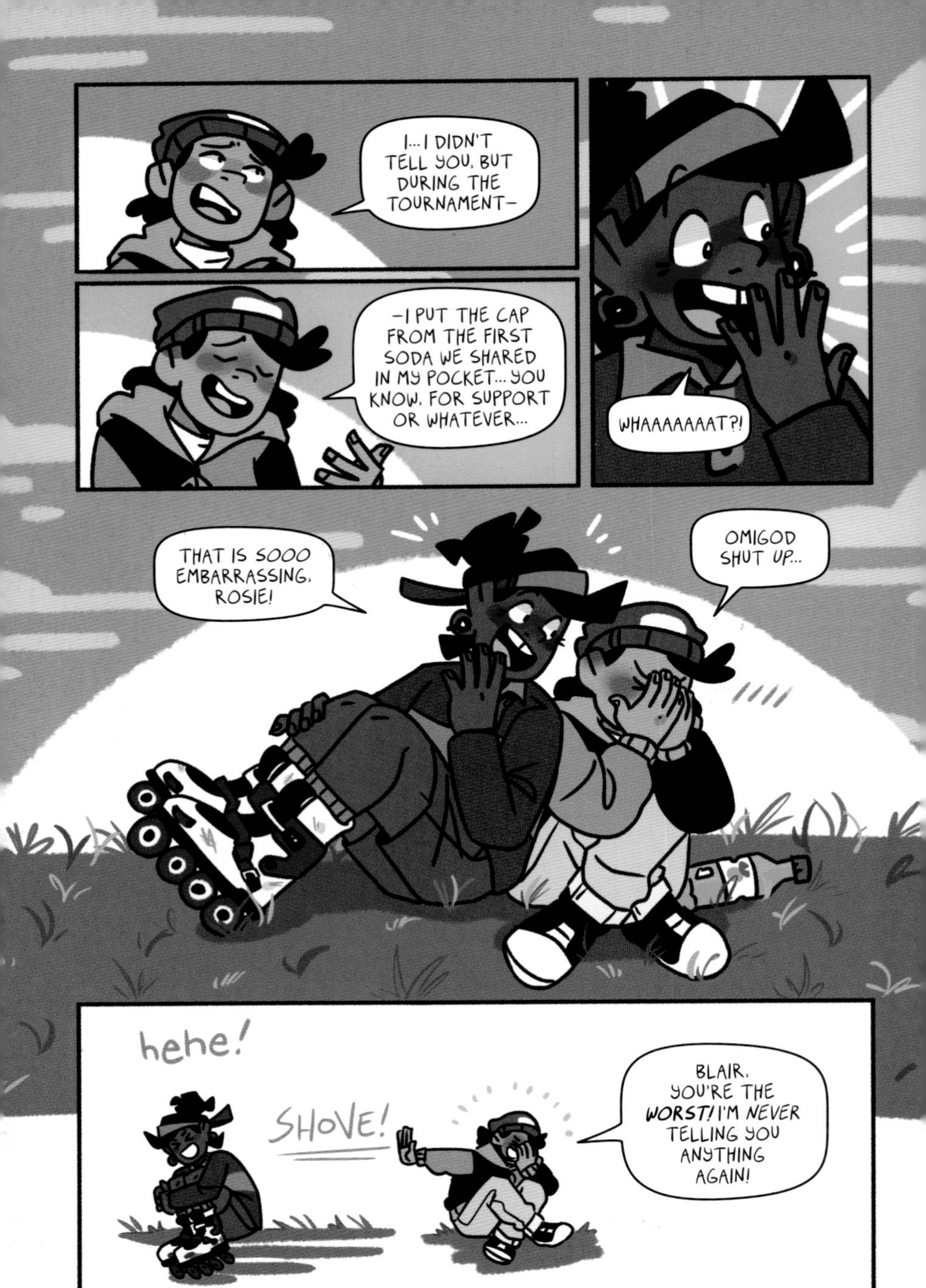
I... I DIDN'T TELL YOU, BUT DURING THE TOURNAMENT—
—I PUT THE CAP FROM THE FIRST SODA WE SHARED IN MY POCKET... YOU KNOW, FOR SUPPORT OR WHATEVER...
WHAAAAAAAT?!
THAT IS SOOO EMBARRASSING, ROSIE!
OMIGOD SHUT UP...
hehe!
SHOVE!
BLAIR, YOU'RE THE **WORST!** I'M *NEVER* TELLING YOU ANYTHING AGAIN!

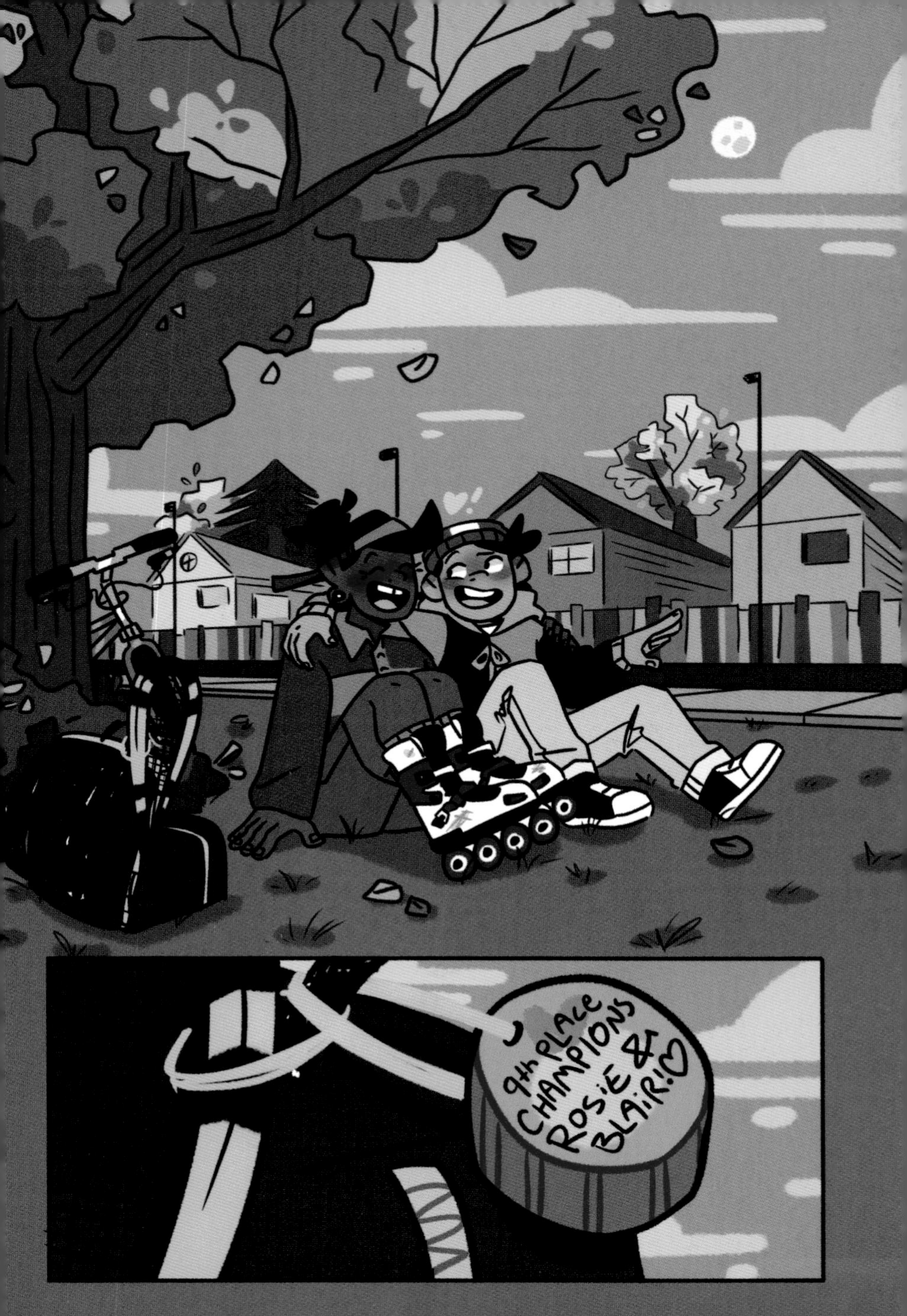
9th PLACE
CHAMPIONS
ROSIE &
BLAIR! ♡

MANY THANKS TO:

My editor, Kiara Valdez, for being with me through every step of the way. You and the entire :01 team were so kind to take a chance on me— I couldn't be more grateful.

John Lowe and John Larrison for pushing my comic abilities all through school and helping me believe in my skills.

Ngozi Ukazu for being the absolute best mentor (and friend) anyone could ask for. Your commitment to helping me (and all the other mentees) is truly incredible. Thank you so much.

My dad for being the best coach in the world and helping me learn that there's always a way to have fun.

My entire family, specifically my mom, nana and papa, Sophie, Sara, and Alex, for never losing faith in me and constantly supporting my dreams. I still can't believe this is real!

Helen Prekker, Violet Chan Karim, Joey Roditis, and Mela Rogers for, year after year, reading and critiquing my various projects and always making time to help my work be the best it can be.

Matthew Terry for always letting me leave work early for anything that had to do with my comics career.

My middle school soccer team, college intramural soccer team, and all my skateboarding homies for showing me the true joy of sports.

And finally, each and every one of my friends who have ever told me they look forward to the things I make. I wouldn't be here without all of you, and I can never be grateful enough to have all of you in my life.

—MADDIE

:01

First Second

Published by First Second
First Second is an imprint of Roaring Brook Press,
a division of Holtzbrinck Publishing Holdings Limited Partnership
120 Broadway, New York, NY 10271
firstsecondbooks.com
mackids.com

Library of Congress Control Number: 2022920390

Our books may be purchased in bulk for promotional, educational, or business
use. Please contact your local bookseller or the Macmillan Corporate and
Premium Sales Department at (800) 221-7945 ext. 5442 or by email at
MacmillanSpecialMarkets@macmillan.com.

First edition, 2023
Edited by Kiara Valdez
Cover design by Molly Johanson
Interior book design by Molly Johanson and Casper Manning
Production editing by Avia Perez

Penciled in Clip Studio Paint. Inked with a textured digital nib and colored digitally
in Clip Studio Paint.

Printed in China by 1010 Printing International Limited, Kwun Tong, Hong Kong

ISBN 978-1-250-78414-8 (paperback)
10 9 8 7 6 5 4 3 2 1

ISBN 978-1-250-78415-5 (hardcover)
10 9 8 7 6 5 4 3 2 1

Don't miss your next favorite book from First Second! For the latest updates go
to firstsecondnewsletter.com and sign up for our enewsletter.

BY ART
WE LIVE